D0427047

THR3E

obsessed

TED DEKKER

THOMAS NELSON
Since 1798

NASHVILLE   DALLAS   MEXICO CITY   RIO DE JANEIRO   BEIJING

Published in Nashville, Tennessee, by Thomas Nelson. Thomas Nelson is a registered trademark of Thomas Nelson, Inc.

Thomas Nelson, Inc., titles may be purchased in bulk for educational, business, fund-raising, or sales promotional use. For information, please e-mail SpecialMarkets@ThomasNelson.com.

Scripture quotations used in *Three* are taken from The Holy Bible, New International Version, © 1973, 1978, 1984 by International Bible Society. Used by permission of Zondervan Publishing House.

This novel is a work of fiction. Names, characters, places, and incidents are either products of the author's imagination or are used fictitiously. All characters are fictional, and any similarity to people living or dead is purely coincidental.

ISBN 978-1-59554-561-9

Printed in the United States of America
08 09 10 11 12 QW 7 6 5 4 3 2 1

THR3E

1

THE OFFICE HAD NO WINDOWS, only electric lanterns to light the hundreds of spines standing in their cherry wood bookcases. A single lawyer's lamp spread its yellow hue over the leather-topped desk. The room smelled of linseed oil and musty pages, but to Dr. John Francis it was the scent of knowledge.

"Evil is beyond the reach of no man."

"But can a man remove himself beyond the reach of evil?" Kevin asked.

The dean of academic affairs, Dr. John Francis, gazed over bifocals at the man who sat opposite him and allowed a small smile to nudge his lips. Those blue eyes hid a deep mystery, one that had eluded him since their first meeting three months earlier when Kevin Parson approached him after a philosophy lecture. They'd struck up a unique friendship that included numerous discussions such as this one.

Kevin sat with his feet flat, hands on knees, eyes piercing and un-moving, hair ruffled despite a compulsive habit of running his fingers through his loose brown curls. Or because of it. The hair was an anomaly; in every other way the man groomed himself perfectly. Clean shaven, fashionably current, pleasantly scented—Old Spice, if the professor guessed right. Kevin's ragged hair begged to differ in a bohemian sort of way. Others fiddled with pencils or twirled their fin-gers or shifted in their seats; Kevin ran his fingers through his hair and

tapped his right foot. Not now and then or at appropriate breaks in
the conversation, but regularly, to the beat of a hidden drum behind
his blue eyes. Some might consider the idiosyncrasies annoying, but
Dr. Francis saw them as nothing more than enigmatic clues to Kevin's
nature. The truth—rarely obvious and almost always found in subtle-
ies. In the tapping of feet and the fiddling of fingers and the movement of eyes.

Dr. Francis pushed his black leather chair back from the desk,
stood slowly to his feet, and walked to a bookcase filled with the
works of the ancient scholars. In many ways he identified with these
men as much as he did with the modern man. Put a robe on him and
he would look rather like a bearded Socrates, Kevin had once told
him. He ran a finger over a bound copy of the Dead Sea Scrolls.

"Indeed," Dr. Francis said. "Can man step beyond evil's reach? I
think not. Not in this lifetime."

"Then all men are condemned to a life of evil," Kevin said.

Dr. Francis faced him. Kevin watched, unmoving except for his
right foot, tapping away. His round blue eyes held steady, stared with
the innocence of a child's, probing, magnetic, unabashed. These eyes
attracted long stares from the secure and forced the less secure to avert
their gaze. Kevin was twenty-eight, but he possessed a strange blend
of brilliance and naiveté that Dr. Francis could not understand. The
full-grown man thirsted for knowledge like a five-year-old. Something
to do with a unique rearing in a bizarre home, but Kevin had never
been forthcoming.

"A lifetime *struggle* with evil, not a life of evil," Dr. Francis
clarified.

"And does man simply choose evil, or does he create it?" Kevin
asked, already many thoughts beyond his initial question. "Is evil a
force that swims in human blood, struggling to find its way into the
heart, or is it an external possibility wanting to be formed?"

"I would say man chooses evil rather than creates it. Human nature's saturated with evil as a result of the Fall. We are all evil."

"And we are all good," Kevin said, tapping his foot. "The good, the bad, and the beautiful."

Dr. Francis nodded at the use of the phrase he'd coined, which referred to the man created in God's nature, the beautiful man, struggling between the good and the bad. "The good, the bad, and the beautiful. Indeed." He stepped for the door. "Walk with me, Kevin."

Kevin ran both hands past his temples and stood. Dr. Francis led him from the office and up a flight of steps to the world above, as Kevin liked to call it.

"How is your paper on the natures progressing?" Dr. Francis asked.

"Guaranteed to raise your eyebrows." They stepped into the empty main hall. "I'm using a story to illustrate my conclusion. Not conventional, I know, but since Christ preferred to use fiction to communicate truth, I figured you wouldn't mind if I borrowed from him."

"As long as it makes the point. I look forward to reading it."

III

Kevin walked with Dr. John Francis down the hall, thinking that he liked this man beside him. The sound of their shoes striking the hardwood floor echoed through the chamber steeped in tradition. The older man strolled casually, his ready smile hinting at wisdom far beyond his words. Kevin glanced up at the paintings of the divinity school's founders along the wall to his right. Bold, gentle giants, Dr. Francis called them.

"Speaking of evil, all men are capable of gossip, don't you think?" Kevin asked.

"Undoubtedly."

"Even the bishop is capable of gossip."

"Of course."

"Do you think the bishop does gossip? Sometimes?"

The dean's answer waited three steps. "We are all human."

They came to the large door that opened to the central campus and Dr. Francis pushed it open. Despite the ocean breezes, Long Beach could not escape periodic stretches of oppressive heat. Kevin stepped out into the bright midday sunlight, and for a moment their philosophical bantering felt trivial in light of the world before him. A dozen seminary students walked across the manicured park, heads bent in thought or tilted back with smiles. Two dozen poplars formed an avenue through the expansive lawn. The chapel's steeple towered over the trees beyond the park. To his right, the Augustine Memorial Library glistened in the sun. The Divinity School of the Pacific, South, was at a glance statelier and more modern than its parent, the Episcopal seminary in Berkeley.

Here was the real world, made up of normal people with sensible histories and ordinary families pursuing an admirable profession. He, on the other hand, was a twenty-eight-year-old convert who really had no business attending seminary at all, much less leading a flock one day. Not because he didn't have honorable intent, but because of who he *was*. Because he was Kevin Parson, who had really only discovered his spiritual side for the first time three years ago. In spite of his whole-hearted embrace of the church, he still felt no holier—and maybe less—than any drunk on the street might. Not even the dean knew his whole story, and Kevin wasn't sure the man would be so supportive if he did.

"You have a brilliant mind, Kevin," the dean said, gazing out at the grounds. "I've seen a lot of people come and go, and few of them have your same tenacity for the truth. But believe me, the deepest questions can drive a man mad. The problem of evil is one of those questions. You'd be wise to court it slowly."

Kevin looked into the graying man's eyes, and for a moment neither spoke. The dean winked and Kevin offered a slight smile. Kevin liked this man as much as he might like a father.

"You're a wise man, Dr. Francis. Thanks. I'll see you in class next week."

"Don't forget your paper."

"Never."

The dean dipped his head.

Kevin took one step down to the concrete landing and turned back. "Just one last thought. In absolute terms, gossip isn't so different from murder, right?"

"Ultimately, no."

"Then the bishop is ultimately capable of murder, isn't he?"

The dean lifted his right eyebrow. "That's a bit of a stretch."

Kevin smiled. "Not really. Neither is more evil."

"You've made your point, Kevin. I'll be sure to warn the bishop against any sudden urges to kill his fellowman."

Kevin chuckled. He turned and walked down the steps. Behind him the door closed with a soft thump. He turned back. The steps were empty.

He was alone. A stranger in a strange world. How many grown men would stare at a flight of steps just vacated by a professor of philosophy and feel utterly alone? He scratched his head and ruffled his hair.

Kevin headed for the parking lot. The sense of solitude left him before he reached his car, which was good. He was changing, wasn't he? The hope of change was why he'd chosen to become a priest in the first place. He'd escaped the demons of his past and begun a new life as a new creature. He had put his old self in the grave and, despite the lingering memories, he was coming to life, like an aspen in the spring.

So much change in so little time. God willing, the past would remain buried.

He swung his beige Sable out of the lot and merged with the steady flow of traffic on Long Beach Boulevard. Evil. The problem of evil. Like traffic—never ending.

On the other hand, grace and love weren't exactly running scared, were they? He had more to be thankful for than he ever imagined possible. Grace, for starters. A fine school with fine teachers. His own home. He might not have a rack of friends to call on at his every whim, but he did have a few. One at least. Dr. John Francis liked him.

He humphed. Okay, so he had a ways to go on the social front. Samantha had called him, though. They'd talked twice in the last two weeks. And Sam was no slouch. Now there was a friend. Maybe more than a—

His cell phone chirped loudly from the cup holder. He'd gotten the thing a week ago and had used it once, placed a call to his home phone to see if it worked. It had, but only after he'd activated the voice mail, which had required a call to the salesman.

The cell rang again and he picked it up. The thing was small enough to swallow if you got hungry enough. He pushed the red button and immediately knew it was the wrong one. Ignore "Send" above the green button. Green is go and red is stop, the salesman had said.

Kevin lifted the phone to his ear, heard silence, and tossed it on the passenger seat, feeling foolish. It was probably the salesman, calling to see if he was enjoying his new phone. Then again, why would a salesman bother to check on a nineteen-dollar purchase?

The phone chirped again. Behind him, a horn honked. A blue Mercedes crowded his bumper. Kevin punched the accelerator and picked up the phone. Red brake lights cut across all three lanes ahead. He slowed down—the Mercedes would have to chill. He pressed the green button.

"Hello?"

"Hello, Kevin."

Male voice. Low and breathy. Drawn out to accentuate each syllable.

"Hello?"

"How are you doing, my old friend? Quite well from what I can gather. How nice."

The world around Kevin faded. He brought the car to a halt behind the sea of red taillights, felt the pressure of the brakes as a distant abstraction. His mind focused on this voice on the phone.

"I . . . I'm sorry. I don't think—"

"It doesn't matter if you know me." Pause. "I know you. In fact, if you really think you're cut out for this seminary foolishness, I must say I know you better than you know yourself."

"I don't know who you think you are, but I don't have a clue what you're talking—"

"Don't be stupid!" the voice yelled into his ear. The man took a deep, scratchy breath. He spoke calmly again. "Forgive me, I really don't mean to yell, but you're not listening to me. It's time to quit pretending, Kevin. You think you have the whole world fooled, but you don't have me fooled. It's time to let the cat out of the bag. And I'm going to help you do it."

Kevin could hardly comprehend what he was hearing. Was this for real? It had to be a practical joke. Peter? Did Peter from Intro to Psych know him well enough to pull a stunt like this?

"Who . . . who is this?"

"You like games, don't you, Kevin?"

There was no way Peter could sound so condescending.

"Okay," Kevin said. "Enough. I don't know what—"

"Enough? Enough? No, I don't think so. The game is just starting. Only this one is not like the games you play with everyone else, Kevin. This one's for real. Will the real Kevin Parson please stand up? I thought about killing you, but I've decided this will be much better." The man paused, made a soft sound that sounded like a moan. "This . . . this will destroy you."

Kevin stared ahead, dumbfounded.

"You may call me Richard Slater. Ring any bells? Actually, I prefer Slater. And here's the game Slater would like to play. I will give you exactly three minutes to call the newspaper and confess your sin, or I will blow that silly Sable you call a car sky-high."

"Sin? What are you talking about?"

"That's the question, isn't it? I knew you'd forget, you stupid brick." Another pause. "Do you like riddles? Here's a riddle to jog your mind: *What falls but never breaks? What breaks but never falls?*"

"What? What's—"

"Three minutes, Kevin. Starting . . . now. Let the games begin."

The phone went dead.

For a moment, Kevin stared ahead, phone still plastered to his ear. A horn blared.

The cars ahead were moving. The Mercedes was impatient again. Kevin pressed the accelerator, and the Sable surged forward. He set the phone down on the passenger seat and swallowed, throat dry. He glanced at the clock. 12:03.

Okay, process. Stay calm and process. Did this really just happen? Of course it just happened! Some madman who called himself Slater just called my cell phone and threatened to blow up my car. Kevin grabbed the cell phone and stared at its face: "Unavailable, 00:39."

But was the threat real? Who would really blow up a car in the middle of a busy street over a riddle? Someone was trying to scare the snot out of him for some maniacal reason. Or some sicko had randomly chosen him as his next victim, someone who hated seminary students instead of prostitutes and really intended to kill him.

His thoughts spun crazily. What sin? He had committed his

sins, of course, but none that stood out immediately. *What falls but never breaks? What breaks but never falls?*

His pulse pounded in his ears. Maybe he should get off the road. Of course he should get off the road! If there was even a remote chance that Slater meant to carry out his threat . . .

For the first time, Kevin imagined the car actually filling with a blast of fire. A shaft of panic ripped down his spine. He had to get out! He had to call the police!

Not now. Now he had to get out. Out!

Kevin jerked his foot off the accelerator and slammed it down on the brake. The Sable's tires squealed. A horn shrieked. The Mercedes.

Kevin twisted his head and glanced through the rear window. Too many cars. He had to find a vacant spot, where flying shrapnel would do the least damage. He gunned the motor and shot forward. 12:05. But how many seconds? He had to assume three minutes would end at 12:06.

A dozen thoughts crowded his mind: thoughts of a sudden explosion, thoughts of the voice on the phone, thoughts of how the cars around him were reacting to the Sable jerking along the road. *What falls but never breaks? What breaks but never falls?*

Kevin looked around, frantic. He had to dump the car without blowing up the neighborhood. *It's not even going to blow, Kevin. Slow down and think.* He ran his fingers through his hair several times in quick succession.

He swung into the right lane, ignoring another horn. A Texaco station loomed on his right—not a good choice. Beyond the gas station, Dr. Won's Chinese Cuisine—hardly better. There were no parks along this section of road; residences packed the side streets. Ahead, lunch crowds bustled at McDonald's and Taco Bell. The clock still read 12:05. It had been 12:05 for too long.

Now true panic muddled his thinking. *What if it really does go*

off? It's going to, isn't it? God, help me! I've got to get out of this thing!
He grabbed at his seat belt buckle with a trembling hand. Released
the shoulder strap. Both hands back on the wheel.

A Wal-Mart sat back from the street a hundred yards to his left.
The huge parking lot was only half-filled. A wide greenway that
dipped at its center, like a natural ditch, surrounded the entire lot.
He made a critical decision: Wal-Mart or nothing.

Kevin leaned on his horn and cut back into the center lane with
a cursory glance in his mirror. A metallic screech made him duck—
he'd clipped a car. Now he was committed.

"Get out of my way! Get out!"

He motioned frantically with his left hand, succeeding only in
smashing his knuckles into the window. He grunted and swerved
into the far left lane. With a tremendous *thump* he crashed over a
six-inch-high median and then into oncoming traffic. It occurred to
him that being rammed head-on might be no better than blowing
up, but he was already in the path of a dozen oncoming cars.

Tires squealed and horns blared. The Sable took only one hit in
its right rear fender before shooting out the other side of the gauntlet.
Something from his car was dragging on the asphalt. He cut off a
pickup that was trying to exit the lot.

"Watch out! Get out of my way!"

Kevin roared into the Wal-Mart lot and glanced down at the
clock. Somewhere back there it had turned. 12:06.

To his right, traffic on Long Beach Boulevard had come to a
screeching halt. It wasn't every day that a car blasted through oncoming traffic like a bowling ball.

Kevin sped past several gaping customers and zeroed in on the
greenway. Not until he was on top of it did he see the curb. The Sable
blew a tire when it connected; this time Kevin's head struck the ceiling. A dull pain spread down his neck.

Out, out, out!

The car flew into the ditch and Kevin crammed the brake pedal to the floor. For a fleeting moment he thought he might roll. But the car slid to a jolting halt, its nose planted firmly in the opposite slope.

He grabbed at the door latch, shoved the door open, and dove to the turf, rolling on impact. He scrambled to his feet and raced up the slope toward the lot. At least a dozen onlookers headed his way from the sea of parked cars.

"Back! Get back!" Kevin waved his arms at them. "There's a bomb in the car. Get back!"

They stared at him for one moment of fixed horror. Then all but three turned and fled, screaming his warning.

Kevin swung his arms furiously at the others. "Get back, you idiots! There's a bomb!"

They ran. A siren wailed through the air. Someone had already called the cops.

Kevin had run a good fifty paces from the greenway before it occurred to him that the bomb hadn't gone off. What if there wasn't a bomb after all? He pulled up and whipped around, panting and trembling. Surely three minutes had come and gone.

Nothing.

Was it a practical joke after all? Whoever this caller was, he'd done almost as much damage through the threat alone as he would have by detonating an actual bomb.

Kevin glanced around. A gawking crowd had gathered on the street at a safe distance. The traffic had stalled and was backing up as far as he could see. Steam hissed from a blue Honda—presumably the one that had hit his right rear fender. There had to be a few hundred people staring at the nut who'd driven his car into the ditch. Except for the growing wail of sirens, the scene had grown eerily silent. He took a step back toward the car.

At least there was no bomb. A few angry motorists and some bent fenders, so what? He'd done the only thing he could do. And really, there still could be a bomb. He'd leave that for the police once he explained his story. Surely they would believe him. Kevin stopped. The car tipped into the dirt with its left rear tire off the ground. From here it all looked kind of stupid.

"You said bomb?" someone yelled.

Kevin looked back at a middle-aged man with white hair and a Cardinals baseball cap. The man stared at him. "Did you say there was a bomb?"

Kevin looked back at the car, feeling suddenly foolish. "I thought there—"

A deafening explosion shook the ground. Kevin instinctively crouched and threw his hands up to protect his face.

The bright fireball hung over the car; boiling black smoke rose into the sky. The red flame collapsed on itself with a soft *whomp*. Smoke billowed from the charred skeleton of what was only a moment ago his Sable.

Kevin dropped to one knee and stared, dumbstruck, wide-eyed.

2

WITHIN THIRTY MINUTES the crime scene was isolated and a full investigation launched, all in the purview of one Detective Paul Milton. The man was well built and walked like a gunslinger—a Schwarzenegger wannabe with a perpetual frown and blond bangs that covered his forehead. Kevin rarely found others intimidating, but Milton did nothing to calm his already shattered nerves.

Someone had just tried to kill him. Someone named Slater, who seemed to know quite a lot about him. A madman who had the forethought and malice to plant a bomb and then remotely detonate the device when his demands weren't met. The scene stood before Kevin like an abstract painting come to life.

Yellow tape marked a forty-yard perimeter, and within it several uniformed police officers gathered pieces of wreckage, labeled them with evidence tags, and stacked them in neat piles on a flatbed truck to be transported downtown. The crowd had grown to well over a hundred. Bewilderment was fixed on some faces; other spectators wildly gestured their version of the events. The only injury reported was a small cut on a teenage boy's right arm. As it turned out, one of the cars Kevin had clipped in his mad dash across the street was none other than the impatient Mercedes. Once the driver learned he'd been following a car bomb, however, his attitude improved significantly.

Traffic on Long Beach Boulevard still suffered from curiosity, but the debris had been cleared.

Three news vans were in the lot. If Kevin understood the situation correctly, his face and what was left of his car were being televised live throughout the Los Angeles Basin. A news helicopter hovered overhead.

A forensic scientist worked carefully over the twisted remains of the trunk, where the bomb had clearly resided. Another detective dusted for prints on what was left of the doors.

Kevin had spilled his story to Milton and now waited to be taken down to the station. By the way Milton glared at him, Kevin was sure the detective considered him a suspect. A simple examination of the evidence would clear his name, but one minor fact haunted him. His account of events omitted Slater's demand that he confess some sin.

What sin? The last thing he needed was for the police to begin digging into his past for some sin. Sin wasn't the point. The point was that Slater had given him a riddle and told him that phoning the newspaper with the riddle's answer would prevent Kevin from being blown sky-high. That's what he'd told them.

On the other hand, willfully withholding information in an investigation was a crime itself, wasn't it?

Dear God, someone just blew up my car! The fact sat like an absurd little lump on the edge of Kevin's mind. The front edge. He smoothed his hair nervously.

Kevin sat on a chair provided by one of the cops, tapping his right foot on the grass. Milton kept glancing at him as he debriefed the other investigators and took statements from witnesses. Kevin looked back at the car where the forensic team worked. What they could possibly learn from that wreckage escaped him. He stood unsteadily, took a deep breath, and walked down the slope toward the car.

The forensic scientist at the trunk was a woman. Black, petite, maybe Jamaican. She looked up and lifted an eyebrow. Pretty smile. But the smile didn't alter the scene behind her.

It was hard to believe that the twisted pile of smoldering metal and plastic had been his car.

"Whoever did this had one heck of a chip on his shoulder," she said. A badge on her shirt said she was Nancy Sterling. She looked back into what was left of the trunk and dusted the inside lip.

Kevin cleared his throat. "Can you tell me what kind of bomb it was?"

"Do you know bombs?" she asked.

"No. I know there's dynamite and C-4. That's about it."

"We'll know for sure back at the lab, but it looks like dynamite. Leaves no chemical signature that ties it to a specific batch once it's been detonated."

"Do you know how he set it off?"

"Not yet. Remote detonation, a timer, or both, but there's not too much left to go on. We'll eventually get it. We always do. Just be glad you got out."

"Boy, no kidding."

He watched her place tape over a dusted fingerprint, lift it, and seal the faint print on a card. She made a few notations on the card and went back to work with her flashlight.

"The only prints we've found so far are in places where we would expect to find yours." She shrugged. "Guy like this isn't stupid enough not to wear gloves, but you never know. Even the smartest make mistakes eventually."

"Well, I hope he made one. This whole thing's crazy."

"They usually are." She gave him a friendly smile. "You okay?"

"I'm alive. Hopefully I don't hear from him again." His voice shook as he spoke.

Nancy straightened and looked him in the eye. "If it's any consolation, if this was me, I'd be in a pool of tears on the sidewalk. We'll get this one, like I said; we always do. If he really wanted to kill you, you'd be dead. This guy's meticulous and calculating. He wants you alive. That's my take, for what it's worth."

She glanced up to where Detective Milton was talking to a reporter. "And don't let Milton get to you. He's a good cop. Full of himself, maybe. Case like this will send him through the roof."

"Why's that?"

"Publicity. Let's just say he has his aspirations." She smiled. "Don't worry. Like I said, he's a good detective."

As if on cue, Milton turned from the camera and walked straight for them.

"Let's go, cowboy. How long you here for, Nancy?"

"I have what I need."

"Preliminary findings?"

"I'll have them for you in half an hour."

"I need them now. I'm taking Mr. Parson in for a few questions."

"I'm not ready now. Half an hour, on your desk."

They held stares.

Milton snapped his fingers at Kevin. "Let's go." He headed for a late-model Buick on the street.

III

The station's air conditioner was under repair. After two hours in a stuffy conference room, Kevin's nerves finally began to lose the tremble brought on by the bomb.

An officer had fingerprinted him for comparisons with the prints lifted from the Sable, then Milton spent half an hour reviewing his story before abruptly leaving him alone. The ensuing twenty minutes of solitude gave Kevin plenty of time to rehash Slater's call while staring at a large brown smudge on the wall. But in the end he could make no more sense of the call than when it had initially come, which only made the whole mess more disturbing.

He shifted in his seat and tapped the floor with his foot. He'd spent his whole life not knowing, but this vulnerability was somehow different. A man named Slater had mistaken him for someone else and very nearly killed him. Hadn't he suffered enough in his life? Now he'd fallen into this, whatever *this* was. He was under the authorities' microscope. They would try to dig into his past. Try to understand it. But even Kevin didn't understand his past. He wasn't about to let them try.

The door banged open and Milton walked in.

Kevin cleared his throat. "Anything?"

Milton straddled a backward chair, slapped a folder down on the table, and drilled Kevin with his dark eyes. "You tell me."

"What do you mean?"

Milton blinked twice and ignored the question. "The FBI's bringing someone in on this. ATF wants a look, CBI, state police—the lot of them. But as far as I'm concerned, this is still my jurisdiction. Just because terrorists favor bombs doesn't mean every bomb that goes off is the work of terrorists."

"They think this is a terrorist?"

"I didn't say that. But Washington sees terrorists behind every tree these days, so they will definitely go on the hunt. It wouldn't surprise me to see the CIA picking through the files." Milton eyed him, unblinking, for a few long seconds, and then blinked three times in rapid succession. "What we have here is one sick puppy. What confuses me is why he picked you. Doesn't make sense."

"None of this makes sense."

Milton opened the file. "It'll take a couple days for the lab to complete their work on what little we found, but we have some preliminary findings, the most significant of which is nothing."

"What do you mean, nothing? A bomb about blew me to pieces!"

"No evidence of real investigative value. Let me summarize for you—maybe it'll shake something loose in that mind of yours." He eyed Kevin again.

"We have a man with a low, raspy voice who calls himself Richard Slater and who knows you well enough to target you. You, on the other hand, have no idea who he could possibly be." Milton paused for effect. "He constructs a bomb using common electronics available at any Radio Shack and dynamite, rendering the bomb virtually untraceable. Smart. He then plants that bomb in the trunk of your car. He calls you, knowing that you're in the car, and threatens to blow the car in three minutes if you can't solve a riddle. *What falls but never breaks? What breaks but never falls?* Right so far?"

"Sounds right."

"Due to some fast thinking and some fancy driving, you manage to drive the car to a relatively safe location and escape. As promised, the car blows up when you fail to solve the riddle and phone it in to the newspaper."

"That's right."

"Preliminary forensics tell us that whoever planted that bomb left no fingerprints. No surprises there—this guy's obviously not the village idiot. The explosion could have caused significant collateral damage. If you'd been on the street when it blew, we'd have some bodies at the morgue. That's enough to assume this guy's either pretty teed off or a raving lunatic, probably both. So we have smart and we have teed off. Follow?"

"Makes sense."

"What we're missing is the most obvious link in any case like this. Motivation. Without motivation, we've got squat. You have no idea whatsoever why anyone would want to harm you in any way? You have no enemies from the past, no recent threats against your well-being, no reason whatsoever to suspect why anyone on this earth might want to hurt you in any way?"

"He didn't try to hurt me. If he wanted to kill me, he could've just blown up the bomb."

"Exactly. So we're not only clueless as to why someone named Slater might *want* to blow up your car, we don't even know why he *did*. What did he accomplish?"

"He scared me."

"You don't scare someone by nuking their neighborhood. But okay, say he just wanted to scare you—we still don't have motivation. Who might want to scare you? Why? But you don't have a clue, right? Nothing you've ever done would give anyone any reason to hold anything against you."

"I—not that I know of. You want me to just make something up? I told you, I really don't know."

"You're leaving us high and dry, Kevin. High and dry."

"What about the phone call?" Kevin asked. "Isn't there a way to track it?"

"No. We can only track a call while it's being made. What's left of your cell is nothing more than a lump of plastic in an evidence bag anyway. If we're lucky, we'll have a shot next time." He closed the file folder. "You do know there'll be a next time, don't you?"

"Not necessarily." Actually, the thought had plagued him, but he refused to give it any serious consideration. Freak occurrences like this happened to people now and then; he could accept that. But a deliberate, drawn-out plot against him was unfathomable.

"There will be," Milton said. "This guy went to great lengths to pull this trick. He's after something, and we have to assume he didn't get it. Unless this was random or some kind of hellacious mistake, he'll try again."

"Maybe he mistook me for someone else."

"Not a chance. He's too methodical. He staked you out, wired the car, knew your moves, and blew it with careful deliberation."

True enough. Slater knew more than even the police knew. "He scared me. Maybe that's all he wanted."

"Maybe. I'm open to anything at this point." Milton paused. "You're sure there's nothing else you want to tell me? We don't have much on you. Never been married, no record, college grad, currently enrolled in seminary. Not the kind of person you'd expect to be involved in a crime of this nature."

Slater's demand crossed his mind.

"If I think of anything else, trust me, you'll be the first to know," Kevin said.

"Then you're free to go. I've put in an order to tap your phones as soon as we can clear the red tape—the boys should be out first thing tomorrow morning. I may also place a black and white outside your house in Signal Hill, but I doubt we're dealing with anyone who would approach your house."

"Tap my phones?" They were going to dig, weren't they? But what was he afraid of, as long as they didn't start prying about his past?

"With your permission, of course. You have any other cell phones?"

"No."

"If this guy makes contact in any other way, I want to hear about it immediately, you understand?"

"Of course."

"And pardon my insensitivity, but this isn't just about you anymore." His eyes twinkled. "We have reporters all over the place and they want an explanation. You might have some media attention. Don't talk to them. Don't even look at them. Stay focused, *capice?*"

"I'm the victim here, right? Why do I get the feeling I'm the one under investigation?"

Milton placed both of his palms on the table. The air conditioning kicked in above them. "Because you are. We have a monster out there and that monster has chosen you. We need to know why. That means we need to know more about you. We have to establish motivation. That's the way it works."

Kevin nodded. Actually, it made perfect sense.

"You're free to go." The detective handed him a card. "Call me. Use the cell number on the back."

"Thanks."

"Don't thank me yet. Do you always stare people down while you're talking to them, or are you hiding something?"

Kevin hesitated. "Has it ever occurred to you that you have a tendency to terrify your witnesses, Detective?"

The man did one of his flash-blink routines—four this time. Paul Milton might have political aspirations, but unless the people decided to turn the country over to vampires, Kevin didn't think the detective had a chance.

Milton stood and walked out.

3

A FRIENDLY COP NAMED STEVE ushered Kevin out the back and took him to the Hertz rental-car agency. Twenty minutes later Kevin held the keys to a Ford Taurus, nearly identical to the Sable that was no more.

"You're sure you're okay to drive?" Steve asked.

"I can drive."

"Okay. I'll follow you home."

"Thanks."

The home was an old two-story that Kevin had purchased five years earlier, when he was twenty-three, using some of the money from a trust fund established by his parents before the car accident. A drunk driver had slammed into Ruth and Mark Little's car when Kevin was only one—their deaths had reportedly been immediate. Their only son, Kevin, had been with a baby-sitter. The insurance settlement went to Ruth's sister, Balinda Parson, who received full custody of Kevin and subsequently adopted him. With a few strokes of a judge's pen, Kevin ceased being a Little and became instead a Parson. He had no memories of his real parents, no brothers or sisters, no possessions that he knew of. Only a trust account beyond anyone's reach until he turned eighteen, much to Aunt Balinda's chagrin.

As it turned out, he had no need to touch the money until he turned twenty-three, and by that time it had grown into a sum in excess of three hundred thousand dollars—a small gift to help him build a new life once he got around to discovering he needed one. He'd called Balinda "Mother" until then. Now he called her his aunt. That's all she was, thank God. Aunt Balinda.

Kevin pulled into the garage and stepped out of the Taurus. He waved as the cop drove by, then closed the garage door. The timed light slowly faded. He stepped into the laundry room, glanced at a full hamper, and made a mental note to finish his laundry before he went to bed. If there was one thing he hated, it was disorder. Disorder was the enemy of understanding, and he'd lived long enough without understanding. How meticulous and organized did a chemist have to be in order to understand DNA? How organized had NASA been in reaching out to understand the moon? One mistake and *boom*.

Mounds of dirty clothes reeked of disorder.

Kevin walked into the kitchen and set the keys on the counter. *Someone just blew up your car and you're thinking about doing laundry.* Well, what was he supposed to do? Crawl into the corner and hide? He'd just escaped death—he should be throwing a party. Let's toast life, comrades. We have faced the enemy and we have survived the bomb blast down by the Wal-Mart.

Please, get a grip. You're babbling like a fool here. Still, in light of the past several hours, it was a blessing to be alive, and gratefulness was warranted. *Great is thy faithfulness. Yes indeed, what a blessing we have received. Long live Kevin.*

He stared past the breakfast nook with its round oak dinette, through the picture window that overlooked the front yard. An oil pump sat dormant on a dirt hill beyond the street. This was his view. It's what two hundred thousand dollars bought you these days.

On the other hand, there was that hill. Kevin blinked. With a pair of binoculars, anyone with a mind to could park himself at the base of that oil pump and watch Kevin Parson organize his laundry in complete anonymity.

The trembles were suddenly back. Kevin rushed over to the window and quickly lowered the miniblinds. He spun around and scanned the main floor. Besides the kitchen and laundry room, there was the living room, the bathroom, and sliding glass doors, which led to a small lawn encircled by a white picket fence. The bedrooms were upstairs. From this angle he could see right through the living room into the backyard. For all he knew, Slater could have been watching him for months!

No. That was stupid. Slater knew of him, maybe something from his past—a demented motorist he'd hacked off on the highway. Maybe even—

No, it couldn't be that. He was just a kid then.

Kevin wiped his forehead with his arm and stepped into the living room. A large leather sofa and a recliner faced a forty-two-inch flat-screen television. What if Slater had actually been *in* here?

He scanned the room. Everything was in its place, the coffee table dusted, the carpet vacuumed, the magazines in their rack beside the recliner. Order. His *Introduction to Philosophy* text sat on the dinette beside him. Large two-by-three-foot travel posters covered the walls in a hopscotch arrangement. Sixteen in all, counting the ones upstairs. Istanbul, Paris, Rio, the Caribbean, a dozen others. An unknowing person might think he ran a travel agency, but to Kevin the images were simply gateways to the real world, places he would one day visit to broaden his horizon.

To expand his understanding.

Even if Slater had been here, there would be no way to tell, short of dusting for prints. Maybe Milton should send out a team.

Easy, boy. This is an isolated incident, not a full-scale invasion. No need to tear the house down yet.

Kevin paced to the couch and then back. He picked up the remote control and turned on the television. He preferred to spin through the channels on the huge Sony picture tube rather than settle on any particular channel for long. The TV was yet another window into life—a wonderful montage of the world in all of its beauty and ugliness. Didn't matter; it was real.

He flipped the channels, one every other second or so. Football, a cooking show, a woman in a brown dress showing how to plant geraniums, a Vidal Sassoon commercial, Bugs Bunny. He paused on Bugs. *I say, what's up, doc?* Bugs Bunny had more truth to speak about life than the humans on the tube. "If you stay in the hole too long, it becomes your tomb." Wasn't that the truth. That was Balinda's problem—she was still in the hole. He flipped the station. The news . . .

The news. He stared at the aerial images, fascinated by the surreal shots of the smoldering car. His car. "Wow," he mumbled. "That's me." He shook his head in disbelief and ruffled his hair. "That's really me. I survived that."

What falls but never breaks? What breaks but never falls? He will call again. You do know that, don't you?

Kevin clicked the tube off. A psychobabblist once told him that his mind was unusual. He'd tested with an IQ in the top one percentile—no problems there. In fact, if there was a problem—and Dr. Swanlist the psychobabblist certainly didn't think there was a problem at all—it was that his mind still processed information at a rate normally found in others during their formative years. Age normally slowed down the synapses, which explained why old folks could be downright scary behind the wheel. Kevin tended to view the world through the eyes of an adult with the innocence of a child. Which was really psychobabble for nothing of any practical value, regardless of how excited Dr. Swanlist got.

He looked at the stairs. What if Slater had gone up there?

He walked to the stairs and took them two at a time. One master bedroom on the left, one guest bedroom that he used as an office to his right, and one bathroom between the two. He headed for the guest bedroom, flipped on the light switch, and poked his head in. A desk with a computer, a chair, and several bookcases, one with a dozen textbooks and the rest heavy with over two hundred novels. He'd discovered the miracles of stories in his early teens, and ultimately they had set him free. There was no better way to understand life than to live it—if not through your own life, then through another's. There was once a man who owned a field. Brilliant, brilliant, brilliant. Not to read was to turn your back on the wisest minds.

Kevin scanned the fiction titles. Koontz, King, Shakespeare, Card, Stevenson, Powers—an eclectic collection. He'd read the books eagerly in his recent renaissance. To say Aunt Balinda didn't approve of novels was like saying the ocean is wet. She would feel no better about his philosophy and theology textbooks.

The travel posters in this room boasted of Ethiopia, Egypt, South Africa, and Morocco. Brown, brown, green, brown. That was it.

He closed the door and walked into the bathroom. Nothing. The man in the mirror had brown hair and blue eyes. Gray in bad light. Somewhat attractive if he was any judge, but generally average looking. *Not the kind of person stalked by a psychopath.* He grunted and hurried to his room.

The bed was made, the dresser drawers closed, the shade open. All in order. *You see, you've been hearing ghosts.*

Kevin sighed and peeled off his dress shirt and slacks. Thirty seconds later he'd changed into a pale blue T-shirt and jeans. He had to get back to a semblance of normalcy here. He tossed the dress shirt into the laundry bin, hung up his trousers, and headed for the door.

A flash of color on the nightstand caught his eye. Pink. A pink ribbon peeked out from behind the lamp.

Kevin's heart responded before his mind did, pounding into overdrive. He walked forward and stared at the thin pink hair ribbon. He'd seen it before. He could swear he'd seen this ribbon. A long time ago. Samantha had given him one exactly like it once, and it had gone missing years ago.

He spun around. Had Sam heard about the incident and driven down from Sacramento? She'd phoned recently but hadn't mentioned coming to visit him. The last time he'd seen his childhood friend was when she'd left for college at age eighteen, ten years earlier. She'd spent the last few years in New York working in law enforcement and had recently moved to Sacramento for employment with the California Bureau of Investigation.

But this ribbon was hers!

"Samantha?" His voice echoed softly in the room.

Silence. Of course—he'd already checked the place. Unless . . .

He snatched up the ribbon, ran for the stairs, and descended them in three long strides. "Samantha!"

It took Kevin exactly twenty seconds to search the house and rule out the possibility that his long-lost friend had paid him a visit and was hiding like they had as children. Unless she had come, left the ribbon, and then departed, intending to call him later. Would she do that? Under any other circumstance it would be a wonderful surprise.

Kevin stood in the kitchen, perplexed. If she'd left the ribbon, she would have left a message, a note, a phone call, something.

But there was no note. His black VTech phone sat on the kitchen counter. Number of messages: a big red "0."

What if Slater had left the ribbon? He should call Milton. Kevin ran a hand through his hair. Milton would want to know about the ribbon, which meant telling him about Samantha, which meant opening up the past. He couldn't open up the past, not after running from it for so long.

The silence felt thick.

Kevin looked at the pink ribbon trembling slightly in his hand and sat slowly at the dinette. The past. So long ago. He closed his eyes.

III

Kevin was ten years old when he first saw the pretty girl from down the street. That was a year before they met the boy who wanted to kill them.

Meeting Sam two days after his birthday was his best present. Ever. His brother, Bob, who was really his cousin, had given him a yo-yo, which he really did like, but not as much as meeting Samantha. He would never tell Bob that, of course. In fact, he wasn't sure he'd tell Bob about Samantha at all. It was his secret. Bob might be eight years older than Kevin, but he was a bit slow—he'd never catch on.

The moon was full that night, and Kevin was in bed by seven o'clock. He always went to bed early. Sometimes before supper. But tonight he'd been under the covers for what seemed like an hour, and he couldn't sleep. He thought maybe it was too bright with the moonlight coming through the white shade. He liked it dark when he slept. Pitch-dark, so he couldn't even see his hand when he put it an inch from his nose.

Maybe if he put some newspapers or his blanket over the window, it would be dark enough.

He climbed out of bed, pulled off the gray wool blanket, and hefted it up to hook over the rod. Wow, it was really bright out there. He glanced back at his bedroom door. Mother was in bed.

The shade hung from a spring-loaded roll at the top, a smudged sheet of canvas that covered the small window most of the time. There was nothing to look out at but the backyard anyway. Kevin lowered the blanket and lifted the bottom edge of the shade.

A dull glow shone over the ashes in the backyard. He could see the doghouse on the left, like it was day. He could even see each board in the old fence that ran around the house. Kevin lifted his eyes to the sky. A bright moon that glowed like a light bulb smiled down at him and he smiled back. Wow!

He started to lower the shade when something else caught his eye. A bump on one of the fence boards. He blinked and looked at it. No, not a bump! A—

Kevin dropped the shade. Someone was out there, staring back at him!

He scrambled off his bed and backed to the wall. Who would be staring at him in the middle of the night? Who would be staring at him period? It was a kid, wasn't it? One of the neighborhood boys or girls.

Maybe he just thought he saw someone. He waited a few minutes, lots of time for whoever it was to move on, and then he worked up the courage for just one more peek.

This time he barely lifted the shade so that he could just see over the sill. She was still there! Kevin thought his chest might explode from the fright, but he kept looking. She couldn't see him now; the shade was too low. It was a girl; he could see that much. A young girl, maybe his age, with long blonde hair and a face that would have to be pretty, he thought, although he couldn't really see any details of her face.

And then she dropped from sight and disappeared.

Kevin could hardly sleep. The next night, Kevin couldn't resist peeking out, but the girl was gone. Gone for good.

He thought.

Three days later he was in bed again, and this time he knew he had been lying awake for at least an hour without being able to sleep. Mother had made him take a very, very long nap that afternoon and he just wasn't tired. The moon wasn't as bright tonight but he had covered up the window to make it darker anyway. After a long time he decided that he might be better off with more light. Maybe if he could trick his mind into thinking it was the next morning already, it would be tired after not sleeping all night.

He stood, tore off the wool blanket, and sent the shade flying up with a flip of his wrist.

A small, round face had its nose against the window. Kevin jumped back and rolled off the bed, terrified. He scrambled to his feet. She was there! Here! At his window! The girl from the other night was right here, spying on him.

Kevin almost screamed. The girl was smiling. She lifted a hand and waved as if she recognized him and had just stopped by to say hi.

He glanced at the door. Hopefully Mother hadn't heard. He turned back to the girl in the window. She was mouthing something to him now, motioning for him to do something.

He could only stand there and stare, frozen.

She was motioning for him to lift the window! No way! And he couldn't anyway; it was screwed shut.

She didn't look frightening, really. In fact, she was actually very nice looking. Her face was pretty and her hair was long. Why was he so scared of her? Maybe he shouldn't be. Her face was so . . . kind.

Kevin glanced again at the door and then slid back onto the end of his bed. She waved again, and this time he waved back. She was pointing at the window sill, motioning again. He followed her hands and suddenly understood. She was telling him to unscrew the window! He looked at the single screw that fastened the sash in place and for the first time realized that he could take it out. All he had to do was find something to turn the screw with. Something like a penny. He had some of those.

Suddenly energized by the idea, Kevin grabbed one of the pennies from an old tin can on his floor and placed it in the screw. It came loose. He unwound it until it was out.

The girl jumped up and down and motioned for him to lift the window. Kevin gave his bedroom door one last look and then yanked on the window. It flew up silently. He knelt on his bed, face to face with the girl.

"Hi," she whispered, smiling from ear to ear.

"H . . . hi," he said.

"Do you want to come out and play?"

Play? Fear replaced excitement. Behind him the house was quiet. "I can't come out."

"Sure you can. Just crawl out the window. It's easy."

"I don't think I'm supposed to. I . . ."

"Don't worry, your mother won't even know. You can just climb back in later and screw the window shut again. They're all sleeping anyway, right?"

"You know my mother?"

"Everyone has a mother."

So she didn't know Mother. She was just saying that she knew mothers didn't like their kids sneaking out. As if all mothers were like his mother.

"Right?" she asked.

"Right."

What if he did go out? What harm would it do? Mother had never actually told him not to climb out of the window at night, at least not in those words.

"I don't know. No, I really can't."

"Sure you can. I'm a girl and you're a boy. Girls and boys play together. Don't you know that?"

He didn't know what to say. He'd never played with a girl before, that was for sure.

"Just hop down."

"Are . . . are you sure it's safe?"

She reached out a hand. "Here, I'll help you."

He wasn't sure what made him do it; his hand just seemed to reach out for hers on its own. His fingers touched hers and they were warm. He had never touched a girl's hand before. The strange sensation filled him with a good feeling he'd never felt before. Butterflies.

Ten seconds later, Kevin was out of the window trembling under a bright moon next to a girl about his own height.

"Follow me," the girl said. She walked for the fence, lifted a loose board, stepped out, and motioned him on. With one last anxious look back at his window, he followed.

Kevin stood beyond the fence shivering in the night, but not from fear so much as from excitement again.

"My name's Samantha, but you can call me Sam. What's yours?"

"Kevin."

Sam stuck out her hand. "Glad to meet you, Kevin." He took her hand and shook it. But she didn't let go. Instead she led him away from his house.

"We moved here from San Francisco about a month ago. I didn't know any children lived in this house, but a week ago I heard my parents talking. Your parents are pretty private people, huh?"

"Yeah, I guess."

"My parents let me walk down to the park at the end of the street where a lot of kids hang out. It's lighted, you know. You want to go down there?"

"Now?"

"Sure, why not? It's safe. My dad's a policeman—if it wasn't safe, believe me, he would know."

"No. I . . . I can't. I really don't want to."

She shrugged. "Suit yourself. I was on my way down the other night when I looked over your fence and saw you. I guess I was spying. Do you mind?"

"No."

"Good, because I think you're cute."

Kevin didn't know what to say.

"Do you think I'm pretty?" She spun away from him and twirled around like a ballerina. She wore a pink dress and pink ribbons in her hair.

"Yes, I think you're pretty," he said.

She stopped her twirling, looked at him for a moment, and then giggled. "I can already tell that we're going to be wonderful friends. Would you like that?"

"Yes."

She skipped back, grabbed his hand, and dragged him into a run. Kevin laughed. He did like her. He liked her very much. More, in fact, than anyone he could ever remember liking.

"Where are we going?"

"Don't worry, no one will know. No one will even see us. I promise."

For the next hour Sam talked to him about her family and their house, which was three down from his. She went to something she called a private school and didn't get home until six every night, she said. Her dad couldn't afford it on his income, but her grandmother had left a trust fund for her and the only way they could use any of the money was if she went to a private school. The kids there weren't really her type. Neither were most of the neighborhood kids. When she grew up, she was going to be a cop like her dad. That's probably why she liked to sneak around, because cops do that to catch the bad guys. She asked Kevin some questions but then backed off when she saw that he was shy.

Sam liked him—he could tell. It was the first time Kevin had felt that kind of friendship from anyone.

At about eight o'clock Samantha told him that she had to get home or her parents would worry. They squeezed back through the fence and she helped him climb back through his window.

"This will be our secret, okay? No one will know. If you hear me tapping on your window at about seven o'clock, you'll know that I can play if you want to. Deal?"

"You mean we can do this again?"

"Why not? As long as you don't get caught, right?"

"Get caught?" Kevin looked at his window, suddenly fighting an urge to throw up. He wasn't sure why he felt sick; he only knew that if Mother found out she wouldn't be happy. Things went funny when Mother wasn't happy. How could he have done this? He never did things without asking. Never.

Sam put her hand on his shoulder. "Don't be afraid, Kevin. No one will know. I like you and I want to be your friend. Would you like that?"

"Yes."

Sam giggled and flashed her bright blue eyes. "I want to give you something." She pulled one of the pink ribbons from her hair and handed it to him. "Don't let your mom find it."

"This is for me?"

"So you don't forget me."

There was no chance of that. No way.

Sam held out her hand. "Until next time, partner. Slip me some skin."

He looked at her, confused.

"My dad says that. It's a street thing. Here, like this." She took his hand and slid her palm on his. "See ya. Don't forget to screw your window down."

Then Sam was gone.

Two nights later she was back. With more butterflies in his stomach and shrill warning bells ringing in his mind, Kevin slipped out his window.

Mother would find out. Sam took his hand and that made him feel warm, but Mother would find out. The ringing in his head wouldn't stop.

III

Kevin snapped out of the memories. A shrill bell screamed. He jerked to the sound. It took him a moment to make the transition from the past.

The black phone on the counter rang. It was a modern contraption with an old-style bell that sounded like an old desk phone. Kevin stared at it, suddenly unsure whether he wanted to pick it up. He rarely received phone calls; few people had reason to call him. Mostly telemarketers.

He'd set the answering machine for six rings. What if it was Samantha? Or Detective Milton?

The phone rang again. *Answer it, Kevin. Of course. Answer it.*

He stepped over to the counter and snatched the receiver from its cradle. "Hello?"

"Hello, Kevin. Did you find my little gift?"

Kevin went numb. Slater.

"I'll take that as a yes. We've had an eventful day, haven't we? First a little phone call and then a little boom and now a little gift. And all within four hours. Makes all the waiting worth it, don't you think?"

"Who are you?" Kevin demanded. "How do you know me?"

"Who am I? I am your worst nightmare. I promise you, you'll agree soon enough. How do I know you? Tsk, tsk, tsk. The fact that you even have to ask justifies everything I have in mind."

It had to be the boy! *God in heaven, save me!* Kevin slumped slowly to the floor. This couldn't be happening. "Oh God—"

"Not God, Kevin. Definitely not God. Now, I want you to listen carefully, because I'm going to give you a lot of information in a short time. Every single bit is critical if you want to survive this little game of ours. Do you understand?"

Kevin's mind raced through the years, searching for someone who might have sounded like this man, anyone who might have any reason at all to speak to him this way. Anyone but the boy.

"Answer me, you creep!" Slater said.

"Yes."

"Yes, what?"

"Yes, I understand."

"Yes, you understand what?"

"That I have to listen carefully," Kevin said.

"Good. From now on you answer me when I ask you a question, and you speak only when I say you speak. Do you understand?"

"Yes."

"Fine. There are only three rules to our game. Remember all of them. One, you say nothing to the cops about my riddles or my phone calls until after the time has passed. Then you may tell them all you want. This is personal—having the whole city coming unglued over a little bomb that might go off wouldn't be useful. Are we clear?"

"Yes."

"Two, you do exactly what I say, or I promise you will pay. Abundantly clear?"

"Why are you doing—"

"Answer me!"

"Yes!"

"Three, the riddles keep coming until you confess. As soon as you do, I go away. It's that simple. One, two, three. Get it through your thick skull and we'll do fine. Understand?"

"Please, if you'll just tell me what to confess, I'll confess. Why are you using riddles? Can I confess without solving riddles?"

Slater remained silent for a moment. "The answer to the riddles and the confession are the same. That's the first clue and that's the last clue. The next time you try to squeeze something out of me, I'll walk in there and cut off one of your ears, or something as interesting. What's the matter, Kevin? You're the brilliant seminary student. You're the smart little philosopher. A little riddle scares you?"

The riddles and the confession are the same. So then maybe it wasn't the boy.

"This isn't fair—"

"Did I ask you to speak?"

"You asked me a question."

"Which requires an answer, not a lecture. For that you will pay an extra little price. I've decided to kill to help you along with your understanding."

Kevin was aghast. "You . . . you just decided—"

"Maybe two killings."

"No, I'm sorry. I won't speak."

"Better. And just so we're clear, you of all people are in no position to talk about being fair. You may have that old fool at the seminary fooled, you may have all the old ladies at that church thinking you're a sweet, young fellow, but I know you, boy. I know how your mind works and I know what you're capable of. Guess what? I'm about to let the snake out of his dungeon. Before we're done here, the world is going to know the whole ugly truth, boy. Open the drawer in front of you."

The drawer? Kevin stood and looked at the utility drawer beneath the counter. "The drawer?"

"Open it and pull out the cell phone."

Kevin eased the drawer out. A small silver cell phone sat in the pencil tray. He picked it up.

"From now on you keep this phone with you at all times. It's set to vibrate—no need to wake up the neighbors every time I call.

Unfortunately, I won't be able to call you on your home phone once the cops bug it. Understand?"

"Yes."

That Slater had been in Kevin's house was no longer open to question. What else did Slater know?

"There's one other little matter that needs our attention before we continue. I have good news for you, Kevin." Slater's voice thickened and his breathing grew heavier. "You're not alone in this. I intend to bring someone else down with you. Her name is Samantha." Pause. "You do remember Samantha, don't you? You should; she called you recently."

"Yes."

"You like her, don't you, Kevin?"

"She's a friend."

"You don't have a lot of friends."

"No."

"Consider Samantha as my insurance. If you fail me, she dies."

"You can't do that!"

"Shut up! Shut up, you foul-mouthed lying punk! Listen carefully. *In life he's your friend, but death is the end.* That's your little bonus riddle for being so dense. You have exactly thirty minutes to solve it or your best friend will indeed go boom."

"What friend? I thought this was about me! How will you even know if I've solved the riddle?"

"Call Samantha. Ask for her help. The two of you can put your stinking heads together and figure it out."

"I'm not even sure I can reach Samantha. How will you know what I tell her?"

Slater's deep chuckle filled the phone. "You don't do what I'm doing without learning the tools of the trade, boy. I have ears and eyes everywhere. Did you know that with the right toys you can understand a man inside a house from over a thousand yards away? Seeing is even easier. The clock is ticking. You're down to twenty-nine minutes and thirty-two seconds. I suggest you hustle."

The line clicked.

"Slater?"

Nothing. Kevin shoved the phone into its cradle and looked at his watch. 4:15. There was going to be another explosion in thirty minutes, this time involving his best friend, which made no sense because he had no best friends. *In life he's your friend, but death is the end.* No cops.

4

FBI SPECIAL AGENT JENNIFER PETERS hurried down the hall, her pulse hammering with an urgency she hadn't felt for three months. The Long Beach bomb report had come in several hours ago, but she hadn't been told. Why? She rounded the corner and shoved the Los Angeles bureau chief's door open.

Frank Longmont sat at his desk, phone pressed to his ear. He didn't bother looking up at her. He knew, didn't he? The weasel had purposefully stalled.

"Sir?"

Frank held up his hand. Jennifer crossed her arms while the chief talked on. Only then did she notice two other agents, whom she didn't recognize, seated at the small conference table to her left. Looked like East Coast stiffs. Their eyes lingered. She turned from them and steadied her breathing.

Her blue business suit had only the smallest of slits up her left leg, but she couldn't shake the certainty that what was decent, even conservative in her mind, still drew frequent glances from men. Her hair was dark, to her shoulders, and her eyes a soft hazel. She had the kind of face others might spend their lives trying to imitate—symmetrical with soft skin and rich color. There was no disguising her physical beauty. *Beauty is a gift,* her father used to say. *Just don't flaunt it.* A gift. Jennifer had found beauty just as often a handicap. Many people of both genders had difficulty accepting both beauty and excellence from the same person.

To compensate, she tried her best to ignore her appearance and instead focus on excellence. *Brains are also a gift,* her father used to say. And God had not been stingy. At age thirty, Jennifer Peters was regarded as one of the best forensic psychologists on the West Coast.

But in the end it hadn't mattered. Her excellence hadn't saved her brother. Which left her as what? A beautiful woman who was much more interested in being smart than beautiful, but who wasn't so smart after all. A nothing. A nothing whose failure had killed her brother. And now a nothing who was being ignored by the bureau chief.

Frank set down his phone and turned to the two men at the table. "Excuse us for a moment, gentlemen."

The two agents exchanged glances, rose, and left. Jennifer waited for the click of the door latch before speaking.

"Why wasn't I told?"

Frank spread his hands. "You obviously were."

She glared at him. "It's been five hours! I should already be in Long Beach."

"I've been on the phone with the Long Beach police chief. We'll be there first thing in the morning."

We'll? He was being cagey. She walked to his desk, hands on hips. "Okay, cut the innuendos. What's going on?"

Frank smiled. "Please, Jennifer, take a seat. Take a breath."

She didn't like the tone of his voice. *Easy, girl. Your life's in this man's hands.*

"It's him, isn't it?"

"We don't have enough yet. Sit." They locked stares. She sat in one of the large chairs facing the desk and crossed her legs.

Frank tapped his finger on the desk absently. "I was thinking of letting Craig take over the on-site investigation. Let you work here in a coordination role."

Jennifer felt her face flush. "This is my case! You can't just remove me!"

"Did I say remove? I don't remember using that word. And if you haven't noticed in your six years with the bureau, we juggle agents quite frequently for a host of reasons."

"No one knows this case like I do," she said. The chief wouldn't actually do this. She was way too valuable on the case!

"One of those reasons is the relationship between agent and critical parties, including victims."

"I've spent a year breathing down this guy's neck," Jennifer said. She let the desperation creep into her voice. "For heaven's sake, Frank. You can't do this to me."

"He killed your brother, Jennifer."

She stared at him. "This suddenly becomes germane? The way I see it, the fact that he killed Roy gives me a right to hunt him down."

"Please, I know this is hard, but you have to try to look at the situation objectively. Roy was the killer's last victim. We haven't heard a peep in the three months since. You ever ask yourself why he chose Roy?"

"It happened," she said. She had, of course. The answer was patently obvious but unspoken.

"He kills four other people in the Sacramento area before you start to close in. You come within five minutes of apprehending him. He takes offense and chooses someone close to you. Roy. He plays his little game of riddles and then kills Roy when you come up short."

Jennifer just stared at him.

The chief held up one hand. "No, that didn't come out like I—"

"You're saying the Riddle Killer killed my brother because of me? You have the audacity to sit there and accuse me of playing a part in my own brother's execution?"

"I said that's not what I meant. But he likely chose Roy because of your involvement."

"And did that fact affect my performance?"

He hesitated.

Jennifer closed her eyes and drew a careful breath.

"You're putting words in my mouth," Frank said. "Look, I'm sorry, really I am. I can only imagine how it was for you. And I can't think of anyone who is more qualified to go after this nut, but the equation changed when he killed your brother. He has it out for you. You're a critical party, and frankly your life's in danger."

She opened her eyes. "Don't patronize me with the danger non-sense, Frank. We signed on for danger. This is precisely what the Riddle Killer wants, you realize. He knows I'm his biggest threat. He also knows that you'll likely pull me for the very reasons you're citing. He *wants* me off the case."

She said it with a strong voice, but only because she'd long ago learned to stuff emotion. For the most part. The bureau did that. The better part of her wanted to scream at Frank and tell him where he could put his objectiveness.

He sighed. "We don't even know this is the same killer. Could be a copy cat; could be unrelated. We need someone here to piece this together carefully."

The Riddle Killer had started playing his little games nearly a year ago. He picked his victims for a variety of reasons and then stalked them until he knew their routines intimately. The riddle usually came out of thin air. He gave the victims a specified amount of time to solve the riddle under the threat of death. Inventive and cold-blooded.

Her brother, Roy Peters, had been a thirty-three-year-old attorney newly employed in Sacramento by Bradsworth and Bixx. A brilliant man with a wonderful wife, Sandy, who worked for the Red Cross. More importantly, Roy and Jennifer had been inseparable right up to college when they'd both pursued law. Roy had bought Jennifer her first bicycle, not because her father couldn't, but because he wanted to. Roy had taught her to drive. Roy had checked out every boy she'd ever dated, often to her feigned chagrin. Her brother had been her soul mate, the standard no other man could measure up to.

Jennifer had replayed the events leading up to his death a thousand times, knowing each time that she could have prevented it. If only she'd pieced the riddle together twenty minutes earlier. If only she'd gotten to him sooner. If only she hadn't been assigned to the case.

Until this moment, no one had even hinted at blame—to do so would be beneath the Bureau. But her own blame had beaten her raw over the last three months. The fact was, if she had not been on the case, Roy would be alive. Nothing would ever change that. In some way she *was* personally responsible for the death of her brother.

Her mission in life was now painfully simple. She would stop at nothing to remove the Riddle Killer from the face of the earth.

If Frank knew the depth of her obsession, he might have pulled her from the case long ago. Her survival depended on her ability to remain calm and reasonable.

"Sir, I'm begging you. You have to let me lead the investigation. He hasn't killed yet. He's growing bold, but if we let him think he can play the FBI, he'll grow bolder. Pulling me from the case would send the wrong message."

The thought dawned on her only as she spoke it. By the look on Frank's face, he hadn't considered that angle yet.

She pressed. "I've had three months to grieve, Frank. Last time I took inventory I was lucid. You owe it to the public to let me go. No one stands a better chance of stopping him before he kills again."

Frank looked at her in silence.

"You know I'm right."

"You've got tenacity; I'll give you that. Tell me that you have no leanings to any kind of personal vendetta."

"I want him out of circulation. If that's personally motivated, so be it."

"That's not what I mean."

"You think I would compromise justice with a quick trigger?" she said with a bite of sarcasm. "Or withhold information from other agencies to get the collar myself? Do you think so little of me?"

"None of us are exempt from strong emotional pulls. If my brother had been killed, I'm not sure I wouldn't turn in my badge and go after him outside the law."

She wasn't sure what to say. She'd considered the same a dozen times. Nothing would give her more satisfaction than pulling the trigger herself when it came right down to it.

"I'm not you," she finally said, but she wasn't so sure.

He nodded. "You don't see the kind of love you shared with your brother much these days, you know. I've always respected you for that."

"Thank you. Roy was an incredible person. No one will ever replace him."

"No, I guess not. Okay, Jennifer. You win. You'll have a half-dozen agencies climbing around; I want you to work with them. I'm not saying you have to spend all day playing footsie with them, but at least give them the respect of keeping them up to date."

Jennifer stood. "Of course."

"Detective Paul Milton will be expecting you first thing. He's not the gun-shy type if you know what I mean. Be nice."

"I'm incapable of anything less."

5

KEVIN CLEARED THE FIRST FOUR STAIRS in his first step. He tripped on the last and sprawled on the landing. "Come on!" He grunted and jumped to his feet. Samantha's phone number was on his desk—please say it was still on his desk. He crashed through the door. His best friend. Who could that possibly be?

He shuffled through papers and knocked a hermeneutics textbook off the desk. He'd left it right here on top; he could swear it! Maybe he should just call Milton. Where was that number!

Slow down, Kevin. Gather yourself. This is a thinking game, not a race. No, a race too. A thinking race.

He took a deep breath and put his hand to his face. *I can't call the cops. Slater will hear the call. He's got the house bugged or something. Okay. He wants me to call Samantha. This is about her too. I need Samantha. Only two minutes have passed. Twenty-eight left. Plenty of time. First thing, find Sam's number. Think. You wrote it down on a white piece of paper. You used it to call her last week and you put the paper somewhere safe because it was important to you.*

Under the phone.

He lifted the desk phone and saw the white slip. Thank God! He grabbed the receiver and punched in the number with an unsteady hand. It rang. It rang again.

"Please, please pick up—"

"Hello?"

"Hello, Sam?"

"Who's calling?"

"It's me."

"Kevin? What's wrong? You sound—"

"I have a problem, Sam. Oh dear God, I've got a problem! Did you hear about the bomb that went off down here today?"

"A bomb? You're kidding, right? No, I didn't hear of a bomb; I have this week off, unpacking from the move. What happened?"

"Some guy who calls himself Slater blew up my car."

Silence.

"Sam?" Kevin's voice trembled. He suddenly thought he might start to cry. His vision swam. "Sam, please, I need your help."

"Someone named Slater blew up your car," she repeated slowly. "Tell me more."

"He called me on my cell phone and gave me three minutes to confess a sin, which he said I would know by a riddle. *What falls but never breaks? What breaks but never falls?* I managed to get the car into a ditch by a Wal-Mart and it blew up."

"Holy . . . You're serious? Was anyone hurt?"

"No. I just—"

"Is the FBI investigating? Good night, you're right—I just turned on the television. It's all over the news up here."

"Samantha, listen! I just got another call from this guy. He says I have thirty minutes to solve another riddle or he's going to blow up another bomb."

Sam seemed to switch into another mode immediately. "Riddles. You've got to be kidding. How long ago?"

He glanced at his watch. "Five minutes."

"You've already reported it?"

"No. He said I can't tell the cops."

"Nonsense! Call the detective in charge right now. Get off the phone with me and call them, you hear me, Kevin? You can't let this guy play his game. Take his game away from him."

"He said that this bomb will kill my best friend, Sam. And I know he can hear me. This guy seems to know everything. For all I know he's watching me right now!"

"Okay, calm down. Slow down." She paused, reconsidering. "Okay, don't call the cops. Who's Slater talking about? Who are your friends down there?"

"I . . . That's the problem. I really don't have any."

"Sure you do. Just give me three people you would consider friends and I'll get the local authorities on them. Come on, let's go."

"Well, there's the dean at the school, Dr. John Francis. The priest at my parish—Bill Strong." He searched his mind for another, but nothing came. He had plenty of acquaintances, but really no one he'd call a true friend, much less a best friend.

"Okay. Good enough. Hold on a second."

She put the phone down.

Kevin lifted his T-shirt and wiped the sweat from his face. 4:24. He had until 4:45. *Come on, Samantha!* He stood and paced. *In life he's your friend, but death is the end. What—*

"Kevin?"

"Here."

"Okay, I put in an anonymous call to the Long Beach police warning that Francis and Strong could be in immediate danger. Enough to get them moved from wherever they are, which is all we can do."

"You talked to Milton?"

"He's the lead? No, but I'm sure he'll get the message. How sure are you that this guy will come unglued if you talk to the authorities?"

"He's already unglued! He said I could only speak when spoken to and he's doing this because I said something."

"Okay. You'll probably get a call any minute from the police, checking on this threat I've just reported. You have call waiting?"

"Yes."

"Ignore the beep. If you talk to the police when they call, Slater will know. What's the riddle?"

"There's something else, Sam. Slater knows you. In fact, he suggested I call you. I . . . I think he might be someone we both know."

The phone sounded hollow for a few breaths.

"He knows me. What's the sin he wants you to confess?"

"I don't know!"

"Okay, we can cover this later. We're running out of time. What's the riddle?"

"In life he's your friend, but death is the end."

"Opposites."

"Opposites?"

"*What falls but never breaks? What breaks but never falls?* Answer: Night and day. What in life is your friend, but death is the end, I don't know. But they're both opposites. Any ideas?"

"No. I don't have a clue." Night falls, day breaks. Clever. "This is *crazy!*" He ground the last word out between his teeth.

She was quiet for a moment. "If we knew the sin, we could infer the riddle. What sin are you hiding, Kevin?"

He stopped pacing. "None. Lots! What do you want me to do, spill my whole life of sins to the world? That seems to be what he wants."

"But there must be something you did that sent this guy to the moon. Think of that and think of this riddle. Anything connect?"

Kevin thought about the boy. But there was no connection between the riddles and the boy. Couldn't be him. Nothing else came to mind.

"No."

"Then let's go back to your best friend."

"You're my best friend, Sam."

"Sweet. But this guy wanted you to call me, right? He knows I would be warned, and if he knows me, he also knows that I have the capability of escaping his threat. I think I'm safe for now. There's another best friend you're missing. Something more obvious—"

"Wait! What if it's not a person?" *That's it!* He glanced at his watch. Fifteen minutes to go. Barely enough time to get there. Call waiting sounded in his ear. That would be the police.

"Ignore it," Sam said. "Such as—"

"I'll call you back, Sam. I don't have time to explain."

"I'm coming down. I'll be there in five hours."

"You . . . you are?"

"I'm on leave, remember?"

Kevin felt a surge of gratitude. "I have to go."

He hung up, nerves buzzing, stomach in knots. If he was right, it meant going back to the house. He hated going back to his aunt's house. He stood in the office, fists clenched by his sides. But he had to go back. Slater had blown up the car, and now he was going to do worse unless Kevin stopped him.

Slater was forcing him back to the house. Back to the past. Back to the house and back to the boy.

III

Kevin's watch read 4:39 when he passed the park at the end of Baker Street and pointed the car toward the white house. The faint sound of children playing on the swing sets faded. Then silence except for the purr of the Taurus. He blinked.

A row of twenty elms lined the left side of the dead-end avenue, one in the front yard of each house, casting a dark shadow over the entire length. Behind the homes, a narrow greenway fed into the park he'd just passed. To his right, warehouses backed up to train tracks. The street had been freshly paved, the lawns were all neatly manicured, the houses modest but clean. By all appearances it was the perfect little street on the edge of town.

He had not visited in over a year, and even then he'd refused to go inside. He needed Balinda's signature for the seminary application. After four failed attempts to secure it through the mail, he finally dragged himself to the front porch and rang the doorbell. She appeared after several minutes, and he addressed her without making eye contact and told her that he had some evidence in his old bedroom that would interest the authorities and would make the police station his next stop if she refused to sign. It was a lie, of course. She turned up her nose and scribbled her signature.

The last time he'd seen the inside of the house was five years ago, the day he'd finally worked up the courage to leave.

Rolling down the blacktop under the canopy of elms wasn't so different from driving through a tunnel. One that led to a past he had no desire to visit.

He passed the houses slowly—the green one, the yellow one, another green one, a beige one—all old, all unique in their own way despite the obvious similarities that came from having a common builder. Same gutters, same windows, same shingle roofs. Kevin locked his eyes on the white house, the fifteenth of the twenty on Baker Street.

Here resides Balinda and Eugene Parson with their thirty-six-year-old retarded son, Bob. Here is the childhood home of one Kevin Parson, adopted son, formerly known as Kevin Little until his mommy and daddy went to heaven.

Five minutes. *Okay, Kevin, time's running out.*

He parked the car across the street. A two-foot picket fence ran around the front yard and then rose to six feet for its run around the back. Here the fence was painted brilliant white, but once you stepped past that gate to the right, it wasn't painted at all, except by years of black ash. A flower bed ran the length of the front porch. Fake flowers, pretty and maintenance-free. Balinda replaced them every year— her idea of gardening.

A gray stone statue of some Greek goddess stood on a pedestal to the right of the Parsons' elm. The front yard was immaculate, the neatest on the street, always had been. Even the beige '59 Plymouth in the driveway had been recently polished so that you could actually see a reflection of the elm in its rear quarter panel. It hadn't been moved in years. When the Parsons had reason to leave the house, they favored the ancient blue Datsun parked in the garage.

The shades were drawn and the door had no windows, making it impossible to see inside, but Kevin knew the inside better than he knew his own house. Three doors down stood the smaller brown house that had once belonged to a cop named Rick Sheer, who had a daughter named Samantha. Her family had moved back to San Francisco when Sam went off to college.

Kevin wiped his palms on his jeans and climbed out. The sound of his door slamming sounded obscenely loud on the quiet street. The shade on the front window separated momentarily, and then closed. *Good. Come on out, Auntie.*

Suddenly the whole notion of coming felt absurd. Slater obviously knew his facts, but how would he have knowledge of Bob's dog? Or that the dog had indeed been Kevin's best friend until Samantha had come along? Maybe Slater was after Dr. Francis or the priest. Sam had made the call. Smart.

Kevin paused on the sidewalk and stared at the house. What now? Walk up and tell Balinda that someone was about to blow up the dog? He closed his eyes. *God, give me strength. You know how I hate this.* Maybe he should just leave. If Balinda had a phone, he would have called instead. Maybe he could call the neighbors and—

The door opened and Bob stepped out, grinning from ear to ear. "Hello, Kevin."

Bob wore a lopsided crew cut, undoubtedly Balinda's doing. His beige slacks hung a full six inches above a pair of shiny black leather wing tips. His shirt was a dirty white and sported large lapels reminiscent of the seventies.

Kevin grinned. "Hello, Bob. Can I see Damon?"

Bob lit up. "Damon wants to see you, Kevin. He's been waiting to see you."

"Is that so? Good, then. Let's—"

"Bobby, baby!" Balinda's shrill voice cut through the front door. "You get back in here!" She appeared out of the shadows wearing red high heels and white pantyhose patched up with streaks of clear fingernail polish. Her white dress was lined with age-stained lace embedded haphazardly with a couple dozen fake pearls, the surviving remnant of what had once been hundreds. A large sun hat perched on jet-black hair that looked freshly dyed. A string of gaudy jewels hung around her neck. But it was the white makeup she applied to her sagging face and her bright ruby red lipstick that planted Balinda firmly in the category of the walking dead.

She glared past heavily shadowed lids, studied Kevin for a moment, and then turned up her nose.

"Did I say you could go out? Get in. In, in, in!"

"It's Kevin, Mama."

"I don't care if it's Jesus Christ, pumpkin." She reached forward and straightened his collar. "You know how easily you catch cold, baby."

She ushered Bob toward the door.

"He wants to see—"

"Be nice for Princess." She gave him a little shove. "In."

God bless her soul, Balinda really did intend good for that boy. She was misguided and foolish, certainly, but she loved Bob.

Kevin swallowed and glanced at his watch. Two minutes. He cut for the gate while her back was still turned.

"And just where does the stranger think he's going?"

"I just want to check on the dog. I'll be gone before you know it." He reached the gate and yanked it open.

"Gone! You've turned running away into a new art form, haven't you, college boy?"

"Not now, Balinda," he said calmly. His breathing came faster. She marched up behind him. He strode down the side of the house.

"At least show a little respect when you're on my grounds," she said.

He checked himself. Closed his eyes. Opened them. "Please, not now, Princess."

"That's better. The dog's fine. You, on the other hand, are not."

Kevin rounded the house and stopped. The familiar yard sat unchanged. Black. Balinda called it a garden, but the backyard was nothing more than one huge ash heap, albeit a fairly tidy ash heap, three feet deep at its center, tapering off to two feet along the fence. A fifty-five-gallon drum smoldered at the center of the yard—they were still burning. Burning, burning, every day burning. How many newsapers and books had been burned back here over the years? Enough for many tons of ash.

The doghouse stood as it always had, in the back left corner. A toolshed sat unused and in terrible need of paint in the other corner. The ash had piled up against its door.

Kevin stepped onto the hardened ash and then ran across the yard for the doghouse. Less than a minute. He dropped to one knee, peered into the doghouse, and was rewarded with a growl.

"Easy, Damon. It's me, Kevin." The old black lab had grown senile and testy, but he immediately recognized Kevin's voice. He whimpered and limped out. A chain was latched to his collar.

"What do you think you're doing?" Balinda demanded.

"Good boy." Kevin stuck his head into the old doghouse and squinted in the darkness. No bomb that he could see. He stood and walked around the small house.

Nothing.

"What is he doing, Princess?"

Kevin turned back to the house at the sound of his uncle's voice. Eugene stood on the back porch, staring out at him. He wore his customary English-style boots and riding pants complete with suspenders and a beret. The skinny man looked more like a jockey to Kevin, but in Balinda's eyes, he was a prince. He'd worn the same outfit for at least ten years. Before that it was a Henry V outfit, awkward and clumsy on such a petite man.

Balinda stood at the edge of the house, watching Kevin with wary eyes. The shade lifted in the window to her left—Kevin's old room. Bob peered out. The past stared at him through those three sets of eyes.

He looked down at his watch. Thirty minutes had come and gone. He reached down and patted the dog. "Good boy." He unleashed him, tossed the chain to the side, and headed back for the gate.

"What do you think you are doing with my property?" Balinda asked.

"I thought he could use some exercise."

"You came all the way out here to let that old bat off his chain? What do you take me for? An idiot?" She turned to the dog, who was following Kevin. "Damon! Back in your house. Back!"

The dog stopped.

"Don't just stand there, Eugene! Control that animal!"

Eugene immediately perked up. He took two steps toward the dog and flung out a flimsy arm. "Damon! Bad dog! Get back. Get back immediately."

The dog just stared at them.

"Try it with your horse training accent," Balinda said. "Put some authority in your voice."

Kevin stared at them. It had been a long time since he'd seen them like this. They'd slipped into their role-playing on the fly. For the moment he didn't even exist. It was hard to imagine he grew up with these two.

Eugene stood as tall as his short frame would allow and expanded his chest. "I say, dog! To the kennel or the whip it'll be. Be gone! Be thou gone *immeeediately!*"

"Don't just stand there; go after him like you mean it!" Balinda snapped. "And I really don't think *thou* is appropriate with an animal. Growl or something!"

Eugene crouched and took several long steps toward the dog, growling like a bear.

"Not like an animal, you idiot!" Balinda said. "You look foolish! He's the animal; you're the master. Act like one. Growl like a man! Like a ruler."

Eugene pulled himself up again and thrust out an arm, snarling like a villain. "Back in the cage, you foul-mouthed vermin!" he cried hoarsely.

Damon whimpered and ran back into his house.

"Ha!" Eugene stood up, triumphant.

Balinda clapped and giggled, delighted. "You see, didn't I tell you? Princess knows—"

A muffled explosion suddenly lifted the doghouse a foot into the air and dropped it back to the ground.

They stood, Balinda at the corner, Bob in the window, Eugene by the porch, and Kevin in the middle of the yard, staring with incredulity at the smoldering doghouse.

Kevin could not move. Damon?

Balinda took a step forward and stopped. "Wha . . . what was that?"

"Damon?" Kevin ran for the doghouse. "Damon!"

He knew before he arrived that the dog was dead. Blood quickly darkened the ash at the door. He looked in and immediately recoiled. Bile crept up his throat. How was it possible? Tears sprang into his eyes.

A screech filled the air. He looked back to see Balinda flying for the doghouse, face stricken, arms outstretched. He jumped back to avoid her rush. On the porch, Eugene was pacing and mumbling incoherently. Bob had his face planted on the window, wide-eyed.

Balinda took one look into Damon's smoking house and then staggered back. Eugene stopped and watched her. Kevin's mind spun. But it wasn't Damon that now made him dizzy. It was Princess. Not Princess—Mother!

No! No, not Princess, not Mother, not even Auntie! *Balinda.* The poor sick hag who'd sucked the life out of him.

She turned to Kevin, eyes black with hate. "You!" she screamed. "You did this!"

"No, Mother!" *She's not your Mother! Not Mother.*

"I—"

"Shut your lying mouth! We hate you!" She flung her arm toward the gate. "Get out!"

"You don't mean that . . ." *Stop it, Kevin! What do you care if she hates you? Get out.*

Balinda balled both hands to fists, dropped them to her sides, and tilted her head back. "Leave! Leave, leave, leave!" she screamed, eyes clenched.

Eugene joined in, chanting with her in a falsetto voice, mimicking her stance. "Leave, leave, leave, leave!"

Kevin left. Without daring to look at what Bob might be doing, he whirled around and fled for his car.

6

THE AIR IS STUFFY. Too hot for such a cool day. Richard Slater, as he has decided to call himself this time, strips out of his clothes and hangs them in the one closet beside the desk. He crosses the dark basement in his bare feet, pulls open the old chest freezer, and takes out two ice cubes. Not really cubes—they are frozen into small balls instead of squares. He found the unusual ice trays in a stranger's refrigerator once and decided to take them. They are wonderful.

Slater walks into the center of the room and sits down on the concrete. A large white clock on the wall ticks quietly. It's 4:47. He will call Kevin in three minutes, unless Kevin himself makes a phone call, in which case he'll remotely terminate the connection and then call Kevin back. Short of that, he wants to give Kevin a little time to digest things. That is the plan.

He lies back, flat on the cool cement, and places one ice ball in each eye socket. He's done a lot of things over the years—some of them horrible, some of them quite splendid. What do you call tipping a waitress a buck more than she deserves? What do you call tossing a baseball back to the kid who mistakenly throws it over the fence? Splendid, splendid.

The horrible things are too obvious to dwell on.

But really his whole life has been practice for this particular game.

Of course, he always says that. There's something about being in a contest of high stakes that makes the blood flow. Nothing quite compares. Killing is just killing unless there's a game to the killing. Unless there is an end game that results in some kind of ultimate victory. Extracting punishment involves making someone suffer, and death ends that suffering, cheating the true pain of suffering. At least this side of hell. Slater shivers with the excitement of it all. A small whimper of pleasure. The ice hurts now. Like fire in his eyes. Interesting how opposites can be so similar. Ice and fire.

He counts off the seconds, not in his conscious mind, but in the background, where it doesn't distract him from thought. They have some pretty good minds on their side, but none quite like his. Kevin is no idiot. He will have to see which FBI agent they send. And of course the real prize exudes brilliance: Samantha.

Slater opens his mouth and says the name slowly. "Samantha."

He's been planning this particular game for three years now, not because he needed the time, but because he's been waiting for the right timing. Then again, the wait has given him more than enough opportunity to learn far more than he needs to know. Kevin's every waking move. His motivations and his desires. His strengths and his weaknesses. The truth behind that delightful little family of his.

Electronic surveillance—it's amazing how technology has advanced even in the last three years. He can put a laser beam on a window at a great distance and pick up any voices inside the room. They will find his bugs, but only because he wants them to. He can talk to Kevin any moment of the day on his own phone without being detected by a third party. When the police get around to finding the transmitter he affixed to the telephone line down from Kevin's house, he will resort to alternatives. There are limits, of course, but they won't be reached before the game expires. Pun intended.

Two minutes have passed and his eyes are numb from the ice.

Water leaks down his cheeks and he reaches his tongue up to touch it. Can't. One more minute.

The fact is, he's thought of everything. Not in a criminal kind of let's-do-a-bank-robbery-and-think-of-everything-so-they-won't-catch-us way. But in a more fundamental way. Precise motivations and countermoves. Like a chess match that will be played in response to another's moves. This method is far more exhilarating than taking a club to someone else's pieces and declaring yourself the victor.

In a few days, Kevin will be a shell of himself, and Samantha . . .

He chuckles.

There is no way they can possibly win.

Time's up.

Slater sits up, catches what's left of the ice balls as they fall from his eyes, tosses them into his mouth, and stands. The clock reads 4:50. He walks across the room to an old metal desk lit by a single shadeless lamp. Thirty watts. A policeman's hat sits on the desk. He reminds himself to put it in the closet.

The black phone is connected to a box, which will prevent tracing. Another remote box hides at the hub that services this house. The cops can trace all they like. He is invisible.

"Are we ready, Kevin?"

Slater picks up the phone, flips a switch on the scrambler, and dials the cell phone he's instructed Kevin to keep with him.

III

Kevin ran to his car and started it before it occurred to him that he had nowhere to go. If he had Samantha's cell number, he would have called her. He almost called Milton but couldn't get past the thought of the cops turning this house into a crime scene. It was inevitable, though—he had to report the bomb. Not telling Milton about Slater's true demand had been one thing; covering up a second bomb was in a whole different league. He considered returning to explain the dog's death to Balinda, but he didn't have the stomach to face her, much less form an explanation that would make any sense.

The explosion had been muffled by the doghouse—none of the neighbors seemed to have heard. If they had, they weren't running around saying so.

Kevin sat in his car, running his fingers through his hair. A sudden fury spread through his bones. The phone in his pocket buzzed loudly against his leg and he jumped.

Slater!

It buzzed again. He fumbled for the cell phone, pulled it out, flipped it open.

"Hello?"

"Hello."

"You . . . you didn't have to do that," Kevin said, voice wavering. He hesitated and then continued quickly. "Are you the boy? You're the boy, aren't you? Look, I'm here. Just tell me what—"

"Shut up! What boy? Did I tell you to lecture me? Did I say, 'I feel badly in need of a lecture at this time, college Kevin?' Don't ever do that again. You've broken the don't-speak-to-me-unless-engaged rule several times now, college boy. The next time, I kill something that walks on two legs. Consider it negative reinforcement. Understand?"

"Yes."

"That's better. And I think it's best not to tell the cops about this one. I know I said you could after the fact, but this little bonus was just something I planned in the event you weren't a good listener, which you were so quick to confirm. Mum's the word on this one. Okay?"

Don't tell the cops? How could he—

"Answer me!"

"O . . . okay."

"Tell Balinda to keep her trap shut too. I'm sure she'll agree. She won't want the cops searching through the house, now, will she?"

"No." So Slater knew about Balinda.

"The games are on. I'm the bat; you're the ball. I keep slugging until you confess. Lock and load."

Kevin desperately wanted to ask him what he meant by that word: *confess*. But he couldn't. He could hear Slater breathing on the other end.

"Samantha's coming down," Slater said in a soft voice. "That's good. I can't decide whom I despise more, you or her." The line clicked and Slater was gone. Kevin sat in silent shock. Whoever Slater was, he seemed to know everything. Balinda, the dog, the house. Samantha. He exhaled and closed his fingers to a fist to steady their trembling.

This is really happening, Kevin. Someone who knows is going to blow the lid off. *What falls but never breaks? What breaks but never falls?* Night and day. *In life he's your friend, but death is the end.* In life the dog was a friend, but death was the end of him. But there was more. Something Slater wanted him to confess was night and day, and life and death. What?

Kevin slammed the steering wheel with his fist. What, *what?*

"What boy?" Slater had said. What boy? So then he wasn't the boy?

Dear God . . . Dear God . . . Dear God what? He couldn't even think straight to pray. He put his head back and took several long, calming breaths. "Samantha. Samantha." She would know what to do. Kevin closed his eyes.

III

Kevin was eleven years old when he first saw the boy who wanted to kill him.

He and Samantha had become the very best of friends. What

made their friendship most special was that their trips into the night remained a secret. He saw other kids now and then, but he never talked to them. Mother didn't like that. But as far as he knew, she never did discover his little secret about the window. Every few nights, whenever they'd planned, or sometimes when Sam would tap on his window, or even sometimes when he went out and tapped on Sam's window, he would sneak out and meet her.

He didn't tell Sam what was happening inside the house. He wanted to, of course, but he couldn't tell her the worst of it, although he wondered whether she might have guessed anyway. His time with Sam was special because it was the only part of his life that *wasn't* about the house. He wanted to keep it that way.

The private school Sam attended held classes year-round, so she was always busy during the day, but Kevin knew he could never sneak out during the day anyway. Mother would find out.

"Why don't you ever want to play at the park?" Sam asked him one night as they walked through the greenway. "You'd get along great with Tommy and Linda."

He shrugged. "I just don't want to. They might tell."

"We could make them swear not to. They like me; they'd promise not to tell. They could be part of our club."

"We have fun together without them, don't we? Why do we need them?"

"Well, you have to start meeting some other people, Kevin. You're growing up, you know. I can't understand why your mom won't let you out to play in the first place. That's kinda mean—"

"Don't talk about her that way!"

"Well, it is!"

Kevin lowered his head, suddenly feeling suffocated. They stood in the quiet for a moment.

Sam put her hand on his shoulder. "I'm sorry."

The way she said it made tears come to his eyes. She was so special.

"I'm sorry," she said again. "I guess just because she's different doesn't mean she's mean. Different strokes for different folks, right?"

He looked up at her, unsure.

"It's a saying." She wiped a tear that had leaked from his right eye. "At least your mom isn't one of those parents who abuse their kids. I've heard my dad talk about some things." She shuddered. "Some people are horrible."

"My mom is a princess," Kevin said softly.

Sam grinned politely and nodded. "She's never hit you, has she, Kevin?"

"Hit me? Why would she hit me?"

"Has she?"

"Never! She sends me to my room and makes me read my books. That's all. Why would anyone hit someone else?"

"Not everyone's as sweet as you, Kevin." Sam took his hand and they started to walk. "I think my dad might know about us."

Kevin pulled up. "What?"

"He's asked a few questions. Mom and Dad talk about your family every once in a while. He is a cop, after all."

"Did . . . did you tell him anything?"

"Of course not. Don't worry. Your secret's safe with me."

They walked for a few minutes, hand in hand.

"Do you like Tommy?" Kevin asked.

"Tommy? Sure."

"I mean, is he your . . . you know . . ."

"Boyfriend? Don't gross me out!"

Kevin flushed and giggled. They came to a large tree behind her house and Sam stopped. She faced him and took both of his hands in hers. "I don't have any boyfriends except you, Kevin. I like you."

He looked into her bright blue eyes. A gentle breeze lifted her blonde hair so that it swam around her, highlighted by the moon. She was the most beautiful thing Kevin had ever seen. He was so taken with her that he had trouble even speaking.

"I . . . I like you too, Sam."

"We're like secret lovers," she said softly, and suddenly her face softened. "I've never kissed a boy before. Could I kiss you?"

"Kiss me?" He swallowed.

"Yes."

Kevin's throat was suddenly dryer than baking powder. "Yes."

She leaned forward and touched her lips to his for a moment.

She pulled back and they stared at each other, wide-eyed. Kevin's heart throbbed in his ears. He should do something! Before he lost his nerve, he bent and returned the kiss.

The night seemed to disappear around him. He floated on a cloud. They looked at each other, suddenly awkward.

"I should go now," she said.

"Okay."

She turned and ran toward her house. Kevin spun around and tore home, and honestly he wasn't sure if his feet really were on the ground. He did like Samantha. He liked her very, very much. Maybe even more than his mother, which was pretty impossible.

The next few days floated by like a dream. He met Sam two nights later and they made no mention of the kiss. They didn't need to. They resumed their playing as if nothing at all had changed between them. They didn't kiss again, and Kevin wasn't sure he wanted to. It might somehow spoil the magic of that first kiss.

Sam didn't come to his window for three straight nights, and Kevin decided to sneak out and go to her house. He took the greenway past the two houses between his and Sam's on light feet, careful not to make the slightest sound. You could never know who might be out at night.

They had hidden from the sound of coming voices and approaching footsteps a hundred times before.

A half-moon sat in the black sky, peeking around slowly drifting clouds. Crickets chirped. Sam's house came into view and his heart thumped a little louder. He eased up to the picket fence and peered over it. Her room was on the bottom floor; he could see the faint glow of light past the tree in front of the window. *Please be there, Sam. Please.*

Kevin glanced around, saw no one, and pushed aside the board Sam had loosened long ago. Her dad might be a cop, but he'd never found this, had he? That's because Sam was smart too. He climbed through and brushed his hands. *Please be there, Sam.*

Kevin took a step. The tree in front of Sam's window moved. He froze. Sam? Slowly a dark head and then shoulders came into view. Someone was peeking into Sam's room!

Kevin jerked back, panicked. The form stood taller, angling for a better view. It was a boy! A tall boy with a sharp nose. Staring in on Sam!

A dozen thoughts screamed through Kevin's head. Who? What was the boy doing? He should run! No, he should yell. Was that Tommy? No, Tommy had longer hair.

The boy spun around, stared directly at Kevin, and then pushed his way past the tree. He stood tall in the moonlight, and a terrible smile twisted his face. He took a step toward Kevin.

Kevin didn't bother with the loose plank—he went over the fence faster than he could have ever imagined possible and ran for a large tree on the edge of the greenway. He pulled up behind it, panting.

Nothing happened. There was no sound of running or of heavy breathing other than his own. He would have run for home but was afraid the boy was waiting by the fence for the first sign of movement. It took him a full five minutes to work up the courage to peek ever so slowly around the tree.

Nothing.

Another five minutes and he was peering over the fence again. Nothing. Whoever the boy was, he'd gone.

Kevin finally worked up the courage to tap on Sam's window. She climbed out, all smiles. She was waiting for him, she said. Waiting for the dashing young man to come to the window of the maiden. That's how it was done in the movies.

He told her about the boy, but she found it funny. One of the neighborhood guys had a crush on her, and her prince charming had sent him packing! Hearing himself tell it, the story did sound funny. They had a good hoot that night. But Kevin had a hard time shaking the image of the boy's horrible smile.

Three nights went by before Kevin saw the boy again—this time in the greenway on his way home. At first he thought it was a dog or some animal running behind the trees, but after he'd climbed into bed, he began to wonder if it was the boy. What if he was going to spy on Sam again? He tossed and turned for half an hour before working up the resolve to go back and check on Sam. He would never go to sleep until he had.

For the first time in a year, he went out for a second time in the same night—prince charming to check on his damsel in distress. He didn't really expect to see anything.

Kevin poked his head over the fence in Sam's backyard and went rigid. The boy! He was there, peering into Sam's window again! He'd waited until Kevin went home and then snuck up to her window to spy on her!

Kevin ducked and tried to calm his breathing. He had to do something! But what? If he yelled and then took off running, the boy wouldn't catch him. At least then he might scare off the boy. He could throw a rock. No. What if he broke Sam's window?

He went up slowly for another peek. The boy was doing

something. He had his face planted against the window and was . . .
he was moving his face around in circles. What was he doing?
Kevin blinked. Was he . . . ? A chill snaked down Kevin's spine. The
boy was licking Sam's window in slow circles.

Something ballooned in Kevin's head. Whether it was rage or just
plain terror, he couldn't be sure, but he spoke while courage strength-
ened him.

"Hey!"

The boy spun around. For one long, still moment, they stared at
each other. The boy stepped forward and Kevin fled. He bolted
through the greenway, pumping his skinny arms and legs as fast as
they would go without tearing loose. He dove through his fence, flew
into his bedroom, and shut the window, surely making enough racket
to wake the house.

Ten minutes later the night slept in silence. But Kevin couldn't.
He felt trapped in the small room. What was the boy doing? Had he
been stalking Sam every night? He had, hadn't he? Kevin had only
stumbled on him twice, but there was no telling how long the boy had
been stalking Sam.

An hour passed, and Kevin could hardly shut his eyes, much less
sleep. That's when he heard the tap on his window. He bolted up in
bed. Sam! He scrambled to his knees and lifted the shade.

The boy stood at the back fence, head and shoulders in plain view.
He stared directly at Kevin, twirling something in his hand. It was a
knife.

Kevin dropped the shade and flung the covers over his head. He
lay trembling for two hours before peeking again, ever so carefully,
just barely lifting the shade. The boy was gone.

The next three days dragged by like a slow nightmare. Each night
he peeked out his window a hundred times. Each night the backyard
remained vacant except for the doghouse and the toolshed. Each night

he prayed desperately for Sam to come for a visit. She'd talked about going to a camp, but he couldn't remember exactly when she was supposed to go. Was it this week?

On the fourth night, Kevin couldn't wait any longer. He paced in his room for an hour, peering out of his window every few minutes, before deciding that he had to check on Sam before the anxiety killed him.

It took him half an hour to work his way up to her house, using the trees in the greenway as cover. The night was quiet. When he finally inched his head over Sam's fence, her light was out. He scanned the yard. No boy. Sam was gone and so was the boy.

He collapsed at the base of the fence with relief. She must be at that camp. Maybe the boy had followed her there. No. That was stupid. How could a boy follow a girl all the way to camp?

Kevin eased his way back to the cover of the greenway and headed home, feeling at ease for the first time in nearly a week. Maybe the boy had moved. Maybe he had found something else to occupy his sick little mind.

Maybe he had snuck into Sam's room and killed her.

He pulled up. No. Kevin would have heard about that. Her father was a cop and—

A blunt object slammed into the side of Kevin's head and he staggered. A groan broke from his throat. Something wrapped around his neck and jerked him upright.

"Listen, you little punk, I know who you are and I don't like you!" a voice snarled in his ear. The arm jerked him around and shoved him against a tree. Kevin wobbled at arm's length from his attacker. The boy.

If his head wasn't throbbing so badly, he might have panicked. Instead he just stared and tried to keep his legs from collapsing.

The boy sneered. Close up, his face reminded Kevin of a boar. He was older than Kevin and a foot taller, but still young, with pimples all over his nose and chin and a tattoo of a knife high on his forehead. He smelled like dirty socks.

The boy brought his face within a few inches of Kevin's. "I'm going to give you one warning and one warning only, squat. That girl is mine, not yours. If I ever see you so much as looking at her again, I'll kill her. If I catch you sneaking out to see her again, I may just kill the both of you. You hear me?"

Kevin just stood dumb.

The boy slapped him across the cheek. "You hear me?"

Kevin nodded.

The boy stepped back and glared at him. A slow lopsided grin split his face at a cruel angle. "You think you're in love with this little tramp? Huh? You're too stupid and too young to know what love is. And so is she. I'm going to teach her love, baby, and I don't need a squat like you messing with our little romance." He stepped back.

Kevin saw the knife in the boy's hand for the first time. His mind cleared. The boy saw his eyes on the knife and he lifted it slowly.

"You have any idea what a nine-inch bowie can do to a squat like you?" The boy twirled the blade in his hand. "Do you know how persuasive a bright shiny blade can be to a young girl?"

Kevin suddenly felt like he was going to vomit.

"Get back to your little room, squat, before I decide to cut you just for looking so stupid."

Kevin fled.

7

KEVIN SAT IN HIS RECLINER, waiting impatiently for Samantha, flipping through the channels to hear the various versions of the "car bomb," as they were calling it. He nursed a warm 7UP in his left hand and glanced up at the wall clock. Nine o'clock—nearly five hours had passed since she'd left Sacramento.

"Come on, Samantha," he muttered softly. "Where are you?" She'd called him halfway down. He told her about the dog and begged her to hurry. She was already doing eighty, she said.

Back to the television. They knew Kevin's identity, and a dozen reporters had tracked down his number. He'd ignored the calls per Milton's suggestion. Not that he had anything to add anyway—their theories were as good as his. Channel nine's suggestion that the bombing might be the work of a well-known fugitive dubbed the Riddle Killer interested him most. The killer had taken the lives of five people up in Sacramento and had vanished three months ago. No more details, but the speculation was enough to plant a knot in Kevin's throat. The pictures of the charred wreckage, taken from the sky, were stunning. Or terrifying, depending on how he thought of them. If he'd been anywhere near the thing when it blew, he'd be dead. Like the dog.

After Slater's call, he'd forced himself to return to the backyard and explain the situation to Balinda, but she wouldn't even acknowledge him. She'd already put the matter behind them by executive order. Poor Bob would somehow be convinced that Damon was alive and well, just gone. Balinda would have to explain her initial screaming flight across the ash after the explosion, of course, but she was an expert at explaining the unexplainable. The only time she even responded to Kevin was when he suggested they not call the police.

"Of course not. We've got nothing to report. The dog's fine. Do you see a dead dog?"

No, he didn't. Eugene had already dumped it in the burn barrel and set it on fire. Gone. What were a few more ashes?

His mind drifted to the call with Slater. *What boy?* Slater didn't seem to know of any boy. *What boy?* The key to his sin was found in the riddles. As far as he could see, the riddles had nothing to do with the boy. So then Slater *couldn't* be the boy. Thank God, thank God, thank God. Some secrets were best left buried forever.

The doorbell chimed. Kevin set down his 7UP and clambered out of his chair. He stopped at the hall mirror for a quick look. Haggard face. Smudged T-shirt. He scratched the top of his head. The bell chimed again.

"Coming."

He hurried to the peephole, peered out, saw that it was Samantha, and unlocked the door. It had been ten years since he'd kissed her on the cheek and wished her well in conquering the big bad world. Her hair had been blonde and long; her blue eyes sparkling like stars. She'd had one of those faces that looked airbrushed all the time, even without a speck of makeup. Smooth rounded cheeks and soft upturned lips, high arching eyebrows and a soft pointed nose. The most beautiful girl he'd ever seen. Of course, he wasn't seeing a lot of girls in those days.

Kevin fumbled with the knob and opened the door. Samantha stood under the porch light, dressed in jeans and smiling warmly. He'd thought of her a thousand times since she'd left, but his mind's eye could never have prepared him for seeing her now, in the flesh. He *had* seen a lot of girls in the last five years, and Sam was still the most beautiful girl he'd ever laid eyes on. Bar none.

"Are you going to invite me in, stranger?"

"Yes. Sorry, of course! Come in, come in."

She walked past him, set down her bag, and faced him. He shut the door.

"My, you've grown up," she said. "Put on a bit of muscle."

He grinned and ran his hand over his head. "I guess."

He was having difficulty not staring at her eyes. They were the kind of blue that seemed to swallow whatever they gazed upon—brilliant and deep and haunting. They didn't reflect the light so much as shine, as if illuminated by their own source. No man nor woman could look into Samantha's eyes and not think that there was indeed a God in heaven. She stood just up to his chin, slender and graceful. This was Samantha, his best friend. His only real friend. Looking at her now, he wondered how he'd survived the last ten years.

She stepped forward. "Give me a hug, my knight."

He chuckled at her childhood reference and hugged her tight. "It's so good to see you, Samantha."

She stood up on her toes and kissed his cheek. Beyond that one blissful kiss when they were eleven, their relationship had remained platonic. Neither of them wanted romance from the other. They were bosom buddies, best friends, almost brother and sister. Not that the thought hadn't crossed Kevin's mind; a friendship had just always been more appealing. She had always been the damsel in distress, and he the knight in shining armor, even though they both knew she had rescued him in the first place. Now, despite the fact that it was she who'd again come to his rescue, their childhood personas came naturally.

Sam turned to the living room, hands on her hips. "I see you like travel posters."

He walked with her and grinned self-consciously. *Quit rubbing your head; she'll think you're a dog.* He lowered his hands and tapped his right foot.

"I'd like to go to all those places someday. It's kinda like looking at the world. Reminds me there's more. Never did like being shut in."

"I like it! Well, you've come far. And I knew you would, didn't I? You just had to get away from that mother of yours."

"Aunt," he corrected. "She never was my mother."

"Aunt. Let's face it, dear Aunt Balinda did you more harm than good. When did you finally leave?"

He walked past her to the kitchen. "Twenty-three. Drink?"

She followed him. "Thanks. You stayed in that house five years after I left?"

"Afraid so. You should've taken me with you."

"You did it on your own—that's better. Now look at you, you have a college degree and you're in seminary. Impressive."

"And you graduated valedictorian. Very impressive." He pulled a soda from the fridge, popped the tab, and handed it to her.

"Thank you," she said. "For the compliment." She winked at him and took a sip. "The drink's nice too. How often do you go back?"

"Where? To the house? As little as possible. I'd rather not talk about that."

"I think that *that* might be tied to this, don't you?"

"Maybe."

Samantha set the can down on the counter and looked at him, suddenly dead serious. "Someone's stalking you. And by the sound of it, me. A killer who uses riddles who's selected us for his own reasons. Revenge. Hate. The baser motivations. We can't shut out the past."

"Right to the point."

"Tell me everything."

"Starting—"

"Starting with the phone call in your car." She walked to the front door.

Kevin followed. "Where are you going?"

"We. Come on, let's take a drive. He's obviously listening to everything we say in here—let's make his life a little more interesting. We'll take my car. Hopefully he hasn't gotten to it yet."

They climbed into a beige sedan and Samantha drove into the night. "That's better. He's probably using lasers."

"Actually, I think you're right," Kevin said.

"He told you that?"

"Something like that."

"Every detail, Kevin. I don't care how insignificant, I don't care what you told the cops, I don't care how embarrassing or stupid or crazy it sounds, I want everything."

Kevin did as she requested, eagerly, with passion, as if it were his first real confession. Sam drove haphazardly and stopped him frequently to ask questions.

When was the last time you left your car unlocked?

Never that I can remember.

Do you lock your car when it's in the garage?

No.

A nod. *Did the police find a timing device?*

Not that he knew about.

You found the ribbon behind the lamp?

Yes.

Did Slater call me Sam or Samantha?

Samantha.

An hour passed and they covered every conceivable detail of the day's events, including the information he'd hidden from Milton.

Everything except his speculation that Slater could be the boy. He'd never told Sam the whole truth about the boy, and he wasn't eager to do so now. If Slater wasn't the boy, which he claimed not to be, there was no need to dig up that matter. He'd never told Sam the whole truth and he wasn't eager to do so now.

"How long can you stay?" Kevin asked after a lull.

Sam glanced at him with a coy smile. "The big boy needs a girl in his court?"

Kevin grinned sheepishly. She hadn't changed a bit. "Turns out girls make or break me."

She arched her brow. "I technically have a week off to finish my move. I have boxes overflowing in my kitchen still. The case I was assigned to when I first arrived a couple months ago has been pretty quiet, but it just heated up. I wouldn't be surprised if they called me in."

"California Bureau of Investigation, huh? Big change from New York."

"Not really, other than being new. I've managed to do a couple things right and have my department head appropriately impressed at the moment, but I still have to earn my stripes with them, if you understand how law enforcement works. Same thing with the CIA before I switched to this job."

"CBI, CIA—gets a bit confusing," Kevin said. "You glad you made the move?"

She looked at him and grinned. "I'm closer to you, aren't I?"

He nodded and turned sheepishly. "You have no idea how much I appreciate this. Really."

"I wouldn't miss it for the world."

"Can't you pull some strings?" He faced her. "Convince them to let you stay down here?"

"Because I know you?"

"Because you're involved now. He *knows* you, for heaven's sake!"

"It doesn't work that way. If anything, that's reason for them to remove me from the case." She stared ahead, lost in thought. "Don't worry, I'm not going anywhere. The CBI is made of a dozen units, roughly a hundred agents in all. My unit is unique—hardly known to most agents. We work outside the system, technically part of the Bureau, but it's directed as much by the attorney general. Trouble-shooting the harder cases. We have some latitude and discretion." She looked at him. "You, my dear, are definitely within the scope of the discretion. More than you know."

Kevin stared out his window. Black. Slater was out there some-where. Maybe watching them now. A shiver ran down his spine.

"So. What do you think?"

Sam pulled the car to the curb a block from Kevin's house and shoved the stick into park. "I think that we have no choice but to fol-low Slater's demands. So far the demands involve no one but you. This isn't like a threat of terror, where either we release a hostage or they blow a building. This is either you confess or he blows up your car. Confession doesn't exactly pose a threat to society." She nodded to herself. "For now we don't involve the police like he wants. But we also take him at his word. He said *cops*—we avoid the cops. That excludes the FBI. We tell the FBI everything."

She cracked her window and stared at the sky. "I also think that Richard Slater is someone one or both of us knew or know. I think his motivation is revenge and I think he means to extract it in a way that will never be forgotten." She looked at him. "There has to be some-one, Kevin."

He hesitated and then fed her part of the truth. "No one. The only enemy I can even remember having is that boy."

"What boy?"

"You know. Remember that boy who was spying on you when we were kids? The one who beat me up?"

She grinned. "The one you saved me from?"

"I asked Slater if he was the boy," Kevin said.

"Did you, now? You omitted that little detail."

"It was nothing."

"I said *every* detail, Kevin. I don't care if you think it's nothing or not. Okay?"

"Okay."

"What did he say?"

"He said, 'What boy?' It's not him."

She didn't respond.

A car drove by. SUV with bright taillights.

"Ever hear of the Riddle Killer?" Sam asked.

Kevin sat up. "On the news tonight."

"The Riddle Killer was given that name for a series of murders up in Sacramento over the last twelve months. It's been three months since his last victim—the brother of an FBI agent who was on his tail. I can guarantee that the FBI will be all over this. Same MO. Guy calls on the phone with a riddle and then executes his punishment if the riddle goes unsolved. Low, gravelly voice. Sophisticated surveillance. Sounds like the same guy."

"Except . . ."

"Except why would he choose you? And why me?" Sam asked. "Could be a copy cat."

"Maybe he's trying to confuse us. Guy like that's obviously into games, right? So maybe this just ups the thrill for him." Kevin lowered his head into his hands and massaged his temples. "Just this morning I had a discussion with Dr. Francis about mankind's capacity for evil. What's the average person capable of? Makes me wonder what I'd do if I met up with this guy." He took a deep breath. "It's hard to believe that people like this actually exist."

"He'll get his due. They always do." She reached over and rubbed his shoulder. "Don't worry, my dear knight. There's a reason I advanced as quickly as I did in the company. I haven't been handed a case so far I couldn't crack." She smirked playfully. "I told you I was gonna be a cop. And I didn't mean street beat either."

Kevin sighed and smiled. "Well, you have no idea how glad I am that it's you." He caught himself. "Not that I'm glad he's after—"

"I understand." She fired the car. "We'll beat this, Kevin. I'm not about to let some ghost from the past or some serial killer push either one of us around. We're smarter than this psycho. You'll see."

"What now?"

"Now we go find some bugs."

Twenty minutes later Sam held six eavesdropping devices in a gloved hand. One from the living room, one from each bathroom, one from each bedroom, and the infinity transmitter from the phone.

Her eyes twinkled like a competitive athlete who'd just scored a goal. Sam had always seemed beyond any kind of discouragement; her optimism was one of her most admirable traits. She carried it around her like a fragrance. As far as Kevin was concerned, Sam had what it took to one day run the CBI or CIA or whatever she so desired.

"Won't slow him down much, but at least it'll let him know that we're engaged. These types tend to get trigger-happy if they think the other side is slacking off."

She filled up the sink, dropped the devices into the water, and peeled off the surgical gloves. "Under normal circumstances I'd take these in, but if I'm right, the FBI has jurisdiction. They would scream bloody murder. First thing in the morning, I'll call my office, explain the situation, and then let Milton's office know of my involvement. Not that they will care—I guarantee that the town will be crawling with agencies by morning. I'd have a better shot working on my own than through them anyway." She was talking to herself as much as to him. "You said they'd be out first thing to sweep for bugs?"

"Yes."

"Tell them you found these lying around. I'll make sure they dust for prints. At this point you have nothing else to tell Milton, so let him do his job, and try to stay out of his way. When the FBI makes contact, cooperate. I've got a few other things I want to run down first thing. We tracking?"

"And if he calls?"

"If I'm not here, you call my cell immediately. We'll go from there." She started for the door and then turned back. "Slater will call. You do know that, don't you?"

He nodded slowly.

"Get some sleep. We'll get him. He's already made his first mistake."

"He has?"

"He pulled *me* into the game." She grinned. "I was born for cases like this."

Kevin walked over, took her hand, and kissed it. "Thank you."

"I think it would be better if I crashed down at the Howard Johnson. No offense, but you don't have a second bed and leather couches remind me of eels. I don't sleep with eels."

"Sure." He was disappointed only because he felt so alive around her. Secure. In his mind, she was absolutely perfect in every way. Of course, he wasn't exactly a Casanova, groomed to judge these things.

"I'll call you."

Then she was gone.

III

Slater sits in a red pickup one block from Kevin's house and watches Sam back out of the driveway then drive south. "There you go; there you go." He clucks his tongue three times slowly, so that he can hear the full range of its sound. There are two sounds, actually—a deep popping as the tongue pulls free from the roof of the mouth, and a click as it strikes the gathered spittle in the base of the mouth. Details. The kind of details most people die without considering because most people are slobs who have no clue what living is really all about.

Living is about clucking your tongue and enjoying the sound.

They had found the bugs. Slater smiles. She has come and he is so very glad she has come quickly, flaunting her skinny little body all through the man's house, seducing him with her wicked tongue.

"Samantha," he whispers. "It is so good to see you again. Give me a kiss, baby."

The interior of the old Chevy is immaculate. He'd replaced the black plastic instrument panel with custom-fitted mahogany that shines now in the moonlight. A black case beside him carries the electronics he requires for his surveillance—mostly extras. Samantha found the six bugs he'd expected the cops to find, but there are still three, and not even the FBI will detect those.

"It's dark down here, Kevin. So very dark."

Slater waits an hour. Two. Three. The night is dead when he eases himself out of the cab and heads for Kevin's house.

8

J ENNIFER CROSSED HER LEGS and stared at Paul Milton across the conference table. She'd made the trip down to Long Beach the previous evening, visited the crime scene where Kevin Parson's Mercury Sable had blown up, made a dozen phone calls, and then checked into a hotel on Long Beach Boulevard.

She spent the night tossing and turning, reliving that day three months earlier when Roy had been killed by the Riddle Killer. The killer didn't use a name, never had. Only a riddle. He'd asphyxiated his first four victims, striking once every six weeks or so. With Roy he used a bomb. She found his body in pieces five minutes after the explosion ripped it apart. Nothing could wash away the image.

After a couple final hours of sleep she'd headed for the station where she waited an hour for the rest to arrive.

With Roy's death the fundamentals of life became stunningly vivid, while virtually all of her aspirations had died with him. She'd taken her relationship with him for granted, and when he was snatched away, she became desperate for every other thing she took for granted. The sweet smell of air. A burning hot shower on a cold morning. Sleep. The touch of another human. The simple things in life sustained her. Life wasn't what it seemed, she'd learned that much, but she still wasn't sure what life really *was*. The parties and the promotions felt plastic now. People rushing around, climbing imaginary ladders of success, fighting to be noticed.

Like Milton. Milton was a walking media package, right down to the bone, complete with a beige trench coat, which now hung in the corner. He was holding a news conference, of all things, just past sunup when she'd first entered the station.

There was no new news; they all knew that. His insistence that the media had a right to know at least that much was no more than smoke blowing. He wanted the camera eye, end of case. Not exactly her kind of man.

Her thinking wasn't exactly professional; she knew that. He was a law enforcement officer with the same ultimate objective as hers. They were in this together, regardless of any personal differences. But Jennifer didn't find the process of putting all the nonsense aside as easy as she had before Roy's death. That was why the Bureau tended to distance agents in her situation from the front line, as Frank had attempted.

Never mind, she would rise above it all.

To her left sat Nancy Sterling, Long Beach's most experienced forensic scientist. Next to her, Gary Swanson from the state police and Mike Bowen from the ATF. Cliff Bransford, CBI, rounded out the gathering. She'd worked with Cliff and found him exceptionally tedious, but smart enough. For him, everything was by the book. Best to stay clear of him unless he approached her.

"I know you all have varying interests in this case, but the FBI has clear jurisdiction—this guy's rap includes kidnapping," Jennifer said.

Milton didn't bat an eye. "You may have jurisdiction, but I've got a city—"

"Don't worry, I'm here to work with you. I'm recommending that we use your offices as a clearinghouse. That puts all the information at your fingertips. We'll coordinate everything from here. I don't know what the CBI or the ATF will want to do about personnel placement, but I would like to work out of this office. Fair enough?"

Milton didn't respond.

"Sounds good to me," Bransford said. "We're fine out of our own offices. As far as I'm concerned, this is your case."

Bransford knew about Roy and was giving her his support. She gave him a slight nod.

"We'll stand off for the meantime," the ATF agent said. "But if explosives show up again, we'll want a larger role."

"Granted," Jennifer said. She faced Milton. "Sir?"

He stared her down and she knew then that her opinion of him wouldn't change. Even if he'd linked this case to the Riddle Killer, which was likely given the profile of the killings in Sacramento, Jennifer doubted he knew of her personal stake in the case. Roy's identity had not been circulated. Even so, she didn't care for his arrogance.

"What's your specialty, agent?" Milton asked.

"Forensic psychology, Detective."

"Profiler."

"Psychological profiles based on forensics," she corrected. She almost spoke the rest of the thought: *That's why they put the word* forensics *in there, for those who grew up in Backwater, Louisiana.*

"Fair enough. But I don't want you talking to the media."

"I wouldn't think of robbing you of all that airtime, sir."

"I think we have an understanding."

"Good. I reviewed your file as of an hour ago." She looked at Nancy. "You do quick work."

"We try," Nancy said. "You might want to take a look at it again. We found a timer."

"Preset?"

"No. A receiver set the timer off, but from what I can gather, there was no way to terminate the timer once it was engaged."

Jennifer glanced at Milton. "So whoever did this had no intention of terminating the detonation, regardless of his threat."

"So it seems."

"Anything else?"

Milton stood and turned to the blinds behind his chair. He parted them and looked down at the street. "So what does your crystal ball tell you on this one, Agent Peters?"

"It's early."

"Humor me."

They were undoubtedly thinking Riddle Killer, but she went with a conservative analysis.

"Best guess, we have a white male who is extremely angry, but not angry enough to compromise his precision or method. He's smart. And he knows it. He knew what kind of bomb to build, how to place it, how to detonate without detection. In fact, he knew that Mr. Parson would escape unharmed, and he knew that his riddle would go unsolved. That's why he didn't bother wasting resources on a termination switch."

"Random victim?" Nancy asked.

"Nothing with this guy is random. If the victim isn't a past acquaintance, then he was selected for specific reasons. His profession, his habits, the way he combs his hair."

"Which is why Parson's insistence that he doesn't know anyone who might hold a grudge doesn't add up," Milton said.

"Not necessarily. You're a cop who can list a hundred people who would take your head off, given the opportunity. The average citizen doesn't have those kinds of enemies. We're dealing with someone who's probably insane—a sideways look on a train could mark you as his next target." She paused. "That's what I would say based solely on what you've given me. But as it turns out, I have more."

"Riddle Killer," Nancy said.

Jennifer looked at her and wondered if she knew about Roy. "Yes. Same MO. The last killing we've attributed to this guy was three months ago in Sacramento, but from every indication, we're dealing with the same man."

"He used riddles, but did he ever *not* kill a victim?" Milton asked.

"You're right; this one's different. All five of his victims were given one riddle and then killed when they failed to solve it. Which means he's not finished with Kevin Parson. He didn't just blow up a car without hurting anyone for the fun of it. He's stretching himself. He's bored. He wants a new challenge. Stringing together multiple riddles is the logical progression, but it also takes more time. He would have to study his mark well enough to sustain continued threats. That means lots of surveillance over many days. It's one thing to pull off one stunt. This guy's planning on doing this again. That kind of planning takes time. Could explain why the Riddle Killer has been so quiet over the last three months."

"This guy gave a name," Bransford said. "Slater. The Riddle Killer remained nameless."

"Again. A progression, in my opinion." Jennifer pulled a thick file from her briefcase and set it on the desk. The tab had two capital letters on it: R. K.

"Don't let the size fool you; we don't know as much as you might think. There's a lot of psychological profile data in here. When it comes to evidence, this guy's as clean as they come. None of the bodies was abused in any way. The first four were asphyxiated; the last was killed with a bomb. All four asphyxiated bodies were reported to the police by the killer himself and left on park benches. For all practical purposes they were evidence-free. This killer finds satisfaction in the game more than the actual killing. The killing is only a prop, something that provides stakes high enough to make the game interesting."

She put her hand on the file. The green edges were worn white from use, mostly her own. She could practically recite the contents, all 234 pages. A full half of the writing was hers.

"A copy of the file is being reproduced for each of you as we speak. I'll be happy to answer any questions once you've had a chance to review it. Has there been any additional contact with the victim?"

"Not today," Milton said. "We have a team on the way to sweep his house. He found some bugs. More accurately, a friend of his found six of them throughout the house. A Samantha Sheer called us this morning. She's connected with the attorney general's office. Just happened to be with him last night and did us a favor. Do you know what falls but never breaks? What breaks but never falls?"

"No."

He grinned disingenuously. "Night and day."

"She gave you that?"

He nodded. "Pretty smart. On the other hand, there are too many fingers in this pot already, and the case is less than a day old."

"The case is a year old," Jennifer said. "She met with him without your knowing? You're not watching the house?"

He hesitated. "Not yet. Like I said—"

"You left him alone overnight?" Jennifer felt her face flush with anger. *Easy, girl.*

Milton's eyes narrowed slightly.

"Who do you think we're dealing with here, a cub scout? Do you even know if Parson's still alive?"

"We are under no standing threat," Milton said. "There is no direct evidence that this is the Riddle Killer. Kevin insisted he was—"

"The victim's in no position to know what's best for himself." Jennifer unfolded her legs and stood. "As soon as I get back, I'd like to get a firsthand look at the evidence, if you don't mind, Nancy."

"Of course."

"Where are you going?" Milton asked.

"To see Parson. As far as we know, he's the only living victim of the Riddle Killer. Our first job is to keep him that way. I'd like to spend a few minutes with him before your people start tearing up his house. An associate of mine, Bill Galager, will be here shortly. Please treat him with the same graciousness you've extended to me."

III

Jennifer left the station and sped for Kevin Parson's house, knowing that she had walked a thin line back in the conference room. Or maybe she was being too self-conscious about her cooperation because of the bureau chief's concerns. All things considered, except for the mistake of leaving the victim unguarded, Milton had handled the case well enough thus far. But one mistake and they would have another dead body on their hands. She wasn't in a position to accept that. Not this time.

Not after she'd led the Riddle Killer to Roy.

Why is that, Jenn? Kevin Parson is a victim, deserving life, liberty, and the pursuit of happiness like every other potential victim, but no more. That was the objective view of her situation.

But, no matter what face she tried to put on the matter, the bureau chief had pegged her. She *had* lost just a bit of objectivity, hadn't she? Regardless of Kevin Parson's makeup, he was now special. Perhaps more special to Jennifer than any other person in any other case, save her brother. He could be a total fool with a habit of running down the 405 freeway naked, and that much wouldn't change.

Fact was, in some small way, Kevin Parson offered her a glimpse of redemption. If Roy had died because of her, maybe Kevin would live because of her.

Because of her. She had to *personally* save him, didn't she? An eye for an eye. A life for a life.

"God, let him be a decent man," she muttered.

Jennifer dismissed the thoughts with a sigh and pulled onto his street shortly after eight. Old track houses, mostly two-story, modest, decent starter homes. She glanced at the file Milton had given her. Kevin Parson lived in the blue house two doors up. She pulled to the curb, shut off the engine, and glanced around. Quiet neighborhood.

"Okay, Kevin, let's see what kind of man he's chosen this time."

She left the file and walked to the front door. A morning newspaper featuring a front-page spread of the car bombing sat on the porch. She picked it up and rang the doorbell.

The man who answered was tall with messy brown hair and deep blue eyes that held hers without wavering. A white T-shirt with a "Jamaica" logo over the pocket. Faded blue jeans. He smelled of aftershave, although he obviously hadn't shaved today. The rugged look worked on him. Didn't look like the kind of man who'd run down the freeway naked. More like a man she'd expect to find featured in *Cosmopolitan*. Especially with those eyes. Ouch.

"Kevin Parson?" She flipped open her wallet to show her badge. "I'm Agent Peters with the FBI. Could I have a few words with you?"

"Sure. Sure, come in." He ran his fingers through his hair. "Sam said you'd probably be coming this morning."

She handed him the paper and walked in. "Looks like you made the news. Sam? That's your friend from the attorney general's office?"

Travel posters covered the walls. Odd.

"Actually, I think she's with the California Bureau of Investigation. But she just started. You know her?" He dropped the paper out on the porch and closed the door.

"She called the police this morning and reported the bugs. Could I see them?"

"Sure. Right over here." He led her to the kitchen. Two soda cans sat on the counter—he'd had a drink last night, presumably with Sam. Otherwise the kitchen was spotless.

"Here." He indicated the sink and placed the two cans in a small recycling bin. Four small eavesdropping devices that resembled watch batteries, one infinity transmitter she'd obviously pulled off the phone, and a device that resembled a common electrical splitter all sat in the water.

"Did Sam wear gloves when she removed these?"

"Yes."

"Good girl. Not that we'll find anything. I doubt our friend's stupid enough to leave prints on his toys." She faced him. "Anything unusual happen in the last twelve hours? Any phone calls, anything out of place?"

His eyes twitched, barely. *You're going too fast, Jennifer. The poor guy's still in shock and you're giving him the nth degree. You need him as much as he needs you.*

She held up her hand and smiled. "Sorry. Listen to me, barging in here and interrogating you. Let's start over. You can call me Jennifer." She reached out her hand.

He searched her eyes, took her hand. Like a child trying to decide whether to trust a stranger. For a moment she felt drawn into his gaze, exposed. They held their grip long enough to make Jennifer feel awkward. There was an innocence about him, she thought. Maybe more. Naiveté.

"Actually, there *is* more."

She dropped his hand. "There is? More than you told the police?"

"He called me again."

"But you didn't call the police?"

"I couldn't. He told me that if I called the police, he'd do something. Carry out his next threat prematurely." He looked around nervously, breaking eye contact for the first time. "I'm sorry, I'm a bit on edge. I didn't sleep that well. Do you want to sit down?"

"That would be nice."

Kevin pulled out a chair and seated her. Naive and chivalrous. A first-year seminary student who graduated from college with honors. Not exactly the kind of guy who wakes up in the morning thinking of ways to make enemies. He sat across from her and ran a hand haphazardly through his hair.

"When did he call you?"

"After I got home last night. He knows when I'm here; he knows when I'm gone. He can hear everything I say. He's probably listening to us right now."

"He may very well be. There'll be a team here in less than an hour. Until then there's not much we can do about surveillance. What we can do is try to get into this man's head. That's what I do, Kevin; I figure people out for a living. But to do that I need you to tell me everything he said to you. You're my link to him. Until we put this guy away, you and I are going to have to work very closely. No secrets. I don't care what he says you can or can't do—I need to hear it all."

"He said I couldn't tell the police anything. He also told me the FBI would be involved, but he didn't seem bothered by that. He doesn't want the city to come unglued every time he calls me."

She nearly broke her professional facade then. The killer expected the FBI. Did he expect Jennifer? It really had started again, hadn't it? He knew that she would come after him again—even welcomed it! The faint taste of copper washed through her mouth. She swallowed.

Kevin tapped his foot and stared at her without breaking eye contact. His gaze was neither piercing nor intimidating. Disarming perhaps, but not in a way that made her uncomfortable—his eyes held a quality she couldn't quite put a finger on. Maybe innocence. Wide, blue, tired innocence.

Not so different from Roy, really. Was there a connection?

You're staring back, Jennifer. Suddenly she was uncomfortable. She felt a strange empathy for him. How could any sane man threaten someone as innocent as this? Answer: *No* sane man.

I'm going to keep you alive, Kevin Parson. I won't let him hurt you.

"One step at a time," Jennifer said. "I want you to start from the phone call after you got home and tell me exactly what he said."

He relayed the phone call in meticulous detail while she asked questions and took notes. She covered every conceivable angle—the choice of words, the sequencing of events, the tone Slater used, the nearly unlimited ways in which Slater might have had access to his life.

"So you think he's been in here on more than one occasion. On one of those occasions he found Samantha's number. He thinks you and Samantha are romantically involved, but you're not."

"That's right."

"Have you ever been?"

"No, not really." Kevin shifted in his seat. "Although I'm not sure that wasn't a mistake on my part."

Obviously Slater had decided that Kevin and Samantha were more than friends. Who was mistaken, Slater or Kevin? She eyed the man before her. How naive was he?

"You should talk to her," Kevin said. "Maybe she could help somehow. She's not a cop."

"Sure." Jennifer dismissed the suggestion even as she spoke. She had no interest in consulting some rookie at this stage. All she needed was one more gunslinger on the case. "How long have you known her?"

"We grew up together here in Long Beach."

She made a note and changed the subject. "So actually Slater called you three times yesterday. Once on your cell phone, once at home here, and once on a cell phone he left for you? The third call just to make sure the phone worked."

"I guess. Yes, three times."

"We have three minutes, three calls, three rules, a riddle with three parts, three months. You think our guy likes threes?"

"Three months?"

She had to tell him. "You ever hear about the Riddle Killer?"

"The guy from Sacramento."

"Yes. We have reason to believe this is him. He killed his last victim three months ago."

"I heard that on the news." Kevin closed his eyes. "You really think it's him?"

"Yes, I do. But he's never let anyone live that we know of. I'm not trying to be crass—there's just no other way to deal with this. We have a chance, an excellent chance, of stopping him before he goes further."

He opened his eyes. "How?"

"He wants to play. It's not the killing that drives him; it's the game. We play."

"Play?" He stared at her desperately and then lowered his head. She wanted to put an arm around him, to comfort him, to hold this poor soul and tell him that everything was going to be okay. But that would be both untrue and unprofessional.

"You ever play chess?"

"A game or two."

"Think of this as a chess match. He's black and you're white. He's made his first move and you've made yours. You lost a pawn. As long as he's interested in the game, he'll play. Your job is to keep him playing long enough for us to find him. It's the only way to beat him."

Kevin ran both hands through his hair. "And what if he's listening right now?"

"We always assume he's listening. He's undoubtedly got the technology to hear what he wants to hear. But for him to hear what I just told you is music to his ears. He's back in some hole right now, rubbing his hands in anticipation of the game. The longer the better. He might not be sane, but he's brilliant. Probably a genius. He'll never toss a match and run scared just because some two-bit FBI agent's on to him."

I hope you are listening, you snake. She clenched her jaw.

Kevin offered an anemic smile. Apparently he understood, but he wasn't in a place to like anything about Slater's game. "The threes could be coincidental," he said. "Maybe."

"Nothing is coincidental with this guy. His mind works on a whole different plane than most. Can I see the cell phone he gave you?"

He pulled it out of his pocket and handed it to her. She flipped it open and scrolled through the activity log. One call at 4:50 yesterday afternoon, as reported.

"Okay, keep this with you. Don't give it to the police, and don't tell them I told you not to give it to them."

That earned her a soft grin, and she couldn't resist returning it. They'd take a crack at tracking Slater's number and triangulating his position, but she wasn't optimistic. There were too many ways to beat the system.

"We'll bug the phone—"

"He said no cops."

"I mean we, the FBI. We'll use a local device that will attach to the cell. I doubt a conventional listening device will do us any good—too easy to scramble and limited on range. The recording device will be noticeable, a small box we'll fix to the back here." She drew her finger through an inch square on the back of the silver phone. "It'll contain a small chip we can remove for analysis later. Not exactly real-time surveillance, but it may be all that we get next time."

He took the phone back. "So I do what he says? Play his game?"

She nodded. "I don't think we have a choice. We'll take him at his word. He calls you; the second you hang up, you call me. He'll probably know about it, and then I guess we'll know what he means by no cops."

Kevin stood and paced to the kitchen counter and back. "Detective Milton grilled me on motivation. Without motivation you have nothing. I can understand that. I think I have an idea."

"Go ahead."

"Hate."

"Hate. That's pretty broad."

"Slater hates me. I can hear it in his voice. Raw contempt. There are few things left in this world that are pure, from my observation. The hate in this man's voice is one of them."

She looked up at him. "You're observant. The question is why. Why does Slater hate you?"

"Maybe not me, but my type," Kevin said. "People tend to react to other people in wholesale rather than detail, right? He's a minister, so I hate him. She's beautiful, so I like her. One month later you wake up and realize you have nothing in common with the woman."

"Do you have firsthand experience on the subject or are you just spinning this from a sociology text?"

Kevin blinked, caught off guard. Unless her intuition was misfiring, he had very little experience with women.

"Well . . ." He ran his hand over his head. "Both, sorta."

"This may qualify as new knowledge, Kevin, but there are men who judge a woman by more than her appearance." She wasn't sure why she felt obligated to say as much; she'd found no offense in his remark.

He didn't bat an eye. "Of course. I see you and you're beautiful, but my attraction to you is based on your caring. I can tell that you really do care about me." He broke eye contact again. "I mean, not in the way it sounds. As your case is what I mean. Not as a man—"

"I understand. Thank you. That was a nice thing to say."

The short exchange felt absurd. Kevin sat back down and for a moment neither spoke.

"But your point is valid," Jennifer said. "Most serial offenders choose victims based on what they represent, not on personal offenses. It's the meticulous thought that Slater has put into this case that makes me wonder if we aren't dealing with personal motivation here. Obsession comes to mind. He's taken a very personal interest in you."

Kevin looked away. "Could be that he's just a very meticulous person." He seemed particularly interested in depersonalizing the motive.

"You're a profiler—what is my profile?" Kevin asked. "Based on what you know, what is there about me that might set off someone?"

"I don't have enough to offer—"

"No, but based on what you do know?"

"My first blush? Okay. You're a seminary student. You take life seriously and have a higher intelligence than most. You're caring and kind and gentle. You live alone and have very few friends. You're attractive and carry yourself with confidence, notwithstanding a couple nervous habits." It occurred to Jennifer as she ran down the list that Kevin was an unusually good person, not merely innocent. "But it's your genuine innocence that stands out. If Slater has no personal stake in you, he hates you for your innocence."

There was more to Kevin than she could see at first glance, much more. How could anyone dislike, much less hate, Kevin Parson?

"You remind me of my brother," she said. Then she wished she hadn't.

What if the Riddle Killer wanted Jennifer to see the similarities between Roy and Kevin? What if he'd chosen Kevin because he intended to make Jennifer live through the hell once again?

Pure speculation.

Jennifer rose. "I have to get back to the lab. The police will be here shortly. If there's anything you need, or if you think of anything else, call. I'll have one of our men watch the house. Promise me you will never leave alone. This guy likes to drop his little bombs when they're least expected."

"Sure."

He looked lost. "Don't worry, Kevin. We'll make it through this."

"In one piece, hopefully." He grinned nervously.

She put her hand on top of his. "We will. Trust me." She once said those same words to Roy to calm him down. Jennifer removed her hand.

They stared at each other for a moment. *Say something, Jennifer.* "Remember, he wants a game. We're going to give him a game."

"Right."

Jennifer left him standing in his doorway looking anything but confident. *Trust me.* She considered staying until the techs arrived, but she had to get back to the evidence. She'd cornered the Riddle Killer once, before he'd gone after Roy, and she'd done it through careful analysis of the evidence. She did her best work when climbing around in criminals' minds, not holding their victims' hands.

On the other hand, Kevin was no ordinary victim.

Who are you, Kevin? Whoever he was, she decided that she liked him.

9

KEVIN HAD NEVER FELT entirely comfortable around women—because of his mother, Sam insisted—but Jennifer seemed different. As a professional it was her job to engender trust, he knew, but he'd seen more than the expected professional facade in her eyes. He'd seen a real woman who'd warmed to him beyond the demands of her job. He wasn't sure how that translated to her capability as an investigator, but he felt certain he could trust her sincerity.

Unfortunately, it did nothing for his confidence.

Kevin walked to the telephone and dialed Samantha's number. She answered on the fifth ring.

"Sam."

"Hi, Sam. The FBI was just here."

"And?"

"Nothing new, really. She thinks it's the Riddle Killer."

"She?"

"The agent. Jennifer Peters."

"I've heard of her. Listen, there's a chance I may need to fly back to Sacramento today. Actually, I have my office on the other line. Can I call you right back?"

"Everything okay?"

"Give me a few minutes and I'll explain, okay?"

He hung up and glanced at the clock. 8:47. Where were the

police? He checked the dishwasher. Half full. He dumped in some detergent and turned it on. It would take him a week to fill the thing up, and by that time it would begin to smell sour.

Slater would have his hands full; that much was good. Surely between Sam, Jennifer, and the Long Beach police he would be safe. Kevin crossed to the refrigerator.

Jennifer thinks I'm nice. I don't care if I'm nice—I want to be alive. And I wouldn't mind if Slater were dead. How nice is that? If a man gossips, is he not nice? The bishop gossips, so he's not nice. Kevin sighed. *Here I am rambling again while the world's blowing up around me.* What would the psychobabblist say about that?

I don't know why I do it, Doctor, but I think the strangest things at the oddest times.

So do all men, Kevin. So do all men. Women don't, of course. The female tends to be the more intelligent or at least the more stable of the sexes. Turn the country over to them and you'll wake up to find the potholes down your street filled in like they should have been a year ago. You're just a man finding his way in a mad world gone madder, madder hatter. We'll break that down next session if you drop another check in the pay box over there. Two hundred this time. My kids need . . .

Kevin twitched. He didn't remember opening the fridge, but now, standing in front of the open door, the milk jug filled his vision. Someone had scrawled a large 3 on the Albertsons jug with a black magic marker, and above it three words:

It's so dark

Slater!

Kevin released the door and stepped back.

When? What's so dark? The *fridge* is so dark? Was this another riddle? He had to tell Jennifer! No, Samantha. He had to tell Sam!

Dread crept into his bones. Where is it so dark? In the cellar. The boy! He stood still, unable to breathe. The world began to spin. *It's so dark.*

Dear God, it *was* the boy!

The door closed on its own. He backed to the wall. But Slater had said he wasn't the boy! *What boy?* he'd said.

The events of that night so long ago swept over him.

III

For a whole week after young Kevin's encounter with the bully, he waited in agony. Dark circles gathered under his eyes and he caught a cold. He made up a story about falling out of bed to explain the bruises on his face. His mother had put him to bed early in the afternoon to fight the cold. He just lay there, sweating on the sheets. His fear wasn't for himself, but for Samantha. The boy had promised to hurt her, and Kevin was sick with worry.

Six days later a tap had finally sounded on his window. He'd eased the blind up, holding his breath. Sam's smiling face stared at him from the backyard. Kevin nearly hit the ceiling in his excitement. As it turned out, Sam had been away at camp. She was horrified by his haggard features, and only after much urging did she convince him to come out to talk. No one would see them; she swore it. He made her search for the boy all around the yard, just to make sure. When he did sneak out, he went only just beyond his own fence, keeping a watchful eye on the greenway. They sat there, hidden in the shadows, and he told Sam everything.

"I'll tell my dad," she said. "You think if he licked my window we'll still be able to see it?"

Kevin shuddered. "Probably. You have to tell your dad. You should go tell him right now. But don't tell him about me sneaking out to see you. Just tell him I was walking by and saw the boy at your

window and he chased me. Don't even tell him that he . . . did anything to me. Your dad might tell my mom."

"Okay."

"Then come back and tell me what he says."

"You mean tonight?"

"Right now. Go home by the street and watch out for the boy.
He's going to kill us."

By now Sam was scared, despite her typical optimism. "Okay." She
stood and brushed off her shorts. "My dad might not let me back out.
In fact, he might even make me stay home for a while if I tell him."

Kevin thought about that. "That's okay. At least you'll be safe;
that's the main thing. But please, come back as soon as you can."

"Okay." She held out her hand and pulled him up. "Friends for
life?"

"Friends for life," he said. He gave her a hug and she ran off toward
the street.

Sam didn't come back to his window that night. Or the next. Or
for three weeks. They were the loneliest weeks of Kevin's life. He tried
to convince his mom to let him out, but she wouldn't hear of it. He
tried to sneak out during the day twice, not through the window, of
course—he could never risk Mother discovering the screw or the loose
board. He went over the back fence, but only got as far as the first tree
on the greenway before Bob began to wail. He barely made it back
onto the ash heap before Mother hurried out in a tizzy. The other time
he went through the front door and made it all the way to Sam's house
only to find, as he had known he would, that she was gone to school.
His mom was waiting for him when he tried to sneak back in, and he
spent the next two days in his room.

Then, on the twenty-second day, the tap came at his window. He
peeked very carefully, terrified that it might be the boy. He would
never be able to describe the warmth that flooded his heart when he

saw Sam's face in the moonlight. He fumbled with the screw and yanked the window open. They threw their arms around each other before he tumbled out and ran with her through the fence.

"What happened?" he asked, breathless.

"My dad found him! He's a thirteen-year-old who lives on the other side of the warehouses. I guess the boy has caused trouble before; Dad knew him when I described him. Oh, you should have seen my dad, Kevin! I've never seen him so angry. He told the boy's parents that they had two weeks to move, or he was going to haul their boy off to jail. Guess what? They moved!"

"He's . . . he's gone?"

"Gone." She raised a palm and he absently high-fived it.

"You sure?"

"My dad let me out, didn't he? Yes, I'm sure. Come on!"

It took Kevin only two outings with Sam to lose his fear of the night again. The boy was indeed gone.

Two weeks later Kevin decided that it was about time he take the initiative to visit Sam. You could only play white knight so many times without actually flexing your muscle some.

Kevin snuck along the treelined greenway toward Sam's house, picking his way carefully. This was his first time out alone in over a month. He made it to her fence easily enough. The light from her window was a welcome sight. He bent down and pulled the loose picket aside.

"Pssst."

Kevin froze.

"Hello, squat."

The horrible sound of the boy's voice filled Kevin with images of a sick twisted smile. He suddenly felt nauseated.

"Stand up," the boy said.

Kevin stood slowly and pivoted. His muscles had turned to water, all except for his heart, which was slamming into his throat. There, ten feet away, stood the boy, grinning wickedly, turning the knife in his right hand. He wore a bandanna that covered his tattoo.

"I've decided something," the boy said. "There are three of us on this little totem pole here. But I'm at the bottom and I don't like that. I'm going to take out the top two. What do you think about that?"

Kevin couldn't think clearly about anything.

"I'll tell you what I'm going to do," the boy said. "First I'm going to cut you in a few places you'll never forget. I want you to use your imagination for me. Then I'm going to come back here and tap on Samantha's window like you do. When she opens the shade, I'm going to stick my knife right through the glass."

The boy chewed on his tongue; his eyes flashed with excitement. He lifted the knife and touched the blade with his left hand. He glanced down and fixated on the sharp edge. "I'll be through the glass and in her throat before she can . . ."

Kevin ran then, while the boy's eyes were still diverted.

"Hey!"

The boy took after him. Kevin had a twenty-foot head start—a fifth of what he needed to outrun the larger boy. At first sheer adrenaline pushed Kevin forward. But behind him the boy began to chuckle and his voice grew closer. Now terror pounded Kevin in unrelenting waves. He screamed, but nothing came out because his throat had frozen shut. The ground seemed to slope upward and then sideways and Kevin lost his sense of direction.

A hand touched his collar. If the boy caught him, he would use the knife. And then he would go after Sam. He might not kill her, but he would at least cut her face. Probably worse.

He wasn't sure where his house was, but it wasn't where he desperately needed it to be. So Kevin did the only thing he knew to do. He turned to his left and tore across the street.

The chuckling stopped for a moment. The boy grunted and doubled his efforts—Kevin could hear his feet pounding with a new determination.

The chuckling started again.

Kevin's chest ached and his breath came in huge gasps now. For a terrible moment he considered just falling down and letting the boy cut him up.

A hand swatted him on the head. "Keep running, squat. I hate it when they just lie there."

Kevin had lost his sense of direction completely. They were coming up to one of the old warehouses in the district across the street. He saw a door in the building directly ahead. Maybe . . . maybe if he could get through that door.

He veered to his right, and then broke for the building. He slammed into the old door, yanked it open, and plunged into the darkness beyond.

The stairwell five feet inside the door saved his life, or at the very least some of his body parts. He tumbled down the stairs, crying out in pain. When he came to rest at the bottom landing, his head felt as though it had come off. He struggled to his feet and turned back to the stairs.

The boy stood at the top, backlit by the moonlight, chuckling. "The end," he said and started down the steps.

Kevin spun and ran. Right into another door. A steel door. He grasped the handle and twisted, but the bulk refused to budge. He saw the deadbolt, threw it open, and plunged headlong into a pitch-black room. He stumbled forward and smacked into a concrete wall.

The boy grabbed Kevin's hair.

Kevin screamed. His voice echoed crazily about him. He screamed louder. No one would hear them; they were underground.

"Shut up! Shut up!" The boy hit him in the mouth.

Kevin summoned all of his fear and struck out blindly into the darkness. His fist connected with something that cracked. The boy hollered and let go of Kevin's hair. Kevin's legs gave way and he collapsed.

It occurred to him in that moment that whatever the boy had initially planned for him could no longer compare to what he would do now.

Kevin rolled and staggered to his feet. The door was to his right, dull gray in the faint light. The boy faced him, one hand on his nose, the other tight around the knife.

"You just lost your eyes, boy."

Kevin bolted without thought. He sprang through the open door, spun around, and slammed it shut. He threw his left hand up and rammed the deadbolt home.

Then it was just him, in the concrete staircase, breathing hard. Silence swallowed him.

A very soft yell reached beyond the steel door. Kevin held his breath and backed up slowly. He lunged up the steps, got halfway up before the sound of the boy reached him again, just barely. He was yelling and cursing and threatening him with words Kevin could barely understand because they were so quiet.

There was no way out, was there? If he left, the boy might die in there! No one would hear his screams. He couldn't leave.

Kevin turned back and slowly descended the stairs. What if he slipped the bolt open and made a break for it? He could make it, maybe.

"I swear I'm gonna kill you . . ."

Kevin knew then that he had only two options. Open the door and get cut, maybe die. Run away and let the boy die, maybe live.

"I hate you! I hate you!" The scream was eerily distant, but raspy and bitter.

Kevin whirled around and flew up the steps. He had no choice. He had no choice. For Samantha, that's what the boy got. It was his own fault anyway.

Kevin shut the outer door behind him and ran into the night. He didn't know quite how or exactly when, but sometime while it was still dark, he made it back into his bed.

III

Something rattled violently. Kevin jerked up. The tabletop reflected the morning sun at eye level. The cell phone vibrated slowly toward the edge.

Kevin scrambled to his feet. *Dear God, give me strength.* He glanced at the clock. 9:00 A.M. Where were the police?

He reached his hand for the phone, hesitated, and then snatched it off the table. Play the game, Jennifer had said. *Play the game.*

"Hello?"

"How is our chess player doing this morning?" Slater asked.

So he *had* been listening! Kevin closed his eyes and focused his mind. His life depended on what he said. Be smart. Outthink him.

"Ready to play," he said, but his voice didn't sound ready.

"You'll have to do better than that. Kevin, Kevin, Kevin. Two little challenges, two little failures, two little booms. You're beginning to bore me. Did you see my little gift?"

"Yes."

"What's three times three?"

Three times three. "Nine," he said.

"Smart boy. Nine o'clock, time to rock. Time for the third. *What takes you there but takes you nowhere?* You have sixty minutes. It'll be worse this time, Kevin."

The phone on the counter rang shrilly. He had to keep Slater on the phone.

"Can I ask a question?" he asked.

"No. But you may answer the room phone. Maybe it will be Sam. Wouldn't that be cozy? Answer the phone."

Kevin slowly lifted the room phone off the hook.

"Kevin?" Sam's familiar voice filled his ear, and despite the impossible situation, he felt a bucket of relief wash over him. He wasn't sure what to say. He held the cell phone against his right ear and the room phone against his other ear.

"Tell her hello from Slater," Slater said.

Kevin hesitated. "Slater says hello," he said.

"He called?" she asked.

"He's on the other line."

"Too bad Jennifer left so early," Slater said. "The four of us could throw a little party. Time's running out. Fifty-nine minutes and fifty-one seconds. Your move." The cell phone clicked.

Sam spoke again. "Kevin, listen to me! Is he still on—"

"He's gone."

"Don't move. I'm turning up your street now. I'll be there in ten seconds." She disconnected.

Kevin stood, immobile, a phone in each hand. Play the game. Play the game. It was the boy; it had to be the boy.

The door flew open. "Kevin?" Sam ran in.

He spun. "I have sixty minutes."

"Or what?"

"Another bomb?"

She stepped up to him and cradled her hands under his wrists. "Okay. Listen to me, we have to think this through clearly." She eased the phones out of his hands and then took him by the shoulders. "Listen to me—"

"We have to call the FBI."

"We will. But I want you to tell me first. Tell me exactly what he said."

"I know who the Riddle Killer is."

She stared, stunned. "Who?"

Kevin sat heavily in a chair. "The boy."

"I thought he told you he *wasn't* the boy."

Kevin's mind began to work faster. "He said, 'What boy?' He didn't say he *wasn't* the boy." He ran to the refrigerator, opened the door, pulled out the milk jug, and slammed it on the counter.

She stared at the thick-stroked letters. Her eyes shifted to him and then back. "When was—"

"He was in here last night."

"*It's so dark.* What's so dark?"

Kevin paced and rubbed his head.

"Tell me, Kevin. Just tell me. We're running out of time here."

"Your dad made the boy leave, but he came back."

"What do you mean? We never saw him again!"

"I did! He caught me on my way to your house two weeks later. He said he was going to hurt you. And me. I ran and somehow . . ." Emotions clogged his head. He glanced at the clock. 9:02. "Somehow we ended up in a storage basement in one of the warehouses. I don't even remember which one anymore. I locked him in and ran away."

She blinked. "What happened?"

"I had to do it, Sam!" He spoke desperately now. "He was going to kill you! And me!"

"It's okay. It's okay, Kevin. We can talk about it later, okay? Right now—"

"That's the sin he wants me to confess. I left him to die in the dark."

"But he *didn't* die, did he? Obviously he's alive. You didn't kill anyone."

He paused. Of course! The dark night flashed through his mind. Unless Slater wasn't the boy, but someone who knew about the incident, a psychopath who'd discovered the truth somehow and had decided that Kevin should pay.

"Either way, I locked a boy in a basement and left him to die. That's intent. That's as good as murder."

"You don't know that this has anything to do with the boy. We have to think this through, Kevin."

"We don't have time to think this through! It's the only thing that makes any sense. If I confess, this crazy game stops." He paced and rubbed his head, suppressing a sudden urge to cry over the thought of actually confessing after all that he'd done to rid himself of his past. "Oh God, what have I done? This can't be happening. Not after everything else."

She stared at him, digesting the new information, her eyes wrinkled with empathy. "So then confess, Kevin. That was almost twenty years ago."

"Come on, Sam!" He whirled to her, angry. "This will blow skyhigh. Every American who watches the news will know about the seminary student who buried another kid alive and left him to die. This will ruin me!"

"Better ruined than dead. Besides, you had reason to lock up the boy. I'll come to your defense."

"None of that matters. If I am capable of attempted murder, I am capable of anything. That's the reputation that will follow me." He gritted his teeth. "This is nuts. We're running out of time. I have to call the newspaper and tell them. It's the only way to stop that maniac before he kills me."

"Maybe, but he's also demanding that you solve the riddle. We may be dealing with the same killer from Sacramento—"

"I know. Jennifer told me. Still, the only way to stop him is to confess. The riddle is supposed to tell me what to confess." Kevin headed for the phone. He had to call the newspaper. Slater was listening—he'd know. This was insane.

"What was the riddle?"

He stopped. "*What takes you there but takes you nowhere?* He said it would be worse this time."

"How does *that* tie in to the boy?" she asked.

The question hadn't occurred to him. *What takes you there but takes you nowhere?* "I don't know." What if Sam was right? What if his confession about the boy wasn't what Slater was looking for?

"What connection is there between the boy and the three riddles he's given?" She grabbed a piece of paper. "Sixty minutes. Yesterday it was three minutes and then thirty minutes. Today it's sixty minutes. What time did he call?"

"Nine o'clock. Three times three. That's what he said."

Her eyes studied the riddles she'd jotted down.

"Call Agent Peters. Tell her about Slater's call and the confession. Ask her to call the newspaper and tell her to get over here as fast as she can. We have to crack these riddles."

Kevin punched in the number Jennifer had left him. The clock read 9:07. They still had fifty-three minutes. Jennifer picked up.

"He called," Kevin said.

Silence.

"He called—"

"Another riddle?"

"Yes. But I think I might know who he is and what he wants."

"Tell me!"

Kevin told her the rest in a halting run-on that ate up several minutes. An urgency he hadn't expected crowded her voice. She was impatient and demanding. But her intensity reassured him.

"So you think you know who he is, and you neglect to tell me about his demand that you confess. What are you trying to do to me? This is a killer we're dealing with!"

"I'm sorry, I was scared. I'm telling you now."

"Any other secrets?"

"No. Please, I'm sorry."

"Samantha's there?"

"Yes. You have to get this confession out," Kevin said. "That's what this is about."

"We don't know that. I don't see the relationship between the riddles and the boy."

"He was here, last night, and he wrote on my milk jug," Kevin said. "It has to be him! You wanted motivation; now you have it. I tried to kill someone. He's mad. How's that? You have to get this confession on the air."

Silence stretched on the line.

"Jennifer?"

"We need more time!" she said and then took a breath. "Okay, I'll put the confession on the wire. Stay put. Do not set foot outside that house, you hear me? Work the riddles."

"Sam—"

But Jennifer had hung up. Now there was a no-nonsense girl. He found comfort in the fact.

Kevin hung up. 9:13. "She'll call the paper."

"Three," Samantha said. "Our guy's tripping over his threes. Progressions. Three, thirty, sixty. And opposites. Night and day, life and death. *What takes you there but takes you nowhere?*" She stared at her page of notes and numbers.

"She wasn't exactly thrilled about you being here," Kevin said.

Sam looked up. "What takes you there? The obvious answer is transportation. Like a car. But he did a car. He won't do a car again. He's into progressions. More."

Kevin's mind spun. "A bus. Train. Plane. But they take you somewhere, don't they?"

"Depends on where somewhere is. I don't think it matters—*there* and *nowhere* are opposites. I think he's going to blow up some kind of public transport!"

"Unless the confession—"

"We can't assume that'll stop him." She jumped to her feet, grabbed the phone from its cradle, and punched the redial.

"Agent Peters? Sam Sheer here. Listen, I think—" She paused and listened. "Yes, I do understand jurisdiction, and as far as I'm concerned, Kevin has always been *my* jurisdiction. If you want to press the matter, I'll get authorization from the attorney gen—" Another pause, and Sam was smiling now. "My thoughts exactly. But how long will it take to evacuate all public transportation in Long Beach?" She glanced at her watch. "By my watch we have forty-two minutes." Sam listened for a while. "Thank you."

She hung up. "Sharp gal. Feisty. The news already has your story. It's going out live on television as we speak."

Kevin ran to his television and flipped it on.

"The next edition of the paper won't hit the street until tomorrow morning," Sam said. "Slater didn't mention the paper this time, did he?"

"No. I'm sure television will work. God help me."

Empathy lit Sam's gentle eyes. "Jennifer doesn't think this will satisfy him. The real game's the riddle. I think she's right." She paced and put both palms on her head. "Think, Sam, think!"

"They're evacuating the public—"

"There's no way they can get them all out in time," Sam said. "It'll take them half an hour just to get the clearances! There's more here. Slater's precise. He's given us more."

The program on the television suddenly changed. The familiar face of Tom Schilling, news anchor for the ABC affiliate, filled the screen. A red "Breaking News" banner scrolled across the picture tube.

The graphic behind Tom Schilling was a shot of Kevin's charred car with the words "Riddle Killer?" superimposed in a choppy font. The anchor glanced off-camera to his right and then faced the audience.

Kevin stared, spellbound. Tom Schilling was about to drop the hammer on his life. Goose bumps rippled up his neck. Maybe confessing *had* been a mistake.

"We have a shocking new development in the case of the car explosion on Long Beach Boulevard yesterday. Kevin Parson, the driver of the car, has come forward with new information that may shed light on the investigation."

When Kevin heard his name, the room faded, the picture blurred, and the words grew garbled, as if spoken underwater. His life was over. Tom Schilling droned on.

"Kevin Parson is a seminary student at . . ."

You're dead.

" . . . the hopeful clergyman has confessed . . ."

This is it.

" . . . locked the boy in an underground . . ."

Your life is over.

He thought it odd that this exposure brought on a sense of impending death even more acutely than Slater's threats had. He'd spent five years pulling himself out of Baker Street's sea of despondency, and now, in the space of less than twenty-four hours, he found himself overboard, drowning again. Someone would start digging into the rest of his childhood. Into the truth behind Balinda and the house.

Here am I. Kevin Parson, a shell of a man who is capable of the most wicked sin conceived of by man. Here am I, a wretched pretender. I am nothing more than a slug, role-playing its way through life in human form. When you learn everything, you will know that and more.

Thank you. Thank you, Aunt Balinda, for sharing this with me. I am nothing. Thank you, you lousy, sick, twisted auntie for slamming this nugget of truth down my throat. I am nothing, nothing, nothing. Thank you, you demon from hell for gouging out my eyes and pounding me into the ground and . . .

"—vin? Kevin!"

Kevin turned. Sam sat at the table, remote in hand, staring at him. The television was off. It occurred to him that he was trembling. He exhaled and relaxed his balled hands, ran them through his hair. *Get a grip, Kevin. Hold yourself together.*

But he didn't want to hold himself together. He wanted to cry. "What?"

"I'm sorry, Kevin. It's not as bad as it sounds. I'll get you through this, I promise."

It's not as bad as it sounds because you don't know the whole story, Sam. You don't know what really happened in that house on Baker Street. He turned away from her. *God, help me. Please help me.*

"I'll be okay," he said and cleared his throat. "We have to focus on the riddle."

A stray thought whispered to Kevin.

"It's the numbers," Sam said. "Public transportation is numbered. Slater's going to blow a bus or a train identified with the number three."

The thought raised its voice. "He said no cops!"

"What—"

"No cops!" Kevin shouted. "They're using cops to evacuate?"

The fear he felt spread through her eyes. "Dear God!"

|||

"I don't care if they have to delay every flight in the country!" Jennifer said. "We have a credible bomb threat here, sir! Get the governor on the line if you have to. Terrorist or not, this guy's going to blow something."

"Thirty-five minutes—"

"Is enough time to start."

The bureau chief hesitated.

"Look, Frank," Jennifer said, "you have to put your neck on the line with me here. The local police don't have the muscle to push this through fast enough. Milton's working on the buses, but the bureaucracy's thicker than molasses down here. I need this from the top."

"You're sure about this?"

"Meaning what? That I'm jumping the gun? We can't afford to risk—"

"Okay. But if this turns out to be a hoax . . ."

"It won't be the first."

She hung up and took a deep breath. It had already occurred to her that they'd violated one of Slater's rules. No cops. But she saw no alternatives. She needed the local police.

A junior detective, Randal Crenshaw, burst through the door. "Milton says they're tracking down the director of local transport now. He should have an answer in ten minutes."

"How long will it take them to clear the buses once they have the word?"

"Dispatch can move pretty quick." He shrugged. "Maybe ten minutes."

She stood and paced the length of the conference table. They now had the first significant lead in the case. The boy. If indeed it was this boy. He'd be how old now? Early thirties? More importantly, someone other than Kevin knew the killer: Samantha Sheer's father, a policeman named Rick Sheer, who'd caught the boy spying.

"I want you to track down a cop who worked Long Beach about twenty years ago," she told Crenshaw. "Name's Rick Sheer. Find him. I need to talk to him. Run a search on any of his logs that mention a boy who was threatening the children in his neighborhood."

The detective scribbled the name across a piece of paper and left.

She was missing something. Somewhere in the notes she'd taken this morning was the identity of the bus or the train or whatever Slater planned on blowing, if indeed they were right about the riddle referring to public transportation.

The target wasn't Kevin, and Jennifer found relief in the realization. For the moment it wasn't *his* life at risk. For now Slater was more interested in playing. Play the game, Kevin. Lead him on. She snatched up the phone and dialed his number.

He picked up on the fifth ring.

"Any thoughts?"

"Just going to call you. It could be a bus or something identified with a three," Kevin said.

That was it! Had to be. "Three. I'll have them put a priority on anything with a three in the identifier."

"How are they doing?"

"Looks good. We should know something in ten minutes."

"That's cutting it pretty close, isn't it?"

"It's the best they can do."

|||

Sam snapped her cell phone closed and grabbed her purse. "That's it, let's go!" She ran for the door. "I'll drive."

Kevin ran after her. "How many?"

"Long Beach proper has twenty-five buses, each identified with several letters and a number. We want number twenty-three. It runs down Alamitos and then back up Atlantic. That's not far. With any luck we'll run into it."

"What about three or thirteen?"

"They started the numbering at five and skipped thirteen."

The tires on Sam's car squealed. She was certain Slater had a bus in mind. The planes were less likely targets for the simple reason that security was far tighter than it once had been. She had checked the trams—no threes. Trains were a possibility, but again, high security. It had to be a bus. The fact that there was only one with three in its designator offered at least a sliver of hope.

Twenty-nine minutes.

They flew across Willow toward Alamitos but were stopped by a red light at Walnut. Sam glanced both directions and sped through.

"Now is one time I wouldn't mind a cop on my tail," she said. "We could use their help."

"No cops," Kevin said.

She looked at him. Two more minutes passed before they hit Alamitos.

"You see a bus, it's probably number twenty-three. You yell."

But they passed no buses. They crossed Third Street through a red. Still no bus.

Ocean Boulevard, right; Atlantic, north. No bus. Horns honked at them on several occasions.

"Time?" she asked.

"Nine thirty-seven."

"Come on! Come on!"

Sam backtracked. When they hit Third again, the light was red and cars blocked the intersection. A bus numbered "6453–17" rumbled by, headed west on Third Street. Wrong bus. The car was stuffy. Sweat beaded their foreheads. The intersection cleared and Sam shoved the accelerator down. "Come on, baby. Where are you?"

She'd cleared the intersection by fifty feet when she slammed on the brakes.

"What?"

She jerked her head around and stared back toward Third Street. She frantically grabbed her cell phone, hit the redial button.

"Yes, could you tell me which bus runs down Third Street?"

Kevin heard the deep male voice from his seat. "The Third Street bus. You need—"

Sam slammed the phone shut, yanked the wheel around, and pulled directly into traffic. She pulled through a screaming U-turn, cutting off a white Volvo and a blue sedan. Horns blared.

"They call the buses by their street names, not their numbers!" Sam said.

"But you don't know if Slater—"

"We know where the Third Street bus is. Let's clear it first and then go for twenty-three." She squealed onto Third Street and honed in on the bus, not a hundred yards ahead. Obviously dispatch hadn't reached the driver yet.

Nineteen minutes.

Sam pulled directly in front of the bus and braked. The bus blasted its horn and ground to a halt behind them.

"Tell the driver to evacuate and stay clear for at least half an hour. Tell them to spread the word to the other cars on the street. Tell them there's a bomb—it works every time. I'm calling Agent Peters."

Kevin ran to the bus. He hammered on the door, but the driver, an older man who must have been three times his recommended weight, refused to open.

"There's a bomb on board!" he yelled, flinging his hands out like an explosion. "A bomb!" He wondered if any of them recognized him from the television. *The kid-killer is now downtown pulling old women off of buses.*

A young man who looked like Tom Hanks stuck his head out an open window. "A what?"

"A bomb! Get out! Clear the bus. Clear the street."

For a moment, nothing happened. Then the door hissed open, and the same young man stumbled out. He yelled back into the bus.

"Get them out, you idiot! He said there's a bomb on this bus!"

A dozen passengers—half by what Kevin could see—bolted from their seats. The driver seemed to catch the fever. "Okay, everyone out! Watch your step. Just a precaution, ladies and gentlemen. Don't shove!"

Kevin grabbed the Tom Hanks look-alike. "Clear this street and stay clear for at least thirty minutes, you hear? Get them all out of here!"

"What is it? How do you know?"

Kevin ran for Sam's car. "Trust me. Just get them clear. The police are on their way." The passengers didn't need any encouragement. Cars stopped and then sped past the bus or backed away.

He slid into the car.

"Hold on," Sam said. She sped off, took an immediate right on the next street, and headed back toward Atlantic.

"One down. Fifteen minutes left."

"This is nuts," Kevin said. "We don't even know if Slater's—"

The cell phone went berserk in his pocket. Kevin froze and stared at his right thigh.

"What?" Sam asked.

"He . . . he's calling."

The phone vibrated again and this time he grabbed it. Samantha slowed.

"Hello?"

"I said no cops, Kevin," Slater's soft voice said. "No cops means no cops."

Kevin's fingers began to shake. "You mean the FBI?"

"Policemen. From now on it's you and Sam and Jennifer and me and no one else."

End call.

Sam had slowed way down. She looked at him with wide eyes.

"What did he say?"

"He said no cops."

The ground suddenly shook. An explosion thundered. They both ducked.

"Turn around! Turn around!"

"That was the bus," Sam whispered. She spun the car around and sped back the way they'd come.

Kevin stared as they rolled onto Third. Boiling flames and thick black smoke engulfed the surreal scene. Three blackened cars parked next to the bus smoldered. God only knew if anyone was hurt, but the immediate area looked vacant. Books lay scattered among the shattered glass of a used bookstore's windows. Its "Read It Again" sign dangled over the sidewalk dangerously. The shop owner stumbled out, stunned.

Sam shoved the gearshift into park and stared at the unearthly scene.

Her cell phone screeched and Kevin started. She lifted it slowly. "Sheer."

She blinked and immediately refocused. "How long ago?" She looked at Kevin and then the bus. A siren wailed. A car Kevin immediately recognized as Jennifer's squealed around the corner and headed toward them.

"Can Rodriguez question him?" Sam asked into her phone. "I'm in a bit of a pinch here." She turned away and lowered her voice. "He just blew up a bus. I'm parked in a car, fifty feet away from it. Yes, I am pretty sure." She listened.

Jennifer roared up and stuck her head out of her car's window. "You okay?"

"Yeah," Kevin said. His fingers were numb and his mind dazed, but he was okay.

Samantha acknowledged Jennifer with a nod, turned to the side, and covered her exposed ear. "Yes, sir. Right away. I understand . . ." She glanced at her watch. "The ten-thirty flight?"

Kevin shoved his door open.

Jennifer stopped him. "No, stay put. Don't move, I'll be right back." She drove toward the bus.

Sam finished her conversation and closed the phone.

"Do you think anyone was hurt?" Kevin asked.

She looked at the bus and shook her head. "I don't know, but we were lucky to find it when we did."

Kevin groaned and ran both hands through his hair.

"I have to go," Sam said. "That was the call I thought I might get. They want me to question a witness. His attorney will have him out by midafternoon. Unfortunately, I can't miss this. I'll explain it when I get—"

"I can't believe Slater did this," Kevin said, staring around again. "He would have killed over twenty people if we hadn't stumbled onto this bus."

She shook her head. "This changes the game. Look, I'll be back on the first flight this evening, okay? I promise. But I have to leave now if I'm going to make the flight." She rubbed his shoulder and looked in Jennifer's direction. "Tell her I'll call and give her my take; she'll take care of you." Three marked police cars had arrived and surrounded the charred bus. "We'll make it, my dear knight. I swear we'll make it."

Kevin nodded. "This is insane."

10

WITHIN FIVE MINUTES OF THE EXPLOSION, a couple dozen law enforcement officials—mostly local police but including some from her own office and several from state agencies—isolated the crime scene and began the forensic investigation. They had quickly located the bomb. By all initial appearances it was the same as the bomb in Kevin's car, only larger.

Jennifer situated Kevin in a coffee shop four doors down from the bus with strict instructions not to move—she'd be back in twenty minutes.

The parameters of the investigation had just changed. Bill Galager from the Los Angeles office arrived, as well as two junior investigators, John Mathews and Brett Mickales. They would work the case from an evidence angle, freeing her to focus on the psychology of it. One conclusion required no degree in criminal psychology—when Slater said no cops, he meant absolutely no cops. And he had the means to know if cops were involved.

According to Kevin, Slater had mentioned her by name. Jennifer. The maniac was drawing her into another trap, wasn't he? By the looks of the bus, he'd graduated into a new class.

No cops. No CBI, except Samantha, who happened to be connected to Kevin by his childhood and the boy. No ATF. No sheriff or state police. Just FBI and, specifically, just Jennifer.

"Still eager to take him on?"

Jennifer turned to Milton, who'd walked up behind her. "Eager?" A touch of defiance glimmered in his eyes, but he didn't elaborate.

"Why did he blow it early?"

"He said no cops. He obviously learned that your department had been informed—"

"They always say no cops. You're not a cop?"

"According to Kevin, he said FBI only."

Milton scoffed.

Jennifer frowned. "No cops. Evidently the history he has with us figures into his game. Bottom line is, he laid down a rule; we broke it; he blew the bus early."

"And what if he said no FBI? Would you back out? I don't think so. This is my city. You don't have the right to cut me out."

"I'm not cutting you out, Milton. Your men are all over the place."

"I'm not referring to mopping up. He's going to call again and the city knows that. They have a right to know."

"The city? You mean the press. No, Milton. The press has a right to know anything that might lend to the city's safety. You're looking at a bus this time; the next time it could be a building. You willing to risk that for the sake of protocol? If you'll excuse me, I have a case to attend to."

Milton's stare grew hot. "This is my city, not yours. I have a personal stake; you don't. Unfortunately, it seems that I'm powerless to do anything about your jurisdiction, but I was assured by your bureau chief that you would cooperate. Slater so much as coughs and you withhold it, I'll have your replacement here in five minutes."

Jennifer was tempted to slap his smug mug. She'd have to call Frank and explain. In the meantime, Milton was a thorn she would have to deal with.

"I don't like you either, Detective. You're too interested in your own good for my tastes, but I suppose that's personal. I'll keep you updated through Galager and I'll expect *your* cooperation in assisting us in any way you can. We're not stupid enough to refuse all the help we can get. But you will do nothing without my authorization. If Slater suspects your involvement, he may do 'your' city more harm than you're willing to take the heat for. Agreed?"

He eyed her carefully and then relaxed. *Didn't expect that, did you, Colombo?* She had no intention of keeping him materially involved, she realized, and the thought surprised her. In fact, in more ways than one, she welcomed Slater's restrictions. This was between her and Slater and Kevin, regardless of how personal Slater wanted to get.

"I want to put a full-court press on his house," Milton said. "Complete electronic surveillance, including wiretaps. You haven't ordered them?"

"Not wiretaps. Slater's not using the landline. The cell wizards have been monitoring the frequency on the cell phone he gave Kevin for the past forty minutes—I put in the request as soon as I left his house this morning. Slater called Kevin thirty minutes ago, just before he blew the bomb. Nothing even registered with our wizards. He's not dumb enough to talk without scrambling. This isn't your typical hack. I have an order in to fix a recording device, an AP301, to his phone ASAP, but we didn't have it on this call."

Milton glared. "I'll put someone on the house."

"No. No cops, or didn't you get that part?"

"For crying out loud, woman! You just chewed me out less than three hours ago for not having someone on him last night!"

"I'll put my own agents on the house. Keep your men clear. If you want to go head-to-head, I'll leak this to the press." She hesitated. "You get anything on the officer I asked about?"

Milton looked away and answered with some reluctance. "Officer Rick Sheer. He moved back to the San Francisco area ten years ago.

Died of cancer five years ago. There's no record that we can find of any incident involving the boy you mentioned. But that doesn't surprise me. Cops routinely deal with neighbors off the record. You say he threatened the boy's father—the incident obviously blew over. No official complaint, no arrest."

Jennifer's heart sank. That left Kevin. And Samantha. Hopefully one of them would recall something that might give them a clue to the boy's identity. All they currently had was Kevin's description, which was practically useless.

"Can you have them look again? What about a personal notebook or—"

"We wouldn't have anything like that."

"Cooperation, remember? Have them look again."

He nodded slowly. "I'll see what I can do."

"Thank you. I assume you've met Agent Galager. You'll be dealing primarily with him from here out."

"And you?"

"I'm going to do what I was trained to do, try to figure out who Slater is. Excuse me, Detective."

She walked past the bus, found Galager. "What do you have?"

"Same guy who did the car." Bill Galager was a redhead with too many freckles to count. He glanced at Nancy, who knelt over fragments of twisted metal at the flash point.

"She's good."

Jennifer nodded. "Work over the evidence in her lab with her and then send it on to Quantico for more testing. Bring this to Milton's attention, and please do your best to keep him off my back."

"Will do. What about any evidence they find at his house?"

A team had arrived at Kevin's house twenty minutes earlier and was scouring the place for anything Slater might have left. She doubted they would find anything. The victims' houses in Sacramento had yielded nothing. Slater might have no scruples, but he had plenty of discipline.

"Same. Let's do our own sweep as well. If you find anything, let me know. I'll be by your office in a couple hours."

He nodded. "You think it's him?"

"Until I find evidence that contradicts it."

"There are some differences. Could be a copy cat."

"Could be. But I don't think so."

"And I'm assuming Kevin matches the victim profile?"

Jennifer searched Galager's eyes. Bill was one of the only agents who'd known Roy well enough to call him a friend.

"He could be Roy in another life," she said. Then she turned toward the coffee shop.

At least five hundred onlookers had gathered behind the police lines now. The news crews were set up, sending live feed across the country. Both Fox News and CNN were undoubtedly running alerts. How many times had the American public seen pictures from Israel of twisted bus wreckage? But this was California. Here, you could count the incidents over the past ten years on one hand.

Milton was giving the vultures an update. Good for him.

11

JENNIFER'S VOICE JARRED KEVIN from his thoughts.
"Hey, cowboy, you want a ride out of here?"

He looked up from the corner table and blinked. "Sure."

"Let's go."

She didn't take him home. Detectives were still searching the place for anything Slater might have left. It would take them a few hours.

"They're not going to dump my underwear drawers, are they?"

Jennifer laughed. "Not unless Slater left his shorts."

"Probably just as well I'm gone."

"You like things neat, don't you?"

"Clean, sure."

"That's good. A man should know how to do laundry."

"Where're we going?"

"You have the phone with you?"

He instinctively felt his pocket. Amazing how small phones could be. He pulled it out and flipped it open. It fit in his palm, open.

"Just checking," she said, turning onto Willow.

"You think he'll call again?" he asked.

"Yes, the confession wasn't what he was looking for."

"I guess not."

"But he does want a confession. You're sure about that, right?"

"That's what he said. When I confess, he goes away. But confess what?"

"That's the million-dollar question, isn't it? What does Slater want you to confess? You have no inkling whatsoever?"

"I just ruined my career and only God knows what else by telling the world that I tried to kill a boy—believe me, if I'd thought of any alternative to that confession, I'd have spilled my guts."

She nodded and frowned. "The demand for a confession's the only part of this puzzle that doesn't fit the Riddle Killer profile. Somehow he dug something up on you that he thinks is significant."

"Like what? How many sins have you committed, Agent Peters? Can you remember them all?"

"Please, call me Jennifer. No, I guess I can't."

"So what does Slater consider significant? You want me to go on television and list every sin I can ever remember committing?"

"No."

"The only thing that makes sense is the boy," Kevin said. "But then the confession should have gotten a response, right?"

"With Slater, yes. I think so. Unless, of course, he *is* the boy, but he wants you to confess something besides your attempt to kill him."

"It wasn't an attempt to kill him. It was more like self-defense. The kid was about to kill *me!*"

"I can accept that. Why did he want to kill you?"

The question took Kevin off guard. "He . . . he was after Samantha."

"Samantha. She just keeps cropping up, doesn't she?"

Jennifer looked out her window and for a few minutes the car remained silent.

III

Kevin was only eleven when he trapped the boy in the cellar and nearly died of fear. He'd left the boy to die—no matter how badly he tried to tell himself otherwise, he knew he had locked the boy in a tomb.

He couldn't tell Sam, of course. If she knew, she would surely tell her father, who would set the boy free and maybe send him to jail, and then he would get out, probably within a couple months, and come back and kill Sam. He couldn't ever tell her.

But he couldn't *not* tell her either. She was his bosom buddy. She was his best, best friend, whom he loved more than he loved his mother. Maybe.

On the third night he meant to go in search of the warehouse, just to take a peek; just to see if it had really, really happened. But after an hour pacing outside his window, he climbed back into his house.

"You're different," Sam told him the next night. "You're not looking me in the eyes like you used to. You keep looking off at the trees. What's wrong?"

"I am not looking off. I'm just enjoying the night."

"Don't try to fool me. You think I don't have a woman's intuition? I'm almost a teenager, you know. I can tell if a boy's bothered."

"Well, I'm not bothered by anything except your insistence that I'm bothered," he said.

"So then you *are* bothered. See? But you were bothered before I said you were bothered, so I think you're not telling me something."

He felt suddenly angry. "I am not!" he said.

She looked at him for a few seconds and then gazed up into the trees herself. "You are bothered by something, but I can see that you're not telling me because you think it might hurt me. That's sweet, so I'm going to pretend you're not bothered." She took his arm.

She was giving him a way out. What kind of friend would ever do that? Sam would do that because she was the sweetest girl in the whole world, no exceptions.

It took Kevin four months of agony to finally work up the courage to go in search of the boy's fate.

Part of him wanted to find the boy's bones in a rotting pile. But most of him didn't want to find the boy at all, didn't want to confirm that the whole thing had really happened.

The first challenge was to find the right warehouse. Guarding a flashlight as closely as he could, he looked through the warehouses for an hour, sneaking from door to door. He began to wonder if he'd ever find it again. But then he opened an old wooden door and there, five feet away, was the dark stairway.

Kevin jerked back and very nearly ran for his life.

But it was only a stairway. What if the boy wasn't there anymore? He could see the latch on the steel door in the shadows below. Seemed safe enough. *You have to do this, Kevin. If you're anything like a knight or a man or even a boy who's already eleven, you have to at least find out if he's in there.*

Kevin played his light down the stairwell and forced his feet down the stairs, one step at a time.

No sound. Of course not—it had been four months. The steel door latch was still closed as if he'd thrown it closed yesterday. He stopped in front of the door and stared, unwilling to actually open it. Visions of pirates and dungeons full of skeletons clattered through his mind.

Behind him the moonlight glowed pale gray. He could always run up the stairs if a skeleton took after him, which was incredibly stupid anyway. What would Sam think of him now?

"Hello?" he called.

Nothing.

The sound of his voice helped. He walked forward and knocked. "Hello?" Still nothing.

Slowly, heart thumping in his ears, palms wet with sweat, Kevin eased the latch open. He pushed the door. It creaked open.

Black. Musty. Kevin held his breath and gave the door a shove. He saw the splotches of blood immediately. But no body.

His bones shook from head to toe. It was real. That was blood all over the floor. Dried and darkened, but exactly where he remembered it should be. He pushed the door again, to make sure no one was behind it. He was alone.

Kevin stepped into the room. A bandanna lay in the corner. The boy's bandanna. He had definitely locked the boy in this cellar, and there was no way out that he could see. That meant one of two things had happened. Either the boy had died in here and someone had found him, or someone had found him before he'd died.

His mind ran through the possibilities. If he'd been found alive, it would have been in the first couple weeks. Which meant he'd been free for over three months and said nothing to the police. If he'd been found dead, of course, he couldn't say anything. Either way, he was probably gone for good. Maybe even alive and gone for good.

Kevin hurried out, slammed the door closed, latched it, and ran into the night, determined never, ever to even think about the boy again. He'd saved Sam, hadn't he? Yes, he had! And he hadn't been arrested or sent to the gas chamber or even accused of doing anything wrong. Because he had done what was right!

Elated and overcome with relief, he ran straight to Sam's house, even though it was past her bedtime. It took him fifteen minutes to wake her and convince her to climb out.

"What is it? My father will kill us if he finds us, you know."

He grabbed her hand and ran for the fence.

"Kevin Parson, I am in my pajamas! What is this all about?"

Yes, what's this about, Kevin? You're acting like a maniac!

But he couldn't help himself. He'd never felt so wonderful in all his life. He loved Sam so much!

He stepped past the fence and she followed him. "Kevin, this is . . ."

He threw his arms around her and hugged her tight, squeezing off her words. "I love you, Sam! I love you so much!"

She stood still in his arms, unmoving. It didn't matter; he was so overwhelmed with joy. "You are the best friend a boy could ever, ever have," he said.

She finally put her arms around him and patted his shoulder. It felt a bit polite, but Kevin didn't care. He pulled back and brushed blonde strands of hair from her face. "I won't ever let anyone hurt you. Ever. Not if I have to die first. You know that, don't you?"

She laughed, caught up in his show of affection. "What's gotten into you? Of course I do."

He looked away, wishing for a response as enthusiastic as he felt. It didn't matter; he was a man now.

Her hand touched his chin and turned his face toward her. "Listen to me," Sam said. "I love you more than anything I can imagine. You really are my knight in shining armor." She smiled. "And I think that it's incredibly sweet of you to drag me out here in my pajamas to make sure I know how much you love me."

Kevin smiled wide, stupidly, but it didn't matter. He didn't have to pretend with Sam.

They hugged tight then, tighter than they had ever hugged before. "Promise to never leave me," Kevin said.

"I promise," Sam said. "And if you ever need me, all you have to do is knock on my window and I'll come flying out in my pajamas."

Kevin laughed. Then Sam laughed, and Kevin laughed at Sam's laughing. It might have been the best night of Kevin's life.

|||

"—Samantha?"

Kevin faced Jennifer. "Pardon?"

She looked at him. "Why was the boy after Samantha?"

"Because he was a demented wacko who found pleasure in cutting up animals and terrorizing the neighborhood. I didn't exactly have the time or the presence of mind to sit him down and run a psychological profile on him. I was scared to death."

Jennifer chuckled. "Touché. Too bad, though. Now we're sitting twenty years beyond that night, and I have the formidable task of trying to do it myself. Whether you like it or not, you may be my best hope of understanding him. Assuming the boy and Slater are one and the same, you're the only person we know who's had any meaningful contact with him, then or now."

As much as the thought of going back to the past made Kevin nauseated, he knew that she was right. He sighed. "I'll do whatever I can." He looked out the side window. "I should have made sure he was dead then."

"You would have done society a favor. In self-defense, of course."

"And what if Slater does show up on my doorstep one of these days? Do I have the right to kill him?"

"We have law enforcement for a reason." She paused. "On the other hand, I might."

"You might what?"

"Take him out. If I knew for sure it was Slater."

"What evil is man capable of?" Kevin said absently.

"What?"

"Nothing." But it was something. It struck Kevin for the first time that he had not only had the capacity to kill Slater, but also the *desire* to do so, self-defense or not. What would Dr. John Francis say to that?

"So. The boy was taller than you, about thirteen, blond and ugly," Jennifer said. "Nothing else?"

The sensation that there was something else nagged at Kevin, but he couldn't remember. "I can't think of anything."

They passed a store that Kevin recognized. "Where are we going?"

Suddenly he knew. His foot began to tap. They drove around a deserted park filled with elm trees.

"I thought I'd take you to your aunt's home. See if we can jog loose a few memories. Visual association can do wonders . . ."

He didn't hear the rest. A buzz lit through his mind and he felt claustrophobic in her car.

Jennifer looked at him but said nothing. He was sweating; she could surely see that. She turned onto Baker Street and drove under the elms toward his childhood house. Could she hear his thumping heart too?

"So this is where it all happened," she said absently.

"I . . . I don't want to go to the house," he said.

She looked at him again. "We're not going to the house. Just down the street. Is that okay?"

He couldn't say no—might as well wave a red flag in front of her. "Sure. I'm sorry. I'm not on the best terms with my aunt. My mother died when I was young and my aunt raised me. We've had our differences. Mostly over college."

"Okay. That's not uncommon."

But she saw more in him, didn't she? And so what if she did? Why did he feel so compelled to hide his upbringing? It was weird but not demented. Samantha said otherwise, but she was biased. It wasn't like he was a victim of physical abuse or anything so horrifying.

He took a slow breath and tried to relax.

"You think the boy chased you into one of those old warehouses across the tracks, that's what you said?"

He looked to his right. The memory of that night came back fresh and raw. "Yes, but I was scared out of my mind, and it was dark. I can't remember which one."

"Have you ever checked any of them? To see if there even is one with a basement?"

Kevin fought a wave of panic. He couldn't let her into the past. He shook his head. "No."

"Why not?"

"It was a long time ago."

She nodded. "There are only a few possibilities. Hopefully nothing's changed. You know we'll have to search."

He nodded. "And what if you find him?"

"Then we know he's obviously not Slater."

"And what about me?"

"We'll know that you killed him. In self-defense."

They drove past the white house. "This is where your aunt lives?"

"Yes."

"And that's the old Sheer residence?"

"Yes."

"None of this jogs your memory of any details?"

"No."

She remained silent to the end of the street, where she turned around and headed back.

Kevin's world felt like it was crumbling around him. Coming here alone was hard enough, but doing it with Jennifer somehow seemed profane. He wanted to tell her what Balinda had really done. He wanted her to comfort him, the little boy who had grown old in this world of madness. Waves of sorrow swept through his mind. His eyes went misty.

"I'm sorry, Kevin," Jennifer said softly. "I don't know what happened here, but I can see it left its mark on you. Believe me, if we weren't up against a clock, I wouldn't have brought you back here in your present state."

She cared for him, didn't she? She really did. A tear slipped from his eye and ran down his cheek. The emotion was suddenly beyond him. He began to cry, and then immediately tried to swallow it, which only made the condition worse. He hid his face in his left hand and started to sob, horribly aware of the foolishness of it all.

She drove out of the neighborhood and then stopped. He looked up through blurred eyes and saw that they were by the park. Jennifer sat still, looking at him with soft eyes.

"I'm . . . sorry," he managed past a tight throat. "It's just . . . my life's falling apart . . ."

"Shh, shh, shh. It's okay." Her hand touched his shoulder. "It's okay, really. You've been through hell these last two days. I had no right."

Kevin put his hands over his face and took a deep breath. "Man. This is crazy. Nothing like making a fool of yourself."

Her hand rubbed his arm again. "Don't be silly. You don't think I've seen a grown man cry before? I could tell you some stories. There's nothing quite like watching a three-hundred-pound, heavily tattooed gorilla sob uncontrollably for an hour. I don't know any decent man who could go through what you've gone through without a good cry."

He smiled, embarrassed. "Is that so?"

"That's so."

Jennifer's smile softened and she looked away. "The Riddle Killer's last victim was my brother. His name was Roy. That was three months ago. He was chosen because I was closing in on the killer."

Kevin wasn't sure what to say. "Your brother?"

"You remind me of him, you know." She faced him. "I won't let this maniac kill you, Kevin. I'm not sure I could survive that."

"I'm so sorry. I had no idea."

"Now you do. Want to go for a walk? I think we could both use some fresh air."

"Okay."

They walked side by side over an emerald green lawn, past a pond with ducks and two large geese. She was laughing and telling him about a goose that had once chased her for the sandwich she held. Next to the horror that had swept over him not five minutes earlier, Kevin felt unusually peaceful, as if he were walking with his guardian angel. He wondered about Jennifer's true intentions. She was a professional, doing her job. All FBI agents talked and laughed like this— it was their way of making someone in his shoes feel comfortable enough to work with them.

The thought made him feel suddenly awkward. Clumsy. Like a three-hundred-pound gorilla. On the other hand, she'd lost her brother.

He stopped.

She touched his arm. "Kevin? What is it?"

"Like a three-hundred-pound, heavily tattooed gorilla."

"That's what he—"

"The boy had a tattoo," Kevin blurted.

"The boy you locked in the cellar? Where?"

"On his forehead! A tattoo of a knife."

"You're sure?"

"Yes! He had it covered with a bandanna that last night, but I saw it the first night."

They exchanged stares. "How many men have a tattoo on their foreheads? Not many." A smile nudged her lips. "That's good," she said. "That's very good."

12

S AMANTHA WAS THE LAST PASSENGER to board the
flight to Sacramento. An hour and a half later she entered a little-
known conference room at the attorney general's headquarters, the
office of the California Bureau of Investigation's "Alpha Division," as
it was known by some. A bulldog of a man named Chris Barston,
who was up on suspicion of aiding terrorists by promulgating bomb-
construction methods on the Internet, sat across the table. They'd
hauled him in last night. His Internet dealings were not her concern,
but the information he had to share evidently was, or Roland, her
boss, wouldn't have insisted she come. Roland sat at the head of the
table, leaning back in his chair. She'd liked the chief from the moment
they were introduced, and when she came to him two days after her
orientation and asked to be assigned to the Riddle Killer case, he'd
agreed. The FBI and the CBI were both active in the case, but
Samantha suggested that the killer had inside connections, and the
possibility had intrigued Roland.

The call from Kevin had blindsided her. She hadn't expected the
Riddle Killer to surface in Southern California at all. She wasn't necessarily convinced that the Riddle Killer and Slater were the same. If
Slater was the Riddle Killer and he was also the boy, it would explain
his ties to her, Kevin, and Jennifer. But certain details about Slater's
calls to Kevin nagged at her.

"Thanks for coming, Sam. Enjoy your holiday?"

"I wasn't aware I *was* on a holiday."

"You're not. Your witness." Roland looked at Chris, who stared past him.

Sam pulled up her chair and opened a blue file Rodriguez had brought to her at the airport. She'd read the contents on the way in.

"Hello, Mr. Barston. My name's Samantha Sheer."

He ignored her and kept his eyes in Roland's direction.

"You may look this way, Chris. I'm going to be asking the questions. Have you ever been questioned by a woman before?"

The man stared at her. Roland grinned. "Answer the woman, Chris."

"I agreed to tell you what I know about Salman. That'll take thirty seconds."

"Great," Sam said. "Then we can limit our exposure to each other so we don't . . . you know, rub off on each other. I think we can stomach thirty seconds, don't you?"

The man's face darkened.

"Tell us about Salman."

He cleared his throat. "I met him in Houston about a month ago. Pakistani. You know, India and all. Speaks with an accent."

"Pakistanis live in Pakistan, not India. That's why they call it Pakistan. Go on."

"You going to mock me for the full thirty seconds here?"

"I'll try to control myself."

He shifted. "Anyway, Salman and I had a mutual interest in . . . you know, bombs. He's clean; I can swear that. He had this tattoo of a bomb on his shoulder. I got one here of a knife." He showed them a small blue knife on his right forearm. "Then he showed me one on his back, a huge dagger. Said he wanted to have it removed because the chicks didn't dig it back in wherever."

"Pakistan."

"Pakistan. He told me he knew a guy who had a tattoo of a knife on his forehead. He didn't tell me nothing about this guy except that his name was Slater and he was into explosive devices. That's it. That's all I know."

"And you think the name Slater interests us why?"

"The news of Long Beach. They said it could be a man named Slater."

"When did your friend know this Slater?"

"I said that's it. That's all I know. That's the deal. If I knew more, I would tell you more. I already wrote down where this Salman guy works last I knew. He's straight up. Talk to him."

Sam looked at Roland. He nodded.

"Okay, Chris. I guess your thirty seconds are up. You're free to go."

Chris stood, glared at her one last time, and left.

"What do you think?" Roland asked.

"I'm not sure what our man would be doing all the way down in Houston, but I think I'm going to Texas. I want to make contact first. For all we know, Salman doesn't even exist. It may take a day or two to track him down. Until then I want to go back to Long Beach."

"Fine. Just keep a low profile down there. If the Riddle Killer's working with someone inside, we don't want him suddenly running scared."

"I'm limiting direct contact to the FBI agent in charge. Jennifer Peters."

"Just watch what you say. For all we know, Agent Peters is Slater."

"Unlikely."

"Just tread lightly."

|||

The prior twenty-four hours had produced more evidence than the entire year combined, but the leads weren't pointing to any quick answers. Meticulous lab work took time, a commodity Jennifer wasn't sure they had enough of. Slater would strike again, and sooner or later they would have bodies to contend with. A car, a bus—what was next?

The city was reeling from news of the bus. Milton had spent half the day preparing and issuing statements to hungry reporters. At least it kept him out of her hair.

She sat at the corner desk Milton had graciously given her and stared at the loose sheets of paper spread before her. It was 4:30, and for the moment she was stuck. A Subway veggie sandwich she'd ordered two hours ago sat on the edge of the desk, and she considered unwrapping it.

Her eyes dropped to the pad under her fingertips. She'd split the page horizontally and then vertically, creating four quadrants, an old technique she used to visually compartmentalize data. Kevin's house, the warehouse search, the knife tattoo, and forensics from the bus.

"Who are you, Slater?" she mumbled. "You're here, aren't you, staring up at me, chuckling behind these words somewhere?"

First quadrant. They'd swept and dusted Kevin's house and turned up exactly nothing. Hundreds of prints, of course—it would take time to work through all of them. But in the high-probability contact points—the phone, the doorknobs, the window latches, the desk, the wood dinette chairs—they had found only Jennifer's and Kevin's prints, and some partials that were unidentifiable. Probably Sam's. She'd been in the house, but according to Kevin she hadn't stayed long or handled anything except for the phone, where they'd found the partials. Either way, the chances that Slater had walked around the place pressing uncovered fingers against dense surfaces had been absurd from the beginning.

No eavesdropping devices turned up either, again not surprising. Slater had used the six bugs they'd uncovered because they were convenient at the time. He had other means of listening in—remote laser transmitters, relayed audio scopes—all of which they would eventually track down, but not likely soon enough. They'd found disturbed ground at the oil rig's base, two hundred yards from Kevin's house, and taken casts of four different shoe prints. Again, the evidence might help them incriminate Slater, but it wasn't identifying him— at least not quickly enough.

The writing on the milk jug was in for analysis at Quantico. Same story. Comparisons could and one day would be made, but not before they actually had Slater in their sights.

They'd affixed the AP301 recording device to Slater's cell phone and were monitoring the house using an IR laser.

Let the games begin.

Jennifer had left Kevin in his house at noon, pleading that he get some sleep. She watched him wander around his living room like a zombie. He'd been pushed beyond himself.

You like him, don't you, Jenn?

Don't be stupid! I hardly know him! I feel empathy for him. I'm attributing Roy's goodness to him.

But you like him. He's handsome, caring, and as innocent as a butter-fly. He has magical eyes and a smile that swallows the room. He's . . .

Naive and damaged. His reaction to driving through his old neigh-borhood had been in part precipitated by the stress of Slater's threats, granted. But there had to be more.

He was similar to Roy in many ways, but the more she thought about it, the more she saw the dissimilarities between this case and the ones in Sacramento. Slater seemed to have a specific, personally moti-vated agenda with Kevin. He wasn't a random victim. Neither was Jennifer nor Samantha. What if Kevin had been the Riddle Killer's prime mark all along? What if the others were just a kind of practice? Warmup?

Jennifer closed her eyes and stretched her neck. She'd made an appointment to see the dean at Kevin's seminary, Dr. John Francis, first thing tomorrow morning. He attended one of those huge churches that held a service on Saturday evening. Jennifer picked up the sandwich and peeled back the wax paper.

Second quadrant. The warehouse. Milton had somehow convinced the bureau chief to speak to her about his involvement. The man was starting to become a major irritant. She'd reluctantly agreed to give him the warehouse search. The fact was, she could use the manpower and they knew the territory. She made it clear that if he breathed one word of his involvement to the media, she'd personally see to it that he took full responsibility for whatever negative consequences resulted. He'd taken four uniformed officers and a search warrant to the warehouse district. The likelihood that Slater was watching the neighborhood was minimal. He might be a surveillance crackerjack, but he couldn't have eyes everywhere.

Based on Kevin's story, he might have stumbled into any of a couple dozen warehouses that night. Milton's team was searching each one now, looking for any that might have a subterranean storage room, an oil pit, a garbage dump—anything similar. Most warehouses today were built on slabs, but some of the older buildings featured underground units that were cheaper to cool.

She could understand Kevin's subconscious erasure of such a traumatic location. It would either be stamped indelibly on his brain or gone, and there was no reason for him to hide any knowledge at this point. Discovery of the basement would be a windfall. If indeed the boy was Slater.

Third quadrant. The knife tattoo. Jennifer took a bite out of the sandwich. Hunger swarmed her with the first taste of tomato. She'd missed breakfast, hadn't she? Seemed like a week ago.

She stared at the third quadrant. Again, assuming the boy was Slater, and assuming he hadn't removed the tattoo, they now had their first bona fide identifier. A tattoo of a knife on the forehead—not exactly something you see on every corner. Twenty-three agents and policemen were quietly working the search. Tattoo parlors that had existed twenty years earlier in the immediate vicinity were first to be scrutinized, but finding one that had any records was near impossible. They were working in concentric circles. More likely was finding a tattoo parlor that remembered a man with a knife tattoo on his forehead. Not all tattoo bearers frequented parlors, but ones with Slater's profile might. For all they knew, he was now covered in tattoos. All he needed was one—a knife in the center of his forehead.

Fourth quadrant. The bus. Another bite. The sandwich was like a slice of heaven.

Same guy, no doubt. Same device: a suitcase bolted behind the gas tank, loaded with enough dynamite to shred a bus, detonated using tungsten leads stripped from an incandescent bulb on a simple five-dollar, battery-operated alarm clock. A mechanical servo could override the clock and either terminate or trigger the detonation. The bomb had been planted days, even weeks ago, based on the dust they'd lifted off one of its bolts. If they could ID what was left of the servo, they might have a shot of tracing its origins. Unlikely.

How long had Slater been planning this?

The phone chirped. Jennifer wiped her mouth, took a quick swallow from a bottle of Evian, and picked up the phone. "Jennifer."

"We think we found it."

Milton. She sat up. "The warehouse."

"We have some blood here."

She tossed the rest of the sandwich in the waste bin and grabbed her keys. "I'm on my way."

III

Kevin looked out between the blinds for the fourth time in two hours. They'd decided to place one unmarked car a block up the street—FBI. Slater seemed ambiguous about the FBI. Either way, the agent behind the wheel would watch only. He would not follow if or when Kevin left at Slater's next beckoning. Static surveillance only.

Kevin released the slats and paced back into the kitchen. In the park, Jennifer had reached out to him and he'd let her. He found her fierce nature compelling. It reminded him of Samantha.

Where was Samantha? He'd called her twice and gotten only her voice mail. He desperately wanted to talk to her about the visit to Baker Street with Jennifer. She would understand. Not that Jennifer didn't, but Sam might be able to help him sort out these new feelings.

He walked to the refrigerator, opened it, and pulled out a liter of 7UP. Feelings. Extremes. The hatred toward Slater that had begun to swell in his gut wasn't so strange. How was he supposed to feel toward someone who had come within a few seconds of taking not only his life, but countless others for undisclosed reasons? If Slater would just quit being so idiotic and tell him what the deal was, Kevin could handle the man. As it was, the imbecile was hiding behind these stupid games, and Kevin was losing patience. Yesterday he'd been too shocked to process his anger. A common form of denial, Jennifer had said. Shock breeds denial, which in turn tempers anger. But now the denial was giving way to this bitterness toward an enemy who refused to show his hand.

Kevin poured half a glass, swallowed the 7UP in several long drafts, and slammed the empty glass on the counter.

He ran his hand through his hair, grunted, and walked to the living room. How could one man wreak so much havoc in the space of one day? Slater was nothing less than a terrorist. If Kevin owned a gun and Slater worked up the stomach to confront him face to face, he was pretty sure he'd have no compunction about putting a slug or two in the man's face. Especially if he was the boy. Kevin shivered involuntarily. Shoulda gone back and made sure the stinking rat was dead. He would have been within his rights, if not according to the law, then in the eyes of God. Turn the other cheek shouldn't apply to sick sewer rats with knives in their hands who licked neighborhood girls' windows.

Slater was listening now, right? Kevin looked around the room and settled on the window.

"Slater?" His voice bounced back at him.

"You hear me, Slater? Listen, you sick scab, I don't know why you're stalking me or why you're too terrified to show your face, but you're only proving one thing. You're toilet water. You're a punk without the guts to face your adversary. Come on, baby! Come and get me!"

"Kevin?"

He whirled around. Sam stood in the rear sliding-glass doorway, staring at him. He hadn't heard the door slide open.

"You okay?" she whispered.

"Sure. Sorry, I was just having a word with our friend, in case he was listening."

Sam shut the door and lifted a finger to her lips. She walked to the front window and pulled the drapes.

"What . . ."

She motioned him quiet again and led him to the garage. "If we talk quietly here, we won't be heard."

"Slater? The car up the street's FBI."

"I know. Which is why I parked two blocks up and came in the back. You don't think Slater's going to see them?"

"He didn't say no FBI."

"Maybe because he is FBI," she said.

"What?"

"We haven't ruled it out."

"We? Who's we?"

She held his gaze for a moment. "Just an expression. They find anything else here?"

"No. Some footprints by the oil rig up the hill. They took a bunch of fingerprints, the milk jug. Jennifer didn't think any of it would help them much."

Sam nodded. "She told me about the tattoo. You never told me about the tattoo."

"I didn't tell you anything about him after that night, remember? He was gone. End of story."

"Not anymore. They'll find the warehouse, and when they do, they'll find more—who knows, maybe the boy."

"Actually, I went back four months later."

"What?"

"He was gone. There was blood on the floor and his bandanna, but he was gone. They won't find him."

Sam looked at him for a few moments. He wasn't sure what she was thinking, but something wasn't quite right.

"You said, *we* haven't ruled it out," he said. "You've always been straight with me, Sam. Who is we?"

She looked into his eyes and put a hand on his cheek. "I'm sorry, Kevin, I can't tell you everything—not now, not yet. Soon. You're right, I have always been straight with you. I've been more than a friend. I've loved you like a brother. A day hasn't gone by these past ten years that I haven't thought about you at least once. You're part of me. And now I need you to trust me. Can you do that?"

The revelation made his head spin. She was somehow involved, wasn't she? She'd been onto Slater before yesterday. It was why Slater knew her!

"What . . . what's going on?"

Her hand slid down his arm and took his fingers. "Nothing's changed. Slater's the same person he was yesterday, and I'm going to do my best to get to him before he hurts anyone. I'm just not at liberty to tell you what we know. Not yet. It wouldn't make any difference to you anyway. Trust me. For old time's sake."

He nodded. Actually, this was better, wasn't it? The fact that she had some inside track and wasn't just blindly feeling her way around this case—that was good.

"But you think the FBI is involved?"

She put her finger on his lips to seal them. "I can't talk about it. Forget I said it. Nothing's changed." She reached up, kissed him on the cheek, and released his hand.

"Can I trust Jennifer?"

She turned. "Sure—trust Jennifer. But trust me first."

"What do you mean, first?"

"I mean if you have to choose between me and Jennifer, choose me."

He felt his pulse thicken. What was she saying? *Choose me.* Did she think he would ever choose Jennifer over her? He wasn't even sure what he felt for Jennifer. She had offered to ease his pain and confusion in a time of vulnerability and he had let her. That was all.

"I would always choose you. I owe my life to you."

She smiled and for a moment he imagined that they were kids again, sitting under an elm with a full moon on their faces, laughing at a squirrel's inquisitive head poking through the branches.

"Actually, I think it's the other way around. I owe you *my* life," she said. "Literally. You saved me from Slater once, didn't you? Now it's my turn to return the favor."

In a strange way, it all made perfect sense.

"Okay," she said. "I have a plan. I mean to flush the snake from his hole." She winked at him and glanced at her watch. "The sooner we get out of here the better. Grab your toothbrush, a change of clothes, and some deodorant if you want. We're taking a trip."

"We are? Where? We can't just leave. Jennifer told me to stay here."

"Until what? Did Slater tell you not to leave?"

"No."

"Let me see the phone."

He fished out the cell phone Slater had left him and handed it to her.

"Did Slater tell you to keep this on?"

Kevin considered the question. "He said to keep it with me at all times."

Sam pushed the power off button. "Then we'll take it."

"Jennifer will have a cow. This wasn't the plan."

"Change of plans, my dear knight. It's time for a little cat and mouse of our own."

13

THE WAREHOUSE was less than a hundred yards from Kevin's old house, two rows back from the road, an old wooden storage facility that had been white before flaking paint revealed its gray underbelly. From the side entrance, none of the houses on Baker Street was visible.

"This it?"

"It's abandoned. Looks like it has been for a while," Milton said.

"Show me."

Two uniforms stood by the door, watching her. One of them handed her a flashlight. "You'll need this."

She took it and turned it on.

The warehouse smelled of a decade's worth of undisturbed dust. Beyond the side door was a single stairwell descending into blackness. The rest of the three-thousand-or-so square feet of concrete sat vacant in dim light filtered by a dozen cracks in the walls.

"Don't they tear these things down?" she asked.

"They used to hold all kinds of goods in these warehouses before the navy moved in just south of here. The government bought this land and hasn't seen fit to rebuild yet. I'm sure they'll get around to it."

A lone cop stood at the bottom of the stairs, shining his flashlight on the threshold. "The door was locked from the outside—took some jarring to get it loose."

Jennifer descended. A steel door led into a ten-by-ten room, concrete, empty. She played her torch over the pitted walls. Exposed floor joists held the ceiling. Most of it. One small section had rotted through.

"The blood's over here," Milton said.

Jennifer directed her light to where he stood looking down at two large dark stains on the concrete. She squatted and studied each.

"The splatter's consistent with blood." The basic position of the stains also matched Kevin's story—both he and the boy had bled. "At this age we probably won't get any reliable DNA evidence, but we can at least verify species. I knew Kevin was hiding something the first time I talked to him."

She glanced at Milton, surprised by his tone.

"And this isn't the last of it. I guarantee he's hiding more," he said.

Milton was a first-class pig. She stood and walked over to a small, almost unnoticeable hole in the ceiling. "The boy's way out?"

"Could be."

So, assuming this read as fact, what would it mean? That Kevin hadn't killed the boy? That they had fought and that Kevin had locked the door from the outside, but then the boy had managed to crawl out through the rotting ceiling? Who knew why he hadn't come back to terrorize Kevin until now?

Or it could mean that the boy actually had died in here, only to be discovered by some passerby years later, body disposed of. Unlikely. Unless a drifter or anyone else had reason to hide the body, it would have been investigated. She'd already run a search for reports and found none.

"Okay, we need to do a bloodstain distribution analysis. I want to know what happened down here. Assuming it is blood, did anyone lie in it? Any blood on the walls or up through the ceiling? I want species identification and, if possible, blood type. Send a sample to the FBI lab immediately. And this stays out of the press."

Milton said nothing. He looked up at the corner and frowned. A shadow passed over his face. It occurred to her that she might actually hate the man.

"Don't get any ideas, Detective. Everything goes through me."

He looked at her for a moment and then walked for the door. "Sure."

III

Kevin drove them along Palos Verdes Drive, west toward Palos Verdes. Slater's bugged phone sat on the dash, turned off.

Sam stared ahead, eyes sparkling. "If Slater can't make contact, how can he play the game? He's driven by the riddles, but if we neutralize his ability to communicate a riddle, then there *is* no riddle, is there? At the least he has to rethink his strategy."

"Or blow up another bomb," Kevin said.

"We're not technically breaking one of his rules. He detonates a bomb and *he's* breaking the rules of engagement. I don't think Slater will do that."

Kevin thought about Sam's plan. On one hand, it felt good to be doing something—anything—besides waiting. The idea made sense on its surface. On the other hand, he didn't trust Slater to follow his own rules. Sam knew him better, maybe, but it was his life they were messing with.

"Why not just turn off the phone and stick around?"

"He'd find a way to communicate."

"He still might."

"Possible. But this way we also get you out of there. The one thing we need now is time. A dozen new leads have surfaced in the last twenty-four hours, but we need time."

There was the *we* word again.

"We should at least tell Jennifer, don't you think?"

"Think of this as a test. We cut off all contact and then we gradually resume contact. Unless Slater's following us now, he'll be lost. His opponent will have disappeared. He may rant and rave, but he won't play the game without you. We add some people to the loop and see if Slater suddenly knows more than he should. Follow?"

"What if he has the car bugged?"

"Then he did it today under the noses of the FBI. They swept it this morning, remember?"

Kevin nodded. The idea was growing on him. "Just like that we're gone, huh?"

She grinned. "Just like that."

"Like sneaking out at night."

It took them half an hour to reach the quaint hotel—an old Victorian mansion that had been converted and expanded to accommodate forty rooms. They pulled into its parking lot at ten after six. A cool, salty breeze drifted off the Pacific, half a mile down green sloping hills. Sam grinned and pulled out her overnight bag.

"Do they have rooms available?" Kevin asked.

"We have reservations. A suite with two bedrooms."

He looked up at the hotel and then back toward the sea. A Conoco station with a Taco Bell stood a hundred yards to the north. Outback Steakhouse, fifty yards south. Cars drifted by, a Lexus, a Mercedes. The madness in Long Beach seemed distant.

"Come on," Sam said. "Let's settle in and get something to eat."

Half an hour later they sat across from each other in a cozy café on the hotel's ground floor, overlooking a dimming horizon. They'd left their cell phones, turned off, in the room. She still wore her office pager, but Slater had no way to reach either of them. It seemed that Sam's simple plan wasn't such a bad idea.

"What would happen if I just disappeared?" Kevin asked, cutting into a thick New York strip.

She forked a small bite of cheese-smothered chicken into her mouth and dabbed her lips with her napkin. "Just up and leave until we find him?"

"Why not?"

"Why not. Leave him high and dry." She took a drink of iced tea and cut another piece. "You could move up to San Francisco."

"He's ruined my life down here anyway. I don't see how I can continue in seminary."

"I doubt you're the first seminary student to have his sins exposed."

"Murder isn't exactly your typical confession."

"Self-defense. And as far as we know, he lived."

"The confession sounded pretty ominous. I think I'm finished."

"And how's murder so different from gossip? Wasn't that your point to the dean? You're no more capable of evil than the bishop, remember? Murder, gossip—what's the difference? Evil is evil."

"Evil is evil as long as you keep it in the classroom. Out here in the real world, gossip doesn't even feel evil."

"Which is why any good detective learns to trust the facts over feelings." She went back to her food. "Either way, I don't think you can run. He'll track you down. That's how his kind works. You raise the stakes and he's likely to come back with higher stakes."

Kevin looked out the window. Darkness had all but swallowed the horizon. Jennifer's words came back to him. Take him out, she'd said.

"Like a hunted animal," he said.

"Except that you're not an animal. You have the same capacities he does."

"Jennifer told me that if I had the opportunity I should blow him away." Anger boiled through his chest. He'd come so far, worked so hard, pulled himself out of the deepest despair, only to be hijacked by some ghost from the past.

He slammed the table with his fist, rattling the dishes.

He met the stares from an older couple two tables down. "I'm sorry, Kevin," Samantha said. "I know this is hard."

"What's to prevent *me* from being the hunter?" he asked. "He wants a game; I'll give him a game! Why don't I throw out a challenge and force *him* to respond to me? Would you do anything different?"

"Fight terror with terror."

"Exactly!"

"No," she said.

"What do you mean, no? Maybe the only way to corner him is to play the game his way."

"You don't fight evil with evil; it just leads to anarchy. We have rules and we have scruples, unlike Slater. What are you going to do, threaten to blow up the convention center unless he gives himself up? Somehow I don't think he'd do anything but laugh. Besides, we have no way of contacting him."

The maître d' approached from Kevin's right. "Excuse me, sir, is everything all right?"

Someone had complained. "Yes. I'm sorry, I'll try to control myself." Kevin flashed him an embarrassed smile. The man dipped his head and left.

Kevin took a deep breath and picked up his fork, but his appetite was suddenly gone. The fact was, when he thought about what Slater was doing to him, he could hardly think of anything but killing him. Destroy the destroyer.

"I know it sounds a bit pretentious right now, but Slater doesn't scare me," Sam said, staring off into the darkness outside, wearing a coy smile. "You'll see, Kevin. His days are numbered."

"And mine might be as well."

"Not a chance. I won't let that happen."

He wasn't brimming with her confidence, but he couldn't resist her infectious smile. This was his Samantha. G.I. Jane.

"Jennifer said that, huh?" Sam asked. "Blow him away."

"Actually, I think she said 'take him out.' Makes sense to me."

"Maybe." She stared at him across the candle flame. "You like her, don't you?"

"Who, Jennifer?" He shrugged. "She seems like a good person."

"I don't mean in a 'good person' kind of way."

"Come on, Sam. I hardly know her. I haven't dated anyone for years." He smiled sheepishly. "Good night, the last girl I kissed was you."

"Is that so? When we were eleven?"

"How could you forget?"

"I haven't. But you do like her. I can see it in your eyes when you say her name."

Kevin felt his face flush. "She's an FBI agent who's trying to save my neck. What's there not to like?" He looked to his right and caught the continuing stare of the older couple. They looked away. "She reminds me of you."

"Really? How so?"

"Kind. No-nonsense. Pretty . . ."

"Like I said, you like her."

"Please—"

"It's okay, Kevin," she said softly. "I want you to like her."

"You do?"

"Yes. I approve." She grinned and placed the last small bite of chicken in her mouth. Even the way she chewed her food was nothing less than spectacular, he thought. Her chin and cheeks were so smooth in motion.

"What about . . ." He trailed off, suddenly self-conscious.

"What about us? That's very sweet, my knight, but I'm not sure we could ever be romantically involved. Don't get me wrong, I love you dearly. I'm just not sure we want to risk what we have for romance."

"Great things always come at great risk," he said.

She stared at him with those intoxicating eyes, caught off guard by his forward statement.

"Isn't that right?" he asked.

"Yes."

"So then don't say we could never be romantically involved. I kissed you once and you sent me to heaven. Didn't you feel something?"

"When you kissed me?"

"Yes."

"I was floating for a week."

"You never told me that."

She grinned, and if he wasn't mistaken, now she was embarrassed. "Maybe I wanted you to make the next move. Isn't that what a knight does for his damsel in distress?"

"I guess I never was a very good knight."

"You've turned into quite a dashing one," Sam said with a twinkle in her eye. "I think she likes you."

"Jennifer? She told you that?"

"Woman's intuition. Remember?"

Sam set down her napkin and stood. "Would you like to dance?"

He glanced around. No one else was dancing, but several colored lights turned slowly on the tiny dance floor. Michael Bolton crooned over the speakers.

"I . . . I'm not sure I know how to—"

"Sure you do. Just like when we were kids. Under the moonlight. Don't tell me you've never danced since then."

"No, not really."

She looked at him gently. "Then we definitely should. Will you?"

He smiled and dipped his head. "It would be my pleasure."

They held each other gently and danced for several long minutes. It wasn't a sensual dance or even romantic. It was just the right thing to do after ten years of separation.

Slater did not call that night.

14

THE WALL IS DARK BROWN, almost black, and pitted. Slightly damp in spots, leaking an odor of mold and mildew and something else he never has been able to place. A single incandescent bulb glows in the bathroom, casting just enough light into the main basement for Slater to see the darkness of the wall.

These are the things he likes: cold, dark, wetness, mildew, and chocolate sundaes with equal portions of ice cream and fudge. Oh, yes, and he likes fascination. In fact, he likes to be fascinating above everything else, and really, in order to be properly fascinating, he has to dispense with the expected and deliver only what they don't expect. This is why confused teenage boys pierce their eyelids and tattoo their foreheads, and why girls out to impress them shave their heads. It is all a pathetic, hopeless attempt to be fascinating.

The problem with doing something so senseless as piercing an eyelid is that it reveals your intentions. *Here am I, a poor teenage slug who requires your attention. Look at me, see how I resemble a puddle of dog vomit? Won't you please throw your fingers to your teeth and be wildly fascinated by me?*

The pitiful first gropings of the dark man.

But Slater knows what they do not. He knows that the dark man is most fascinating when he moves in complete obscurity. Hidden. Unknown. That's why he is called the *dark* man. That's why he has started in the dark. That's why he does all of his best work at night. That's why he loves this basement. Because for all practical purposes, Slater *is* the Dark Man.

Someone famous should write a comic book based on him.

Slater stands from his stool. He's been looking at the pitted wall for over an hour without moving. He finds it fascinating. Darkness is always fascinating. He's never quite sure what he's looking at, unlike a piece of white paper, which only grows fascinating if he puts a black pen to it.

It's light outside—he knows this because of the single crack in the corner. Samantha has taken Kevin and gone into hiding. Which means that after all these months, she's learned something new.

Slater hums softly and walks toward a small vanity. The secret of being the Dark Man is not looking like a dark man at all. That is why the world looks at stupid little teenagers with rings in their noses as idiots. It's like walking around school, stripped to the waist in a Charles Atlas pose all day. Please. Too obvious. Too stupid. Too boring.

Now the angel of light routine—those who pile on the white to obscure the Dark Man, like Sunday school teachers and clergy, like priests—not a bad instinct really. But these days, a white collar is no longer the best disguise.

The best disguise is simply obscurity.

Slater sits and tilts the mirror so that it catches enough light from the bathroom to cast his reflection. You see, now there is a Nobody. A strongly built man with blond hair and grayish eyes. A wedding band on his left hand, a closet full of pressed shirts and Dockers and a silver Honda Accord out on the street.

He could walk up to any Betty in the mall and say, "Excuse me, do I look like the Dark Man to you?"

"What on earth are you talking about?" she would say. Because she wouldn't associate him with a name like Dark Man. She, along with ten thousand other mall flies, would be fooled. Blind. Shrouded by darkness.

That is his secret. He can walk under their noses without the slightest hint of guilt. He is virtually transparent, for the very reason that he is so much like them. They see him every day and don't know who he is.

Slater frowns at himself and wags his head in mockery. "I like you, Kevin. I love you, Kevin." Sam can be such a cockroach. He should have killed her when he had the chance, long ago.

Now she's in the thick of things again, which is good because he can finish the job, once and for all. But her audacity makes him nauseated.

"Let's run away and play hide-and-seek," he mocks again. "What do you take me for?"

The fact is, Sam knows more about him than any of the others. True, her little disappearing act will gain them nothing, but at least she's made a move, which is more than he can say for the rest. She's trying to flush him out. She might even know that he's been under their noses all along.

But the Dark Man isn't that stupid. They can't hide forever. Kevin will eventually stick his slimy head out of his hole, and when he does, Slater will be there to bite it off.

He leans the mirror against the wall and crosses to the room he's prepared for his guest. It is slightly larger than a closet, encased in concrete. A steel door. Leather restraints lay on the floor, but he doubts he'll need them. The game will end here, where it's been designed to end. The rest of this cat-and-mouse foolishness is only a smoke screen to keep them in the dark, where all good games are played. If the newspapers think they have a hot story now, they are about to be reeducated. The occasional destruction of a car or bus by

way of explosion a story hardly makes. What he plans will be worthy
of a book.

"I despise you," he says softly. "I loathe the way you walk and the
way you speak. Your heart is vile. I will kill you."

|||

The anger had worked its way up to a seething through the night.
Kevin tossed and turned in a fitful attempt at sleep. Sam's optimism
sat like a light on the horizon of his mind, but as the night wore on,
the light grew dim until it faded altogether, obscured by bitterness
toward the man who had stomped into his life uninvited.

Fury was a good word for it. Rage. Indignation. They all worked.
He relived that night twenty years ago a hundred times. The boy
sneering at him as he turned the knife in his hands, threatening to
shove the blade through Sam's chest. The boy's name was Slater—had
to be. How he'd escaped was beyond Kevin. Why he'd waited so long
to come after him made no sense either. He should have killed Slater
then.

His pillow felt like a wet sponge. His sheets clung to his legs like
mildewed leaves. He couldn't remember a time when he was so upset,
so distraught, since the boy had first threatened him so many years
ago.

Sam's plan was brilliant, except for the obvious fact that it only
delayed the inevitable. Slater wasn't going away—he would wait out
there in the dark, biding his time while Kevin slowly dehydrated
beneath the sheets. He couldn't do this. He couldn't just wait and
waste away while Slater chuckled under his rock.

The idea ignited in his mind with the sky's first graying. *Buy a
gun.* His eyes sprang open. Of course! Why not? Become the hunter.

Don't be absurd. He closed his eyes. *You aren't a killer.* The discussion with Dr. Francis was one thing—all that talk about gossip and

killing being the same thing. But when it came right down to it, he could never kill another human. He couldn't line up a man in the gun's sights and send a slug through his head. *POW!* Surprise, creep.

Kevin slowly opened his eyes. Where would he get a gun anyway? A pawnshop? Not with today's laws. Not legally, anyway. On the other hand, for the right price . . .

Forget it. What was he going to do, shoot the phone if Slater called again? The man was too good to walk into danger. How could he lure Slater into a confrontation?

Kevin rolled over and tried to put the idea from his mind. But now the notion began to grow, fed by his own loathing. In the end Slater would kill him—nothing else made any sense. So why not take the fight to him first? Why not demand a meeting? Face me, you slime bucket. Come out of the shadows and look me in the eyes. You want a game?

Suddenly the thought of anything less seemed weak. He had to at least try.

He wrestled off the sheets and slid to the floor. Sam wouldn't agree. He would do this without her, now, before she awakened and stopped him. He quickly pulled on his jeans and a T-shirt. The details didn't seem so critical at the moment—where he'd find a gun, how he'd hide it, how he'd use it. With enough money . . .

Kevin grabbed his wallet off the nightstand and fumbled through it. It would have to be cash. He'd stuffed his emergency cash, the four hundred dollars from under his mattress, into his wallet before leaving the house. Still there. Surely with that much he could buy a gun on the black market.

Kevin eased out of his room, saw that Sam's door was still closed, and walked for the door before pulling up. He should at least leave a note. *Couldn't sleep, went to put a slug in Slater's head, be back soon.*

He found a pad of paper with the hotel's insignia stenciled across the top and scribbled a note. *Couldn't sleep, went for a drive, be back soon.*

The morning air felt cool on his clammy skin. Six o'clock. The underworld was undoubtedly still stirring. He had to get out before Sam awoke or he wouldn't be going anywhere. She would worry if he didn't return quickly. As soon as the night crawlers made their appearance, he would pull over and ask one of them the dreaded question: Where can I buy a gun to blow away the man who's after me?

He started the car and headed south.

And what if the night crawler recognized him? His face had been plastered on the news. The jarring thought made Kevin flinch. He swerved. A white sedan on his tail flashed its lights. He quickly pulled over, as if it had been his intention all along. The car sped by.

Maybe he should have brought a sock to pull over his head. Kmart special over here—one bad man with a stocking over his head, holding up a night crawler with a wallet. Give me your gun, buster.

Twenty minutes later he emerged from a 7-Eleven with a pair of dark glasses and an orange Broncos baseball cap. With a day's stubble, he looked nothing like the man he'd seen on television the previous day. But he decided to take the drive up to Inglewood just to be sure. Probably more guns to be had up there anyway.

An accident on 405 stretched the hour trip into two hours. It was eight-thirty before he'd pulled onto Western Avenue in Inglewood. He had no idea where to begin looking. Sam would be up now.

He drove aimlessly, palms sweaty on the steering wheel, telling himself he had no business asking anyone where to buy a gun, much less buying one. If he headed back over to Hawthorn and headed south, he could be back in Palos Verdes in under an hour.

But Palos Verdes was within spitting distance of Long Beach. And Slater was waiting in Long Beach. He had to find himself a gun. Maybe a knife would be better. Definitely easier to find. Then again, killing with a knife somehow felt more evil than killing with a gun, and harder, assuming he could do either.

What would Jennifer say to this sudden madness that had overtaken him? Take him out. No, that was figurative, Kevin. He swallowed, suddenly swamped with the foolishness of what he was doing. He didn't even have a plan! *God, help me.*

For someone studying to be a priest, he sure hadn't prayed much in the past two days. He'd been too busy confessing his sin to the world. He wasn't sure he even believed that God *could* save him. Could God really reach in and save his people? He imagined a huge finger flicking the head off Slater's shoulders. For that matter, what did it take to become one of God's people? How was the soul truly regenerated? Through the sinner's prayer? *Take my heart, take my soul; wash my mind as white as snow. And if anyone comes after me with a gun, please put him in a place where there is no sun—preferably six feet under in a concrete tomb.*

He'd never really prayed like that. Oh, he'd prayed plenty in church. He'd committed himself to vocation and to ministry. He'd said what he needed to say to become who he was trying to become, and he was doing what he needed to do to help others become like him. But he was no longer sure what he'd become. He'd broken with his past and started fresh.

Or had he?

Sure he had. Out with the old, in with the new, yippee-kie-ay, yabba dabba doo. *Are you regenerated, Kevin? Are you saved? Are you worthy of feeding at the trough with the others in the flock? Are you fit to shepherd the sheep grazing in God's green pastures?*

I was three days ago. At least I thought I was. At least I was successfully pretending to think I was.

Praying to a heavenly Father filled his mind with images of Eugene, dressed in his riding boots, issuing commands in a phony

English accent. Fathers were silly men who went about pretending they were important.

Kevin cleared his throat. "God, if anyone ever needed your help, I do. However you do it, you have to save me. I may not be a priest, but I do want to be your . . . your child."

Tears filled his eyes. *Why the sudden emotion?*

It's coming because you never were anyone's child. Just like Father Strong used to say. God's waiting with outstretched hands. You never really took that seriously, but that's what becoming a child is all about. Trust him at his Word, as the good reverend would say.

Kevin pulled into a Burger King. Three young men walked out in baggy jeans with chains that hung from their belt loops to their knees.

A gun. Right now he didn't need God's Word. Right now he needed a gun.

III

Jennifer picked up her phone, dialed Kevin's number, and let it ring a dozen times. Still no answer. He'd been gone since five o'clock last evening, and she had hardly slept.

They had set up audio surveillance with a single laser beam, which when placed on any one of Kevin's windows could turn the glass into an effective diaphragm for sounds beyond. Slater had probably used a similar device. The problem with the laser technology was that it picked up sounds indiscriminately. A digital-signal processor decoded the sounds and filtered voice, but the settings had to be adjusted whenever the operator changed windows, or when conditions—such as the closing of drapes—changed sufficiently to interfere with the acoustics of the room. For some reason Kevin had decided to close the drapes just before his departure.

A young agent named McConnel was resetting the laser receiver when Kevin had come out. McConnel said he heard a barrage of static in his earphone and looked up to see the garage door open and the rented Ford Taurus pull out. He'd reported the incident immediately, but his hands were tied. No following.

The fact that McConnel had heard nothing resembling a phone call before Kevin's departure was somewhat comforting, but the call could have come while the agent was adjusting the receiver.

Jennifer had tried to reach Sam at the Howard Johnson hotel, on the whim that she might know Kevin's whereabouts. No luck. The agent wasn't picking up her cell and the hotel clerk said that she'd checked out yesterday morning. She remembered Sam because she'd been tipped twenty dollars. Any agent who'd leave a tip for a desk clerk was unusual at the least.

Jennifer only hoped that Slater would have as much difficulty reaching Kevin as she did. If so, the disappearing act might actually offer some benefits. No bombs. So far. Hopefully the statewide bulletin on the Taurus wouldn't trigger one. She wasn't sure why Kevin had left—most probably a reaction to the stress—but in doing so he may have inadvertently stalled Slater.

Jennifer called the agent on duty by the house and learned, as expected, nothing new. She decided to try the dean a few minutes early.

Dr. John Francis lived in an old brick house on the edge of Long Beach, two blocks west of Los Alamitos. She knew that he was a widower with doctorates in both psychology and philosophy who'd lived in the same house for twenty-three years. Other than that all she knew was that he had taken Kevin under his wing at the seminary. And that he liked to drive fast, judging by the black Porsche 911 in his driveway.

Five minutes after pulling up to his house, Jennifer sat in a cozy living room, listening to quiet strains of Bach, nursing a hot cup of green tea. Dr. Francis sat opposite her in an armchair, legs crossed, smiling without trying to. He was quite distressed over all the news he'd heard about his student, but she would never guess it with a glance. The professor had one of those faces that couldn't help but reflect God's goodness, regardless of what might be happening.

"How well do you know Kevin?" she asked.

"Quite well as far as students go. But you must understand, that doesn't qualify me to pass any judgment on his past."

"His past. We'll come back to that. This may sound like a simple case of revenge based on what the media is pumping over the air, but I think it's more complicated than that. I think whoever's after Kevin sees his life as it is now and takes exception to it. That's where you come in. It appears that Kevin's a quiet man. Not a lot of friends. In fact, he evidently considers you his best. Maybe his only, other than Sam."

"Sam? You mean his childhood friend, Samantha? Yes, he's spoken of her. He seems quite taken with her."

"Tell me about him."

"You're looking for something in his life today that might elicit anger in someone from his past?"

She smiled. The psychologist in him was speaking. "Exactly."

"Unless Kevin comes forward with his confession, which he did, the man will extract a price."

"That's the basic story."

"But the confession missed the mark. So now you dig deeper, in search of that which so offends this Slater."

She nodded. Dr. Francis was a quick study. She decided to deal straight with the man. "On the surface it seems obvious. We have a student pursuing a holy vocation. As it turns out, his past is filled with mystery and murder. Someone takes exception to that dichotomy."

"We all have pasts filled with mystery and murder," Dr. Francis said.

Interesting way to put it.

"In fact, it's one of the aspects of the human condition Kevin and I have discussed before."

"Oh?"

"It's one of the first things an intelligent man like Kevin, who comes to the church later in life, notices. There is a pervasive incongruity between the church's theology and the way most of us in the church live."

"Hypocrisy."

"One of its faces, yes. Hypocrisy. Saying one thing but doing another. Studying to be a priest while hiding a small cocaine addiction, for example. The world flushes this out and cries scandal. But the more ominous face isn't nearly so obvious. This is what interested Kevin the most. He was quite astute, really."

"I'm not sure I follow. What's not so obvious?"

"The evil that lies in all of us," the professor said. "Not blatant hypocrisy, but deception. Not even realizing that the sin we regularly commit is sin at all. Going about life honestly believing that we are pure when all along we are riddled with sin."

She looked at his gentle smile, taken by the simplicity of his words.

"A preacher stands against the immorality of adultery, but all the while he harbors anger toward the third parishioner from the left because the parishioner challenged one of his teachings three months ago. Is anger not as evil as adultery? Or a woman who scorns the man across the aisle for alcoholic indiscretions, while she routinely gossips about him after services. Is gossip not as evil as any vice? What's especially damaging in both cases is that neither the man who harbors anger nor the woman who gossips seriously considers the evil of their own actions. Their sins remain hidden. This is the true cancer in the church."

"Sounds like the same cancer that eats away at the rest of society."

"Exactly. Although in the church it makes every attempt to

remain hidden, where it is left alone to grow in the dark. You ever wonder why incidences of divorce and gluttony and virtually all of evil's fruits are as high in the church as in society at large?"

"Actually, I didn't know that."

"Though being freed from sin, most remain slaves, blinded and gagged by their own deception. 'The good that I would, that I do not do and that which I would not, that I do.' Welcome to the church in America."

"And you're saying you've discussed this with Kevin?"

"I discuss this with every class I teach on the subject. Kevin, more than most students, understood it."

"Based on what you're saying, what Slater's doing isn't so different from what every old lady in the church does when she gossips?" *And killing Roy was no different either,* she almost said.

"Assuming that old ladies have a proclivity for gossip, a false assumption, actually. On the other hand, Saint Paul drew a distinction between some sins and others. Although he did place gossip in the most vile category."

Jennifer set down her cup on a cherry wood end table. "So you're suggesting that the Riddle Killer is interested in Kevin confessing his true nature, not necessarily some particular sin. Seems like a stretch. To what end? Why would Slater single out Kevin, unless Kevin somehow wronged him?"

"Now you're out of my league, I'm afraid."

"You're pushing theory way beyond what feels reasonable, Doctor. My brother was murdered. I hardly see any similarities between his killer and an old lady in a church."

"I'm so sorry. I didn't know." His compassion appeared thoroughly genuine.

"Even naysayers accept the brilliance of the teachings of Jesus," he said. "You do know what he said on the matter?"

"Tell me."

"That to hate a man is the same as killing him. Perhaps the gossipers are murderers after all."

The notion struck her as absurd. Jennifer sighed. "So Slater, who was once wronged by Kevin, studies him today and sees this great inconsistency—that Kevin lives a life of minor sins—anger, resentment, gossip. But Slater believes, as you seem to, that minor sins are no less evil than the greater sins. Kevin decides to become a priest. This upsets Slater and he decides to teach Kevin a lesson. That the gist of it?"

"Who's to say how a demented mind works?" The professor smiled. "Really, it's beyond me how anyone could do this to another man, especially a man like Kevin. Regardless of his past sins, Kevin is a walking testimony of God's grace. You'd think he's been through his share of difficulties. To have become the man he is today is nothing short of amazing."

She studied Dr. Francis. "He is quite unusual, isn't he? I didn't know his type still lived on the West Coast."

"His type?" the professor asked. "You mean his innocence?"

"Innocent, genuine. Maybe even naive, in a nonoffensive way."

"You're aware of his past?"

"Sketchy. I haven't exactly had the time to dig past his file these last two days."

The doctor's brow went up. "Perhaps you would do well to pay a visit to the home of his childhood. I don't know the entire story, but from what Father Strong told me, Kevin's childhood was anything but normal. Not necessarily terrible, mind you, but I wouldn't be surprised to find more there than Father Strong or any of the rest of us suspects, particularly in light of these recent events."

"So you don't know the details of his past. Still, you say he's been through his share of difficulties."

"His parents died when he was one. He was raised by an aunt who despises his pursuit of higher education. As you say, he acts like a man who has recently walked off an island to discover that there is a rest-of-the-world. Naive. I think there's something in Kevin's past that haunts him. It may shed some light on this man you call Slater."

"The boy," she said.

"I'm afraid I don't know about any boy."

She would take a trip to Baker Street as soon as she left. "Nothing else comes to mind? No other students or faculty might have any motive to hurt Kevin?"

"Heavens, no. Not unless all of our gossiping students are becoming murderers to flush out the truth." He grinned.

"You sound like a wonderful teacher, Dr. Francis. Do you mind if I call on you again?"

"Please." He tapped his chest. "There's a special place in here for Kevin. I can't place it or explain why I am so taken by the boy, but I think we all have something to learn from his story."

She stood. "I pray you're right."

"I didn't know you were a religious woman."

"I'm not."

15

THE YOUNG MEN WITH THE CHAINS didn't look like they were carrying any weapons. Not that criminals made a habit of hanging guns around their necks from shoestrings for all to see. Either way, Kevin gave them a pass and pulled back onto Western.

Maybe looking in less obvious spots would fare better. Side streets. Any beer-drinking slug wearing a wife-beater would be packing one, right? Or at least have a piece tucked under the mattress nearby. The fact was, Kevin had no clue what he was doing and the growing realization pushed his nerves into overdrive.

He drove several neighborhoods before working up the courage to park in one particularly seedy-looking lane and take to foot. Wouldn't it be ironic if he were held up at gunpoint minding his own business? Why play games with a serial killer when you could take a stroll down misery lane and get offed any day of the week? Just like in the movies. Or was the other more like a movie?

He walked down the street, past houses with prying eyes. Maybe now would be a good time to pray. On the other hand, considering his intentions, praying felt inappropriate. A ball rolled out on the sidewalk three feet in front of him. He glanced at the house to his right and saw a boy, maybe three feet tall, staring at him with wide brown eyes. A large, shirtless man covered in tattoos, bald except for a black goatee, stood in the doorway behind the boy, watching him from under bushy eyebrows. Kevin picked up the ball and tossed it awkwardly back into the brown lawn.

"You lost?" the man asked.

That obvious? "No," he said and turned away.

"You look lost to me, boy."

Kevin was suddenly too terrified to respond. He walked on, not daring to look back. The man humphed, but made no other comment. Half a block later he glanced back. The man had retreated into his house.

Now, that wasn't so bad. You go, boy. Kevin the player.

Kevin the fool. Here he was, wandering a strange neighborhood, pretending to have a clue, scheming nondescript plans, while the real game awaited its star player twenty miles south. What if Slater had called in the last couple hours? What if he'd called Jennifer or the police with the next threat? Or what if Sam had awakened, found him gone, turned on the phone, and received a call?

Kevin stopped walking. What on earth did he think he was doing? Sam. Sam had a gun. She'd never shown it to him, but he knew she carried it in her purse. Why not just take her gun? What was she going to do, throw him in jail for—

"Excuse me."

Kevin spun around. The man from the doorway stood five feet away. He'd pulled on a white T-shirt that barely managed to contain his bulging shoulders.

"I asked you a question."

Kevin's heart pounded. "I'm . . . I'm not lost."

"I don't believe you. I see a Wall Street punk walking down the sidewalk at ten in the morning and I know he's lost. You trying to score?"

"Score? No. Gosh, no."

"Gosh?" The man grinned and savored the word. "Gosh, no. Then what are you doing so far from home?"

"I'm . . . just walking."

"This look like Central Park to you? Not even the right state, boy. I can hook you up."

A cool sweat ran down Kevin's back. Ask him. Just ask him.

He glanced around. "Actually, I'm looking for a weapon."

The man's eyebrows went up. "And you think this is where weapons grow on trees, is that it?"

"No."

The man studied him. "You a cop?"

"Do I look like a cop?"

"You look like a fool. Is there a difference? What kind of idiot walks around a strange neighborhood looking for a piece?"

"I'm sorry. I should probably leave."

"I guess so."

The man was blocking the sidewalk, so Kevin sidestepped to the street. He took three steps before the man spoke again.

"How much you got?"

He stopped and faced the man. "Four hundred dollars."

"Let me see it."

What if the man robbed him? Too late now. He pulled out his wallet and spread it open.

"Follow me." The man turned and walked back toward his house without checking to see if Kevin followed.

He did. Like a puppy. How many prying eyes watched the sucker from Wall Street slinking along behind Biff?

He followed the man up to his porch. "Wait here." He left Kevin with his hands in his pockets.

Thirty seconds later he was back with something wrapped in an old white T-shirt. "Give me the money."

"What is it?"

"It's a thirty-eight. Cleaned and loaded." Biff glanced up the street. "Worth six, but it's your lucky day. I need the cash."

Kevin fished out his wallet with a trembling hand and handed the contents to the man. He took the bundle. Where was he going to put it? He couldn't just walk down the street with a bundle that had *gun* written all over it. He started to shove it down his pants— too bulky.

The man finished flipping through the bills and saw Kevin's dilemma. He grinned. "Boy, you are a case, aren't you? What're you gonna do, hold up your dog? Give me the shirt."

Kevin unwrapped a shiny silver pistol with a black handle. He gripped the butt with his fingertips and handed the shirt to the man.

The man looked at the gun and smirked. "What do you think you have there? A pastry? Hold it like a man."

Kevin snugged the gun in his palm.

"In your belt. Pull your shirt over it."

Kevin shoved the cold steel barrel past his bellybutton and covered it with his shirt. Still looked pretty obvious to him.

"Suck your gut in. For another hundred I'll show you how to pull the trigger." Grin.

"No thanks."

He turned and walked back out to the sidewalk. He had a gun. What on earth he was going to do with it, he still had no idea. But he had the piece. It was okay to pray now, maybe.

God, help me.

III

Baker Street. It was the third time in two days Jennifer had driven down the narrow lane under the elms. The warehouse where they'd found the blood couldn't be seen from the street itself—it was in the second row of buildings. She imagined a young boy racing across the street toward the clustered warehouses with a bully at his heels. Kevin and the boy.

"What is here that you want to hide, Kevin?" she murmured. "Hmm?" The white house loomed to her left, immaculate, with the shiny beige Plymouth in its driveway. "What did Aunt Balinda do to you?"

Jennifer parked her car on the street and walked up to the porch. A slight breeze rustled through the leaves. The green lawn appeared freshly mowed and trimmed around the edges. She didn't notice until she stepped up on the porch that the red roses in the flower beds were imitation. For that matter, so were all the flowers. It seemed Aunt Balinda was too tidy a person to mess with the natural flaws of nature. Everything about the house was perfectly finished.

She rang the bell and stepped back. A curtain to her left parted; a middle-aged man with a crew cut looked out. Bob. Kevin's retarded older cousin. The face stared, smiled, and disappeared. Then nothing.

Jennifer rang the bell again. What were they doing in there? Bob had seen her . . .

The door cracked and filled with an old, heavily painted, saggy face. "What do you want?"

Jennifer flipped open her badge. "Agent Peters, FBI. Just wondered if I could come in and ask you a few questions."

"Certainly not."

"Just a few—"

"Do you have a search warrant?"

"No. I didn't think I would need one."

"We all make mistakes, dear. Come back with a search warrant." The woman started to close the door.

"Balinda, I presume?"

She turned back. "Yeah? So what?"

"I will be back, Balinda, and I'll bring the police with me. We'll turn the place inside out. Is that what you want?"

Balinda hesitated. Her eyelashes flapped several times. Ruby red lipstick glistened on her lips, like glossy putty. She smelled of too much talcum powder.

"What do you want?" Balinda asked again.

"I told you. Just a few questions."

"Then ask them." She made no move from the door.

The woman was begging to be properly engaged. "I don't think you understand me. When I come back in an hour, I'll have a half-dozen blue suits with me. We'll have guns and microphones. We'll strip-search you if we have to."

Balinda just stared.

"Or you can let me in now, just me. Are you aware that your son Kevin is in trouble?"

"Doesn't surprise me. I told him he'd end up in trouble if he went off."

"Well, it seems that your warning had some merit."

The woman made no move.

Jennifer nodded and stepped back. "Okay. I'll be back."

"You won't touch anything?"

"Not a thing." She lifted both hands.

"Fine. But I don't like people invading our privacy, you understand?"

"I understand."

Balinda walked inside and Jennifer pushed the door open. A single glance into the dimly lit house washed away her understanding.

She entered a hallway of sorts, formed by stacks of newspapers that ran nearly to the ceiling, leaving a passage just wide enough for a slight man to walk through without getting newsprint on his shoulders. Two faces peered at her from the end of the makeshift hallway—Bob's and another man's—both craning for a view.

Jennifer stepped in and closed the door behind her. Balinda whispered urgently to the two men and they retreated like mice. Grayed carpet had been worn to the wood subfloor. The edge of a newspaper to Jennifer's right stuck out far enough for her to read the headline. *London Herald.* June 24, 1972. Over thirty years old.

"Ask your questions," Balinda snapped from the end of the hall.

Jennifer walked toward her, mind swimming. Why had they stacked all these papers in tall neat stacks like this? The display gave eccentricity a whole new meaning. What kind of woman would do this?

Aunt Balinda wore a white dress, high heels, and enough costume jewelry to sink a battleship. Behind her, backlit by a window that overlooked a dirt yard, Eugene stood in riding boots and what appeared to be a jockey's outfit. Bob wore plaid knickers that revealed the tops of knee-high socks. A polo shirt hugged his thin frame.

The hall directed her into what appeared to be the living room, but again, its dimensions had been altered by floor-to-ceiling stacks of paper. Newspapers alternated with books and magazines and the occasional box. A foot-wide crack between two of the stacks allowed light in from what had once been a window. For all of its mess, the room had an order to it, like a bird's nest. The stacks stood several rows deep, allowing just enough room for old Victorian furniture placed just so between smaller mounds of paper in the middle of the floor. These appeared to be in the process of being sorted.

To Jennifer's right, a small kitchen table was piled high with dishes, some clean, most dirty. A collection of empty TV dinner packages sat on one of the chairs. The boxes had been cut with a pair of blue-handled scissors, which rested on the top box.

"Are you going to ask your questions?"

"I'm . . . I'm sorry, I just didn't expect this. What are you doing here?"

"We live here. What do you think we're doing here?"

"You like newspapers." They weren't complete papers, but sections and clippings from newspapers, she saw, categorized according to subject by placards set into the stacks. People. World. Food. Play. Religion.

Bob stepped away from where he'd cornered himself in the kitchen. "Do you like to play?" He held out an old Game Boy in his hand, a monochrome model that looked like it might play Pong with enough persuasion. "This is my computer."

"Hush, Bobby, honey," Balinda said. "Go to your room and read your books."

"It's a real computer."

"I'm sure the lady isn't interested. She's not from our world. Go to your room."

"She's pretty, Mom."

"She's a dog! Do you like dog hair, Bobby? If you play with her, you'll get dog hair all over you. Is that what you want?"

Bob's eyes widened. "The dog is gone."

"Yes, she will be. Now go to your room and sleep."

The boy started to walk away.

"What do you say?" Eugene said.

Bob turned back and dipped his head at Balinda. "Thank you, Princess." He flashed a grin, hurried off through the kitchen, and shuffled down another hall, this one stacked with books.

"I'm sorry, but you know children," Balinda said. "Minds full of mush. They only understand certain things."

"Do you mind if we sit?"

"Eugene, get our guest a chair."

"Yes, Princess." He grabbed two chairs from the table, set one beside Jennifer, and held the other for Balinda to sit. When she did, he lowered his head with the respect of an eighteenth-century butler. Jennifer stared. They had created a world out of their newspapers and all of this paraphernalia—shaped to fit their lives.

"Thank you."

"You're welcome, madam," Eugene said, dipping his head again.

It wasn't unheard of for adults to create their own realities and then protect them—most people clung to some form of illusion, whether it be found in an extension of entertainment or in religion or simply in a self-propagated lifestyle. The lines between reality and fantasy blurred for every human at some level, but this—this was a case study to be sure.

Jennifer decided to slip into their world. When in Rome . . .

"You've created your own world here, haven't you? Ingenious." She looked around, awed. Beyond the living room stood another doorway, maybe leading to the master bedroom. A stair banister ran along one wall. The same Sunday *Times* Jennifer had read earlier was spread out on the coffee table. The cover story, an article on George W. Bush, had been neatly cut out. The picture of Bush was at the bottom of a discard box. A stack two feet deep sat untouched next to the *Times,* topped by the *Miami Herald.* How many papers did they receive each day?

"You cut away what you don't like and keep the rest," Jennifer said. "What do you do with the clippings?" She turned to Balinda.

The old woman wasn't sure what to think of her sudden change. "What clippings?"

"The ones you don't like."

She knew with one look at Eugene that she'd guessed right. The man glanced nervously at his princess.

"What a brilliant idea!" Jennifer said. "You create your own world by clipping out only those stories that fit your idyllic world and then you discard the rest."

Balinda was speechless.

"Who's the president, Eugene?"

"Eisenhower," the man said without hesitation.

"Of course. Eisenhower. None of the others are worthy to be president. Any news of Reagan or the Bushes or Clinton just gets cut out."

"Don't be silly," Balinda said. "Everyone knows that Eisenhower is our president. We don't go along with the pretenders."

"And who won the World Series this year, Eugene?"

"Baseball isn't played anymore."

"No, of course not. Trick question. What do you do with all the baseball stories?"

"Baseball isn't played—"

"Shut up, Eugene!" Balinda snapped. "Don't repeat yourself like a fool in a lady's presence! Go cut something up."

He saluted and stood at attention. "Yes, sir!"

"Sir? What has gotten into you? You're losing your mind just because we have a visitor? Do I look like a general to you?"

He lowered his hand. "Forgive me, my princess. Perhaps I should save us some coin by cutting some coupons. I should love to take the carriage to the shop for stores as soon as I do."

She glared at him. He did an about-face and walked for the stack of fresh newspapers.

"Don't mind him," Balinda said. "He gets a bit strange when he's excited."

Jennifer glanced out the window. A thin ribbon of smoke drifted skyward from a barrel. The yard was black . . .

They burned them! Whatever didn't fit neatly into the world Balinda wanted went up in smoke. Newspaper stories, books, even pictures on TV dinner boxes. She looked around for a television. An old black and white sat dusty in the living room.

Jennifer stood and walked toward it. "I have to hand it to you, Balinda; you take the cake."

"We do what we are entitled to in the privacy of our home," she said.

"Of course. You have every right. Frankly, it would take tremendous strength and resolve to sustain the world you've managed to build around yourself."

"Thank you. We've given our lives to it. One has to find a way in this chaotic world."

"I can see that." She eased through the living room and peered over the banister. The staircase was filled in with reams of old papers. "Where does this lead?"

"The basement. We don't use it anymore. Not for a long time."

"How long?"

"Thirty years. Maybe longer. It frightened Bob, so we nailed it shut."

Jennifer faced the hall Bob had disappeared down. Kevin's room was down there somewhere, hidden behind piles of books—probably butchered—and magazines. She walked down the hall.

Balinda stood and followed. "Now wait a minute. Where—"

"I just want to see, Balinda. I just want to see how you managed it."

"Questions, you said. You're walking, not talking."

"I won't touch a thing. That's what I said. And I won't."

She passed a bathroom on her right, cluttered and filthy. The hall ended at the doorways of two rooms. The door on the right was shut—presumably Bob's room. The door on the left was open a crack. She pushed it open. A small bed sat in one corner, strewn with loose clippings from children's books. Hundreds of books stood against one wall—half with their covers torn off, altered, or trimmed to meet Balinda's approval. A small window with a pull-down shade looked into the backyard.

"Kevin's old room?" she asked.

"Until he abandoned us. I told him that if he left he'd end up in trouble. I tried to warn him."

"Do you even want to know what kind of trouble he's in?"

Balinda turned away. "What happens out of this house is not my concern. I told him he had no business running off with the serpent. Sss, sss, sss. It's lies, lies, all lies out there. They say we came from monkeys. You're all fools."

"You're right, the world is full of fools. But I can assure you, Kevin isn't one of them."

Balinda's eyes flashed. "Oh, he's not, is he? He was always too smart for us! Bob was the dumb one and Kevin was God himself, come to enlighten the rest of us poor idiots!" She took a breath through her nostrils.

She'd hit a button in the old hag. The adopted nephew wasn't retarded like her own son and Balinda had taken exception to the fact.

Jennifer swallowed and walked to the window. It was fastened down with one screw. What kind of mother would raise a boy in an environment like this? The thought of Kevin crying as they passed by the house yesterday came with new understanding. *Dear Kevin, what did she do to you? Who was the small boy who lived in this room?* The screw was loose in its hole.

Balinda followed Jennifer's stare.

"He used to crawl out of that window. He didn't know that I knew, but I did. Nothing happens around here without my knowing."

Jennifer turned back and brushed past Balinda. Nausea swept through her stomach. In a twisted way, Balinda had probably raised

Kevin with noble intentions. She'd protected him from a terrible world full of evil and death. But at what price?

Slow down, Jennifer. You don't know what happened here. You don't even know that this wasn't a wonderful environment for a child to be raised in.

She stepped into the living room and calmed herself.

"I knew he was sneaking out," Balinda was saying. "But I just couldn't stop him. Not without beating him raw. Never did believe in that kind of discipline. It may have been a mistake. Look at where it got him. Maybe I should have beaten him."

Jennifer took a shallow breath. "What kind of discipline *did* you use?"

"You don't need discipline when your house is in order. Life is discipline enough. Anything more is an admission of weakness." She said it all with her chest puffed, proud. "Isolate them with the truth and they will shine like the stars."

The revelation came like a cool balm. She looked around. So Kevin's rearing had been weird and distorted, but maybe not terrible.

"A man has been threatening Kevin," she said. "We believe it's someone your son—"

"He's my nephew."

"Sorry. Nephew. Someone Kevin might have known when he was ten or eleven. A boy who threatened Kevin. He had a fight with this boy. Maybe you remember something that might help us identify him."

"It must have been the time he came home all bloody. I do remember that. Yes, we found him in bed in the morning and his nose was a mess. He refused to talk about it, but I knew he'd been out. I knew everything."

"What kind of friends did Kevin have at that age?"

Balinda hesitated. "His family was his friend. Bob was his friend."

"But he must have had other friends in the neighborhood. How about Samantha?"

"That fool girl? They sneaked around. Don't think I didn't know. He let it slip a few times. She was the one who may have ruined him in the first place! No, we tried to discourage him from keeping friends outside the house. This is an evil world. You don't just let your children play with anyone!"

"You didn't know *any* of his friends?"

Balinda stared at her for a long time and then walked for the door. "You're starting to repeat your questions. I don't think we can help you more than we have." She opened the door.

Jennifer took a last look around the house. She pitied the poor boy who grew up in this distorted world. He would enter the real world . . . naive.

Like Kevin.

But Balinda was probably right. There was nothing more to learn here.

16

S AMANTHA PACED THE FLOOR of the hotel room for
the hundredth time. She'd anticipated almost every eventuality,
but not Kevin's disappearance.

Roland had paged her and she'd called him from the room phone.
He wasn't thrilled about her having turned off her cell but agreed that
her plan had some merit. Meanwhile they had set up a meeting with
the Pakistani, Salman, in Houston. This evening. Removing Kevin
from the game by pulling him out of Slater's reach might have been
the best way to stall the killer until her return tomorrow. But she
hadn't considered the possibility that Kevin would disappear. Now she
was due to catch a flight in a few hours, and Kevin was gone.

Jennifer Peters would be burning up the phone lines by now, trying to find them, but Sam couldn't bring herself to tip her hand—not
yet. Something about the whole investigation bothered her, but she
couldn't put a finger on it. Something wasn't right.

She reviewed the facts as she knew them.

One. Someone, probably a white male, had terrorized Sacramento
over the last twelve months by selecting seemingly random victims,
giving them a riddle to solve, and then killing them when they failed.
He'd been dubbed the Riddle Killer by the media and the name had
stuck with law enforcement. Jennifer's brother, Roy, had been his last
victim.

Two. She had opened an undercover CBI investigation under the premise that the killer had or was an inside man. Nothing indicated that the killer knew of her investigation.

Three. Someone with almost the same MO as the Riddle Killer was now stalking both Kevin and her in a game of riddles.

Four. A concrete connection had been established between this same killer and a boy who'd threatened both her and Kevin twenty years earlier.

On the surface, it all made perfect sense: A boy named Slater takes to torturing animals and terrorizing other children. He's nearly killed by one of those children, Kevin, when Kevin locks him in a cellar to protect a young girl Slater intends to harm. But Slater escapes the cellar and grows up to become one of society's worst nightmares—a man void of conscience with a lust for blood. Now, twenty years later, Slater learns that the two children who tormented him so long ago are alive. He stalks them and devises a game to deal with both in one fell swoop. Obvious, right?

No. Not in Sam's mind. For starters, why had Slater waited so long to go after both her and Kevin? Did the small incident in the cellar just skip his mind for twenty years? And what was the likelihood that she, employed by the CBI, just happened to be assigned to a case involving the same person who tried to kill her twenty years ago?

And now, in the eleventh hour, this new lead from Sacramento—someone in Houston who claimed to know Slater. Or more accurately, the Riddle Killer. If she was right, they were all barking up the wrong tree.

Sam glanced at her watch. Two-thirty and still nothing. She had a plane to catch for Dallas at five. "Come on, Kevin. You're forcing my hand here."

She sighed and picked up her cell phone. She reluctantly switched it on and dialed Jennifer Peters's number.

"Peters."

"Hello, Agent Peters. Samantha Sheer—"

"Samantha! Where are you? Kevin's gone. We've been trying to track him down all morning."

"Slow down. I know Kevin's gone. He's with me. Or was with me, I should say."

"With *you?* This isn't your investigation. You have no right this side of hell to act without our approval! You trying to get him killed?"

Wrong, Jennifer, I don't need your approval. "Don't insult me."

"Do you have any idea how crazy things are down here? The media's gotten wind, presumably through that deadhead Milton, that Kevin's disappeared, and they're already suggesting Slater kidnapped him. They've got cameras on rooftops, waiting for the next bomb, for heaven's sake! A killer's loose out there, and the only man who may be able to lead us to him has gone AWOL. Why didn't you call? Where is he now?"

"Take a breath, Jennifer. I have called, against my better judgment. I've put in a request to share what we know with you, but only you, do you understand? What I share with you, no one else hears. Not Milton, not the FBI, no one."

"Put in a request with whom?"

"With the attorney general. We've been working this case from a new angle, you might say. Now you know, but no one else does."

Silence.

"Agreed?"

"I swear, the way these bureaucracies work, you'd think we still lived in caves. I've been busting my butt for a year on this case, and now I learn that some crackpot agency is doing an end run? Do you have any information that might be useful, or is that a secret too?"

"We have reason to suspect an inside link."

"Inside. As in law enforcement?"

"Maybe. We would have shared files a long time ago if we didn't suspect that someone inside may be tracking with Slater."

"Meaning?"

"Meaning we're not sure who we can trust. For reasons I can't go into today, I don't think Slater is who you think he is."

"You mean the boy? *I* don't even know who I think he is!"

"That's not what I mean. He probably is the boy. But who's the boy?"

"You tell us. He threatened you, didn't he?"

"That was a long time ago, and we have no ID. For all we know, he's the director of the FBI now."

"Please, don't patronize me."

"You're right. He's not the director of the FBI. All I'm saying is that we can't eliminate the possibility that he's someone on the inside. I'll know more tomorrow."

"This is ridiculous. Where are you now?"

Sam paused. She had no choice now. Withholding information from Jennifer would only hamper her investigation at this point. She needed the FBI to focus on their own investigation, not meddle in hers. And there was this little fact that Kevin was missing.

She explained her rationale for taking Kevin, and Jennifer listened patiently, interrupting occasionally with pointed questions. Sam's reasoning finally won her a grunt of approval. The news of Kevin's disappearance didn't.

"So as far as we know, Slater does have him," Jennifer said.

"I doubt it. But it does look like I've made a mistake. I didn't expect this."

Jennifer let the apology go, which from Sam was as good as an acceptance. The FBI agent sighed.

"Let's hope he comes in. Soon. How well did you know him when he was a boy?"

"We were close. I didn't have a better friend."

"I visited his aunt's house this morning."

Sam sat on the bed. How much did Jennifer know? Kevin had never shared the details of his life in the house with Sam, but she knew much more than he suspected.

"I never did see the inside of the house," Sam said. "His aunt wouldn't allow it. It was hard enough sneaking around the way we did."

"Was there abuse?"

"Physical, no. Not that I saw. But in my book Kevin suffered severe, systematic psychological abuse from the day he entered that twisted house. You talked to Balinda?"

"Yes. She's created a sanctuary for herself in there. The only realities that make it past the cutting floor are the ones she decides are real. God only knows what the house was like twenty years ago. Manipulation of a child's learning process isn't unheard of—it's even broadly accepted in some arenas. Military school comes to mind. But I've never heard of anything like Balinda's little kingdom. Judging by Kevin's reaction to the place, I would tend to agree. He suffered abuse in that house."

Sam let the phone line remain silent for a while.

"Be careful, Jennifer. This is a case about a hurting man as much as it is a hunt for a killer."

Jennifer hesitated. "Meaning?"

"There's more. There are secrets behind the walls of that house."

"Secrets he hasn't shared with you, his childhood sweetheart?"

"Yes."

By the sound of Jennifer's breathing, Sam knew she felt uncomfortable with the tone of the conversation. She decided to expand the agent's mind a little.

"I want you to consider something that's nagged me for the last two days, Jennifer. No one hears, understand? This is between us. Agreed?"

"Go on."

"I would like you to consider the possibility that Kevin and Slater are really the same person." She dropped the bomb and let Jennifer respond.

"I . . . I don't think that's possible." Jennifer chuckled nervously. "I mean that would be . . . the evidence doesn't support that! How could he pull off such a crazy stunt?"

"He's not pulling anything off. Please, understand me, I'm not suggesting it's true, and God knows even considering the idea terrifies me, but there are elements to this case that just don't sit right. I think the possibility is at least worth some thought."

"He would have to be calling himself. You're suggesting he was in Sacramento, blowing up victims three months ago?"

"If he is the Riddle Killer. I'm working on that."

"And if he is Slater, who's the boy? We found blood in the warehouse, consistent with this story. There was a boy."

"Unless the boy was really Kevin. Or there was no boy."

"You were there—"

"I never actually saw the boy, Jennifer."

"Your father forced the family to leave! What do you mean you never *saw* the boy?"

"I mean I told my father the boy was there—there was plenty of evidence at my window and I believed Kevin for the rest. Call it a white lie. Regardless, I actually never saw the boy. We forced the family of a bully to move, but thinking back on it, the boy ran off before my dad could apprehend him. He accused a local bully based on my testimony, and I based my testimony on Kevin's. But there was no definitive evidence that it was someone *other* than Kevin. I didn't even know Kevin had locked the boy in the warehouse until yesterday."

"The physical evidence for Kevin being Slater doesn't add up. He blew up his own car?"

"I'm not saying that he *is* Slater. I'm only positing a possibility. Considering his childhood, Multiple Personality Disorder may not be out of the question—the Kevin we know wouldn't necessarily even know that he's Slater. Everything that we have so far could fit the scenario; that's all I'm saying. There are no inconsistencies. Think about it."

"Neither is there any evidence to support it. Highly unlikely. MPD results only in very limited cases of severe childhood abuse. Almost always physical abuse. Balinda might be a witch, but she doesn't fit the profile for physical abuse. You said so yourself."

"You're right, there wasn't physical abuse. But there are exceptions."

"Not any that fit this scenario. At least not that I know of, and it is my field of study."

Probably right. Highly unlikely, but in cases like this every possibility had to be considered. Something was not what it seemed, and as disturbing as her suggestion was, Sam couldn't just discard it. If Kevin was Slater, exposing the fact would be the greatest favor she could do for her childhood friend.

On the other hand, hearing herself say it out loud, the notion sounded absurd. A simple voice or handwriting analysis would settle the matter.

"Have the lab run a handwriting comparison from the jug."

"We already have. Standard procedure. It was negative."

"It's technically possible for multiple personalities to have varying motor characteristics."

"In this case, I don't think so."

"Then start comparing it with everyone else connected to the case. Someone on the inside's working this, Jennifer. Someone's not who we think they are."

"Then get me your file."

"It's on the way."

"And if Kevin contacts you, call me. Immediately." To say that the agent sounded agitated would be like saying the sky was big.

"You have my word."

"As much as your plan to isolate Kevin may have made sense, having Slater's voice on tape could be invaluable. Particularly in light of your suggestion. Turn it on and leave it on."

Sam picked up Slater's silver phone and switched it on. "Done."

"The recording device is still active?"

"Yes."

A knock sounded on the door. Sam started.

"What is it?" Jennifer asked.

"Someone's at the door." She walked for the door.

"Who?"

She turned the deadbolt and pulled it open. Kevin stood in the hallway, blinking and haggard.

"Kevin," Sam said. "It's Kevin."

| | |

Jennifer lowered the phone and sat hard. The notion that Kevin and the Riddle Killer might be the same man wasn't only absurd; it was . . . wrong. Sick. Deeply disturbing.

Galager walked by her desk, headed for the lab. She couldn't bring herself to look at him. Was it possible?

Her mind spun back to the scene of Roy's death. Was it possible that Kevin—

No! It made no sense.

And why is this such an infuriating prospect, Jennifer? You can't imagine Kevin killing Roy because you like Kevin. He reminds you of Roy, for heaven's sake.

Jennifer rehearsed the facts quickly. If Kevin was Slater, then he would have to be calling himself, possible but unlikely. He would also have to have an alter ego of which he was clueless. She had interviewed enough witnesses over the years to recognize sincerity, and Kevin had it in spades. He would have had to plant the bombs long ago, possible, but in both cases he would have had to detonate them without his own knowing.

No. No, this was too much. She began to relax. The man she had comforted in the park yesterday was no killer. The boy, whose blood they'd found in the cellar, on the other hand, could be.

Point was, she had panicked at the thought that Kevin might be the killer, hadn't she? She should have been ecstatic at the mere prospect of uncovering the killer's true identity. Which said that she cared far too much for Kevin, an absurdity in itself given the fact that she hardly knew him!

On the other hand, she was bound to him in a way few people ever are. They shared the death of her brother in common—she as the victim's survivor, he as the next victim.

Jennifer sighed and stood. She was too emotionally wrapped up in this whole thing. The bureau chief was right.

"Galager!"

The man paused at the door across the room. She motioned him back.

"What's up?"

"We found Kevin."

Galager pulled up. "Where?"

"Palos Verdes. He's okay."

"Should I get Milton?"

He was the last person she wanted to bring in. But she had her marching orders, didn't she? At least she didn't have to deal with him directly. She scribbled the information on a notepad, ripped the page off, and handed it to Galager.

"Fill him in. Tell him I'm tied up."

It was the truth. She was tied up, in knots that refused to loosen.

|||

They sat on the bed in a stalemate. Kevin was hiding something; that much Sam had known since she'd first talked to him. Friday night. Now his lying was more blatant, but try as she may, she could not coax the truth out of him. His story that he'd been wandering through his old neighborhood, thinking, for the past eight hours was simply unbelievable. True, given his circumstances, almost any behavior was possible. But she knew Kevin too well; she could read those clear blue eyes, and they were shifting. Something else was bothering him.

"Okay, Kevin, but I still don't think you're telling me everything. I have a plane to catch in a couple hours. With any luck, Slater will take the day to revel in his little victory yesterday. God knows we need the time."

"When will you be back?"

"Tomorrow morning." She stood, walked to the window, and pulled back the curtain. "We're closing in, Kevin. We're right on this guy's tail; I can feel it in my bones."

"I wish you weren't going."

Sam turned back. "Jennifer will be here. She'll want to talk to you."

He looked past her out the window. "Yeah."

Dark circles hung under his eyes. He seemed distracted.

"I need a drink," he said. "You want one?"

"I'm fine. You're not going to run off again, are you?"

He grinned. "Come on. I'm here, aren't I?"

"Yes, you are. Hurry back."

He opened the door to leave.

The beige phone on the nightstand rang shrilly. She glanced at the clock beside it—3 P.M. They had overstayed their checkout.

"Go ahead," she told Kevin. "It's probably the front desk."

Kevin left and she picked up the phone.

"Hello?"

"Hello, Samantha."

Slater! She whirled to the door. So Kevin *couldn't* be Slater! He'd been in the room when the killer had called.

"Kevin!" He was gone.

"Not Kevin. It's your other lover, dear."

How had Slater gotten their number? The only person who knew where they were was Jennifer. *Jennifer* . . .

"They want my voice, Samantha. I want to give them my voice. Have you turned the cell phone back on, or are you still playing your idiotic cat-and-mouse game?"

"It's on."

The line clicked. Slater's cell began to ring. She grabbed it and answered.

"There, that's better, don't you think? The game won't last forever; we might as well make this more interesting."

It was the first time she'd actually heard his voice. Low and gravelly.

"What good is a game that you can't lose?" she asked. "It proves nothing."

"Oh, but I can lose, Sam. The fact that I haven't proves that I'm smarter than you." Short heavy breath. "I came within a single pane of glass of killing you once. This time I won't fail."

The boy. She turned and sat on the bed. "So that was you."

"Do you know why I wanted to kill you?"

"No." Keep him talking. "Tell me."

"Because all nice people deserve to die. Especially the pretty ones with bright blue eyes. I despise beauty almost as much as I despise nice little boys. I'm not sure who I hate more, you or that imbecile you call your lover."

"You make me sick!" Samantha said. "You prey on innocence because you're too stupid to realize it's far more fascinating than evil."

Silence. Only heavy breathing. She'd struck a nerve.

"Kevin confessed, as you demanded," she said. "He told the whole world about that night. But you can't live by your own rules, can you?"

"Yes, of course. The boy. Was that me? Maybe it was, maybe it wasn't. Kevin still hasn't confessed his sin. He hasn't even hinted at it. The secret's much too dark, even for him, I think."

"What? *What* sin?"

He chuckled.

"The sin, Samantha. *The* sin. Riddle time. *What wants to be filled but will always be empty?* I'll give you a clue: It's not your head. It has a number: 36933. You have ninety minutes before the fireworks begin. And please remember, no cops."

"Why are you so afraid of the cops?"

"It's not who I'm afraid of; it's who I want to play with." The line clicked.

He was gone.

Sam stood still, mind reeling. He'd called on the hotel room phone. Could he have tracked them down so quickly? Or the phone— could he have a way of tracking it once she turned it on? Unlikely. She paced to the end of the bed and back. Think, Sam! Think! Where was Kevin? They had to—

"Sam?" Kevin's muffled voice sounded beyond the door. He knocked.

She ran for the door. Opened it.

"He called," she said.

"Slater?" His face went white.

"Yes."

Kevin stepped in, can of 7UP in his hand. "What did he say?"

"Another riddle. *What wants to be filled but will always be empty?* With some numbers. 36933." The most obvious solution had already run through her mind. She ran to the coffee table and grabbed the telephone book.

"Call Jennifer."

"How much time?"

"Ninety minutes. Threes. This guy's obsessed with threes and progressions of threes. Call her!"

Kevin set his drink down, jumped for the phone, and punched in her number. He relayed the information quickly.

"On the room phone," he said.

"No, he called back on the cell," Sam corrected him.

"He called back on the cell," Kevin relayed.

Sam spread the phone directory map open and searched the streets. Thirty-third. A warehouse district.

"No cops. Remind her no cops. If she has any ideas, call, but keep the others out of it. He was very clear."

She closed her eyes and took a deep breath. It was the only answer that made immediate sense. But why would Slater choose such an obvious riddle?

She looked up at Kevin. "Tell Jennifer that I was wrong about Slater. You were in the room when Slater called."

Kevin looked at her with a raised eyebrow, passed on the message, listened for a moment, and then addressed Sam. "She says she's on her way. Don't move."

Only Jennifer could know specifically where they were. She would have picked up the caller ID when Sam called her on the room phone. How had Slater tracked them down so quickly?

Sam stepped forward and took the phone from Kevin. "Don't bother coming, Jennifer. We'll be gone. Work the riddle. I'll call you as soon as we have something."

"How will leaving help you? I want Kevin back in my sights where I can work with him. You hear me?"

"I hear you. We're out of time now. Just work the riddle. I'll call you."

"Sam—"

She hung up. She had to think this through.

"Okay, Kevin. Here we go. Slater's into threes; we know that. He's also into progressions. Every target is larger than the one before. He gives you three minutes, then thirty minutes, then sixty minutes, and now ninety minutes. And he gives this number, 36933. The 369 follows the natural progression, but the 33 doesn't. Unless they're not part of the 369. I think we have an address: 369 Thirty-third Street. It's in a warehouse district in Long Beach, about ten miles from here. *What wants to be filled but will always be empty?* A vacant warehouse."

"That's it?"

"Unless you can think of anything better. Opposites, remember? All of his riddles have been about opposites. Things that aren't what they want or seem to be. Night and day. Buses that go around in circles. A warehouse that is designed to hold things but is empty."

"Maybe."

They stared at each other for a few seconds. They had no choice. She grabbed his hand.

"Come on, let's go."

17

THE WAREHOUSE IDENTIFIED AS 369 on Thirty-third Street stood among a dozen others in northern Long Beach, all constructed from the same corrugated tin, all two stories high, all addressed with the same large black numbers above the doors. Years of neglect had worn most of them down to a dull gray. The 369 was hardly more than a shadow. No sign identifying a business name. Looked vacant.

Kevin slowed the car and peered ahead at the looming structure. Dust blew across the sidewalk. A faded Mountain Dew bottle, the two-liter plastic variety, bumped up against a single-entry door to the right of the loading bay.

He stopped the car thirty yards from the corner and eased the gearshift into park. He could hear several sounds—the purring of the engine, the blower blasting air over their feet, the thumping in his chest. They all sounded too loud.

He glanced at Sam, who stared at the structure, searching.

"What now?"

He had to get the gun out of the trunk; that was what now. Not because he thought Slater would be here, but because he wasn't going anywhere without his new purchase.

"Now we go in," she said. "Unless the fire codes were nonexistent twenty years ago, the building will have a rear entrance."

"You take the back," Kevin said. "I'll take the front."

Sam's right eyebrow lifted. "I think you should wait here."

"No. I'm going in."

"I really don't think—"

"I can't sit around and play dumb, Sam!" The aggression in his tone surprised him. "I have to do something."

She faced 369 Thirty-third Street again. Time was ticking. Sixty-two minutes. Kevin wiped a trickling line of sweat from his temple with the back of his hand.

"Doesn't seem right," Sam said.

"Too easy."

She didn't respond.

"We don't have a key—how are we getting in?" he asked.

"Depends. Getting in isn't the concern. What if he's rigged it to blow upon entry?"

"That's not his game," Kevin said. "He said ninety minutes. Wouldn't he stick to his own rules?"

She nodded. "Has so far. Blew the bus ahead of schedule but only because we broke the rules. Still doesn't seem right." She cracked her door. "Okay, let's see what we have here."

Kevin got out and followed Sam toward the building. As far as he could see in both directions, the street was empty. A warm late afternoon breeze lifted dust from the pavement in a small dust devil twenty feet to his right. The plastic Mountain Dew bottle thumped quietly against the entry door. Somewhere a crow cawed. If Jennifer had figured out the riddle, at least she wasn't making the mistake of swarming in with the cops. They walked up to a steel door with a corroded deadbolt.

"So how *are* we getting in?" Kevin whispered.

Sam eased the plastic bottle aside with her foot, put a hand on the doorknob, and twisted. The door swung in with a creak. "Like that."

They exchanged stares. Sam stuck her head into the black opening, looked around briefly, and pulled back. "You sure you're up to this?"

"Do I have a choice?"

"I could go in alone."

Kevin looked at the dark gap and squinted. Black. The gun was still back in the trunk.

"Okay, I'm going around back to see what we have," Sam said. "Wait for me to signal you. When you go in, find lights and turn them on, but otherwise touch nothing. Look for anything out of the ordinary. Could be a suitcase, a box, anything not covered in dust. I'll work my way through the warehouse in the dark just in case someone's in there. Unlikely, but we'll take the precaution. Clear?"

"Yes." Kevin wasn't sure how clear it was. His mind was still on the gun in the trunk.

"Go easy." She edged to the corner, looked around, and then disappeared.

Kevin ran for the car on his tiptoes. He found the shiny silver pistol where he'd hidden it under the carpet behind the spare tire. He shoved it into his belt, closed the trunk as quietly as he could, and hurried back to the warehouse.

The gun handle stuck out from his belly like a black horn. He pulled his shirt over the butt and flattened it as best he could.

Darkness shrouded the warehouse interior. Still no signal from Sam. Kevin poked his head in and peered through the oil-thick blackness. He reached in and felt for a light switch along the wall. His fingers touched a cool metal box with a plastic switch on its face. He flipped the switch.

A loud hum. Light flooded the warehouse. He grabbed at his midsection and withdrew the gun. Nothing stirred.

He peeked again. A vacant foyer with a receiving desk. Lots of dust. The smell of mildewing rags filled his nostrils. But nothing like a bomb that he could see. Beyond the receiving area, stairs led up to a second floor. Offices. A panel of switches was mounted to the wall at the foot of the stairs. Marks broke the dust directly up the middle of the steps. Footprints.

He instinctively pulled his head from the door. Slater! Had to be. Sam was right; this was it!

Still no signal from her. Unless she'd called him and he'd missed it. With all these walls it was possible.

Kevin held his breath and slipped through the door. He stood still for a moment and then walked on the balls of his feet toward the receiving desk. Behind the desk—could be a place for a bomb. No, the footprints went up . . .

Clunk!

Kevin whirled around. The door had swung shut! The wind? Yes, the wind had—

Click. The lights went out.

Kevin started in the direction of the door, blinded by darkness. He took several quick steps, stuck out a hand, and groped for the door. His knuckles smashed into steel. He fumbled for the handle, found it, and twisted.

But it refused to turn. He gripped hard and jerked the handle first to the left and then to the right. Locked.

Okay, Kevin, stay calm. It's one of those doors that stays locked. Except that it had opened for Sam. Because she was on the outside.

Wasn't it normally the other way around?

He turned and yelled. "Sam?" His voice sounded muted.

"Sam!" This time the word echoed from beyond the stairs.

He'd seen a light panel by the stairs. Maybe they operated other lights? Kevin turned and walked toward the stairs, but his knees found the reception desk first. The crash sent a bolt of electricity through his nerves and he nearly dropped the gun. He stepped to the side and shuffled up to where he remembered the light switches.

"Samantha!"

He slapped the wall, found the switches, and palmed them on. No lights.

The floor above him creaked. "Sam?"

"Kevin!" Sam! Her voice sounded distant, from the back, as if she was still outside the building.

"Sam, I'm in here!"

His eyes had adjusted to the darkness. Light glowed from the upper level. Kevin glanced back toward the door, saw only darkness, and mounted the stairs. Light glowed faintly above him, a window maybe.

"Sam?"

She didn't respond.

He had to get to some light! Another floorboard creaked and he whipped around, gun extended. Was the weapon cocked? He snugged his thumb over the hammer and pulled it back. *Click.* Easy, Kevin. You've never shot a gun in your life. You shoot at a shadow and it might be Sam. And what if the gun doesn't even work?

He headed up the stairs on weak legs.

"Kevin!"

Sam's voice came from his right and forward, definitely outside. He paused halfway up the steps, tried to still his breathing so that he could hear better, but finally gave up and hurried toward the light at the top.

The glow came from a doorway at the end of a barely visible hallway. His breathing came hushed and low now. Something thumped down the hall. He held his breath. There it was again, a step. Boots. Directly ahead and to his right. From one of the other rooms along the hall. Sam? No, Sam was still outside! *Dear God, give me strength.*

He felt exposed standing in the hall. What was he thinking, waltzing up the stairs as if he were some kind of gunslinger?

Frantic, Kevin stepped to the faint outline of a doorway on his right. The floorboards protested under his feet. He cleared the doorway and slid back against the wall on his left.

Boots. There was definitely someone else on the upper floor with him. Could be Sam if the acoustics had misdirected her voice. Could it be her? Sure it could.

It is, Kevin. It's Sam. She's in the next room, and she's found the bomb. No, her voice had been distant. And she didn't walk like that. No way.

Her voice suddenly came again, faint. "Kevin!"

This time there was no mistake, Sam was yelling at him from below, out near the front door now. Her fist pounded on the steel door.

"Kevin, are you in there?"

He took one step back toward the doorway. The boot again. Thumping in the next room.

Someone was in there! Slater. He gripped the pistol tightly. Slater had lured him in. That's why the riddle was so simple. A dread spread through his bones.

Sam was at the front door. The deadbolt wasn't engaged—she should be able to either break it or pick it.

Another thought occurred to him. The bomb was probably set to go off—what if he was trapped in here when it did? What if the cops came and Slater detonated the bomb early? But Sam would never allow the cops anywhere near the warehouse now.

But what if she couldn't get the door open?

Panicked, Kevin slid along the wall, met a corner, and felt his way along the back wall. He put his ear on the plaster.

Breathing. Slow and deep. Not his. Slow shuffling.

A low voice reached through the wall. "Kevinnnn . . ."

He froze.

"Forty-six minutesss . . . Kevinnnn."

III

The difference between innocence and naiveté has never registered in Slater's mind. The two are synonymous. In fact, there is no such animal as innocence. They are all as guilty as hell. But he can't deny that some are more naive than others, and watching Kevin creep up the stairs like a mouse has reminded Slater of how utterly naive his nemesis really is.

He'd been sorely tempted to kick the man in the head then, while Kevin was still four steps from the top. Watching him tumble and break would have held its appeal. But place-kicking has always struck him as one of sport's more boring moments.

Welcome to my house, Kevin.

The man has gone and gotten himself a gun. He holds it like he might hold a vial of the Ebola virus and probably hasn't thought to cock it, but he's at least gathered the resolve to arm himself. And he is undoubtedly packing without Samantha's knowledge. She would never allow a civilian to stumble around with a loaded weapon. Kevin has found a sliver of manhood. How fun! The man may actually try to kill him, as if he's become the stalker instead of the victim.

In ways not even Kevin can yet know, this isn't such a new thing. Kevin has tried to kill him before. Their lives are inseparably intertwined, each bent on killing the other. To think that this man who's crept up the stairs holding his big shiny pistol has the stomach to pull the trigger, much less kill, is absurd.

Now the fool has wedged himself in the next room down and is undoubtedly wetting himself. If he only knew what lay in store for him in the hours to come, he might be lying in a puddle of his own vomit.

Here, kitty, kitty.

"Forty-six minutesss . . . Kevinnnn . . ."

| | |

Kevin nearly pulled the trigger then. Not with calculated aim, but out of sheer terror.

"Sam?" His voice sounded like a wounded lamb's bleating. He was briefly revolted by his weakness. If this was Slater, he was getting exactly what he wanted. A face to face. A chance to blow him away.

The doorway stood opposite him, its gaping hole darker than the black surrounding it. If he were to run now, he could bound down the stairs and reach the front door, right?

A new sound reached into the room—the sound of something sharp scraping along the wall outside. Down the hall toward his door.

Kevin gripped the pistol in both hands, pointed it at the doorway, and slid down to his seat. If Slater stepped through that space, he'd do it. He'd see the dark form and start pulling the trigger.

The scraping continued, closer, closer. Closer.

"Kevinnn," a voice whispered.

God, help me! His mind started to go fuzzy.

Take him out, Kevin. Jennifer's voice echoed through his mind. Blow the scumbag away!

He could hardly see the gun in front of him to aim it, but he could point. And whoever walked through that door wouldn't be able to see him, right? Not in this darkness. Kevin would only see a shadow, but he had that advantage.

The scraping closed in on the door.

Sweat slipped into Kevin's eyes. He held his breath.

Sam's voice yelled distant. "Kevin, you stay put! You hear me?"

He couldn't respond.

"Stay right there."

She was going to get something to force the door. Pick the lock. A brick, a crowbar, a gun. A gun! She had a gun in her purse. *Hurry!*

The whisper came again. "Kevinnnn . . ."

The doorway suddenly filled with the dark shape of a man. Kevin's finger tightened on the trigger. What . . . what if it wasn't Slater? A bum, maybe.

The form stood still, as if staring at him. If it moved . . . If it even flinched, Kevin would pull the trigger.

Blood pounded through his head as if pumps had been shoved in his ears and were trying to suck him dry. *Whoosh, whoosh.* He couldn't move other than to tremble slightly in the dark. He was eleven years old again, facing the boy in the cellar. Trapped. *That'll cost you your eyeballs, punk.*

A metal object clanged against the front door. Sam!

The figure didn't flinch.

Now, Kevin! Now! Before he runs. Pull the trigger!

Clang!

"Why would I do something so senseless as blow up an old abandoned warehouse?" Slater's voice asked.

"It's so nice to meet you again face to face, Kevin. I like the dark, don't you? I thought about bringing candles for the occasion, but I like this better."

Shoot! Shoot, shoot, SHOOT!

"We've only been at this three days and I'm already tired of it. Practice is over. We start the real game tonight," Slater said.

The sound of steel against steel echoed from the front door.

"We'll be seeing you."

The figure moved.

The pressure Kevin had exerted on the trigger finally sprang the hammer at the same instant. The room ignited with a brilliant flash chased by a horrendous thunder. He saw Slater's black coat as he cleared the doorway.

"Aaaahhhh!" He fired again. A third time. He scrambled to his feet, leapt for the opening, and spun into the hallway. A door at the end of the hall swung closed. The man was gone. Darkness surrounded Kevin.

He whirled around, grabbed the railing, and stumbled down the stairs.

"Kevin!"

The door burst open to daylight before Kevin reached it. Sam jumped clear and he spilled out onto the sidewalk.

Sam had her weapon drawn. She took one look at Kevin and spun into the doorway, gun extended.

"He's gone," Kevin panted. "Out back. A window or something."

"Wait here." Sam ran to the corner, shoved her head around, and then disappeared.

The ground felt uneven under Kevin's feet. He gripped a telephone pole and steadied himself. Why had he waited? He could have ended the whole thing with one shot, right there in the room. On the other hand, he had no proof that the figure was Slater. Could've been an idiot playing . . .

No, it was Slater. Definitely. You spineless punk! *You let him walk. He was right there and you whimpered like a dog!* Kevin grunted and closed his eyes, furious.

Sam reappeared thirty seconds later.

"He's gone."

"He was just there! Are you sure?"

"There's a fire escape with a ladder. He could be anywhere by now. I doubt he's hanging around for an encore." She glanced back, considering.

"There's no bomb, Sam. He wanted to meet me. That's why the riddle was so easy. I saw him."

She stepped up to the door, looked inside, and flipped the switches. Nothing happened.

"How did the door lock?"

"I don't know. I was just in there and it slammed behind me."

She stepped just beyond the door and looked up. "It's rigged. He used a pulley with a string . . ." She followed the string with her eyes.

"What is it?"

"The string ends by the counter. He was down here when he pulled the door closed."

The revelation struck Kevin as absurd. "In the lobby?"

"Yes, I think so. String's pretty well hidden, but he was here. I don't want to contaminate the scene—we need to get some light in there." She walked back out and opened her cell phone. "You sure it was him?"

"He spoke to me. He stood right there and asked me why he'd be so senseless as to blow up an abandoned building." Kevin's legs felt like putty. He abruptly sat on the sidewalk. The gun hung from his right hand.

Sam eyed it. "This is what you found wandering your old neighborhood this morning?"

Kevin set the gun down. "Sorry. I can't just let him push me around anymore."

She nodded. "Put it back in the trunk or wherever you had it stashed, and please, don't use it again."

"I shot at him. You think maybe I hit him?"

"I didn't see any blood. But they'll find evidence of the shots." She paused. "They may want you to surrender the gun. I don't suppose it's legal."

He shook his head.

"Just get it out of sight before the others get here. I'll talk to Jennifer."

"Others?"

She glanced at her watch. "It's time for her to take over here. I have a plane to catch."

18

THERE WAS NO BOMB and Slater had met his objective forty minutes early. They had solved their first riddle within the allotted time, but it still had served the killer. He'd made contact with Kevin in person and escaped without a trace.

Sam had called Jennifer with the details while waiting for her cab to arrive. She was still unsettled about something—was even a little reluctant to call Jennifer, but she said that she had no choice. Of all the authorities, she trusted Jennifer the most. No cops until the ninety-minute mark had passed; that much she'd insisted on.

Jennifer was on her way with an FBI team to begin the investigation. Sam would be lucky to catch her flight; Kevin watched the cab's taillights as it sped down the street and around the corner.

Yes indeed, they had solved the riddle. Or had they? He should be swimming in relief about now—he'd come nose to nose with a madman and survived. Chased him away with a few shots to boot. Sort of.

But his head still felt like it was caught in a vise. He agreed with Sam; something wasn't right.

What was it about this appointment in Houston that was so important to her? And why wasn't she forthcoming on the actual nature of the meeting? She knew the Riddle Killer was here. What was there in Houston?

And why wouldn't she just tell him? Here in Long Beach the city was terrorized by the man the media had dubbed the Riddle Killer, but Sam was off on a tangent in another city. Made no sense.

A black car swung onto the street and roared toward him. Jennifer.

Two other agents climbed out with her, one with weapon drawn, both armed with flashlights. Jennifer spoke quickly to them, sending one around back and the other for the front door, which still stood open in a splintered frame. Sam had taken the car jack to it.

Jennifer approached him, dressed in a blue suit, hair flowing around her shoulders in the warm breeze. "Are you okay?" she asked.

She glanced at the warehouse, and for a brief moment Kevin imagined that her question was only a courtesy—her real interest lay in whatever awaited her prying eyes beyond the door. A new crime scene. Like all of them, she loved the crime scenes. As well she should—the crime scene led to the criminal, in this case Slater.

She turned her attention back to him.

"As okay as I can be, I suppose," he said.

She walked up to him and looked into his eyes. "I thought we understood each other."

He ran a hand through his hair. "What do you mean?"

"I mean we're on the same side here. I mean you tell me everything, or did our conversation yesterday not make an impression on you?"

He suddenly felt like a silly schoolboy standing in the principal's office. "Of course we're on the same side."

"Then make me a promise you can live by. You don't disappear unless we agree for you to disappear. In fact, you do *nothing* unless we agree you do it. I can't do this without you, and I certainly don't need you following someone else's lead."

An unreasonable sorrow swept over Kevin. He felt a knot in his throat, as if he might cry, right here in front of her. Again. Nothing would be so humiliating.

"I'm sorry. Sam said—"

"I don't care what Sam tells you. You're my responsibility, not hers. Heaven knows I need all the help I can get, but until you hear differently from someone besides Sam, you follow my lead. Regardless of whose idea it is, you talk to me. Okay?"

"Okay."

She sighed and closed her eyes momentarily. "Now what did Sam suggest?"

"That I should do everything you say."

Jennifer blinked. "She's right." She looked past him at the warehouse. "I want this creep as much as you do. You're our best shot . . ." She stopped.

"I know. You need me to get him. Who gives a rip about Kevin as long as we get what we need out of him; is that it?"

She stared at him, whether angered or embarrassed, he couldn't tell. Her face softened.

"No, that isn't it. I'm sorry you're living through this hell, Kevin. It's beyond me why innocent people have to suffer, but try as I have, changing the fact is beyond me." She held his eyes with her own. "I didn't mean to sound so harsh. I just . . . I'm not going to let him get to you. He killed my brother, remember? I lost Roy, but I'm not going to lose you."

Kevin suddenly understood. It explained her anger. Maybe more.

"And yes, as a matter of fact, I do need you," she said. "You're our best hope of apprehending a very demented nut case who happens to be after you."

Now Kevin felt more like a clumsy freshman than anyone who might be hauled into the school office for discipline. *Stupid, Kevin. Stupid, stupid.*

"I'm sorry. I'm so sorry."

"Apology accepted. Just don't run off again, okay?"

"Guaranteed." He lifted his eyes and saw the same strange look he'd seen in Sam's eyes at times. A cross between concern and empathy. *Stupid, stupid, Kevin.*

Jennifer dropped her eyes to his mouth and took a deep breath. "So. You saw him."

He nodded.

She glanced back at the door. "He's progressing."

"Progressing?"

"He wants more. More contact, more danger. Resolution."

"Then why doesn't he just come out and ask me for whatever it is he wants?"

She held a flashlight in her hand. "Are you up to walking through it with me? We'll wait until my men come out—I don't want to compromise any evidence. I realize you're frazzled, but the sooner I know how this went down, the greater our chances of using any information we come up with."

He nodded. "The cops know yet?"

"Not yet. Milton can't seem to keep his trap shut. He knows we found you and so does the media. As far as the public is concerned, this didn't happen. Tensions are high enough as it is."

She looked at her watch. "We still have eighteen minutes left in his ninety-minute window. Somehow that doesn't add up. Honestly, we were thinking library rather than warehouse."

"Library. *What wants to be filled but will always be empty?* As in empty knowledge."

"Yes."

"Hmm."

"We're getting evidence; that's what counts. We have his voice on tape; we have his presence in this building; we have more background. He's had several chances to hurt you and he hasn't. Sam told me that you spoke with him. I need to know exactly what he said."

"More background?" Kevin asked. "What background?"

An FBI agent walked toward them. "Excuse me, just wanted to let you know that the lights are back on. Fuse was pulled."

"No explosives?"

"Not that we can find. There's something here I think you should see."

She looked up at Kevin. "I'll be right back."

"Do you want me to show you what happened?"

"As soon as they're finished securing the scene. We don't want any more footprints or trace evidence than necessary. Hold tight." She hurried for the door and disappeared into the warehouse.

Kevin shoved his hands into his pockets and ran his fingers over Slater's cell phone. He was a klutz, no doubt about it. Maybe that was the sin Slater wanted him to confess. Kevin Parson is a fool and a klutz, a man incapable of entering society in any normal way because his Aunt Balinda beat his intellect against an imaginary wall for the first twenty-three years of his life. His mind is scarred beyond recognition.

He glanced back at the building, and the image of Jennifer walking for the door replayed itself. Sam was right; she liked him, didn't she?

Liked him? How could he know whether she liked him? *You see, Kevin. That's the way first-class losers think. They have no shame. They find themselves pinned down by an assassin's knife and their mind is drawn to the FBI agent they've known for all of three days.* Two days if he subtracted the day he ran off with Sam, the stunning CBI agent.

The cell phone vibrated at his fingertips and he jumped.

It went off again. Slater was calling and that was a problem, wasn't it? Why would Slater call now?

The phone rang a third time before he managed to unfold it. "H . . . hello?"

"H . . . hello? You sound like an imbecile, Kevin. I thought I said no cops."

Kevin spun to the warehouse. The agents were inside. There was a bomb in there after all, wasn't there? "Cops? We didn't call cops. I thought FBI were okay."

"Cops, Kevin. They're all pigs. Pigs in the parlor. I'm watching the news and the news says the cops know where you are. Maybe I should count to three and blow their guts to kingdom come."

"You said no *cops!*" Kevin shouted. There was a bomb in the warehouse and Jennifer was in there. He had to get her out. He ran for the door. "We didn't *use* the cops."

"Are you running, Kevin? Quick, quick get them out. But don't get too close. The bomb might go boom and they'll find your entrails on the walls with the others'."

Kevin shoved his head in the door. "Out!" he screamed. "Get out! There's a bomb!"

He ran for the street.

"You're right, there is a bomb," Slater said. "You have thirteen minutes left, Kevin. If I decide not to punish you. *What wants to be filled but will always be empty?*"

He slid to a stop. "Slater! Come out and face me, you . . ."

But Slater was gone. Kevin snapped the phone shut and whirled to the warehouse just in time to see Jennifer emerge, followed by both agents.

Jennifer saw the look on his face and stopped. "What is it?"

"Slater," he said dumbly.

"Slater called," Jennifer said. She rushed up to him. "We're wrong, aren't we? This isn't it!"

Kevin's head began to spin. He placed his hands on his temples and closed his eyes. "Think, Jennifer. Think! *What wants to be filled but will always be empty?* He knew we would come here so he waited for us, but this isn't it! What wants to be filled? What!"

"A library," the agent named Bill said.

"Did he say how much time?" Jennifer asked.

"Thirteen minutes. He said he may blow it early because the cops talked to the press."

"Milton," Jennifer said. "I swear I could wring his neck. God help us." She yanked a notepad from her hip pocket, stared at the page filled with writing, and began to pace. "36933, what else could have a number associated—"

"A reference number," Kevin blurted.

"But from which library?" Jennifer asked. "There's got to be a thousand—"

"The school of divinity," Kevin said. "Augustine Memorial. He's going to blow up the Augustine Memorial Library."

They stared at each other for a moment frozen in time. As one, the three FBI agents ran for the car. "Call Milton!" Bill said. "Evacuate the library."

"No cops," Jennifer said. "Call the school."

"What if we can't get through to the right people fast enough? We need a squad car over there."

"That's why we're going. What's the fastest way to the school?"

Kevin ran for his car across the street. "Down Willow. Follow me."

He slid behind the wheel, fired the engine, and squealed away from the curb. Eleven minutes. Could they reach the library in eleven minutes? Depended on traffic. But could they find a bomb in eleven minutes?

A horrifying thought strung through his mind. Even if they did reach the library, they would have no time to search without risking being caught inside when the bomb blew. There was this matter of seconds again. They could be forty seconds off and not know it.

A car was one thing. A bus was worse. But the library—God forbid that they were wrong. "You sick coward!"

They roared down Willow, horns blaring, ignoring the lights

completely. This was becoming a bad habit. He swerved out of the path of a blue Corvette and swung onto a smaller surface street to avoid the sea of traffic. Jennifer followed in the big black car. At each intersection the street dips pounded his suspension. He would make Anaheim Street and cut east.

Seven minutes. They were going to make it. He considered the gun in the trunk. Running into the library waving a gun would accomplish nothing but the confiscation of his hard-earned prize. He only had three bullets left. One for Slater's gut, one for his heart, and one for his head. *Pow, pow, pow. I'm gonna put a slug in your filthy heart, you lying sack of maggot meat. Two can play this game, baby. You picked the wrong kid to tick off. I bloodied your nose once; this time I'm gonna put you down. Six feet under, where the worms live. You make me sick, sick . . .*

Kevin saw the white sedan in the intersection ahead at the last possible moment. He threw his weight back into the seat and shoved the brake pedal to the floor. Tires screeching, his car slid sideways, barely missed the taillight of an ancient Chevy, and miraculously straightened. Hands white on the wheel, he punched the accelerator and sped on. Jennifer followed.

Focus! There was nothing he could do about Slater now. He had to get to the library in one piece. Interesting how bitter he'd become toward the man in the space of three days. *I'm gonna put a slug in your filthy heart, you lying sack of maggot meat?* What was that?

The moment Kevin saw the arched, glass face of Augustine Memorial Library, he knew that Jennifer's attempts to clear the place had failed. An Asian student ambled by the double doors, lost in thought. They had between three and four minutes. Maybe.

Kevin crammed the gearshift into park while the car was still rolling. The car bucked and stopped. He burst out and tore for the front doors. Jennifer was already on his heels.

"No panic, Kevin! We have time. Just get them out as quickly as possible. You hear?"

He slowed to a jog. She pulled up beside him, then took the lead.

"How many study rooms are there?" she asked.

"A few upstairs. There's a basement."

"PA system?"

"Yes."

"Okay, point the way to the office. I'll make an announcement; you clear the basement."

Kevin pointed out the office, ran for the stairs, and took them in twos. How long? Three minutes? "Get out! Everyone out!" He ran down the hall, spun into the first room. "Out! Get out now!"

"What's up, partner?" a middle-aged man asked lazily.

He couldn't think of a nonpanicky way to tell the man. "There's a bomb in the building."

The man stared for a second, then bolted to his feet.

"Clear the hall!" Kevin shouted, breaking for the next room. "Get everyone out!"

Jennifer's voice came over the PA, edgy. "This is the FBI. We have reason to suspect that there may be a bomb in the library. Evacuate the building calmly and immediately." She began to repeat the message, but yells echoed through the basement, drowning out her voice.

Feet pounded; voices cried out; panic set in. Maybe it was just as well. They didn't have enough time for order.

It took a full minute, at least, for Kevin to satisfy himself that the basement was clear. He was putting himself in danger, he realized, but this was his library, his school, his fault. He gritted his teeth, ran for the stairs, and was halfway up when he remembered the supply room. Unlikely anyone would be in there. Unless . . .

He stopped four paces from the top. Carl. The janitor liked to listen to his Discman while he worked. He liked to joke about how there was more than one way to fill the mind. Books were fine, he said, but music was the higher culture. He took his breaks in the supply room.

You're cutting it close, Kevin.

He whirled and ran back down. The supply closet was to his right, in the back. The building lay in silence now except for the urgent padding of his feet. What was it like to be caught in an explosion? And where would Slater have planted the charges?

He threw the door open. "Carl!"

The janitor stood by a stack of boxes with the words *New Books* written on pink sheets of paper.

"Carl! Thank God!"

Carl smiled at him and nodded his head to whatever music pumped into his ears. Kevin ran over to him and pulled the headphones off. "Get out of here! They've evacuated the building. Hurry, man! Hurry!"

The man's eyes widened.

Kevin grabbed his hand and shoved him toward the door. "Run! Everyone else is out."

"What is it?"

"Just run!"

Carl ran.

Two minutes. There was a second, smaller closet to his right—overflow supplies for administration, Carl had once told him. Mostly empty. Kevin leapt for the closet and pulled the door open.

How much explosive did it take to blow a building this size? Kevin was staring at the answer. Black wires protruded from five shoeboxes and met in a contraption that looked like the inside of a transistor radio. Slater's bomb.

"Jennifer!" he yelled. He twisted for the door and yelled again, at the top of his lungs. "Jennifer!"

His voice echoed back. The building was empty. Kevin ran his hands through his hair. Could he carry this thing outside? It'll blow there. That's where the people are. You have to stop it! But how? He reached for the wires, paused, and pulled back.

Pulling the wires would probably set it off, wouldn't it?

You're going to die, Kevin. Any split second it could go. He could set it off early.

"Kevin!" Jennifer's scream carried down the stairs. "Kevin, for God's sake, answer me! Get out!"

He fled the supply room in a full sprint. He'd seen the movies a hundred times—the explosion behind, the billows of fire, the diving hero rolling to freedom just out of the blast's reach.

But this wasn't a movie. This was real and this was now and this was him.

"Kevin—"

"Get out!" he yelled. "The bomb's in here!" He cleared the first four steps, and his momentum carried him to the top in two more bounds.

Jennifer was at the door, holding it open, face white. "What are you thinking?" she snapped at him. "It could go early. You'll get us both killed!"

He ran out and tore for the parking lot. Jennifer kept pace.

A huge arc of onlookers stood a hundred yards off, watching them run. "Get back!" she yelled, sprinting for them. "Farther back! Get—"

A deep, dull *whomp* cut her off. Then a louder, sharp blast and the crash of shattering glass. The ground shook.

Jennifer grabbed Kevin by the waist and pulled him down. They landed together and rolled. She threw her arms over his head. "Stay down!"

He lay smothered by her for a few long seconds. Screams rolled across the lawn. Jennifer pushed herself halfway up and looked back.

Her leg was over the backs of his legs and her hand pressed into his back for support. Kevin twisted and followed her gaze.

Half of the Divinity School of the Pacific's crown jewel lay in a heap of smoking rubble. The other half jutted to the sky, stripped of glass, naked.

"My God, my God, help us all," Jennifer said. "He blew it early, didn't he? I could kill Milton."

Still breathing hard from the run, Kevin dropped back down and buried his face in the grass.

19

T HE LIBRARY EXPLOSION on the heels of the bus bomb put Long Beach at the world's center stage. All the networks played and replayed live footage of the library being blown to smithereens, courtesy of an alert student. Helicopters circled the hole that had been a building and relayed stunning images to millions of glued viewers. The world had seen this before and everyone had the same question on their minds: Terrorism?

But the explosion was the work of a madman known only as the Riddle Killer, the networks all said. Miraculously, no one had been hurt in the blast; in fact, no life had been taken by any of the three incidents. Nevertheless, they all knew it was only a matter of time. He'd killed in Sacramento; he would kill in Long Beach. Unless the authorities stopped him first. Unless his intended victim, Kevin Parson, confessed what the killer demanded he confess. Where was Kevin Parson? He'd last been seen running from the building with a woman, an FBI agent by some accounts. They had them on the student's video. Stunning footage.

The ATF had entered the fray after the first bomb; now they came in force. The state police, local police, sheriff, a half-dozen other task forces all poured over the library.

Jennifer did her best to keep Kevin beyond the reach of the media's long tentacles while making sense of the scene. She avoided Milton, for the simple reason that she didn't trust herself in his presence. He'd come within a few seconds of killing Kevin and countless others by talking to the press. If she'd been frustrated with him before, the sight of him running to and fro made her seethe now.

Still, he was an integral part of the investigation, and she couldn't avoid him once he finished his rounds with the press.

"You knew this was coming?" he demanded.

"Not now, Milton."

He took her arm and steered her away from the onlookers, squeezing with enough force to hurt her. "You were here. That means you knew. How long did you know?"

"Let go," she snapped.

He released her arm and glanced over her shoulder, smiling. "The word *negligence* mean anything to you, Agent Peters?"

"The word *carnage* mean anything to you, Detective Milton? I knew because he wanted me to know. You didn't know about the library because he said that if you were told, he'd blow the building early. In fact, he did blow it early, because you had to announce to the world that we'd found Kevin. You, sir, are lucky we got out when we did or you'd have *at least* two dead bodies on your hands. Don't ever touch me again."

"We could have put a bomb squad in there."

"Is there something with the air down here that messes with your hearing? What part of 'he told us he'd blow the building early' didn't penetrate that thick skull of yours? You almost killed us!"

"You're posing a danger to my city, and if you think I'm just going to stand by and let you, you're naive."

"And you're posing a danger to Kevin. Take it up with the bureau chief."

His eyes narrowed for a brief second, then he smiled again. "We're not through with this."

"Sure we are." She walked away. If not for the fact that half the world was watching, she might have taken the man's tie and shoved it down his throat. It took her thirty seconds to put the man out of her mind. She had more important things to dwell on than an over-zealous fool. So she told herself, but in reality Milton sat in her gut like a sour pill.

Two questions soon preoccupied her mind. First, had anybody seen a stranger enter the library in the past twenty-four hours? And second, had anybody seen *Kevin* enter the library in the last twenty-four hours? Samantha had raised the question of Kevin's involvement, and although Jennifer knew the idea was ridiculous, the question raised others. Samantha's theory that someone on the inside might be somehow tied to Slater bothered her.

The Riddle Killer was remarkably elusive. The last three days were no exception. Sam was in Texas, flushing out something that had her hopes high. No doubt she'd come waltzing in tomorrow with a new theory that would set them back to square one. Actually, the CBI agent was beginning to grow on her, but jurisdiction had a way of straining the best relationships.

As it turned out, no one had seen a stranger around the library. And no one had seen Kevin. The front desk receptionist would have remembered Kevin—he was an avid reader. Short of bypassing the security system, of which there was no evidence, the likelihood of any-one entering the library unseen was small. Carl had been in the closet yesterday morning and there'd been no bomb, which meant Slater had found a way in since then, either at night or under their noses, un-recognized. How?

An hour after the explosion, Jennifer sat across from Kevin in a small Chinese restaurant and tried to distract him with small talk while they ate. But neither of them was good at small talk.

They went back to the warehouse at nine, this time armed with high-powered halogens that lit up the interior like a football field. Kevin walked through the scene with her. But now it was nearing midnight, and he was half-asleep on his feet. Unlike the library, the warehouse was still silent. No police, no ATF, only FBI.

She hadn't bothered to tell Milton about the incident at the warehouse. She would as soon as she was done with it. She'd explained the situation to Frank, and he'd finally agreed to her reasoning, but he wasn't happy with it. He was getting an earful from a dozen different sources. The governor wanted this tied up now. Washington was starting to apply pressure too. They were running out of time. If another bomb went off, they might take the case from her.

Jennifer glanced at Kevin, who leaned his head back against the wall in the reception area, eyes closed. She entered a ten-by-ten office storage room where they were compiling evidence for delivery to the lab. Under other circumstances, she would probably be doing this back at her desk, but Milton would be breathing down her neck. Besides, proximity favored the storage room, so Galager had transferred what he needed from the van and set up temporary shop here.

"Any conclusions, Bill?"

Galager leaned over a drawing of the warehouse floor plan, on which he'd painstakingly redrawn the footprints as they appeared.

"Best as I can tell, Slater entered and left through the fire escape. We have a single set of footprints coming and going, which correlates with the testimony. He walks up and down the hall a half-dozen times, waiting for Kevin to show, descends the stairs at least twice, springs his trap, and ends up in this room here." He tapped the room next to Kevin's hiding place.

"How did he lock the door? He shut it with the string, but Sam told me it was open when they first arrived."

"We can only assume that he had the lock rigged somehow. It's feasible that with a hard knock the lock could engage."

"Seems thin," Jennifer said. "So we have him entering and leaving through the fire escape. Kevin enters and leaves through the front door. What about the footprints themselves?"

"When all is said and done, there are only four clear prints, all of which we've casted and photographed. Problem is, they're all from the hallway and the stairs where both Kevin and Slater walked. Same size. Same basic shape. Both hard-soled and similar to what Kevin is wearing—impossible to visually determine which is which. The lab will break it down."

Jennifer considered his report. Sam hadn't entered the building, which was good thinking. But she hadn't seen Slater come or go either.

"What about the recording?" Galager had already transferred the data to a tape, which he had in a small recorder on the table.

"Again, the lab will have to tell us what they can come up with, but it sounds clean to me. This is the first recording from the hotel room." He punched the play button. Two voices filled the speaker. Slater and Samantha.

"There, that's better, don't you think? The game won't last forever; we might as well make this more interesting."

Low and gravelly. Breathy. Slater.

"What good is a game that you can't lose? It proves nothing."

She recognized Sam's voice. The tape played to the end of the conversation and clicked off.

"Here's the second recording, made while we were here earlier this evening." Galager punched it up. This time it was Kevin and Slater.

Kevin: *"H . . . hello?"*

Slater: *"H . . . hello? You sound like an imbecile, Kevin. I thought I said no cops."*

The recordings were clear and clean. Jennifer nodded. "Get them to the lab with the footprints immediately. Any word yet on the dagger tattoo or the blood work from the warehouse?"

"Blood's too old for anything but type. They're having trouble even with that, though. Twenty years is a long time."

"So it is twenty years old?"

"Best estimate, seventeen to twenty. Follows his confession."

"And the type?"

"They're having a hard time typing it. On the other hand, we do have something with the tattoo. A parlor in Houston says they have a large man with blond hair who comes in on occasion. Same tattoo as the one Kevin drew us. Says he's never seen a tattoo like it except on this man." Galager grinned deliberately. "The report came in about an hour ago. No current address, but the parlor says the man was in last Tuesday around ten o'clock."

"In Houston?" That's where Sam had gone. "Slater was in Houston last week? Doesn't sound right."

"Houston?" Kevin asked behind her. They turned to see him standing in the door. He walked in. "You have a lead in Houston?"

"The tattoo—"

"Yeah, I heard. But . . . how could Slater be in Houston?"

"Three-hour flight or a very long day's drive," Galager said. "Possible he's going back and forth."

Kevin's brow furrowed. "He has a dagger tattoo? What if this guy turns out to be the boy, but not Slater or the Riddle Killer? You pick him up and now he knows about me, where I live. All I need is another wacko after me."

"Unless this guy lives in a cave," Galager said, "he's heard the confession and seen your face on television. There's a chance he *is* Slater. And there's an even better chance that Slater is the boy. We have a man threatening you who all but admits that he's the boy; a boy who has reason to threaten you, identified with a very unique tattoo. And now we have a man with the same tattoo. Circumstantial, I realize, but it sounds pretty plausible to me. We make busts on less."

"But can you put someone behind bars with that?"

"Not a chance. That's where the physical and forensic evidence comes in. As soon as we have a suspect in custody, we measure him up against the evidence we've gathered, which is substantial. We have Slater's voice on tape. We have his shoe print. We have several bombs, all of which were made somewhere. We have six bugs—all this in three days. A virtual windfall in cases like this. I'd say Slater's getting sloppy."

And more so today than yesterday. "He's at least pushing the pace," Jennifer said. "Getting caught doesn't seem to concern him. Which isn't good."

"Why?" Kevin asked.

She looked at his haggard face. A blade of grass from the library lawn was still stuck in his shaggy hair. His blue eyes looked more desperate than enchanting now. He didn't tap his foot or rake his hair as frequently. The man needed rest. "Based on his profile, my guess is that he's closing in on his objective."

"Which is what?"

Jennifer glanced at Galager. "Good work, Bill. Why don't you wrap it up and call the locals?" She took Kevin's arm and led him out. "Let's take a walk."

Two of the streetlights nearest the warehouse were either shut down on energy conservation timers or burned out. A cool ocean breeze drifted over Long Beach. She'd shed her jacket and wore a sleeveless gold blouse with a black skirt—it was actually a bit chilly at this hour.

She crossed her arms. "You okay?"

"Tired."

"Nothing like fresh air to clear the mind. This way." She led him toward the fire escape in the back.

"So, what is Slater's objective?" Kevin asked again, shoving his hands in his jeans pockets.

"Well, that's a problem. I've been giving it a lot of thought. On the surface it seems simple enough: He wants to terrorize you. Men like Slater do what they do for a variety of reasons, usually to gratify some twisted need they've grown into over many years, but almost without exception they prey on the weak. Their focus is on their own need, not on the victim."

"Makes sense. And Slater's different?"

"I think so. His objective doesn't seem to be himself as much as you. I mean you specifically."

"I'm not sure I understand."

"Take your typical serial offender. Say a pyromaniac bent on burning down houses. He doesn't care whose house it is as long as it fits his needs. He needs to see the flame engulfing this structure—it excites him and gives him a feeling of power beyond his reach in any other way. The house is important—it has to be a certain size, maybe a certain build, maybe a symbol of wealth. In the same way a sex offender might prey on women he considers appealing. But his focus is on himself, not the victim. The victim is almost incidental."

"And you're saying that Slater hasn't chosen me for what I can do for him, but for what he can do to me. Like he did with your brother."

"Maybe. But this is playing out differently than Roy's murder. The Riddle Killer filled his thirst for bloodshed by killing Roy and killing him quickly. Slater is playing with you, over three days now. I'm beginning to question our initial assumption that Slater and the Riddle Killer are the same person." The Riddle Killer didn't seem to know his victims, other than Roy, whom he'd selected for her benefit. She rubbed her arms against the cold.

"Unless all that was just a cover-up for what he's doing now. Unless extracting revenge for what I did to him was the game all along."

"That's the obvious assumption. I'm not sure anymore. Revenge would be a simple matter. Assuming Slater is the boy you locked up, he could have found a hundred opportunities over the years to extract his revenge. His most obvious course would have been to hurt or kill you. I don't think Slater's interested in killing you. Not anytime soon, anyway. I think he wants to change you. He wants to force your hand somehow. I don't think the game's the device; I think the game's the objective."

"But that's crazy!" Kevin stopped and put both hands into his hair. "What is there about me? Who? Who would want to . . . to force my hand?"

"I know it doesn't all fit yet, but the sooner we narrow down Slater's true motivation, the higher our chances of getting you out of this mess."

They were at the back, by the fire escape. A ladder reached up to the second floor and curved into a window. Jennifer sighed and leaned against the tin siding.

"Bottom line is that if I'm right, then the only way to understand Slater's true motivation is to understand you, Kevin. I've got to know more about you." He was pacing, staring at the concrete, hands still in his hair.

"I want to know about the house," she said.

"There's nothing to know about the house," he said.

"Why don't you let me judge that?"

"I can't talk about the house!"

"I know you don't think you can, but it may provide our best clues now. I know it's hard—"

"I don't think you have a clue about how hard it is! You didn't grow up there!" He paced and smoothed his hair frantically, and then flung his arms wide. "You think any of this means anything? You think this is reality? A bunch of ants running around the globe, hiding their secrets in their deep dark tunnels? We *all* have our secrets. Who's to say that mine have anything to do with anything? Why don't the rest of the ants have to crawl out of their tunnels and broadcast their sins to the world?"

Kevin was baring himself, and Jennifer needed him to do just that. Not because she would ever exploit him, but because she needed to understand his secrets if she hoped to help him.

And she did hope to help him. More now than a day ago, even if Slater wasn't her brother's killer after all.

"You're right," she said. "We're all fallen, as my priest used to say. I'm not interested in your sin. I wasn't even in favor of the initial confession, remember? I'm interested in you, Kevin."

"And who am I?" He was desperate. "Huh? Answer me that. Who am I? Who are you? Who is anybody? We are what we do! We are our secrets. I *am* my sin! You want to know me, then you have to know my sin. Is that what you want? Every little dirty secret out on the table so that you can dissect it all and know Kevin, the poor tormented soul?"

"That's not what I said."

"You might as well have, because it's true! Why is it fair that I should spill my guts when the pastor next-door has as many nasty secrets as I do? Huh? If we want to know him, we have to know his secrets, is that it?"

"Stop it!" Her anger surprised her. "You're *not* your sin! Who ever told you that lie? Aunt Balinda? I've seen you, Kevin. You asked me what my profile for you was. Well, let me be more specific. You are one of the kindest, gentlest, most interesting, appealing men I know. That's who you are. And don't insult my intelligence or my feminine discernment by dismissing my opinion." She took a breath and a guess. "I don't know what Slater's up to, or why, but I guarantee you're doing exactly what he wants you to do when you start to believe that you're trapped. You've come out of that. Don't go back."

She knew by his blink that she was right. Slater was trying to pull him back to the past, and the thought so terrified him that he was breaking down. Which was exactly how Slater would accomplish his objective. He would trap Kevin in his past.

Kevin stared at her, stunned. It occurred to her then, looking back into his wide eyes, that she didn't merely like Kevin, she cared for him deeply. She had no business caring for him; she didn't even *want* to care for him, not in that way. Her empathy had risen to the surface, unbidden. She'd always been a sucker for the downtrodden. She had always had a soft spot for men who were hurting in some way. Now her soft spot had found Kevin.

But this didn't feel like a soft spot. She actually found him appealing, with his ragged hair and his charming smile. And those eyes. That wasn't empathy, was it?

She closed her eyes and swallowed. *God forbid, Jennifer. And when was the last time you dated a man, anyway? Two years ago? That hillbilly from Arkansas who came from good stock, so says Mom?* She'd never known the full meaning of boring until then. She would prefer a man with a goatee who rode a Harley and winked frequently.

Jennifer opened her eyes. Kevin was seated on the concrete, cross-legged, head in his hands. The man never ceased to surprise her.

"I'm sorry, I'm not sure where all that came from," she said.

He lifted his head, closed his eyes, and took a deep breath. "Please, don't be sorry. That was the nicest thing I've heard in a long time." His eyes fluttered open, as if he'd just heard himself. "Maybe *nicest* is the wrong word choice. It was . . . I think you're right. He's trying to pull me back, isn't he? That's his objective. So who is he? Balinda?"

Jennifer sat down beside him and folded her legs to the side. Her skirt wasn't exactly dress of choice for concrete sitting, but she didn't care.

"I need to tell you something, Kevin. But I don't want it to upset you."

He stared ahead and then turned to her. "You went to the house, didn't you?"

"Yes. This morning. It took a few threats to convince Balinda to let me in, but I saw the place and I met Eugene and Bob."

Kevin lowered his head again.

"I know it's hard, but I need to know what happened in that house, Kevin. For all we know, Slater could be someone Balinda hired. That would fit the profile. She wants to change you. But without knowing the whole story, I'm floundering here."

"You're asking me to tell you something no one knows. Not because it's so horrible—I know I'm not the only one who's had a few challenges along the way. But it's dead and buried. You want me to bring it back to life? Isn't that what Slater's trying to do?"

"I'm not Slater. And frankly, it doesn't sound dead and buried to me."

"And you really think this whole game has to do with my past?"

She nodded. "I'm assuming that Slater has an objective that is tied to your past, yes."

Kevin remained quiet. The silence stretched, and Jennifer sat beside him feeling his tension, hearing his breathing. She wondered if it would be appropriate to put a hand on his arm but immediately decided it wouldn't.

He suddenly groaned and rocked. "I don't think I can do this."

"You can't slay the dragon without luring it out of its hole. I want to help you, Kevin. I need to know."

For a long time he just sat there rocking. Then he stilled and his breathing slowed. Maybe it was too much too fast. He'd faced more than most could stomach these last three days and she was pushing him even further. He needed sleep. But she was running out of time. Slater was escalating.

She was about to suggest that they get some rest and consider it in the morning when he turned his face to the night sky.

"I don't think Balinda's intentions were necessarily evil." He spoke in a soft monotone. "She wanted a good playmate for Bob. He was eight when they adopted me; I was one. But Bob was retarded. I wasn't, and Balinda couldn't accept that reality."

He paused and took several deep breaths. Jennifer shifted and leaned on her arm so that she could watch his face. His eyes were closed.

"Tell me about Balinda."

"I don't know her story, but Balinda creates her own reality. We all do, but Balinda only knows absolutes. She decides what part of the world is real and what part isn't. If something isn't real, she makes it go away. She manipulates everything around her to create an acceptable reality."

He stopped. Jennifer waited a full thirty seconds before prodding him. "Tell me what it was like to be her son."

"I don't know it yet, because I'm too young, but my mom doesn't want me to be smarter than my brother. So she decides to make me retarded too because she's already tried to make Bob smarter but she can't."

Another stall. He was switching tenses, dipping into the past. Jennifer felt her stomach turn.

"How does she do that? Does she hurt you?"

"No. Hurting is evil in Balinda's world. She won't let me out of the house because the world outside isn't real. The only real world is the one she makes inside the house. She is the princess. She needs me to read so that she can shape my mind with what she makes me read, but she cuts up stories and makes me read only things she decides are real. I'm nine years old before I know there are animals called cats because Princess thinks cats are evil. I don't even know there is evil until I'm eleven. There's only real and unreal. Everything real is good and everything good comes from Princess. I don't do anything bad; I only do things that aren't real. She makes the things that aren't real go away by starving me of them. She never punishes me; she only helps me."

"When you do something that's not real, how does she punish you?"

He hesitated. "She locks me in my room to learn about the real world or makes me sleep so I'll forget the unreal world. She takes away food and water. That's how animals learn, she says, and we are the best animals. I can remember the first time because it made me confused. I was four. My brother and I are playing servant, folding dishtowels for Princess. We have to fold them over and over until they're perfect. Sometimes it takes all day. We don't have toys because toys aren't real. Bob asks me what one plus one is because he wants to give me two towels, but he doesn't know what to call it. I tell him that I think one plus one is two and Princess overhears me. She locks me in my room for two days. Two towels, two days. If Bob doesn't know how to add, then I can't either, because it isn't real. She wants me to be dumb like Bob."

An image of Balinda seated under a stack of clipped newspapers filled Jennifer's mind and she shivered.

Kevin sighed and changed tenses again. "She never held me. She hardly even touched me unless it was by mistake. Sometimes I went without food for days. Once a whole week. Sometimes we couldn't wear clothes if we did unreal things. She deprived us both of anything she thought might feed our minds. Mostly me, because Bob was retarded and he didn't do as many things that weren't real. No school. No games. Sometimes no talking for days. Sometimes she made me stay in bed all day. Other times she made me sit in the bathtub in cold water so I couldn't sleep all night. I could never ask her why, because that wasn't real. Princess was real, and if she decided to do something, anything else was unreal and couldn't be talked about. So we couldn't ask questions. Even questions about real things, because that would question their reality, which was unreal."

Jennifer filled in the blanks. The abuse wasn't primarily physical, not necessarily even emotional, although there was some of both of those. It was primarily psychological. She watched Kevin's chest rise and fall. She desperately wanted to reach out to him. She could see the boy, sitting alone in a bathtub of cold water, shivering in the dark, wondering how to make sense of his horrible world that he'd been brainwashed to think was good.

She fought back tears. *Kevin, dear Kevin, I'm so sorry!* She reached out her hand and put it on his arm. Who could do such terrible things to a little boy? There was more, details, stories that could undoubtedly fill a book to be studied by universities across the country. But she didn't want to hear more. If she could only make it all go away. She might be able to stop Slater, but Kevin would live with this past until the day he died.

A brief absurd image of her lying down beside him and holding him gently in her arms ran through her mind.

Kevin suddenly groaned and then chuckled. "She's a twisted, demented lunatic."

Jennifer cleared her throat. "Agreed."

"But you know what?"

"What?"

"Telling you about it makes me feel . . . good. I've never told anyone."

"Not even Samantha?"

"No."

"Sometimes talking about abuse helps us deal with it. Our tendency is to hide it, and that's understandable. I'm glad you're telling me. None of it was your fault, Kevin. It's not your sin."

He pushed himself up. His eyes were clearer. "You're right. That old goat did everything in her power to hold me back."

"When did you first realize that Balinda's world wasn't the only one?"

"When I met Samantha. She came to my window one night and helped me sneak out. But I was trapped, you know. I mean mentally. For a long time I couldn't accept that Balinda was anything but a loving princess. When Samantha left to study law, she begged me to go with her. Or at least somewhere away from Balinda, but I couldn't leave. I was twenty-three before I finally worked up the courage to leave. Balinda went ballistic."

"And you've done all this in five years?"

He nodded and grinned softly. "Turns out that I was fairly intelligent. It only took me a year to get my general education papers, and four years to graduate from college."

It occurred to Jennifer that she was treating him like a patient with these short, probing questions, but he seemed to want it now.

"Which is when you decided to become a minister," she said.

"That's a long story. I suppose because of my strange rearing the subject of good and evil held unusual fascination for me. Naturally I gravitated toward the church. Morality became somewhat of an obsession, I guess. I figured the least I could do was spend my life showing some small corner of the real world the way to true goodness."

"As opposed to what?"

"As opposed to the false reality we all create for ourselves. Mine was extreme, but it didn't take me long to see that most people live in their own worlds of delusion. Not so different from Balinda's, really."

"Observant." She smiled. "Sometimes I wonder what my delusions are. Is your faith personal?"

He shrugged. "I'm not sure. The church is a system, a vehicle for me. I wouldn't say that I know God personally, no. But my faith in a God is real enough. Without an absolute, moral God, there can be no true morality. It's the most obvious argument for the existence of God."

"I grew up Catholic," she said. "Went through all the forms, never did quite understand it all."

"Well, don't tell Father Bill Strong, but I can't say I do either."

Sitting next to him now, just a few minutes since his confession, Jennifer had difficulty placing Kevin in the context of his youth. He seemed so normal.

He shook his head. "This is incredible. I still can't believe I just told you all that."

"You just needed the right person," she said.

The sound of feet running on the pavement sounded behind them. Jennifer twisted around. It was Galager.

"Jennifer!"

She stood and brushed her skirt.

"We have another riddle!" Galager said. He held a sheet of notebook paper in his hand. "Mickales just found this on the windshield of Kevin's car. It's Slater."

"My car?" Kevin jumped to his feet.

Jennifer took the note. Yellow pad. The scrawling was black, familiar. The milk jug from Kevin's refrigerator. She read the note quickly.

$3+3 = 6$.

  Four down, two to go. You know how I like threes, Kevin. Time's running out. Shame, shame, shame. A simple confession would do, but you force my hand.

  Who escapes their prison but is captive still?

  I'll give you a hint: It isn't you.

  6 A.M.

Kevin gripped his hair and turned away.

"Okay," Jennifer said, turning for the street. "Let's get moving."

20

SAMANTHA WAS TIRED. The Pakistani had insisted they meet at a Mexican restaurant five miles out of town. The light was too low, the music was too loud, and the place smelled of stale cigarettes. She stared the witness directly in the eye. Chris had sworn that Salman would cooperate and he had. But what he had to say wasn't exactly what Sam wanted to hear.

"How do you know it was a dagger if you never saw it?"

"He told me it was. I have the tattoo on my back, and he said he had one like it on his forehead."

"Did you see any scarring or discoloration that might indicate he had the tattoo removed?"

"Perhaps. He wore his hair over his forehead. Didn't matter—he said he had it removed and I believed him."

They'd been over all of this at least once; he'd already described the tattooed man with remarkable detail. Salman was a tailor. Tailors notice these things, he said.

"And this was while you were in New York, four months ago. And you saw him five or six times at a bar named Cougars over the course of about a month?"

"That is what I have said. Yes. You may check with the bar owner; he may remember the man as well."

"So according to you, this man who had a dagger tattoo and who called himself Slater was in New York while the Riddle Killer was killing victims in Sacramento."

"Yes, definitely. I remember watching the news while I was in New York the very night after I had talked to Slater."

Salman had spilled enough details in the previous hour to make his testimony credible. Sam had been in New York four months ago. She knew the pub Salman referred to, a low-class joint frequented by your typical mix of unsavory characters. A CIA task force had set up a sting at the joint to flush out an Iranian whom they suspected had ties to a bombing in Egypt. The man had exonerated himself.

"Okay." She turned to Steve Jules, the agent who'd accompanied her from the Houston office. "I'm done. Thank you for your time, Mr. Salman. It was invaluable."

"Perhaps I could make you a suit," he said with a grin. "I have a new shop here. There aren't so many tailors in Houston as in New York."

She smiled. "Maybe next time I'm in Houston to escape the heat."

They left the bar in Steve's car. This wasn't what she'd wanted to hear. In fact, it was downright dreadful. What if she was right about the rest of it? *Dear God, dear God.*

She wanted only one thing now: to be with Kevin. Kevin needed her more now than ever. The despondent look on his face as she sped off to the airport haunted her.

Her childhood friend had grown into quite an incredible man, hadn't he? Tormented by his past, perhaps, but he'd escaped that hell-hole he called a home and flourished. Part of her wanted nothing more than to run back to him and throw herself in his arms and beg him to marry her. Sure he had his demons; everyone did. Yes, he had a long struggle ahead of him; didn't they all? But he was the most genuine man she'd ever known. His eyes shone with the excitement and wonder of a child, and his mind had absorbed the world with stunning capacity. His progress was nearly superhuman.

On the other hand, she could never marry Kevin. Their relationship was too valuable to compromise with romance. He saw that too, otherwise he never would have allowed room for any attraction to Jennifer. Their occasional romantic innuendo was simply teasing. They both knew that.

She sighed.

"Tough interview," Steve said beside her.

She picked up her cell phone and punched in her boss's number. It would be late, but she had to get this to him. "I thought it went pretty smoothly," she said.

Roland picked up the phone on the fourth ring. "It's midnight."

"He was two hours late," Sam said.

"And?"

"And he knew Slater."

"Our guy?"

"Very possible. Tattoo like that is extremely unusual. But he claims to have known Slater in New York."

"So."

"So it was four months ago. Over a period of about a month. The Riddle Killer was in Sacramento then, killing Roy Peters."

"So Slater's not the Riddle Killer."

"That's right."

"Copy cat?"

"Could be."

"And if Slater is the boy, he's no longer walking around with a dagger tattoo on his forehead because he had it removed."

"So it seems."

Roland covered the phone and spoke to someone—probably his wife unless he was in a late meeting, which was entirely possible.

"I want you back in Sacramento tomorrow," he said. "If Slater isn't the Riddle Killer, he's not your concern."

"I know, sir. I have three days left on my leave, remember?"

"We called you back in, remember?"

"Because we believed that Slater was the Riddle Killer. If he's not, the trail's cold."

Roland considered her argument. He wasn't the most reasonable man when it came to time off. He put in eighty hours a week and expected his subordinates to do the same.

"Please, sir, I go way back with Kevin. He's practically family to me. I swear, three more days and I'll be back in the office. You have to let me do this. And there's still the chance that I'm wrong about Salman's testimony."

"Yes, there is."

"It's still possible that Slater knows the Riddle Killer."

"Possible."

"Then give me more time."

"You heard about the library?"

"The whole world heard about the library."

He sighed. "Three days. I expect to see you at your desk Thursday morning. And please, tread lightly down there. This is unofficial. From what I've heard the whole scene is one big snake pit. Every agency in the country has a stake in this."

"Thank you, sir."

Roland hung up.

Sam considered calling Jennifer but decided it could wait until morning. She could tell her only that Slater wasn't the Riddle Killer. She needed to satisfy herself as to the rest before she said anything that might do Kevin more harm than good.

She'd already checked on flights back. No red eyes, one at 6 A.M. and one at 9 A.M. She needed sleep. The nine o'clock United flight would have to do. It would take her through the Denver hub and put her in Long Beach at noon.

|||

"Okay . . ." Kevin watched Jennifer pace the warehouse floor. They'd delayed plans to share details of the warehouse with the police and instead decided to use the place as a staging area. It was the only way to keep Milton off her back, Jennifer said.

"Let's review what we *do* know."

Agents Bill Galager and Brett Mickales straddled chairs by the table, chins in their hands, focused on Jennifer. Kevin leaned against the wall, arms crossed. It was hopeless. They were beat; they were clueless; they were dead. They'd rehashed a hundred ideas in the two hours since Slater's note had been discovered.

"We know that he's escalating. Car, bus, building. We know that all of his other threats made reference to damage of some kind. This one did not. We know that we have until 6 A.M. to solve or . . . or what we don't know. And we know the riddle. *Who escapes their prison but is captive still?*"

Jennifer spread her hands.

"You're forgetting the most crucial bit of knowledge," Kevin said.

"Which is?"

"The fact that we're toast."

They stared at him as if he'd just walked in and flashed his pecs. A wry grin crossed Jennifer's face. "Humor's good."

"People," Mickales said. "He's gonna do people this time."

"There were people every time."

"But he went after a car, a bus, and a building. This time he goes straight after people."

"Kidnapping," Kevin said.

"We've suggested that. It's a possibility."

"If you ask me, it's the best one," Mickales said. He stood up. "It fits."

Jennifer crossed to the table, eyes suddenly wide. "Okay, unless anybody has a better idea, we'll chase that."

"Why would Slater kidnap anyone?" Kevin asked.

"For the same reason he threatened to blow up a bus," Mickales said. "To force a confession."

Kevin stared at the man, suddenly overwhelmed. They'd been at it ad nauseam and they kept coming up with the same thing, which was essentially nothing. In the end it always came back to his confession.

"Look." He could feel the heat rising up his spine. He shouldn't be doing this—he was beyond himself. "If I had the slightest clue as to what this wacko wanted me to confess, you think I would hold out?"

"Easy, man. Nobody's suggesting—"

"I don't have the foggiest notion what his crazy confession is! He's nuts!" Kevin stepped toward them, aware that he'd crossed a line already. "They're out there screaming bloody murder for Kevin's confession. Well, I gave them one, didn't I? I told them I killed someone as a kid. But they want more. They want real blood. They want me to bleed all over their gossip columns! Kevin, the kid killer who brought down Long Beach!"

His fingers were trembling. They looked at him in silence.

He ran his fingers through his hair. "Man . . ."

"Nobody's screaming bloody murder out there," Jennifer said.

"I'm sorry. I'm just . . . I don't know what to do. This isn't all my fault."

"You need rest, Kevin," Jennifer said. "But if Slater's planning to kidnap someone, you may be a target. I know he said it wasn't you, but I'm not sure what that means." She turned to Galager. "Keep the watch on the house, but I want a transponder on him. Kevin, we're going to give you a small transmitting device. I want you to tape it where it won't be found. We'll leave it inactive—this guy's into electronics; he may scan for signals. Anything happens, you turn it on. The range is roughly fifty miles. Fair enough?"

He nodded.

She walked toward him. "Let's get you home."

Galager headed for the van, which was still parked on the street. Kevin walked outside with Jennifer. The weight of two days without sleep descended on him. He could hardly walk straight, much less think straight.

"I'm sorry. I didn't mean to blow up."

"No apology needed. Just get some sleep."

"What are you going to do?"

She looked off to the east. The helicopters were down for the night. "He said no cops. We could put a guard on likely targets, but for all we know, he's planning on kidnapping the mayor. Or it could be another bomb." She shook her head. "You're right, we're pretty much toast."

They stopped at the car. "It meant a lot," he said. "Talking to you tonight. Thank you."

She smiled, but her eyes were tired. How much sleep had she gotten in the last three days? He suddenly felt terrible for her. Flushing out Slater was more than a job for her.

"Go home and get some sleep," she said, squeezing his arm. "Galager will follow you home. We have someone outside. If Slater makes contact—if *anything* happens—call me."

Kevin looked up to see Galager pull up in the black car. "Somehow I doubt it'll be me. That's not what he wants. I'll be fine. The question is, who won't be?"

What if it was Jennifer? Sam was in Houston.

"What about you?" he asked.

"Why would he want to kidnap me?"

Kevin shrugged. "It's not like I have a lot of friends."

"I guess that makes me a friend. Don't worry, I can handle myself."

By the time Kevin finished with Galager's little lecture on the operational procedures for the transmitter and climbed into bed, the three o'clock hour had come and gone. His head was numb before it hit the pillow. He fell into an exhausted sleep within the minute, lost to the horrors of his new life.

For an hour or three.

III

Slater stands by the fence, stock-still in the darkness. He's given them until six, but this time he will be done before six, before the first light grays the sky. He said six because he likes threes, and six is three plus three, but he can't risk doing this in the light.

No one has stirred in the house since his arrival thirty minutes ago. When he first conceived the plan, he considered just blowing up the house with all its occupants trapped inside. But after thinking very carefully about his ultimate objective, because that's what Slater does the best, he settled on this plan. Putting this woman in a cage will send the city through the roof. It's one thing to wonder which unnamed citizens might be the next to discover a bomb under their bed; it's far more disturbing to know that Mrs. Sally Jane who lives on Stars and Stripes Street and buys her groceries at Albertsons is locked up in a cage, waiting desperately for Kevin Parson to fess up.

Besides, Slater's never kidnapped anyone before. The thought brings a chill to his spine. The sensation of pleasure so intense that it runs up and down the spine is interesting. It is not boring like teenagers poking holes in their noses.

Slater looks at his watch. 4:46. Is 4:46 divisible by three? No, but 4:47 is. And that's one minute away. Perfect. Perfect, perfect, perfect. The pleasure of his brilliance is so intense that Slater now begins to shiver a little. He stands by the fence with perfect discipline, resisting a desperate urge to run for the house and drag her out of bed. He is perfectly disciplined and he is shivering. Interesting.

He's waited so long. Eighteen years. Six times three. Three plus three times three.

The two minutes crawl by very slowly, but Slater doesn't mind. He is born for this. He glances at his watch. 4:47. He can't stand it any longer. It's one minute early. Three is divisible by one. Close enough.

Slater walks up to the sliding glass door, pulls out the pick with a gloved hand, and disengages the lock in less than ten seconds. His breathing comes thick, and he pauses to still it. If the others wake, he will have to kill them, and he doesn't want to mess with that. He wants the woman.

He eases into the kitchen and leaves the door open. They have no dogs or cats. One child. The husband is Slater's only concern. He stands on the tile floor for a full minute, adjusting his eyes to the deeper darkness, breathing in the home's smells. The senses are the key to living life to its fullest. Tastes, sights, smells, feelings, sounds. Eat what you like, watch what you can, touch who you want. That's what he wants Kevin to do. To taste and touch and smell his true self. It will destroy him. The plan is perfect. Perfect, perfect, perfect.

Slater takes one deep breath, but very slowly.

He walks through the living room and puts his hand on the door-knob to the master bedroom. It opens without a sound. Perfect. The room is dark. Pitch-black. Perfect.

He walks slowly to the bed and stands over the woman. Her breathing is quicker than the man's. She faces him, mouth slightly parted, hair tangled on the pillow. He reaches out a hand and touches the sheet. Soft and smooth. Two hundred thread count at least. He could stand here over them for an hour and breathe in their smells without being seen. But the light is coming. He doesn't like the light.

Slater reaches into his shirt pocket and withdraws a note, which he sets on the dresser. For Kevin. He slips his hand into his coat and takes out a roll of gauze and a bottle of chloroform. He unscrews the bottle and dips the roll into the liquid. The smell fills his nostrils and he holds his breath. It has to be strong enough to put her under without a struggle.

He replaces the lid on the bottle, drops it into his pocket, and eases the roll of soaked gauze in front of the woman's nose, careful not to touch it. For a moment she doesn't stir, then she whimpers in her dreams. But she doesn't move. He waits twenty seconds, until her breathing slows enough to persuade him that she's unconscious. He shoves the roll into his jacket.

Slater settles to his knees, as if bowing before his victim. A sacrifice for the gods. He lifts the sheet and slips his hands under the body until his elbows are directly under her. She lies limp, like a noodle. He gently pulls her toward his chest. She slides off the bed and sags in his arms. The husband rolls half a turn and then settles. Perfect.

Slater stands and carries her out of the house without bothering to shut the doors. The clock in his car reads 4:57 when he settles behind the wheel with the woman breathing slowly in the backseat.

Slater starts the car and drives away. He could have carried her to the hiding on foot and returned later for the car, but he doesn't want to leave the vehicle in front of the house any longer than absolutely necessary. He's too smart for that. It occurs to him that this will be the first time he's ever brought a guest to the hiding. When she awakes, her eyes will be the first besides his own to see his world. The thought brings a moment of panic.

So then, all the more reason not to let her out. It's what will happen anyway, isn't it? Even if Kevin confesses, Slater has always known that she will have to die. His exposure to another human being will be temporary. He can live with that. Still, why hasn't this detail occurred to him earlier? It isn't a mistake, just an oversight. But oversight can lead to mistakes. He chides himself and turns down the dark street.

Slater doesn't bother with stealth now. The woman is stirring, so he gives her another healthy dose of chloroform, yanks the body out of the rear seat, and heaves it over his shoulder. He hurries for the door, opens it with a key, and enters the small room. Close door, feel for chain, pull on overhead light.

A dim light exposes the space. Down a flight of steps. Another chain, another light. Through the tunnel. Open the second door with a second key. The hiding. Home, sweet home.

The thought of sharing his home with another person for a little while suddenly doesn't seem so bad. In fact, it holds its own excitement. Everything he needs is here. Food, water, a bathroom, a bed, clothing, the electronics—of course, she won't be sharing any of those amenities.

The woman is stirring again.

He crosses to the room he's prepared. The walk-in closet once stored materials he's used in his games, but he's cleared it for her. Can't take the chance that she knows how to set off dynamite now, can he? The room is seven by seven and solid concrete all around except the ceiling, which is heavily insulated wood. The door is steel.

He places her onto the cement floor and steps back. She groans and rolls to one side. Good enough.

He closes the door, locks it with a deadbolt, and stuffs a rolled-up rug into the crack at the bottom. Lights out.

21

KEVIN HEARD THE RINGING long before he awoke. It sounded like a high-pitched laugh. Or an intermittent scream. Then there was the pounding, a thumping that could be his heart. But it sounded more like banging on the door.

"Sir?" Someone was yelling, calling him sir.

Kevin's eyes somehow managed to open. Light shone through the window. Where was he? Home. His mind started to drift. He would have to get up eventually and go to class, but at the moment he felt as though he'd met the wrong end of a rhino charge. He closed his eyes.

The muffled voice came again. "Kevin? The phone . . ."

His eyes snapped open. Slater. His life had been turned upside down by a man called Slater who called on the phone. The phone was ringing.

He spilled out of bed. The clock said 7:13. Slater had given them until 6 A.M. He ran to the bedroom door, twisted the lock, and yanked it open. One of the agents watching his house stood there, the cordless phone from the kitchen in hand.

"I'm sorry to wake you, but your phone's been ringing on and off for fifteen minutes. It's a pay phone. Jennifer told us to wake you."

Kevin stood in his pinstriped boxer shorts. "Has . . . has anything happened?"

"Not that I've heard."

Kevin took the phone absently. "Okay. I'll answer it this time."

The agent hesitated, expressionless, and then walked down the stairs for the door. Kevin didn't even know his name. He wore a dark navy jacket and tan slacks; black hair. Walked stiffly, like maybe his underwear were too tight. But the man had a name and maybe a wife and some kids. A life. What if Slater had gone after this man instead of Kevin? Or gone after someone in China, unknown to the West? For that matter, how many men or women were facing their own Slaters throughout the world? It was an awkward thought, standing there at the top of his stairs, watching the agent leave through the front door.

Kevin walked back into his bedroom. He had to call Jennifer. Six o'clock had come and gone—something had to have happened.

The phone suddenly rang. He picked up the receiver.

"Hello?"

"Kevin?" It was Eugene. Kevin felt himself shutting down immediately. The sound of that voice. They didn't have a phone in the house. He was calling from a pay phone.

"Yes."

"Thank God! Thank God, boy. I don't know what to do! I just don't know what I should do . . ."

You could start by drowning yourself. "What's wrong?"

"I'm not sure. It's just that Princess isn't home. I woke up and she was gone. She never leaves without telling me. I thought maybe she went down for some dog food because we threw it away, you know, but then I remembered that we burned the dog and—"

"Shut up, Eugene. Please, just shut up and try to make some sense for once. Her name is Balinda. So Balinda left without telling you. I'm sure she'll be back. You can live without her for a few hours, can't you?"

"This isn't like her. I have a very bad feeling, Kevin! And now I've gotten Bob worried. He keeps looking in all the rooms, calling for Princess. You have to come—"

"Forget it. Call the police, if you're so worried."

"Princess won't allow that! You know . . ."

He talked on but suddenly Kevin wasn't hearing. His mind had turned over a stone. What if Slater had kidnapped Balinda? What if the old hag was really gone?

But why would Slater take Balinda?

Because whether you like it or not, she is your mother, Kevin. You need her. You want her to be your mother.

A cold sweat broke out on his temples and he wasn't sure why. He had to call Jennifer! Where was Samantha? Maybe Jennifer had heard from her.

He interrupted Eugene's rambling. "I'll call you back."

"You can't call me! I have to go home!"

"Then go home."

Kevin hung up. Where was Jennifer's number? He ran downstairs, still in his boxers, snatched her card from the counter with a trembling hand, and dialed the number.

"Good morning, Kevin. I'm surprised you're not still sleeping."

"How did you know it was me?"

"Caller ID. You're on your home phone."

"Have you heard anything?"

"Not yet. I just got off the phone with Samantha. It seems we were wrong about Slater being the Riddle Killer."

"We may have a problem, Jennifer. I just got a call from Eugene. He says that Balinda's missing."

Jennifer didn't respond.

"I was just thinking, do you think Slater could have—"

"Balinda! That's it. It makes perfect sense!"

"It does?"

"Stay put. I'll swing by in ten minutes."

"What? Where are we going?"

She hesitated. "Baker Street."

"No, I can't! Really, Jennifer, I don't think I can go in there like this."

"Don't you see? This could be the break we need! If he took her, then Slater's tied to Balinda and Balinda is tied to the house. I know this may be hard, but I need you."

"You don't know that."

"We can't risk me being wrong."

"Why can't you just go?"

"Because you're the only one who knows how to beat him. If Slater did take Balinda, then we know that this whole thing goes back to the house. To the past. There has to be a key to it all, and I doubt that I'm the one who's going to find it."

He knew what she was saying, and it sounded more like psychobabble than truth. But she could be right.

"Kevin? I'll be there with you. It's paper and boards; that's all it is. I was there yesterday, remember? And Balinda's gone. Ten minutes?"

Balinda was gone. Bob wasn't the problem—he was a victim in this mess. Eugene was just an old fool without Balinda. The witch was gone.

"Okay."

III

The white house stood as ominously as always. He stared at it through the windshield, feeling silly next to Jennifer. She was looking at him, knowing him. He felt naked.

Balinda wasn't in the house. Unless she'd come back. If so, he wouldn't go in. Jennifer might want him to. She seemed pretty convinced that there was more to this than he'd told her, but in all honesty, he couldn't think of anything. Slater was the boy and the boy had nothing to do with the house.

"When is Sam coming?" he asked, stalling.

"She said noonish, but she has a few errands to run."

"I wonder why she didn't call me?"

"I told her you were sleeping. She said she'll call you as soon as she can." Jennifer looked at the house. "You didn't tell Sam about locking the boy in the cellar—how much does Sam really know about your childhood, Kevin? You two have known each other for years."

"I don't like to talk about it. Why?"

"Something's bothering her. She wouldn't tell me, but she wants to meet later this afternoon. She's convinced that Slater isn't the Riddle Killer. I can buy that, but there's more. She knows something else." Jennifer hit the steering wheel. "Why do I always feel like I'm the last to know what's going on here?"

Kevin stared at the house. She sighed. "I had to tell Milton about this. He wants to talk to you this morning."

"What did you say?"

"I said he would have to take it up with the bureau chief. We still have official jurisdiction. The rest are still running their investigations, but on the ground everything goes through us. The thought of Milton interviewing you gives me the creeps."

"Okay, let's go," Kevin said, distracted. They might as well get this over with. She would never know how much better he felt with her here. On the other hand, she was a psychologist—she probably *would* understand. He opened his door.

Jennifer put her hand on his arm. "Kevin, I need you to know something. If we discover that Slater did take Balinda, there's no way we can keep it from the media. They'll want to know more. They can be nosy."

"So then my whole life gets dissected by the press."

"Pretty much. I've done my best this far—"

"That's what Slater wants. That's why he took her. It's his way of exposing me." He dropped his head and ruffled his hair.

"I'm sorry."

Kevin stood from the car and slammed the door. "Let's get this over with."

Walking across the street and up the steps to the front door, Kevin made a firm decision. Under no circumstances would he blubber or show any more emotion in front of Jennifer. He was leaning on her too much already. The last thing she needed was a basket case. He would walk in, give Bob a hug, slug Eugene, do his I'm-looking-for-the-key-to-Slater routine, and leave without so much as batting an eye.

His foot crossed the threshold for the first time in five years. The tremble started in his fingers. It spread to his knees before the door closed behind him.

Eugene let them in. "I don't know. I just don't know where she could have gone. She should have been back by now!"

Bobby stood at the end of the hall, grinning wide, beaming. He started to clap and hop in place without leaving the ground. A lump the size of a boulder filled Kevin's throat. What had he done to Bob? He'd abandoned him to Princess. He'd been punished his whole life in part because of Bob, but that didn't make Bob guilty.

"Kevin, Kevin, Kevin! You came to see me?"

Kevin quickly walked to his brother and hugged the man tight. "Yes. I'm sorry, Bob. I'm so sorry." The tears were leaking already. "Are you okay?"

Eugene watched dumbly; Jennifer wrinkled her brow.

"Yes, Kevin. I'm very good."

He didn't seem so concerned about the old bat's disappearance.

"Princess has gone away," he said, smile suddenly gone.

"Why don't you show me your bedroom," Jennifer said to Eugene.

"My, my, my, my. I don't know what I'll do without Princess," Eugene said, heading off to the left.

Kevin let them go. "Bob, could you show me your room?"

Bob lit up and skipped through the narrow passage between the stacks of newspapers. "You want to see my room?"

Kevin walked down the hall on numb legs. It was surreal, this world he'd escaped. An issue of *Time* poked out of the stack to his right. The face on the cover had been replaced by a smiling image of Muhammad Ali. Only God, the devil, and Balinda knew why.

Bob hurried into his room. He snatched something off the floor. It was an old beat-up Game Boy, a monochrome version. Bob had himself a toy. Balinda had softened in her old age. Or was it because Kevin had left?

"It's a computer!" Bob said.

"Nice. I like it." Kevin peeked into the room. "Do you still read stories that Bal—Princess gives you to read?"

"Yes. And I like them a lot."

"That's good, Bob. Does she . . . make you sleep during the day?"

"Not for a long time. But sometimes she won't let me eat. She says I'm getting too fat."

Bobby's room looked just as it had five years earlier. Kevin turned back into the hall and pushed open the door to his old room.

Unchanged. Surreal. He set his jaw. The flood of emotions he'd expected didn't come. The window was still screwed down and the bookcases were still full of bogus books. The bed he'd spent half his childhood in was still covered by the same blanket. It was as if Balinda was waiting for him to return. Or maybe his leaving didn't fit into her reality, so she refused to accept it. With her mind there was no telling.

No keys to Slater here.

A wail—Eugene—carried through the house. Bob turned and ran for the sound. So it was true.

Kevin walked back out to the living room, ignoring the sounds of lament issuing from the back bedroom. He should take a torch to this place. Burn out the rat's nest. Add a few more ashes to the backyard. The stairwell to the basement was still choked off with a mountain of books and magazines, stacks that hadn't been touched for years.

Jennifer stepped out of the master bedroom. "He took her."

"So I gathered."

"He left a note." She handed him a blue slip of paper. Three words were scrawled in the familiar handwriting.

Fess up, Puke.

"Or what," he said. "You'll dump her in the lagoon?"

Kevin stared at the words, numb from four days of horror. Part of him didn't care, part of him felt sorry for the old hag. Either way, all of his deepest secrets would soon be on the table for the world to pick through. That was the point. Kevin wasn't sure how much he cared anymore.

"Can we go now?"

"Are you finished?"

"Yes."

She looked around. "The health department is going to have a field day once this gets out."

"They should burn it."

"That's what I was thinking," she said. Her eyes settled on his. "Are you okay?"

"I feel . . . confused."

"As far as the rest of the world is concerned, she's your mother. They may wonder why you don't seem to care. She may be a witch, but she's still human. Only God knows what he'll do to her."

The emotions came from his gut, unexpectedly and in a rush. He suddenly felt suffocated in the small, dark space. She was his mother, wasn't she? And he was horrified by the fact that he even *thought* of her as a mother, because in reality he hated her more than he hated Slater. Unless they were one and the same and she had kidnapped herself.

A confusing mixture of revulsion and sorrow overcame Kevin. He was falling apart. His eyes swam with tears and his face wrinkled.

Kevin turned for the door. He could feel their stares on his back. *Mommy.* Fire burned through his throat; a tear spilled from his left eye.

At least they couldn't see. He would never allow anyone to see this. He hated Balinda and he was crying for her and he hated that he was crying for her.

It was too much. He hurried for the door, crashed through with far more noise than he wanted, and let out a soft sob. He hoped Jennifer couldn't hear; he didn't want her to hear him acting this way. He was just a lost boy and he was crying like a lost boy and he really just wanted to be held by Mommy. By the one person who had never held him.

"Kevin?" Jennifer was running after him.

He only wanted to be held by Princess.

22

THE QUESTIONS HAD NAGGED at Samantha through the night. The scenario fit some unseen hand like a glove; the question was, which hand? Who was Slater?

She'd talked to Jennifer upon waking and heard about the note on Kevin's windshield. She should have taken an earlier flight! Jennifer suspected kidnapping, but as of seven this morning there had been no evidence of foul play.

Sam told Jennifer about Salman. If the Pakistani Salman had indeed met with Slater in New York, then whoever the FBI had located with a tattoo could not be Slater, because Slater's had been removed. Furthermore, Slater couldn't be the Riddle Killer—he'd been in New York at the time of Roy's murder. Jennifer hadn't been ready to accept her conclusion out of hand, but the two cases did have a few significant disparities that were obviously weighing on her mind. She talked about objectives. She was beginning to suspect that the Riddle Killer and Slater weren't similarly motivated.

As for the tattoo, they would know within a few hours.

Sam's plane landed at LAX at 12:35. She rented a car and headed south for Long Beach. Traffic on 405 was as bad as it got for a weekday. She called Jennifer. The agent answered on the first ring.

"Hi, Jennifer, it's Sam. Anything?"

"As a matter of fact, yes. The tattoo is a bust. Our man works on an oil rig six months a year. He's been out on one for the last three weeks."

"Makes sense. Any word on a kidnapping?"

Jennifer hesitated and Sam sat up. "Balinda was taken from her home last night," Jennifer said.

"Balinda Parson?" Sam's pulse spiked.

"One and the same. No contact, no leads, nothing but a note left in Slater's writing: 'Fess up, Puke.' Kevin took it pretty hard."

Sam's mind was already whirling. Of course! Taking Balinda would force media attention on Kevin's family. His past. "Does the media know?"

"Yes. But we're keeping them away from Baker Street under the claim that it could trigger Slater. There's wall-to-wall coverage on this thing. I've spent the last hour handling interagency concerns. The bureaucracy's enough to drive me nuts. Milton's ticked off, the ATF wants the evidence from Quantico—it's a mess. Meanwhile we're dead in the water."

Jennifer sounded tired. Sam braked and came to a stop behind a pickup truck billowing black smoke. "How is he?"

"Kevin? He's dead to the world. I left him at his house about two hours ago, sleeping. God knows we could all use some rest."

Sam pulled around the truck. "I have some ideas, Jennifer. Is there a chance we could meet sooner?"

"What is it?"

"I . . . I can't explain right now."

"Come by the station. Unless something breaks, I'll be here."

"Okay. But I have to chase something down first."

"If you have information that's pertinent to the investigation, I expect to be told. Please, Sam, I can use all the help I can get here."

"I promise you I'll call the second I know anything."

"Sam. Please, what's on your mind?"

"I'll call you," Sam said and hung up.

Without evidence her fears would have to remain the paranoia of a close friend, desperate for answers. And if she was right? God help them. God help Kevin.

She drove south, ticking off the facts. Slater had been in New York at the same time she'd been there. Slater knew her, a small detail she'd withheld from the CBI. Knowing Roland, he'd yank her from the case.

Slater was obsessed with Kevin's past; Slater was the boy; Sam had never seen the boy; all of the riddles had to do with opposites; all demanded a confession. Slater was trying to force Kevin back into his past. Who was Slater?

A chill snaked down her arms.

Samantha approached Kevin's house from the west, parked two blocks down, and took to foot, careful to keep yard fences between herself and the black car parked up the street. She had to do this without causing a fuss, and the last thing she wanted to do was wake Kevin if he was asleep.

Dread swelled in her chest as she neared. The notion that Kevin might indeed be Slater refused to budge from her tired mind.

She had to wait for the agent up the street to turn his head before crossing from the neighbor's fence into Kevin's backyard. She hurried up to the sliding glass door and knelt so that Kevin's picket fence blocked her head from the car's line of sight. Working quickly above her head, she inserted a thin pick into the lock and worked it with as much precision as she could from the awkward angle. The pin fell and she pried up the latch. She wiped a bead of sweat from her cheek, glanced back at the black car, slid the glass door open a foot, and slipped past the pulled blinds. She reached back through and closed the door.

If they'd seen her, they would be moving already. They hadn't.

Sam looked around the house. A two-by-four-foot travel poster of a bikini-clad native walking down a white beach said that New Zealand promised paradise. *Dear Kevin, you want so much. I should have known how badly you were hurting, even when we were children. Why did you hide it from me? Why didn't you tell me?*

The house's silence engulfed her. So peaceful, so quiet, asleep while the world crumbled. She crossed to the stairs and took them on her tiptoes. Kevin's bedroom was to the left. She eased the door open, saw him on the bed, and walked quietly up to him.

He lay sprawled on his belly, arms above his head, as if surrendering to some unknown enemy beyond the mattress. His head rested on its side, facing her, lower cheek bunched, mouth closed. His face didn't speak of surrender, only sleep. Deep, deep, sweet sleep.

He was dressed in street clothes; his tan Reeboks sat on the floor, nudging the bed skirt.

Sam briefly wondered if Jennifer had stayed with him until he fell asleep. Had she seen him like this? This sweet boy of hers? This stunning man who bore the weight of a hundred worlds on his shoulders? Her champion who'd slain the wicked boy on Baker Street?

What did Jennifer see when she looked at him? *She sees the same as you do, Sam. She sees Kevin and she can't help but to love him as you love him.*

Sam reached out, tempted to brush his cheek. *No, not as I love him. No one can love him as I love him. I would give my life for this man.* She withdrew her hand. A tear broke down her right cheek. *Oh, how I love you, dear Kevin. Seeing you these last three days has reminded me how desperately I love you. Please, please tell me that you will slay this dragon. We will, Kevin. Together we will slay this beast, my knight.*

The childhood role-playing reference flooded her with warmth. She turned away and walked into his closet. She wasn't sure what she was looking for. Something that Slater had left. Something that the

FBI missed because they wouldn't have guessed that it belonged to Slater.

Kevin had ordered his clothes neatly. Slacks and shirts hung in a row, jeans and cargo pants folded and stacked, shoes on a rack. Seminary dress to the right, casual dress to the left. She smiled and ran her fingers through the slacks. She smelled the shirts. His scent lingered. Amazing how she recognized it after so many years. He was still a boy. *A man, Sam. A man.*

She searched the closet and then slowly worked her way through the rest of his room, walking around him, careful not to make any sound. Other than the rise and fall of his back, Kevin did not move. Sam found nothing.

The bathroom proved no better, and her spirit lightened. She didn't want to find anything.

His study. Sam shut the door and sat at his desk. She ran a finger over his books: *Introduction to Philosophy. Sociology of Religion. Hermeneutics Revealed.* Two dozen others. He was in his first semester at the divinity school but he'd bought enough texts for two years, easily.

On the floor beside the desk she saw a small pile of paper, which she picked up. A paper he'd titled "The True Natures of Man." He was a true man.

Please, Sam, let's cut the romantic drivel and do what you came to do.

She was less concerned about noise; there were two doors between her and Kevin. She searched the drawers and removed the books one by one. This is where Slater would leave a clue. This was the room of the mind. He was obsessed with numbers and mind games. The mind. Somewhere, somewhere.

A small stack of business cards, topped by a slip of paper bearing her own number, sat by a calculator that looked fresh out of the box, perhaps never used. The first card belonged to John Francis, Ph.D.,

Academic Dean, Divinity School of the Pacific, South. Kevin had spoken at length about the man. Surely Jennifer had already interviewed him.

And what if she hadn't? The last four days rushed by without time for standard procedure or a thorough investigation. She picked up the phone and called the number on the card. A receptionist with a nasal voice asked her if she wanted to leave a message. No, thank you. She hung up, turned over the card, and saw that Kevin had scribbled another number with the same prefix. She dialed it.

"Hello, this is John."

"Hello, Dr. John Francis?"

"Yes, this is he."

"This is Samantha Sheer with the California Bureau of Investigation. I'm working with an agent Jennifer Peters on the Kevin Parson case. Are you familiar with it?"

"Of course. Agent Peters was here yesterday morning."

"Kevin speaks highly of you," Sam said. "You have a doctorate in psychology, isn't that right?"

"Correct."

"What is your assessment of Kevin?"

"That's a bit like asking which animals live in the sea. Kevin's a wonderful man. I can't say there's anyone else I'd rather tangle my wits with. Extraordinary . . . genuine."

"Genuine. Yes, he is genuine. Nearly transparent. Which is why it's strange he can't remember this sin Slater demands he confess, don't you think? I'm wondering, is there anything that's occupied him in these last few weeks? Any reoccurring themes, projects, papers?"

"As a matter of fact, yes. He was quite interested in the natures of man. You might say consumed with the subject."

Sam picked up the rough draft of the paper. "The true natures of man," Sam said. "And what are the natures of man? Or what would Kevin say are the natures of man?"

"Yes, well, that's the mystery, isn't it? I'm not sure I can tell you what Kevin would say. He told me he had a new model, but he wanted to present them cohesively in his paper."

"Hmm. And when is this paper due?"

"He was scheduled to turn it in this Wednesday."

"For what class?"

"Introduction to Ethics."

"One more question, Doctor, and I'll let you go. You're a religious man with an education in psychology; would you say that the natures of man are primarily spiritual, or psychological?"

"I know that Freud would turn in his grave, but in my mind there's no doubt. Man is primarily a spiritual being."

"And Kevin would agree to that?"

"Yes, I'm sure he would."

"Thank you for your time, Doctor. You sound like a reasonable man."

He chuckled. "They pay me to be; I do try. Anything else, don't hesitate to call."

She set the phone down. Ethics. She scanned the paper and saw that it was hardly more than the recitation of several theories on man's natures. It ended with a new heading: "The True Natures." She set the pages down. Where would Kevin keep his notes on the natures of man?

She stepped over to the bookcase and reached for a large gray book titled *Morality Redefined.* The book was used, frayed around the edges, pages yellowing. She lifted the cover, saw that it was a library book. Copyright 1953.

Sam flipped through the pages, but there were no notes. She was about to replace the book when the back cover fell open. Several loose sheets of white paper dropped to the floor. On the top of one in Kevin's handwriting: *The True Natures of Man, an Essay.*

Samantha withdrew the pages and sat down at the desk. They were only notes. Three pages of notes. She scanned them, a simple outline with headings that fit the subject. Summaries.

We learn as we live, and we live what we learn, but not so well.

How can a nature be dead and yet live? He is dead in the light, but thrives in the dark.

If Good and Evil could talk to each other, what would they say?

They are all pretenders, who live in the light but hide in the dark.

Insightful. But there was nothing here that Slater would have . . .

Sam froze. There at the bottom of page four, three small words.

I AM I.

Sam recognized the handwriting immediately. Slater! "I am I."

"Dear God!"

Sam set the pages on Kevin's desk with a trembling hand. She began to panic.

No. Stop. *What does "I am I" even mean, Sam? It means Slater is Slater. Slater snuck in here and wrote this. That proves nothing except that he has his nose in every part of Kevin's life.*

If Good and Evil could talk to each other, what would they say?

Then how had Kevin and Slater talked to each other? The FBI had a recording. How, how? Unless . . .

A second cell. He's using another cell phone!

Sam ran for Kevin's room. *Dear God, let me be wrong!* He hadn't moved. She crept up to him. Where would he keep the phones? The one Slater had left him was always in his right pocket.

There was only one way to do this. Quickly, before she awakened him. Sam slipped her hand into his right pocket. He wore cargo pants, loose, but his weight pressed her hand into the mattress. She touched the phone, felt the recording device on the back. Slater's.

She rounded the bed, crawled up for better access, and slid her hand into his left pocket. Kevin grunted and rolled to his side, facing her. She stayed still until his breathing returned to a deep slow rhythm and then tried again, this time with his left pocket exposed.

Her fingers felt plastic. Sam knew then that she was right, but she pulled it out anyway. A cell phone, identical to the one Slater had left for Kevin, except black instead of silver. She flipped it open and scrolled through the call history. The calls were to the other cell phone. One to the hotel room phone. Two to Kevin's home phone.

This was the cell phone Slater had used. To talk, to detonate the bombs. Sam's mind throbbed. There could be no doubt about it.

They would crucify him.

23

SAM ROLLED OFF THE BED, closed Kevin's door, and flew downstairs. She gripped the phone Slater had used to make his calls in her right hand—for now Slater wouldn't be making those calls, at least not on this phone. She didn't bother being discreet on her exit but walked right out the back, turned up the street, and ran for her car.

I, Slater, am I, Kevin. And that had been Samantha's greatest fear. That her childhood friend had a multiple personality disorder as she'd suggested to Jennifer a day earlier, and then immediately rejected because Kevin was in the room when Slater called. But it struck her as she lay trying to sleep last night that Slater had not *talked* to her while Kevin was in the room. The phone had only rung while he was in the room. Kevin was in the hall before she picked up and heard Slater. Kevin could have simply pushed the send button in his pocket and then talked to Sam once in the hall. Could multiple personalities work that way?

She'd been with Kevin in the car when Slater called, just before the bus blew. But she had no proof that Slater was actually on the line then. They had no recording of that call.

It was absurd. It was impossible! But try as she might in sleepless fits, Sam couldn't account for a single definitive situation that necessarily proved they couldn't be the same man. Not one.

Mere conjecture! It had to be coincidence!

Now this.

If Good and Evil could talk to each other, what would they say?

Sam reached her car, stomach in knots. This might not be enough. She'd been irresponsible to suggest the possibility to Jennifer in the first place. The man you think you might be falling in love with is insane. And she'd said it so calmly for the simple reason that she didn't believe it herself. She was only doing what she was trained to do. But this . . . this was an entirely different matter.

And Kevin *wasn't* insane! He was merely role-playing, as he had learned to do with Balinda for so many years. He had split into a divergent personality when he first began to comprehend true evil. The boy. He had been the boy! Only he didn't know that he was the boy. To Kevin at age eleven, the boy was an evil person who needed to be killed. So he killed him. But the boy had never died. Slater had simply remained dormant until now, when somehow this paper on the natures of man had allowed him to resurface.

She could still be wrong. In true cases of multiple personality disorders, the subjects were rarely conscious of their alternate personalities. Slater wouldn't know that he was Kevin; Kevin would not know that he was Slater. Actually they *weren't* each other. Physically, yes, but in no other way. Slater could be living right now as Kevin slept, plotting to kill Balinda, and Kevin wouldn't have a clue. Some things Slater did would be merely imagined; others, like the bombs and the kidnapping, would be acted out.

She tossed Kevin's phone on the seat and punched Jennifer's number into her own.

"Jenn—"

"I need to meet you! Now. Where are you?"

"Sam? I'm down at the PD. What's wrong?"

"Have you gotten the lab reports on the shoe prints and the recordings yet?"

"No. Why? Where are you?"

"I was just in Kevin's house and I'm headed your way." She pulled onto Willow.

"How's Kevin?"

Sam took a deep breath and let it out slowly. "He's asleep. I found a second phone on him, Jennifer. It was the phone used to call the cell with the recording device. I don't know how else to say this. I think Kevin is Slater."

"That's . . . I thought we'd already been over this. He was in the room when Slater—"

"Listen, Jennifer, I've come at this from a hundred different angles in the last twelve hours. I'm not saying that I can prove it; God knows I don't want it to be true, but if it is, he needs help! He needs you. And he's the only one who can take us to Balinda. Kevin won't know, but Slater will."

"Please, Sam, this is crazy. How could he have pulled this off? We've had people on the house. We've been listening to him in there! How did he get out to kidnap Balinda?"

"It's his house; he knows how to get out without your boys catching on. Where was he between 3 A.M. and 5 A.M. last night?"

"Sleeping . . ."

"Kevin may have thought he was, but was he? I don't think he's had six hours' sleep in the last four days. Trace it back. He hasn't gotten any phone calls while you were listening, at least not in the house. I hope I'm wrong, I really do, but I don't think you'll find a discrepancy. He's too intelligent. But he wants the truth out. Subconsciously, consciously, I don't know, but he's getting sloppy. He wants the world to know. That's the answer to the riddle."

" *What falls but never breaks? What breaks but never falls?* Night and day," Jennifer said. "Opposites. Kevin."

"Kevin. *Kevin* was the boy; that's why I never saw the boy when we were kids. He was in that warehouse cellar, but only him, no second boy. He hit himself. Check the blood type. The confession Slater wants isn't that Kevin tried to kill the boy, but that he *was* the boy. That Kevin is Slater."

"I am my sin," Jennifer said absently. There was a tremor in her voice.

"What?"

"Something he said last night."

"I'll be there in ten minutes," Sam said. "Don't let Kevin leave the house."

"But only Slater knows where he has Balinda? Kevin truly doesn't know?"

"That's my guess."

"Then we need Slater to find Balinda. But if we send the wrong signal, Slater may go into remission. If he does and Kevin doesn't know where Balinda is, we may have our first actual victim in this case. Even if we hold Kevin in a cell, she could starve to death." Jennifer was suddenly sounding frantic. "He's not the Riddle Killer; he hasn't killed anyone yet. We can't let that happen."

"So we let him walk out?"

"No. No, I don't know, but we have to handle this with kid gloves."

"I'll be right there," Sam said. "Just make sure Kevin doesn't leave that house."

III

The sound of his bedroom door closing pulled Kevin from sleep. It was 3:00. He'd slept over four hours. Jennifer had insisted that he not be bothered unless absolutely necessary. So why were they in his house?

Unless *they* weren't in his house. Unless it was someone else. Someone like Slater!

He slid out of bed, tiptoed to the door, eased it open. Someone was opening the sliding glass door to the back lawn! *Just ask who it is, Kevin. It's the FBI, that's all.*

But what if it wasn't?

"Hello?"

Nothing.

"Is anyone here?" he called, louder this time.

Silence.

Kevin descended the stairs and stepped cautiously into the living room. He ran over to the window and peered out. The familiar Lincoln was parked half a block down the street.

Something was wrong. Something had happened. He walked to his kitchen phone and instinctively felt for the cell phone in his right pocket. Still there. But something wasn't right. What?

The cell phone suddenly vibrated against his leg and he jumped. He shoved his hand back into the pocket and pulled out the silver phone. The other phone, the larger VTech, was in his left hand. For a moment he stared at them, confused. *Did I pick that up?* So many phones, his mind was playing tricks on him.

The cell vibrated madly. *Answer it!*

"Hello?"

Slater's voice ground in his ear. "Who thinks he's a butterfly but is really a worm?"

Kevin's breathing smothered the phone.

"You're pathetic, Kevin. Do you have knowledge of this obvious fact yet, or am I going to have to beat it out of you?" Slater breathed heavily. "I have someone here who wants to hold you and for the life of me I can't understand why."

Blood flushed Kevin's face. His throat felt as though it was locked in a vise. He couldn't speak.

"How long do you expect me to play tiddlywinks, Kevin? You're obviously too dense for the riddles, so I've decided to up the ante. I know how conflicted you are about Mommy, but by now I have it under reliable advisement that you aren't so conflicted about me. In fact, you hate me, don't you, Kevin? You should—I've destroyed your life."

"Stop it!" Kevin screamed.

"Stop it? Stop it? That's all you can manage? You're the only one with the power to stop anything. But I don't think you have the guts. You're as yellow as the rest of them; you've made that abundantly clear. So here's the new deal, Kevin. *You* come and stop me. Face to face, man to man. This is your big chance to blow away Slater with that peashooter you obtained illegally. Find me."

"Face me, you coward! Come out and face me!" Kevin shouted.

"Coward? I'm petrified. I can hardly move, much less face you." Pause. "Do I have to chisel it on your forehead? You find *me!* Find me, find me! The game ends in six hours, Kevin. Then I kill her. You fess up or I slit her throat. Are we properly motivated now?"

The detail about the six hours hardly registered. Slater wanted to meet him. Kevin shifted on his feet. He actually wanted to meet him. But where?

"How?"

"You know how. It's dark down here. Alone, Kevin. All alone, the way it was meant to be."

Click.

For an endless moment Kevin stood glued to the linoleum. Blood throbbed through his temples. The black VTech phone trembled in his left hand. He roared and slammed it on the counter with all of his strength. Black plastic splintered and scattered.

Kevin shoved the cell phone in his pocket, whirled around, and flew up the stairs. He'd hidden the gun under his mattress. Three bullets left. Two days earlier the thought of going after Slater would have terrified him; now he was consumed with the idea.

It's dark down here.

He shoved his hand under the mattress, pulled out the gun, and crammed it behind his belt. Dark. Down. *I've got a few ideas about dark and down, don't I? Where the worms hide their nasty little secrets. He knew, he knew!* Why hadn't he thought of this earlier? He had to get out unseen and he had to go alone. This was now between him and Slater. One on one, man on man.

The FBI car was still somewhere down the street. Kevin ran out the back and sprinted east, the opposite way. One block and then he cut south. They would know that he'd left. In fact, they would have recorded Slater's last call to him through the home surveillance. What if they came after him? He had to tell Jennifer to stay away. He could use the cell phone, but the call would have to be short, or they would triangulate his position.

If *dark* and *down* was where he thought it might be . . . Kevin ground his teeth and grunted. The man was a pervert. And he would kill Balinda—empty threats weren't part of his character.

What if the FBI sent out helicopters? He turned west and hugged a line of trees by the sidewalk. The gun jutted into his back.

He started to jog.

III

"Now! I need some facts now, not in ten minutes," Jennifer snapped.

Reports normally came in from Quantico at intervals established by the agents in charge. The next report window was in ten minutes, Galager had explained.

"I'll call, but they've only had the evidence for a few hours. This stuff can take up to a week."

"We don't have a week! Do they know what's happening down here? Tell them to turn on the television, for heaven's sake!"

Galager dipped his head and left.

Her world had collapsed with the call from Sam two minutes ago. She still didn't want to accept the possibility that Kevin could have blown up the bus or the library.

From her corner station Jennifer could see the exit across a sea of desks. Milton barged out of his office, grabbed his coat, and headed for the door. Where was he going? He paused, glancing back, and Jennifer instinctively turned her head to avoid eye contact. When she glanced back, he was gone. An inexplicable rage flashed through her mind. But really none of this was Milton's fault. He was simply doing his job. Sure he liked the cameras, but he arguably had a responsibility to the public. She was directing her frustration and anger at him without appropriate cause—she knew this but it didn't seem to calm her.

It wasn't Kevin, she reminded herself. Even if Kevin was Slater, which hasn't been established, the Kevin she knew wouldn't blow anything up. A jury would take one look at his past and agree. If Slater was Kevin, then he was part of a fractured personality, not Kevin himself.

A thought smacked her and she stopped. Could Slater be framing Kevin? What better way to drag the man down than to frame him as the lunatic who tried to blow up Long Beach? She sat behind the desk, grabbed a legal pad, and penciled it out.

Slater is the boy; he wants revenge. He terrorizes Kevin and then convinces the world that he is Kevin, terrorizing himself because he is Slater. Kevin is ruined and Slater escapes. It would raise the bar for perfect crimes.

But how could Slater pull that off? Sam had found *two* phones. Why would Kevin be carrying around two phones without knowing it? And how could the numbers that Slater called be on that second phone? An electronic relay that duplicated the numbers to make it look like the phone had been used. Possible. And how could Slater have placed the phone in Kevin's pocket without Kevin's knowledge?

It would have had to be while Kevin slept, this morning. Who had access to Kevin . . .

Her phone rang and she snatched it up without thinking.

"Jennifer."

"It's Claude, surveillance. We have a situation at the house. Someone just called Kevin."

"Who?" Jennifer stood, knocking her chair back.

Static. "Slater. We're pretty sure. But that's not all."

"Hold on. You have the recording from Kevin's cell phone?"

"No, we have a recording from inside the house. Someone who sounded like Slater called Kevin from *inside* Kevin's house. I . . . uh, I know it sounds strange, but we have both voices inside the house. I'm sending the recording down now. He threatened to kill the woman in six hours and suggested that Kevin meet him."

"Did he say where?"

"No. He said Kevin would know where. He said it was dark down here, that's it."

"Have you talked to Kevin?"

"We made the decision to enter premises." He paused. "Kevin was gone."

Jennifer collapsed in her chair. "You let him *walk?*"

Claude sounded flustered. "His car's still in the garage."

She closed her eyes and took a calming breath. What now? "I want that tape here now. Set up a search in concentric circles. He's on foot."

She dropped her phone on the table and closed her fingers to still a bad tremble. Her nerves were shot. Four days and how much sleep? Twelve, fourteen hours? The case had just gone from terrible to hopeless. He was going to kill Balinda. Inevitable. *Who* was going to kill Balinda? Slater? Kevin?

"Ma'am?"

She looked up to see one of Milton's detectives in the door. "I have a call for you. He says he tried your personal line but couldn't get through. Wouldn't give his name."

She nodded at the desk phone. "Put it through."

The call transferred and she picked up. "Peters."

"Jennifer?"

It was Kevin. Jennifer was too stunned to respond.

"Hello?"

"Where are you?"

"I'm sorry, Jennifer. I'm going after him. But I have to do this alone. If you come after me, he'll kill her. You're recording the house, right? Listen to the tape. I can't talk now, because they'll find me, but I wanted you to know." He sounded desperate.

"Kevin, you don't have to do this. Tell me where you are."

"I *do* have to do this. Listen to the tape. It's not what you think. Slater's doing this to me. Don't bother calling me; I'm throwing this phone away." He abruptly clicked off.

"Kevin?"

Jennifer slammed the phone in its cradle. She ran her hands through her hair and picked up the phone again. She dialed Samantha's number.

"Hello?"

"Kevin's gone, Sam," Jennifer said. "He just received a call from Slater threatening to kill Balinda in six hours. He baited Kevin to meet him, said he would know where and that it was dark. As far as I know, that's it. The tape's on the way down."

"He's on foot? How could they let him walk out?"

"I don't know. The point is, we're now on a very tight time line and we've lost contact."

"Slater's cell—"

"He said he was getting rid of it."

"I'll go back," Sam said. "He can't get far."

"Assuming you're right about Kevin, Slater's drawing him to a place they must both know from their childhood. Any ideas?"

Sam hesitated. "The warehouse?"

"We'll check it out, but it's too obvious."

"Let me think about it. If we're lucky, we pick him up. Concentrate the search to the west—closer to Baker Street."

"There's another possibility, Sam. I know it may sound like a stretch, but what if Slater's framing Kevin?"

The phone was quiet.

"Forensics will give us a better picture, but the cell could have been planted and the call log duplicated by relay. The objective fits: Kevin is branded a psychopath who terrorized himself, he's ruined, and Slater skips free. Childhood grudge revenged."

"What a tangled web we weave," Sam said quietly. "Get the data on the recordings; hopefully it'll tell us more."

"I'm working on it." Galager walked in and sat down, file in hand. Jennifer stood. "Call me if you think of anything."

"One last thing," Sam said. "I talked to Dr. John Francis and he mentioned that you'd spoken to him already, but you might want to consider breaking this down with him. He knows Kevin well and he's in your field. Just a thought."

"Thank you, I will."

She set the phone down. Galager was back. "Well?"

"Like I said, not done. But I do have something. Ever hear of a seismic tuner?"

"A what?"

"Seismic tuner. A device that alters voice patterns."

"Okay."

"Well, I could record my voice and program this thing to match it to yours."

"So? The sample we sent them of Kevin's voice sounds nothing like Slater's—what's your point?"

"I talked to Carl Riggs at the lab. He says that even if they do determine that both Slater's voice and Kevin's voice have the same vocal patterns, someone who knew what they were doing could manufacture the effect with a seismic tuner."

"I'm not following. Bottom line, Galager." Her frustration was overflowing now.

"Bottom line is that Slater could have altered his voice to make it sound like a derivative of Kevin's voice. He could have obtained a sample of Kevin's voice, broken it down electronically, and then reproduced its vocal patterns at a different range and with different inflections. In other words, he could be speaking through a box that makes it sound like he's Kevin, trying not to be Kevin. Follow?"

"Knowing that we would analyze the recording and conclude that both voices were Kevin's." She blinked.

"Correct. Even though they aren't."

"As in, if he wanted to frame Kevin."

"A possibility. Riggs said there's an open case in Florida where a guy's wife was kidnapped for a ransom of a million dollars. The community came together in a fund drive and raised the money. But it turns out the kidnapper's voice was a recording of the husband's, manipulated by a seismic tuner. He evidently kidnapped his own wife. It's going to trial next month."

"I didn't know there was such a thing as a seismic tuner."

"There wasn't until about a year ago." Galager stood. "Either way, even if both voiceprints match Kevin's, we won't know if both really are his until we rule out the use of a seismic tuner. Riggs won't have the voice report until tomorrow. They're on it, but it takes time."

"And the shoe prints?"

"Should have that this evening, but he doesn't think it'll help us either. Not distinctive enough."

"So what you're telling me is that none of this matters?"

"I'm telling you none of this may matter. In the end."

He left and Jennifer sagged into her chair. Milton. She would have to depend on him now. She needed every available patrol car in the city to join the search for Kevin, and she needed the search conducted without risking a leak to the media.

Jennifer closed her eyes. Actually, none of that mattered. What mattered was the fact that Kevin was lost. The boy was lost.

She suddenly wanted to cry.

24

KEVIN KEPT TO THE SIDE STREETS, jogging as naturally as he could despite the pounding in his head.

When cars or pedestrians approached, he either changed directions or crossed the street. At the least lowered his head. If he had the luxury of a direct route, the crosstown jog would be half what it was with all of his side jaunts.

But Slater had said alone, which meant avoiding the authorities at all costs. Jennifer would have the cops out in force this time. She would be desperate to find him before he found Slater because she knew that Kevin didn't stand a chance against Slater.

Kevin knew it too.

He ran with the dread knowledge that there was no way he could face Slater and survive. Balinda would die; he would die. But he had no choice. Although he thought he'd freed himself, he'd really been slumping around in that dungeon of the past for twenty years. No longer. He would face Slater head-on and live, or die in this last-ditch effort to reach freedom.

What about Jennifer? And Sam? He would lose them, wouldn't he? The best things in his life—the only things that mattered now— would be ripped away by Slater. And if he found a way to escape Slater this time, the man would be back to hunt him down again. No, he had to end this once and for all. He had to kill or be killed.

Kevin swallowed hard and ran on through unsuspecting residential neighborhoods. Helicopters chopped through the sky. He couldn't quickly differentiate the police from others, so he hid from them all, which slowed his progress even more. Eleven police cars crossed his path, each time forcing him to alter direction. He ran for one hour and still was only halfway there. He grunted and pushed on. The hour stretched into two. With every step, his determination increased until he could almost taste his bitterness toward Slater, the coppery taste of blood on his dry tongue.

The warehouse district dawned on him without warning. Kevin slowed to a walk. His wet shirt clung to his torso. He was close. His heart began to pound, as much from his nerves as from exertion now.

Five P.M. Slater had given them six hours. Three plus three. The ultimate in this sick little game of threes. By now the whole city would be on a desperate manhunt to find Balinda before the nine o'clock deadline. The FBI would have listened to the surveillance from the house and, with Sam, they would be pounding their collective skulls against the wall trying to decode Slater's cryptic message. *You'll know, Kevin. It's dark down here.*

Would Sam figure it out? He'd never told her about the place.

Kevin crossed railroad tracks and slipped into a patch of trees sequestered away here on the outskirts of the city. Close. So close.

You're going to die, Kevin. His skin felt like a pincushion. He stopped and looked around. The city noise sounded distant. Birds chirped. A lizard scurried over dead leaves to his right, stopped, craned a bulging eye for a view of him, and then darted for the rocks.

Kevin walked forward. What if he was wrong? It could have been the warehouse where he'd trapped the boy, of course—that was dark down here. But Slater would never be so obvious. Cops would be crawling all over the place, anyway. No, this had to be it.

He caught sight of the old toolshed through the trees and stopped.

What little paint remained flaked gray with age. Suddenly Kevin wasn't sure he could go through with it. Slater was probably hidden behind one of the trees at this very moment, watching. What if he did run, and Slater stepped out from his hiding place and shot him? He couldn't call for help—he'd dumped the cell phone in an alley behind a 7-Eleven five miles east.

Didn't matter. He had to do this. The gun dug into his belly where he'd moved it when it rubbed him raw at his back. He touched it through his shirt. Should he pull it out now?

He eased the gun from his belt and walked forward. The shack sat undisturbed, hardly more than an outhouse. Breathing deliberately through his nose, Kevin approached the rear door, eyes glued to the boards, the cracks between them, searching for a sign of movement. Anything.

You're going to die in there, Kevin.

He crept up to the door. For a moment he stood there, shaking badly. To his right, deep tire marks ran through the soft earth. A rusted Master Lock padlock hung from the latch, gaping. Open. It was never open.

He eased the lock out of the latch and set it on the ground. Put his hand on the handle and pulled gently. The door creaked. He stopped. A small gap showed pitch-blackness inside.

Dear God, what am I doing? Give me strength. Did the light even work anymore?

Kevin pulled the door open. The shack was empty. *Thank God.*

You came to find him, and now you're thanking God that he isn't here?

But if he's here, he's under that trapdoor, down the stairs, through the tunnel. That's where "dark down here" is, isn't it?

He stepped in and pulled a chain that hung from a single light bulb. The bulb glowed weakly, like a dim lounge lamp. Kevin closed the door. It took him a full five minutes, trembling in the dim yellow light, to work up enough courage to pull the trapdoor open.

Wood steps descended into black. There were footprints on the steps.

Kevin swallowed.

III

A mood of pending doom had settled over the conference room and two adjacent offices in the Long Beach police headquarters where Jennifer and the other FBI agents had worked feverishly over the past four days.

Two hours of methodical searching, both on the ground and from the air, had turned up nothing. If Slater's *dark down here* place was the warehouse cellar, he would walk in to find two uniformed policemen with weapons drawn. Sam had called in twice, the last time after giving up her ground search. She wanted to check into something that she didn't elaborate on. Said she would call back. That was an hour ago.

The forensic report on the shoe prints had come in—inconclusive. Jennifer had retraced every detail of the past four days, scrutinizing them for clues to which of the two new theories held more water. Either Kevin was Slater, or Slater was framing Kevin by seeding evidence to make it appear that he was Slater.

If Kevin really was Slater, then at least they had their man. No more games for Slater. No more victims. Unless Slater killed Kevin, which would be tantamount to suicide. Or unless Slater killed Balinda. Then they'd have two dead bodies lying in a place that's dark down here. Even if Slater didn't kill Balinda, Kevin would have to live with what he did as Slater for the rest of his life. The thought brought a lump to Jennifer's throat.

If Slater were someone else, Kevin would merely be the poor victim of a horrible plot. Unless he was killed by Slater, in which case he'd be the dead victim of a horrible plot.

The clock ticked on. 5:30. Jennifer picked up the cell phone and called Sam.

"Sam, we're dead down here. We don't have a thing. The shoe prints came back inconclusive. Please tell me you have something."

"I was just going to call. Have you talked to John Francis yet?"

"No. Why?"

"I've been at Kevin's house digging through his writings, papers, books, anything where he might have made reference to his past, a clue to a place that's dark. I knew Kevin was intelligent, but I never expected quite this—mind blowing. No obvious references at all to Slater or anything that even hints at multiple personalities."

"Which could support our theory that he was framed," Jennifer said.

"Maybe. But I did find this in a periodic journal he keeps on his computer. Listen. Written two weeks ago.

"'The problem with most of the best thinkers is that they dissociate their reasoning from spirituality, as if the two exist in separate realities. Not so. It's a false dichotomy. No one understands this more than Dr. John Francis. I feel like I can trust him. He alone truly understands me. I told him about the secret today. I miss Samantha. She called . . .'"

"It continues about me," Sam said. "The point is, I think Dr. John Francis may know more than he may realize."

"The *secret*," Jennifer said. "Could be a reference to something he never told you. A place he knew as a child."

"I want to talk to him, Jennifer."

It was the only glimmer of light Jennifer had seen in two hours. "You have his address?"

"Yes."

Jennifer grabbed her coat. "I'll meet you there in twenty minutes."

|||

The descent into the bomb shelter and through the tunnel had wrung a gallon of sweat from Kevin's glands. The door at the bottom of the stairwell into the basement stood wide open. Kevin leaned forward and peered into the room for the first time in twenty years, numb on his feet.

A shiny black floor with patches of concrete showing through. A chest freezer to the right, next to a white stove and a sink. A metal desk to the left, piled with electronics. Boxes of dynamite, a file cabinet, a mirror. Two doors that led . . . somewhere.

Kevin held the gun out with both hands, breathless. Sweat stung his eyes. This was it! Had to be. But the room was empty! Where was Slater?

Something bumped against the door to his right and Kevin jerked the gun toward it. Gray carpet had been rolled and stuffed into the crack at its base.

Thump, thump, thump. A muffled cry.

Kevin's body went rigid.

"Is someone there?" He could barely make out the words. "Pleeeease!"

Balinda. The room started to move. He shoved a foot forward and steadied himself. Frantic, he searched the room again. Where was Slater?

"Pleeeease, please." She sounded like a mouse. Kevin took another step. Then another, gun wavering before him.

"I don't want to die," the voice wept. "Please, please, I'll do anything."

"Balinda?" Kevin's voice cracked. The sounds stopped. A thick silence settled.

Kevin struggled to breathe. Slater had left Balinda here for him to find. He wanted Kevin to save his mommy, because that's what little boys do for their mommies. He had deserted her, and now he would rescue her to make up for the horrible sin. Kevin's world started to spin.

"Kevin?" The voice whimpered. "Kevin?"

"Mommy?"

Something scraped the concrete behind him. He whirled, gun extended.

A man stepped out of the dark shadows, sneering. Blond hair. *No shirt.* Beige slacks. White tennis shoes. *No shirt.* A tattoo of a heart over his left breast with the word *Mom* stenciled in black. He held a large silver gun at his side. *No shirt.* His naked torso struck Kevin as obscene. Slater, in the flesh.

"Hello, Kevin," Slater said. "I'm so glad you found us." He edged to his right.

Kevin followed him with the gun, finger tightening. *Do it! Shoot. Pull the trigger.*

"I wouldn't shoot just yet, Kevin. Not until I tell you how you can save Mommy. Because I swear if you kill me now, she's dead meat. Do you want Mommy to be dead meat?" Slater grinned and moved around slowly, gun still at his side. "Well, yes, I suppose you might want Mommy to be dead meat. That would be understandable."

A fist thumped into the door. "Kevin! Help me!" Balinda's muffled voice cried.

"Shut up, witch!" Slater yelled, face flushed red. He caught himself and smiled. "Tell her it isn't real, Kevin. That the darkness isn't really dark. Tell her that if she's a good girl, you'll let her out. Isn't that what she told you?"

"How do you know me?" Kevin asked, voice cracking.

"You don't recognize me?" Slater exposed his forehead with his left hand. "I had the tattoo removed."

He was the boy, but Kevin already knew that. "But . . . how do you know about Balinda? What are you doing?"

"You still don't get it, do you?" Slater edged closer to the door Balinda was thumping on. "Four days of crystal-clear clues and you still are as stupid as you look. Do you know how long I've waited for this? Hmm? Planned for this. It's brilliant. Even if you think you know, you don't. Nobody will know. Ever. That's the beauty of it."

Slater giggled. His face twitched.

"Drop the gun," Kevin said. He had to know what Slater meant. He wanted to shoot the man. He wanted to send a piece of lead through his forehead, but he wanted to know what Slater was saying.

"Drop the gun."

Slater reached for the doorknob, twisted it, pushed the door open. Balinda sat on the floor, hands bound behind her back, foot against the door. Slater calmly pointed his pistol at her white, stricken face.

"Sorry, Kevin," Slater said. "Toss me the peashooter, or I shoot Mommy."

What? Kevin felt his face flush with heat. He could still shoot and Slater would be dead before he could kill Balinda.

"Drop it!" Slater said. "I've got this trigger milled down to a hair. You shoot me and my finger twitches and she's dead."

Balinda started to cry. "Kevin . . . honey . . ."

"Now! Now, now, now!"

Kevin lowered the gun slowly.

"I know how fond you are of it, but when I say drop, I really do mean drop. Now!"

Kevin dropped the gun and stepped back, panicked.

Slater slammed the door shut on Balinda, stepped forward, and scooped up the gun. "Good boy. Mommy will be proud of you." He shoved Kevin's gun into his own belt, walked toward the door to the stairwell, and shut it.

"There."

Balinda's feet thumped the door again. "Kevin? Pleeeease . . ."

"Ahhhhh!" Slater screamed and ran at the door. He kicked it hard enough to put a dent in the steel. "Shut up! One more peep and I'll staple your mouth shut!"

Slater stood back, panting. Balinda quieted.

"Don't you hate these women who don't know how to keep their yappers shut?" Slater turned around. "Now, where were we?"

A strange resolve settled over Kevin. He was going to die down here after all. He really had nothing to lose. The twisted boy had grown up into a pathetic monster. Slater would kill both him and Balinda without a fleeting thought of remorse.

"You're sick," Kevin said.

"Now there's a novel thought. Actually, you're the sick one. That's what they suspect now and, believe me, by the time I'm done here, they won't have any reason to think differently."

"You're wrong. You've already proved your insanity. You've torn this city to shreds and now you've kidnapped an innocent—"

"Innocent? Hardly, but that's not the point. The point is, *you* kidnapped her." Slater grinned wide.

"You're not making sense."

"Of course not. I'm not making any sense to you because you're not thinking. You and I both know that I did all those nasty things. That Slater called Kevin, and Slater blew up the bus, and Slater is holding the old witch in a cement box. Problem is, they think that Kevin is Slater. And if they don't yet, they will soon enough. Kevin is Slater because Kevin is crazy." Grin. "That's the plan, puke."

Kevin stared, mind numb. "That's . . . that's not possible."

"Actually, it is. Which is why it'll work. You don't think I'd go for something implausible, do you?"

"How could I be you?"

"Multiple Personality Disorder. MPD. You're me without even knowing that you are me."

Kevin shook his head. "You're actually stupid enough to think that Jennifer—"

"Sam believes it." Slater walked over to the desk and touched a black box that looked like an answering machine. He'd lowered the pistol to his side, and Kevin wondered if he could rush him before he had a chance to lift it and shoot.

"She found the cell phone I used in your pocket—that alone's enough for most juries. But they'll find more. The recordings, for instance. They'll show that my voice is really your voice, manipulated to sound like a terrible killer named Slater." Slater feigned horror and shivered. "Oooo . . . chilling, don't you think?"

"There are a thousand holes! You'll never get away with it."

"There are no holes!" Slater snapped. Then he grinned again. "And I already *am* getting away with it."

He picked up a picture. It was a photograph of Sam, taken at a distance with a telephoto lens. "She's really quite beautiful," he said, lost in the image for a moment. He reached up and ripped down a large black sheet that hung on the wall. Behind it, fifty or sixty pictures had been affixed to the concrete.

They were all of Samantha.

Kevin blinked and took a step forward. Slater's gun came up. "Stay back."

Pictures of Sam on the street, New York, Sacramento, through a window, in her bedroom . . . Heat spread down Kevin's neck.

"What are you doing?"

"I wanted to kill her once." Slater slowly faced Kevin, eyes sagging. "But you know that. You wanted her, so you tried to kill me instead."

Slater's lips began to quiver and his breathing came in short quick drags. "Well, now I *am* going to kill her. And I'm going to show the world who you really are, because you're no better than I am. You're the pretty boy down the street she loves to play with. But does that make you better? No!" He screamed the last word and Kevin jumped.

"Hang out with me for a while and we'll see how sweet you are." He leaned forward and tapped Kevin's chest with the gun barrel.

"Deep down inside you're no different than I am. If you'd met me before you met Samantha, we'd both have been at her window, licking the glass. I know that, because I was just like you once."

"That's what this is about?" Kevin demanded. "A jealous schoolboy come back to butcher the boy across the street? You're pathetic!"

"And so are you! You're sick like the rest of them." Slater spat a thimbleful of saliva at the cement. It landed with a smack. "Sick!" He took two steps forward and shoved the gun into Kevin's cheek. Pain flashed up his jaw. "I should just end this now. You and all the freaks who pretend to be so sweet on Sundays! You may not be me but really you are me, you slug."

Slater's body shook against Kevin's.

Kevin's mind began to shut down. *You're going to die, Kevin.*

III

Slater fights a desperate urge to pull the trigger. He knows that he can't do it. This isn't the plan. Not this way. Not yet.

He stares at Kevin's round eyes. The smell of fear and sweat wafts through his nostrils. Impulsively he sticks out his tongue and presses it firmly against Kevin's jaw. He draws it all the way up his cheek to his temple, as if he's licking an ice-cream cone. Salty. Bitter. Sick, sick, sick.

Slater shoves Kevin and steps back. "Know what I taste? I taste Slater. I'm going to kill her, Kevin. I'm going to kill both of them. But that's not what the world will think. They're going to think that you did it."

Kevin straightens and glares at him. The man has more spunk than Slater estimated. Enough to come here, he'd guessed as much. But he can't forget that this man also locked him in that cellar once, when he was still a boy. They might be more alike than even Slater realizes.

He takes a deep breath. "Now, let's calm down, shall we? I have a new game I would like to play."

"I'm not going to play any more games," Kevin says.

"Yes, you are. You'll play more games or I'll cut up Mommy, one finger at a time."

Kevin glances at the door that holds the old woman.

"And if we still aren't properly motivated, I'll start on *your* fingers. Are we still all stuffed and cocky?"

Kevin just stares at him. At least he isn't whimpering and crying like the old hag.

"Let's face it, Kevin. You came here with one thing on your mind. You wanted to kill. Kill, kill, kill. That's another way you and I are alike." Slater shrugs. "True, the object of your blood lust is me, but when you cut away all the face-saving, it's the same instinct. Most humans are truly murderers, but I didn't bring you here to lecture. I brought you here to kill. I'm going to give you your wish. You came to kill me, but that doesn't suit my tastes, so I've chosen to flip things a bit."

Kevin doesn't flinch.

"We already have one, but we need the other." Slater looks at the wall, the collage of pictures. It's in part her beauty that he hates so much. It's why he keeps the photographs covered. By nine o'clock she will be dead.

"Kill me," Kevin says. "I hate you." He speaks the last words with such contempt that Slater feels a sliver of shock.

But Slater doesn't show shock. He shows anger and hatred, but not shock, because shock is weakness.

"So courageous. So noble. How can I refuse such a sincere request? Consider yourself dead already. We all die; yours will be a living death until you finally do kick the bucket. In the meantime, we must lure in our second victim. She will fly to your rescue. Her knight is in peril."

"I despise you."

"You will help me or Mommy will begin to scream!" Slater says.

Kevin glares at him and then closes his eyes slowly.

"Just a simple call, Kevin. I would do it, but I really need her to hear your voice."

Kevin shakes his head and is about to speak, but Slater doesn't want to hear it. He steps forward and slams the gun against the side of Kevin's head.

"I'll kill her, you perverted little brat!"

Blood oozes down Kevin's face. This excites Slater.

Kevin's face wrinkles and he begins to cry. Better, much better. He sinks slowly to his knees and for the first time since his nemesis entered the room, Slater knows he will win.

III

Samantha raced through Long Beach. Secret. What secret? Kevin had hidden his dealing with Slater as a boy and he'd remained quiet about his home life, but the journal entry had to be something else. Something the professor knew.

She was a block away when her cell phone rang. She couldn't imagine how investigators had managed before the advent of cellular technology. On the other hand, criminals took advantage as well. Slater certainly had.

"Sam."

"This is Kevin."

"Kevin!"

" . . . no one else. Do you understand?" His voice sounded flat—horrible. He was reading, being forced. Sam veered for the curb, ignoring a honk behind.

"Kevin, if you're with Slater keep talking and don't cough. If you're not, cough. Yes, I do understand." Actually, she'd missed what she was supposed to understand. And she quickly considered asking him to repeat it, but that might endanger him.

Kevin didn't cough.

"We're playing a new game," he said. "This game's for you, Sam. If you can find us before nine, he'll set me and Mommy free." His voice wavered. She heard a muffled voice in the background. Slater.

"I will give you the first clue. If you find it, there will be another one. No authorities can be involved, including that wench, Jennifer." Slater chuckled in the background. His voice suddenly filled the phone, loud and eager.

"First clue: *Who loves what he sees, but hates what he loves?* You might find a clue in his house; you might not. Hurry to the rescue, Princess." The phone went dead.

"Slater? Kevin!" Sam threw the phone against the windshield. "Aaaahh!"

Who loves what he sees, but hates what he loves? Her mind was blank. 6:27. Less than three hours. She had to get back to Kevin's house. The answers had to be in his papers. His journal. Somewhere!

She roared through a U-turn and headed back north. What was the chance that Slater had found a way to monitor her phone calls? If he knew electronics well enough to pull off a frame on Kevin, he knew more than she. No authorities involved, he'd said.

Sam bent for her cell on the floor and swerved badly enough to force a second attempt. She caught the phone, fumbled with the battery, which had jarred loose. Power on. Redial.

|||

"Thank you again for your time, Dr. Francis. As I explained on the phone—"

"Yes, yes, of course." The professor waved her in. "Please come in, dear. Believe me, I will do whatever I can for that boy."

Jennifer paused. "You understand why I'm here? It seems that you know more about Kevin than you first suggested. At least Kevin believes you do."

"I know him better than most, yes. But nothing that I haven't told you."

"That's what we're going to find out. With your help." She stepped into the house. "We're running out of time, Professor. If you can't help us, I'm afraid no one will be able to. You talked to Samantha Sheer from CBI earlier today; she'll be here shortly." Her cell went off and she pulled it from her waist. "Excuse me."

It was Sam. She'd heard from Kevin. Jennifer instinctively turned back toward the door and listened while Sam ran through the details.

"So you're headed *back* to the house?"

"Yes. Review the clue with Dr. Francis. *Who loves what he sees, but hates what he loves?* You got it? Review *everything* with him. He has to know something."

"I have to report this."

"Slater said no cops, and he mentioned you by name. You won't be out of the loop. Just stay where you are. Don't brief Milton. Let me work alone; that's all I ask. If you think of anything, call me. But this is between us now. Kevin, Slater, and me. Please, Jennifer."

Jennifer hesitated. "Okay. I'll give you an hour. Then I call this in, understood? I'm over my head here."

"I'll call you."

"One hour." She closed the cell.

"Anything wrong?" Dr. Francis asked.

"Everything's wrong, Doctor."

25

WHO LOVES WHAT HE SEES, but hates what he loves?"
Dr. Francis said. "Every man, every woman, every child
beyond the age of accountability."

"He loves the ice cream, but hates the fat it puts on his waist,"
Jennifer said.

"Yes. She loves the wrong man, but hates what he does to her life.
The dilemma goes back to Eve and the apple in the garden. Sin."

"I don't see how that helps us," Jennifer said. "The reference has
to be personal, something that only Sam or Kevin might know.
Something the three of them knew when they were children."

"Three children? Or two? Sam and Kevin, who had his alter
ego—the boy?" Dr. Francis sat in a large leather recliner and leaned
forward. "Tell me everything. From the beginning. Time is slipping."

He listened, eyes sparkling, with only the occasional frown to
betray his anxiety over Kevin's predicament. In many ways he reminded Jennifer of Kevin, genuine to the bone and thoroughly
intelligent. It was the first time she'd run through the last four days
aloud and with such comprehensive minutiae with anyone except
Galager. The first call, the car bomb, the second call regarding the
doghouse. Then the bus, Kevin's flight with Sam to Palos Verdes, the
warehouse, the library, the kidnapping, and now this death threat.

She told it all in one long run-on, interrupted only by his prodding for further detail. He was a thinker, among the best, and he seemed to like playing detective. So did most people. His questions were insightful. How do you know that Kevin was inside his house when the second phone call was made? Is there a way to intercept a laser signal? All the questions lent themselves to whether Kevin could logically be Slater.

Twenty minutes and Sam still hadn't called. Jennifer stood and paced, hand on chin. "I can't believe it's coming down to this. Kevin's out there somewhere in the dark with a madman and we're . . ." She ran her hands through her hair. "It's been like that since I got down here. Slater's always one step ahead, and we're running around like a bunch of toy monkeys."

"You remind me of Kevin when you do that."

He was looking at her hands, still in her hair. She sat down on the couch and sighed. "So now I'm Kevin as well."

He chuckled. "Hardly. But I do agree that the primary question is who, not what. Who is Kevin? Really."

"And?"

He leaned back and crossed his legs. "Multiple Personality Disorder. It's referred to as Dissociative Identity Disorder these days, isn't it? Where two or more personalities inhabit a single body. As you know, not everyone acknowledges such an animal. Some spiritualize the phenomenon—demon possession. Others discount it outright or think of it as commonplace, a gift even."

"And you?"

"While I do believe in spiritual forces and even demon possession, I can assure you that Kevin is not possessed. I've spent many hours with the boy, and my own spirit isn't so callous. The fact of the matter is, all of us experience some level of dissociation, more so with age. We suddenly forget why we walked into the bathroom. Or we have strange déjà vu. Daydreaming, highway hypnosis, even losing yourself in a book or movie. All forms of dissociation that are thoroughly natural."

"A far cry from the kind of dissociation that would be required for Kevin to be Slater," Jennifer said. "As you said, you've spent time with him, so have I. Kevin doesn't have a trace of Slater in him. If both personalities share the same body, they are completely unaware of each other."

"*If.* That is the operative word here. If Kevin is also Slater. Frankly, your theory that Slater may be framing Kevin makes as much sense. But . . ." Dr. Francis stood and paced to the fireplace and back. "But let's assume Kevin is Slater for the moment. What if there was a child, a boy, who from a very young age was isolated from the real world."

"Kevin."

"Yes. What would that child learn?"

"He would learn whatever he was taught from his surroundings: the environment he could touch, taste, hear, smell, see. If he were alone on an island, he would think the world was a small piece of dirt floating on the water, and he would wonder why he didn't have fur like the rest of his playmates. Like Tarzan."

"Yes, but our child does not grow up on an island. He grows up in a world of shifting realities. A world where realities are merely slips of paper cut up into truth. There are no absolutes. There is no evil and, by extension, there is no good. Everything is pretend, and only that which you decide to be real is actually real. Life is merely a string of role-playing adventures."

Dr. Frances lifted his hand to his beard and pulled lightly at the gray strands. "But there *is* an absolute, you see. There is good and there is evil. The boy feels a void in his soul. He longs for an understanding of those absolutes, good and evil. He is abused in the most mentally strenuous ways, causing his mind to separate into dissociative realities. He becomes a master role-player, and finally, when he is old enough to understand evil, he subconsciously creates a personality to play the part. Because that's what he's learned to do."

"The boy. Slater."

"A walking, living personification of man's dual nature. The natures of man could be playing themselves out through personalities he's created. It does follow, doesn't it?"

"Assuming man has more than one nature. It could also be a simple fracture—common dissociation."

"Man does have more than one nature," the professor said. "The 'old man,' which is our flesh, and the fingerprint of God, the good."

"And for those of us who don't necessarily believe in the spirit of God? Who aren't religious?"

"A person's inner natures have nothing to do with religion. They are spiritual, not religious. Two natures battling. Good and evil. They are the good that we would do but do not do, and they are that which we would not do, but still do. The apostle Paul. Romans chapter seven. The capacity for good and evil is within every person from birth, I think. The spirit of God can regenerate man, but it is the human spirit I'm talking about here. Not a separate nature, although I would say that the struggle between good and evil is hopeless without divine intervention. Perhaps that's what you think of when you say 'religious,' although really religion has little to do with divine intervention either."

He offered a quick smile. For the second time in as many days he was tempting her to discover his faith. Right now, however, she didn't have the time.

"So you're thinking Kevin, as a young boy, simply struggled to make sense of the conflict within him, between basic good and evil. He dealt with it the way he learned to deal with all reality. He creates roles for each persona and plays them out without knowing that he's doing it."

"Yes, that's exactly what I'm thinking," the professor said, standing and pacing to his right. "It's possible. Entirely possible. It may not even be classical Dissociative Identity Disorder. Could be Post-traumatic Stress Disorder, which is even more likely for this kind of unconscious role-playing."

"Assuming Kevin is Slater."

"Yes, assuming Kevin is Slater."

| | |

Sam poured through Kevin's journal, searching desperately for a key to the riddle. *Who loves what he sees, but hates what he loves?* When that yielded no answer, she paged through his class notebooks.

The most obvious answer was mankind, of course. Mankind looks and sees and loves and then hates. The story of humanity in one sentence. Not quite up there with Descartes's "I think therefore I am," but obvious enough.

Who loves what he sees, but hates what he loves? Who, who? Slater. Slater was who. Despite Jennifer's theory, Kevin had to be Slater. If so, Slater was the hater of the two.

She sighed. Something common to all three of them triggered this riddle. But what? She had only two hours to win this mad game. And even if she did find them, Slater surely wouldn't let them all go. Someone would die in the next two hours. Kevin had saved her from the killer once; he'd risked his life. Now it was her turn.

6:59. And this riddle was only the first clue.

She mumbled through gritted teeth. "Come on, Kevin! Tell me something."

| | |

"Then Slater's the boy, stalking Sam, but he's really Kevin's evil alter ego," Jennifer said.

"And Kevin doesn't like the evil boy, so he kills him," the professor said.

"But isn't that evil? To kill?"

"God killed a few men in their time. Read the Old Testament. Kevin tries to kill the boy because the boy threatens to kill his childhood friend."

"But the boy is really Kevin. So Kevin would have killed Samantha if he hadn't dealt with the boy?"

"Think of it—a personality that embodies only evil would be quite a little monster. Slater, the evil in Kevin, sees that Samantha favored Kevin over him. Slater decides he must kill Sam."

"And now that monster has come back to life and is stalking Kevin," Jennifer said. "In this scenario of yours."

"That monster never died. That would require more than Kevin was capable of on his own. Death to the old self." Dr. Francis paused and then continued. "As Kevin matured, he recognized Balinda's folly, but he didn't recognize his dual nature. He did, however, successfully climb out of his past, leave the house, and embrace the real world."

"Until three months of seminary and discussions of his one obsession, the natures of man, finally brings Slater back to the surface," Jennifer finished.

The professor lifted an eyebrow. "It's possible."

As a clinical theory the possibilities were interesting, but Jennifer was having difficulty accepting it as reality. Theories abounded in the study of the mind, a new one every month, it seemed. This was a theory. And time was still ticking away, while the real Kevin possibly sat at the real Slater's gunpoint, praying desperately for someone to burst through the doors and save him.

"But why the game? Why the riddles?"

"I don't know." His eyes glimmered mischievously. "Perhaps the whole thing was really Kevin's idea."

"I don't follow."

"Evil only survives in the dark. This isn't religious either, by the way. The simplest way to deal with evil is to force it into the light of truth. Expose its secret. Sun on the vampire. Sin thrives in the dungeon, but slap it on the table for all to see, and it withers rather quickly. It was one of Kevin's greatest complaints about the church, actually. That everyone hides their evil. Their sin. Pastors, deacons, bishops—they perpetuate the very nature they are in business to destroy by covering it up. No confession allowed except in secret."

"Now you sound like a skeptic."

"I'm a skeptic of religious systems, not of the faith. Someday I will be happy to discuss the difference with you."

"How does this make the riddles Kevin's idea?"

"Perhaps subconsciously Kevin knows that Slater still lurks. What better way to destroy him than to expose him? Kevin could be forcing Slater's hand, forcing him to reveal himself. Ha! I'm telling you, Kevin is genuine enough to conceive of just such a plan! Slater thinks he has Kevin where he wants him by forcing a confession, when it's the very confession that will destroy Slater, not Kevin! It's like the cross all over again."

Jennifer rubbed her temples. "I can just hear the court case now. This all assumes Slater isn't framing Kevin."

"Yes. But either way, we've pieced together his framework. At least the logic of it." Dr. Francis sat and faced her with his fingers touching each other in a tepee. "My goodness. You came here to find out who Kevin really is. I think I've just stumbled on it, my dear."

"Tell me, who is Kevin?"

"Kevin is every man. And woman. He is you; he is me; he is the woman who wears a yellow hat and sits on the third pew every Sunday. Kevin is the natures of humanity personified."

"Please, you can't mean that everyone's a Slater."

"No, only those who do as Slater does. Only those who hate. Do you hate, Jennifer? Do you gossip?"

| | |

Who loves what he sees, but hates what he loves? The simplicity of it hit Sam midstride, as she paced Kevin's living room, staring at the travel posters. The windows to the world. It wasn't *who;* it was the *seeing!* Who had *seen?* Slater had seen her and wanted her. But where had he seen her?

The window. Her window! The boy Slater had watched her from the window and seen what he desperately wanted but could not have. And he hated her.

The answer to the riddle was her window!

Sam stood still, stunned, then ran for her car. She fired the engine and roared down the street. 7:23.

Sam punched in Jennifer's cell number.

"This is—"

"I think I have it! I'm on my way now."

"What is it?" Jennifer demanded.

Sam hesitated. "This is for me—"

"Just tell me where, for heaven's sake! I know it's for you, but time's running out here!"

"The window."

"Kevin's window?"

"My window. That's where Slater saw me. That's where he hated me." She glanced in her rearview mirror. Clear. "I need more time, Jennifer. If Slater even gets a whiff of anyone else snooping around this, he may pull the trigger. You know that."

No response.

"Please, Jennifer, there's no other way."

"We could have a dozen of the best minds on this."

"Then get them on it. But no one from the investigation and, without question, no locals. We can't risk a leak. Besides, no one's going to know these riddles like I do. This is about me now."

Silence.

"Jennifer—"

"Just hurry, Samantha."

"I'm doing sixty in a thirty-five as it is." She hung up.

Hold on, Kevin. Please don't do anything stupid. Wait for me. I'm coming. I swear I'm coming.

26

WHETHER THE BOY WAS IMAGINARY OR REAL, he knew Sam and he wants her to come," Dr. Francis said as Jennifer closed her phone. "He's luring her in. You see that, don't you? The riddles are only to continue the game."

Jennifer sighed. "And if Sam finds them? He'll kill them all and I'll have done nothing."

"What can you do?"

"Something. Anything! If I can't save him, then I should report this."

"Then report it. But what can any of your colleagues do?"

He was right, of course, but the idea of sitting here in his living room discussing the natures of man was . . . impossible! Roy had been killed in similar circumstances by the Riddle Killer. True, Slater probably wasn't the same man who'd killed Roy, but he represented the same kind of man. Unless Kevin was Slater.

Did Slater live in her? Do you hate, Jennifer? Milton?

"Perhaps the most you can do is try to understand, so that if an opportunity does come, you're better equipped," the professor said. "I know how frustrating it must be, but now it's up to Sam. She sounds like someone who can handle herself. If I'm right, Kevin will need her."

"How so?"

"If Kevin is Slater, he'll be powerless to overcome Slater on his own."

Jennifer looked at him and wondered what movies he watched.

"Okay, Professor. We still don't know if Kevin is Slater or not. Theories are fine, but let's try the logistics on for size." She pulled out her notebook and crossed her legs. "Question: From a purely logistical and evidentiary perspective, could one person have done what we know to have happened?"

She opened the book to the list she'd made two hours earlier, after Sam's call suggesting for the second time that Kevin was Slater. She ticked the first item with her pencil. "Kevin gets a call in his car."

"Although you said there's no evidence of that first call, correct? The cell phone was burned. The entire call could have been in Kevin's mind, two voices talking. Same with any unrecorded conversation he had with Slater."

She nodded. "Number two. The car blows up three minutes after the call, after Kevin has escaped."

"The personality that is Slater carries a sophisticated cell phone in his pocket—Kevin's pocket. This device is a secure telephone and a transmitting device. After the imaginary conversation giving him three minutes, the Slater personality triggers a bomb he's planted in the trunk. It explodes, as planned. He detonates all of the bombs in similar fashion."

"The second phone Sam found."

"Follows," Dr. Francis said.

"Where does the Slater personality make all these explosives? We found nothing." Jennifer had her own thoughts but she wanted to hear the professor.

He smiled. "Maybe when I'm done playing scholar, I'll apply for a job with the FBI."

"I'm sure we would welcome you. Understanding of religion is a hot recruitment criterion these days."

"Slater obviously has his hiding place. Likely the place he's hidden Balinda. Kevin takes frequent trips to this location as Slater, totally unaware. The middle of the night, on the way home from class. He remembers nothing of them because it is the Slater personality, not Kevin, who is actually going."

"And his knowledge of electronics. Slater learns, but not Kevin."

"So it would seem."

She looked at her list. "But the warehouse is different because he calls the room phone and talks to Samantha. It's the first time we have him on tape."

"You said the phone rang while he was in the room, but Slater didn't speak until Kevin was out. He reaches into his pocket and presses send on a number he's already entered. As soon as he's in the hall, he begins to speak."

"Sounds far-fetched, don't you think? Somehow I don't see Slater as a James Bond."

"No, he's probably made his mistakes. You just haven't had the time to find them. For all you know, the recording will bear that out. We're just reconstructing a possible scenario based on what we do know."

"Then we can assume he planted the bomb in the library the night before last somehow, while he was supposedly in Palos Verdes with Samantha. Maybe he slipped out at night or something. The library's not exactly a high-security facility. He, meaning Slater, did everything either while our eyes were off him or remotely using the cell phone."

"If Kevin is Slater," the professor said.

She frowned. The scenario was plausible. Too plausible for her own comfort. If it bore out, the scientific journals would be writing about Kevin for years.

"And the Riddle Killer?" she asked.

"As you said earlier. Someone Slater imitated to throw the authorities off. What do you call it—copy cat? It's only been four days. Even the wheels of the FBI can turn only so fast. Perpetuating the double life beyond a week might be impossible. Four days is all he evidently needed."

Jennifer closed the notebook. There were a dozen more, but she saw with a glance that they weren't so unique. What they really needed was the analysis of the two recordings from Kevin's cell phone. It was the second call that interested her. If this theory held water, the same person had made and received the call that had sent them running for the library. It couldn't have been imagined by Kevin because it was recorded.

She sighed. "This is way too complicated. There's something missing here that would make all of this much clearer."

The professor ran his fingers over his bearded chin. "Maybe so. Do you rely on your intuition very often, Jennifer?"

"All day. Intuition leads to evidence, which leads to answers. It's what makes us ask the right questions."

"Hmm. And what does your intuition tell you about Kevin?"

She thought about it for a moment. "That he's innocent, either way. That he's an exceptional man. That he's nothing like Slater."

His right eyebrow went up. "This after four days? It took me a month to conclude the same."

"Four days of hell will tell you a lot about a man, Professor."

"'Yea, though I walk through the valley of the shadow of death, I will fear no evil.'"

"If he is Slater, do you think Kevin's afraid?" she asked.

"I think he is petrified."

III

Baker Street was black and still, shrouded in the long line of elms standing like sentinels. The drive had sliced twenty-one minutes off the clock, thanks to an accident on Willow. 7:46. She passed Kevin's old house—light glowed behind the drapes where Eugene and Bob might very well still be crying. Jennifer had kept the media at bay for the day, but it wouldn't last. By tomorrow there would probably be at least a couple vans parked out front, waiting for a snapshot of the crazies inside.

What loves what it sees? She slowed the car to a crawl and approached her old house. A porch light glared angrily. The hedges were ragged, not trimmed like her father had kept them years earlier. She'd already decided that she wouldn't bother the residents for the simple reason that she couldn't think of a decent explanation for why she would want to snoop around the bedroom window without causing alarm. She hoped they didn't have a dog.

Sam parked the car across the street and walked past the house, then cut into the neighbor's yard. She rounded the house and headed for the same old fence she and Kevin had wriggled through on a hundred occasions. Unlikely the boards were still loose.

She crouched by the fence and ran along it toward the east side of the yard, where her old bedroom faced. A dog barked several houses down. *Settle down, Spot, I'm just going to take a peek.* Just like Slater used to take peeps. Life had come full circle.

She poked her head over the fence. The window was opaque, slightly obscured by the same bushes she'd crawled over as a child. Vacant? No dog that she could see. The boards she'd once been able to slip through wouldn't budge. Up and over—the only way.

Sam grabbed the fence with both hands and vaulted it easily. She had a body built for gymnastics, a coach had told her in law school. But you don't start taking gymnastics at age twenty and expect to make the Olympics. She had opted for dance classes.

The lawn was wet from a recent watering. She ran for the window and knelt by the hedge. What was she looking for? Another clue. A riddle maybe, scratched in the ground. A note taped to the brick.

She slid in behind the bushes and felt the wall. The musty smell of dirt filled her nose. How long had it been since anyone had climbed through this window? She eased her head up and saw that the window not only was dark, but had been painted black on the inside.

Her pulse spiked. Did Slater live here? Had he taken residence in her old house? *I can't have you, so I'll take your house.* For a moment she just stared at the window, caught off guard. Someone laughed inside. A man. Then a woman, laughing.

No, they'd probably just turned the room into a darkroom or something. Photography buffs. She exhaled and resumed her search. Time was ticking.

She felt along the ledge, but there was nothing she could feel or see. The ground was dark at her feet, so she knelt and groped around in the dirt. Her fingers ran over a few rocks—he could have written a message on a rock. She held them up to what little light reached her from the warehouses across the street. Nothing. She dropped the rocks and stood again.

Had she been wrong about the window? There was a message here; there had to be! The dial on her watch glowed green, 7:58. She felt the first tendrils of panic tickle her spine. If she was wrong about the window, she'd have to start over—the game would be lost.

Maybe she shouldn't be looking for a written message.

She groaned and stepped back into the lawn. The panic was growing. *Take a breath, Sam. You're smarter than he is. You have to be. For Kevin's sake. Play his game; beat him at his own game.*

She paced the lawn, uncaring of her exposure now. She wore black slacks and a red blouse, dark colors that wouldn't easily be seen from the street. Time was running out.

Sam walked to the fence and faced the window. Okay, is there something in the bushes? An arrow? That was stupid movie stuff. She followed the roofline. Did it point anywhere? There were two second-story windows above the one down here, forming a triangle of sorts. An arrow.

Enough with the arrows, Sam! This is something that you couldn't mistake. Not something cute out of a Nancy Drew mystery. What's changed here? What is altered to make a statement? What's altered that could make a statement?

The window. The window is painted black, because it's now a darkroom or something. So really it's not a window any longer. It's a dark sheet of glass. No light.

It's dark down here, Kevin.

Sam let out a small cry and immediately swallowed it. That was it! *No* window. What used to have light but does no more? What has no window?

Sam ran for the fence and slung herself over it, spilling to the ground on her landing. Was it possible? How could Slater have pulled it off?

She felt for her gun. *Okay, think. One hour.* If she was right, she didn't need five minutes, much less sixty, to find Kevin.

|||

"And how is a man or a woman set free from this hideous nature?" Jennifer asked.

"You kill it. But to kill it you must see it. Thus the light."

"So just like"—Jennifer snapped her fingers—"that, huh?"

"As it turns out, no. It needs a daily dose of death. Really, the single greatest ally of evil is darkness. That is my point. I don't care what faith you have or what you say you believe, whether you go to church every Sunday or pray to God five times a day. If you keep the evil nature hidden, like most do, it thrives."

"And Kevin?"

"Kevin? I don't know about Kevin. If he is Slater, I suppose you would need to kill Slater the way you kill the old self. But he can't do it alone. He wouldn't even know to kill him. Man cannot deal with evil alone."

|||

Kevin had never shown her the inside of the old shed because he said it was dark inside. Only he hadn't just said inside, he said *down* there. She remembered that now. Nobody used the useless old shack in the corner of the lawn. The old bomb shelter turned toolshed on the edge of the ash heap.

The window that wasn't really a window had to be Kevin's window. In Slater's mind he might have used another riddle: *What thinks it's a window but really isn't?* Opposites. As a boy, Kevin thought he'd escaped his tortuous world through his window, but he hadn't.

The old toolshed in the corner of Kevin's lawn was the only place Sam knew of that had a basement of sorts. It was dark down there and it had no windows, and she knew that she knew that she knew that Slater was down in that bomb shelter with Balinda.

Sam held the nine millimeter at her side and ran for the shack, bent over, eyes fixed on its wood siding. The door had always been latched and locked with a big rusted padlock. What if it still was?

She should call Jennifer, but therein lay a dilemma. What could Jennifer do? Swoop in and surround the house? Slater would do the worst. On the other hand, what could *Sam* do? Waltz in and confiscate all illegally obtained firearms, slap on the handcuffs, and deliver the nasty man to the county jail?

She had to at least verify.

Sam dropped to her knee by the door, breathing heavily, both hands wrapped around her gun. The lock was disengaged.

Just remember, you were born for this, Sam.

She stuck the barrel of her gun under the door and pulled, using the gun sight as a hook. The door creaked open. A dim bulb glowed inside. She pushed the door all the way open and shoved her weapon in, careful to stay behind the cover of the doorjamb. Slowly, the opening door revealed the shapes of shelves and a wheelbarrow. A square on the floor. The trapdoor.

How deep did the shelter go? There had to be stairs.

She stepped in, one foot and then the second. The trapdoor was open, she could see now. She edged over to the dark hole and peered down. Faint light, very faint, from the right. She pulled back. Maybe calling Jennifer would be the wisest course of action. Just Jennifer.

8:15. They still had forty-five minutes. But what if she waited for Jennifer and this *wasn't* the place? That would leave them with less than half an hour to find Slater. No, she had to verify. Verify, verify.

Come on, Sam, you were born for this.

Sam shoved the gun into her waistband, knelt down, gripped the edge of the opening, and then swung one leg into the shaft. She stretched her foot, found a step. She mounted the stairs and then swung back up. The shoes might make too much noise. She took them off and then settled back on the stairs.

Come on, Sam, you were born for this.

There were nine steps; she counted them. Never knew when she might have to run back up full tilt. Knowing when to duck to avoid a head-on with the ceiling and when to turn right to exit the shack could come in handy. She was telling herself this stuff to calm her nerves, because anything in the dread silence was better than facing the certainty that she was walking to her death.

Light came from a crack below a door at the end of a concrete tunnel. The tunnel led to a basement below Kevin's house! She'd known that some of these old bomb shelters were connected to houses, but she'd never imagined such an elaborate setup beneath Kevin's house. She'd never even known there *was* a basement in his house. Wasn't there a way to the top floor from the basement? Jennifer had been in the house, but she hadn't said anything about a basement.

Sam withdrew her gun and tiptoed down the shaft.

"Shut up." Slater's voice sounded muffled behind the door. Sam stopped. Verified. She could never mistake that voice. Slater was behind that door. And Kevin?

The door was well insulated; they would never hear her. Sam walked to the door, nine millimeter up by her ear. She reached for the doorknob and slowly applied pressure. She didn't plan on bursting in, or entering at all, for that matter, but she needed to know a few things. Whether the door was locked, for starters. The knob refused to turn.

She backed up a foot and considered her options. What did Slater expect her to do, knock? She would if she had to, wouldn't she? There was only one way to save this man, and it was on the other side of that door.

Sam eased down to her belly and pressed her left eye to the crack beneath the door. On the right, white tennis shoes walked slowly toward her. She stilled her breathing.

"Time is most definitely winding down," Slater said. The feet were his, white tennis shoes she didn't recognize. "I don't hear your lover breaking down the door."

"Sam's smarter than you," Kevin said.

The tennis shoes stopped.

Sam jerked her eye to the left, where the voice had come from. She saw his feet, Kevin's shoes, the tan Reeboks she'd seen by his bed a few hours ago. Two voices, two men.

Sam pulled back. Kevin and Slater weren't the same person. She'd been wrong!

Sam flattened herself again and peered, breathing too loudly but not caring now. There they were, two sets of feet. One to her right, white, and one to her left, tan. Kevin tapped one foot nervously. Slater was walking away.

She had to tell Jennifer! In case something happened to her, she had to let Jennifer know who stood behind that door.

Sam slid back and stood. She hurried to the end of the hall. Going up the stairs might be prudent, but at this distance, there was no way Slater could hear. She lifted her phone and hit redial.

"Jennifer?"

"Sam! What's going on?"

"Shh, shh, shh. I can't talk," Sam whispered. "I found them."

A barely audible ring pierced the silence, as if a gunshot had discharged too close to her ear within the last half-hour.

Jennifer seemed incredulous. "You . . . you found Kevin? You actually located them? Where?"

"Listen to me, Jennifer. Kevin's not Slater. Do you hear me? I was wrong. It has to be a frame!"

"Where are you?" Jennifer demanded.

"I'm here, outside."

"You're absolutely positive that Kevin isn't Slater? How—"

"Listen to me!" Sam whispered harshly. She glanced back at the door. "I just saw them both; that's how I know."

"You have to tell me where you are!"

"No. Not yet. I have to think this through. He said no cops. I'll call you." She hung up before she lost her nerve and dropped the phone into her pocket.

Why didn't she just call Jennifer in? What could she possibly do that Jennifer couldn't? Only Slater knew the answer to that. The boy she'd never seen. Until today. *Kevin, dear Kevin, I'm so sorry.*

A shaft of light suddenly cut through the tunnel. She whirled around. The door was open. Slater stood in the doorframe, bare-chested, grinning, gun in hand.

"Hello, Samantha. I was getting worried. So nice of you to find us."

27

SAM'S FIRST INSTINCT WAS TO RUN. Up the stairs, duck, to the left, into the open. Come back with a flamethrower and burn him out. Her second instinct was to rush him. The rage that flooded her mind seeing him backlit by the light surprised her. She could feel her gun at her waist and she grabbed for it.

"Don't be so predictable, Sam. Kevin thinks you're smarter than me. Did you hear him say that? Prove it, darling." He brought the gun up and aimed it inside to his right. "Come on in here and prove it to me, or I'll cap the kid where he stands."

Sam hesitated. Slater stood with a cocky grin. She walked down the hall. *You were born for this, Sam. You were born for this.*

Slater backed up, keeping his gun aimed to his right. She stepped past the steel door. A single bulb cast dim light over the basement. Shades of black and gray. Stark. Kevin stood in front of a wall of pictures, face ashen. Pictures of her. He took a step toward her.

"Not so fast," Slater snapped. "I know how badly you want to be the hero again, boy, but not this time. Take the gun out slowly, Samantha. Slide it toward me." There wasn't a trace of doubt on Slater's face. He had them precisely where he'd intended.

Sam slid the gun across the concrete, and Slater scooped it up. He walked to the door, closed it, and faced them both. It struck Sam, staring at the man's smirk, that she'd committed a kind of suicide.

She'd stepped into the lair willfully, and she'd just given the dragon her gun.

You were born for this, Sam. Born for what? Born to die.

She turned from him purposefully. *No, I was born for Kevin.* She looked at him, ignoring Slater, who stood behind her now.

"You okay?"

Kevin's eyes darted over her shoulder and then settled on hers. Trails of sweat glistened on his face. The poor man was terrified.

"Not really."

"It's okay, Kevin." She smiled. "I promise you, it'll be okay."

"Actually, it won't be okay, Kevin," Slater said, walking briskly to her right. He wasn't the monster she'd imagined. No horns, no yellow teeth, no scarred face. He looked like a jock with short blond hair, tight tan slacks, a torso cut like a gymnast's. A large, red tattoo of a heart branded over his breast. She could have met this man a dozen times over the years and not taken notice. Only his eyes gave him away. They were far away, light gray eyes, like a wolf's. If Kevin's eyes swallowed her, Slater's were the kind she might bounce off of. He even smiled like a wolf.

"I'm not sure you're aware of what we have here, but the way I see it, you're both in a bit of a pickle," Slater said. "And Kevin is fit to be tied. He's made three phone calls to his FBI girlfriend, and I just sat back and let him do it. Why? Because I know how hopeless his situation is, even if he doesn't. No one can help him. Or you, dear Samantha."

"If you wanted to kill Kevin, you could have done it a dozen times," Sam said. "So what *is* your game? What do you hope to accomplish with all of this nonsense?"

"I could have killed you too, my dear. A hundred times. But this way it's just so much more fun. We're all together like a happy little family. Mommy's in the closet, Kevin's finally come back home, and now his little girlfriend has come to save him from the terrible boy down the street. It's almost like old times. We're even going to let Kevin kill again."

Slater's lips fell flat. "Only this time he's not going after me. This time he's going to put a bullet in your head."

Sam took this in and faced Kevin. He looked so frail in the yellow light. Afraid. Slater was going to force his hand to kill. Her. It all made perfect sense now, although exactly what Slater had in mind, she didn't know.

Surprisingly, Sam felt no fear. In fact, she felt somewhat buoyed, even confident. *Maybe this is how you feel just before you die.*

"So. He's the boy, after all," Sam said to Kevin. Both men were watching her. "How does a big, strong, handsome man like this become so jealous of you, Kevin? Think about it. How could such a powerful, intelligent man be driven to such insane fits over one man? Answer: Because underneath that big, bold, red tattoo and all that bulging muscle, he's only a pathetic little weasel who's never managed to make a friend, much less win a girl."

Slater stared at her. "I'll keep your predicament in mind and for-give the rest of your desperate insults, but I don't think *jealous* is the right word, Samantha. I am not jealous of this piece of meat."

She faced him slowly, wildly bold and unsure why. "Then forgive me for such poor word choice. You're not insanely jealous; you're delighted with the sweet bond of love that Kevin and I have always shared. The fact that I would have shoved a toilet plunger into your face if I'd ever caught you peeping and licking at my window doesn't bother you, does it?"

His mouth was a thin, straight line. He blinked. Again.

"The fact is, *I chose Kevin,*" Sam said. "And Kevin chose me, and neither of us wants anything to do with you. You can't accept that. It drives you crazy. It makes you see red."

Slater's face twisted. "And Kevin doesn't see red?"

Silence settled. Balinda was in the closet. A clock on the wall read 8:35. She should have told Jennifer where they were. Her cell phone was still in her pocket, and she didn't think Slater knew. Could she call Jennifer? If she could slip her hand into her pocket and press the send button twice, it would automatically dial the last number. Jennifer would hear them. A tingle ran through her fingertips.

"You really think Kevin is any different than me?" Slater waved the guns around absently. "You really think this little puke here doesn't want exactly what I want? He'll kill and he'll lie and he'll spend the rest of his life pretending he won't, just like the rest. That's better than me? At least I'm honest about who I am!"

"And who are you, Slater? You're the devil. You're the sickness of this world. You're vile and you're vomit. Go on, tell us. Be honest—"

"Shut up!" Slater screamed. "Shut your disgusting pie hole! This little piece of trash sits in the pew every Sunday, swearing to God that he won't keep doing his secret little sins when he knows as well as I that he will. We know he will because he's made this promise a thousand times and breaks it every time. He's the liar." Spittle flew from his lips. "*That's* the truth!"

"He's nothing like you," Sam said. "See him? He's a terrorized victim whom you've tried desperately to pound to a pulp. See you? You're a revolting monster pounding whoever threatens you into a pulp. See me? I'm neither terrorized nor frightened, because I see you and I see him and I see nothing in common. Please, don't be such a snail."

Slater stared at her, lips parted, stunned. She had pushed him beyond himself with the simple truth, and he was writhing inside already. She shoved her fingers into her pockets and confidently hooked her thumbs.

"Where do they breed your kind, Slater? Is that a mask you're wearing? You look so normal, but I have this unshakable suspicion that if I pulled your ear, the whole mask would come off and—"

Gunfire crashed through the room and Samantha jerked. Slater had fired the gun. A muffled wail cried through the door. Balinda. Sam's pulse quickened. Slater stood without flinching, gun ex-tended to the ground where his bullet had chipped a divot from the concrete. "That hole below your nose is starting to bother me," he said. "Maybe you should think about closing it."

"Or maybe you should consider putting a hole in your head," Sam said.

Slowly a smile formed on his lips. "You have more spunk than I would have guessed. I really should have broken your window that first night."

"You're demented."

"How much I loved to hurt little girls like you."

"You make me very, very sick."

"Take your hands out where I can see them."

He'd noticed. She pulled her hands out of her pockets and re-turned his glare. Neither backed down.

"Enough!" Kevin yelled.

Sam faced him. Kevin scowled at Slater, whose face was red and quivering. "I've always loved her! Why can't you just accept that? Why have you hidden away all these years? Why can't you find some other poor sucker and leave us alone?"

"Because none of them interests me like you do, Kevin. I hate you more than I hate myself, and that, puke face, is quite interesting."

III

Slater sounds confident, but he's never felt so much unease in all of his life. He has underestimated the strength of the girl. If his plan depends on bending her will, he will have significant challenges ahead. Fortunately, Kevin is more pliable. He'll be the one pulling the trigger.

What is it about her? Her nerve. Her unyielding conviction. Her arrogance! She really does love the fool and she flaunts that love. In fact, she is all about love and Slater hates her for it. He'd seen her smiling, combing her hair, bouncing around her bedroom as a child twenty years ago; he'd seen her run around, locking up criminals in New York, like some kind of superhero on steroids. Happy, happy and snappy. It makes him sick. The look of disdain in her eyes now brings small comfort—it's born out of her love for the worm to his right. So then, all the more reason for Kevin to put a bullet through her pretty white forehead.

He glances at the clock. Nineteen minutes. He should forget the timing and just do it now. A bitter taste pulls at the back of his tongue. The sweet taste of death. He should do it!

But Slater is a patient man, most excellent in all of the disciplines. He will wait, because it is his power to wait.

The game is down to the last test. The last little surprise.

Slater feels a surge of confidence sweep through his bones. He chuckles. But he doesn't feel like chuckling. He feels like shooting his gun again.

Say what you want now, little girl. We'll see who Kevin chooses.

|||

Kevin watched Slater, heard him chuckle, knew with awful certainty that things were going to get worse.

He couldn't believe that Sam had actually come in and given up her gun like that. Didn't she know that Slater would kill her? That was his whole point. Slater wanted Sam dead, and he wanted him to kill her. Kevin would refuse, of course, and then Slater would just kill her himself and find a way to frame Kevin. Either way, their lives would never be the same.

He looked at Sam and saw that she was watching him. She winked slowly. "Courage, Kevin. Courage, my knight."

"Shut up!" Slater said. "Nobody talk! My knight? You're trying to make me gag? *My knight?* What rubbish!"

They stared at him. He was losing himself in this game.

"Shall we begin with the festivities?" Slater asked. He shoved Samantha's gun into his waistband, took two long steps to Balinda's door, unlocked it, and threw it open. Balinda sagged against a wall, bound and wide-eyed. Black smudges covered her white lace nightgown. Stripped of makeup, her face looked quite normal for a woman in her fifties. She whimpered and Kevin felt a pang of sorrow knife through his chest.

Slater bent down and hauled her to her feet. Balinda stumbled out of the room, lips quivering, squeaking in terror.

Slater shoved her against the desk. He pointed to the chair. "Sit!"

She collapsed to her seat. Slater waved his gun at Sam. "Hands up where I can see them." She lifted her hands from her waist. Keeping his gun pointed in Sam's general direction, Slater pulled a roll of duct tape from the top drawer, ripped off a six-inch slab with his teeth, and plastered it over Balinda's mouth.

"Keep quiet," he mumbled. She didn't seem to hear. He shoved his face up to her. "Keep quiet!" he yelled. She jumped and he chuckled.

Slater removed the second gun from his pants and faced them. He cocked the guns, raised them to his shoulders. Sweat covered his white chest like oil. He grinned, lowered his arms, and twirled each pistol like a gunslinger.

"I've thought about this moment for so long," Slater said. "The really big moments in life are never as inspiring as you imagine them—I'm sure you've both figured that out by now. What happens in these next few minutes has run so many laps around my mind that I swear there's a groove an inch deep in there. I've taken way too much pleasure from the thoughts already; nothing can possibly compare. That's the downside of dreaming. But it's been worth it. Now I'm going to make it happen, and of course I'll try to spice it up as much as possible to keep things interesting."

He spun each gun again, the left, then the right. "I've practiced, can you tell?"

Kevin looked at Sam, who stood five feet from Slater, staring at the madman with a quiet fury. What was going through her mind? Slater had shifted his focus to her the moment she'd come in. With Kevin, the man showed no fear, but now facing Sam, Slater was trying to hide his fear with this show of his, wasn't he? He was actually afraid. Sam just stared at him, undaunted, hands limp by her hips.

Kevin's heart swelled. She was the true rescuer, always had been. He wasn't the knight; she was. *Dear Sam, I love you so. I've always loved you.*

This was the end; he knew that. They couldn't save each other this time. Had he told her how much he really did love her? Not with romantic love—with something much stronger. A desperate need. The need to survive. The way he loved his own life.

Kevin blinked. He had to tell her how precious she was to him!

"The game is simple," Slater said. "No need confusing the common folk. One out of two people will die"—he glanced at the clock—"seventeen minutes from now. The old woman"—Slater shoved one of the guns to her temple—"who has evidently mistaken life for a Froot Loops commercial. Actually, I like that about her. If you're going to pretend, you might as well do the whole enchilada, right?"

He smiled and slowly aimed the other gun toward Samantha. "Or the bright young maiden." Both arms were fully extended at right angles now, one toward Balinda, the other toward Sam. "Our executioner will be Kevin. I want you to begin thinking about which wench you'll kill, Kevin. Killing neither isn't an option; that would ruin the fun. You must choose one."

"I won't," Kevin said.

Slater tilted the gun and shot him in the foot.

He gasped. Pain throbbed through to his sole and then spiked up his shin; nausea rolled into his gut. The Reebok on his right foot had a red hole in it and was trembling. His horizon tipped.

"You will." Slater blew imaginary smoke from the barrel. "I promise you, Kevin. You most definitely will."

Sam ran for him and caught his sagging body. He let her support him and adjusted his weight to his left foot.

Sam jerked her head toward Slater. "You're sick . . . You didn't need to do that!"

"A hole in the foot, a hole in the head; we'll see who ends up dead."

"I love you, Sam," Kevin said softly, ignoring the pain. "No matter what happens, I want you to know how lost I am without you."

|||

Jennifer paced. "I could *strangle* her!"

"Call her," Dr. Francis said.

"And risk exposing her? She could be right outside his door and her cell goes off? Can't do it."

He nodded. "Something doesn't sit right."

She picked up her phone. "I had myself firmly convinced that Kevin was Slater."

"And he isn't."

"Unless—"

Her cell phone chirped. They both looked at it. Jennifer flipped it open.

"Hello?"

"We have the report from Riggs," Galager said. But Jennifer already knew that Slater and Kevin weren't the same person.

"Bit late. We already know. Anything else?"

"No. Just that."

She sighed. "We have a problem, Bill. What's the mood over there?"

"Gloomy. Frantic without direction. The director just called for you. He's getting an earful from the governor. Expect a call any second. They want to know."

"Know what? We don't know where he's stashed Balinda. We're down to a few minutes and we don't have the faintest idea where he's taken her. Tell them that."

Galager didn't respond right away. "If it's any consolation, Jennifer, I think he's innocent. The man I talked to wasn't a killer."

"Of course he isn't a killer," Jennifer snapped. "What do you mean? Of course . . ." She turned to the professor. His eyes were fixed on her. "What did the report say?"

"I thought you said you knew. The voices on the recording are from the same person."

"The seismic tuner—"

"No. The same person. In Riggs's estimation, if the recording is Kevin and Slater, then Kevin is Slater. There's an echo in the background that barely surfaces on the second tape. Both voices are from the same room. Riggs's guess is he's using two cell phones and the recording picks up a faint reproduction of what he's saying on the other phone."

"But . . . that's impossible!"

"I thought it was the prevailing theory . . ."

"But Sam's with them, and she called us. Kevin isn't Slater!"

"And what makes you think you can trust Sam? If she's with them, didn't she tell you where they are? I'd bank on Riggs."

Jennifer stood frozen to the carpet. Was it possible? "I have to go."

"Jennifer, what do I—"

"I'll call you back." She snapped the phone closed and stared at the professor, dumbstruck.

"Unless Sam *didn't* see them both."

"Did you ever meet with Sam?" Dr. Francis asked. "Actually see her with your own eyes?"

Jennifer thought. "No, I didn't. But . . . I talked to her. So many times."

"So did I. But her voice wasn't so high that it sounded necessarily female."

"Could . . . he do that?" Jennifer scrambled for understanding, searched for something, anything Sam had done that might contradict the notion. None came immediately to mind. "Cases of many more than two personalities have been documented."

"What if Slater isn't the only one who's Kevin? What if Samantha is also Kevin?"

"Three! Three personalities in one."

28

SAMANTHA WATCHED THE SECOND HAND tick relentlessly through its slow arc. Kevin sat on the floor, head in hands, distraught. Balinda slumped in her chair five feet to his left, mouth taped gray, eyes flittering over Kevin. If Kevin's aunt could talk now, what would she say? *I'm so sorry, Kevin! I beg your forgiveness! Don't be a coward, Kevin! Get up and kick that man where he'll remember it!*

Balinda never looked at Slater. It was as if he didn't exist. Or she couldn't bear to look at him. For that matter, the woman didn't look at Sam either. Her attention was consumed by Kevin and Kevin alone.

Sam closed her eyes. *Easy, girl. You can do this.*

But in all honesty she was no longer feeling like she could do this or anything. Slater had two guns and a big smile. She had only her cell phone.

"Uh, uh, uh, hands where I can see, darling."

|||

Jennifer ran her hands through her hair. "This is crazy!" Her head hurt and time was running out. *Think!*

"She was always disappearing! She—he could have made it all up. The CBI, the task force, the interview with the Pakistani, all of it! They were all things she could have created in her mind based on information Kevin already knew."

"Or that Kevin simply fabricated," Dr. Francis said. "Kevin concludes that Slater can't be the Riddle Killer because deep in his subconscious he knows that *he* is Slater. Sam, his alter ego, concludes the same. She's working to free Kevin without knowing that she *is* him."

"She kept suggesting that there was someone on the inside! There was—Kevin! He was on the inside. And she was the one who first concluded that Kevin was Slater!"

"And to Kevin, both Slater and Samantha are as real as you and me."

They were running over each other with their words now, connecting dots that formed a perfect picture.

Or did they?

Jennifer shook her head. "But I just talked to Sam and she saw Kevin and Slater while she was *outside* the door. You're saying that I was actually talking to Kevin, and that he was simply imagining himself as Samantha, sneaking up on him and Slater?"

"It's possible," the professor said, excitedly. "You've read the case studies. If Kevin is truly split, Sam would have her own personality. Everything she's done has been done completely in Kevin's mind, but to both of them, it has been completely real."

"So it was Kevin I just talked to."

"No, it was Sam. Sam is distinct from Kevin in his mind."

"But physically, it was Kevin."

"Assuming she is him, yes."

"And why didn't Slater stop him? If Slater was there as well? Kevin picks up the phone and calls me, and in his mind he's really Samantha, outside the door. Makes sense. But Slater's there too. Why doesn't he stop the phone call?"

"I don't know," the professor said, turning with hand on chin. "You'd think he'd stop Kevin. So we could be wrong."

Jennifer massaged her temples. "But if they *are* all Kevin, it would mean he never even had a childhood friend named Samantha. He created her as an escape to fill the void in his life. Then he created Slater, and when he discovered that Slater hated Sam, he tried to kill Slater. Now Slater's come back and so has Sam." She turned. "But her father was a cop! He lived in the house three down from Kevin's."

"Kevin could have known that a cop named Sheer lived in that house and simply built Samantha's reality on that. Do you know whether Officer Sheer even had a daughter named Samantha?"

"Never checked." Jennifer paced, sorting through the tide of thoughts. "It does make sense, doesn't it? Balinda wouldn't let Kevin have a best friend, so he fabricated one. He role-played her."

"This is what Kevin could have meant when he told me he had a new model for the natures of man," Dr. Francis said. "The three natures of man. Good, evil, and the man struggling between! 'The good that I would, that I do not, but that which I would not, that I do.' There are really three natures in there! One, *the good*. Two, *that which I would not*. And, three, *I!*"

"The struggle between good and evil, embodied in a man who is role-playing both good and evil and yet is still himself as well. Kevin Parson."

"The noble child. Every man."

They stared at each other, transfixed by the enormity of it all.

"It's a possibility," the professor said.

"It almost makes perfect sense." Jennifer glanced at her watch. "And we're almost out of time."

"Then we have to tell her," Dr. Francis said, walking for the kitchen. He turned back. "If Sam is Kevin, then she has to be told! *He* has to be told! He can't deal with this on his own. No one can deal with evil on their own!"

"Call Sam and tell her that she's Kevin?"

"Yes! Sam's the only one who can save him now! But she's power-less without you."

Jennifer took a deep breath. "What if we're wrong? How do I tell her without sounding like an idiot? Excuse me, Sam, but you're not a real person. You're just part of Kevin?"

"Yes. Tell her as if we know it's a fact, and tell her quickly. Slater may try to stop the call. How much time?"

"Ten minutes."

|||

"This is going to be delightful, Samantha," Slater said, clicking the barrels of the two pistols together like drumsticks. He squirmed. "It's starting to give me shivers all over."

The phone was her only hope, but Slater kept insisting that her hands remain where he could see them. If he knew about the phone, he would have insisted she give it up. Either way, it sat like a useless lump in the folds of her slacks. She'd thought through a dozen other possibilities, but none presented themselves as viable. There would be a way—there was always a way for good to triumph over evil. Even if Slater did kill her . . .

A high chirping sound cut through the silence. Her cell!

Slater spun, glaring. She acted quickly, before he could respond. She snatched it from her pocket and flipped it open.

"Hello?"

"Sam, listen to me. I know this may sound impossible to you, but you're one of Kevin's personalities. Both you and Slater, do you hear me? That's why you can see them both. You—we—have to save Kevin. Tell me where you are, please, Sam."

Her mind rocked crazily. What had Jennifer said? She was one of Kevin's . . .

"What . . . what do you think you're doing?" Slater demanded.

"Please, Sam, you have to believe me!"

"You saw me in the car at the bus explosion," Sam said. "You waved."

"The bus? I saw Kevin. I waved to Kevin. You . . . you'd already left for the airport. Listen to me . . ."

Sam didn't hear any more. Slater had recovered from his shock and bounded for her.

"Below the screw," Sam said.

Slater's hand crashed against the side of her head. The cell phone dug into her ear and clattered to the concrete. She instinctively reached for it, but Slater was too quick. He slapped her arm away, scooped up the cell phone, and threw it across the room. It skipped off the floor and shattered against the wall.

He faced her and shoved a pistol under her chin. "Below the screw? What does that mean, you filthy little traitor?"

Sam's mind hurt. *You are one of his personalities,* isn't that what Jennifer had said? *I am one of Kevin's personalities? That's impossible!*

"Tell me!" Slater yelled. "Tell me or I swear I'll put the hole in your head myself."

"And forgo the pleasure of seeing Kevin do it?" Sam asked.

Slater looked at her for a moment, eyes working over her face. He jerked the pistol back and grinned. "You're right. Doesn't matter anyway; they're out of time."

III

"It was her?" Dr. Francis asked.

"Sam. Call was terminated. Sure didn't sound like Kevin to me. She said she saw me at the bus, but I never saw her." Jennifer swallowed. "I hope we didn't just put a bullet in Sam's head."

Dr. Francis sat slowly.

"She told me they were below the screw," Jennifer said.

"The screw?"

Jennifer whirled to him. "The screw that held Kevin's window closed. Below the window, below the house. There's . . ." Could it be so close, right under their noses? "There's a stairwell in the house, clogged with piles of newsprint now, but it leads to a basement."

"Below the house."

"Kevin has Balinda in the basement of their house! There has to be another way in!" Jennifer ran for the door. "Come on!"

"Me?"

"Yes, you! You know him better than anyone else."

He grabbed his coat and ran after her. "Even if we find them, what can we do?"

"I don't know, but I'm done waiting. You said he can't do this without help. God, give us help."

"How much time?"

"Nine minutes."

"My car! I'll drive," the professor said and veered for the Porsche in the driveway.

|||

Samantha had never felt more distracted from the mission at hand than now. What was the mission at hand? Saving Kevin from Slater.

She thought back to her years in college, to her law enforcement training, to New York. It was all fuzzy. Broad sweeps of reality without detail. Not the kind of detail that immediately surfaced when her mind wandered to the past, as a child, sneaking around with Kevin. Not the specifics that flooded her mind when she considered these past four days. Even her investigation of the Riddle Killer now seemed distant, like something she had read, not actually engaged in.

If Jennifer was right, she was really Kevin. But that was impossible because Kevin sat on the floor ten feet away, rocking, deeply withdrawn, holding a red foot, bleeding from his left ear.

Bleeding from his ear. She took a step around for a better view of Kevin's ear. Her cell phone lay in several pieces twenty feet away on the concrete where Slater had hurled it. That was real enough. Was it possible that Kevin had made her up? She looked at her hands—they seemed real, but she also knew how the mind worked. She also knew that Kevin was a prime candidate for multiple personalities. Balinda had taught him how to dissociate from the beginning. If Kevin was Slater, as Jennifer insisted, then why couldn't *she* be as well? And Sam could see Slater because she was there, in Kevin's mind where Slater lived. But Balinda was real . . .

Sam walked up to Balinda. If Jennifer was right, there were only two bodies here—Kevin's and Balinda's. She and Slater were only personalities in Kevin's imagination.

"What's with you?" Slater snapped. "Back off!"

Sam turned to face the man. He had the barrel of his weapon trained on her knee. Did he really have the gun if he was just in her mind? Or was that Kevin, and he only looked like Slater to her?

Slater grinned wickedly. Sweat wet his face. He glanced at the clock behind her. "Four minutes, Samantha. You have four minutes to live. If Kevin chooses to kill his mother instead of you, then I'm going to waste you myself. I just decided that, and it feels pretty good. How does it feel for you?"

"Why is Kevin bleeding from the ear, Slater? You hit me in the ear, but did you hit him in his ear?"

Slater's eyes shifted to Kevin and then back. "I love it. This is the part where the clever agent begins to play mind tricks in a last-ditch effort to confuse the nasty assailant. I really do love it. Back away from the bait, precious."

Sam ignored him. Instead she reached out and pinched Balinda on the cheek. The woman clenched her eyes and made a squeak. Thunder crashed through the chamber; white-hot pain seared through Sam's thigh. Slater had shot her.

Sam gasped and grabbed her thigh. Blood spread through her black capris. Her head swam. The pain was real enough. If she and Slater weren't real, then who was shooting whom?

Kevin jumped to his feet. "Sam!"

"Stay!" Slater said.

Sam's mind climbed from the pain. Kevin was shooting himself? Any normal person viewing this would see that he'd just shot himself in the thigh.

The details began to fall into order, like dominoes slowly toppling in a long line. So then if Kevin shot Sam in the head, he'd really kill whom? Himself? He was going to kill either Balinda or himself! And even if Slater killed Sam, he would really be pulling the trigger on Kevin, because all three of them occupied the same body. No matter who shot whom, Kevin's body would receive the bullet!

Sam felt a swarm of panic. *Tell Kevin,* Jennifer had said.

"When I say back off, I mean back off—not pinch her, not lick her, not spit on her," Slater said. "Back off really does mean back off. So . . . *back off!*"

Sam took a side step away from Balinda. *Hurry, Jennifer, please hurry! Beneath the screw. That means the basement; you know about the basement, don't you? Dear God, help them.*

"Hurts, doesn't it?" Slater's eyes danced around. "Don't worry, a bullet to the head does wonders for the odd surface wound. *Pow!* Works every time."

"He's bleeding in the ear because you hit *me* in the ear," Sam said. "He's bleeding in the leg too, isn't he?" She followed Slater's glance. Kevin stood, weaving on his feet, stricken with empathy. Blood soaked both his shoe and his right pant leg. He didn't feel the pain because in his mind it hadn't happened to him. Their personalities were completely fragmented. And what about Slater? She dropped her eyes to his thigh—a red spot was spreading on his tan slacks. Slater had shot Sam, but the wound appeared on both Kevin and Slater. She looked at Slater's ear. Then at his shoe. Blood there too.

"I'm so sorry, Sam," Kevin said. "This isn't your fault. I'm sorry I got you into this. I . . . I shouldn't have called you."

"You called her because I told you to call her, you idiot!" Slater said. "And now you're going to kill her because I'm telling you to kill her. Don't slip into Mommy's land of Froot Loops on me, Kevin. I swear I'll kill every one of you if you don't play nicely."

The truth of the matter struck Sam as she watched the deepening lines of sorrow in Kevin's face. This was the confession that Kevin had to make. The whole game was really *Kevin's*, a desperate attempt to flush his evil nature out of its hiding place. He was trying to expose the Slater in him. He'd reached out to her, the Samantha in him, the good in him. He was exposing the good and the bad in him to the world, in a desperate attempt to be rid of Slater. Slater thought he was winning, but in the end Kevin would be the victor.

If he survived. He'd already shot himself twice, once in the foot and once in the thigh.

"I have a theory," Samantha said, voice unsteady.

"The old Colombo trick," Slater said. "Let's stall the nasty man with the I've-got-a-theory routine. Can it! Time's ticking."

Sam cleared her throat and pressed on. "My theory is that I'm not really real."

Slater stared at her.

"I'm a childhood friend Kevin created because that's what he learned to do when he was a child." She looked into his eyes. "You made things up, Kevin. Only I'm not really made up—I'm part of you. I'm the good part of you."

"Can it!" Slater said.

"Slater isn't real either. He's another personality, and he's trying to trick you into killing either me or your mother. If you choose me, you'll be killing the good in you, maybe even yourself. But if you choose Balinda, you'll be murdering another living person. Your mother, for all practical purposes."

"That's a lie, you foul-mouthed, sick . . ." Slater's tirade sputtered short. His eyes bulged from a red face. "That's the stupidest thing I've ever heard!"

"That's not possible," Kevin said, face round in confusion. "That can't be, Sam! Of course you're real! You're the most real thing I've ever known."

"I *am* real, Kevin. I'm real and I love you desperately! But I'm part of you." Hearing herself say it, she sounded foolish. How could she possibly not be real? She felt and looked and even smelled real! But it did make sense on some unspeakable level.

"Look at your leg. You're bleeding because I was shot," she said. "I'm you. And so is Slater. You have to believe me. You've taken the good and the evil in you and turned them into imaginary people. Personalities. It's not really that strange, Kevin. You're acting out the struggle between good and evil every human being engages in. Slater and I are only the players in your own mind. But neither of us can do anything unless you give us the power to do it. He can't pull that trigger unless you do. Do you—"

"Shut up! Shut up, you lying piece of trash!" Slater jumped across the room and shoved a gun into Kevin's hand. He lifted the hand and pointed it toward Samantha.

"You have fifty seconds, Kevin. Fifty, tick, tick, tick." He lifted his own pistol and pressed the barrel against Balinda's temple. "Either you shoot Sam or I shoot Froot Loops."

"I can't shoot her!" Kevin cried.

"Then Mommy dies. Of course you can! You pull that trigger, or I swear I'm going to take care of Mommy and then finish you off for being a bad sport, you hear me? Forty seconds, Kevin. Forty, tick, tick, tick."

Slater's face glistened in the dim light. Kevin held the gun by his side. His face wrinkled; tears hung in his eyes.

"Point the gun at Samantha, you idiot! Lift it up. Now!"

Kevin lifted it slowly. "Sam? I can't let him kill Balinda, right?"

"Please don't get all sentimental on us," Slater said. "It's good for the mood, I realize, but it makes my stomach turn. Just put a bullet through her forehead. You heard her, she's not real. She's a figment of our imaginations. Of course, so am I; that's why you have two bullet holes in your leg." He chuckled.

Sam's mind hurt. What was really happening? What if she was wrong? Never before had she held a notion to be so utterly impossible and so utterly true at once. And she was now telling Kevin to gamble his very life on that notion. *Dear God, give me strength.*

"Look at your leg, Kevin," Sam said. "You shot yourself. Please, I'm begging you. Don't let Slater kill her. He can't shoot unless you give him the power. He's you."

29

T HE DOOR at the end of the tunnel was unlocked. Jennifer could hear Sam's voice begging inside. She wasn't sure what she would find when she crashed in, but time was gone. Dr. John Francis breathed raggedly behind her.

They'd come to the house, barged past Eugene to find the stair-well still blocked with books. After frantically searching the perimeter, they found the stairs in the old bomb shelter. No telling how often or how long Kevin had been here over the years thinking he was Slater.

"Here we go."

She twisted the knob, took a deep breath, and threw her weight forward, gun extended.

The first thing she saw was Balinda, seated in a wooden chair, bound and gagged with gray duct tape. The second was the man standing over her. Kevin.

Kevin had a gun in each hand, one outstretched and pressed into Balinda's temple, and the other crammed against his own head like a man about to commit suicide. No Samantha, no Slater. Just Kevin.

But she knew that Kevin wasn't seeing what she saw. His eyes were clenched tight and he was hyperventilating.

"Kevin?"

He jerked his head toward her, eyes wide.

"It's okay, Kevin," Jennifer said. "I'm here." She held out a hand, urging calm. "Don't do anything. Please, don't pull that trigger."

Sweat covered his upper lip and cheeks. He stood, torn, terrified, furious. Blood leaked from wounds on his right thigh and foot. He'd shot himself! Twice.

"Kevin, where is Samantha?" Jennifer asked.

His eyes jerked to his left.

"Shut up," he snarled. Only it was in Slater's voice, which she now clearly recognized as Kevin's voice, but lower and grating.

"You're not real, Slater," Jennifer said. "You're only a personality Kevin created. You have no power on your own. Sam, do you hear me?"

"I hear you, Jennifer," Sam said—only it wasn't Sam; it was Kevin speaking in a slightly higher voice. Unlike over the phone, Jennifer heard the resemblance now.

"You don't see me, do you?" Sam asked.

"No."

"Listen to her, Kevin," Sam said. "Listen to me. I would die for you, my knight. I would gladly give my life for you, but it's Slater you have to kill, not me. Do you understand? We are you. Only you. And now that you've flushed him out, you have to kill him."

Kevin clenched his eyes and began to shake.

"Shut up!" Slater screamed. "Everyone, shut up! Do it! Do it, Kevin, or I swear I'll put this round in Mommy's forehead! Time's up!"

Jennifer felt frantic. "Kevin—"

"Shoot Slater, Kevin," the professor said, stepping past her. "He can't kill you. Put the weapon on Slater and kill him."

"Won't he shoot himself?" Jennifer demanded.

"You have to separate yourself from Slater, Kevin."

Kevin's eyes fluttered open. He'd recognized the professor's voice. "Dr. Francis?" Kevin's normal voice.

"There are three natures, Kevin. The good, the bad, and the poor

soul struggling between them. Remember? You're role-playing those
three roles. Listen to me. You have to kill Slater. Take your gun off
Sam and point it at Slater. He can't do anything to stop you. Then,
when you are sure that you have your gun on Slater, I want you to
shoot him. I'll tell you. You have to trust me."

Kevin turned his head, staring to his left and then back to his right.
From Kevin's perspective he was looking between Samantha and Slater.

"Don't be a fool!" Slater said. Kevin swung the gun that was on
Balinda toward Jennifer. "Drop the gun! Out!" It was Slater and he
was frantic.

"Do what the professor says, Kevin," Sam said. "Shoot Slater."

III

Kevin stared at Slater and wondered why he hadn't fired. The man
had swung his gun from Balinda and aimed it at Jennifer, but he
wasn't pulling the trigger. The time had come and gone and still Slater
hadn't shot.

It occurred to him that he still had the gun in his hand, trained
on Sam. He lowered his arm. They wanted him to shoot Slater.

But . . . if Sam and Jennifer were right, that was him over there,
threatening Jennifer. And they wanted him to shoot himself? He'd
flushed the man out of his hiding and now he was to kill him.

Kevin turned to Sam. She looked so tender, so lovely, eyes drawn
with sympathy. *Dear Sam, I love you so.* Her eyes reached into his
mind, his heart, melting him with their love.

She took a step toward him. "I should go now, Kevin."

"Go?" The thought frightened him.

"I won't be gone. I'll be with you. I *am* you. Shoot Slater."

"Stop!" Slater screamed. "Stop!" He stepped out and swung his
gun on Samantha.

"I love you, Kevin," Samantha said. She stepped up to him, smiled gently, knowingly. "Shoot him. His kind is powerless when you understand who holds the true power. I know you're the one who feels powerless, and on your own, you are. But if you look to your Maker, you'll find enough power to kill a thousand Slaters, wherever they crop up. He will save you. Listen to Dr. Francis."

She reached out and touched his hand. Her finger went through his skin, into his hand. Kevin watched, mouth gaping. Samantha stepped into him, her knee into his knee, her shoulder into his shoulder. He couldn't feel her. Then she was gone.

Kevin gasped for air. She was him! She'd always been him! The realization fell into his mind like an anvil dropped from heaven. And she was gone, wasn't she? Or maybe closer than ever. A buzz circled his mind.

And if Sam was him, then Slater . . .

Kevin turned to his right. Slater shook from head to foot, gun aimed at Kevin's head now. But that wasn't a real person over there; it was only his evil nature, right?

Kevin looked at Jennifer. Her eyes were begging him. She couldn't stop Slater because she couldn't see him. She only saw him—Kevin.

If he was Slater, then the gun was really in his hand, wasn't it? He could force Slater to lower the gun by lowering it himself, in his mind.

Look to your Maker, Sam had said.

Open my eyes.

Kevin looked at the pathetic man who called himself Slater. He closed his eyes. It occurred to him then that he had two guns in his hands—one at his side and one at his temple. That would be Slater. He lowered the gun; now he had two guns by his side, one in each hand. He opened his eyes.

Slater faced him, gun lowered, face twisted with fury. "You'll never succeed, Kevin. Never! You're just like me, and nothing will ever change that. You hear me? Nothing!"

"Now, Kevin," Dr. Francis said. "Now."

Kevin lifted his right arm, pointed the nine millimeter at Slater's head, and pulled the trigger. The shot echoed loudly. At this range he could hardly miss.

But he did miss. He missed because suddenly there was no target to hit. Slater was gone.

Kevin lowered the gun. The bullet had buried itself in the metal desk behind the spot where Slater had stood, but it hadn't penetrated any flesh and blood. Slater wasn't flesh or blood. He was dead just the same. At least for now.

For a few long seconds the room rang in the aftermath of the detonation. Balinda began to sob. Kevin looked at her and pity, not anger, washed through his mind. She needed help, didn't she? She was a wounded soul, like him. She needed love and understanding. He doubted she would ever be able to return to the false reality she'd created.

"Kevin?"

The world seemed to collapse at the sound of Jennifer's voice. He wasn't certain what had just happened, but if he wasn't mistaken, he'd blown up a bus and a library and kidnapped his aunt. He needed help. Dear God, he needed help!

"Are you all right, Kevin?" Jennifer's voice broke.

He lowered his head and began to cry. He couldn't help it. *Dear God, what have I done?*

An arm settled on his shoulders. He could smell the musty scent of her perfume as she pulled him close.

"It's okay, Kevin. Everything's okay now. I won't let them hurt you, I promise."

He dissolved in sobs at her words. He deserved to be hurt. Or was that Slater's old voice?

Listen to Dr. Francis, Samantha had said. He would. He would listen to Dr. Francis and let Jennifer hold him. It was all he had now. Truth and love.

30

J ENNIFER LOOKED THROUGH the glass door at Kevin, who stood by the flowers in the professor's lawn, touching and smelling the roses as if he'd newly discovered them. Dr. John Francis stood beside her, gazing out. Kevin had spent the last seven days in a prison cell, awaiting an extended bail hearing that had ended three hours earlier. Persuading the judge that Kevin wasn't a flight risk was a simple matter; convincing her that Kevin wasn't a threat to society wasn't. But Chuck Hatters, a good friend to Jennifer and now Kevin's attorney, had managed.

The press had slaughtered Kevin that first day, but as the details of his childhood leaked out over the next week, their tenor had changed— Jennifer had seen to that. She'd held a news conference and revealed his past in all of its horrifying detail. Kevin was simply role-playing as only a child who'd been severely abused and fractured could role-play. If even a single person had been hurt or killed, the public would probably have continued screaming retribution until another earth-shattering event distracted them. But in Kevin's case, pity quickly took precedence over a few destroyed buildings. The Slater personality would never have blown up any bus before it had been evacuated, Jennifer argued. She wasn't sure she believed it, but enough of the public did to swing the tide of outrage. Kevin still had his significant detractors, of course, but they no longer dominated the airwaves.

Was he insane? No, but she couldn't tell them that yet. The courts would put him through the wringer, and legal insanity was his only defense. In many ways, he *had* been legally insane, but he seemed to have emerged from the basement with a full grasp of himself, perhaps for the first time in his life. Patients who suffered from Dissociative Identity Disorder typically required years of therapy to pull themselves free of their alternate personalities.

For that matter, even the diagnosis would take some time. Kevin's admittedly enigmatic behavior didn't fit any classical disorder. Dissociative Identity Disorder, yes, but there were no cases of three personalities carrying on a conversation as she herself had witnessed. Posttraumatic Stress Disorder, perhaps. Or a strange blend of Schizophrenia and DID. The scientific community would undoubtedly argue over this one.

The good news was that Kevin could hardly be better. He would need help, but she'd never seen such a sudden shift.

"I'm curious," Dr. Francis said. "Have you unraveled Samantha's part in all this?"

Samantha? He spoke as if she were still a real person. Jennifer looked at him and caught the smile in his eyes. "I think you mean how Kevin managed to play Samantha without tipping his hand, don't you?"

"Yes. In the public places."

"You were right—another day or two and we'd have caught on. There were only three places where Sam was supposedly exposed to the public. The Howard Johnson hotel, the hotel in Palos Verdes where they spent the night, and when they cleared the bus. I talked to the clerk at the Howard Johnson where Sam stayed. She did remember Sam, if you recall, but the person who she remembers was a man with brown hair and blue eyes. Sam."

"Kevin," the professor said.

"Yes. He actually went over there and checked in as Sam, thinking he really was her. If he'd signed in under Samantha instead of Sam, the clerk would have raised a brow. But to her he was Sam."

"Hmm. And Palos Verdes?"

"The maître d' from the restaurant will be a good witness. Evidently some of the customers complained about the strange behavior of the man seated by the window. Kevin. He was staring directly across the table and speaking to an empty chair in hushed tones. Raised his voice a couple times." Jennifer smiled. "The maître d' approached and asked if everything was okay, and Kevin assured him it was. But that didn't stop him from walking to the dance floor a few minutes later and dancing with an invisible partner before leaving the room."

"Sam."

"Sam. According to Kevin, the only other time they were together in public was when they cleared the bus that blew up. Kevin insisted that Sam was in the car, but none of the passengers remember seeing another person in the car. And when I drove by a few minutes after the explosion, Kevin was alone, although he clearly remembers Sam sitting beside him, talking on her phone to her superiors. The California Bureau of Investigation has no record of her, of course."

"Of course. And I suppose Kevin chose to imitate the Riddle Killer because it offered him a fully fleshed persona."

"Don't you mean *Slater?*"

"Pardon me—Slater." The professor smiled.

"We found a stack of newspaper clippings on the Riddle Killer in Slater's desk. Several were addressed to Kevin's home. He never remembers receiving them. He can't remember how he got into the library undetected or how he planted the bombs in his car or the bus, although the evidence in the basement leaves no doubt that he built all three bombs."

Jennifer shook her head. "Kevin himself, as himself, wasn't aware that he was carrying both Sam's and Slater's cell phones most of the time. You'd think when he wasn't in their personas, he'd be aware of that much, but somehow the alter egos managed to shut off his mind to those realities. Amazing how the mind works. I've never heard of such a clear fragmentation."

"Because the personalities Kevin spun off were so diametrically opposed," Dr. Francis said. "*What falls but never breaks; what breaks but never falls?* Night and day. Black and white. Evil and good. Kevin."

"Night and day. Evil. Some in your camp are calling him possessed, you know?"

"I've heard."

"And you?"

He took a deep breath and let it out slowly. "If they want to attribute his evil nature to a demonic presence or a stronghold, they may do so without argument or endorsement from me. It sounds quite sensational, but it doesn't change the fundamental truth. Evil is evil, whether it takes the form of a devil with horns or a demon from hell or the gossip of a bishop. I believe Kevin was merely playing out the natures that reside in all humans from birth. Like a child might play Dorothy and the Wicked Witch of the West. But Kevin really believed he was both Slater and Samantha, thanks to his own childhood."

The professor crossed his arms and looked back out at Kevin, who was staring at a cloud formation now.

"I do believe that we all have Slater and Samantha living within us as part of our own nature," he said. "You could call me *Slater-John-Samantha.*"

"Hmm. And I suppose that would make me *Slater-Jennifer-Samantha.*"

"Why not? We all struggle between good and evil. Kevin lived that struggle out in dramatic fashion, but we all live the same struggle.

We all struggle with our own Slaters. With gossip and anger and jealousy. Kevin said his term paper was going to be a story—in more ways than one, I think he just lived his paper out."

"Forgive my ignorance, Professor," Jennifer said without looking at him, "but how is it that you, supposedly a 'regenerated' man, devoted servant of God, still struggle with evil?"

"Because I am a creature of free will," Dr. Francis said. "I have the choice at any given moment how I will live. And if I choose to hide my evil in a basement, as Kevin did, it will grow. Those who populate America's churches may not be blowing up buses and kidnapping, to be sure, but most hide their sin just the same. Slater lurks in their dungeons and they refuse to blow the lid off them, so to speak. Kevin, on the other hand, most certainly blew the lid off, no pun intended."

"Unfortunately, he took half the city with him."

"Did you hear what Samantha said in the basement?" the professor asked.

Jennifer had wondered if he would bring up Samantha's words. "'You are powerless on your own. But if you look to your Maker, you'll find enough power to kill a thousand Slaters,'" she said. The words Samantha spoke to Kevin had haunted Jennifer for the last week. How had Kevin known to say that? Was it really as simple as his good nature crying out the truth?

"She was right. We are all powerless to deal with Slater on our own."

He was talking about man's dependence on God to find true freedom. He'd spent long hours with Kevin in his prison cell—Jennifer wondered what had passed between them.

"After seeing what I've seen down here, I'm not going to even try to argue with you, Professor." She nodded at Kevin. "You think he's . . . okay?"

"Okay?" Dr. Francis's right eyebrow went up. He smiled. "I'm sure he'll be delighted to hear the news you have, if that's what you mean."

Jennifer felt exposed. He could see more than she meant for him to see, couldn't he?

"Take your time. I have some calls to make." He walked for his study.

"Professor."

He turned back. "Yes?"

"Thank you. He . . . we . . . *We* owe our lives to you."

"Nonsense, dear. You owe me nothing. You may, however, have a debt to Samantha. And to Samantha's Maker." He grinned deliberately and entered his study.

Jennifer waited until his door closed. She slid the glass door open and stepped onto the patio. "Hello, Kevin."

He turned, eyes bright. "Jennifer! I didn't know you were here."

"I had some time." As much as she tried to ignore the fact, there was a unique bond between them. Whether it was her natural reaction to the sympathy he engendered or her own generous spirit or more, she didn't know. Time would tell. The Riddle Killer was still at large, and yet she somehow felt she'd found herself for the first time since Roy's death.

Kevin glanced back at the roses. His eyes couldn't hold hers unwaveringly as they had before—he'd lost a certain innocence. But she preferred him this way.

"I'm taking a sabbatical," she said.

"From the FBI? You are?"

"I am. I just came from a hearing with Judge Rosewood." Jennifer couldn't contain herself any longer. She smiled wide.

"What?" he asked. Her elation spread to him. "What's so funny?"

"Nothing. She's going to consider my request."

"The judge? What request?"

"You do know that I'm a licensed psychotherapist, don't you?"

"Yes."

"Even if we win your acquittal, which I think we will, the court will insist on therapy. In fact, your treatment will likely begin much sooner. But I don't think we can trust just any psychotherapist to pry around your head."

"Psychobabble," he said. "They . . ." His eyes widened. "You?"

Jennifer laughed. If the judge could see her now, she might reconsider. But she couldn't. In fact, no one could. The professor had retired to his office.

She walked up to him, pulse quickening. "Not your psychotherapist, exactly. But I'll be there, every step of the way, monitoring. I don't intend to let anyone mess with your mind any more than they have to."

He stared into her eyes. "I think I'd let you mess with my mind."

Everything in Jennifer's being wanted to reach out to him then. To touch his cheek and tell him that she cared for him more than anyone she'd cared for in a very long time. But she was an FBI agent, for heaven's sake. The agent in charge of his case! She had to remember that.

"Do I really need a psychotherapist?" he asked.

"You need me." That sounded a bit forward. "I mean you need someone *like* me. There are a lot of issues . . ."

Kevin suddenly leaned forward and kissed her on the cheek. "No, I don't need someone like you," he said. "I need you."

He pulled back, then looked away and blushed.

She couldn't help herself anymore. She stepped forward and kissed him very lightly on his cheek.

"And I need you, Kevin. I need you too."

I do not understand what I do. . . . It is no longer I myself who do it, but it is sin living in me. . . . For what I do is not the good I want to do; no, the evil I do not want to do—this I keep on doing. . . . I find this law at work: When I want to do good, evil is right there with me. . . . I delight in God's law; but I see another law at work in the members of my body, waging war against the law of my mind and making me a prisoner of the law of sin. I myself in my mind am a slave to God's law, but in the sinful nature a slave to the law of sin.

From a letter written by Saint Paul to the church in Rome, A.D. 57.
ROMANS 7:15–25

obsessed

This one's for The Circle

1

ROTH BRAUN SLOWLY TWISTED THE DOORKNOB AND GAVE THE door a slight shove. A familiar medicinal odor stung his nostrils. Outside, the sun warmed a midsummer day, but here in the dungeon below the house, the old man lived in perpetual twilight.

Roth imagined a Jew stepping into a delicing shower and let himself relish the horror he might feel in that moment of realizing that more than lice were meant to die in this chamber.

Roth was in a very good mood.

The smothering quiet was broken by the sound of the old prune's tarred, seventy-eight-year-old lungs rasping for relief. Gerhard's wheezing annoyed Roth, ruining his otherwise perfect mood.

The only living soul he despised more than the Jew who'd stolen his power was Gerhard, who had allowed the Jew to steal his power.

He glanced at Klaus, the gangly male nurse who had tended his father for three years. The white-smocked man hovered over Gerhard in the corner of the room, refusing to meet Roth's eyes. Gerhard Braun sat in a dark-red leather recliner, blue eyes glaring over the nasal cannula protruding from each nostril.

"Good morning, Father," Roth said. He closed the door quietly and stepped into the room, pushing aside a curtain of tinkling glass beads that separated it from the entryway. "You wanted to see me?"

His father looked at a servant, who busied himself over the table in the adjacent dining room.

"Leave us."

By the trembling in his voice, either Gerhard really was dying, or something was upsetting him, which invariably sowed its own sort of death. How many men alive today had been responsible for as many deaths as his father? They could be counted on two hands.

Even so, Roth hated him.

The servant dipped his head and exited through a side door. The steel door closed and the nurse flinched. Glass in a cabinet behind the table rattled despite the room's solid-concrete walls. The nineteenth-century Russian crystal—one of dozens of similar collections pilfered during the war—had once belonged to the czar. The Nazis' defeat should have sent Gerhard to the gallows; instead, the war had left his father with obscene wealth. The paintings alone had netted him a significant fortune, and these he owned legally. He'd shipped them to Zurich, where a hotly contested law made them his after remaining unclaimed for five years. Compliments of the Swiss Federation of Art Dealers.

Until the day I suck the energy from your bones, I will love you for showing me the way.

Until the day I suck the energy from your bones, I will despise you for what you did.

Gerhard held up a newspaper. "Have you read this?"

Roth walked across the circular rope rug that covered the black cement slab and stopped five feet from Gerhard. A hawk nose curved over his father's thin, trembling lips. Wispy strands of gray hair backlit by a yellow lamp hovered over his scalp. Skeletal, blue-veined fingers clutched what appeared to be a *Los Angeles Times*. A stack of newspapers—the *New York Times, Chicago Tribune,* London's *Daily Telegraph,* and a dozen others—sat a half-meter thick on the small end table to his left. Gerhard routinely spent six hours each day reading.

Gerhard flung the paper with a flick of his wrist, never removing his eyes from Roth. It landed on the floor with a *smack.*

"Read it."

The male nurse pretended to fiddle with the oxygen tank. Roth stood still. This attitude of Gerhard's was no longer simply ruining his mood, but destroying it altogether.

"I said, 'Read it'!"

Roth calmly bent and picked up the paper. The *Los Angeles Times* was folded around an article in the Life section, "Fortune Goes to Museum." Roth scanned the text. A wealthy woman, a Jew named Rachel Spritzer, sixty-two years of age, had died three days ago in Los Angeles. She'd been survived by no one and had donated her entire estate to the Los Angeles Museum of the Holocaust.

"So another Jew's dead." Roth lowered the paper. "Your legacy lives on."

His father clutched the arms of his chair. "Read the rest." His chest sounded like a whistle.

If Roth wasn't a master of his own impulses, he might have done something stupid, such as kill the man. Instead, he set the paper on the windowsill and turned away. "You've read it, Father. Tell me what it says. I have a ten o'clock engagement."

"Cancel it."

Roth walked to the bar. Control. "Just tell me what has you so concerned."

"The Stones of David have me concerned."

Roth blinked. He poured a splash of cognac into a snifter.

"I'm finished chasing your ghosts." He swirled the brandy slowly before sipping it. "If the Stones still exist, we would have found them long ago."

Gerhard managed to stand, trembling from head to foot, red as a rooster around the neck.

"They *have* been found. And you know what that means." He launched into a coughing fit.

Roth's pulse quickened a hair and then eased. If the man wasn't dying, he was losing his mind. Surely the Stones hadn't been found after all this time.

Gerhard staggered three steps to the windowsill, pushing his startled nurse out of the way, and grabbed the newspaper. He leaned on the wall with one hand and held the paper up in the other. He threw the paper toward Roth. It fluttered noisily and landed on the black slab.

"Read it!" Gerhard's eyes drilled him. So then maybe there was something to this.

Roth picked up the paper, found the article, and slowly read down the column. What if Gerhard was right? What if the relics did exist after all? They would be priceless. But the Stones' monetary value didn't interest Gerhard—he already had enough wealth to waste in his final years.

Gerhard's obsession was for the journal that had gone missing with the Stones.

And Roth's obsession was for the power that had gone missing with the Jew who'd taken the journal.

He had spent nearly thirty years tracking down innumerable leads, searching in vain. There was no telling how much wealth had been stripped from the Jews when Hitler had gathered them up and sent them to the camps. Much of the fortune had been confiscated by the gestapo and recovered after the war, but a number of particularly valuable items— priceless relics that belonged in museums or in vaults—had disappeared. Some of those treasures could be found in this very house. But any well-heeled collector knew that the most valuable collection had vanished for good in 1945.

The Stones of David.

One stunning item in Spritzer's collection is an extremely old golden medallion, better known as one of the five Stones of David. According to legend, the medallions are the actual stones selected by David to kill the giant Goliath. The smooth stones were subsequently gilded and stamped with the Star of David. The collection was last verified in 1307, when they were held by the Knights Templars. The collection was rumored to be held by a wealthy Jewish collector before World War II but went missing before the claim could be verified.

Alone, each medallion may be worth over $10,000,000. But the collection in its entirety is valued at roughly $100,000,000. The relic will be displayed in a museum yet to be disclosed with the following cryptic caption at Rachel Spritzer's request: "The Stones are like the lost orphans. They will eventually find each other."

Sweat cooled Roth's palms. He set the paper on the bar, set an unsteady finger in its margin, and scanned to the end.

> *Rachel Spritzer lived alone in an apartment complex she owned on La Brea Avenue and died a widow. The complex will be sold by the estate, along with much of Spritzer's noncollectible property.*
>
> *Rudy and Rachel Spritzer immigrated to the United States sixteen years ago, five years before Rudy was killed in an automobile accident. (See B4.)*

For a moment Roth's vision clouded. His mouth went dry.

"Now I have your attention?" Gerhard demanded.

Roth read the article again, searching for any phrase that might undermine the possibility that this Jew could be anyone other than whom Gerhard was suggesting.

"She was sixty-two," Gerhard said. "The right age."

Roth's mind flashed back to those war years when he was only twelve. Even if the connections were only circumstantial, he could hardly ignore them.

"I *knew* the Jew survived," Gerhard said.

"She donated only one Stone. There were five."

"If one Stone exists, then the journal exists. Someone has that journal!"

"She's dead."

"You will make her speak from the grave." Gerhard swayed on his feet, right fist trembling. His eyes looked black in the basement's shadows. "She knew. She knew about the journal."

"She's dead!" Roth snapped. He took a deep breath, irritated with himself for losing control. The fact was, Gerhard's history with the Stones gave him knowledge that no one else could possibly have.

"You know well enough that the journal implicates the entire line of elders. It lists each of our names and the names of the women we killed. It must be found!"

Mention of the women triggered a coppery taste in the back of Roth's mouth. The last time he'd seen the journal, it contained 243 names. Roth would one day surpass that number, he had vowed it.

But even a thousand or ten thousand would not compensate for the one that had escaped Gerhard.

"That woman would toy with me even in her death," the old man said. "In her house, in her belongings—somewhere, the old bat left a trail. You will go to Los Angeles." The nurse, Klaus, moved to assist Gerhard back to his seat, but the old man shook him off. Klaus retreated.

Gerhard was right. The Stones could lead to the journal. The journal could lead to the Jew. The Jew would lead to power, a supernatural power that his father had never attained. But Roth would.

The prospect of finding the Jew after so many years felt delightfully obscene.

Roth realized that his fingers were trembling.

"The United States," Roth said absently. "We don't have the same liberties there."

"That's never stopped you before."

The notion swarmed Roth like bees from a disturbed hive. Hope. More than hope—a desperate urgency to possess. Pounding heart, dry mouth. He was no fool. He would neither fight the emotion nor show it. After lingering so long on the edges of his mind, the desire to possess this one lost hope swallowed him. This is what Roth lived for, the purest form of power found in the very emotion that at this very moment raged through his body.

In his mind's eye he was already flying to America. He would have to move quickly, set the trap immediately. There was no telling how long they would keep the old Jew's collectibles in Los Angeles.

Roth stared into his father's blue eyes for a few long seconds, torn between the man's mad obsession with the past and his own with the future. What Roth did for tomorrow, Gerhard did because of yesterday. Who was the better man?

He remembered the first dead Jew he'd seen in the camps twenty-eight years ago. He'd been eating fresh eggs and sausage prepared by one of the Polish servants from the village for breakfast. It was the most delicious breakfast he'd ever tasted. Perhaps leaving his mother in Germany to spend the summer with his father up in Poland would be a good thing after all. He was twelve at the time.

"Papa?"

"What?" his father asked, walking toward the window overlooking the concentration camp.

"Why do Polish eggs taste better than German eggs?"

His father pulled back the curtain, and Roth saw a woman hanging from the main gate. Gerhard answered him, but Roth didn't hear the response. The year was 1942, and hers was the first of many dead bodies Roth would see in Poland. But there was something about the first.

Roth let the memory linger, then returned his mind to the Stones. His father's eyes glistened with tears; his face wrinkled.

"The Jew took my soul. *She* took my soul! I beg you, my son." Roth felt a terrible pity for him. A single tear broke free and ran down Gerhard's right cheek.

"If the Jew is alive, she will be drawn by the Stone," Roth said.

"Forget the Jew. I must have the journal. You see that, don't you? More than anything, I must have it." He held out a spindly arm laced with bulging veins. "Swear it to me. Swear you'll bring me what is mine."

Roth looked at the large swastika on the gray wall, sickened by Gerhard's weakness. He would make it right, because the Stones meant far more to him than they could possibly mean to his father.

"Come here," Roth said to the nurse.

Klaus glanced at Gerhard then stepped out from the shadows.

Roth backed up and stepped off the rug. There was the right way and the wrong way to do this, and the purest in mind knew the difference.

"Farther, to the middle of the rug," he said.

Klaus took another step so that he stood near the center of the rug.

"I would like to repay you for your care of my father," Roth said. "Few men could put up with a whining old man the way you do. Is there anything you would like?"

No response. Of course not.

"Anything at all?"

The nurse lowered his head. "No sir."

Roth pulled out his gun and shot Klaus through the top of his head while he was still bent over. The slug likely ended up in his throat.

The man dropped in a pile.

Roth looked at his father. "You should have sent him out."

"You're working against your own kind," Gerhard said. "He was pure."

"Then I did him a favor by sending him to his grave pure."

2

STEPHEN FRIEDMAN MARCHED ALONG THE SOUTH EDGE OF THE vacant Santa Monica parking lot, mind whirling. This was a primo deal, baby. Definitely, absolutely, one of the most primo deals he had come across in the seven years he'd played the real-estate market.

His partner on occasion, Dan Stiller, followed closely at Stephen's heels, black portfolio under his arm.

Stephen leaped over a chain and kept an energetic pace along the uneven asphalt. Tufts of stubborn brown grass grew among the cracks. The crumbling brick wall across the lot had been decorated by hundreds of white droppings. Seagulls. Someone had scrawled some word art on the wall: BIG DADDY ROCKS. To any ordinary pedestrian, the parking lot would have looked desolate, and perhaps worthless.

To Stephen, this piece of ground looked like a slice of potential paradise.

He smiled at Dan, who'd walked around the chain. Prevailing Santa Ana winds slapped at the wide lapels of Dan's plaid polyester blazer and whipped his hair back. The effect accentuated his sloping forehead and turned his bulbous nose into something that might have fit a Boeing 747. But behind that nose, Dan's brain was proportionally as large. They made a good team for the odd investment—two young Jews, both immigrants, carving out a new life in this magnificent land of opportunity. Where Dan's conservatism held them in check, Stephen's enthusiasm drove them on.

"It's a natural," Stephen said.

"Like the condo in Pasadena was a natural?" Dan referred to the complex Stephen had insisted they convert to a neighborhood amusement park. But the notes came due before construction could begin.

"I got us out of that, didn't I?" Stephen said.

"Involving a crook like Joel Sparks isn't exactly my idea of getting us out."

"The mob rap is totally hearsay. He's a businessman; he has money. He bailed us out."

"We lost a hundred thousand dollars."

"You've never lost a hundred thousand before? You win some, you lose some." Stephen turned to the vacant lot. "Besides, this one's a winner, guar-an-teed." He took a long whiff of the air. "I can practically smell it. You smell that, Dan? That's money you smell."

"Actually, that's exhaust I smell. And it's the carbon monoxide in the exhaust, the stuff you *can't* smell, that worries me."

"It may just be me, but I get the distinct impression you have some doubts. You don't trust my nose?"

Dan wiped his brow. "I don't doubt your ability to choose them, Stephen. But, yes, I'm struggling with this particular idea."

Stephen had made and lost a million dollars a dozen times already— and they both knew as much. The very same impulsive passion that pushed him to seize opportunity also landed him in trouble from time to time. He made a million dollars easier than most. He also lost it easier than most.

Never mind. The fact that he now understood this about himself tipped the scales in his favor. He was up at the moment—eight hundred thousand up. Not bad for a thirty-one-year-old immigrant from Russia. Dan, for all his cautiousness, was only liquid to the tune of half that much. Which was why he needed Stephen. The only real issue separating them was what to do with the property.

Stephen tapped his temple. "You have to imagine it, Daniel. Open your mind!" He scanned the property and spoke with animated gestures. "Americans love entertainment. Cotton candy, ice cream, a roller coaster." He pointed to the deteriorated brick wall. "Right over there you see gull droppings; I see balloons. This lot is most definitely a coastal amusement park begging to be built."

Three teenagers passing by on the sidewalk turned to look at Stephen as his voice grew louder.

"I'm not saying that it couldn't happen, but a museum is more reasonable, if not to you, then to the city planners. Stephen, think. We have to submit our intentions with the down payment by next Wednesday. There are two other parties bidding. If the city rejects our plan, we lose the deal. All I'm suggesting is that we go with a more conservative plan."

"And I say the people here are secretly crying out for a roller coaster. They're praying every night for us to put thoughts of museums and office buildings out of our minds, because they want clowns and the sound of laughing children to invade their neighborhood."

Dan stared at him.

Stephen saw an opportunity and seized it. He stepped toward the teenagers and motioned to a boy with long blond hair and a pooka-shell necklace. "Excuse me, Sir Hamlet, there. Could I get your opinion on something?"

The blond boy glanced at a younger rail-thin girl with large freckles and an embroidered blouse, and a skinny boy who towered over both of them.

Stephen fished out a ten-dollar bill. "I'll give you ten bucks for five minutes of your time."

"Ten bucks?"

"Ten bucks."

"For what?"

"Just to act something out for me and my business partner here."

Dan objected. "Come on, Stephen."

"Act what out?" the blond kid asked.

"We're investors, and we're trying to decide if this parking lot should be an amusement park or a museum." Stephen pointed to the freckled girl. "I want you to stand over there"—he pointed, then gestured toward the other two—"and you two over there and there."

"Ten bucks for each of us?" the boy asked in a small voice.

Stephen saw that they were sloppily dressed. Not *cool* sloppily, but poor sloppily. The girl's sandals were tied together with string, and the tall skinny kid's bell-bottoms were ankle-high. For a moment he just stared at them, struck by an odd sense of empathy that he couldn't place. The city was full of kids like this—why these three suddenly pulled at his heart, he didn't know.

No, he did know. At this moment they were him. They were decent, wide-eyed kids mesmerized by the possibility of making a quick ten dollars.

"What's your name?" Stephen asked the blond boy.

"Mike." If the boy were a smart aleck, Stephen might have changed his mind. But no snot-nosed kid would have answered the question so innocently. Several others on the sidewalk had stopped and were watching.

"I'll tell you what, Mike. I'll give you each *twenty* dollars if you help me out here. That's a lot of money for five minutes, but my friend and I are going to make a bundle on this piece of property, so I think it's fair. What do you say?"

"You mean it? Twenty dollars?" the small girl asked, eyes wide.

"I mean it."

One last glance at each other, and they scrambled over the chain to their posts.

"What do we do?"

"I want you to pretend you're an amusement park." He pointed to each in succession. "You're a Ferris wheel, you're a merry-go-round, and you're a roller coaster. Just stick your arms up like this"—he threw his hands up over his head—"or like this"—he waved them out at his sides—"and when I tell you to, pretend you're machines."

"You better not be pulling our legs about the twenty dollars," the blond boy said.

"Scout's honor," Stephen said.

The kids adjusted their arms.

"Perfect!" Stephen faced Dan. "Okay, Dan, now you stand over here—"

"I'm not doing this, Stephen."

"You have to! I need you to do this. You need to stand over there like a statue. How else are we going to compare?"

"No way."

Stephen took his arm, turned him from the kids, and whispered. "Be a good sport, Dan. For their sakes. Look, you need my five hundred grand, right? Just go along with me here."

Dan looked at the three kids and then walked to one side.

"Act like a statue, Dan," Stephen said.

"I am like a statue."

"Stick an arm up or something, so you look more like a statue."

Dan hesitated and then raised an arm and went stiff, like a German soldier saluting.

The gawking crowd on the sidewalk now included a dozen kids and several adults. Stephen faced them.

"Ladies and gentlemen, we're conducting a quick survey here. We have to decide whether we want to build an amusement park or a museum here. You guys are the judges."

He spun and faced the three kids like a conductor cuing up his orchestra. "Ready?"

The freckled girl chuckled. "You're pretty crazy, mister."

"You'd better believe I am. Ready?"

"Ready."

"Okay, make like an amusement park." He waved his arms.

The tall skinny kid was the roller coaster. He stuck his arms out like a cross, which wasn't Stephen's idea of how to show a coaster, but at least the boy was playing along. The girl turned in a slow circle like a merry-go-round, and the blond boy made a circle with his arms. Ferris wheel. They grinned wide.

"Sound! Sound!" Stephen called.

"Sound is an extra five bucks," the blond boy said.

"Make it ten," Stephen said. Shoot, he'd probably give them forty if they wanted it. "Give me some sound!"

"*Vroom, vroom. Whir.*" Wasn't much, but it earned some laughs from the gathering crowd. "*Honk honk,*" snorted the girl.

"Excuse me," Stephen said. "What's *honk honk*? If I'm paying ten bucks for a noise, I need to know what it is."

"It's the line of cars waiting to get in," the girl said.

Stephen smiled wide, delighted. "There you go, then. Cars waiting to get in to the amusement park!" He faced the crowd. "All in favor of the amusement park, raise your hands."

Two dozen hands went up amid chuckles.

"All those in favor of a museum"—Stephen pointed to Dan—"raise your hands."

A middle-aged couple walking by raised their hands and grinned.

"There you go. Case settled. Thank you for your cooperation. You're dismissed." Some loitered, some moved on.

The kids ran up to him and Stephen handed each thirty dollars.

"That's it?" Mike asked. "We're done?"

"You're done. Don't blow it all at once."

They hurried off, looking back over their shoulders.

Dan shook his head. "Okay, Mr. Hot Shot. So you have a bit of charm with the locals. I can assure you that the bank, which holds the papers on this lot, doesn't care about your antics. And I guarantee the city will look more favorably on a museum than on a playground. Especially a museum that already has its backers. You know the Jewish Public Affairs Committee has talked about bringing the Holocaust museum under its umbrella and then relocating it. Why not here? If they follow through, we'll do well. That was the whole idea."

"Just because we're Jewish doesn't mean everything we do has to promote the Jewish cause," Stephen said. "This is nothing but business."

"Of course. But you *are* a Jew. A secular Jew without much sentimentality for our history, maybe, but still a Jew. You can't ignore that. You're irrevocably tied to the war."

Stephen's morning paled. Dan's problem was that he knew too much.

"No, Dan, nothing is irrevocable. Especially not memories of the war. This is the United States of America, not Poland. Just because my great-great-great-great-grandmother dug potatoes in Poland or wherever doesn't mean I have to build a monument to her here."

Stephen had left both Russia and his past at age twenty to find a new life, and for the most part he'd succeeded. Anything that threatened to take him back, even if only in his mind, offended him.

"You're being unfair," Daniel said quietly. "You owe your life to your mother. And you know very well that she probably gave her life in one of the camps. How can you turn your back on that?"

"Because I don't *know* that she died in a camp," Stephen snapped. "I don't even know who she was. Why do you bring this up? I'll give you money for your museum. Just don't pretend we're crusaders here. I spent twenty years trying to find my mother and finally came here to give up that search. I don't have the stamina for that kind of thing."

"Seek and you will find—"

Stephen flung an arm into the air, his irritation flaring to anger. "Don't patronize me. For all I know, my mother and father *were* killed in some gas chamber. Whoever brought me into this world obviously suffered enough—is it incumbent on me to suffer too? As far as I'm concerned, it never happened. I don't have a mother. I'm not even Jewish anymore."

He paused, surprised by the emotion shortening his breath.

"And if there's a God in heaven who cares that I should seek, then I challenge him to create something . . ." He pinched his thumb and forefinger together. "Even a small morsel of some goodness worth seeking. Anything but the death that turns up everywhere I look."

Dan blinked at his outburst. "I'm sorry—"

"Then leave it. Give me some breathing room. Build your museum, but don't exploit my conscience."

Dan held up both hands.

For a few seconds that stretched into twenty, they stood in the vacant lot, making a good show of studying it. How they had managed to go from amusement parks to prison camps was beyond Stephen. Why, he wasn't entirely sure, but the subject never failed to resurrect ugly feelings he couldn't deal with.

Actually, he could deal with them. By burying them. Burying them deep and letting them lie dead in an unmarked grave. Certainly not by building a monument to them.

"You know, you may be right," Dan said. "An amusement park could transform this neighborhood."

"Forget it," Stephen said. "You already have backing for the museum. It's the safer plan. Though not as much fun, you have to admit."

"No, not as much fun. Your call."

"Couldn't we build a museum as part of an amusement park?"

Dan chuckled. "Now, there's an idea. I have three hundred thousand. We need eight by Tuesday. Can I count on you for the five?"

"Yes. And forget the amusement park for the time being. I'll run some comps and get the money to you by Tuesday."

"Okay." They shook hands.

"Sorry, huh?" Stephen said. "I can get carried away sometimes."

"Don't be ridiculous. I shouldn't have brought it up." He nodded at Stephen's blue Chevy Vega. "Go buy yourself a new car; it'll help you feel better."

"What, you don't like my car?"

"It's a bucket of bolts."

"It's my friend. Maybe the only one I have. Other than you and Chaim, of course. And I just installed an eight-track." He snapped his fingers to a few bars from James Taylor's "You've Got a Friend."

They stared at each other. For some strange reason a great sadness crept into Stephen's chest. He suddenly felt very lonely. He was standing in the middle of a parking lot in Santa Monica, surrounded by pedestrians and cars, contemplating a deal that could make him hundreds of thousands of dollars, and he felt oddly abandoned.

Like an outcast. Or like a child who couldn't find his mother. Both.

Stephen swallowed. *Bury it.* He grinned and slapped Dan on the back. "Man, you have got to stop being so serious. I'll see you later."

Dan smiled back. "Okay."

ROTH BRAUN STOOD ATOP THE GUTTED BUILDING ACROSS THE street from Rachel Spritzer's apartment. The warm California breeze swept over his face, through his hair, around his arms. He hated America, but he loved the purity of nature, and despite the smell of exhaust, the wind held some of the power that came with that purity. Even those who thought they understood the psychic energy in nature rarely really understood its true unspoiled power.

It was the energy of a million nuclear detonations.

It was the force of a billion dying babies crying out at once.

It was the substance of creation—raw, staggering. A plea to reverse the chaos suffered at the hands of ruined humanity.

Purity. This was the true meaning behind the Nazi swastika.

Roth unbuttoned the top three buttons on his black silk shirt and let the breeze reach inside. The others were waiting in the car with the agent who would show them Rachel Spritzer's building. Roth had insisted they wait while he scouted out the neighborhood. The Realtor had objected, and Roth wanted to crush his windpipe, but his practiced and generous self-control had allowed him simply to repeat the demand and thereby receive a nod.

The Realtor undoubtedly assumed that Roth was walking around the buildings to get a feel for the value of the adjacent land. Instead, he had climbed the stairs of this abandoned building opposite the Spritzer place and now stood unseen above them all.

Like a god.

Still, they were waiting; otherwise he might have performed a ritual to the spirit of the air, right here on the black tarred roof.

He'd slept less than four hours since shooting the male nurse in Gerhard's flat, but he felt as though he could go another week without closing his eyes. This time, the success of his mission was within reach.

Roth put his hands on his hips and walked to his right, keeping his eyes on Rachel Spritzer's apartment.

"Who are you, Rachel Spritzer?" He spoke low. "What secrets do you hold? Hmm? Who will come to find you? Who, who, who? I know who."

He did not doubt that this rather plain-looking four-story apartment complex held the secret to more power than most of the neighbors who'd lived like rats around it for the last thirty years could imagine. He knew this because he had disciplined his mind to connect with the psychic energy that said it was so.

The Stones had surfaced through the death of yet another Jew. Fitting. There was Gerhard's fortune to be found, yes. But more. Much more.

Roth lifted his eyes and scanned the city stretching into the haze. He breathed deeply and closed his eyes. In his younger days, before he'd perfected his exquisite self-control, he might have succumbed at a time like this to the compulsion to kill. The discovery of Rachel's Stone called for a celebration, no doubt about that. But he would wait until the sun was down. What he had in mind here could not be compromised by weak-minded indulgences.

What he had in mind here would make an indiscriminate killing laughable. He would discriminate with utmost care.

Roth exhaled completely, allowed a shiver of eagerness to work its way through his body, and turned to the roof access.

Let the game begin.

4

TWO OR THREE TIMES A WEEK, STEPHEN CAME HOME FOR LUNCH. Today was one of those days, and Chaim Leveler was glad. The boy was clearly troubled by an altercation he'd had with Dan Stiller.

Evidently, Stephen had said a few things he now regretted. For all his ambition, the lad was actually quite sensitive. He tried to cover up the deep wounds of a hapless past, but no spin could change what had happened. Stephen would always be a war child: subject of all worlds, master of none. Lost in the folds of history without a true mother, a true father, or a true home.

Stephen sat at the chrome-rimmed dining-room table, spreading mayonnaise on his bread. "You should spend less time figuring out how to make money and more time thinking about love," Chaim said, laying a hand on Stephen's shoulder as he walked to his green vinyl chair. "Look at you. You are smart, good-looking. Although you could use a haircut, never mind what is culturally accepted. Either way, what woman can resist a dimpled smile? You're thirty-one. You should have three children already."

"Yes, of course. Sylvia."

"Now that you mention it . . ." Chaim had always thought Stephen and his bright young niece, as he insisted on calling her, would make a handsome pair.

"Please, Rabbi, I don't need a matchmaker."

Chaim wasn't technically a rabbi, at least not in the eyes of the synagogue. No Messianic Jew could truly be a rabbi. But the retired fire marshal had never been able to suppress his spiritual fervor. Not that he ever tried. He smiled at Stephen's term of endearment and rounded the table, stroking a full beard. The smell of fresh mint tea and salmon sandwiches whetted his appetite more than he cared to admit. Age had snuck up on him like a wolf on a rabbit; he had to stay fit enough to flee the snapping fangs. He touched his belly.

Chaim had left Russia immediately after the Second World War. Two years in the Sobibor prison camp had exhausted his interest in Europe. His brother, Benadine Leveler, had survived the war fighting with a Polish resistance group. Afterward, Benadine had stayed in Russia and opened the orphanage where Stephen was deposited as a child. At times, Chaim felt guilty for coming to this land of plenty, but how could he feel bad with Stephen at his table? The lad may never have come to America if Chaim hadn't blazed the trail.

The call from his brother, informing him that Stephen was coming to America, had been one of Chaim's brightest moments. It had been a pleasure to help Stephen, no longer a child, find his feet. As it turned out, Stephen hardly needed help. He'd completed his studies with honors and entered the lucrative world of real estate at the age of twenty-four. Still, Chaim felt he could take some credit for that.

The boy had elected to live in Chaim's two-bedroom home all these years despite the alternatives his considerable earnings provided. Even in the best years, Stephen never ran out and bought a new Mercedes or otherwise advertised his wealth. America had a difficult time understanding Stephen. He didn't run through women, didn't drive fast cars, didn't spend half his earnings on parties and clothing. But not because he was too frugal or conservative.

Stephen could walk into a Las Vegas casino and drop a thousand dollars in a game of craps inside of ten minutes. He was as impetuous and bold as they came.

Stephen didn't flaunt his success for the simple reason that the trappings of American life didn't appeal to him. At least not the kind of trappings a few million dollars could buy. When Stephen dreamed, he dreamed of owning jets and buying islands. Of obscuring the past and buying himself a new future. He was a tie-dye dreamer; he dreamed big, audacious, colorful dreams that held certain appeal, even if they were absurd fantasies to most.

"What you need, dear Stephen, is some love in your life," Chaim said again.

"You don't give up, do you?"

"Why should I? Pass me the mayonnaise, will you?"

Stephen passed the jar.

"It wasn't so long ago that I was in love, you know," Chaim said. "Sofia. A beautiful Jewish girl in St. Rothsburg. When she entered my life, the rocks began to smell like chocolates. Nothing became everything overnight."

Stephen shook his head. "Enough."

Chaim acquiesced. They made small talk and ate their fish sandwiches. Delicious.

Stephen finally wiped his mouth and stood. "Speaking of love, didn't you invite Sylvia to supper tonight?"

"Dear me, I had forgotten!" Chaim stood and hurried to the sink. "And I'm cooking, yes?"

"We could order—"

"Nonsense! She loves my cooking. Did I promise her anything in particular?"

"Veal parmesan, wasn't it? Or was it fondue?"

"You're not sure?"

"I had more on my mind at the time than the menu." Stephen lifted his chin, stepped onto the kitchen floor, and began dancing with an imaginary partner. His lips twisted into that whimsical, dimpled smile. "Love, dear Rabbi. Remember? Love is in the air, and I am caught in its draft."

"Nonsense. I don't think you would know love if it smacked you upside the ear. Seriously, Stephen. Was it veal?"

Stephen spun around once. "Love, Rabbi. The food of life itself. Cook us love for dinner."

"Be serious, boy! I've forgotten what I told her!"

"It won't matter what we eat. Feed us stones, and we'll think they're chocolates, Rabbi. You do remember love, don't you?"

"Ha! I was born for love." Chaim impulsively stepped around the counter, grabbed the taller man's upheld hand, and swung into his dance. "Although I doubt I make a suitable partner."

Stephen didn't miss a beat. He spun Chaim around and feigned a swoon. "Abandon yourself, Rabbi. Tonight, I will feed on love."

Chaim dropped Stephen's hand, suddenly embarrassed. "Oy, what has become of us? What am I going to do about dinner?"

Stephen spun into the living room and abruptly dropped his arms. He walked to the stereo and punched the power button. "Veal sounds wonderful. I'm certain it was veal. In fact, I was sure all along. I just wanted to see your moves."

"My moves! Please!"

The telephone rang shrilly and Chaim picked it up.

―――

THE RABBI was right, Stephen thought. He really could use a little romance in his life. He spun the radio dial. Stopped on the alto voice of Carly Simon. Stephen returned the mayonnaise to the refrigerator while Chaim spoke into the phone. Of course, it meant finding the right woman to romance or, more to the point, finding a woman who wanted to be romanced by him. He'd had one major love fresh off the boat as a freshman in college. *"You gave away the things you loved, and one of them was me,"* Carly drawled. A girl named Betsy who had been utterly infatuated with him for two weeks before moving on to some other prey. The experience had left him less than confident. *"You're so vain, you're so vain."*

"Are you sure?" Chaim's tone caught Stephen's attention. "How is it possible?"

"What?" Stephen asked, closing the fridge.

Chaim responded by turning his back.

Something had happened. Stephen walked to the table to clear off the remaining dishes. Perhaps it was Marjorie Stillwater, the old lady from Chaim's church. She'd died? Or was this Joel Sparks, insisting that Stephen owed him money? What if something had happened to Sylvia?

The suggestions trotted through his mind, but none paused. It was probably nothing.

"Thank you, Gerik." The rabbi set down the phone.

"Well? What was that about?"

Chaim still didn't turn.

Alarm spread through Stephen. This wasn't like Chaim. Not at all.

"What's going on? For heaven's sake, tell me."

When the rabbi turned, the blood had faded from his already pale face—he looked like a ghost. He reached for the newspaper, flipped through the sections, stared at a page for a moment, then showed it to Stephen. "Did you hear about this?"

The page was open to the story about Rachel Spritzer's death. They had all heard of the reclusive woman, of course, at least of her reputation. Stephen glanced at the paper and shifted his eyes back to Chaim.

"I heard of it, yes. She lived alone in an old, vacant apartment complex off La Brea. The property is worth roughly five hundred thousand dollars, demolition costs factored. Why? You know something I don't?"

"She had in her possession one of the Stones of David, which she donated to the museum."

Stephen looked up. "No, I hadn't heard that." Surprising. Even stunning. But this information wouldn't have turned Chaim white. "You're serious? The Stones of David?" He reached for the paper. It came out of Chaim's limp hand.

Stephen glanced down the article, settled on the part about the relic, and read. His interest in the Stones of David had been started by his foster father. He glanced up, saw that Chaim was staring at him, and returned his eyes to the paper.

"I knew about the listing," he said. "But I didn't know about the Stone. This is proof, then. They do exist." Stephen quoted from the article: "The Stones are like the lost orphans. They will eventually find each other."

The rabbi was still quiet. Stephen closed the paper and dropped it on the table. "What gives?"

"She was an emigrant from Hungary," Chaim finally said. "A very wealthy emigrant who had in her possession one of the Stones of David. Not too many wealthy Jews survived the war."

"I can read that much for myself."

"She used to visit Gerik down at his antique shop. She left a note with him to be opened in the event of her death." Chaim stopped. "Evidently, she'd been sick for some time."

"And?"

"Do you mind . . . would you mind showing me your scar, Stephen?"

Odd request. He had a scar below his collarbone—a crude half circle with three points inside it, like a half-moon some creature had taken a bite out of. He'd searched for the meaning of the mark. Chaim had asked Gerik about it once, and the old man drew a blank. It was a mark from the war; they guessed that much, but no more.

Stephen pulled down his collar, revealing the scar.

Chaim stared and seemed to shrivel.

Stephen released the shirt. "What? Tell me—what!"

"Stephen, Rachel Spritzer's note says that she branded her son—who was born in a Nazi labor camp—with the image of half a Stone of David."

The words made no sense to Stephen. Rachel Spritzer marked her infant son. Half a Stone of David. Surely this wasn't connected to him.

Tears filled the rabbi's eyes. "She had been searching for her son since the war, but she had to be very secretive."

"You're not saying . . ."

Stephen felt the air slowly vacate his lungs. Heat washed down his neck and back.

"I'm saying that I think you've found your mother, Stephen. I think that Rachel Spritzer was your mother."

The room shifted out of focus. Stephen reached out to steady himself on a chair.

He couldn't breathe.

5

Poland
April 24, 1944
Early Morning

MARTHA PRESSED HER EYE AGAINST THE THIN CRACK BETWEEN the two boxcar planks for the thousandth time in four days. Outside, dawn colored Poland's horizon gray. Where in Poland, she didn't know. Why to Poland, she didn't know. But she was certain if they didn't stop soon, some of the women in this car never would know.

How long could a human live in a cramped box without food or water?

There was this gray sky above them, and there was this constant *clank, clank, clank* of railroad tracks below them, and there were vacant stares inside, and there was enough heartache to have wrung the tears from every one of them days ago, and that was the sum of the matter. Nothing to say, nothing to do, not much even to feel anymore.

Except for the baby. She had to feel for the sake of the baby inside her.

Martha clenched her jaw, turned back to the dark car, and slid to her seat. She hadn't urinated for two days, but the dull pain was manageable for the time being. There were three waste buckets on the far side, all full after the first day. Having nothing to eat or drink did have its advantages, however small.

The freight car held roughly seventy women, made up of two groups: a motley crew of fifty who'd accompanied her from the prison in Budapest, and another twenty who'd joined them much later, well inside Poland. Late on her second night in the car, the train had pulled into a large plant with huge smoking stacks. Martha had stared through the cracks at hundreds, maybe thousands of men, women, and children. They wore gaunt faces and walked slowly in long lines to the big brick buildings near the train's caboose. Music floated over the compound—Bach. Something felt horribly wrong with the scene, but she couldn't put her finger on it.

Soldiers swapped out the buckets, hustled the new prisoners on board, slammed the gate shut, and locked it tight. The boxcar began rolling again about an hour later.

Ruth had been in the second group, which was mostly comprised of Jews from Slovakia. The petite young woman had eyed Martha for a full day before edging past the others to her side. She'd taken Martha's arm at the elbow and stood in silence.

Martha smiled as best she could and placed her hand on Ruth's. They remained like that for several hours. No need for talk. Human touch was all the young woman seemed to want, and Martha found it indescribably comforting. *Everything will be all right because I can feel you, and you are all right. See, it's not so bad—your arm is warm.*

Ruth had finally stretched up on her toes and whispered into Martha's ear. "Are you from Hungary?"

Martha nodded. "Yes."

"I am Ruth Kryszka," she said in decent Hungarian. "They took my husband a week ago from a farm where we were hiding in Slovakia. I think they may have killed him." Her voice trembled slightly, but she seemed brave.

Martha drew her closer and felt compelled to kiss her on top of her head.

"Who are you?" Ruth asked.

The question was Martha's first normal exchange in four weeks, and it made her want to cry.

"I am Martha," she whispered. "Martha Spieller." She wasn't entirely sure why they were whispering. Perhaps because they clung to their own histories as the last bastion of meaning in a world gone mad. Sharing it was like sharing the deepest secret.

"I am from Budapest," Martha said.

"I studied in Budapest once," Ruth said. "It's a beautiful city. They are killing Jews in Hungary?"

Killing Jews? She said it as if she spoke of eating bread.

"Some. Not so much in Budapest, but my father was well-off. The gestapo came with the gendarmes three or four weeks ago. They confiscated our house and my father's collections. I was taken to the prison outside of Budapest, and now I'm here."

"Are you married?"

Martha had cried herself to sleep for two straight weeks in prison, remembering the brutality of that day. They'd been eating lunch—imported Swiss cheese and strawberries with a wonderful white wine—listening to Father talk confidently about the return of better days, when the pounding came on the door. Not just a knock, but smashing fists and shouts. For a moment they'd all frozen, even Father. Then he'd dabbed his lips, pushed back his chair, and assured them it would be all right. Yes, of course, he'd set things up with Kallay's high-ranking officials. No harm would come to his family.

But they all knew that one day harm would come. Most able-bodied Jewish men already had been sent to labor camps. All Jewish property had been legally confiscated.

Martha closed her eyes, doubting whether she could share this particular secret of hers. "My husband and father were killed in our home," she said with an ease that surprised her. "They took my mother and younger sister, but I haven't seen them."

It was enough for a few hours. After a period of rocking quietly with the clanking train, Martha rested her cheek on the shorter woman's head and quietly cried for the first time since boarding.

They whispered above the sound of the tracks several times over the next day, exchanging precious secrets that were really not secrets at all. They were both Jews. They had both lost their husbands and their homes. They were both young—Ruth twenty-five and Martha thirty-two—and above all, they were both on the same train, rolling and grunting and whistling its way steadily closer to some unknown destination.

Now, the dawn outside marked Martha's fourth morning aboard the cattle car, and still the train rumbled north, always north. Ruth sat next to Martha, knees bunched up to her chin, brown eyes bright, a fighter who'd accepted whatever comfort Martha could offer.

Ruth faced her and whispered. "Do you think we will both be in the same place?"

"I don't know where we're going."

"To a labor camp."

"A labor camp? You know this?"

"I think so." Ruth hesitated. "Do you know what they are doing? The Germans?"

"In the war?"

"No, to us. To the Jews."

Martha had heard rumors, hundreds. "They are killing some and forcing the rest to work."

"They are exterminating us," Ruth said. "It's why Paul and I went into hiding. The station where I was put on the train—I think that was a camp called Auschwitz, where they kill us like cattle. There are other death camps, but not this far north, I don't think."

Martha stared into the darkness. Surely Ruth was exaggerating. "They can't just kill like that."

"But they do. I heard it from someone who escaped from a camp called Sobibor. They kill with gas and then burn the bodies."

A chill swept over Martha. Gas?

She felt Ruth's eyes on her. "You're pregnant?"

"What?"

"You're pregnant, aren't you?"

Martha sat up, terrified that her secret was known. Was it so obvious? A cotton shirt and a loose wool sweater hid her belly well. This was her first child, and even without the loose shirt she wasn't showing much.

"I am also," Ruth whispered.

"You . . . you're pregnant?"

"I don't think we should let them know."

Martha was at a loss for words. If Ruth could see that she was pregnant in this dim light, surely others would see it as well. She'd refused to consider what the Germans might do to her when they learned of it, but she couldn't escape the certainty that they would eventually discover her child.

"How did you know?" she finally asked.

"Don't worry, it's not so obvious. I see these things."

"And they won't?"

"If they do, they'll know that I'm pregnant too," Ruth said. There was a comforting sweetness in her voice. She had a heart of gold, this one.

"How many months are you?" Martha asked.

"Six."

"Six? I am almost six!"

"Five then? You hardly show! It's your first? It must be your first."

Martha wondered if any of the others could hear their excited whispers. She lowered her voice.

"Yes, my first. And yours?"

"Yes."

For a minute, the secret lives they carried within them overshadowed any sense of pending doom. Martha could feel Ruth glowing beside her.

"What will you name it?" Ruth asked.

"I . . ." Now the desperation of their plight surfaced again. Martha looked away. "I don't know."

Ruth placed her palm on Martha's belly. "He feels like a David to me," she said.

"And if it's a girl?"

Ruth hesitated. "Esther. David or Esther."

THE TRAIN'S whistle pierced the silence. The cadence of the wheels immediately slowed. Martha tensed, then stood and peered through the thin crack.

"What is it?" Ruth asked over her shoulder. "We're stopping?"

"I don't know."

"Do you see buildings?"

"Yes. Yes, there are buildings!"

Murmurs swept through the boxcar. A woman to their left demanded that someone tell them what was going on. It occurred to Martha that the question was directed at her. She had the best eye-level view out of this box.

"I think we're stopping," she said. "There are buildings and a fence."

"A fence?"

Voices bubbled up in the car. A loud hissing confirmed her suspicions. The train was stopping.

Martha's palms were wet already. Good news might greet them here. A drink of water. Some soup and bread—stale, soggy, moldy; it wouldn't matter. There would be a toilet. Even a hole in the ground would be a welcome sight.

Ruth laced her fingers with Martha's and squeezed tight. "This is it! This has to be it."

"I think so."

The air felt electric.

Only Martha and another woman, who poked her head past Martha's knees, could see clearly. The train passed guards who held back dogs straining against their leashes. Soldiers lined a road beside the tracks, rifles slung, some staring casually, others smoking. A tall fence topped with rolls of barbed wire ran along the perimeter of a compound, which housed dozens of long rectangular buildings.

Martha glanced over her shoulder. The women who could stand had done so. They'd grown quiet again, eyes wide in the dim light, staring at her or at the cattle gate. Their door to freedom.

Ruth leaned into Martha's ear and whispered. "The strong are allowed to work. Stand tall and suck your belly in."

Martha put her arm around the woman and drew her tight. "Thank you, Ruth." She kissed her head again.

She wasn't sure why she was thanking young Ruth.

"Promise you won't leave me," Ruth said.

"I won't."

The car jerked to a standstill.

They heard the dogs then, a chorus of barks that seemed to have started on command. The lock rattled. Martha's heart hammered at twice its normal rate.

The gate swung open, and light flooded the car. Martha strained for a view.

The first thing to catch her attention was a German officer standing thirty feet away beside a line of trucks. He wore a freshly pressed SS uniform with a bright red-and-black armband, arms folded behind his back, legs spread in bulging slacks, shiny black holster at his side. But more riveting than these were his eyes. Even at this distance, she saw them clearly. They were blue. And they were dead.

The next thing Martha saw was the sign above the gate.

TORUŃ

"Out. Step off the train and line up by the trucks." A guard pointed at a caravan of seven or eight flatbed transport trucks behind him.

For a moment, none of the women moved.

"No need to be afraid. Hurry!"

They surged out of the train as quickly as aching joints would allow. Ruth released Martha's arm, and they walked down the ramp into the crisp morning air side by side. All the way down the train, women emerged from the freight cars, which were fewer now than Martha remembered from when she had boarded in Hungary. Maybe ten cars remained.

"Make a line. Make a line!" The guards hustled the women into a long line, several deep. They weren't beating or shooting, simply bringing order to a situation that required it. This was not the way soldiers intent on extermination behaved.

Martha hurried for the line, Ruth by her side. The morning air felt fresh; she could smell something, maybe baking bread. They might even have hot showers. It had been a month since her last hot shower.

Or perhaps they would be gassed.

"Follow the guards into the camp. We have food and blankets. Follow the guards into the camp."

They hurried as best they could past the gate and into the camp called Toruń. Martha gazed at the sprawling compound and tried to remain calm. The other women weren't hysterical. Ruth wasn't crying or showing fear. She had to be strong. Martha straightened her back against the terror.

The yard was a slab of brown mud beaten into submission by thousands of feet. Not a blade of green grew between the buildings. Four guard towers rose above the fence, each manned with three guards. Overlooking the entire yard, a red house stood on a rise to the right. A large German flag rolled lazily on a pole from the highest gable.

"Form a line, form a line!"

"I think we might be in for some trouble," Ruth said, staring at the large brick buildings to the left.

"Silence! Single file!"

The women extended their line until they stood shoulder to shoulder at the center of the yard. A dozen women dressed in frayed shirts and slacks, women who apparently lived here, walked past the new group in single file, watching. Several others dressed in gray uniforms worked with the new arrivals, jostling them into order, issuing commands even though they looked to be prisoners too.

Martha saw an SS officer from the corner of her eye; she turned. Ruth glanced over, saw the man, and stood still. It was the officer Martha had first seen, the one with dead eyes.

The officer strode toward the group from the left, a long overcoat now draped over his shoulders, a stick gripped in both hands. He walked to the middle of the yard and faced them.

"You have arrived at Toruń, subcamp of Stutthof, in Poland. My name is Gerhard Braun, and I am god." He spoke in Hungarian, and his eyes remained flat. They settled on Ruth and lingered there as he spoke.

"I have selected each one of you. For that you should feel fortunate. Your train came through Auschwitz, yes? In Auschwitz, you would never receive such personal service.

"Now, I imagine that most of you would love a bowl of hot soup and the opportunity to relieve your bladder. Am I right?"

None of them responded.

"Answer me when I speak!" The officer's face flushed.

"Yes," Ruth said loudly. Martha hesitated, unnerved by her friend's bold response, then mumbled the same with the others.

He paced, calming himself. "I was sent to this stink hole only because I speak Hungarian fluently, and I will tell you that this place easily can put me in a bad mood. In fact, most of the time I am in a bad mood. There's no need to exasperate me. At this very moment, my twelve-year-old son is watching us from the window of my house. He's visiting from Germany. His name is Roth. I would like all of you to wave at him."

Martha glanced at Ruth and then up at the red house a hundred meters away. First a few, then all of the women waved at the window, though they could see no one behind the glass.

"Good. Now, I have a decision to make," Braun said. "I can send you to the barracks where you'll be assigned duties and then fed. Or I can send you to the building to your left." Without turning, he let his stick flop in the direction of a large brick building. "This building is where we give you a shower. Has anyone heard of the showers?"

Martha felt her muscles stiffen, but she dared not speak.

"No? The showers at Auschwitz are ten times as large as ours. They say you should never hold your breath while taking a shower." He paced, lifted his face to the sky, and then faced them.

Martha's stomach twisted. Surely he didn't mean to kill them. Birds were chirping in a huge poplar by the gate; the morning sun was bright on the horizon; they'd done nothing wrong. Besides, he surely wouldn't toy with them in this manner if he intended to kill them. She let out a slow breath.

None of the women had spoken.

"Take your clothes off and leave them on the ground with your belongings. Now!"

"Suck your belly in!" Ruth whispered.

Martha quickly pulled off her shirt and then her slacks, holding her belly as tight as possible. In less than thirty seconds, they were naked.

Braun stretched his arm toward the showers. "Move!"

They turned and filed through the mud like a flock of white geese. Two female guards hurried them on each side. The dead-eyed commandant watched them go.

Martha refused to let her mind assess the situation. Thoughts of warm showers and hot soup had fled. Perhaps being treated as cattle on a cattle car had been better.

They marched into the brick building, past a line of square wooden toilets, and into a large cement room with a dozen shower heads protruding from one wall. Martha felt a wedge of panic rise in her chest. She had to be strong!

She bumped into Ruth, who had stopped in front of her.

"Keep moving!" one of the guards yelled. "Move!"

Ruth spun, eyes wide. "It's a shower!" She ran to one of the shower heads that dribbled a steady stream of clear liquid, cupped her hand to catch some, sniffed it, and whirled about.

"Water! It's water, Martha!"

The showers suddenly began to spit and spray. Ruth grabbed handfuls of water and splashed her face and mouth. Martha stood rooted to the concrete as the women rushed to the flowing water, crying out with delight. How many of them had suspected something other than water, she didn't know, but she felt their rapture.

To her right, two expressionless female guards watched.

"Martha!" Ruth called.

Martha ran into the cool streams. Life flooded her skin and reached into her soul. She lifted her hands and shrieked with exuberance. She couldn't remember feeling so alive.

There was a God in heaven, and he was kissing them with this water. Or was he?

6

Los Angeles
July 18, 1973
Wednesday Afternoon

S TEPHEN AND CHAIM APPROACHED RACHEL SPRITZER'S ABANDONED apartment building from the north. Ordinarily, Stephen drove with the ease of someone who'd found a thousand addresses in Los Angeles— one hand on the wheel, the other on the listing; one eye on the map, the other on street signs. Today, the nervous twitches of a new driver ran through his bones. Both hands on the wheel, both eyes glued to the windshield.

They'd stopped by Gerik's antique shop to retrieve the note, an unexpectedly innocuous note written on white paper with thin blue lines. The words still bounced around Stephen's head.

> *I have searched all of Europe for my son. An orphan after the war, perhaps.*
> *His name is David, and his father died during the war. I placed half of*
> *David's Stone on his right shoulder, under his collarbone.*

That was what the note had said just above a sketch identical to Stephen's scar.

And, *They must not know that he is my son. I would fear for his life if they were ever to find out.*

And, *I had hoped he would come because of the Stones, but I could not*

*make it widely known. This note is my only remaining hope. Tell no one
unless it is he. May God forgive me.*

That was it.

So who was Rachel Spritzer?

How had she come into possession of a Stone of David?

For that matter, who was *he?* Stephen's foster father had named him,
upon collecting him from an orphanage in Poland. But his name was
really David. It simply had to be.

Gerik had been little help. He had been as surprised as anyone that
Rachel had harbored such a treasure all these years. Rachel had given
Gerik the note six months earlier when her health began to fail. But he
hadn't opened it until after her death, as instructed. If Chaim hadn't made
a comment about the scar on Stephen's chest, Gerik never would have
connected the note to Stephen.

Whatever had prevented Rachel Spritzer from revealing her connection to a lost child had held power over her until the day she died.

Stephen had received the note with a trembling hand and paced for
fifteen minutes, asking unrelenting questions. But there were no answers.
Not from Gerik, who knew Rachel better than most, he said. Rachel was
a private woman.

Three blocks off La Brea, the traffic thinned considerably. Amazing
how neighborhoods changed from one street to the next. Here stands a
million-dollar home with elegant palms and a mermaid fountain in its
front lawn. There, a mere slingshot's distance off, stands a home surrounded by lumps of clay.

"It could be coincidence," Stephen said.

"Yes, it could," Chaim responded. "I can't see it though. Can you?
The mark on your chest matches the sketch in her note."

"Still. Could there be any proof?"

"They've already buried her. I don't know."

"What about the will? Maybe she mentioned something in the will?"

"Gerik said no."

Stephen nibbled on a fingernail and tried to think clearly. All these years his mother lived not twenty miles away? He wasn't sure whether it was preposterous or tragic. Why hadn't she found him? Why hadn't he found *her*?

This couldn't be his mother. Not this rich woman who'd died and made the local news. The woman may have abandoned him in Poland, then gone on to live a life of luxury while he scraped to build a life from scratch. The woman quite possibly had given birth to him, but she could not be his mother.

"It should be up ahead on the left," Chaim said.

Stephen fought a sudden urge to turn back, afraid of what he might find. Or what he might not find.

You are my Stone of David, his foster father, Benadine, used to say, kissing him on the forehead. He asked Benadine what it meant. His foster father had smiled. "You are a survivor, Stephen. No Goliath can touch you." That was enough to make any boy of six walk around with a puffed chest for the day.

You are my Stone of David.

But he'd never been Rachel Spritzer's Stone of David.

A tall, gray structure loomed ahead. He glanced at the listing and scanned the building again. Four stories high. Cracked and discolored stucco siding. Chipped red-tile roof. Mexican tiles displaying the building numbers embedded in the stucco under an exposed light bulb. A Caldwell Realty sign in the lawn.

"This is it," Chaim said. "I have the distinct feeling that your denial has been compromised. Perhaps this is all for the best."

"I'm not in denial," Stephen said. "I'm living beyond the past."

Chaim didn't respond.

Stephen pulled to the curb and peered up at the structure. Dying vines spilled from flower boxes below dirty windows. A lone palm tree listed slightly, its dead, bushy fronds in desperate need of a trim. Concrete steps led to a single brown entrance door. A patchy brown lawn surrounded the corner lot, separating it from the nearest structure—a dilapidated apartment building with boarded windows across the street.

The buildings looked to have been built at the same time, although Rachel's building was in far better condition than its twin.

They climbed out of the car, Stephen clutching the newspaper with its old black-and-white photograph of Rachel Spritzer and her husband, Rudy, shortly before his death. Three yards to his right sat a dog, stubby tail madly twitching, tongue hanging limply out of its jaw. It was a cocker spaniel, not fully grown, perhaps a year old or so.

"Are you okay?" Chaim asked.

Stephen gazed up at the four-story building. "Yes."

"Arrff!"

"Easy, boy."

The dog offered a brief whine, bounded toward him, stretched up on its hind legs, and tried to lick his hand with a large wet tongue.

Stephen glanced around, saw no sign of the dog's owner, and tentatively petted the spaniel behind its ears, welcoming the distraction.

Stephen straightened and flipped his hand "Go home. *Shoo.*"

The dog sat on its haunches, tilted its head, and stared at him with big brown eyes.

"Go on now. *Shoo!*"

The dog turned away and bounded a few feet before turning back and sitting again. Good enough.

"Maybe it would be best to come back later, after you've had more time to digest this news," Chaim said.

"No." Stephen let out a long breath. "I don't know why I'm so nervous. It's just a house."

Chaim said nothing, but Stephen was sure he was thinking *denial.*

They walked to the entry. Chips in the stucco and small cracks in the door's brown paint showed the building's age. A lock box hung on the door handle. According to the article, Rachel Spritzer had spent the last month of her life in a hospice facility, where she'd made preparations to settle her estate. The complex had been on the market for a week. Stephen entered his code, removed a corroded brass key, and opened the front door.

Chaim poked his head in, then studied Stephen. "I think I'll wait in the car."

"There's no need for that."

"Yes, I think there is. You should be alone."

Stephen nodded. "Okay. I won't be long."

"Take your time." He descended the steps. "Please, take your time."

The dog suddenly barked and bounded up the steps and into the building.

The dog had no business inside, but the moment Stephen stepped in, a sense of wonder swept away any thought of issuing the canine out. The entire entry level had been converted into a parking garage similar to those found under office buildings. Three rows of bare steel posts stood in the place of load-bearing walls. Judging by two large cobwebs, the garage door hadn't been opened in at least a month. He noticed a single elevator to his right, next to a door that read, "Stairs."

This was his mother's house?

The dog had stopped ten feet in and once again stared at Stephen, head tilted.

Stephen shut the door behind him. "You can't be in here," he said. But again, he welcomed the dog's presence. Despite Chaim's insistence, Stephen wasn't sure he wanted to be alone.

The dog bounded for the elevator, sat by the door, and stared eagerly at the call buttons. Seemed to know the building. What was the chance that this was Rachel's dog? Surely she would have made arrangements for it, as she had for the rest of her estate.

Stephen walked toward the elevator, breaking the silence with the *clack* of his shoes on hard concrete. With a whole lot of remodeling, the apartment building could be restored. Then again, if the rusted pipes overhead were any indication, the entire infrastructure would need an overhaul. Cheaper to start over.

See, it didn't feel like his mother's house to him. He was a Realtor examining a building, not a son coming home. Maybe because he wasn't really her son.

A twinge of guilt pricked his mind. He should feel more like a son.

"You stay here," he told the dog. But the moment he cracked the door to the stairwell, the cocker spaniel bolted for it, squeezed between Stephen's legs, and disappeared down a flight of steps.

"Hey!" His voiced echoed through the stairwell. He considered following the dog into the darkness below. "I'm going up." He was talking to this dog as if it could understand. "You hear me? I'm going up. Don't you dare poop down there."

Stephen headed up the concrete steps. He would deal with the dog before leaving. Letting it wander around the basement for a few minutes wouldn't hurt anyone.

The second floor still housed three apartments, but they looked as if they'd been abandoned for a decade, maybe two. Green carpet, fifties all the way.

Third floor, same as the second. Musty, dark, and vacant. She had lived in the building only a month ago, but where? Caldwell may have removed her belongings, but the first three floors had been vacant for a long time.

Stephen walked up the last few steps, saw the heavy oak door that led into the fourth floor, and stopped. This was it. His hammering heart was driven as much by nerves as by the climb.

The dog sat by the door. Must have run up while he was on the third floor. Maybe this really was Rachel's dog. Did that make it his dog? It really was a beautiful dog, and by the look in its eyes, quite intelligent. No, this wasn't his dog. Rachel had left everything to someone else. To a museum.

"You poop down there?"

The dog barked and Stephen jumped. "Hush."

This was ridiculous. He should just go in there, see what this Rachel Spritzer had left, and then be on his way.

He gathered himself, transferred the newspaper to his left hand, pushed the door open, and stepped into the fourth floor. A smell that reminded him of cherry blossoms tinged with licorice filled his nostrils. The odor of . . . Russia. His foster grandmother's apartment in Moscow. If he was right, he would find some mothballs hanging around somewhere as well.

The dog ran around him and headed straight for the back of the apartment. Stephen peered through the dim light. He was breathing through his nostrils. Loudly. He opened his mouth. Better.

The entire level had been converted into a single apartment. Plush carpet, textured gold wallpaper, lavender drapes—Turkish, if he was right.

A light switch to his right brought a large crystal chandelier to life in the entryway. He walked farther in, taken by the contrast between the floors below and this one. Judging by a scattering of empty picture hangers leaning against the walls, someone had selectively removed some of the paintings. Undoubtedly, the museum had picked through her belongings and taken what they considered truly valuable. There certainly weren't any Stones of David lying around.

You are my Stone of David.

Stephen stood in place for a full minute, gazing about the room, trying to decide what it meant to him. Was there some deep, mysterious connection between the apartment and his life? He tried to imagine Rachel Spritzer living here. He lifted the paper and stared at the picture of Rachel and Rudy Spritzer. The black-and-white photograph was slightly out of focus. Dark hair pulled up in a bun. A kind face. Thin. Before coming to the United States, and during his first year here, he had searched for any record of his true parents. Nothing. Not a scrap of information in the hundreds of war records he'd pored over.

He folded the paper, took a deep breath, and walked into the room. He would look around, sure. It would be good to know who had given him birth. But to pretend there was any meaningful relationship between this woman and him was nothing more than misguided sentimentality. He'd shut this door once and had found a certain amount of peace in doing so. He couldn't afford to open that door now. This was about closure, not a new beginning.

Stephen walked slowly through the sprawling five-bedroom apartment, feeling distant from it all.

Some of her clothes still hung in the master-bedroom closet, clearly the source of the mothballs he'd smelled. A king-size canopy bed sat draped in lace. The kitchen boasted the latest appliances. A cookie jar with a rose inlaid in gold leaf still held sugar biscuits. Although the museum evidently had no interest in the furniture, most of the pieces in the living room were antiques, probably from Europe, and would fetch some money with the right dealer. The dinner table was hand carved from cherry.

History seemed to leak from every knickknack and every doily. But Stephen didn't want to engage that history right now. The trappings of unmistakable taste were everywhere. No photographs though. She hadn't even left him a photograph.

Stephen stopped in the middle of the room, struggling against a terrible urge to cry. He couldn't, of course. He was a grown man. He didn't even know if she really was his mother. And even if she was his mother . . .

A wellspring of sorrow rose through his chest. He struggled to hold back tears and failed.

He stood straight, sniffed hard. It was enough. He'd come, he'd seen, and he'd cried. He couldn't afford any more.

Stephen walked to the dining room table, slapped down the paper, and cracked his knuckles. All right, then. There you have it. Finished. Chaim was waiting. He headed for the door.

The dog.

"Hey, do—" His voice cracked and he cleared it. "Hey, puppy?" He headed back to the master bedroom. "Hello? Puppy?"

A brown nose poked out from under the bed skirt. No eyes, just the nose. "Come on, Spud, time to go."

In response, the spaniel eased its head out, still flat to the carpet, eyes rolled back for a view of Stephen. The dog was certainly no stranger to this apartment. If it wasn't Rachel's, it had to be one she'd befriended.

"Come on." Stephen turned and walked into the living room, hoping the dog would follow. It bounded past him, pulled up by the elevator, and barked.

"You want to ride the elevator? Is that the way you normally go?" He punched the call button. "Sure, why not?" He was feeling better already.

He punched the call button, stepped in behind a happy cocker spaniel, and pressed the lowest button before realizing it had a B on it. Basement. The number on the button above was worn off, and when he pushed it, no light illuminated. The car rumbled slowly for the basement. Stairs would have taken half the time.

Stephen rested his head against the wood paneling. What would he tell Chaim? He would be reasonable. He had found some closure. Maybe they could come back later and walk through the apartment together. Maybe they should take a closer look at her will—she may have left something for him in the fine print. Something that had meaning.

He tried again to imagine the Jewish woman who had carefully packed her precious treasures and crossed the seas in search of a new life. Rachel Spritzer. She'd survived Hitler's reign of terror. He'd spent the last ten years pushing it from his mind.

The car reached the bottom, and its door slid open. He hit the close button, but the dog leaped through the gaping doors.

"No, Spud, not here! Hey!" Stephen stepped from the elevator, hit the switch to his right, and let his eyes adjust.

The dog stood by a door across the empty room, swapping expectant looks between the door and Stephen.

"You know this place, don't you? Is this where you slept?"

Curious, Stephen quickly poked his head into three other doorways. Two led to empty storage rooms, the other to an old coal room. He cracked the door Spud had fixated on—utilities. The dog hurried toward a plump, black cast-iron boiler that sat against the far wall, then found an old blanket in the corner. Spud had obviously slept here on more than one occasion.

Stephen scanned the room. The building had been constructed in the forties or fifties, before electricity dominated the water-heating industry. Black water pipes ran out of the boiler and disappeared into the ceiling. A newer electric water heater stood in the corner. Several fifty-five-gallon drums lined the wall next to the black boiler. The room smelled a bit like kerosene. Or was that charcoal he smelled?

He walked to the drums and tapped them. Two gonged loudly, empty. The third thudded, and the liquid caught in its rim vibrated. It smelled stagnant. A drop splashed on the drum, and Stephen glanced up. The culprit appeared to be a slowly leaking pipe.

He grunted and was about to turn when the dog caught his eyes. Spud was sniffing at a round plate set in the concrete floor behind the boiler. Something like a manhole cover, only smaller, maybe eighteen inches in diameter.

"You find something?" He crossed the room and leaned over the dog for a better view. Spud was pawing the edges of the cover now. Careful not to rub against the boiler, Stephen squeezed behind, bent down beside the dog, and examined the dirt-encrusted surface. A pattern had been stamped into the steel, but he couldn't make sense of it. The cover probably gave entry to a sewer system or a large drain. Of course, you never knew with these old buildings.

He straightened, dug for his keys, and scraped at the dirt. No luck. A screwdriver or crowbar would probably do the trick, but he didn't make a habit of lugging around either in his back pocket. Interesting though. The dog was certainly taken by it.

It occurred to him that he was squatting over a sewer grate behind a potbellied boiler with a dog. The day's revelations had messed with this mind. He grunted and stood. Black dust covered his right hand, and he wiped it as best he could against the cement wall.

He found a certain quality about the utility room appealing. The fact that it had survived all these years, maybe. Its utter silence, perhaps. Peace and bliss at the bottom of a hole. Or was it isolation and death? Abandonment. Misery loves company.

"That's it, Spud."

The dog looked up wistfully; returned a longing gaze to the circle.

"If only my life were as simple as yours. Let's go."

Amazingly, Spud obeyed.

They opted for the stairs this time. The ancient elevator deserved a wrecking ball through its gut. It was amazing that the thing still worked. Stephen pushed his way into the garage and stopped.

The rolltop door was open. A black Cadillac with tinted glass gleamed under the lights—a rental from California Limousine Service, according to the insignia on its doors.

"Stephen Friedman, what on earth are you doing in a dump like this?"

Stephen turned to face Mike Ryder, a Realtor he'd bid against on a piece of property in Hollywood last year. The dog ran past Mike and through the garage door.

"Hey, Mike. Never know where you'll find the deals. You showing the place?"

"Second time today. To the same party. That mutt follow you in?"

"It slipped in before I could stop it," Stephen said. No sign of Chaim. "Know who he belongs to?"

"I think he's a she," Mike said. "Used to belong to the owner, but I guess she found another home. Been meaning to call the pound."

"Who's the lucky prospector?" Stephen asked, glancing around.

"German investor. Working on an offer."

Stephen arched an eyebrow. "Just like that? How much?"

"Asking price. He's on the top floor now with two business associates. Forget this place, Stephen—no short-term money in this one."

The thought of someone buying the building struck Stephen as profane. He may not have a legal right to the place, but if Chaim was right and he was Rachel's son, his own history was tied to this building.

Stephen nodded and looked at the limousine again. Odd for a foreign investor to snap up a property like this so quickly.

"Your listing, right? Can you give me a day on this?"

"You really interested?" Mike wore a crooked grin. He shrugged and headed for the elevator. "Nothing's going to happen in a day anyway. You got it. But don't tell me I didn't warn you. You may have a nose for a deal here or there, but trust me, this ain't one of them."

"Appreciate it."

Stephen left the building feeling dazed and confused, and clueless as to why. It was just a building from the past. Like the Holocaust, he should just leave it for history.

The thought made him sick.

7

THE RICH AROMA OF VEAL GREETED STEPHEN WHEN HE STEPPED into the house at five thirty. He'd dropped Chaim off after their visit to the apartment and gone for a long drive before making some inquiries at the courthouse and the museum that had acquired Rachel's estate. In the end, he'd learned nothing new. The afternoon had been a complete waste of his time. He had to get beyond this crazy assault on his emotions.

But Chaim and Sylvia would want to talk about it. Maybe it would be for the best.

He stood by the door and gathered his resolve; the last thing he wanted to do was spoil the evening with his problems. The fact was, he really didn't have any problems. Nothing had changed, really. Only history. So he'd been born to a woman named Rachel Spritzer. Maybe. So what?

He walked toward the sound of voices in the kitchen.

"The carrots and onions do the trick, I'm telling you," Chaim was saying.

"Smells delicious." Sylvia's soft voice. "You really didn't have to go to so much trouble for—"

"Nonsense. Besides, Stephen insisted."

She chuckled. "I hate to break it to you, dear Rabbi, but Stephen is only a friend. And I think the feeling is mutual."

Stephen pulled up short.

"Are you accusing me of meddling?" Chaim objected. "How does an old man like me propose to meddle in the lives of two young pups?"

A pot boiled gently on the stove.

"Two lovely, beautiful young pups, I might add." Chaim said. "A lonely man and a lonely woman, searching for love, practically ordained for each other."

"Please! I don't know where you get the idea that I might be interested in Stephen. As a friend, sure. But trust me, he's not my type."

"Oh? And what is your type? You're both Jewish."

"There's more to a relationship than religion."

"You don't find him physically attractive? And he's ambitious, smart, strong willed—you could never go wrong with a man like him."

"Don't get me wrong, I like him, I really do. I just can't imagine him as any more than a brother."

There was a pause. Long enough for Stephen to realize that he'd started to sweat.

"I think you're wrong about him," Chaim said.

"Please, what's wrong with a brother?"

Stephen backed up a few paces then walked forward, hoping they could hear him. He rounded the corner, saw Sylvia kiss Chaim on the forehead. Brown hair fell to her shoulders. She had a small nose, dwarfed next to the rabbi's. Chaim was no beast, but Stephen couldn't help but think that Sylvia was indeed the beauty kissing the beast.

"And you're like a father to me," Sylvia said.

"What is that incredible smell?" Stephen asked, stepping into their view. Chaim and Sylvia both started.

He winked at them. "Is this the talk of love that I smell? Or is it veal parmesan?"

"Hello, Stephen." Sylvia exchanged a quick glance with Chaim. "It seems that God has informed the rabbi that you and I should fall madly in love and raise a dozen children in marital bliss."

"Oy, I said no such thing!"

Stephen stepped to Sylvia and kissed her on the cheek. "Thank you for coming."

"My pleasure."

Stephen withdrew a box from under his arm and handed it to Sylvia. "In case the rocks still taste like dirt."

"Chocolates." Chaim arched an eyebrow.

"Rocks?" Sylvia asked.

"Chaim was telling me this morning how even the rocks taste like chocolates when you fall madly in love. From his own vast experience, of course."

Sylvia took the box. "Thank you. These look wonderful."

Chaim eyed him. "Are you okay?"

"Fine? Why wouldn't I be? Today I found my mother. Her name was Rachel Spritzer. She was a very wealthy woman. A few days ago she died and left me nothing." He shrugged. "So what has changed? Nothing."

"She was your mother," Sylvia said.

"Was she? And what is a mother?"

They both looked at him.

"How is the district attorney today?" Stephen said. "Keeping our streets safe from thugs?" He made no secret of his skepticism when it came to her boss, Ralph Ferguson, the bald, potbellied DA who'd come to Los Angeles from the East Coast seven months earlier. Sylvia still hadn't committed to liking or not liking the man, even after going on four months as one of his attorneys fresh out of law school.

"That would be the police chief's department," she said. "We only lock them up."

"Lock 'em up . . . take 'em off the street . . . same thing. People don't give you enough credit. That whole department would fall apart without you."

She laughed. "Last I checked, I was still chained to the research desk, but thanks for the vote of confidence."

They avoided the subject of Rachel Spritzer for the next twenty minutes. They were all thinking about it, Stephen knew. It was in their eyes and on the tips of their tongues. But they were giving him the space he demanded.

The veal smelled wonderful, but Stephen hardly tasted a bite. They made small talk about the church Chaim attended, about Sylvia's research, about the deal Stephen was working with Dan Stiller.

"I visited the Holocaust museum," Stephen finally said after a stretch of silence.

Chaim set down his fork. "You did?"

"Yes. And the will makes no provision for any other party."

"You told them who you were?" Sylvia asked.

"I told them I was Stephen Friedman."

"But they knew you're related?"

"Of course not. How am I supposed to prove that? 'Hi, my name is David Spritzer, son of Rachel Spritzer; hand over the goods'?"

"There has to be a way."

"I don't even know if I *am* her son."

"You must be," Chaim said. "How could she ever know about the scar? No, there is no doubt."

"Legally there could be," Stephen said.

"Hire an attorney," Sylvia said.

"I don't *want* to hire an attorney. I want closure. And I think I have it now. She was my mother; I can probably accept that. End of story."

"It can't be the end of the story," Chaim said. "She alluded to some danger. Sylvia, can't you talk to the police about this?"

"Please, no," Stephen objected. "Really, whatever was in her past is in the past. Finished. I just want to get on with my life."

Stephen pushed a piece of meat into his mouth. "I'm not the only one she abandoned. Her dog's on the street as well." He immediately regretted the remark.

Chaim raised his eyebrows. "That was her dog?"

"I think it might live in the basement."

"The building has a basement?"

"Not so uncommon for a building that size. Nothing but an old boiler and utilities down there."

"How old is the place?"

"Built in 1947. The boiler isn't in use, of course. Maybe she stashed all her gold in the sewer." He couldn't seem to stop this flood of spiteful comments.

Sylvia looked up from the meat she was cutting. "What sewer?"

"There was a manhole in the boiler room. I assume it leads to an old drainage sewer of some kind."

Chaim glanced at Sylvia and then back. "A manhole? How big?"

Stephen set down his empty fork and indicated with his hands. "About so." It was absurd to think that Rachel Spritzer would put anything in a sewer. Besides, the cover hadn't been touched in years.

"Since when do they put entrances to public sewers in private buildings?" Chaim asked. "In Russia maybe, but not here."

"They don't," Stephen said. "But if the sewer predated the building, it's possible. I've seen it. These days, they would simply collapse the sewer and reroute it, but not in the forties."

"Could be submerged utility valves," Sylvia said.

The rabbi began to eat again. "Could be a bomb shelter."

"It could be a secret entrance to Fort Knox," Stephen said. "Please. It was in the utility room."

"How big did you say?" Chaim asked.

"Eighteen inches?"

"I would think that was a floor safe," Chaim said.

"No, it was a manhole cover of some kind," Stephen insisted.

"How do you know this?"

"Well, I don't."

"There you go, then. A floor safe."

"Makes sense to me." Sylvia winked. "You walked away from a fortune without knowing it."

"The cover was caked with an inch of grime," Stephen said. "No keyhole either."

"Still, I like the idea of a safe. A woman who owned one of the Stones of David would like the idea too."

Stephen rolled his eyes. "Don't be ridiculous. Nobody has touched it for years—does that sound like a safe to you? I can't believe we're even talking this way."

Chaim nodded. "You're right. It was a drain." He sliced into a potato. "I'm very sorry about all of this, Stephen. Maybe Sylvia is right. You should hire an attorney."

"I don't need an attorney. I have Sylvia. Honestly, I don't have a case, do I?"

"No telling without digging deeper," Sylvia said.

"But from what you know."

"No, probably not. But you never know until you dig deeper."

The image of that manhole cover, or whatever hid behind the pot-bellied boiler, fixed itself in Stephen's mind.

"I don't think I could handle digging deeper. I'll just . . . things will be fine. I'm working on a very good deal with Dan; I have a wonderful home. Wonderful friends." He attempted his best smile. "This will all pass, and things will be fine. You'll see."

———

SYLVIA LEFT at nine, and Stephen retired to his room at ten.

He climbed under the sheets and turned off the lamp, but he could not sleep. What if Chaim was right about the safe? Absurd. Eighteen inches—about right for a safe. A big safe, anyway. Too small for a manhole, really. Floor safes weren't that uncommon, although a safe behind a boiler was odd. Maybe he should return with a few tools and clean off the lid. Settle the matter. A safe would have a lock of some kind.

He tossed and turned. The hour hand on the white-faced alarm clock by his bed crept past midnight.

Say, for the sake of argument, that there was a safe behind the boiler. And say that there was more to Rachel's estate than what her will revealed. Wasn't it possible she would have left it in a safe? Maybe for her real son to find? He considered the note.

I had hoped he would come . . .

Even if the circle behind the boiler did belong to a safe, there might be no way to open it. Short of owning the building, breaking into the compartment was out of the question. Had she hidden a key in the basement? Or in her apartment?

Stephen crawled out of bed at one, went to the bathroom and returned, careful not to slough off what little grogginess had set in after three hours in the dark. *Sleep. Please, let me sleep.* He plopped into bed and shut his eyes.

What would she hide in a safe anyway?

The Stones of David.

No, she'd donated the one Stone in her possession to the museum. If she would have had two or three or all five, she would have donated the entire collection.

She'd had a month to settle her estate before dying—surely she would have itemized her estate. Rachel hardly seemed the kind who would lock up a treasure in a floor safe and then forget to list it among her assets. Especially something so valuable as the Stones of David.

Unless she wanted her son to find them without tipping off whomever she was afraid of. There was a thought. A silly, stupid thought. But a thought that kept him awake.

—⁓—

ROTH BRAUN sat in the black sedan and peered into the night. It was now well past midnight, and the long journey from Germany had worn him thin. If not for his anticipation of the satisfaction that lay ahead, he would have collapsed long ago.

But Roth wasn't fueled by regular flesh and blood and muscle and sinew. He drew his power from the blackest part of night.

He picked up the penlight with his gloved hand and snapped it on. A round circle of light lit the book that lay on his lap.

A telephone directory of greater Los Angeles. A monstrous thing that he would have preferred to leave back at the hotel. But he needed options in the event that the Jew he'd selected was unavailable or hard to reach.

There was always the possibility that he might select the wrong woman. Name alone couldn't confirm heritage. For all he knew an American Indian married a Jewish man and now bore the name Goldberg. But that didn't really matter. The selection of a Jew as opposed to an Indian or a German wasn't critical, though certainly more rewarding.

It did have to be a woman. His father had selected women. A woman had been his father's undoing. Yes, it had to be a woman.

His penlight illuminated the first name he'd chosen. Hannah Goldberg. Sounded like a Jew. Certainly a woman. Hopefully living alone.

According to the phone book, she lived across the street from where he was parked now. The number on her mailbox read 123423. Such a big number for an address. The Americans were far too many.

By night's end they would be at least one fewer.

Roth snapped the light off and set the book on the passenger seat. His fingers were trembling, but he knew he could subdue this visible anticipation with a single squeeze. He had this power. For the moment he would indulge the slight physical response.

Roth picked up a red scarf, ran the silk under his nostrils, inhaled slowly, then tucked the long scarf into his pocket.

He opened the car door, stood in the night, glanced up and down the vacant street, pushed the door closed. He rounded the hood and headed across the street. A single porch light lit the entryway. Otherwise the house was dark.

It was going to be a good night.

8

BLINDING RAYS STREAMED THROUGH THE WINDOWS WHEN Stephen pulled himself from sleep the next morning. He swung his legs to the floor. Nine o'clock. When had he fallen asleep?

He hurried to the shower. First stop, Rachel Spritzer's apartment. He considered running the comps he'd promised Daniel first but decided that could wait. He had to get this other business out of his blood.

He'd go, find nothing, and be done with his mother's apartment. End of story.

He couldn't remember ever feeling so knotted up. The obscure hope that had kept him awake last night now demanded that he get into the apartment complex and down to the safe.

What if?

No, Stephen, not what if. Impossible, crazy, stupid.

But what if?

From his clock radio, Diana Ross was belting out "Ain't No Mountain High Enough."

THE REALTOR'S sign was missing from Rachel Spritzer's yard when Stephen pulled up an hour later. Huh. Even if the Germans had made an acceptable offer, the sign usually remained until closing.

A single brown car Stephen recognized as Mike Ryder's waited along the curb. No pedestrians. And no cocker spaniel. Probably off licking someone else's hand.

Stephen got out of the Vega, grabbed a hefty screwdriver and a hammer from the floor behind the driver's seat, shoved the first in his slacks' front pocket, and slid the hammer into the inside pocket of his blazer. The folds of his pants easily concealed the screwdriver; the hammer wanted to lean out. He tried to flip the hammer around so the head would sit in his pocket. No luck. He would have to hold it in place with his left forearm.

He patted his left breast pocket and headed toward the front door. If he was lucky, he would miss Mike. A quick trip down to the basement, and he would be gone. He was a Realtor with legal access—he wasn't exactly breaking and entering. Still, sweat glistened on his brow. Hot day.

Stephen stopped at the door. No lock box. No sign; no lock box. For a brief moment, he actually panicked. How could . . .

The door swung open and Mike stood in the frame. "Stephen!" He clearly hadn't expected anyone. "Whoa, too strange. I was just going to call you." He stepped out and shut the door behind him, then donned a pair of mirrored aviator shades. "Sorry, man. It's off the market."

"What do you mean, 'off'? Pulled?"

"Sold."

"Sold?"

"Closes tomorrow morning. Impossible, I know, but true. What can I say? Sometimes they go your way; sometimes they don't." A slight smile curved his mouth.

"How can it close tomorrow?" Stephen asked, seeking a new angle. He still wanted in, to satisfy his curiosity if nothing else. "Paperwork takes longer than that."

"Not necessarily. Clean title, cash deal."

"The German?"

"Roth Braun. Asking price. Paid for the furnishings too. Signed the papers yesterday."

"He's here?"

"Not at the moment, but I'm sure he will be. Sounds like he intends to live out of the top floor for a few days while he finishes his business here in the States." Mike locked the door and walked down the steps.

"Any chance you could let me in?" Stephen asked.

"In? Why? It's sold."

"Not technically. It'll be sold tomorrow morning. If they make closing. Either way, I think I left my wallet somewhere inside."

"As far as I'm concerned, it is closed," Mike said. "They put half down in earnest money. Two hundred fifty thousand smackaroos, my friend. That sound anything but done to you? I'm not sure I'd want to be caught inside the property when Braun shows up. Considering the size of the deposit, we're giving him access. I'm surprised he's not here already."

Stephen almost walked away then—he really had nothing to gain at this point.

Except maybe an inheritance that was rightfully his. Except maybe four more Stones of David.

"I'll be sure to hurry. Just let me in. I'll lock up. I'm a Realtor, for heaven's sake. This is what I do. Five minutes max. For my wallet." The hammer felt heavy in his jacket, and he turned slightly away.

"If he shows up—"

"My *wallet*, Mike! He won't."

Mike looked around and shrugged his shoulders. He pulled out a key, jogged up the stairs, and unlocked the door. "Locks from the inside. Make it quick. Trust me, you don't want to run into Braun. The dude gives me the creeps."

"If it becomes an issue, I'll tell him I entered the building while you were still inside. You left without knowing I'd come in, and I left shortly after."

"Yeah. Okay. You have a hammer in your pocket?"

Stephen froze briefly. Recovered. "Oh, yeah. I forgot it was still there." He pulled it out, thinking it was impossible to forget such a bulky object. "Pounded in a sign just a bit ago."

Mike stared at him for a moment. "You always keep hammers in your jacket pockets?"

"Gosh, no. I don't know what I was thinking. I was in a hurry." He pushed his way past the door. "You sticking around?"

"Not a chance. You're on your own. Don't forget the door."

Mike left wearing a puzzled expression. Stephen closed the door and let out a sigh. Not exactly the smoothest of cover-ups. A few white lies. He *was* going to pound a stake, if he could call the screwdriver a stake. Hadn't exactly done it yet, but he wouldn't call it a bold-faced lie. Never mind, this was his mother's house. Or had been.

He took the stairs to the basement, flipped the light switch, and gazed around. A single caged incandescent bulb cast a yellow hue over the four doors, all closed. Had the German been down here yet? He crossed to the boiler room, stepped in, and lit the room with another switch.

Three fifty-five-gallon drums, large water heater, potbellied boiler. Nothing had changed. The smudge marks where he'd wiped his hand yesterday stood out on the wall behind the boiler. A small hiss from the water heater broke the stillness.

Stephen pulled out the screwdriver and walked to the boiler. The circle in the concrete hadn't been disturbed. He moved one of the empty drums to gain working space. Settling to one knee, he chipped at the dirt that encrusted the lid. It broke off in small, crusty chunks. At this rate, cleaning the lid would take ten minutes at least.

He paused to listen. Silence. What was he doing? This was nuts. An image ran through his mind—him spilling out of the building, smeared with dirt and sweat. *Hello, Mr. Braun. The boiler works just fine, just fine. No need for a plumber. Yeah, that's what I am, a plumber.*

He attacked the lid with determination, needing to be done with this madness. The screwdriver kept catching on the pattern's small edges. Could be anything. He cleared the edges and saw that the lid was indeed just that, a steel lid set into the concrete.

Questions racked his mind as he worked. Why would anyone put a safe here? Assuming it was a safe, which it probably wasn't. But then why would anyone put a sewer entrance here? Unless it wasn't a sewer entrance or a drain or anything of the sort. Unless it was really a safe . . .

He shook his head and used his fingertips to brush the surface clear. The relief appeared to be a single insignia stamped into the metal. Still no keyhole, which meant it probably wasn't a safe. Not a chance this thing was a—

And then, suddenly, there was a keyhole.

A dime-sized slab of dirt flipped off the lid, revealing a round cylinder and the telltale zigzag of a key slot.

Stephen knelt over the lid and blinked. He ran his eyes around the edges and then refocused on the keyhole. His heart pounded. It had to be a safe!

He stuck the screwdriver into the slot and tried to turn it but gave up immediately. There had to be a key.

So, it was an old floor safe, hidden here behind an ancient boiler. Didn't mean it held anything but air. On the other hand, what if? What if there really was something hidden in there? For him. Rachel's son.

Stephen stood and hurriedly looked around for a key. The wall, the boiler, the furnace. Nothing. He paused to listen. Nothing. How long had he been here? Ten minutes at least.

He took a deep breath and sighed. Now what? He stepped up to the safe. The overhead light bulb glared on it. He'd actually managed to clear most of the grit from the surface. Small dirt chunks now ringed the safe. Anyone setting foot in the room would see it immediately. *Here I am; open me and find hidden riches.*

The least he could do before leaving was sweep away the dirt and make some attempt at hiding his hack job. He was about to look for a broom when the steel edges of the lid's pattern suddenly tripped a wire of recognition in his brain. Something familiar. Letters?

Stephen fell to his knees, snatched up the screwdriver, and attacked the dirt with renewed vigor.

The dirt came up in stubborn flakes but slowly revealed letters and then words. He tossed the screwdriver in favor of his fingernails. He clawed at the surface, brushed the dirt off again, and jumped up.

The Stones are like the lost orphans. They will eventually find each other.

Stephen's heart rose into his throat. A high-pitched ring sounded on the edge of his consciousness. *The Stones.* At his feet was a hidden safe that made specific reference to the Stones of David. He was a Stone of David. He was David. This meant what?

His breathing sounded loud in the chamber. *You're jumping to conclusions, Stephen. This is where she once kept the single Stone she owned. You're letting your imagination run wild down here.*

A faint *hum* ran through the walls. Stephen spun. The garage door! It had to be the German. And unless he was blind, he would have noticed the blue Vega parked out front.

Sweat covered Stephen's face. He instinctively wiped it away and then swore when his hand came away smeared black. He dived for the safe. Landed on his knees hard enough to send pain up his spine.

Using his arms as two brooms, he swept all the loose dirt back over the lid. Never mind the huge smudges that dirtied his blazer; he had to hide what he'd done here. The building might belong to some German named Braun, but as far as he was concerned, this safe belonged to him.

Footsteps sounded faintly above. He jumped to his feet, grabbed one of the empty drums, and drag-rolled it along the wall as quietly as possible, which was far too noisily.

If they barged in on him, what would he say? The plumber thing wouldn't have a prayer. Maybe he was from the city inspector's office, checking on compliance issues. A requirement for closing on the property. Cross the t's and dot the i's and all that rot. Unfortunately, he'd gotten a tad involved, thus the painted face and smudged arms.

Stephen grunted and maneuvered the drum directly over the floor safe. He stepped back. Looked natural enough, except that now a ring showed on the concrete from where he'd taken the drum. He brushed at it with his feet and managed to at least confuse the issue.

He ran from the room. Doubled back, grabbed his hammer and screwdriver, checked the room one last time, and headed back out. He hung out at the bottom of the stairwell for several minutes, begging a God he didn't really believe in to make the people upstairs disappear.

They ascended in the elevator. *Thank God, thank God.* Good enough, then.

Stephen crept up the stairs on his toes, poked his head into the garage, saw no one, took a deep breath, and headed for the front door.

He made it all the way without taking a breath. Unfortunately, he was forced to breathe before he got out. His gasp echoed through the garage. Perfect stealth.

Stephen ran for his car. If the German was to look out the window at the moment, he would see a dirtied man making a break for the blue Vega. Let him draw his own conclusions. At least Stephen was in disguise of sorts.

"Arf!"

He pulled up ten yards from his car. The dog sat by his door, stubby tail wagging furiously.

"Shoo! Shoo!"

Spud did not shoo.

Stephen leaned over him and unlocked the door. He expected the dog to bolt then. Instead, Spud licked his hand.

The dog had bad timing. At any minute someone would begin yelling out the door for Stephen to get back in there and explain what in tarnation he'd been doing in the basement.

"Okay, okay, go easy on me. I'm not a salt lick or whatever it is you guys—I mean gals . . ."

The dog jumped into the car, hopped into the passenger's seat, and looked away.

"Out." He didn't want to yell or make a scene. "Get out, dog!" he whispered harshly.

Spud refused to acknowledge him.

"Get out!" he whispered again.

No luck.

Stephen slid in, closed his door, and leaned across to open the passenger door so he could shove the mutt out the other way. Now Spud turned huge, eager eyes on him. The dog licked his hand as Stephen reached for the lock.

Maybe he should take the dog. Stephen straightened and gripped the steering wheel. Mike planned to call the pound, which meant the cocker spaniel might find a new home. Or an early grave.

Now was not the time to weigh his options.

Spud barked.

"Okay, but just for a day. That's it." He fired up the car and pulled into the street.

The dog looked forward, apparently pleased.

"And if you poop in the car, you're out for good. You got that?"

She whined and lay down on the seat. If Stephen didn't know better, he would think Spud here could actually read his intentions.

Which were what?

To find out what was in that safe. Rachel's safe. Mother's safe.

A tremble in his fingers refused to settle. He studied them. He didn't think he was prone to shaking.

He fought a sudden desire to wheel the car around, slip back into the apartment, and have at the safe. But he rejected the idea immediately. His eagerness might have landed him a case of the shakes, but he hadn't lost his mind to this thing. Right?

9

Toruń
April 25, 1944
Near Midnight

B E THANKFUL," GOLDA SAID IN A SOFT, HUSKY VOICE. SHE MUST have heard Martha's hushed cry. Only one day had passed, and Martha doubted she could survive another.

Moonlight cast gray shadows on the wall opposite the small window. A hundred women crowded Block D, the barracks reserved for Jews. Most of them slept, exhausted from a long day's work at the soap plant. Martha couldn't remember ever feeling quite so hopeless, lying here on the planks they called beds. At least in Budapest, she was in a familiar city. Here, she was abandoned and so far from home. Golda was right, she should be thankful, but she couldn't bring her emotions in line with her reason.

"You're alive," the barracks leader said. "Full trains leave Stutthof for Auschwitz all the time. And you came on a train *from* Auschwitz. There will be no crying in my barracks."

Martha could not answer. An apology seemed unwarranted, and any defense would be insensitive to the hardship they all faced.

On the bunk opposite Martha's, Ruth rolled over, rose to her elbows, and faced Golda. "Your body's alive, but maybe they've killed your heart. Who ever heard of such a rule, no crying?"

"In another week, you'll be begging for a dead heart," Golda snapped under her breath. "When the war is over, you may cry all you like. In here, you will keep your driveling to yourself. You aren't the only one trying to survive this madness."

Ruth didn't retreat, but she didn't respond either. Martha could see the whites of her eyes glancing from Golda's bunk to hers. Maybe she was tempted, as was Martha, to tell the hard woman that pregnant women couldn't afford to shut down their hearts, for fear it would shut down the child's heart within them.

Toruń was a labor camp for about five thousand women, mostly Polish dissidents and political prisoners from the Baltic region, but quite a few Jews lately as well. The food, a daily helping of a liquid they had the nerve to call soup and one slice of a white cardboard substance they called bread, was not enough to keep both mother and child alive. Martha had spent her first day at the plant, thinking the problem through until her head throbbed. As long as a woman could work, she was spared death, but between disease and malnutrition, life expectancy was only a few months at best. Between disease, malnutrition, and a growing baby, she couldn't expect to live more than half as long.

Unless she and Ruth found a way to eat more, neither would likely bear their babies.

Ruth's eyes returned to Golda. "Don't think that because we're new here, we don't know the meaning of suffering in silence," she said. "But if you can't protect your passions in this life, then stepping into the next might be better, don't you think?" Ruth, the brave one. "What good is surviving if you survive with a dead heart?"

Golda hefted herself to one elbow and studied Ruth. "What, you're a rabbi? There *is* no passion in this place! It was the first thing the Nazis stole from us."

"Not from me. The desire to live and thrive is a drive granted by God. Fine, we will learn not to cry, but you waste your time trying to kill our passions."

The leader squared off with Ruth in silence.

"She's right," a voice said quietly from above Martha. Rachel, another Jew from Hungary who'd been here for a month already, leaned over the bunk. "It's the most sensible thing I've heard since coming here. If we can't have hope, then why live at all?"

"Animals don't feel hope," Golda said.

When no immediate response came, Golda lay back down, satisfied she'd made her point. "We should be thankful for one thing only, and that is that we are alive," she said. "Braun might be the devil in white skin, but if you play by his rules, you may actually live awhile. Talking of hope and passion will only get you killed."

"Some things are worth dying for," Ruth said.

"Not your passions. Trust me, you can't afford to be passionate."

"I can't afford not to be passionate," Ruth said, soft and sweet, like an angel. "I'm pregnant."

Martha felt her pulse surge in the sudden vacuum created by Ruth's statement.

Golda sat up, swung her feet from the bunk, and stared at Ruth.

Rachel slid to the floor. She sat on Ruth's bed. "You're with child?" she whispered.

"Yes."

"I have a child. A three-year-old boy. They took him away in another holding camp."

Martha could hold her tongue no longer. "I'm pregnant too," she said. They turned to her as one.

"Six months," Martha said. Her voice held a slight tremor.

"*Both* pregnant?" Rachel asked.

"Yes," Ruth and Martha said together.

"Do you know what this means?" Golda demanded.

"It means that we both carry joy and passion in our bellies," Ruth said.

"Don't be a fool! You'll likely be dead by tomorrow evening!"

"Don't be so harsh, Golda!" Rachel said. "You can't know that."

"I'm required to report this immediately. You have no idea what this means to the barracks."

"You have no right—"

"If they are discovered without my reporting it, five of us will be shot for hiding it!"

Martha felt a welcome resolve sweep through her. She could only hide so much without sacrificing her sanity. "Then tell him," she said. "I can't hide forever. Report me—"

"Report both of us," Ruth said. "We're not afraid, are we, Martha?"

Martha considered the question. "I'm scared to death."

Ruth stared back, white. "So am I."

Rachel and Golda did not move and offered no words of comfort. Were they so insensitive? Martha could understand Golda's dilemma, but the woman's silence sent a chill through her bones.

"What has the commandant done to others who are with child?" she finally asked.

"He sends some away." Golda's voice sounded tempered, perhaps by Ruth and Martha's display of strength. "He's allowed only one to have her child. This one finds some twisted pleasure in exercising power over life. Letting one live extends hope. He uses your hope as a weapon, to make the suffering worse for everyone."

Martha took a deep breath, fighting to hold on to courage. "Even if he does allow us to live, we don't have enough food to keep the babies alive."

"We will depend on God's will," Ruth said.

"God's will?" Golda said. "God's lost his will. I'm not sure God hasn't lost *himself* in this war."

"No, Golda," Ruth said. "Don't mistake man's weakness for God's."

She humphed. "Braun will want to see you." She sighed impatiently. "Whatever you do, don't slouch or look stupid. Don't anger him. And don't try to seduce him. If he tries to seduce you, resist, but not too much. It's a dangerous game. He's not permitted to touch a Jew, but that doesn't mean he won't."

The thought nauseated Martha. "I . . . I couldn't."

"Think of the little bundle of passion in your belly, and you can do anything." Golda faced Ruth. "There's your sentiment for you." She swung her legs back onto the bunk and lay still.

"I would pay any price to keep my child," Rachel said. She paused and looked at her hands. "I marked my son before they took him away." Her lips began to quiver with emotion, and she lifted her fingers to cover them. She stifled a cry and whispered. "I burned him. What else could I do? He's too young to remember his name. How will he know I am his mother? I had to mark him so maybe one day I could tell him that mark means he's my son. I could write letters and search for him that way. I wanted to tattoo him, like they do with all of us, but I didn't have the ink, and they were going to send me away the next day."

Martha wondered what could drive a woman to burn a mark on her baby. There must have been a better way. She could never imagine doing anything so painful to her own child. But to question this tormented woman who'd lost her boy felt scurrilous.

Rachel glanced up, anxious, as if realizing how shocking her confession must seem. "It's not so different from giving a baby a shot, is it? You poke a needle into the child so that he won't become ill. He screams today, but you've saved his life. It's all I did."

"Yes," Ruth said, rubbing Rachel's back. "It's exactly what you did, Rachel. And it's what I would do too. These are not normal times. We must cling to each other—to our children, our families—no matter what the cost. It's all we have left. This is our hope."

Martha lay back, empty of the courage she'd felt less than a minute earlier. If only she weren't pregnant. What had she and Paul thought, even considering bringing a child into this cruel war? It had been her idea. She'd practically begged him, and now look at her! What a fool she had been, thinking that a baby would make her feel alive again.

Martha stared at the pitted bunk boards above her, blinded by bitterness. She hated herself; she hated the war; she hated Golda; she hated the baby.

The baby? Tears sprang to her eyes. Dear God, what was she thinking? No! She could never hate the life that grew within her body. *Never!*

10

THE NEXT DAY CREPT BY, TORMENTED BY THE BURDEN OF THE unknown. Golda had made the report to one of the guards before the eight o'clock work bell. Ruth and Martha were assigned to the fat vats, a hot, grueling place that would have sweated the women dead in a single day if not for the extra rations of water.

The bell signaling the end of the workday customarily rang at six. At five, when one of the guards signaled for her and Ruth to follow him, Martha rose from her stool with terrible anxiousness.

The guard marched them to the red house on the hill.

The air felt cool, promised rain. Birds chirped, full of life, a far cry from the deathlike hissing of the fat vats. Martha glanced over her shoulder at the camp below. From this vantage point, it looked crisp and clean, except for the huge mud hole in the center yard. It could easily be a Hungarian factory or a large college for boys.

A prisoner tended a flower bed that lined the walkway to the porch. Her eyes caught Martha's for the briefest of moments and then turned away. Did she know something? No, how could she? Except perhaps that few prisoners who entered the house fared well.

Martha swallowed and climbed the steps, legs weak and shaking.

Be strong. Don't slouch. He likes pretty women.

Both she and Ruth were pretty. Maybe that would give them favor. A petite doll from Slovakia and a tall brunette from Hungary. The thought sickened her.

Ruth took her hand and squeezed. She could feel a slight tremble in the fingers of the younger woman, who was brave not because she didn't feel fear, but because she faced it with surprising strength. Little Ruth needed her, didn't she? It was why she'd found Martha on the train. It was why she had taken Martha's hand now.

Martha squeezed back. "Be brave," she whispered. "He will never send away two such beautiful women. We are in God's hands, remember?" She didn't know which hope would prove true, that they'd find themselves in God's hands or that the commandant would find something in them to favor. Maybe both, maybe neither.

The guard opened the door and pushed them in. A young boy standing behind a chair, perhaps Braun's twelve-year-old son, stared at them for a moment and then ran down the hall.

The door shut behind them. They faced a spacious living room, handsomely decorated with crystal and paintings and golden velvet drapes, not unlike her father's country home outside Budapest. Leather couches surrounded a large, turquoise Oriental rug, well-worn but tightly woven. A long dining table was set with silver goblets and tall red candles.

Without warning, Braun stepped into the room from the kitchen. He'd been waiting there, staring at them with his dead, blue eyes.

It occurred to Martha that her hand was still in Ruth's. She tried to pull it free, but Ruth clung too tightly. The commandant wore his uniform slacks and knee-high black leather boots, but above his waist, only a white undershirt. His eyebrows arched.

His eyes drifted over them. "The two pretty ones." He walked to a cabinet and withdrew a bottle of red wine. "Would you like to join me in a drink?"

Martha heard the question, but she felt as though she were trying to breathe through syrup. Her heart sounded too loud in her ears. Her hand was still in Ruth's tight grip. They should decline, right?

"That would be nice," Ruth said evenly, finally releasing Martha's hand. "Thank you."

"Wonderful. It's not exactly German wine, but it is quite fine." Braun pulled out the cork and sniffed the bottle. "When in Poland, do as the Polish." He grinned, poured three shallow glasses, and stepped forward with two.

Ruth and Martha each took a glass.

"Thank you."

"Thank you." Martha thought her voice sounded like a mouse, and she determined to be stronger.

Braun retrieved his own glass. "So I understand that these two feisty Jews are pregnant. Honestly, I never would have guessed. You're both so"— he turned—"*fresh* looking."

Ruth lowered her eyes. "Thank you, sir."

Thank you? Was Ruth going too far?

Braun regarded Ruth with a pleasantly surprised look. Maybe her friend was onto something. What if the commandant chose to let her live, but sent Martha away?

"You're too flattering," Martha said, lowering her eyes as Ruth had done.

"Hmm. Yes, I suppose I can be. But you should know that I detest the fat guts of pregnant women. Especially bloated Jewess guts. If I know that the pure Aryan race is to be extended by a birth, I can stomach the sight. Otherwise I find myself wanting to vomit."

Martha stared into her glass. For a moment, he had seemed almost human. Now, she resisted a sudden urge to throw his wine at him and scratch out his eyes. Not even Ruth had a quick answer.

Braun was watching them carefully. "Which is why, whenever I oversaw the execution of Jews before being sent here, I personally shot the pregnant women. Himmler insists that no more than two bullets be used for each Jew. When I shoot a pregnant whore, I can take out two Jews with one bullet. How does that strike you?"

"It strikes me as inhuman," Martha said evenly.

Ruth glanced at her, then back at the SS officer. "It strikes me as diabolical. Only a coward would even find such a thing admirable."

Braun's grin seemed to stick in one place. They'd surely committed themselves to death.

He suddenly grinned wide and set down the glass. "Fortunately for you, neither of you has a pig gut. Lift your shirts, please."

Martha hesitated only a fraction of a second before lifting her shirt to reveal her belly. Ruth did the same.

"Amazing. You can hardly see it. They tell me six months."

"Yes."

"I like children, of course. I love children, actually. Even, dare I say it, the odd Jewish child. Young, impressionable minds waiting to be formed. Innocence. Innocence can be intoxicating. That's why we sometimes kill a hundred Jews at once, you know. So that when we kill only twenty, we are practicing a kind of innocence."

"I can see the logic," Ruth said. "But wouldn't killing *no* Jews lend itself to an even purer innocence?"

Braun stared at her, as if considering the argument for the first time. "But then we are confronted with another evil," he said.

"Allowing Jews to live?"

"Precisely." He held her gaze. "Sometimes the death of one satisfies the wrath of a just God. Isn't that why God demanded blood sacrifice from the Jews?"

"The death of a lamb," Ruth said. "Not a human. A long time ago."

"The last sacrifice of the Jews wasn't a lamb. It was a man. Jesus Christ. You don't remember?"

"You use the indiscretion of a few men to justify a slaughter?"

He stared at her and then abruptly diverted his gaze. "You will both live. You will be given double rations and allowed to give birth, should you survive so long. In exchange for this, I ask only that you visit me on occasion. You don't need to be afraid; I won't touch you, although I do find you both very beautiful. I would just like your company from time to time."

Ruth dipped her head without removing her eyes from his. "Thank you, sir. You can be very kind."

"Well, I suppose we all have it in us." He walked to the wall and plucked a red scarf from a hook and handed it to Ruth. "I would like you to do me a favor. Take this scarf into your barracks and place it on the bed five down from your own. The woman will know what it means."

Ruth took the scarf. "Just place it on the bed?"

"Yes. Just drape it over the bed. Will you?"

"Of course."

Braun smiled. "Good. Good, then. You may leave."

Ruth folded the scarf and tucked it under her waistband.

Martha wasn't sure how to feel about their good fortune.

The barracks were still empty when they arrived. Together they ran to the window and watched the guard walk away. Ruth was clearly more elated than Martha. She lit up like a Christmas bulb and threw her arms around her friend.

"See what Golda says to that!" Ruth said. "You see what passion can do?"

"It's not over, Ruth. It's a beginning, but—oh, you're right! Thank you!" She kissed Ruth on the cheek. "Thank you, thank you, thank you."

Ruth pulled out the scarf and walked to the bunk five down from hers—Rebecca's, if Martha remembered right—and unfolded it over the corner of the bed.

"Come, let me show you something," Martha said. She led Ruth to her bunk and slid onto the bed, where she'd scratched ninety small marks into the wall. "This is how we will know when the baby is due. Each day, I will cross one off."

"I can hardly believe he's agreed."

A morsel of doubt tempted Martha. Golda had insisted that the commandant only lifted hope to crush it. She pushed the thought aside.

"The end of July."

The door suddenly creaked open. Women began filing in, worn to the bone. Ruth and Martha exchanged a glance and then bounded out of the bed.

"Where's Golda?"

Golda was the eighth person to step through the door. The first seven had stopped and were staring. They knew? Golda had frozen in the doorway. They knew already? They *all* knew?

But Golda wasn't staring at her, was she? Not at all. Her eyes were fixed past Martha's shoulder, down the aisle. They were all staring down the aisle.

She turned with Ruth, but there was nothing to see. Only the red scarf.

Martha faced Golda. "What?" The woman's face had drained of blood. "What is it?"

"The scarf," Golda said matter-of-factly. "It's on Rebecca's bed."

"The commandant told me to put it there," Ruth said. "Is—what does it mean?"

Golda walked past them, picked up the scarf, stared at it for a second, and then set it back on the bed. Two dozen women now crowded the aisle by the door, all eyes fixed on the red scarf. A few lowered their heads and walked off.

"What is it?" Ruth cried.

"It's Braun's game," Golda said softly. "Every few days, he orders a guard to place the scarf on a bed. The selected woman is required to visit the commandant at six thirty for dinner."

"For dinner? Oh, my dear, poor Rebecca. I had no idea! I didn't—"

"The woman does not return. The next morning she is found dead, hanging by her neck from the front gate." Martha felt the blood drain from her face.

Ruth lunged for the scarf, but Golda stopped her short. "You can't do anything! Stop it!"

A loud gasp silenced the group. There in the doorway stood Rebecca, eyes fixed wide on the red scarf. She slowly lifted a trembling hand to her mouth. Her face went white like paste. Nobody moved.

Then three women converged on her. They placed their arms around her neck and began stroking her hair in a kind of silent ritual that struck terror in Martha's heart. No one made a sound.

Except Rebecca. Rebecca suddenly sagged and began to whimper.

———

"YOU'RE TWELVE—grow up! This isn't a world made from fairy tales. It's a world where lions eat sheep and powerful men eat inferior animals like Jews."

Roth watched his father, terrified and in awe at the same time. He lowered his eyes to his knees, bared between his shorts and knee socks. No matter what Father said, thinking of other boys his age as animals was still a little strange, although he wouldn't dare admit such a thing.

This was his third visit to the camp, and each time the sights became easier to accept, but he doubted very much that young boys were meant to see the things he saw. His friends back in Berlin walked around all proud in their uniforms, but they hadn't seen what he'd seen.

"Come here," his father said in a softer tone, stepping toward the window. He stretched out his arm and beckoned with his fingers. "Come on, I want to show you something."

Roth approached and looked out at the work camp below them. It was brown everywhere. Mud and dirty buildings and women plodding around in brown clothes. Some of them wore white scarves on their heads.

Father placed a calloused hand on Roth's shoulder. "What do you see?"

Roth thought about it. "Jews?"

"Yes, that's what most would say. Jews. But when I look I see more than Jews. What I see separates me from most men."

Roth looked up. There was something almost magical about the way his father looked at him with those mesmerizing blue eyes.

"What do you see?" Roth asked.

Father lifted his eyes. "What I see isn't for children."

Roth felt a stab of disappointment. The feeling quickly changed to humiliation.

"But I'm not a child," he said. "How can I grow up if you don't let me see things that other children don't see?"

His father considered this.

"Once you cross the threshold, there's no turning back. Are you sure you're ready for that?"

He wasn't sure. Not at all. But he nodded anyway. "Yes."

Father stepped back and arched one eyebrow. His eyes dropped to Roth's feet then up his body. Roth stood tall, uncomfortably aware that he was quite short for such a bold statement.

But judging by the look on his father's face, Gerhard was proud of his answer. He'd stood there like a man and said yes.

The commandant stepped forward and smoothed Roth's blond hair. "You come from good stock, boy." He paced in front of the window, one hand stroking his chin. "Do you remember what I told you about the swastika?" he asked.

"Yes."

"Tell me."

"That it is an old symbol that has been changed."

"The Sanskrit word, *svastika*, means good fortune. It's a spiral spinning with the sun. Only those who have a clear understanding of the occult know that a chaotic force can be evoked by reversing the symbol. This is behind the design of our swastika."

His father stopped and turned to him. "This war—all that the Third Reich is doing," he stretched his hand out to the camp below, "in camps like these—is about power. It's about reversing the effect of a terrible degeneration that has ruined civilization over thousands of years. This is the führer's primary objective. Do you understand?"

His father had tensed and his hand shook a little. It made Roth nervous.

"Do you understand?"

"Yes, Father."

Father stared at the camp. "When I look at that mud hole down there, I don't see Jews. I see degenerated humanity. I see a wrong that needs to be righted. And I see the perfect solution. In ridding the world of them, yes, but not in the same way I did at Auschwitz. They are killing enough Jews each day to satisfy our objective. Marching them into the chambers like zombies, ignorant of their fate." The man's lips twisted in disgust. "Here . . . here our task is far nobler. Here we are finding a way to power the new world."

Roth followed his stare. How Father saw a way to power the world with the sad-looking Jews below was beyond him, so he said nothing.

"They are like batteries," his father said.

"Batteries?"

"Psychic fuel cells. If you know how to take that power, it becomes yours and makes you strong. Like taking the power out of one battery and putting it in your own."

His father had closed his eyes. His lips trembled. Roth quickly lowered his eyes, afraid to be caught looking.

"Do you know what hope and fear have in common?"

Was he meant to answer? Roth wondered briefly if his father was speaking to him, or to himself.

"They both hold great power. But that power is dependent on both fear and hope together. Think about it. Without the fear of something terrible, you cannot have the hope that it won't happen, you see? Without having hope for something wonderful, you can't have any fear of losing it. They work together, the two most powerful forces we possess."

Father turned from the window, walked to the bar, and poured a drink into a glass. "I play a game of high stakes here, Roth. I play for the kind of power that few men will ever have. Not the power of deciding who will live and who will die—that's child's play. But the power of taking another human being's power. The power to harvest their souls."

He paused, eyes glimmering, as if this was a great revelation that should impress Roth. And indeed it did. His heart was beating very fast.

"I lift their hopes to the heavens"—he lifted his hand high in the air, then swung it down hard—"then dash them. *Why?* you may want to know. I'll tell you why. The anguish they feel in that moment weakens their will. Their resolve turns to putty. Their anguish becomes my power."

Then his father said one more thing that would never leave Roth.

"This is how the Prince of Darkness has always gained his power—through the suffering of his victims. That's how he took the life of the Christian God, Jesus Christ. Raised him up and dashed him to the ground. And he was a Jew too."

Father chuckled, took a drink, then set the glass down with a satisfied sigh.

"There are many of us, Roth, not just me. Our work is meticulously recorded, and one day I will show you what we have done. The deaths of our enemies—these Jews—is a happy bonus. But it is the power that feeds us. Does this excite you?"

Only then did Roth realize that he was squeezing his hand into a fist. He relaxed, but he found that he couldn't speak.

Father smiled reassuringly. "Not to worry. It was all quite strange to me as well. I still remember the first ritual I witnessed. It scared me to death. But the power, Roth . . . the power was intoxicating!"

He laughed and Roth joined, glad for the relief.

"Would you like to join me tonight?" his father suddenly asked.

"Join you?"

"Well, not join me. You can watch me through the slit in the door. I've picked a woman. At this moment she's down there in the camp, plumbing the deepest wells of her soul, dredging up horror. Tonight I will ravage her soul. Don't worry, it won't be gory or brutal. I have no need for theatrics. A little blood is all."

Roth said the only thing that came to mind. "Okay."

Father beamed his pride, a look irreversibly seared into Roth's mind. "That's my boy!"

11

S TEPHEN RETURNED HOME TO FIND THE RABBI GONE. YES, OF course; Chaim always spent Thursday afternoons down at the mission, serving soup and spreading good cheer. But this was good. Stephen couldn't tell anyone about the safe, not even Chaim.

Two things had changed during his last visit to Rachel's apartment. The first had to do with secrecy. Some things in life had to remain private. Matters of love. Matters that were deeply sacred. If Rachel was his mother, and if she had gone to the grave with some deep, dark secret, then he should pursue that secret with reverence.

The second change had to do with objective. The scales of his desire had tipped from a simple need to discover to a surprising need to possess. If Rachel, being his mother, had searched for him as the note to Gerik claimed; and if taking out a full-page advertisement in search of her son placed him—David—in terrible danger; and if, failing to find him, she'd secretly hidden something for him, then it was his right to possess this last remaining link to his mother.

The Stones are like the lost orphans. He was an orphan. The other orphans would be the other four Stones of David. Either way, he had the mark; the safe had the mark, or at least the words. The safe should be his.

Stephen left Spud on the front porch. He brought the dog a bowl of water and some lunch meat, which Spud gulped down without chewing. "Stay here." Stephen pointed a finger. "Don't move."

He hurried into the bathroom and stopped in front of the mirror.

434

He'd forgotten about the black dust. He looked like a native warrior trapped in a business suit. It was a wonder Spud hadn't barked at him all the way home. Now that he thought about it, several drivers had peered at him quizzically on the trip home. *What's wrong, never seen a treasure hunter before? Just returning from a coal mine where I've found a stash of diamonds.*

He stripped off his shirt and paused to trace the small scar near his left breastbone. Whatever he'd speculated about it before, he now knew the truth.

Stephen showered, dressed, and drove straight to the library with Spud in the passenger seat. "You have to stay in the car, you know. No way I can take a dog into the library."

He parked in the shade of a jacaranda and cracked the window. "I'll be back."

His first challenge was to research without tipping his hand. He couldn't very well run around conducting interviews about his mother without bringing attention to the possibility that she had hidden the other four Stones in her apartment.

A series of searches through the periodicals turned up nothing on Rachel Spritzer. As Gerik had said, she'd lived privately. She had been hiding her secret.

Who were you, Mother?

Stephen turned to the Stones of David. He flipped through library cards, found dozens of titles that contained information on the Stones, and pulled five of them. Settling in a quiet corner, he began to read.

None of them told him any more than he already knew. He'd done a research project on the Stones for a history class nearly a decade ago. But now he read the coverage in each book with renewed interest.

Although the biblical record made no mention of what happened to the five stones David chose to slay Goliath, historians' first note of their existence cropped up in 700 BC, when they were taken to Babylon along with other treasures from the kingdom of Judah.

They next appeared in AD 400 in Alexandria. Christian folklore claimed the Stones represented the seed of David, the purest surviving symbol of Israel, which was Christ. According to Genesis, God put enmity between the serpent's seed and the woman's seed, and the woman's seed would crush the head of the serpent. David had crushed the head of Goliath with a stone, and the Messiah had come to deliver the final deathblow.

Nevertheless, most Christians weren't even aware of the relics. They'd been lost again in AD 700, and for a thousand years their very existence was in dispute. Here the record became somewhat fragmented. Various rumors surfaced and then faded, until the Knights Templars claimed to hold them for almost two hundred years before the order's sudden demise in 1307, when the French king Philip IV drove them into obscurity. *You are my little Stone of David.* Why would his foster father use that particular phrase of endearment for Stephen?

Most experts valued the collection at between $75 and $150 million. The idea caused the slight tremble to return to Stephen's fingers.

Rachel had donated a Stone of David to the Los Angeles Museum of the Holocaust. He returned to the library's newspaper section. Virtually every major newspaper in the country had picked up the story, and several already debated the existence of such a relic. Others doubted the authenticity of Rachel's Stone. But to think that a World War II survivor such as Rachel would lie about the Stone seemed somehow profane. It *had* to be genuine.

As for the Spritzers, they had immigrated to the United States sixteen years ago from Hungary. They spent their time working with orphanages around the world. Low-profile. Wealthy. That was all he could determine.

Stephen checked out three of the volumes and headed home, nerves taut. He'd learned nothing new.

The rabbi still wasn't back. Stephen led the dog into his room and ordered her to stay in the corner. Spud jumped onto his bed, eyed him as if asking permission, and, when Stephen made no objection, curled up by the pillow.

Stephen looked at the books. Who was he trying to fool? There was only one way to do this. He had to get back into the building, find a key, and open the safe. He was just delaying the inevitable, subconsciously trying to work up the courage.

But he couldn't just waltz up to the front door and demand they let him look for a key. The moment the owner sniffed anything remotely like a safe, he'd slap the crazy Realtor with a restraining order and take the treasure for himself.

"Stephen?"

Stephen whirled. Chaim stood in the doorway.

"Sorry, didn't mean to startle you." The rabbi looked at him questioningly. "You okay today?"

"Why wouldn't I be? Sure. Why, what's up?"

"That's what I was just asking you. Isn't that the dog from the apartment?"

"I'm just watching over her for a day or so."

"So you went back?"

Stephen shrugged. "Just to collect the dog. I'm okay, Rabbi. Really."

The rabbi shifted his gaze to his left and Stephen followed it. The books lay on his desk, one cracked open to a chapter titled "Stones of David: Fact or Fiction?"

"Maybe you should take a few days off," Chaim said. "Your mother has died. You missed the funeral, but you should grieve in your own way."

"Grieve what? I didn't know my mother."

"Then grieve the fact that you didn't know her."

"I've spent my whole life grieving that fact already."

"I think you may be in a bit of denial."

"That's what you keep saying." Maybe he should confide in Chaim. Only Chaim. Caution argued against it, but since when had he let caution guide his path?

"I want to tell you something, Rabbi. But I want you to swear to secrecy. Can you do that?"

"Have I ever broken your confidence?"

"No, you haven't, but this you have to swear to. No matter what, you have to agree not to breathe a word. Do I have your word?"

The rabbi smiled. "Do I have to prick my finger?"

"I'm not kidding." Stephen leaned back against the desk. "I just need your confidence on this."

They held stares. "Then you have it."

"You swear?" Stephen asked.

"Swear by neither heaven nor—"

"Just swear it."

"I swear, then."

"You won't tell a soul?"

"Stephen, I won't tell a soul that you went back to Rachel Spritzer's apartment and discovered a floor safe in the basement." Chaim arched an eyebrow.

"You know?"

"Simple deduction. And a few filthy clothes." Chaim glanced at the coal-blackened blazer on the floor.

Stephen let his enthusiasm rise to the surface. He ran both hands through his hair. "Okay, you were right; it's a safe."

"Doesn't surprise me. I know Jews. Especially Jews from the era. I'm going to eat. Would you like something?" The rabbi turned and walked toward the kitchen.

Stephen hurried after him, incredulous at the man's ambivalence. "It's a floor safe, Rabbi! My mother's floor safe!" The dog jumped from the bed and pattered along behind him.

"I don't mean to be insensitive, Stephen. But I don't think you should do anything without proper legal representation. Rachel Spritzer went to great lengths to hide the Stone she donated to the museum."

"The Stone should be mine! I could contest the will."

"If you could prove you were her son, perhaps. But why was your mother so careful to hide it? There are those who would stop at nothing for something so valuable. Rachel was frightened. You have to be careful."

Chaim's wariness made Stephen pause. Telling him had been a mistake. Though the rabbi did have a point.

"Involving attorneys could take months. It's hopeless. How could I ever prove that I'm her son?"

"That would be for the courts." Chaim sighed. "Although you're probably right in the long run. She's donated everything to the museum."

"But not"—Stephen's mind spun—"not necessarily what is in the safe. Not if the safe wasn't listed among her assets. I can find that out. But trust me, if it was listed, the museum would have made the claim already. They obviously haven't."

"Perhaps because it's empty." Chaim pulled out the leftover veal and set it in the oven. "I know these may be hard days for you, but you must be careful."

Stephen decided then not to tell the rabbi about the inscription on the safe. If anything, he would have to divert attention away from the safe now.

"There might be another way," Chaim said.

"Another way to what?"

"To take possession of whatever is left in Rachel's apartment. Who's handling the estate?"

"The building's sold," Stephen said.

"Already? We were just there yesterday."

"A German investor."

Chaim studied Stephen with an amused expression. "Then buy the place from this German investor."

The suggestion hit Stephen like a bucket of ice water. Yes. He could offer the investor a quick turnaround profit. Once the building was in his name, he could open the safe.

He turned away, worried that the rabbi might note his eagerness. He had to downplay the whole thing.

"Maybe. Ah, you're probably right. I should just forget it. What do I have to gain? I've seen what's there, right?"

"I'm not suggesting that you forget it," Chaim said. "She was your mother. You need space and time to deal with that. And your true inheritance should be yours. But you must walk very carefully."

"You're right." Stephen clapped his hands and squinted at the oven. "Veal sounds great."

"That's my boy. Now. The reception at the Board of Realtors is formal?"

Stephen looked at him, not understanding.

"The reception you invited Sylvia and me to?" Chaim said. "Tomorrow night? It's a formal affair, right?"

That reception. It was this weekend? "Formal, yes, I think so."

They ate veal together.

Ten came before they retired. "Good night, Stephen. Sleep well."

"Good night. I will."

But he didn't. He hardly slept a wink. The dog, on the other hand, slept like a baby nestled against his shoulder.

12

THE SLEEPING MIND WORKS IN STRANGE WAYS WHEN HUNG UP somewhere between out-like-a-light and bright-eyed, Stephen had always believed. In this no-man's-land, the challenges of the next day's plans walk about like relentless trumpeters. IRS agents and bill collectors loiter. A few hastily spoken words of a friend echo and transform themselves into vile threats.

On this night, Stephen's no-man's-land was populated by his mother, a faceless German crook, Chaim Leveler, and a hole in the ground filled with black air. He himself was mysteriously absent. The rabbi spent most of the night walking around inside the safe, waving his arms like a leprechaun, insisting that danger lay ahead. Rachel Spritzer spent most of the time holding her one golden Stone up to the light, asking it to lead David home. The German stood guard at the boiler room, his rocket launcher aimed at the elevator. And the hole . . .

The hole was just an empty hole, apart from the munchkin rabbi.

Stephen awoke late, at eight. He stumbled out of bed, pulled on a pair of olive-green slacks and a white shirt. No time to shower. A shave was in order, but a bit of scruff wouldn't hurt. He had plans for this day.

The dog! Where was Spud? He ran out to the living room. The cocker spaniel sat by the front door, waiting patiently. "There you are." The rabbi must have heard her whine and let her out. What was Stephen going to feed her? "Come on, let's take a ride."

Stephen hopped into the Vega after Spud and fired the engine before realizing he'd forgotten to brush his teeth. "Wait here, dog. I have to brush my teeth." Spud eyed him smugly. "*You* should try it sometime." The dog turned away.

Stephen left the car purring, ran into the house, gave his teeth a quick scrub, and returned. The prospect of the deal he was set to propose ran through his veins as hot as any he could remember. Purchasing a building that held a secret treasure trove in the basement was nothing less than the stuff of fantasies. And yet that was precisely what he was about to do.

The German had purchased Rachel Spritzer's apartment building for four hundred ninety thousand dollars. With a little work, the building could easily go for six or seven hundred thousand. Maybe more. The bank might just finance the deal without a down payment, based on his portfolio. This would accomplish two things. One, he would still have the money he had promised to Dan. And two, he would have unfettered access to that safe.

Assuming the German would sell.

The whole plan was perhaps a tad impulsive, but really it involved little more than shifting a few funds around.

And if the German didn't want to sell?

He would. He just would.

He pulled up to the curb in front of the apartment. It seemed as familiar to him as his own home now, even though this was only his third visit.

"Okay, dog, here's the deal. I can either leave you here or let you out, but if you get out, no running around getting into trouble."

Spud whined and glanced through the windshield. These were her stomping grounds. She would probably just run off, which could be a good thing. For all Stephen knew, someone else had taken the dog in and was waiting for her to return.

"Come on, let's have a look."

He got out and walked up to the door. Spud trotted proudly alongside. Stephen pressed the intercom buzzer. Butterflies took flight in his belly.

He pushed the call button. "Hello? Anyone home?"

Nothing.

The doorknob twisted freely in his hand. The building was open? He hadn't locked the door behind him yesterday—maybe they hadn't noticed. They used the garage door for access.

Stephen glanced up the street before stepping into the garage with Spud. It was empty. He scanned the room. Like a tomb. Hallowed. His pulse quickened. Where would Rachel hide a key to the safe?

"Let's go," he whispered. They walked toward the elevator in tandem, the son and the dog. Stephen's shoes clacked loud on the concrete and he rose to his tiptoes. Next time, he would wear sneakers.

He winced when the elevator started its grinding ascent. The four-story climb took twice the time a climb up the stairs would take. When the doors finally clanged open, empty space greeted him. Silence rang in his ears.

"Hello?" A faint echo from the elevator. He poked his head into the flat. "Hello?"

Unless he was hiding to pounce on him, the German was gone. The closing, perhaps.

Spud stepped cautiously past the door, ears perked, mouth closed, testing the air with her nostrils.

"What is it?" Stephen whispered. The dog relaxed and trotted for the bedroom as she had yesterday.

The scent of licorice filled Stephen's nose. "Hello?" Empty. If the new owner was at the closing, then the transaction hadn't been completed, had it? The building was still technically for sale. As a Realtor, he had the right to inspect the place. Find a key, maybe. Open the safe.

He walked slowly into the living room, taken once again by the unspoken history here. He'd left the first time determined to leave this history behind him, but now, inexplicably, he felt the irresistible urge to seek it out. To embrace it. To hear his mother speak to him from beyond the grave.

He ran his fingers over a white doily and then gently picked it up. His mother had purchased this doily, perhaps in a small shop somewhere in Budapest. He set it down.

And there, that painting of a young girl smelling a rose. Why had it attracted Rachel? Had it been a careful purchase, or one made simply to fill a hole? The former, probably. Rachel struck him as a careful person.

He walked on the carpet in a daze. He looked for a brass or silver key in all the places people normally hid keys—kitchen cupboards, jars of potpourri, dresser drawers, bookcases—but really he was looking past it all to find his mother. Did she hum while she worked in the kitchen? What kind of food did she cook? Did her sweet breads and rich stews fill the apartment with their aroma? He inhaled deeply and tried to smell her over the scents of licorice and cherries.

The walls creaked. He jerked up. Wind? Or just the frame expanding with the warming sun? He returned to his search.

Rachel had left signs of a careful life everywhere. Silver bells and crystal butterflies lined a bookcase, perfectly positioned in small groupings. Intricately designed rugs, woven in rich reds and blues, lay precisely where he would have placed them. A painting of a yellow daisy growing out of a bleak, rocky landscape hung above the couch.

If the new owners had spent the night here, there was no sign of it. Why?

Stephen had finished a full round of the apartment and was tiptoeing through the master bedroom when he noticed an odd strip of molding behind the window drapes. He stepped around the bed, drew the curtain back. A door? Here, to the left of the window, was a door. He turned the handle and eased the door open.

A sunroom. Stephen walked in.

White curtains were drawn on three windows. A single rocking chair sat beside a doily-covered oak lamp table. Dozens of framed photographs lined the wall, mostly black-and-white. Hundreds. They were pictures of the war. Of concentration camps. Of people, some in prison clothes, others in street clothes.

It was a sanctuary. Rachel's special room.

History charged the air, electric enough to lift the hair on his arms when he moved.

A photograph to his right showed a mass grave filled with hundreds of emaciated bodies, tangled as they had fallen. The fuzzy image showed a woman, two children, and two men standing in their underwear with their backs to the pit, hugging themselves. One of the children was looking back into the grave. The caption above read, *Jews await execution in Belzec.*

Stephen's vision blurred. He tried to move his foot, but he stood rooted to the carpet. He'd seen similar pictures before but refused to engage them. He'd come to America to start over, not to wallow in this horrible chapter of history. But here . . .

Here in Rachel's shrine, this chapter of his mother's history—of his history—grabbed him by both arms, yanked him in, and would not let go. She was here, one of the faces in these pictures. He might be here.

His eyes moved to a picture of a young girl, maybe ten, mouth open and toothless. Round, innocent eyes. Legs and arms crossed, preserving her modesty. Hardly more than a skeleton. She was bald and she was naked.

The picture said she was Greta's daughter, Susan. *Medical labs.* He'd heard that the Nazis had conducted experiments on children, but he'd never seen them, not like this. What had they done to this child?

Stephen lifted both hands to his cheeks, as if that would somehow quell the nausea in his gut. These were Jews. His people. How could any sane human do this to another living person? He wanted to run from the room, but his legs refused to move. Part of him hated Rachel Spritzer for leaving this grotesque monument.

But no, it was also lovely, a lovely thing. It was a monument to love. By showing this picture of the toothless girl, Rachel was speaking to her through time. *I will not forget you, Susan. You are not ugly to me. You are beautiful, and I will cherish you forever.*

And Mother would surely say the same to him. I love you, David. I will cherish you forever. Tears filled his eyes. To think that he'd turned his back on the memories of his mother's own suffering . . .

He searched the walls for a picture that resembled the picture from the newspaper. He wanted to cry out, *Mommy, Mommy.* And the fact that he wanted to cry out brought a fresh flood of tears to his eyes.

Stephen's eyes stopped on an eight-by-ten frame that sat beside the lamp on the oak table. The black-and-white photo captured a woman with long black hair. Rachel? He stumbled forward on numb legs and lifted the photograph.

The woman seemed to stare through him. Round, melancholic eyes. Innocent lips. She was beautiful.

He turned the photo over and saw that there was no backing. He read the black cursive.

My dearest Esther, I found this picture in Slovakia after the war. It is your mother, Ruth, one year before your birth.

Not an hour passes without my begging God that you and David will find each other. I will never forget. You are the true Stones of David.

Stephen's heart bolted. *You are the true Stones of David?* He flipped the picture over. The woman's name was Ruth. Her daughter was Esther. Esther was also a Stone of David? But the daughter of Ruth, not Rachel Spritzer.

Esther and David were meant to find each other.

Stephen sank into the rocker and stared at Ruth's picture. For a moment he imagined that Ruth was actually Esther. Was Esther alive? A secret bound them all together. Ruth and Rachel and Esther and David. He stared into the eyes of the young Ruth, and he knew with unequivocal certainty that his life had just been irrevocably changed.

His own destiny stared him in the face. Nothing would ever matter as much as understanding what secrets lay behind these eyes. He vowed it silently.

The air felt thick. He wiped his eyes and drew long breaths.

The Stones are like the lost orphans. They will eventually find each other.

The safe.

A hum ran through the floorboards. Elevator?

Hands shaking, he pried the photograph out of the frame with his fingernails, slipped it into his shirt, shoved the empty frame under the end table, and hurried out of the room.

The key. He hadn't searched the room for a key.

Spud scrambled from under Rachel's bed, went rigid for a moment, and then raced from the room.

Stephen ran after the dog. "Spud! Get back here."

But the dog already stood on guard by the door. She uttered a low growl. "Down, girl!"

———

THE ELEVATOR doors slid open. Stephen leaned nonchalantly against the wall and took a settling breath. Two men dressed in dark suits stepped out and stopped at the sight of the dog.

"Well, it's about time," Stephen said. "Don't mind Spud. She doesn't bite."

They looked up at him, unfazed.

He unfolded his arms and straightened. "Hope you don't mind—the door was open, and I was looking for the owner." He reached out a hand. "Name's Stephen Friedman. I'm a Realtor. Sit, Spud."

The man ignored his hand.

Spud growled and bared her teeth. "No, Spud. Relax, girl."

Amazingly, Spud quieted and backed up.

"You're trespassing." Heavy German accent.

Stephen lowered his arm. "I'm sorry, maybe you don't understand. I'm here with an offer. I have a client who is willing to pay a substantially higher price than what you paid for this building. I realize it's a bit unusual, but—"

"We really have no interest in selling," the man said with an amused smirk. "You said the door was open?"

"Yes. I was looking for a Roth Braun."

"I can assure you Mr. Braun has no interest in selling. I apologize for the inconvenience, but you really should leave now. He will be here soon."

"Then I'll wait for him," Stephen said.

"You're not listening. Please leave. Now."

"I'm offering—"

"I don't care if you're offering twice what was paid; we're not interested."

Stephen stared at them, taken off guard by their dismissal. "You hear that, Spud? They aren't interested in the million dollars I was going to offer them." He had no intention of offering a million dollars, of course. But saying it might make them think twice. "May I ask what Mr. Braun's interest in the building is?"

"Actually, no; that would be completely inappropriate," the dark-haired man said. His friend looked on without expression. He was white enough to be an albino. Blond hair and eyebrows. Pale blue eyes that forced Stephen's stare away. They obviously weren't impressed.

"Is he going to tear it down?" Stephen asked.

The dark-haired man glanced at the blond, then back to Stephen, apparently amused. "Are all Americans as dense as you?"

Perhaps the man was more incensed than amused.

"I will now give you precisely thirty seconds to vacate the property, or I will personally show you the door," the German said.

Stephen lifted both hands in a sign of surrender. "Easy. I'm just a businessman interested in business. It's a simple matter of money. How could any sane man refuse to double his investment in a day? It makes me wonder what you're doing here. In America."

"That is none of your concern. Now, please"—the man bowed his head in an unsuccessful attempt at graciousness—"leave."

He wore thick gold rings on several fingers, one with an onyx carved in the shape of a lion. A heavy gold chain hung on his neck. And under his jacket? Stephen would be surprised if the man didn't wear a gun.

"Okay. I'm leaving." He turned to the stairs, paused, and turned back. "Does the owner have any interest in Rachel Spritzer?"

The man stepped forward, grabbed Stephen above his elbow, drew him roughly toward the stairs, and shoved him down the first two steps. "Now you're trying my patience. Get out!"

Pain flared up Stephen's arm. "Ouch! I'm going."

Spud barked and dodged a swift kick. She ran deftly past them and into the stairwell.

"I know you're going. And I'm going with you."

Stephen twisted his arm away and hurried down, stunned by their treatment of him. When had he ever been physically removed from a building by a bodyguard? *Ouch?* Had he actually said "ouch"?

"This is crazy. You're actually physically throwing me out of the building?"

"I'm protecting the interests of my employer. You, on the other hand, are breaking the law."

Braun's bodyguard pushed him across the garage floor, ignoring Spud, who'd found her courage again and was hopping to their left, barking furiously. The man pulled the front door open, swung his foot at Spud, who bolted out in a hasty retreat, and shoved Stephen through.

"The door was open—"

"Forgive the confusion. You won't find it open again." The door slammed in his face.

"Uh! You . . . *idiot!*" Stephen turned to find an elderly lady on the sidewalk watching him.

He forced a grin and shrugged. "Brothers."

She smiled knowingly and went on her way.

Stephen hurried for his car, trailed by an indignant dog. They climbed in and sat side by side, staring out the front window. He hadn't actually talked to Braun, but somehow he doubted the treatment would have been any different.

"What do you think, Spud? Maybe we overdid it a bit?"

He pulled out Ruth's picture and stared into her eyes for a long minute.

"Well, I don't think we did," he said. "I'm going to find a way in, Spud. One way or another, I'm going to find out what's in that basement."

The dog whimpered.

A black limousine drove by, took a left at the stop sign and rounded the apartment. Braun. Stephen slipped the picture between the seats and gripped the wheel with both hands.

Several thoughts flashed through his mind. His deal with Dan Stiller. The reception tonight. Chaim and Sylvia, whom he'd invited to the reception tonight.

All were distant distractions from the driving urge to get to the bottom of Rachel Spritzer's apartment complex. Literally.

Stephen decided then that he would cancel the rest of his plans for the day and apply his energy to one end and one end only: getting at that safe.

He started the engine and angled for La Brea.

—ᵛᵛᵛ—

"A REALTOR named . . ." Claude turned to Lars.

"Stephen Friedman," Lars said.

"Stephen Friedman. Don't worry, he won't be back."

"He was inside?"

"Yes. Up here, in fact. He claimed to have a client willing to pay a million dollars for the property."

"How did he get in? I said no one enters. Is that too complicated for you?" Roth wanted to hit one of them. Not because the man had come in, but because Claude and Lars had broken his trust. He immediately set the impulse aside.

"He said the front door was open," Claude said. "I can promise you, he won't be back."

On second thought, reprisal of some kind was in order. And the appearance of the Realtor confirmed that the game was in full swing.

Could it be the Jew?

He had to play the game perfectly now. One slip and all would be lost.

"If anyone else enters, kill them. We have too much riding on this to risk exposure."

"Killing a Realtor will draw attention," Lars said.

"Not the Realtor. Kill anyone else. The Realtor, bring to me."

Roth turned away and walked to the living room. He withdrew a white handkerchief and dabbed at the sweat that had gathered on his forehead. He couldn't remember ever feeling so terrified over the prospect of failure.

The Stones were here. They called out to him. But also, more than mere fortune. With calculating, deliberate moves, he would finish what Gerhard had started in Toruń.

"We have to move quickly. Start in the kitchen. I want every drawer emptied of every spoon and fork." He faced Claude and Lars, who waited with folded arms. "Every word she wrote, no matter how insignificant it seems, comes to me." He looked around at the remaining artwork and sniffed at the air. "They're here, I can smell them. Can you smell them?"

They exchanged glances. Fools, pawns, oblivious to the game. "I can smell Jew," Claude said, the corner of his mouth lifting slightly.

Roth ignored the bourgeois response and glanced out the window. He'd expected more activity around the building. The wench had possessed one of the Stones of David, for heaven's sake. He'd half-expected the museum to be out here with a wrecking ball, searching for the others. Their assumption that someone who'd gladly donated her entire estate would not cunningly hide a greater fortune betrayed them for the fools they were. They'd picked through the apartment and removed a number of valuables but conducted no thorough search. Like most men, they were psychically impaired.

All the better for him.

He stripped off the black silk jacket. His shirt was also silk. Black silk. He loved the way it felt on his skin, smooth and slick. He draped the jacket over a chair. They would blockade the entry door, bring in only food and what tools they needed, and live on the third floor while they worked.

"Take off your jackets," he said.

Claude and Lars stripped down to white undershirts.

"Place your guns on the table where we can get to them. Just as a precaution."

They did so.

"What about the sunroom?" Lars asked. The man's gray eyes had always fascinated Roth. You could look in his eyes and guess that he was ruthless, but at other times those eyes seemed as innocent as a child's.

"I will work in the sunroom," Roth said. Rachel Spritzer's own private museum had been a delightful surprise. The pictures excited Roth, gave him the unexpected thrill of reliving his formative years.

He turned and headed for the master bedroom.

Toruń
May 25, 1944

EVEN WITH DOUBLE RATIONS OF THE BROTH AND BREAD, MARTHA didn't know how her baby would survive another two months. She and Ruth had both lost weight in their arms and legs—everywhere but in their bellies, which had grown slowly to show the life curled up within.

Prisoners came and went, most bearing long expressions of desperation and hopelessness. News of the outside world filtered in with the new arrivals, but separating the rumors from the truth was nearly impossible.

Warplanes flew high above, presumably on bombing runs to the south. Rumors of the Russians advancing with their allies, advancing to crush the Germans, rippled through the camp but provided little hope. Here in Toruń, such possibilities could not rise above the resignation of five thousand women plodding on dry mud, clinging to a life few were sure they wanted anymore.

They said the Germans were gathering all the Hungarian Jews in the camp at Kistarcsa, outside Budapest, but Martha could hardly remember what her homeland looked like, much less cry over what was happening in the bleak landscape of her distant memory. The exceptions were her sister, Katcha, and Antonette, her mother. She pressed every prisoner from the south for news of the two women, but no one had any. How could they? Trainloads of Jews shuttled here and there, and they were supposed to remember a face or a name among them all?

Martha stood outside the barracks and stared at the gray sky. Heavy clouds stretched from horizon to horizon, dark like the mud under her feet. To her right, the gate to Toruń, where she'd seen eighteen women hanged with bags over their heads over the past month, stood exposed to the gathering storm. To her left, the commandant's house rose like a monument painted red with the blood of his victims.

Rebecca was the first she'd seen hanging from the gate, but always, every two days, or three at most, the camp awoke to another body, swinging like a sack of rocks. It wasn't enough for Braun to kill the women. He insisted on this inconceivable torture before the slaughter, of dining them and God only knew what else. The wails of some victims cut through the camp at midnight. But the cries would always end abruptly, cut off by the sudden snap of the noose.

Martha heard movement behind her. She turned to see Ruth walking toward her from the barracks, smiling. No other woman in the compound could smile as much as the young mother-to-be from Slovakia. Unfortunately, her optimism was lost on most of the others. At times even Martha felt a hint of contempt, perhaps a bit of jealousy as well. Ruth's talk of passion and joy sometimes struck Martha as offensive in this place of death.

Ruth slipped her arm around Martha's and pulled her close. "It's getting warmer," she said. "Summer will be here soon."

On the other hand, Ruth exhibited an unrelenting need for companionship. Since their meeting on the train, she had been more like a sister to Martha than a friend. When they stood side by side like this, as they often did before the evening roll call, Martha felt more alive, and more hopeful, than at any other time during the day.

"It's going to rain again," Martha said.

"Hmm. Look at the flowers out there," Ruth said, gazing at the field.

"They've painted the guard towers," Martha said. "Why would they paint the guard towers?"

"Perhaps they want to brighten the guards' mood."

Her optimism was incorrigible. Martha nearly laughed, but the gray skies held her back.

"Little David's been kicking me silly today," Ruth said. She put her hand on Martha's belly. "Yours?"

"Quiet. I think he has the days and nights mixed up. I could hardly sleep last night. Anyway, how do you know yours is a David?"

"Then she's an Esther, and yours is a David. Or they are both Esthers."

"Or both Davids."

"But it would be better if one is a David and one is an Esther."

"Why?"

Ruth smiled wide. "So they can fall in love and be married, of course. Wouldn't that be something?"

Martha had to chuckle. "You're impossible. Women are being hung from the gate, and your mind is skipping through the daisies, planning weddings."

Ruth's smile faded. She reached up and swept a strand of hair from Martha's cheek. "If you have a daughter, she will be very beautiful, like you. She'll run through fields of daisies and marry my beautiful David."

"Aren't you forgetting something?"

"That dead babies can't grow up to be married men and women?"

"Yes."

Ruth looked out at the field, shifting to one of her rare, somber moods. "You're right. That's the problem with this world. But do David and Esther know that? They're warm and snug in our bellies, jumping for joy, oblivious to the trains and the camps. We should take a lesson from them."

"We're not oblivious to the stink of death, though."

"No. But we aren't oblivious to the joy that awaits us either."

"Joy? You mean the possibility of a noose around our necks? Or a train ride back to Auschwitz?"

"No, I mean what awaits us when we are born into the next life."

Martha sighed. "Yes, of course, how silly of me. The next life. After we've been killed."

"Or after we have lived long and full lives. Death is the one thing that happens to every person. So what if our passing is a little strenuous? What awaits will be no less delightful."

Ruth had never spoken so frankly about death, and Martha wasn't sure she liked it much.

A guard approached them from the commandant's hill. Ruth looked his way, silenced for a moment. Braun had asked both of them to his house only once since that first meeting—a ridiculous social affair during which they sat on his couch and talked nonsense. Ruth had been called up on three other occasions, by herself.

"He likes you," Martha said, still watching the guard.

"I'm not sure I can go again." Emotion crowded Ruth's voice.

"You have to. But please tell me you won't let him touch you."

"There's a letter opener on his desk. I would stab him in the heart before I let him touch me."

"Maybe you should do it anyway."

"I've been tempted."

Ruth turned to Martha. "I would like to ask you something. If anything were to happen to me after my child is born, will you take him as your own?"

"Of course. I would think of nothing else."

"And if anything happens to you, I will care for your child." Ruth's eyes searched hers, concerned, which alarmed Martha.

"What is it, Ruth? Do you know something?"

"No. No, of course not. I swear it, Martha. I will care for your child as if it were my own."

Martha nodded. "And I will take care of yours."

"At all costs. Forever. Swear it."

"At all costs, forever. I swear it."

"As do I," Ruth said.

The guard stopped twenty feet away. "You. The short one. The commandant wants to see you."

Ruth squeezed Martha's hand. "Thank you."

"Be strong," Martha whispered.

The admonition was more for herself than her friend.

14

C HAIM LEVELER SCANNED THE RECEPTION HALL AGAIN, BUT Stephen was nowhere to be seen. He hadn't seen or heard from the boy since they'd retired last evening. The Realtors' semiannual reception had started an hour ago, and still no sign. This wasn't entirely unlike Stephen, but given the circumstances of the last two days, Chaim worried.

Three hundred voices of realty professionals and their significant others filled the room with a steady murmur. Guests dressed in black jackets and trendy maxis surrounded a few dozen tables, each decorated with miniature homes—whether edible or not, the rabbi wasn't sure. The crab cakes and truffles certainly were edible, and quite good too.

"Hello, Rabbi."

He turned to see Sylvia, dressed in a long black gown and smiling softly. "My, you look stunning, dear." He took her hand and kissed it. "Have you seen Stephen?"

"No. He's not here yet?"

"Not that I've seen. He's distracted. I think this discovery of his mother is getting to him." He'd given his word not to breathe a word about the safe, not even to Sylvia. "Not that I blame him."

"He's not doing anything stupid, is he?"

Chaim looked at her, surprised. She'd touched on his fear exactly, but to say it so plainly seemed insensitive. "No, no. Why would you say that?"

"Stephen is unpredictable and impulsive. I wouldn't put anything past him. You talk to Gerik again?"

"Yes," Chaim said.

"And he's worried about Stephen's safety?"

"You know Gerik. Sure he's concerned, but he also sees this as a private matter. And he thinks Stephen should follow his heart to whatever resolution awaits him."

"Well, if any danger does exist, Stephen is the type to find it."

"Listen to us. It's probably nothing." Chaim smiled. "We're seeing ghosts. Stephen is a grown man, not a child. Maybe Gerik is right—let him follow his heart."

Sylvia sighed. "Probably right. I'm a bit uptight. All this talk about a serial killer has the office in knots."

"Serial killer? What are you talking about?"

"You should turn on the television more often, Rabbi. Two women killed in two nights, each found with their wrists slit."

"That's reason to assume it was a serial killer?" Chaim asked. "It's a big city—"

"Both women were Jewish. Both were left in identical states. A red scarf was draped over the face of both women. These are deliberate killings."

"My, my." The rabbi shook his head slowly.

"The mayor isn't too thrilled that the information was leaked to the press. Last thing we need is panic among Jewish women."

"Does it concern you?" he asked.

"What? That I'm Jewish?" She scanned the floor. "Honestly, I hadn't thought about it."

"Well, I'm sure a good party is just what you need to get your mind off work."

Chaim patted her hand and took a step before stopping short. She followed his gaze. Stephen angled toward them from the main entrance. He wore a white shirt without a jacket. No tie. His dark, thinning hair had been hastily slicked back.

Sylvia watched him approach. "Distracted, you said?"

Stephen zigzagged his way around curious stares, mounted the steps into the hall, and hurried to them, winded. A light sheen of sweat coated his unshaved face.

He cracked a boyish grin. "Hey. Boy. Sorry I'm late. I've been tied up doing some"—he paused and shifted his eyes—"research."

Chaim stared.

"I feel a bit underdressed," Stephen said. "It was either that or miss the whole thing." He looked around. "Whole gang's here."

"Daniel Stiller is looking for you," Chaim said. "Something about the Santa Monica property. Where have you been?"

"Stiller . . ." Stephen stared off in a daze.

"You okay?" Sylvia asked.

"Right. Fine. I just lost track of time. Do I look okay? I tried to freshen up a bit in the restroom."

"A jacket wouldn't hurt," Sylvia said. "But hey, who's looking? Nothing wrong with the . . . earthy look."

"You think someone has a jacket I could borrow?" He attempted to smooth his rumpled shirt.

"I doubt it," Chaim said. They stood in silence for a moment. He'd never seen the lad so frazzled. It was hardly his business, but Chaim felt compelled to ask the question again. "So, where were you?"

Stephen looked from him to Sylvia and then back. He glanced around, bright-eyed now. He took them both by their arms and eased them around so their backs were to the main hall.

"Did Chaim tell you, Sylvia?"

"Tell me what?"

"About the safe. That's good, Rabbi. I knew you were a man of your word. Promise me you won't tell a soul, Sylvia." He glanced over his shoulder. Evidently, the coast was still clear.

"How can I promise you what—"

"Just promise me."

"Fine. I promise," Sylvia said.

"It *is* a safe. And she has a room in her house filled with pictures of the camps. She had to be a camp survivor. I found a note on a picture—there's a girl she referred to as a Stone of David. Her name's Esther. I think she may still be alive. My foster father used to call me his Stone of David."

He looked at them as if expecting this information dump to fill their minds with amazement. Chaim heard it all, but he'd been so distracted by Stephen's near-rabid performance that he'd missed the point. He caught Sylvia's eye. She took Stephen by the arm.

"Stephen, I don't have a clue what you just said, but I think you need some rest. Maybe we should go."

"What do you mean, you don't have a clue? Aren't you listening?" Another quick look over his shoulder. He whispered harshly. "It's a *safe!* And I swear the people who bought the building know something's there. Don't you see? I'm an orphan from the war. *The orphans will find each other.* She wants me to find the safe. For all we know, it just might have the other four Stones."

He stopped midgesture, looked from Sylvia to Chaim, and lowered his arms. "You don't see it, do you?"

Chaim finally found his voice. "We see that you are quite taken with this thing, my boy. But this is neither the time nor the place to show the world your interest."

"You're right. You're right. I don't know what came over me. Sorry."

"Don't be," Sylvia said.

He closed his eyes. "I must look like a fool."

"Don't be silly. A crazed maniac, maybe, but not a fool." She smiled.

Stephen grinned. "Okay. Sorry. Not another word about it tonight. I swear."

"Honestly, you have to be careful," Chaim said.

"Not to worry, Rabbi." He patted Chaim on the shoulder. "How's the food?"

"The crab cakes are among the best I've tasted."

"You've both had a chance to meet some new people?"

"Not yet," Sylvia said. "But I'm sure there are plenty of Realtors who'll willingly serve an attorney her drink. Would you mind?"

"Not at all," Stephen said.

But Stephen didn't move to get Sylvia her drink.

"Listen." Stephen stroked his chin and glanced around furtively. "I'm not sure this was a good idea. I shouldn't have come in the first place, and the thought of having to mingle is giving me the shivers."

"Please, Stephen, we didn't mean to suggest that—"

"No, Rabbi." He held up his hands. "I really, really think I need to go. I'm not dressed right." He winked and put a hand on Chaim's shoulder. "Do me a favor, will you? If you run into Dan Stiller again, tell him I'll get in touch with him in the morning."

"Actually, I was thinking of leaving myself. It—"

"No. Absolutely not. I forbid it! You will stay and enjoy yourself. I have a few errands to run, and then I'll be home."

"Errands? It's nine o'clock."

Stephen grinned deliberately. "Exactly. Need to buy some shampoo and a razor. Thank you for coming, Sylvia. I would love to stay and chat, but the shower is bellowing my name. Stay and have some fun."

"Don't worry about me. I'm just getting started."

He cocked his finger at her like a gun. "That's the spirit. Show the rabbi how an attorney parties, will you?" He began to back away. "Good night."

He turned and hurried toward a side door, leaving Chaim and Sylvia staring after him with raised brows.

—⁘⁘⁘—

STEPHEN RAN out of the building, more relieved than he could remember feeling in a long time. He hadn't been roped into a conversation with a single one of his peers—luck was definitely on his side. It was going to be a good night. Even the dog seemed eager, perched on the edge of the passenger's seat.

"Don't worry, Rabbi," Stephen muttered. "If you knew what I know . . ."

Which was? That he had indeed done some research, if stalking Rachel Spritzer's apartment building from every conceivable angle and setting every last cell in his brain to the task of getting at that safe could be classified as research. As a result, he'd stumbled upon information only a fool could ignore: the contents of the safe did not belong to the museum.

At least that's the way he read the provision buried in the will.

He'd left the apartment and visited Caldwell Realty, where he'd persuaded a secretary named Sally to let him take a peek at the documents. No harm—they would soon be part of the public record in a transaction like this anyway. He found the portions of Rachel Spritzer's will that dealt with the apartment. According to the document, in addition to the building itself, Rachel Spritzer had donated to the museum all of her earthly possessions "currently located in the fourth-floor apartment of #5 Thirty-second Street . . . including but not limited to . . ." The document contained an inventory of her most valuable possessions.

The contents of the safe weren't in the fourth-floor apartment. They were in the basement. And they weren't technically part of the building. The safe itself was, but not the contents.

True, the specific mention of her residence may have simply been intended to address her living quarters in general, but as far as Stephen was concerned, that was open to debate. Which could mean there *was* something in that safe Rachel Spritzer didn't want the museum to possess. He was no attorney, but considering everything else, the implications read like absolute fact to Stephen.

He'd also taken the time to flesh out the man who'd bought the building on such short notice. Roth Braun. A German investor with no ties to the United States that he could find. Not one. He had a name in Germany, owned a bunch of businesses that read like Mafia cover-ups to Stephen, especially in light of his earlier exchange with Braun's henchmen. Still, the man looked clean on paper. Maybe he really had purchased the building as a legitimate investment.

Not a chance. Braun knew something. Specifically, something about Rachel Spritzer. It struck Stephen that the man could be the very danger his mother alluded to in her note. All the more reason to get into that safe.

Stephen had spent three hours thinking through a dozen ways to get into the building. He watched as a woman, apparently someone from the city, approached the front door, spoke briefly to the dark-haired German, had him sign something, and then left. An inspector, maybe, getting a waiver.

His challenge was to get in without them knowing he was in. No matter how he broke down the problem, this meant the front door was out of the question. A dozen times he told himself that he was charting dangerous waters. And a dozen times the photograph of Ruth reached into his soul, demanding he liberate the Stones of David. The authorities were out, absolutely out. He had no claim against the Germans. Retaining an attorney was even more impossible. If Braun learned about the safe, he and the treasure would be long gone before any court could even hear a case.

Stephen's only option was to move alone, and quickly. He felt sick—or was it giddy?—with the impossibilities of the situation.

And then one thought healed his sickness.

A plan.

An improbable, highly creative plan that no one would suspect of anyone but a fool. Improbable enough to actually work.

He returned to the apartment building, drove around it three times, each time gathering his resolve, and finally settled on his course. A visit to the hardware store ate up the remaining daylight and the first hour of darkness. But the time proved invaluable. He refined options and details by careful calculation until the plan was perfect.

Skipping out of the reception without talking to Dan Stiller may not have been wise, but they still had ample time to submit their proposal to the city. Next Wednesday was still a long ways off. He had to get this small matter of history and destiny and several hundred million dollars off his chest before he could really concentrate on the Santa Monica property anyway.

Chaim and Sylvia no doubt believed him a tad whacked-out, but he'd covered well enough. They couldn't possibly understand the true significance of the safe.

Stephen glanced at his watch. A little over two hours before midnight. Perfect.

15

S URPRISINGLY, LA BREA AVENUE SEEMED TO HAVE MORE TRAFFIC near midnight than midday. Stephen parked the Vega on a side street two blocks south of his mother's apartment. He pulled a backpack from the back seat, checked to see that no one was watching, and hefted the bag over his shoulders. *Natural. Look natural.* Just an ordinary Joe taking a midnight stroll with a pack strapped to his back.

"You stay put, Spud. I'll be back before you know it."

The dog jumped out before Stephen could shut the door. "Spud!" But the dog ran up the street and disappeared. This was getting to be a bad habit.

Stephen locked the car and turned north, searching for the dog on his way. Surely she would come back. He felt oddly lost without the dog's carefree presence.

The sidewalk was deserted except for a woman walking directly toward him, half a block up. Where had she come from? *Avoid eye contact. Natural.* They passed each other without incident. Had she seen his car?

He cut east at the next street and then turned left into an alley that approached the rear of the abandoned complex across the street from Rachel's building. Darkness swallowed him. He hurried his pace. So far, so good, but still no sign of Spud. Maybe just as well for the time being.

Stephen stopped at the end of the alley and poked his head around the corner. The windows of what he'd decided to call "Building B" were patched up with plywood. Graffiti covered the back wall. How many pimps and drug pushers frequented these shadows each night? He hoped not to encounter any. Beyond Building B, across the street, stood Rachel's apartment. If he could get into Building B, he might be able to find a window with a view of her apartment. He glanced at his watch—11:30. Half an hour to burn. He looked down the empty alley and then stepped lightly toward the back door.

Something clattered noisily on the asphalt and he jumped. His foot had hit a bottle. Enough of this. He ran for the building, pulled up beside a rear service entrance, and twisted the knob. To his surprise, it opened. He slipped in, shut the door, and heaved a sigh of relief.

His breathing sounded like billows in the hollow chamber. The lines of walls slowly grew out of the darkness. A long hall and stairs. Couldn't use the light yet.

He mounted the stairs and felt his way up one flight, then two, then three. Fourth floor. He pushed on the door exiting the stairwell and stepped cautiously through it.

Moonlight shone through a single window on the opposite wall. The rooms had been gutted—sections of framing lay in tangled heaps in every direction. But the floor seemed sound enough. He picked his way across the room to the window.

There it was, illuminated by a bright moon—Rachel's apartment. Stephen's pulse surged. The lights in her fourth-floor suite were still on. The lights of her master bedroom. The sunroom.

He instinctively pulled back from the window. Rachel's curtains were drawn. Made sense—the men who'd thrown him out didn't seem the kind to walk around in their underwear with the drapes wide open.

Stephen slid the backpack off and settled to one knee. They were up there all right, picking through her belongings. How dare they? But on the bright side, if they were preoccupied with the fourth floor, they wouldn't be in the basement.

If.

Thank God he'd taken the picture of Ruth from the sunroom. He straightened, struck by a terrible thought. The picture! Where had he put it?

He remembered immediately and relaxed. He'd left it on his desk.

For a brief moment, he considered retracing his steps, racing home, retrieving the photo, and returning. What if the rabbi entered his room and found it? He could trust Chaim. After all, it was only a picture.

Stephen studied his mother's building. The real trick was to get in and out without dropping any clues. Leaving a trail to the boiler room would only proclaim that it possessed something noteworthy. In the unlikely event that he failed tonight, he couldn't afford to tip his hand. He was smarter than that.

Eleven thirty-five. His fingers trembled with anticipation. There was nothing magical about midnight. It had just seemed a good time. The neighborhood was already quiet; maybe he should just go now.

No. He had to follow the plan, and the plan was midnight.

Was it illegal, this plan of his? Maybe. Maybe not.

On second thought, absolutely. But at times, principle should supersede the law, and this was one of those times.

The sum of the matter was this: if Rachel had intended the museum to have the contents of the safe, she would have specified as much in her will. The fact that she hadn't meant its contents were for someone else. Someone like him. That's why she'd inscribed the safe with words that would have meaning only to an orphan branded with a Stone of David.

An element of danger trailed Rachel, a secret that put her son's life at risk. She had hoped that her son would recognize the caption in the paper—"the Stones are like the lost orphans"—and figure out the rest. As he was doing.

As Chaim would say: *If you want to have what others do not have, you must be willing to do what others are unwilling to do.* If ever there was a time to prove such an axiom, it was tonight.

One hundred million dollars—more money than he'd ever dreamed about. The idea made his mind hurt. He could walk down Sepulveda slipping hundred-dollar bills to the down-and-out and watch their eyes light up. He could buy an island with a yacht parked in the slip down by the shore.

On the other hand, his passion for this safe was as much about principle, about his mother and her secret, and about a little girl named Esther who'd been lost to Ruth. Put together—the safe, the Stones, Rachel, Esther—the sum was too much to ignore. As a Stone of David, he had an obligation. A calling.

It occurred to him that his liberation of this treasure was, in some convoluted way, not terribly unlike the liberation of a concentration camp by the Allied soldiers. He was redeeming what belonged to the Jews. Restoring their inheritance. His inheritance. This would be his part in the war. Stephen's mind reeled with a dozen thoughts, some completely reasonable, others admittedly less.

Desperate times; desperate measures.

Watch. Eleven forty. Time was crawling.

Something thumped softly across the room. Stephen started, nearly choking on his heart. He pressed himself against the wall and gazed into the shadows.

A dog bounded silently over the rubble, grinning wide, tongue flopping. Spud! She jumped up and stretched to lick his face. "Where'd you go? Okay, enough. Enough!" Stephen hugged the dog. "Boy, am I glad to see you."

No, he wasn't. What was he going to do with her now?

"She likes you," a woman's voice said.

Stephen bolted up, knocking the dog to the ground. "What?"

"I said, she likes you." A petite woman in her twenties stepped out of the shadows. She wore torn bell-bottom jeans with a light-colored blouse and beads. Hundreds of beads: on her wrists, on her neck, in her braided hair.

"What are you doing up here?" she asked.

"I was . . . I was just looking around."

"Is that right?"

What was he supposed to say? Nothing came to mind.

"The last time I saw anyone wearing those kind of duds up here was three months ago when they put this building up for sale. But nobody's buying. You know why? Because it belongs to us."

"Oh."

She stared at him, uncertain, then a smile slowly formed on her lips. "Well, the dog likes you, so maybe I do too. You can call me Melissa."

"Okay." She was a hippie type. Stephen had only one thing on his mind now. Get past this and pretend she'd never seen him. This wasn't in the plan. "Groovy," he said.

"Groovy." Melissa walked around him, wearing a whimsical smile, smelling like jasmine tea. "Groovy. Well, Mr. Groovy, you are in the wrong building. This building belongs to the Brotherhood of Bohemia. What's in the backpack?"

"Nothing."

"Mr. Groovy, whose bulging backpack has nothing in it, and who doesn't like to talk. That about cover it?"

He just nodded, then glanced out the window over his shoulder. Street still empty. Almost midnight.

Melissa suddenly started to chuckle, and Stephen smiled with her. "What's so funny?"

"You."

Her laughter grew until it echoed around the room. He stepped forward and tried to wave her down. "Could you hold it down? The whole place will hear you!" Across the street, the curtains were still drawn.

"There's no one in the building right now but us, baby." She controlled her laughter. "I think you just might do. You could play the city slicker who wants to be groovy but doesn't have a clue."

He had no idea what she meant.

"Okay, you can stay for a bit. But I've gotta cruise—city's just coming alive for us bohemians. Wanna join us?"

"No thanks. I've got some stuff to do."

She looked out the window. "They moved in a few days ago. Friends of yours?"

"Who?"

"The people you're looking at. You know, Rachel's place."

"You . . . you knew Rachel?"

"Not really. She was friendly, and she asked me to take care of Brandy here." Melissa bent and rubbed the dog's back. "But that's about it. You knew her?"

"No."

Melissa nuzzled the dog playfully, cooing. She jumped up. "Gotta go. Come on, girl." She hurried off. Spud—no, Brandy, the dog's name was Brandy—gave Stephen a long, indecisive gaze, then bounded after the girl.

It took ten minutes for Stephen to recover from the intrusion. He wasn't sure how he felt about Melissa's attachment to the dog. A constant companion like little Brandy, although something he never would have sought, appealed to him. But there Brandy went, bounding after the girl.

Stephen surveyed the street one more time. Not a soul had walked by in ten minutes. Time for Mr. Groovy to boogie.

16

S TEPHEN MADE HIS WAY DOWN THE STAIRS, STOPPING ON EVERY floor to listen. Apart from his own pounding heart, he heard nothing. Melissa and Brandy were gone.

Every Special Forces movie he'd ever watched barked the same mantra: *Get in quick, and get out.* Made sense. In his case: Get in quick, secure the fortune, and get out. Without leaving a calling card, of course. Or, better yet, leave a calling card with the wrong address.

Stephen huddled at the base of the gutted building for a full minute, trying to overcome an acute case of hesitation. Once he went to work there would be no backing out, no explanation that any cop would buy.

A hundred million dollars.

Esther.

He headed toward the apartment. *Natural. Look natural.* But when his foot hit the lawn, he couldn't resist hunching over and scurrying for the apartment's dark shadows, natural or not. He squatted at the wall and looked back. Coast clear.

Keeping low, Stephen rounded the corner and walked to the metal garage door. As he saw things, the garage was the best way in, because it faced the side street rather than the main thoroughfare, and also because it was hidden from view. The most brilliant break-in artists always found the weak holes, however unexpected. Besides, the windows were high and covered with wrought iron—no easier to deal with than the garage door.

He fell to his knees, unzipped the backpack, and yanked out a roll of heavy, dark gray plastic. Gray, same color as the building's stucco. The plastic unfurled noisily with a whip of his wrists. He shoved his hand into the pack, pulled on a pair of gloves, withdrew a roll of duct tape, and quickly taped the plastic onto the garage door over his head, so that it covered him like a lean-to. Working under the crackling plastic, he was sure half the neighborhood could hear him. It was possible that from the street he looked like a gray ghost, flailing under the plastic sheeting in the moonlight. No, he'd made sure the plastic was thick, hopefully thick enough to block the light. Of course, the plastic was thick enough to prevent him from noticing whether a crowd had gathered to watch the specter.

The roll of tape slipped out of his sweaty fingers. He drew back the plastic and peered toward the street just to make sure. No one.

He fumbled for the roll and completed his disguise. Now he crouched under the plastic lean-to, taped above him and on both sides. The idea was to blend in, but he couldn't shake the suspicion that he was doing more poking out than blending in.

Cutting torch. He'd used one once, in Russia many years ago, a monster consisting of twin bottles on a dolly. The largest part of the setup he'd purchased today was the torch itself, a foot-long silver tube with a ninety-degree cutting tip. Green and red hoses fed into two football-sized canisters in his backpack. One oxygen, one acetylene. He fired up the device in an alley after buying it—seemed simple enough despite the clerk's warning that it wasn't a toy. No, of course not.

Stephen cracked the acetylene valve and lit the cutting tip with a lighter. Yellow light filled his hideout. Safety glasses. He reached into the bag, came out with a set of dark glasses, and tried to fix the band around his head with one hand. No go. Sweat snaked past his left eye. He raised his right hand to nudge the goggles into place.

The plastic to his left sizzled. He jumped back and inadvertently dropped the torch. Flame licked at his legs and he cried out, kicking at the torch. The plastic to his right pulled free, exposing him to the world.

Stephen dived for the pack and twisted the canister's knob. The flame died. He sat on his knees, shaking. He'd burned a hole in the plastic and singed his leg hair.

It took him a minute to calm down, resecure the plastic camouflage, and set up for a second, informed attempt. Goggles on, nerves under control, flame down. With dark goggles on, he found he couldn't see to light the thing, and his nerves were anything but under control. Bringing focus to bear, he finally managed to light the torch, pull his glasses into place, and set up for the burn.

He took a deep breath. This was insane.

The words of his foster father blazed through his mind. He'd spoken them a hundred times during Stephen's adolescence: *Try to see trouble as you would see a brick wall, Stephen. Then try not to run smack into it at every turn. Seriously, son, I worry for your life at times.*

He felt like a fifteen-year-old boy at the moment, running straight for a brick wall.

Then again, there was Chaim: *If you want to have what others do not have, you must be willing to do what others are not willing to do.*

Like run straight at the brick wall.

He cranked the oxygen, adjusted the flame until it was bright blue, and tested the pressure trigger. The miniature jet flared to life. Stephen leaned forward on his knees and committed an irrevocably criminal act.

He cut into the building. That was the *breaking* part of *breaking and entering.*

But he was smart about his breaking. Cutting too close to the plastic would melt the tape. He cut a foot in, slicing right through the thin sheet metal as if it were butter. With any luck, he didn't look like a glowing Christmas bulb from the street. He shielded the light with his body as much as possible.

If Braun was in the garage at the moment, watching red sparks spray over his floor, Stephen would be toast. And if the metal fell inward onto the concrete, it might wake the world. But if he could cut this hole without setting off any alarms, the plastic would hide the hole while he did his real business.

Halfway through the long arc, Stephen concluded that his idea wasn't so brilliant after all. No doubt he *did* look like a glowworm. No doubt the metal *would* fall in.

As it turned out, the sheet did fall inward, despite his attempt to pry it toward him with the torch's cutting tip. But the sound it made wasn't so much a *clang* as a *whap*.

Stephen yanked off his goggles and held his breath. A dome-shaped hole led into the dark garage. No Braun. Only the black limousine parked on the right-hand side.

He wrapped a rag around the hot torch, shoved it into his pack, and pulled the bundle into Rachel's garage behind him. The plastic settled into place, masking the ragged opening.

He let his eyes adjust to the deeper darkness. If they came down now, he would roll under the Cadillac. Or maybe he'd just dive back out the hole. Out the hole, he decided, definitely out the hole.

Now for the car. He had to make it look like some local hoodlum had seen the car and broken in to steal it. Sleight of hand. Get their attention on the garage so the real damage in the basement would go unnoticed.

He pulled out a screwdriver and approached the Cadillac's driver-side door. It was unlocked. And the key was on the front seat. His first real stroke of pure fortune.

He left the car door wide open for his return later, cut across to the garage, and eased through the door. The stairwell was an echo chamber. He tiptoed down into the basement.

A buzz grew louder in his mind. He'd made it into Rachel's basement. His plan was unfolding in brilliant fashion. Had his pulse eased even a beat or two since breaking and entering, it would have surged now, but his heart already was maxed out.

No windows down here. He hit the light, acquired the boiler room, turned the light off, and angled for the door. He found it with his forehead in ten strides. Good to remember that—ten strides.

He opened the door, closed it behind him, flipped on the light. New gas water heater, black potbellied boiler, empty fifty-five-gallon drum. And under the drum . . .

The safe.

Stephen stared, mesmerized. The room was black and gray and

smelled musty from concrete and dust and water. But the bland colors were inviting and the musty smell intoxicating. He'd let his mind walk into this small room a hundred times over the last forty-eight hours, and to actually be here again . . . the feelings of comfort and accomplishment surprised him.

For several long seconds, Stephen stood immobilized with anticipation. His world was spinning in a new direction, and this room was its axis.

He crossed the floor and tugged at the drum. It scraped loudly against the concrete. Could they hear that? He had to get the torch out first. Get the torch out, pull the drum off, slice through the safe's metal lid, extract the treasure, flee.

He grabbed at his backpack and then abandoned it in favor of the drum again. He had to see the safe, just to be absolutely sure that it hadn't been opened by the idiots upstairs. The drum slid with another wake-the-dead scrape. Stephen tilted it on edge and froze.

Exactly as he remembered. Undisturbed beyond his own work. An irresistible sense of urgency swarmed him. He released the drum and yanked the backpack from his shoulder. The drum clanged to the concrete. The fact that he was now making enough noise to wake Braun from a coma occurred to him as a distant abstraction. The man was four stories above him anyway.

Stephen dragged the drum out of the way, pulled out his tools, donned the protective goggles, and lit the cutting torch with the confidence of an experienced journeyman. No problem. *Whoosh* goes the acetylene, *pop* goes the oxygen, and we're in business. He could cut through Fort Knox with a big enough one of these, right?

His unsteady fingers betrayed his frayed nerves.

He dropped to one knee and lowered the cutting tip to the lock. If he could cut out the bolt, hopefully the lid would lift out. The torch eased into the hard steel with a blast of oxygen. Not exactly like cutting through butter, but the metal melted away and fell inside.

He jerked back, struck by a horrifying thought. What if the glowing steel fragments melted the gold on the Stones of David? Too late. Surely Rachel had protected whatever she'd hidden in the safe.

Drawing the full molten circle around the lock took Stephen several minutes, time enough to heighten his fears that he was ruining the safe's contents. He finished the cut, turned the torch off, and pulled off the goggles. A ragged but complete gap ringed the two-inch lock.

He flipped the torch over and tapped the circle. It fell in and landed with a dull *thunk*. Stephen reached for the hole and jerked back from the heat before he made contact with the metal. He hooked the cutting tip into the hole and pulled up, but the lid refused to budge.

"Come on . . ."

Stephen jumped to his feet and jerked back as hard as he could. The lid suddenly released, sending him back two steps and then to his rear end. He stared at the safe, lid dislodged, half covering a hole in the concrete.

He'd done it.

He was afraid to look.

Slowly he rose, hardly aware of the dull pain in his tailbone. He bent over the hole but saw only darkness. He tested the metal for heat, felt it quite cool opposite the cut, and shoved the lid aside. A hole, eighteen inches wide and maybe two feet deep, opened up before his eyes.

And at the bottom of the safe, an object.

His movements seemed too slow. The buzzing settled in his ears. There was something in the safe. There was a shallow metal cookie box down there. And there was a picture taped to the top of the box. Several black burn holes spotted the picture.

Ruth's picture. Only it said "Esther" on it.

Stephen stared into her eyes. Esther was a Stone of David. But was there more? *See, there's a tin can under that picture, and in that tin can is something your mother left for you. A hundred million dollars' worth of something.* He could hardly breathe.

Far above Stephen's head, a voice yelled.

Stephen jerked his head up. They'd found his hole in the garage door!

He plunged his hand into the safe and grabbed the box, but immediately a warning bell clanged in his head. If the Germans were in the garage at this moment, there was a decent chance they would discover him—bad enough. But what would happen if they discovered him *with* the box under his arm or shoved into his pack?

For the first time that night, true-blue panic flooded Stephen's veins. He reacted without conscious thought, like a finely tuned machine masterfully created for a single purpose.

To hide the treasure.

He dropped the box back into the hole, shoved the lid over the top, kicked at it until it clanked into place, and then spun the drum back over the whole mess.

The car. He had to make them think someone had broken in for the car. If they found him down here, they would want to know why a man had broken into the building with a cutting torch and made straight for the boiler room.

It was all he could do to ignore the whispers in his head that demanded he take the box now. There was a fortune in that box, for heaven's sake!

Not a chance. Not that dumb.

He donned the backpack, grabbed the cutting torch, and scanned the floor. To his eye, it looked undisturbed. At this juncture, he was more concerned with the safe's well-being than his own. If they found the safe— end of story. If they found him, he still had a chance.

Stephen turned off the light, slipped out of the room, then poked his head back in and hit the switch one last time just to be sure he'd left no clue. Reason should have him fleeing for safety already, he realized. But he was beyond reason. He slapped off the light and closed the door.

Now what? Instinct vacated him. Footsteps sounded on the concrete over his head. He had to get out of the basement. Anywhere but down here with the safe.

Stephen ran for the stairwell and took the steps two at a time. The hum of the elevator told him they were using it rather than the stairs. Maybe he could wait them out here. He pressed up against the wall behind the door into the garage.

No. He had to get closer to the car—away from the stairs.

He stepped up to the door and cracked it. Two large forms dressed in T-shirts stood by the large hole in the garage door, backs to him. How far could he get in his tennis shoes before they heard him? The front door had been chained—no exit there. Apart from the Cadillac, thirty yards away, the garage offered no cover.

The sound of his heart, pounding like a tom-tom, might give him away before his footsteps did. He took a careful breath, squeezed into the garage, and eased the door closed.

He moved quietly on the edges of his soft-soled shoes, rolling from heel to toe. A shadow in the night, gliding toward the car. He couldn't bring himself to look up, as if doing so might alert them. He had to reach the car. Every step was one closer to freedom.

This was idiotic! He was out in the open! At any moment they would glance back and see the thief strolling across their garage, armed to the teeth with his cutting torch. He almost turned to retreat.

Then again, they hadn't seen him yet. If they'd seen him, they'd be yelling—

"Hey!"

Stephen jerked up. "Hey!" he yelled back.

The two bouncers he'd met earlier stared at him. Maybe if he distracted them with some clever move, like torching one of the car's tires, he could buy himself enough time to sprint between them and dive through his hole to freedom.

The smaller of the two, if "small" could be used in reference to either man, walked toward him. In a moment of lucidity, it struck Stephen that this man was no ordinary thug. No insults, no demands to know what he was doing in their garage, no cautious approach or gun. The man pulled out a cigarette and lit it as he walked. He stopped by the car and leaned on the hood. His friend walked up casually beside him. Neither spoke.

"You're leaning on my car," Stephen said.

The larger man, the blond, spoke quietly into a radio. German.

"Get *off* my car. If you don't get off the car, I'm going to call the police," Stephen said. "I don't know who you think you rented it from, but this limousine belongs to me. My employer. She's my wife." That was stupid. "I only came to take what does not belong to you."

They appeared not to have heard him. A voice crackled on the radio.

"I have to talk to your boss. I know this may look a bit out of the ordinary, but it's imperative that I talk to Roth Braun."

They just stared at him. The man with the radio spoke into it again.

They were probably discussing how to dispose of his body. "Do you recognize me?" Stephen demanded. "I'm the guy who was here this morning, claiming to be a Realtor. Well, I must confess, I'm not a Realtor. But what I am will definitely interest Roth Braun."

The quiet blond stepped forward and indicated the elevator across the room. "Please step into the elevator."

Stephen hesitated. This was unquestionably one of those life-or-death junctures.

The man on the hood tossed his cigarette and stood up. "Move."

Stephen turned and walked toward the elevator.

17

ROTH BRAUN SAT AT RACHEL SPRITZER'S DINNER TABLE DRESSED in a black silk shirt. A heavy gold chain hung around his neck. Stephen stood before the man, unable to hold his eyes. The blond German had blue eyes too, but his were soft, distracted. Braun's were cold, still. Like death.

Stephen's backpack sat on the floor, contents dumped out and thoroughly examined. Piles of kitchenware were stacked neatly on the dinette. The knickknacks so carefully arranged by Rachel Spritzer had been taken from the walls and shelves along with the paintings. They were conducting a methodic search of the apartment.

"What's your name?" Braun asked.

"Parks," Stephen said, and cleared a croak from his voice. "Jerry Parks."

Braun looked at the blond man. "You said his name was Friedman?"

"That's what he told us this morning."

Back to Stephen, eyes bland. "Well?"

"Do you mind if I have a drink?" Stephen asked. "Surely the old woman left some scotch around here."

"You burn a hole in the side of my building and ask me for a drink?" A slight grin curved Braun's wet lips. "Sure, why not? Lars?"

The blond went to the cupboard and returned with a bottle and a glass. He poured Stephen a finger of amber liquid and then stepped back.

"Scotch," Braun said.

Stephen never touched the stuff, and he barely managed to throw it back without gagging. He set the glass on the table, mind scrambling. One look at Braun, and he knew this man wouldn't hesitate to do him bodily harm. But he hadn't betrayed the boiler room, had he? The safe was . . . safe.

He glanced at his knapsack. "I know this looks a bit strange to you." Insane was more like it. Stephen forced a tentative smile. "I mean, it's not every day someone lies about his identity, offers a million dollars for a gutted building, gets thrown out, and then returns at midnight to burn a hole in the garage door, right?"

Braun's right eyebrow arched.

"Well, it makes perfect sense when you know what I know." Stephen walked to his right and stared around at the bare walls. He was about to make a very big gamble. "Trust me, it does."

"Trust doesn't come naturally to me," Braun said.

Stephen had abandoned his theft story during his climb, somewhere around the third floor. Depending on who Braun really was, he would either turn him over to the police or worse.

"For starters, I'm not a Realtor and I'm certainly not a thief," he said. "Do I honestly strike you as being desperate enough to risk my life for a Cadillac? I'm interested in the building, not the car."

"And what about a rundown building interests you?"

"You'll have to ask my employer. Maybe the same thing that interests you."

Braun looked amused. Stephen cleared his throat and pushed ahead. "I mean, you have to admit, burning a hole in a garage door might be strange, but refusing an offer of one million dollars for this heap is just as strange, don't you think?"

The German studied him for a moment. "Claude."

The dark-haired man walked forward. His hand flashed out and struck Stephen on the cheek with enough force to drop an ox. Stephen fell to his seat.

"You broke into my building, Mr. Parks," Braun said. "I believe it would be within the law to shoot you."

Stephen struggled to his feet. "Then I've succeeded, haven't I?" The night's emotion suddenly surged in him. "Stop being so dense." *Too much, Stephen, way too much.*

Braun took the insult without any visible reaction, which for some reason unnerved Stephen more than if he'd whipped out a gun. Stephen felt as if he might fall if he didn't sit. He put a hand on a chair to steady himself. "My employer will pay you two hundred thousand dollars for a three-day lease of the building."

His mind worked furiously. He had to get their attention completely off the basement. If he rented the top floor, he could find a way to the basement unnoticed. "Actually, two hundred thousand for a three-day lease of the top two floors."

Braun smiled softly. "You burned a hole in my garage door to tell me this? Why don't you call my Realtor?"

Stephen hesitated. "Your Realtor doesn't do property management. His work on this deal is done."

"I'm not interested."

"That's . . . that's ridiculous! Two days, then."

"Ridiculous? I would say that offering two hundred thousand for two days is ridiculous."

If Braun took him up on the offer, he might actually pay. The Stones of David were in that cookie tin down in the safe—they had to be. He could take them and be on his way. Actually, he needed only fifteen minutes, but he had to consider what impression he would leave if the offer failed. He had to persuade them there was something on the upper floor that would require a two-day search.

"I think he wants to search this flat," Stephen said. "Something of sentimental value—your guess is as good as mine. Maybe the pictures. Humor him."

"Pictures?"

"The ones in the sunroom. I saw them the last time I was here."

"Out of the question."

"There's another hundred thousand in it for me. I'll give you half of my take. That's two hundred and fifty—"

"No." Braun stood, almost as tall as the man he called Lars, but broader in the shoulders. "Take our guest down to the basement and show him our hospitality," he said, turning.

Stephen stepped back. The basement? They were going to hurt him. "If I'm not back by two, my employer will call the police," he said. He meant to sound matter-of-fact, but his pitch sounded more scared-to-death.

"I doubt it," Braun said, turning back.

"He said you might say that. He also said you were even less likely to want the police involved. You touch me again, and I swear I'll have the police crawling through this building like bees in a hive. My employer assures me his motivations were purely sentimental. Somehow, I doubt yours are."

For several long moments they faced off. A thin smile finally curved Braun's mouth.

"Claude, Lars, please excuse us."

The two men left and descended the stairs.

"Jerry Parks?" The man walked up to him. There was enough power in his arms to snap Stephen's neck with a single twist. He was breathing heavily, deliberately, and Stephen got the impression that he was enjoying himself.

Braun walked around him. Circled him slowly, arms clasped behind his back. He stopped behind Stephen, lingered for a few seconds, then stepped easily to Stephen's left.

The man seemed delighted and doing his best to hide it. *Whoever he was, Roth Braun was a man possessed by evil,* Stephen thought.

"There's nothing to be found here except some old photographs of Jews who deserved to die," he eventually said.

A strange brew of emotions bubbled in Stephen's chest. The picture of the toothless young girl in Rachel Spritzer's sunroom filled his mind.

He looked back at Braun. "You won't know that until you've taken a wrecking ball to these walls," he said, then added, "Up here."

"You're dancing on your own grave." Roth spoke in a low, gravelly voice. "I can smell it on you. Fear. Sorrow. Desperation. Hope. The most powerful forces known to man. You stink of them all."

Stephen barely managed the fear that gripped his mind. Roth's heart was as black as his shirt.

"If you ever set foot on my lawn again, I will track you down in your home and burn you along with it. Tell your employer to search for pictures of dead Jews somewhere else. These are mine."

Braun turned and walked toward the master bedroom. "Claude will see you out."

The tremble that overtook Stephen's limbs should have been triggered by relief. Braun was setting him free. But the shaking was full of dread. Fear, sorrow, desperation, hope. As Braun had said.

Susan. Toothless Susan. She might just as easily have been Ruth's daughter, Esther. For all he knew, Esther had ended up in the same medical lab, and this beast Braun took some kind of demented pleasure in it all.

Stephen scooped up his backpack and hurried to the door. He wanted out nearly as much as he wanted that safe in the basement. He met Claude in the stairwell and the man escorted him to the hole he'd burned in the garage door.

The moment the plastic fell into place behind him, Stephen began to run.

He couldn't go home. What if they followed him? Could he dare risk exposing Chaim to these people?

Stephen ran east, away from the neighborhood, but the moment he was out of Claude's sight, he doubled back through the alley toward Building B, yanked open the same back door he'd used earlier, and climbed the stairs to the fourth floor. He sat down by the window that overlooked Rachel's apartment. The sunroom was right there, across the street, nearly at eye level. He lowered his head between his knees and began to cry.

Understanding didn't seem important. Emotion shouted down reason. Anguish, horror, anger. In a strange way, he felt that he had to right what had been wronged for little Susan, the victim of his mother's oppressors. He had to become what the Jews couldn't become in their cages. For Susan's sake, his mother's sake, Esther's sake, he had to take back what was theirs.

He had to possess that tin box left for him in the safe.

My little Stone of David.

If he'd been eager to get to the treasure before, he was now desperate for it. His urgency made no sense; his desire had become a compulsion. How he'd gone from reasonable Realtor to manic desperado in the space of three days, he had no clue.

He stood, paced, bit his fingernail, and stared at that building across the street.

Stephen had once heard that over half of the homeless suffered from some sort of mental delusion. Many were once-successful people who'd vacated reason for a small spot in one abandoned building that over-looked another.

He finally slumped in the corner and rested his head against the wall. The last thing Stephen remembered thinking was that he was losing his mind.

18

S HE HEARD MOANING AND WHISPERS AND THE SOUND OF pattering feet, but these were common fragments in many of Martha's dreams. But when whispers hissed into her left ear and hands began to jerk her body, she knew this was no dream.

"Martha! Ruth's giving birth; wake up! Hurry, hurry, wake up!"

She bolted up in the darkness, rolled out of bed, and began to run before her feet hit the floor. "Ruth?"

Three steps along, she realized she was running the wrong way. She spun.

Ruth lay in her bed, knees bent, moaning softly. Half a dozen women were huddled around her.

"Water!" Golda stood up and barked the order. "Bring a bucket from the showers!"

Martha slid up close to Rachel and knelt by Ruth's head.

"Give Ruth room," Golda bossed. "Stand back, some of you. Let her breathe, for heaven's sake. Who's getting water?"

"I am," someone said. The door banged behind the voice as someone ran to the showers for water.

"And blankets. Someone else, hurry."

"Martha!" Ruth suddenly buckled with a spasm. "The pain . . . Martha!"

Martha grabbed Ruth's hand. "It's okay, dear. I'm right here. Breathe. Breathe."

Ruth rolled her eyes and looked at Martha. The early morning moon shone through the windows and gently reflected the sweat glistening on her face.

"Martha." She smiled. "Martha."

"Shh, shh. Save your strength." She turned to Golda. "We need more light."

Normally, light was prohibited. Golda hesitated, then said, "Get some candles, Rachel." Rachel ran for three small candles they saved for special occasions. This indeed qualified. Golda shooed the women away from the bunk. "Stand back. You'd think none of you had ever seen a woman give birth before. And keep yourselves quiet, or the guards will hear."

"Let the guards hear," Martha said. "What do they expect, a nice calm Sabbath affair?"

"No, but they may want to take her to the clinic. Believe me, we don't want her to give birth in the clinic."

Martha hadn't considered the possibility that the camp doctor would not share the commandant's feelings about Ruth giving birth. He could easily kill the child and claim it was dead at birth!

"Okay, then we have to keep quiet," she said.

"We are quiet," Rachel objected. "But she's in pain; you can't just muzzle—"

"Shut up, all of you!" Ruth gasped.

They stared at her, silenced. The scene was both terrifying and wonderful at the same moment, Martha thought. She herself would soon be in this position, lying on her back begging God for mercy.

The women went to work like a flock of hens intent on the coop's only chick. Rachel lit the candles. Golda slid blankets under Ruth. Martha rubbed Ruth's back and spoke softly in her ear. They set the bucket of water at the foot of the bed.

Some of the others spoke in hushed tones or watched from a distance. But even the most jaded women could not completely ignore the bustle about Ruth's bunk.

A baby was being born. New life was coming into the world.

Here, perhaps more than any other place on earth, the wonder of it felt monumental. Martha knew that some of the women despised her and Ruth because the commandant had favored them. Or because they intended to bring their babies into this horrible war. Some even murmured that an abortion, however crude, would be better than a delivery.

For three months, Ruth had talked to them about joy and passion, scolding them for their long faces as she rubbed her belly. She'd upset more than one woman along the way, but she'd lightened the hearts of many others. There was not one woman in the barracks who didn't have some stake in this baby.

The women piled up on the nearby bunks and peered at the scene as if it were a theatrical play unfolding before their eyes. An hour later, well after Ruth's water had saturated the blankets, Martha ran through the barracks for dry ones. She saw that only one woman remained in her bunk at the far end of the barracks—Latvina, a twenty-year-old from Russia who'd been beaten the day before for spilling a bucket of mud in the brick factory.

"Is she having the baby?" Latvina asked.

Martha spun back. "Yes!"

"It's . . . alive?"

The simple question frightened her. "I think so. Lie down and get your rest; we'll bring the baby to you later." Then she ran for the blankets, suddenly panicked for not being at Ruth's side. Why hadn't she let someone else get the blankets?

"Blankets!" She held them over her head.

"Let her through!" Golda barked. "Let Martha through!"

The women parted like the Red Sea, and Martha edged through the narrow aisle, brushing half of them with her own pregnant belly. She gave Rachel the blankets and knelt beside the bed.

Tears ran down Ruth's face, and Martha grabbed her elbow in alarm. "Ruth? Ruth, what's happening?"

Ruth opened her eyes and smiled through her tears. "I'm having a baby, Martha." She gripped her belly with both hands and cried it out, an impossible blending of pain and gratitude. "I . . . am having . . . a baby!"

"A baby." Martha put her hand on top of Ruth's and smiled with relief. "Yes, you are having a baby." She faced the others, flooded with joy. "She is having a baby," she cried through a sudden burst of laughter.

Several dozen women stared at her, some smiling wide, others lost in their own thoughts.

Ruth's body began to quiver, and Martha turned back. Her friend's mouth was open in silent agony. And then it wasn't silent at all. She began to scream, long and loud. Loud enough for the whole camp to hear.

The final push lasted only thirty seconds, with Golda and Rachel easing the new life into the world, and Ruth wringing Martha's hands until they were white.

It happened almost unexpectedly. First there was only Ruth, screaming on the bed. And then there was Ruth and a baby, cradled in Rachel's arms, covered in fluid.

The room fell silent under the gaze of a hundred women stretching for a clear view of the birth. Then one question cut through the silence, braved by someone too far away to see. Latvina.

"Is it alive?"

As if in answer, the baby's cry sliced through the room.

Pandemonium swept the barracks, dozens of voices piled on top of each other.

"It's a girl!" Rachel announced, working quickly. She wiped away most of the fluid and handed the child to Martha, who carefully laid her in her mother's waiting arms.

Ruth was crying again, this time with loving eyes on the new life in her arms. She held the baby tenderly and began to shake with sobs.

Martha wept with her, unable to speak. Behind them, the women had quieted to sniffles and soft sobs. The barracks was held captive to the emotion bound up in the miracle of this new life. For a few minutes, no one spoke.

"Do you have a name?" Rachel asked.

Ruth caught her breath, wiped her eyes, and drew a finger down the tiny girl's cheek. "Her name will be Esther. She—"

The name passed through the room on the lips of the women, covering Ruth's next words.

"Hush!" Golda ordered. "Please, have some respect."

The women grew quiet.

"What is it, Ruth?" Golda asked.

"Let every woman here look at my child and see that there is hope. She is a star in the sky, pointing the way." She started to cry again, but stopped herself. "What price can you place on this treasure? Esther is the hope of our people. The seed of Israel."

A young woman pushed her way through the others. Latvina.

"May I hold her?"

Golda held out her hand. "This is no time—"

"No, it's okay," Ruth said.

Latvina stepped forward and gingerly lifted the child. She smiled, kissed little Esther on the forehead, and began to sing a soft lullaby in Russian. This young woman who perhaps wondered if she would ever complete her womanhood by bearing a child held tiny Esther as if she were the mother herself.

Then another woman, Margaret, wanted to hold her, and Ruth again overturned Golda's objection. Margaret held the child delicately. She'd lost her two-year-old daughter at Auschwitz before being shipped here to work. A surreal calm settled on the barracks in the dim glow of first light. The candles flickered silently as the six or seven women closest to Ruth took turns holding the baby. Hushed tones of awe and wonder rippled through the onlookers. Quiet tears of hope and love.

Martha silently questioned the wisdom of exposing the child to so many so soon, but one look at Ruth's beaming face, and she knew it was the right thing. Allowing these women to hold this moving, breathing hope was life-giving. Its own kind of birth.

The baby came to Golda, who hesitated at first but then reluctantly took the child. The woman stared into Esther's tiny, wrinkled face. Her own face slowly knotted, and a tear made its way down her right cheek. "Hope," she whispered, and kissed the baby on the head. "Ruth's hope."

"Our hope," Ruth said.

Golda stepped forward and passed Esther into Martha's arms. "Israel's hope."

19

Los Angeles
July 21, 1973
Saturday Morning

S TEPHEN AWOKE TO A HOT SHAFT OF SUNLIGHT ON HIS RIGHT cheek. A warm, musty-smelling towel licked his cheek. For a moment, nothing else registered except this most peculiar sensation and the ache in his neck.

The dog. It had to be the dog.

He pushed himself to his elbow and stared into the mug of Brandy, who stood over him grinning wide and wagging her tail. Behind the dog stood Melissa, now clad in a halter top and gauchos. Beside her were two men, both dressed in corduroys and army jackets. Hippies.

"Welcome to the world of the living, Mr. Groovy," Melissa said.

The man on her left reminded Stephen of Shaggy from the *Scooby Doo* cartoon, only with longer hair. The other was squatty with a touch of Asian in his face. All three looked at him as if he were a specimen to be studied, but he doubted this motley crew would threaten a flea.

"Stephen," he said. "My name's Stephen."

"Excuse me. Stephen. I thought I told you this building belongs to us."

Stephen looked around. He was lying on what had once apparently been carpet, worn thin and so packed with dirt that it now resembled concrete. Portions of an old wall clung to steel supporting posts, but someone had taken an ax or a chain saw to most of the rest. He could see straight through the building to an empty elevator shaft thirty yards away. A pile of twenty or thirty old tires leaned against one wall. The room smelled like mud.

He stood unsteadily, trying to remember why he hadn't gone home.

Then he remembered. He turned to the window, ignoring the pain in his neck. The morning sunlight bathed Rachel's building across the street. The night's events crowded his mind.

"Hey, dude. Did you hear the lady? We're not offering a lease on this spot, dig?"

He turned back and faced Shaggy. "I was just resting."

"You running?"

"No."

"He's interested in Rachel Spritzer's building," Melissa said.

The gangly man looked out the window. "That so?" He walked up and peered across the street. "Why's that?"

"I'm a Realtor," Stephen said.

"That so? And why would a Realtor sleep in a dump like this, watching a building that's already sold?"

"Why would an intelligent man like yourself take leave of his senses and claim to own a building like this?" Stephen asked.

The man's eyebrow arched. He grinned. "What makes you think I'm intelligent?"

Stephen hesitated. "Your choice of jacket?"

Melissa chuckled.

The gangly man winked. "We got us a Realtor with spunk, dudes." He stuck out his hand. "Name's Sweeney."

Stephen shook the hand. "Nice to know you, Sweeney."

"You've met Melissa, and that's Brian. And for the record, intelligence can be overrated. I should know. I not only attended UCLA, I graduated with honors. Believe it or not, under this skin I'm really an architect, although I haven't actually worked as one in the fake world. Melissa's old man runs a law firm downtown, and Brian's just hanging with us for the day."

He walked back to his friends, crossed his arms, and turned around. "So what are you really doing here?"

Stephen wasn't sure he knew. He'd broken into the apartment last night and come out empty-handed. But he *had* come out. And he knew some things now. He was sure that Braun knew about the Stones of David. Nothing else explained his intense and unreasonable interest in the building. He was also quite sure that Braun *didn't* know about the safe.

And he was sure the safe wasn't empty.

"I'm not sure," he said.

They held stares.

"Why are you here?" Stephen asked. "You throw it all away?"

"No, my man. I'm finding what I couldn't find in the books. Life, love, and the pursuit of happiness. The second bohemian revolution."

"Sounds interesting." Brandy was sniffing through a pile of wood ten feet away. Stephen suddenly felt tightness in his chest, and he wasn't sure why. He looked back out the window.

"It has its downsides," Sweeney said, "but in the end, we're all just children chasing after the rainbow."

"Maybe that's why I'm here, then," Stephen said. "Chasing the rainbow."

"Looks like some idiot tried to break into Rachel's building last night. Cut a hole in the garage. You know anything about that?"

Stephen blinked. "You're kidding. Cut a hole?"

"That's what it looks like. Cutting torch or something."

"How stupid is that?"

"Definitely not the intelligent way to approach life's problems. Some druggies will try anything for a fix."

"Idiots," Stephen said.

"What do you say, kids? Should we let Mr. Groovy hang?"

Melissa winked at Stephen. "Sure. Why not?"

Brian just shrugged.

Sweeney spread his hands. "There you go. You can hang. But don't tell anyone about this place—it's quiet and far enough out of the main drag to stay that way. We on?"

"Sure."

"Gotta split."

Stephen watched them go. Brandy eyed him cockeyed for a few seconds. "Hey, Brandy," he whispered.

The dog trotted over to him and licked his hand eagerly.

Melissa whistled. "Come on, puppy. Let's leave him in peace."

"No—"

The dog galloped for the hippies, stopped at the stairs for one last look, and then disappeared.

Stephen stared at the stairwell until the sound of their footsteps faded. The door slammed far below. Gone. He was alone in the world—even the dog had left him again.

He sighed and faced the window once more. The image of the tin box with Ruth's picture, which he was now thinking of as Esther's picture, loomed in his mind. Like mother, like daughter. The woman he'd been destined for.

He stared at the sunroom across the street, transfixed by the drawn curtains, wondering what Roth Braun was doing in secret over there.

Who are you, Esther?

The perplexing obsession that had taken him out of his game yesterday taunted him again. Now, in retrospect, it felt rather childish. He really had to get back to being normal. The thought of trying to explain why he'd spent the night in an abandoned building made him cringe.

But with each passing second, Rachel Spritzer's apartment continued to draw him, like a wraith beckoning a man to his appointed death; like a siren seducing a fool to his destruction.

Only it wasn't a wraith or a siren; it was a tin box with a picture of Esther. Stephen sat heavily against the wall.

That and the Stones of David, which, incidentally, were worth millions.

He closed his eyes and swallowed. Maybe he had gone over the edge last night, but he couldn't just dismiss his connection to the Stones of David.

His mind drifted. If he was right, no one knew how valuable that safe really was. He was faced with the kind of opportunity that presented itself to one lucky soul maybe once every century. Like stumbling onto a lottery ticket worth ten million dollars. Only this was far more significant.

How far to the Spritzer building? Thirty yards. Then straight down about another thirty yards in the corner of the boiler room.

He should've grabbed the tin box last night. Stephen gritted his teeth. No, they would have found it on him. But he could have at least opened the box and stuffed its contents in his pockets, right? No, too risky.

With any luck, he'd stalled Braun with the bit about the upper floors. How long before the creep made his way into the basement? Then again, even if he did search the basement, there was no guarantee he would find the safe. If Stephen was lucky, he had a couple of days. Maybe three.

Stephen stood slowly, determined to fight off waves of gloom. He looked around, dazed. The thought of going home to the rabbi made him queasy.

A thought struck him. The picture of Ruth was still on his desk at Chaim's house. He really should have brought it with him, really should get it and keep it with him. Besides the note from his mother, it was his only tangible link to his past. And perhaps to his future.

He would go home, get that picture, and then decide on a reasonable course of action.

Stephen turned and headed for the stairs. Maybe he could show the picture to Gerik. The old Jew knew everything about everybody from the war. But could he trust Gerik with more than the antique dealer already knew? Not a chance. He couldn't trust anyone. Even if he could, he didn't want to. This was solely his business. Besides, you trust one person with your once-in-a-lifetime, and it becomes someone else's once-in-a-lifetime.

On the other hand, what if the antique dealer actually knew Ruth? Or Esther? Unlikely, but possible. Stephen stepped up his pace to a jog.

The Vega sat where he'd parked it. If anyone saw the haggard man climbing in, they might guess he was stealing it. Stephen eased the car into traffic. At least he hadn't forgotten how to drive. How to comb his hair, perhaps, and how to sleep in his own bed, but out here on the streets he was incognito. On a mission. To do nothing more than retrieve a photograph from his own desk, true enough, but at least he was making progress again.

The Beatles insisted he let it be, let it be. Stephen ejected the tape from his eight-track and threw it on the floor of the passenger seat. Whispered words of wisdom, please. They had no idea.

His next bit of progress was to get into his bedroom unseen. Facing Chaim's scrutiny at this juncture was as unappealing as chewing quinine tablets.

The plan was simple. He was getting pretty good at sneaking into buildings. If Chaim wasn't home, he would just walk in the front door, clean up a bit, take the picture, and leave—five minutes max. If the rabbi *was* home, then Stephen would climb in through his bedroom window, which he was quite sure he'd left open. The trick would be to get in without the neighbors seeing his butt hanging out the window.

He parked the car a block from the house. Chaim's old Peugeot was in the drive.

Stephen sat in silence for a good minute before stealthily climbing out of the car. He ducked into the backyard and crept as naturally as possible along the wall toward his window. He reconsidered the plan—walking in and explaining himself to the rabbi would be so much simpler. On the other hand, the thought of baring his soul really was unnerving. What was he going to say? *Oh, good morning, Rabbi. Yes, well, I look like a vagabond because I've decided to become one. To kick things off in the right spirit, I torched a hole in the German's garage door last night and then spent the night in the dump across the street.*

He reached the window, glanced around, and pushed it up. He'd forgotten about the screen, but a hard punch put his hand right through it. A few more, and the mesh sat in tatters. Another quick look, a kind of pull-up dive, and Stephen spilled into his room, no worse off than a bruised hip bone, compliments of the windowsill.

He had to move quickly. The unframed photograph sat on his desk next to several phone messages left in Chaim's handwriting. He couldn't read Ruth's piercing eyes, a mysterious blend of resilience and tenderness. She was perhaps the most beautiful woman he'd ever seen.

He shoved the photo into his shirt and immediately withdrew it. His sweat would ruin it. Besides, he was going to take a shower. He tiptoed for the bathroom. No. Running water might alert the rabbi. Maybe he should skip the shower. He really didn't have time anyway.

Stephen stood before the mirror, photograph in hand, and looked at himself. His hair stood on end, and his face was coated with dust. He quickly patted his hair and reached for the faucet, but stopped before twisting the knob. The house had noisy pipes that were known to even groan on occasion.

He really should just walk out into the living room and tell Chaim he was home. He'd gone out with some friends last night, partied until dawn, and come home for a shower. Fun, fun, fun. And the hole in the screen? Well, a bird must have crashed through.

Stephen grunted. This was ridiculous. He had to get out.

Using some water from the tank behind the toilet, he managed to clean his face. He took a stab at fixing his hair and brushed his teeth without using water. Three minutes in the bathroom, and he suddenly felt sure the rabbi would walk in on him at any moment. He wrapped his treasured picture in a towel, stuffed it under his shirt, and climbed back out the window.

"I DON'T know what he's up to," Lars said, "but his name *is* Stephen Friedman, and he *is* a Realtor. He lives up north with an old Jew."

"Another Jew," Roth said.

"Both father and mother dead. Has connections with the DA through a friend. A Jewish girl named Sylvia Potok."

"Married?"

"Stephen, no. The woman, I don't know."

Roth suddenly wanted off the subject. It wasn't an issue that Lars or the others should concern themselves with.

"He should be easy enough to deal with if he becomes a problem," Lars said.

Three more men had arrived from Germany this morning to join the deconstruction project. They were carefully removing the plaster from the walls in the kitchen and would work their way through the entire floor. The task would take them a couple of days, coincidentally the term of the Realtor's suggested lease. If either the journal or the other four Stones were in this house, they would find it.

But Roth had already found what he had come for. Stephen Friedman.

The boy had come home. Exactly as Rachel Spritzer had wanted. The game. The game was on.

Roth had spent the first part of the night in the sunroom, desperate to coax secrets from the pictures. So much pain. But like hope and fear, pain and pleasure yielded the most power when they could be found together.

Afterward he satisfied himself by selecting another Jewish woman, this one from Pasadena. Toruń had come to Los Angeles. And soon, if the powers of the air were smiling on him, he would take Los Angeles back to Toruń.

"We move on the grave site tonight and the museum tomorrow night," he said. "How much will the grave cost us?"

"Half a million U.S. dollars to exhume the body, leave us alone with it for an hour, and return the grave to normal by morning. The guards at the museum, on the other hand, can't be bought."

He had expected this. "We only want to look at the contents. Surely we can find someone there who will accept a million dollars for a few hours alone with some old trinkets. We don't want to see the Stone, just her belongings." He paused. "Offer two million if you have to. If all else fails, we'll go in with gas."

Lars didn't respond.

"I want access to every last item from her estate, every scrap of paper, every photograph, and I want it within the next forty-eight hours. Frankly, I don't care what it costs."

"Understood."

"And the next time Gerhard calls, tell him I'm occupied. I will not speak to him again."

"Of course."

Roth was an unusually patient man, but he'd never been in a posi-tion quite like this, with such high stakes and on foreign soil. He stood and slowly paced.

In under a week, he would finish what his father should have finished thirty years ago.

The fact that his plans were proceeding exactly as he'd envisioned was almost too much to bear. His success made him feel warm. He wanted to look at the pictures again.

20

FROM THE STREET, GERIK'S ANTIQUE SHOP LOOKED LIKE NOTHING other than one more flea-infested hole that might sell used clothes, half of which had been soiled and never properly cleaned. But step past the bell that clanged upon entry, and even an amateur would know this shop was unique.

The store ran long and narrow, crowded by hundreds of antiques that sat and hung and leaned and balanced in every conceivable space. The walls could be plastered with mud or coated in gold and no one would know, because there was no wall to see. Instead, there were Queen Anne chairs and ornate mirrors and huge brass plates and myriad paintings. A large cherry four-poster bed purportedly once owned by Thomas Jefferson himself hung from the ceiling.

Stephen stood at the door and peered into the shadows for a glimpse of Gerik Dlugosz, "Gary" to all who frequented his store. A middle-aged woman with a splotchy red face and a blue silk blouse glanced up at him from some silver vases. She was looking at the towel wrapped under his arm, he just knew it. *What does that man have under his arm, pray tell? It looks valuable. It looks secretive. I wonder if he'll show it to me.*

Stephen hurried up the left aisle, past long glass cases stuffed with coins and copper figurines and sprawling collections of silverware. If it was old and valuable, it belonged here. The floor creaked with each step. You'd think that with all the money Gerik made, he could invest in a new place.

"Stephen?"

Stephen instinctively gripped his wrapped picture and jerked at the sound of Gerik's voice.

The thin man walked toward him with an outstretched hand. A scraggly gray beard hung off his chin. "So good to see you again." He put an inviting hand on Stephen's shoulder and steered him to the side. "And how are you holding up?"

"Fine. Good."

"Excellent. Excellent." The proprietor stopped by a case and ran curious eyes over Stephen. "You've been to Rachel's apartment, then?"

"Yes."

"And?"

"Nothing much. The museum had already been through."

"Yes, of course. I am very sorry, Stephen. I wish I could help you. You've contacted an attorney?"

"No."

"No. I don't blame you. You should follow your own heart until things become clear."

They stood in silence.

"Maybe I could help you in some other way," Gerik said.

"No, nothing." Stephen was feeling hot under the neck. It had been a mistake to come. "I just came by for a visit."

"Is that so?" Gerik smiled softly. "I don't believe you. But I'm willing to pretend. So then, let's visit."

A mistake. Definitely a mistake. The shop had four or five other customers at the moment, and Stephen was sure they were all at least curious about him, if not downright fixated on him. His hair was a mess, his clothes wrinkled and dirty, his face haggard, and he clung to a bundle under his arm as if it were his last worldly possession. He relaxed and leaned on the counter, determined to appear somewhat normal.

"Business good?" he asked.

"Always."

Stephen looked at an old pocket watch in the case. A handwritten tag hanging off it read 3000. Nothing else. Surely that couldn't be the price. Twin horse heads graced either side of the silver piece. He dared a glance at one of the other customers and saw that the man wasn't staring at him after all. But if he knew what Stephen knew, his eyes would be popping out of his skull. *Fess up, boy, where are the other four Stones? You have no right to them. They are for a serious collector with millions to spend.*

"Three thousand," Stephen said. "What does that mean?" Question sounded dumb, but he had to say something before making a retreat.

"It means that someone will give me three thousand dollars for a watch I paid five hundred dollars for," Gerik said.

Stephen looked up, surprised. "Three thousand dollars? It's worth that much?"

"It's worth what someone will pay for it. What's the value of a diamond? Whatever someone is willing to pay for a pretty stone that makes him feel important."

"And someone will want that old watch enough to pay three thousand dollars? Amazing."

"They aren't buying an old watch, my boy. They're buying an idea. The value of an idea is determined by how appealing the idea is to someone. If you want something desperately, you will pay desperately. Isn't that true?"

"Yes. Yes, I suppose so."

"I sell ideas. Actually, if you think about it, everything is really no more than idea. The past is nothing more than a memory, which is one kind of idea. The future is still a hope, another kind of idea. The present is fleeting and becomes a memory before you can put your hands on it. All ideas. I sell ideas."

"That's a bit cynical, isn't it? Am I just an idea?"

"No. But what I think of you is." Gerik grinned. "And, of course, there's the greatest of ideas," he said with a twinkle in his eyes. "Love. You could even say that I sell love. Obsession. A good thing."

Stephen chuckled nervously and looked at the three-thousand-dollar watch. "Sure—love. I would say that's stretching things a bit."

"Is it? Last week, I sold a brass masquerade mask with red feathers to a woman from Hollywood. It is said the mask was worn by a wealthy French nobleman known for his extravagant parties. She'd been seeking that mask for seven years, and I was fortunate enough to track it down for her. I honestly think she might have parted with her husband for it. She loved it as much as she loved anything. Another collector offered me ten thousand dollars for the mask. She paid me twenty-five. What was it worth? Twenty-five."

"Most people associate love with other people," Stephen said.

"And I associate it with any object of desire. People who buy from me are in love with what they purchase. Many are obsessed. I'm not sure some wouldn't risk their lives for a particular obsession. Which isn't all that crazy—some ideas are actually worth dying for." Gerik winked. "I think Rachel was such a person."

Stephen looked at him, taken off guard. He couldn't think of a response.

"Life is hardly worth living without an obsession. God himself is obsessed."

Stephen stared on dumbly. What was this man talking about?

"With his creation. With humans. With the love of humans. You think he created with nonchalance? Let's throw some mud against the sky and see if any of it sticks? Not a chance. We are created for love, for obsession. So we do indeed obsess, though usually not over the right idea." He hesitated and eyed Stephen's shirt again.

"I had a rough night." The words about this obsession business echoed through Stephen's head. "Is that . . . Judaism?"

"What? That we are created to obsess? Sure, why not? What do you have there?"

Stephen shifted nervously. "This? Nothing. Really. Just some stuff I picked up. Some, you know, personal effects that I picked up from my place and wrapped here. In this towel. For safekeeping. You know." *You babbling fool!* He looked around again. "This is a beautiful place, Gerik. A wonderful . . . little place. You should be proud of what you've done here in this . . . place."

"Thank you." The man was eyeing him without a break now. "Would you like to clean up in the back?"

"Me? Why would I want to clean up? I'm fine. I just picked up some things, and I wanted to stop by and see, you know, all this things." *This things?* "I'm fine, really."

"Fine."

"Good."

Stephen felt terribly exposed. As if he were in one of those dream sequences in which he walked out onto a stage, only to realize that he was naked. He was chewing on his fingernail without remembering exactly when he'd lifted his finger to do so.

"Okay, so I'm not completely good," Stephen finally said. The antiques dealer arched an eyebrow. "Do you mind if I have a word with you?"

"Not at all," Gerik said.

Stephen glanced around. "Not here."

Gerik hesitated, then turned and walked deeper into the store, where the furniture hung lower and the shadows were darker. He stopped and turned around.

"This is private?" Stephen asked.

"We might as well be in a vault," the old man assured him.

"Our voices might carry."

"No one can hear us."

"No, but voices can travel."

"I've practically lived in this room for twenty years, and I can assure you—"

"Please, Gerik."

Stephen looked back at the man browsing thirty feet away and saw that they'd attracted his attention.

"I'm sorry, where are my manners? Please, I'm not thinking clearly. Follow me."

They walked past the last of the stacked furniture way in the back and stepped into an office cluttered with books and papers. Gerik closed the door, picked up a pipe, and lit it. A blue cloud billowed over his head. Stephen held the wrapped photograph against his chest now.

"You found something at the apartment," Gerik said.

Stephen didn't respond.

"May I see it?"

"This?"

"You did want to show me, didn't you?"

"I guess so, yes." He began to unwrap the picture, suddenly unsure if he wanted to show it. "I . . . came across this." The picture of Ruth stared up at him, mesmerizing.

He hadn't noticed it before, but her hair was swept back so that it exposed her left ear. That would be her right ear if the photo had reversed her image. A nice ear. A stunning ear actually, one that looked as if it had been painted on with a skilled—

"And?"

Stephen looked up and blinked.

"I . . . I found this photograph and thought maybe you could take a look at it."

Gerik held out his hand. The towel fell to the floor. Stephen gave him the picture. "Her name's Esther."

Gerik puffed on the pipe and studied the image. He turned the picture over. "It says her name is Ruth."

"Right. I mean Ruth."

"Taken before or during the war." He read the note on the back. "Stone of David," he said, and glanced up at Stephen. "Taken before the war. Esther would be your age, if she survived."

"Exactly," Stephen said. "That's exactly my point!"

"It is?"

Was it?

"You found this in her apartment?"

Stephen cleared his throat. "It was with some other pictures of . . . of victims. Maybe I shouldn't have taken it, but I just . . . it was quite moving."

"Of course you should have taken it. She would have wanted you to have it. Most of the world wants to forget the Holocaust, you know."

Gerik knew nothing about the safe; he was speaking from his heart only. He set his pipe down and examined the edges of the photograph with a trained eye.

"Did Rachel tell you anything else? About Ruth."

"No, nothing," Gerik said. "She asked about the Stones, of course. Do you know what one Stone of David is worth?"

"Millions."

"Like I said earlier, it's worth what someone will pay for it, which means twenty million as of this morning."

"Someone offered twenty million to the museum?"

"A group of Jewish moguls who insist the relic belongs in Israel. I'm not sure I disagree. But Christians also lay claim to the Stones, as you may know. The seed of Adam to strike Lucifer on the head, in the line of David. Christ. I know of collectors in Rome who would pay well over one hundred million for the collection. Perhaps even two hundred."

Stephen felt his heart thump a little harder. "Hmm." He was chewing his fingernail again.

Gerik handed the picture back and Stephen took it carefully.

"Thank you."

"I doubt they'll be found in our lifetime," Gerik said.

"No? Why not?"

"Because they were part of some Nazi's war spoils. No one knows which officer took them, but it's rumored that they were pillaged from a wealthy Polish collector's home in Warsaw. If the Nazi survived the war-crimes trials, he won't be eager to show off his loot, I can promise you that."

"Maybe Rachel had all five."

"Unlikely."

Stephen went rigid. Did Gerik know something definitive, or was he just guessing?

"Think so?"

"Why give one Stone and not five?"

"Exactly! That's exactly what—no, that makes sense."

"I really should get back to the store. Half of my inventory could be gone by now." Gerik walked toward the door, and Stephen followed him.

"You're right to treasure the picture, Stephen," the old man said, turning back. "Wherever she is now, little Esther is worth more than all the

Stones of David together. Now, there would be an obsession worth dying for, don't you think?"

Stephen felt his face blush, and he shifted his gaze. "I don't know. It's just a picture."

"No. It's an idea. A memory. Perhaps a hope, but not simply a picture. I'm sorry I can't help you find her."

"That's not—"

"Of course it is. If I'm not mistaken, you're quite taken by her, which is understandable. I'm a Jew. I was there. She deserves your obsession, dead or alive. Your obsession gives her life value." Gerik smiled politely and left.

Stephen didn't remember actually leaving the antique shop. He drifted rather than walked. The old man was right about some things and wrong about some things. Right about Esther deserving someone's obsession, wrong about the Stones not being found.

Unless they weren't in the tin box.

He wasn't willing to dwell on that possibility.

He drove to Rachel's apartment. Still there. Still alone on the lot, towering in the midday sun while the busy beavers scurried through the upper floor, chewing, chewing, chewing. He drove around it once, then twice, doubling back three blocks away so as not to be too obvious. Too many passes of a blue Chevy Vega, and someone might raise an eyebrow. Or a gun.

Shades were pulled. The hole in the garage door had been sealed with boards. They wouldn't leave the bottom floor unguarded this time, not a chance.

That's right. This time. He had no choice but to go again.

They probably had men or dogs or machine guns rigged to go off upon unauthorized entry. This time it would take more than a torch and a lighter to get in.

Fifteen minutes. Fifteen minutes alone in the basement, and he would be finished.

He finally parked the Vega on a side street and crept back up the stairs to his hiding spot on the fourth floor of Building B. He had to think this through. There was a way. There had to be a way.

He leaned against the wall beside the window and slid to his seat. There was always a way. This one hid in the dark corners of his mind and refused to step into the light, but Stephen knew he could eventually coax it out. With enough patience, with enough focus, the right plan would present itself.

He unfolded Ruth's picture and gazed into her eyes. "Speak to me, Esther. Tell me."

21

S YLVIA SAT AT HER DESK STUDYING THE PHOTOGRAPHS IN THE
file. Forty in all, taken from every conceivable angle. They were dupli-
cates from homicide, a precaution that the DA insisted on.

"I want a parallel file compiled now, and I want you to build that file
with every last bit of evidence that you can scrounge from every detective
on this case. Baby-sit them if you have to, but I need that file to be up-
to-the-minute."

It was Sylvia's first high-profile case. No telling how long before they
apprehended the killer, or when it would eventually go to trial, assuming he lived that long. But if and when the time came to prosecute, the
DA would be ready. Sylvia would make sure of it.

Three nights; three victims; same MO.

She stared at the bodies. Blood pooled around each. Enough to
conclude that whoever had killed the women had wanted them to
bleed out.

Why?

The last victim had struggled more than the first two, according to the
preliminary investigative reports. Bruises on the wrists.

The sight sickened her. She'd become an attorney to protect the rights
of victims, not analyze their brutal deaths.

Jewish women across the city were double bolting their doors or moving in with relatives. The fact that the case had gone public was a good
thing, despite the fear it caused. Better fear than death.

And what about you, Sylvia? She glanced at the office door. The rest of the staff had already gone home. How easy would it be for a killer to break into the DA's office?

But really. What were the chances that she would be singled out? Besides, all three had been killed in their homes.

Still, the quiet was disconcerting.

The phone rang shrilly and she jumped. She snatched up the receiver.

"Hello?"

"I'm worried, Sylvia." It was Chaim. "Very worried. This isn't like Stephen. Something's wrong."

She reoriented her attention from the killer to Stephen.

"Sylvia?"

"I'm thinking, Rabbi." She sighed. "He's probably out on a hot date. What did you expect with all of your love talk?"

"A hot date is the farthest thing from his mind. I would have thought at least he'd call."

"Maybe he did and the line was busy. Maybe he has something he wants to surprise you with. Maybe he's at that Santa Monica property."

"He tore out his own window screen, for heaven's sake!"

That silenced her for a moment. "Like I said, he can be irrational at times."

"Impulsive, not irrational," he said.

He had a point.

"Really, Sylvia, I'm worried, and this conversation isn't helping me."

"Look, I'm sure he's fine. He may be reeling from this news about his mother, and God knows he can do some crazy things when he puts his mind to it, but he's not an idiot."

"This from the same woman who insisted that if anyone could find danger, Stephen could?"

"Well, maybe I was wrong."

"And maybe you weren't."

"He's smart, Rabbi. Like you said, he really is. Let him follow his heart."

"Now you sound like Gerik."

"Would you like me to come over? I could bring some Chinese."

"Would you? Yes, I would like that."

—⁓—

STEPHEN HAD reviewed the situation a hundred times. Maybe a thousand, counting all the subconscious assessments. The long of it was that he was in a vicious circle of dilemmas; the short of it was that the dilemmas ended at an impasse. He just couldn't see a way out.

Still he paced in front of the window and rehashed his problem.

His head hurt, and he wasn't sure he was thinking so effectively anymore. Nevertheless, he was thinking: he was thinking that Gerik was much smarter than he'd imagined. His words of wisdom had set Stephen free.

He was thinking he had wasted the day pacing and driving and avoiding the house.

He was thinking he was avoiding the house because he didn't want to answer to Chaim.

He was thinking involving Chaim could be dangerous for the rabbi.

He was thinking Roth Braun knew the Stones were in Rachel's house and would kill for them.

He was thinking he would either go home tonight or get a motel room. He might be a tad whacked-out, but he wasn't loony enough to sleep here again.

He was thinking he really should go to the police.

Then again, he knew a few things too: he knew he couldn't go to the police because he, not Braun, was the one committing crimes here.

He knew the Stones of David were in the basement over there.

He knew the Stones in the basement were his.

He knew there had to be a way into that basement to take the Stones that were his.

Stephen peered out the window. A city worker walked up to Rachel's building. His heart skipped a beat, but then he saw that she was only reading the meter on the back wall. Maybe he could take her place and demand to read the meters in the basement. Were there any meters in the basement? He couldn't remember. Of course, they would see his face and end it right there. He had no reason to doubt their threats.

He resumed his pacing.

He also knew that nothing he knew was really for certain, except the fact that he couldn't go to the police.

There had to be a way into the building.

He did know how *not* to get into the building. Not with a cutting torch.

Not with a truck through the garage door.

Not on a hang glider to the rooftop.

Not via a helicopter pounding above their heads.

Not through the front door.

Not in a huge wooden horse, or in a cake, or in a massive scrumptious pizza delivered for the Wolfmeister.

Not through the front door. Said that already.

Not on a rocket . . .

Stephen stopped. Not through the front door. Why was that again? Why not?

His heart bolted. Could it work? He jumped to the window again. The meter reader was down the street now, climbing into a black Datsun. Why not?

He resumed pacing, frantically now. It was bold. It was daring. It was the kind of thing no one could possibly expect.

It was lunacy!

Which made it perfect.

He glanced at his watch. Almost seven. Almost dark. That was even better.

But where would he get an outfit at this hour? His mind revved into overdrive. It was Saturday night.

He knew something else. He knew that every Saturday night, Marjorie Stillwater played bingo.

—⁓—

THE CHURCH Chaim attended was a small interdenominational affair, a study in cultural diversity. Black, white, Korean, Jewish—you name it—

a hodgepodge of seekers who'd found their answer in Christianity. The old church building had a steeple on the outside and exactly thirty pews on the inside. Two hundred or so managed to squeeze into the sanctuary every Sunday.

They were a friendly lot, a little too friendly for Stephen's tastes. Hugs and kisses and smiles, smiles, smiles. They seemed genuine enough, but to an outsider like Stephen, who didn't want to care about God, much less Christianity, their sincerity came across as a pressing invitation to join them. Fine for the meek and mild, not so fine for the headstrong.

Stephen had attended services on three separate occasions, and each time he'd left feeling both welcomed and repelled by the oddity of it all. The fact that he suspected some truth in Chaim's assertions that Jesus of Nazareth was more than a man only complicated the matter.

He'd always seen religion as a function of some folks' need for meaning and a moral compass. Whatever it was, it was not an object of personal faith. Father had led him and his foster brothers through the seven feasts, spring and fall, with an emphasis on Passover, and Stephen had dutifully followed the course expected of all non-Orthodox Jewish boys until he'd come to the United States.

He'd found in Chaim a different kind of religion altogether. His was born less out of tradition than simple faith. The rabbi still was attracted to much of Judaism, but he also believed the Messiah had already come. He'd put his faith in Jesus of Nazareth, and he talked regularly about falling madly in love with him. Christianity: faith, love, and lots of wet kisses on the cheek from old ladies who wore wigs.

Actually, *one old lady* would be more truthful, and *one* wet kiss even more so. He'd met Marjorie Stillwater within a few minutes of entering the church the first time, and he'd spent at least half the service watching her. Her big, flowing, blond wig had slipped to one side, and no one but him seemed to notice or care.

One of the pastor's teachings suddenly returned to Stephen. He'd heard it on his second—or was it his third?—visit. The pastor recounted a story Jesus had apparently told, about a man who was walking in someone else's field one day, found a treasure, and basically went ballistic.

That was the way the pastor had put it. Ballistic. In the parable, the man hadn't told the landowner about the treasure on his land. No, he was far too focused on the treasure to do any such decent thing. Instead, he'd hidden it again, snuck out and sold all that he owned, approached the owner, and bought the field without telling the man about the treasure. A tad deceptive, to be sure. Surprising that Jesus would tell such a story. All things considered, one might think he was trying to say that man's passion for God needs to look more like desperation than reason.

Stephen nibbled on a fingernail and made a connection. His own ordeal with his mother's building wasn't so different from the man's ordeal with the field, was it? Stephen might not be after the kingdom of God, but then neither was the man in the story. They really weren't so different, he and this man. Neither was a Christian, both were after a treasure, and both were singularly focused on the task.

The thought gave him some courage.

Stephen had been to Marjorie's tiny house six blocks from the Santa Monica Pier only once, but he'd seen enough to know precisely what he had to do now.

He slowed the Vega to a crawl in front of the house. Light glowed through the living-room curtains, but he couldn't tell if she was home. He had to either get her out of the house or verify that she already was. Pay phone.

He found a phone three blocks over, searched the directory for her number, and made the call. The plan was simple enough—if she answered, he would call Marjorie to the church for an emergency. *Come quick, Miss Stillwater! Don't have time to explain, just get down here as fast as you can. It's life or death.* Click. That would send her scrambling.

But ten rings later, she hadn't answered, which meant she was probably at bingo, exactly as he'd suspected. Perfect. Bingo ended . . . when?

Probably not before eight o'clock. That gave him almost an hour. Very perfect.

Stephen drove to within a block of Marjorie's house and approached her front porch on foot. He was getting in the habit of parking his car a block away from all his destinations these days, a noteworthy but not necessarily incriminating fact. He walked straight, without daring to look left or right. Nothing that would make him look suspicious to neighbors. Just nephew Stephen coming for a visit.

The trusting old woman had locked her keys inside and used a spare from under the third flowerpot when Stephen had visited. The flowerless pot sat where he remembered it, full of dirt that had spilled to the wood porch more than a few times, judging by the stains. Stephen bent, withdrew the key, unlocked her door, and returned the key.

And if she was still here?

He stepped in. "Marjorie?"

Her bedroom door stood open to a dark interior. Stephen closed the front door. "Marjorie?"

The tiny house rang of silence. She was gone. Which meant she would be back sooner or later. With his luck, probably sooner. Stephen hurried into the bedroom, found the sliding doors that presumably led into her closet, and slid the door open.

Two dozen dresses hung organized by color—reds and blues and purples. He had absolutely no business being here, staring at Marjorie Stillwater's dresses. They smelled like talcum powder.

Stephen ran his hand lightly down the row of hangers, parting each dress for a better view. This was how women shopped at Sears. For hours, inexhaustibly running their hands down the rows and around the carousels, imagining what, only God could really know. He'd gone shopping once with Sylvia and was exhausted after the first rack.

A business suit of some kind would be best, but Marjorie just wasn't a business-suit kind of person. He wasn't sure he cared for her selection of colors. Lots of purples. Dresses might be too . . . feminine. A pantsuit would be better. At least it had pants and a jacket thing. Question was, did Marjorie own any pantsuits? He continued down

the row and stopped three outfits from the end at a lime-green polyester pantsuit, freshly pressed. Maybe she'd bought the outfit in a
moment of youthful extravagance and not yet worked up the courage
to actually wear it.

He wrestled the suit jacket from its hanger and held it up to his
shoulders. Marjorie wasn't thin, and he wasn't large—should work. The
idea was preposterous, but that was exactly the point. No one would
suspect this woman could possibly be Stephen Friedman. Dressing as a
man in disguise would be nearly impossible without the help of someone who knew what he was doing. Arriving as a woman, on the other
hand . . .

Still, he wasn't thrilled with the prospect of donning Marjorie's lime-
green pantsuit. He walked to her dresser and started rummaging through
the drawers for the rest of his outfit. What else? Nylons—definitely nylons.
Couldn't walk in with hairy ankles. Maybe socks would work. Depended
on the shoes.

He bounded over to the closet again, dropped to his knees, and
scanned her shoes. High heels, mostly. They'd never fit. Working women
did wear men's shoes on occasion, didn't they? Shoes that looked like
men's? He stared down at the tassels on his own black leather shoes and
tried to imagine them with Marjorie's lime-green pants.

He really had no choice but to split the difference—he'd go for the
nylons and wear his own shoes. It wasn't unbelievable that a woman in
his occupation might wear comfortable shoes on the job.

Stephen hauled his bundle into the bathroom and plopped it down
on the floor. Flared lime-green polyester pants, matching suit jacket,
lavender shirt with paisleys, white pantyhose or nylons (he wasn't sure
what this particular variety was called), white gloves, and the crowning
element of this disguise—the reason Marjorie had been a brilliant selection—a blond wig.

He dropped his pants and pulled on one leg of the nylons. Tight,
but they were supposed to be tight. The hair on his legs was still visible,
but the pants would take care of that. He stood and hopped into the second leg.

This particular method of donning nylons proved to be less brilliant than he'd imagined. He had his leg halfway in before it occurred to him that things were going wrong. He started to fall forward, hopped once, tried to free his leg, and succeeded only in catapulting himself headlong toward the wall.

After betraying him so boldly, his masculine prowess came to his aid. He performed a duck/roll/flip and hit the wall with his back instead of his head. The whole house shook with the impact. A shelf full of knick-knacks slipped off the wall and crashed over his head before he could get his arms up to protect himself.

Stephen lay on the floor, one leg still half-caught in the nylons, and took quick stock of the situation. Silence. No one banging on the door, demanding to know who was in there trying to get into a pair of pantyhose.

A broken plate lay in pieces a foot from his head—not unheard of with all the earthquakes that rolled through these parts. All in all, he'd averted any real setback.

Stephen rolled to his back and tugged on the second leg of the nylons. He felt as if he was being strangled from the ankles up. Why women quietly suffered in these contraptions, he couldn't imagine.

The rest of the outfit slid on with ease—lime-green pants, lavender paisley shirt, lime-green jacket. His own shoes. No need for a bra, not with the jacket. See, that was smart too; judging by his battle with the pantyhose, he might very well hang himself trying to don a bra. Stephen slipped his shoes back on and stood in front of a full-length mirror behind the door.

Lime green was clearly not his color, but the lavender blouse actually brought a glow to his face. He tugged at the jacket sleeves and managed to extend them another inch, enough to cover what hair the gloves would miss.

The weakest link in the disguise was clearly the length of the pants, which flared wide and hung short, six inches above his ankles. Three-quarter-length pants—he was sure he'd seen a model or two wearing an outfit something like this. They might even pass for gauchos. His black shoes looked a bit out of fashion—maybe he would leave them in the car.

Now for the second reason Marjorie Stillwater was a brilliant solution—makeup. Even if he had bought a new outfit at Woolworth's, he needed makeup and the dressing room to apply it.

He walked into the bedroom and glanced at the dresser clock. Seven thirty. Plenty of time.

He fished in her shower, found a razor, and shaved his face as clean as the dull blade would allow. Patted his skin dry with a towel. Face powder, lots of face powder. A touch of reddish stuff he found in her third drawer that he thought might be rouge or perhaps blush. He examined himself in the mirror.

More. More makeup.

Five minutes later, he pulled on the blond wig and stood back for a view. His image was actually quite frightening, with all the hair and the red lipstick. He looked like a stick of celery with blond leaves. But apart from the heavy eyebrows, there wasn't a hint of man on him. The heavy eyebrows and the square jaw. And the shoes.

On the other hand, he imagined he might look quite sexy to someone who didn't know. He would kick off his shoes before entering and walk light on his feet. In the dim light, he would easily pass for a city inspector. He cleared his throat and tried out a fitting voice.

"Hello?" Too low. Sounded nothing like a lime-green celery stick.

He tried again, leaning on his falsetto. "Hello. My name is Wanda."

A door slammed. She was home early!

For one eternal second, Stephen froze. The bathroom drawers were open, his clothes were in a pile behind him, the fallen shelf and its broken plate lay scattered to his left. He tore himself from terror's grip and flew about the room, scrambling to hide his tracks. The broken plate went in the laundry hamper; the fallen shelf went under the sink with a little brass elephant that had plunged with it; the lipstick went back in the third drawer down. Or was it the second?

No time. He scooped up his clothes and ran for the bedroom, slapping off the lights as he passed. He evaluated the bedroom window. Short of burning holes in garage doors, diving out windows was one of the best ways to enter and leave other people's buildings unawares.

Unless they were covered with wrought iron.

So Stephen did what any man in his situation would do: he dropped to his hands beside the bed and rolled under the mattress in one smooth motion. Immediately, two problems presented themselves. One, his feet were sticking out of the bottom. This he remedied with an instinctive jerk/curl. His left knee slammed into the box spring, bumping the whole bed a few inches into the air. He reacted to the sharp pain up his leg by dropping his knee. The box spring *thumped* softly back to the frame.

The second problem he saw while the bed was momentarily elevated: he'd dropped his clothes upon rolling under the bed. They sat in a mound just beyond the bed skirt. He snatched them into darkness not a moment too soon.

The lights popped on. "Hello?"

Stephen held his breath in the stillness, but his heart was echoing down here.

Apparently satisfied, Marjorie hummed a few notes and walked into the bathroom. He couldn't see her, which meant she couldn't see him. He should slip out now.

Stephen began to execute his turn, but Marjorie walked back into the bedroom, still humming. At least she hadn't discovered the evidence in the hamper. Or, for that matter, the shelf missing from her wall.

She tossed something on the bed and headed back for the bathroom. Stephen waited a few seconds and resumed his turn toward the foot of the bed, where he would roll/spring/run stealthily from the bedroom.

But Marjorie, who'd graduated from humming to opera, came back before he could get even halfway around. She sat heavily on the edge of the bed, opera voice now gaining volume.

Stephen knew that beds with poor frames and cheap springs bowed under weight, but he had an awful premonition that *bow* would be far too gracious a term to describe—

Marjorie catapulted herself into the air and slammed into the bed with a shrill, high-pitched vibrato. The mattress pounded into his chest, and he grunted. Her virtuoso halted abruptly. After a few moments of silence, she humphed, shifted her weight for comfort, and turned off the light.

Turned off the light? It was what—seven thirty? Who went to bed at seven thirty? This was not good. A celery stick with blond leaves pinned in the darkness under the body of a woman who went to bed before the sun did.

Stephen considered his predicament. Not even Gerik with all his talk of obsession would approve of this.

Did I say go stark-raving mad? he would ask the jury. *No, I said we were created to obsess. Not to don women's clothing and crawl under strangers' beds.*

Stephen waited ten minutes before a soft snore put him at ease. He put both palms flat on the springs and carefully pushed up. Like a bench press. How much? Felt like two hundred if it was an ounce. Dead, heavy, sagging weight that—

Marjorie rolled over, and Stephen slid three inches to his right, masked by the motion. That was it! Move when she moved.

He waited a minute and then pushed up again. She lay like a log, so he pushed harder. She shifted, and he slid another inch or two. It was working. Five pushes later, he was free.

Stephen tucked his own clothes under one arm and crawled from the room on his remaining limbs like a thieving monkey.

The moment he stepped on the porch, he regretted his decision to park the car a block down. There were streetlights out here! He would be strutting his stuff down the sidewalk, exposed for the whole neighborhood to see. On the other hand, it would be an opportunity to practice. He needed a crash course on walking confidently, like a woman. This was nothing less than an unexpected gift.

Stephen headed out to the sidewalk. He tried several gaits and decided the short-step one, with cocked arms and a limp wrist, did the trick as well as any.

A whistle cut through the air. He jumped. A man leaned against the streetlight across the road, staring at him. Her. Stephen hurried for the Vega.

By the time he slid behind the wheel, Stephen was feeling quite buoyant. He was on a roll. His plan was going to work; he had a feeling about this. The dashboard clock read a quarter of eight—a bit late for a city inspector, but time wasn't something he had to play with.

22

HE MADE TWO STOPS ON HIS WAY TO THE APARTMENT AND ARRIVED at eight thirty, later than expected, but he had the angle covered.

Stephen grabbed a black leather doctor's bag, took a deep breath, adjusted his wig in the rearview mirror, and stepped out. From here on out, it was purely professional. Confident. Purposeful. He turned and strutted up the sidewalk, up the steps to the porch, and pushed the doorbell.

He cleared his throat and tested the voice he'd used for the duration of the ride. Sounded thoroughly male, but with a good half hour's practice he managed to capture a decidedly female quality.

He quickly reached into the bag, withdrew a round plastic lemon, and squirted a shot of juice into his mouth. He'd bought the lemon juice with his other supplies, thinking it might help his voice.

Chains rattled. Startled, he tossed the lemon over the rail and did his best to ignore the waves of heat washing over his skull. From now on, he was a her. Remember that. Her, her, her.

The door parted a crack; the one called Claude stood in the gap. "Yes?"

"Alicia Ferguson with the city," Stephen said in his practiced falsetto. "I'm here for the pest inspection."

Claude's eyes swept down his body. Her body. They stopped at her shoes. Stephen glanced down. He'd forgotten to take them off. They looked absurd, sticking out all black and gangly.

"Feet kill me on this job," Stephen said. "I can't afford to care about fashion."

"It's night," Claude said. "I was told nothing about an inspection. We can't accept any visitors at this hour."

"I'm afraid you don't have a choice; 5031CBB isn't something we debate. I'll need to come in and run a few tests, and then I'll be out of your hair."

Five minutes alone in the basement was all he needed.

"We were told nothing of this."

"Doesn't surprise me," Stephen said. "I spend half the day explaining myself to owners, which is one reason I'm so late today." He pulled a sheaf of paperwork from the bag. "Had a guy on Thirty-fourth who made me call the authorities in. Set me back two hours." He flipped open the pages. "Here it is, city ordinance 5031CBB. *The city shall at its election inspect any building suspected for pest contamination within seven days of the sale of such property.* It goes on, but that's the gist of it. Ten, fifteen minutes is all I should need."

Claude eyed the paperwork suspiciously and pulled a walkie-talkie off his hip. He spoke to someone in German. A dog barked in the garage. Two dogs.

Claude lowered his radio. "I'm sorry. You can't enter at this time. Come back on Monday."

"I don't think you're hearing me, sir. I will inspect the building now. If you refuse me, I will be back with the police and several colleagues."

"It's after eight o'clock. Why are you working so late?"

"I thought I told you why. I had another stubborn foreigner who forced me to call in the police. I don't have a choice on this; they give me ten properties, I have to finish ten properties. Any less and it affects my bonus, and I'm not about to let you cost me any money." Claude just stared and Stephen wondered if he'd heard. He spread his hands, careful to appear as delicate as possible. "Fine. I'll be back in a few minutes with the LAPD."

He turned to go. Claude spoke quickly into the radio. A static-filled response came back.

"Where do you need to run your tests?" Claude demanded.

"Five basic pest groups," Stephen said. "I'll have to take a look."

Another quick exchange on the radio.

Claude pushed the door open. "Please be quick. We will be leaving soon."

"Is that so? Don't wait on my account. Go ahead and leave—I'll be happy to lock up."

"Just hurry your tests. Please."

Stephen stepped in and looked around the huge garage. Two large dobermans growled at him from a spot halfway across the room, where they'd been tethered to a metal pole.

To the right, the stairs.

"Okay, why don't you leave me to run a few tests," he said. "Say, fifteen minutes?"

"I would rather watch."

"Well, I would rather be home in bed, off these poor feet. I'll tell you what, Claude, why don't you sit down here and let me do what they pay me—"

"How do you know my name?"

Stephen blinked. "You are Claude, aren't you? Associate to a Mr. Roth Braun, I think the paperwork said."

Claude hesitated. "Yes."

"Well, Claude, if you don't mind, I'd rather do what I do without you breathing over my shoulders. Now, where are there pipes in this rats' nest?"

"Everywhere—"

"Does this thing have a basement?"

"Yes."

"Then I suppose I'll start there. How do I get down?"

Claude motioned at the staircase.

Stephen gripped his bag and walked without further hesitation. Any luck, and Claude would stay put. No further hints necessary.

He reached the door and stepped into the stairwell. No Claude. A tremble coursed through him. He was going to make it! Just stay here, big boy. He ran down to the first landing. Just stay—

The door pushed open; Claude stood above him. Stephen felt his heart drop to his heels. If he'd had a gun, he might have pulled it and winged the guy then.

"Don't you have something better to do?"

Claude descended the stairs without responding.

"Fine," Stephen said, turning back up the stairs. He wasn't about to lead the man anywhere near the safe. He'd have to regroup above.

He mounted the steps and walked up briskly, mind racing. This wasn't the plan. "If you're going to insist on badgering me, I'll come back tomorrow with more help. This is absolutely ridiculous. I have to say, I've never . . ."

Cool air flooded the crown of his head. His hair suddenly felt liberated.

Stephen jerked around and saw that a few loose hairs from the wig had caught on a splintered wooden beam above. It swung by the strands, six inches from his matted hair.

For a moment they stood in silence, struck by the sight of the blond furry ball swinging in space above Stephen's dark head of hair. Their eyes met.

Stephen threw the bag at Claude, hurled himself up the stairs, and slammed past him while he clutched the bag. The German yelled, stumbled, and came after him. Had Stephen elected to wear the heels, he would be dead now. But he had a head start, and he was dressed in pants. He flew across the garage, a streak of green.

The front door was still open. Stephen crashed through it and fled toward his Vega.

Claude stopped on the porch and yelled something in German, but Stephen could hardly make out the words, much less the meaning.

He threw the car into drive before his door was properly closed and squealed for La Brea. It took him two blocks to fully realize what had just happened.

He'd survived. This was good.

He'd failed. This was bad.

23

ROTH BRAUN DESCENDED THE STEPS ONE AT A TIME, FEELING destiny and purpose course through his veins like liquid gold. The man had played his cards as expected.

With this latest charade, the Jew had given away more than he had intended: he was after the basement. From the beginning he had been interested in the basement.

It was why he drew attention to the top floor. It was why he'd broken into the garage and then emerged out of thin air from below. It was why he had tried to descend the stairs then reverse course when Claude insisted on following.

The Jew's heart was in the basement.

He stepped into the garage and stared at the dogs. Their eyes shone yellow in the dim light, but they didn't move. They sensed something in him. They perceived his power, like a high-pitched sound inaudible to the human ear.

He *tsked* and was rewarded with their soft whines.

Roth opened the door to the stairwell and walked down, not bothering to turn on the lights.

In the basement he elected to flip the light switch. His breath sounded hollow and welcoming in the concrete chamber. The Jew had been here—he could feel the emotions in the air. Excitement. Fear. Hope.

The scent of the room reminded him of the basement in his father's house at Toruń. Mildew and dirt. Not so different from a grave.

This was an unexpected little treat, wasn't it? Here in America, so far from home, yet home after all.

Roth Braun felt compelled to sing. He shut the door behind him, stared at the gray room with its sealed steel doors and sang the German war anthem. His voice echoed with vibrato and he pumped his fist and sang louder, the whole song, just as he had as a child.

Gratified, he twisted his head, stretched his neck, and walked toward the door directly opposite him.

It was his third time in the boiler room. The other rooms were made of concrete and had no furnishings, so if anything had been hidden in the basement, it would likely be in the utility room. The previous two visits had been cursory, but this time he would look for evidence of the Jew.

The potbellied stove looked undisturbed. No sign of anything that . . .

Roth caught himself. The drum behind it had been moved. He could sense it as much as see it, although a thin line of dust a centimeter from the base confirmed the same.

Roth stepped forward and pulled the drum aside. A steel lid sat in the floor. It had been scraped clean.

A floor safe.

Rage overcame him. The Jew had beat him to it. In this delicate game, Roth had been outmaneuvered. By a Jew.

Just as his father had been.

The feelings that had warmed him while singing the anthem were gone. He tightened his fists and closed his eyes. Control.

Not all was lost, of course. The Jew hadn't been down here on his last unbelievable visit as a city employee. Claude had assured him of that much. Whatever Stephen had found earlier was still here, or he wouldn't have risked so much to come back for it.

Roth bent down, pulled the steel lid to one side and stared into the hole. He withdrew the tin box and stared at the picture of a woman whom he immediately recognized.

Seeing her here, on this box in America, offended him. The fact that they'd managed to smuggle even a picture of her out was an insult to his father. To him.

Roth demonstrated considerable restraint in not tearing the picture from the lid. Instead he pried the cover off with a controlled hand. Inside, a piece of cloth wrapped around Rachel's treasure.

But was it his father's treasure?

He set the tin box down and carefully unwrapped the cloth.

Heat gathered at the top of his skull and rushed down his head, making him momentarily dizzy.

The journal.

No Stones, but that didn't really surprise him. A relic as valuable as the Stones of David would never present itself so easily.

The journal was treasure enough for now. It was true then. She had smuggled the journal out with the Stones. The journal that could incriminate not only Gerhard, but dozens of others. She'd hid it all these years knowing that if Gerhard were executed for crimes, her hope of finding her son would be dashed.

She was a smart one.

Roth lifted the old leather cover and gazed at the contents. Every woman that Gerhard had ever killed was listed, by date of execution. Details of the ritual and a small smudge of their blood by each name.

With the journal was a letter. The letter told the rest of the story. Rachel's story.

Roth sank to his knees and began to weep with gratitude. There was so much hope here. So much fear and desperation and longing. So much power. His resolve to finish what he'd started when he'd bought this building crashed through him like a waterfall.

Gerhard wanted the journal because it threatened his very life. But Roth knew that the journal would call to Stephen. Roth hadn't come to Los Angeles for the Stones, no. Nor the journal.

Roth had come for Stephen.

He spent an hour with the treasure, soaking in its meaning, plotting his next move. This was good. This was very good. It confirmed everything he'd guessed. He was perhaps the most fortunate man alive at this moment. But fortune had little to do with his success. He was here because he had earned his good fate and been patient in the working for it.

Thirty long years.

He set the journal back into the cookie tin as he'd found it, replaced the box in the safe, pulled the lid over the hole, and slid the drum back into place.

Stephen must find the treasure, and he must find it on his own, in a way that elevated his hope to the highest heavens.

He stood to his feet. A celebration was in order.

Roth walked from the basement, determined to find not one, but two women this night.

24

T HE BIRTH OF LITTLE ESTHER HAD FILLED MARTHA'S BARRACKS with a surreal hope that lingered against all odds. The rumors of mass gassings at Auschwitz came so regularly now that none of the women doubted them any longer. Hungary had been all but emptied of its Jews, they said, and most of them had vanished into the camp at Auschwitz. Only the strongest were occasionally spared and sometimes sent north, to Stutthof. Martha could hardly bear to think of what had happened to her mother and sister. Part of her insisted that she couldn't afford to think about them—she had to think about one thing only: giving birth to the child within her. Any day now, maybe even tonight. A few days at the most.

Her heart hammered every time she thought about going into labor. Imagine, not one baby in the barracks, but two! Esther and David. Or if she had a baby girl, Esther and Esther. Two stars of hope.

Ruth and Martha hurried from the factory and walked quickly to the barracks, where Rachel had been given charge of the baby today. The commandant had allowed Ruth to stay with Esther for ten days before issuing the order that she return to work.

"She's going to be famished," Ruth said breathlessly. "It's been eight hours since I fed her. He's a beast!"

"Of course he is," Martha said. "But he's been good to you. And Esther is alive." She looked up at a group of women passing the other way. "Half the women in this camp grumble about how you're favored."

"Not in our barracks."

"No, not those who know you, but they all see you walking up to his house every day with Esther. It drives them mad. They think he likes you."

"Then they should try to spend some time with him! He insists I go; what am I supposed to do, slap him in the face? I have Esther to think about now. He hasn't touched me. Do they know that?"

"I've told them. Keep your voice down."

Streams of women crisscrossed the camp, making their way back to their barracks or the bathrooms before the roll call. Here in Toruń, roughly five thousand women, over half of them Jews, clung to the hope that they might be spared, yet they all knew a single order could change everything. The Russians were advancing from the east. If they could just hang on a little longer, surely the nightmare would end. Little Esther had been spared and allowed a new life outside her mother's womb—perhaps they, too, would be spared.

Martha imagined an army advancing over the fields to the east, coming to liberate them. What a day that would be. She and Ruth holding their tiny babies bundled in blankets, being whisked away to begin a new life. They rounded the showers and angled for the barracks where Rachel waited with baby Esther. Fifty yards. Ruth quickened her pace.

"This waiting is making me crazy," Martha said.

Ruth faced Martha, eyes bright. "Oh, Martha, you will be so excited. It's a miracle. You can feel the new life coming from you, and nothing else in the world matters."

Martha laughed. "Except for the pain."

"No, the pain tries to distract you, but the baby is stronger than the pain, Martha! A baby! You're giving birth to a baby, and the whole world stops for that." Ruth touched Martha's belly. "Can't you feel it?"

"Yes. Honestly, I'm terrified."

Ruth took her hand and squeezed it. "I was too. I was so scared that I couldn't breathe right. You were telling me to breathe, and while part of me was thrilled with what was happening, the other part was terrified." She smiled wide, as if her confession had been a secret.

But Martha knew her friend too well. Ruth, the courageous one who spoke the truth with chin held high, needed comfort and assurance as much as any woman in the camp. She was like a little girl in some ways—wise and confident, as long as Martha was by her side to hold her hand.

Ruth began to skip.

"Stop it, Ruth. Do you want to rub salt in their wounds?"

"They could use a touch of salt now and then. The red scarf hasn't touched one of their beds since Esther was born. Don't they see that? They should be grateful for my skipping and all my trips up the hill. Little Esther and I stand between them and that monster. He does like her, you know. It horrifies me to think about it, but that pig is actually fond of my baby."

She hurried the last twenty meters, threw open the door, and ran in with Martha on her heels. "Rachel?"

Ruth pulled up three paces in, and Martha nearly ran her over. Down the aisle between the bunks Rachel faced them, holding the baby in her arms, tears streaming down her cheeks.

"What's wrong?" Ruth ran for her baby. "What did they do?" she demanded.

Something had happened to Esther? Martha felt her heart bolt. She ran after Ruth, who carefully took the bundle from Rachel.

"Is she okay? Please, tell me she's okay."

Rachel's lips were quivering. She still said nothing. Ruth peeled the blanket from her baby's face. The child cried. So she was alive!

"Shh, shh. It's okay now. Mommy's here." Ruth cradled the child and rocked her gently. "What is it, Rachel? She's hungry?"

Rachel didn't respond. Why should she? It was a rhetorical question. Several others entered the barracks behind them.

Ruth pulled her shirt up and let the baby suckle. The child quieted and began to eat noisily. "You see, Rachel? She's fine. What is it?"

Someone gasped behind them. "The scarf!"

Martha looked past Rachel and saw the scarf immediately. The bright red material was draped on a lower bed, six or seven bunks down the aisle.

The first thing Martha thought was that Ruth had been wrong about the commandant.

The second thing was the realization that the red cloth lay terribly close to her own bed.

On her bed.

She blinked, unable to process the meaning. This silk scarf angled across the corner of her bed. This splash of red against the drab gray blanket. There was a mistake, of course. That bunk was her bunk. She was about to give birth to her baby. The commandant had promised it.

The barracks filled with more women. Questions—What is it? What's going on? Why is everyone standing here?—then silence.

Martha stared, still stunned.

Ruth's baby suckled quietly beside her.

"Ruth?" Martha faced her, suddenly very worried. "What . . . ?"

"I'm sorry," Rachel said, weeping. "The guard, he came in and asked me which was Martha's bed. I didn't know; I swear, I didn't know. He put the scarf there and then left." She fell to her knees and gripped Martha's dress. "I'm so sorry, Martha. I'm so sorry."

"Stop it!" Ruth snapped. "Stop your blubbering, Rachel."

Golda pushed through the gathered women. "What's going on?" Then she saw the red scarf and her lips formed a grim line.

All of this ran through Martha's mind: Rachel's weeping, Ruth's anger, Golda's silence. They all meant the same thing.

She would be hanged tonight, before her child was born.

Her legs started to give way, and she reached out to break her fall, but Rachel and Golda both held her up. She wanted to scream, but she was suddenly hyperventilating. The others were silent, and she hated them for it. A breathy moan escaped her lips.

They would come for her at six thirty, in ten minutes. But the baby! No, he couldn't do this! It was inhuman! Why had he placed this cloth on her bed? Didn't he love little David as he loved little Esther?

"Ruth." She touched her belly. "Ruth!" Her voice sounded distant, inhuman. She could see her friend still staring at the scarf, baby cradled in her arms.

"Hold Esther, Rachel," she heard Ruth say.

"Where are you going?"

"To the commandant."

"No!" Golda objected. "You can't just go—"

"He's going to kill her!"

"And if you go, he may kill you as well."

"It's my life!" Ruth yelled.

"Stop it!" Martha cried. Her limbs trembled, but she couldn't bear these women screaming at each other. She sat heavily on the nearest bunk. "Please, don't argue. Ruth, you know you can't go up there. You have to think of Esther."

Ruth stared at her, face flushed. She looked at the scarf then back at Martha. Slowly, she relaxed.

"I know this is a horrible thing," Golda said, "but he's killed dozens of women this way already."

"She's pregnant!" Ruth snapped. "He gave his word!"

"We have to accept it."

Martha knew she was right, but the truth did nothing to temper a sudden urge to claw the woman's eyes from her face. How many pregnant women had the commandant hanged from his gallows? How many within a day of their child's birth?

"No," Ruth said. "We don't have to accept it."

She walked up the aisle, took the scarf in her hands. "He told me once that the woman presented to him wearing the red scarf was the Jews' sacrificial lamb. She would die for the whole camp, to appease his wrath."

What she did next could not have been anticipated by any of them. She walked to her own bed, lay the red cloth across the corner, and smoothed it.

"Now the scarf is on my bed. I will go."

What was she saying? A sliver of hope sliced through Martha's heart. Ruth would make an argument for Martha's life? What if the commandant would listen? There was some hope in that, wasn't there?

"What do you mean, you will go?" Golda asked.

Ruth looked at Martha and then at her own baby. Tears misted her eyes, and she raised her hand to her lips.

Then Martha understood. "No! No, Ruth!"

Her friend wasn't listening. Ruth returned to Rachel, took her child lovingly. Kissed the baby on her forehead and then on her lips, tears dripping on the infant's cheek. She sniffed softly and then swallowed back her tears.

"I love you, dear Esther. I love you so much."

Martha was horrified by this display. She staggered to her feet. "Ruth—"

Ruth put a finger on her lips. "Shh. Listen to me, Martha."

"What are you doing? You can't take the scarf!"

"Listen to me! This is the only—"

"No!" Martha sobbed. She couldn't hear this. The panic she'd felt only a moment ago felt small next to the notion that Ruth would follow through with her plan.

"No, you can't—"

"Listen to me!" Ruth shouted. "They'll be coming soon."

Martha blinked.

"I'm sorry, I don't mean to shout." Tears slipped from Ruth's eyes again. "This is the only way to save both of our babies, Martha."

"He will never allow it."

"Your child will die with you," Ruth cried. "How can we allow that? Your child has as much right to live as I do. Should both of you die so that I can live?"

"Yes! I was chosen, not you."

"And now I choose."

"You don't even know if he will accept your choice."

"He will. I know him. He will, and he will let you live and have your baby." She kissed her infant again, several times, all about the face. "Promise me, Martha. Raise her as your own."

She handed the child to Martha, who took her, fingers numb. "Ruth . . ."

The women stared at the scene, dumbstruck. Not even Golda found the courage to object. Martha didn't know what to say. She didn't want this to be happening any more than she wanted to die herself. She should stop Ruth. Push the baby back into her arms and run up the hill to demand that Braun hang her.

She could do none of these.

For an endless minute, Ruth and Martha stared into each other's eyes. Then Ruth's show of bravery slowly began to fold. Her lips began to curve downward and quiver. Her breathing came quicker and sounded forced. She was trying to be courageous, but she couldn't stand against this terrible onslaught of fear and sorrow on her own.

This was Ruth, the young woman with more courage than the whole camp put together. But this was Ruth, the girl who'd edged her way through the train to find Martha's comfort in a time of loneliness.

Martha gave the baby to Rachel and wrapped her arms around Ruth's shoulders. The younger woman hugged Martha's pregnant belly, buried her face in her neck, and began to sob.

The pain in Martha's heart threatened to tear a hole through her chest. She wanted to die. She had to say something, anything that would stop Ruth from what she was going to do.

Golda's cheeks glistened with tears, and she made no attempt to wipe them away.

"Please, Ruth. Please . . ."

The door banged open. "Get back! What is going on?"

Martha began to panic. "Please, Ruth."

The women parted, and there stood the guard, the same young blond who'd come on several occasions to lead away women. She was accustomed to some emotion, but this scene made her hesitate.

"Whose bed is that?" she demanded, pointing her stick at the red scarf.

"If you have a boy, tell him to marry my Esther," Ruth whispered. She faced the guard and wiped her tears. "That's my bed."

She retrieved the scarf and glided down the hall, past Martha's clinging hands, passed her baby with one last kiss and one last sob, and past the guard, out the door.

Martha slumped to the bed, curled into a ball, and began to cry uncontrollably.

25

THINK, THINK, THINK. HE'D PRACTICALLY THOUGHT HIMSELF TO death these last five days.

Stephen had returned to the hiding place in Building B two nights before, stripped off the green pantsuit, donned his old dirty slacks, paced, and made an important decision.

He would not go home tonight.

He would rent a motel room.

And so he had. An old, flea-infested room seven blocks down on La Brea. Sunday, he'd made another important decision.

He would not rent a motel room that night.

He would sleep here overlooking Rachel's apartment on the off chance that the German entourage would vacate the building for a spell. Monday, he would go home. After he found a way into that basement. But Monday had come, and he had neither found a way into the basement nor gone home.

He'd lost his mind to this thing, and he no longer cared.

Braun had made a threat, and Stephen had dared to defy him. For the first time, he feared for Chaim's life. He couldn't go home. As long as he stayed out of reach, Braun couldn't hurt him or endanger Chaim.

Besides, Stephen didn't want to go home.

On the other hand, he had to at least let Chaim know that all was well, even if it wasn't. He'd made a phone call from a booth on La Brea. The conversation lasted less than a minute.

Where are you? Are you okay? What are you doing?

I'm in a . . . motel. I'm okay. I'm taking a few days to think things
through. Are you okay?

Of course I'm okay. When will you be home?

Soon. Don't worry. Please don't worry.

But he knew from Chaim's tone that the rabbi was worried, so he
added the warning. *Be careful, Rabbi. Promise you'll be careful.*

Stephen looked around the ten-by-ten living space he'd pulled together
while thinking. He'd scavenged wood and some tires from the piles
around the room and built up a semblance of walls to cordon off his area.
Two walls, each stabilized by nothing more than its own weight, leaned
against trusses and angled from the floor to the building's outer wall. A
few tires added stability. It was a lean-to of sorts.

Some might think he'd flipped his lid. Sylvia, for example. The rabbi
even. But it wasn't madness that drove him. He was no more mad than
the rest of God's children, chasing after their rainbows.

*See, Stephen, even that sounded a bit mad. Your reasons for not being
mad are mad.*

In a bohemian kind of way, what he was doing made perfect sense. He
was pursuing an idea that really mattered. The safe was his pot at the end
of the rainbow. Until some dramatic breakthrough would put his hands
on that safe, he would carefully block out any part of the world that took
his attention off the goal. Did that sound like madness? Of course not.
The greatest achievements in history were accomplished by men willing
to do what others were not willing to do.

The antique dealer, Gerik, had said that man was created to obsess.
The rabbi had said that the only thing worse than not getting what you
desperately want is not desperately wanting anything at all. Well then?

Stephen straightened from his work over the left wall. What was that
diatribe the rabbi had once delivered at the breakfast table?

*You can have nothing to die for until you first have something to live for.
The Holocaust did that for Jews. It revealed the incomparable value of another
idea. Life. Love! Love, Stephen. We should be daily ravaged by love. The Nazis
hated us. If from this we do not learn to love, we dishonor the lives of six million Jews.*

"That's right, Rabbi," he muttered. "So then I will desperately want and I will love. This is my labor of love."

He nudged a two-by-four into place—an extra brace required because the wall swayed every time he touched it—and stood back.

"Lovely," he mumbled.

Another preposterous idea had been brewing over the last twenty-four hours, and with each passing hour its preposterousness faded. The notion that Joel Sparks could be his salvation seemed counterintuitive, given the man's less-than-honorable character. But Stephen was in pursuit of love, not necessarily reason.

Stephen reached into his backpack, carefully pulled out the eight-by-ten photograph of Ruth, and looked into her eyes. In his mind's eye, this woman was Esther. As Gerik had said, the daughter of this woman would today be about the age of her mother in the picture. She would look like her mother, perhaps.

This was Esther. This was the woman he was meant to find. She was an orphan, a true Stone of David, and her picture was in the safe, on top of the tin box that Stephen would soon have.

He had stared at Esther's picture for hours in these last three days.

He was meant for her.

Honestly, he thought he might be falling in love with the woman in this picture. Her daughter, Esther. Chaim would call it infatuation, but Stephen knew the difference.

"You have ruined me," he whispered lovingly, and he kissed the picture lightly.

He stood and looked around. The two haphazardly erected walls bordered the window that overlooked Rachel's apartment. A piece of plywood layered with some insulation made a bed in the left corner. Three cans of beans and two cans of corn stood in a neat pile in the right corner. A crate with a candle, some matches, a spoon, a can opener, and a comb he hadn't yet used sat dead center.

He'd slept on his bed here last night, if *slept* could be broadly defined. *Moaned* and *rolled about* and *stared* at the sagging ceiling might be more accurate word choices. He tried to walk the beach yesterday, figuring a bit of sun and a change of scenery might do him some good. The walk lasted fifteen minutes. He'd fled the crowds in a near panic, desperate to be alone to think things through, as if he hadn't done enough of that.

Think, think, think. The thinking was driving him loopy.

On the bright side, the short exposure to the real world had stimulated his appetite. The idea of going to a restaurant unnerved him, so he made one stop at a grocery store, gathered a handful of necessities, endured the checkout line, and retreated to safety here.

Stephen approached the wall to the left of the window, dropped to his knees, and carefully taped the corners of the photograph to the drywall with duct tape. He stepped back, sat cross-legged, rested his elbows on his knees, and stared at the picture.

Was there another woman in the world as beautiful? Was it even physically possible for the world to produce not one, but two women as stunning as the woman who gazed at him from this black-and-white photograph? The sweep of her hair; the subtle curve of her jaw; soft, steady eyes. He could swear the photo had been touched up with a skilled brush. No nose could be that perfect, no lips so symmetrical. But he knew that no artist had retouched this photo. This was Ruth, who was Esther, who was perfect.

Stephen closed his eyes and swallowed. Time was running out. He had to make contact with Joel Sparks. Illegal, insane, impossible.

But he had to do this. For Ruth's sake. For his mother's sake.

He opened his eyes and stared at the picture. For Esther's sake.

Stephen grunted and rose quickly to his feet.

GREAT WESTERN Bank was bustling with a late-morning crowd when Stephen walked through its doors just before noon. To say he felt conspicuous sporting two days' growth of stubble and a rumpled shirt was only half-true. The crowd, not his appearance, was to blame for his anxiety.

The white Converse tennis shoes he'd bought to replace his impractical wing tips stood out like fluorescent bulbs. Maybe he should have dirtied them a bit. Still, he was doing nothing illegal. He really had no reason to be nervous.

Wait. What if Sweeney and gang returned to the fourth floor and stole his picture of Ruth? Some vagabond could ransack his shrine and disappear without a trace. He should have brought the picture with him. Too late.

Stephen made a halfhearted attempt to smooth his shirt and walked straight for the closest banker's desk. A middle-aged woman with a ball of blond hair, meticulously shaped by curlers, looked up. A gold nameplate on her desk read "Nancy Smith." Her eyes scanned him from head to toe.

"May I help you?" she asked, her politeness all but forced.

Stephen slid into a chair, glanced around, and leaned forward. "I would like to make a withdrawal," he said.

"You need to go to one of the tellers for a withdrawal—"

"No, I need to withdraw a lot of money."

Her face slowly turned white. "I . . . we don't keep money in our desks."

"Of course not. But you have it in the vault. I need a hundred thousand. Surely you keep that much on hand."

Her eyes shifted with a look of panic. What was her problem? He knew that banks didn't like to shell out large sums of cash without prior arrangements, but her reaction was uncalled for. It wasn't like he was holding her up.

"I'm . . ." She swallowed. "Please . . ."

Understanding came in a flash. "You think I'm trying to rob you?"

Her look was answer enough.

He found it within him to laugh kindly. "Don't be ridiculous," he said. "I have money in this bank, and I need to withdraw some of it."

"You do?"

"Yes." Her eyes dropped to his shirt, and he pulled the tails to straighten the wrinkles. "I'm sorry, I . . . I got mugged in the alley, and the . . . people got my shirt dirty." He felt his face flush, and he grinned. "Druggies. They'll do anything for a fix these days."

She just looked at him.

"I need a hundred thousand dollars," he said.

"Wait here, please."

She stood and walked toward the manager's office. Stephen hunched down and watched her speak to a balding bank manager. Both looked out at him, and he looked away until he sensed someone approach.

"My name is Bruce Spencer; I'm the bank manager. Can I help you?"

"Do you have cash in your vault?"

The manager grinned. "We're a bank—we always have money."

"Then you can help me. I have an account with your bank—just over eight hundred thousand. I need a hundred thousand in twenties. Can you do that?"

The man's left eye twitched. "That's a lot of money."

True enough. Any normal investor would have put it to work in more aggressive ways than what a bank could offer. But Stephen's rearing on foreign soil had given him this incongruous conservative streak when it came to saving money.

"Which is why I have it in your vault rather than stuffed under my mattress." He pulled out the check he'd prepared and handed it to the man. "If you don't mind, Mr. Spencer, I'm in a bit of a hurry."

Spencer glanced at the check. "Are you in some kind of trouble?"

"Do I look like I'm in some kind of trouble?"

"Frankly, yes."

"There you go, then. I'm in a spot of trouble, and I need some money. Isn't that what money's for?"

"That's a lot of money," Spencer repeated.

"I think we've already established that." He had no reason to treat the manager with condescension, but he was growing impatient.

The manager handed the check to Nancy. "Please verify the funds and get Mr. Friedman his money." Then to Stephen, "This will take a few minutes, I'm sure you understand. Most large withdrawals are arranged in advance."

"I'll wait. No problem. But please don't take all day. I am in a hurry."

Stephen walked out twenty minutes later, sweat leaking down his back, big bag of cash under his right arm. So far so good.

26

JOEL SPARKS WAS A DEVELOPER IN PASADENA KNOWN FOR HIS low-income housing developments. But a closely held rumor suggested that Sparks had more than casual Mafia ties. The possibility had nearly paralyzed Dan Stiller two years earlier, when Stephen had proposed Joel bail them out of their deal gone bad. After all, the Mafia bit was only a rumor, Stephen had insisted. But judging by the way the man carried himself, Stephen thought the rumor might have some credence.

He drove north, nibbling on a nail, knowing that he was about to plunge into very deep waters.

Then again, there was no guarantee the man was even available on this particular Monday afternoon.

Sparks's large white mansion stood against a hill in north Pasadena, surrounded by palms and a sweeping red-brick driveway. Stephen leaned out his window and punched the call button at the main gate.

"Yes?"

"Uh . . . yes, Stephen Friedman here to see Joel Sparks."

The intercom remained silent. He pushed the button again.

"Hello?"

"You have an appointment?"

Not good.

"Uh . . . well, yes. Better, I have business he won't be able to refuse."

The wait was longer this time, but just as Stephen was again reaching for the call button, the gates began to swing inward.

Okay, baby. Calm and collected. He drove up to the house, parked the

Vega, and walked up the steps to the front door. The cash would stay in his trunk for now. One step at a time.

A bodyguard who passed himself off as a butler led Stephen over marble floors to a spacious office. Details registered in his mind but didn't stay—the paintings on the walls, the crystal chandelier, the floor-to-ceiling cases of leather-bound books. Then his attention was consumed by the large man at the sliding glass doors, back to Stephen, phone plastered to his ear.

"Of course, don't I always?"

The butler-bodyguard closed a door behind Stephen, and Joel Sparks turned. His deep-set eyes tried to hide behind pronounced cheekbones. He smiled, but to Stephen it looked more like a grimace. He had nasty written all over him. Amazing he wasn't locked up yet.

Or was Stephen just imagining things?

"Good. I'll call as soon as I hear." He set down the phone. "Well, well. If it isn't the man who sold me that overpriced piece of junk on Wilson." He stepped forward and offered his hand. "How's business these days?"

"Good." Stephen took the hand. "Yeah, good."

"Really? You're driving a Vega and you're dressed like a schmuck. Can't be that good. Have a seat."

Stephen sat on a black leather couch. "Yeah, I know. I didn't have time to change."

"What can I do for you?"

Right to business. Just like any deal. Stephen crossed his legs, then set his foot back down.

"I need a favor."

"You owe me a favor. What makes you think I'm in the mood to give you even more credit?"

"This one will make up for both."

Sparks leaned against his desk. "I'm listening."

"Let's say you left something important in a building, but when you went back to get it, the owners wouldn't let you in."

"And?"

"How would you go about getting it?"

Sparks's plastic smile softened. "I'm not sure I understand. I deal in real estate, not the law. I think you have the wrong party. Come back with a building to sell me at half price, and we'll do business." He reached for a call button on his desk.

"It's worth a lot to me," Stephen said, "this thing that I left behind. Family heirloom that dates back to the war."

Sparks withdrew his hand and studied Stephen for a few long seconds. "Just out of curiosity, how much is it worth to you . . . this heirloom? I may know a good lawyer."

"I'm not sure. A lot of cash."

"How much cash?"

"You tell me."

"Tell you what? You're the one with the heirloom, not me. Lawyers don't come cheap these days."

"Twenty?"

"Twenty thousand."

"Twenty thousand cash."

"Tell you what, I'll mention this to a lawyer I know, and maybe he'll give you a call."

"I need to retrieve the heirloom tonight."

Sparks sighed. "Then I'm afraid I can't help you. Try the yellow pages."

"How about fifty?"

"Exactly what kind of heirloom are we talking about here? You walk into my office looking like you fell off a cliff, offer me fifty thousand dollars in cash to break into a building, and I have to wonder if you're on the wrong side of the law. I don't mess with the law."

"Of course not. I'm just trying to get something that belongs to me without having to go through a lengthy process. I may not look like it now, but I've done quite well for myself these last few years. Some things are more important than money. I'll pay you fifty thousand in cash to distract the owners long enough for me to take what's mine. Totally copacetic. No harm, no foul."

"Paying for something like this could be illegal."

"Why? I'm not stealing anything."

"You have fifty thousand cash?"

"In the car."

Sparks took a deep breath. "Well, God knows I could always use fifty thousand cash, but this is just not something I do."

"It so happens that these guys have guns. They're in an abandoned apartment complex—five of them now, I think. German Mafia types. Considering the circumstances, how about seventy-five thousand?"

"I'm not sure you realize what you're asking."

"I pay you, and I'm the one incriminated in any crime, right? But this isn't even a crime per se. I've got seventy-five thousand dollars in a bag that says you know someone who can help me out."

"What's the heirloom?"

"Some photographs."

Sparks stood and walked toward the sliding glass door that led out to a pool. He stood, hands on hips, doing what mafioso types do best, making a judgment call. Stephen could practically hear his thoughts. *Do I trust this punk with my true identity? Do I let him into the inner circle of the unlawful? Do I tell him that I look like a bat because I am one, feeding at night on the weak and the lonely, like this poor sap?*

Then Stephen thought to himself *I'm already in your circle, mafioso. I've lost my mind and I'm chasing after a rainbow, and I've gone too far to turn back now. Take your best shot, baby.*

"If you double back on me, I will destroy you." Sparks turned around, lips drawn tight. His transformation from aboveboard businessman to underworld criminal was complete. "Do you understand me?"

"Absolutely."

"Something goes wrong—someone gets hurt and you even sneeze— I guarantee, you'll spend your life regretting it."

The sincerity of Sparks's tone sent a chill down Stephen's back. He could hardly have hoped for more. If the man who stood before him now couldn't distract the Germans for a few minutes while Stephen retrieved his treasure, it couldn't be done.

He smiled. "Nothing will go wrong."

"Bring me a hundred thousand and we'll talk."

"A hundred?"

"Not a penny less."

Stephen stood. "Okay. I have it in the car."

———~~~———

TWO DAYS and nothing but one short, cryptic phone call from Stephen. Chaim had taken nineteen messages for Stephen, eight from a desperate Dan Stiller. The rest were from a variety of sources, mostly related to real estate.

The rabbi stood and walked into the kitchen. He decided against a glass of orange juice, breathed a prayer, and headed for the phone.

His initial alarm slowly had been replaced by curiosity. Stephen was no doubt disturbed by the discovery of his mother and her death, but if Chaim was right, this recent strange behavior wasn't connected to remorse. Stephen was after what he believed was his. He was maybe even after the Stones of David, and, apparently, he believed he could get them.

Gerik answered on the third ring.

"Hello, Chaim! So pleased you called."

"Hello, Gerik. Have you heard from Stephen lately?"

"Not since last Friday. He's missing?"

"You saw him Friday?"

Gerik relayed his encounter with Stephen and the photograph without the slightest hint of concern.

"This doesn't worry you?" Chaim asked.

"What? That a young Jew has discovered something worth throwing his life into? Not in the least."

"The something is a *picture*—"

"Hardly, Chaim. That something is a girl named Esther who may or may not have survived the death camps. His passion is for Esther and everything she represents. Grace in the face of horrible suffering. Love. Let him run. Let him redeem her. Let him obsess. God knows, we could use a few hundred thousand more like him."

"Yes, of course, let him obsess. Have you ever considered the dangers of obsession? Just because you love someone doesn't mean you have the right to break the law in their name."

"I don't think Stephen is planning on breaking the law, do you?"

"I truly can't say. But I'm worried. He has a tendency for this, Gerik. He's done it before."

"He's gone after his mother's inheritance before?"

"No. But there's more here. He's a war child, an abandoned orphan, an immigrant without a true home. He compensates for his loneliness with some of his antics. But at times like this, I fear he retreats into isolation, searching for meaning. For belonging. Family. He becomes the lost child again, and he doesn't follow reason."

"Maybe becoming a child again isn't so bad," Gerik said. "He needs time to work through this, Chaim. Let him search for his identity. Let him feel his need to belong to someone. We all might consider the same with God."

Chaim took a deep breath and nodded. "I think he may be after more than his identity. There are the Stones of David."

"If he is so fortunate to have stumbled on information leading to the other Stones, he should go after them. Especially if they are his rightful inheritance."

Chaim didn't necessarily disagree. "Rachel's note mentioned danger. I'm thinking of calling the police."

"The police would put an end to whatever hope Stephen has for finding what he's searching for. Surely you know that."

"The police could save his life."

"How many times have you told me your Christ taught that man should abandon this kingdom for the next?"

"These are Stones, not the kingdom of God. The passionate dedication that Christ requires of his followers can destroy a man if misdirected."

"But this isn't really about the Stones," Gerik said. "It's about love. Isn't the kingdom of God about love?"

"Yes."

"There you go, then."

"I'm still worried."

"Then you don't trust him," Gerik said.

"Exactly. I don't trust him. Passion has a way of making people do stupid things. Especially people like Stephen."

There was kindness in Gerik's laughter. "Yes, passion is dangerous, but it's also a requirement for good living."

"This isn't God he's pursuing, Gerik."

The antique dealer turned somber. "Then help him, Chaim. Be with him to keep him from falling over himself. But don't kill his passion."

Chaim let the man's suggestion settle in. "Maybe."

"Perhaps we should all be so obsessive of love."

Chaim didn't answer.

27

Los Angeles
July 23, 1973
Monday Night

STEPHEN MET FIVE OF SPARKS'S THUGS IN THE ALLEY AT NINE AND led the black-clad men to the fourth floor of Building B as agreed. The leader, Bert, was a burly man with a pitted face who looked as though he'd grown up on a diet of thumbtacks.

The other four were no more congenial. Three had each survived a tour in Vietnam. This pleased Stephen more than he would ever admit. They were his salvation, and he welcomed them with a giddiness he didn't know he was capable of.

"What's this?" Bert asked, motioning to Stephen's makeshift hiding place.

"This place? I don't know. Looks like a . . . hangout. I found it here."

"Someone lives here. What if they come back?"

"No one lives here," Stephen said. "It's been abandoned."

"Doesn't look abandoned to me. Picture on the wall, food cans in the corner. No way." Bert eyed Stephen. "You do this?"

"You take me for an idiot? Why would I do this? Forget it. Doesn't matter anyway. You do your thing, and I watch from here like we planned. If someone comes, it's my problem, not yours."

"I don't like it," one of the others said. "You should wait somewhere else."

"Fine. I'll find another window." He had no intention of doing any such thing. The fact that these thugs were tromping all through his place was annoying enough without them ordering him around in his own home. Who did they think they were?

"Let's get going," he said.

Bert lifted his binoculars and peered across the street. "Top floor's lit, the rest are dark. Looks simple enough. You're sure there's only two dogs?"

"Does it make a difference? You're using a stun grenade—that should knock them all out."

"Everything matters. Joey, you think you could get the gas canister through one of those windows from here?"

Joey eyed the top floor. "Should be easy enough. But a ground-level shot will be just as easy. That puts me in position when we go in."

Bert nodded and lowered the glasses. "Okay, everyone follows the plan. We gas the top floor, knock out the dogs in the garage, and hold the stairwell and the elevator for seven minutes from the all-clear. That means you"—he jabbed a finger at Stephen—"have exactly seven minutes from the time we signal three short flashes to get your butt across the street, into the basement, collect these . . . heirlooms of yours, and get out. Two long flashes, and we abort. Clear? You see two, and we're out of here, no questions, no refunds."

"What if I fall or get delayed somehow? I know we agreed on seven minutes, but—"

"Seven means seven. What you do in those seven minutes is up to you. Any longer and we'll have cops swarming the place, especially if whoever's in there starts firing off unsilenced rounds."

They'd been over this several times already. Their entry would be relatively painless, but there was no telling what the Germans would do if they got off the fourth floor before the gas knocked them out. If one of the neighbors called in gunshots, it would take the nearest precinct seven minutes to show, less if a squad car happened to be nearby—a risk they would have to accept. If a cop did show before the seven minutes were up, they would blow a hole in the back of the garage and vanish into the night. Stephen would be on his own.

That was the plan, and Stephen thought it was stupendous. The way he figured it, three minutes would be all he really needed to drop into the basement, move the barrel, scoop up the tin box, and do his own vanishing act.

"Let's do this," Bert said. He caught Stephen's attention, brought two fingers to his eyes, and then pointed them at the building. "Don't take your eyes off the target."

"Not a chance."

"Seven minutes."

"Seven minutes."

They pounded down the stairs, and Stephen took up his position at the window. He lifted the binoculars and strained to see shapes beyond the drawn curtains. Nothing. If someone pulled back a curtain and saw a man staring at them through binoculars from across the street . . .

He lowered the glasses and edged to his left. A dark shadow crossed the street to the right—that would be Joey with the grenade launcher. Stephen's pulse pounded. He scanned the neighborhood for pedestrians. All clear.

Could this actually work? What if the gas canister from Joey's launcher bounced off the window? No, these guys knew what they were doing. They were in the zone, man. They would crash the party and put Braun out of business.

The other four men broke for the side of the building and slid into the shadows below one of the ground-floor windows. He could hardly believe this was happening. Should've done this three days ago.

The curtains suddenly parted at one of the fourth-floor windows. Stephen jerked back. They'd been spotted!

No, not necessarily. Maybe the Germans had only heard something. Stephen sneaked another peek. A man stood at the window, studying the street. Come on, Joey! Light them up! Do it, do it now!

But Joey was out of sight, and the south side of the building remained dark. The man in the window didn't seem satisfied. Stephen dismissed a sudden temptation to stick his head out the window and direct their attack.

A dull *thump* sounded, followed by a crashing window. Joey had fired. And hit.

The curtain dropped shut. Stephen leaped to the center of the window and strained for a view of the attack. Another crash, this one from ground level. A definite *whump!* Maybe more than definite. Maybe thundering. The stun grenade. The cops were probably already on their way.

Stephen watched five men hoist themselves into the window and disappear. Still no sign of anything from the top floor. Maybe they were all unconscious. Or racing down the stairwell bearing arms.

"Come on," he growled. "Come on!"

"What's up, Groovy?"

Stephen spun. Sweeney and Melissa!

"Lotsa commotion out there tonight," Sweeney said. "You in on it?"

"What are you doing here?" Stephen demanded.

"I asked first."

Stephen whirled back to the window. What had he missed? He had to watch for the flashes! Nothing seemed to be happening.

The bohemians had walked up beside him and peered out. "You looking at anything in particular or just gazing at that missed opportunity over there?" Sweeney asked.

Stephen turned sideways, keeping the building in his peripheral. He could feel sweat snake past his right temple.

"I need some privacy right now."

Melissa looked at his flimsy walls. "You want us to knock before entering, is that it? Come on, dude, let's knock." She led Sweeney out of Stephen's square with a straight face and lifted her fist to knock. "Oops, no door, Groovy. I would knock on the wall, but it might fall if I do."

This could not be happening.

―⁂―

ROTH BRAUN was seated on what was left of Rachel Spritzer's leather sofa when the canister crashed through the dining-room window, rolled to a stop under the table, and hissed white gas.

A sliver of fear immobilized him momentarily before his training took over, returning to him his full power of control.

The Jew had returned. This was good.

He bolted from the couch. "Gas!"

The effects were surprisingly quick—three men seated at the table were on their knees already, gasping for air. Roth was far enough away to escape its initial effects. Surely it wasn't lethal. Or had he misjudged the man?

A dull *thump* shook the floors below them.

Lars ran from the master bedroom, stared at the scene with wide eyes, and stepped aside just in time to avoid Roth's rush.

"A blanket!" Roth said. "Hurry!"

They'd shredded the bed to its springs. Lars grabbed a blanket from the floor and threw it at Roth, who quickly stuffed it into the crack at the bottom of the door.

"It'll seep around the door," Lars said.

"Give me an ax." Braun shoved the closet doors leaning against the wall to the floor. "The stairwell's behind this wall."

Axes were one thing they weren't short on, and they'd already taken the plaster off the bedroom side of the wall. They wouldn't find anything by tearing down the walls—the treasure was in the basement. But Stephen had to believe that he was in a race against time to retrieve the treasure. So Roth would keep up the charade. He would play the game until Stephen found his own way in. There was no point in crushing the Jew's hopes until they had been elevated to a point of fanaticism.

Roth caught the ax with his left hand and broke a two-by-four with his first swing.

"They will be coming up the stairs." He cursed himself for leaving the masks on the third floor and swung again. The ax shattered two timbers this time.

Roth grinned and swung again. This time, the entire wall sagged. Nothing was so satisfying as the game. They were coming to the finish line, neck and neck.

"Come on, Jew!" Roth bellowed, swinging again. "Come on!"

Another three quick chops, and a three-foot portion splintered off and fell out.

Roth dropped the ax, shoved his head into the stairwell, saw a clear path, and crawled out. He dropped to the third-floor landing, followed by Lars. The attackers were still below, waiting for the gas to complete its work. He slammed through the door and ran for a cache of supplies in the first bedroom.

"The ventilation system. Flood the building with tear gas."

Lars tore through a large black duffle bag, yanked out two gas masks, and tossed one to Roth. Gas masks secure, they each grabbed three small canisters. Lars snatched up a rifle.

"Gas first," Roth snapped. He shoved a crowbar at Lars. "Use the return vents." He ran into the hall, turned the thermostat to manual vent, dropped the canisters, and crammed his crowbar under a large return vent above his head. The grill popped off in two attempts. He could hear Lars doing the same in the adjacent hall.

Roth popped the tabs on all three canisters and dropped them into the vent. Perhaps the men below already had gas masks in place, but with any luck they would wait to don the gear until they secured the stairwell. Masks limited field of vision.

It would take no more than a minute for the gas to work its way through the building. Without another word, they collected their weapons and reentered the stairwell.

Roth motioned Lars to cover. The blond German swung his rifle over the rail. "Clear."

So, they were still in the garage? Or was this the work of a lone fool, firing off a canister of gas with the intent to crawl up after half an hour to collect his treasure?

"No killing," he ordered. "Not now."

He descended the stairs to the second-floor landing and covered for Lars. They took up positions on the first landing, weapons trained on the door to the garage. If anyone cracked that door, Roth would put a bullet in his gut.

⎯⎯⎯⎯

THE FIRST *clunk* came while Melissa's hand was still raised, and for a moment Stephen thought she'd stomped her foot to imitate a knocking sound. The noise came again, distant.

All three of them looked out the window together. The sound was hardly more than a knock, but there it came again. Stephen froze. Someone was taking a hammer or an ax to one of the walls in Rachel Spritzer's apartment.

"What's that?" Sweeney asked.

They'd entered his hiding place without knocking again.

"I . . . I don't know." Stephen was desperate. He turned and held up both hands to ward them off. "Please! I have to do something here."

"What's up, man? Something's going down and—"

"Just leave!" Stephen shouted.

They flinched.

He flung his arm toward the door. "Can't you take a hint? Leave!"

"Now you've gone and hurt my feelings, man," Sweeney said. "What gives you the right? And after we extended our hospitality to you?"

"Is that what you call this? Hospitality? You're hurting my feelings by being here. I'm telling you, I have something real important to do, and you can't be here!"

"Then maybe you should apologize," Melissa said, crossing her arms.

Stephen stared at her, mouth open. The whole scene felt surreal. He glanced back at the building. No flashes, right? He would have seen the light from the corner of his eye. Nothing but black on the garage level. What was keeping Bert? They should have given the all-clear by now. He swung back.

"I'm sorry!" He was frantic, and he knew that they knew he was frantic. "Believe me, I'm so sorry."

"For kicking us out of your little shrine here."

"Yes! For kicking you out of—"

"What was that?" Sweeney asked.

Stephen turned back to the window. "What?"

"I thought I just saw some flashes."

"You did? How many?"

"I don't know. Two, I think. Maybe it was three."

"Well, was it two or three?" Stephen demanded.

"I don't know. Lighten up."

Stephen turned on Sweeney. "It was either two or three, it couldn't be both! And they were either long flashes or short flashes. Two long flashes or three short ones. Tell me!" he yelled.

Sweeney stared back, shocked.

"Sorry. I'm sorry for that. Look, I just need to know exactly what you saw. You have no idea how important it is to me."

"That your signal?" Melissa asked. "That's why you're looking over there. You're waiting for a signal from someone inside. You've been holding out on us."

"You're right, I have. And I'm sorry, okay. Just tell me what—"

"I think it was three short," Sweeney said. "But I saw only two."

"Then why is it three?"

"Because the two flashes I saw were short. You said three short or two long right? These were short, so there must have been three. I just saw the last two."

He had seven minutes! He'd already wasted at least one. Stephen bolted for the stairs.

"Hey, someone's climbing out the window down there," Sweeney said.

Stephen slid to a stop. "What?"

"No, two! Check that, make it three . . . five! Five people dressed in black just dived out that window down there."

Stephen ran for the window. Sure enough, Bert and gang were out of the building, along the wall, bent over.

Two long flashes blazed from one of their flashlights.

"What?"

"Are they okay?" Melissa asked.

"What happened?" Stephen asked, disbelieving. "What are they doing?"

The men ran to the east, crouched low. They rounded a building and were gone. Stephen faced the apartment, still not comprehending exactly what had just happened. There had been three short flashes followed by two long flashes. The team had entered, secured, and then been beaten back by Braun somehow.

But how?

It didn't matter how. The fact was, they were gone.

The desperation came quickly, pummeling him like a breaking wave.

He spun from the window, suddenly panicked. He should go anyway! He should run over there, dive through the window, zip into the basement, and grab the tin box! For all he knew, Sparks could have told his men to shut it down before he got in.

But Braun had managed to beat back five trained soldiers. He was either a lot smarter or a lot stronger than Stephen previously assumed.

He slowly lowered himself to the crate. The world faded. Five days of pent-up frustration flooded his chest. It was time to give up. It was time to go home and explain everything to the rabbi. To crawl out of this hole and rediscover the land of the living. Tears blurred his eyes, and he fought to contain himself.

"You okay, man?" Sweeney asked.

No, man, I'm dying here. Can't you see that? Of course I'm okay. I'm a successful Realtor with eight hundred thousand dollars in the bank. Make that seven.

Melissa put her hand on his shoulder. "It's okay, honey. We all have bad days."

He lowered his head and tried to shake off the emotion. The attempt failed miserably. Silence swallowed them for a few minutes.

"Man, you have it bad, don't you?"

Stephen cocked his head to see Sweeney sitting cross-legged in the corner of his hiding place.

"I have what bad?"

"The desires. You've got a case of the desires, and you have it bad. Maybe that's good."

Stephen didn't bother with a response.

"That's what I'm looking for, you know. It's why I left the world behind and took on the bohemian ideals. I don't know what about Rachel Spritzer's place has you like this, but you've given yourself to it. Know what happens when you abandon yourself to something like that?"

"No, tell me."

"It either ruins you or makes you. Drugs, for example. There's something that you give yourself to, and it ruins you. But give yourself to love, and it makes you."

"Whatever."

Sweeney stood. "Come on, Melissa, let's leave Groovy to figure things out. He's got me all inspired again."

"Take care, Stephen," she said. They looked at him from his doorway that wasn't, and he knew that somewhere in his breaking down he'd earned their respect. Somehow, the realization comforted him. His new family was embracing him.

They left, and Stephen curled up on his bed.

———

"TEAR IT apart!" Roth thundered. "Every wall, every post, every carpet, the whole building, from top to bottom, starting with the third floor. We begin now!"

"It's midnight," Balzer said.

Roth glared at the man.

"We're still recovering," Balzer said.

The gas had rendered them unconscious for an hour before its effects faded. From what they could tell, four or five men had orchestrated the attack and been driven out by the tear gas. One of them had dropped a magazine of 627 rounds in their quick exit, most likely from an M-16. A stun grenade had killed one dog and knocked the other out.

The attackers had used a grenade launcher for the gas canister. Whoever they were, they didn't lack resources.

Roth was pleased with the Jew's efforts. It was critical that he find his own way in. Then, and only then, could Roth make his next move. If Stephen suspected at any point that he was being played for a fool, he would be compromised. He might even quit.

And what if the Jew actually outwitted him as his mother had outwitted Gerhard?

Roth would have to take that risk.

Suddenly angered, he lifted his pistol and shot Balzer through the head.

"Balzer was ill," Roth said. "We don't have time for illness. Is anyone else ill?"

No one challenged him.

"Good. I want this building stripped to the basement in two days."

He faced Lars. "What was the name of the woman at the district attorney's office?"

"Which woman?"

"The friend of the Realtor."

Lars hesitated. "I don't . . . maybe Sylvia. Yes. Sylvia Potok."

"I need her address," Roth said.

28

RUTH'S FIRST MOMENT OF REDEMPTION CAME WHEN SHE STEPPED through the door to Braun's house on the hill.

She'd been here at least a dozen times, and always she was greeted with a coy smirk, a look that said, *Aren't you fortunate to be in my presence?* Tonight, the commandant stood by his dinner table, dressed in full dashing uniform, and his look went from coy to shocked in the space of two seconds. Ruth took a tiny measure of comfort in his surprise.

The guard shut the door behind her, and she faced Braun with as much courage as she could muster. Bitterness and fury had marched her up the hill, but now, looking at him blinking in his silly uniform, she felt more ill than angry.

"What are you doing here?" he demanded. His eyes shifted to the red scarf hanging from her arm. "I didn't send for you."

"You sent for a woman who is pregnant. Of course you would. Why waste a rope on one when you can hang two with the same rope?"

He stared at her, unmoving. "You think this is a joke?"

"Is it?"

Behind him, the table was set with two place settings of Dutch china, crystal glasses, white serviettes rolled in silver rings, and a single red rose.

Braun walked around the table, fingers dragging lightly on the silk tablecloth. "I sent for Martha, not you. There has been a mistake. I'll send a guard—"

"I took the scarf." She said it with her usual confidence, as if her visit was just another contest of wills. But she knew this one was different.

"You don't have the right." His face darkened. "I sent for Martha."

"You insist on your sacrificial lambs. What kind of sacrifice does an unwilling victim make? I'm here willingly. Or don't you have the courage to match mine?" She walked toward the table and met his eyes. "We'll see who has more courage tonight, a small Jewish girl with a gun to her head, or a big, strapping Nazi thug."

Ruth stepped past the commandant, lifted the lid on the white porcelain dish. Steam rose, scented of chicken and celery with a touch of ginger. She paused, gripped by the incredible sensations that ran through her mind with this single, delightful odor. She hadn't smelled real food in many months, but this . . . this tantalizing scent seemed to spread right through her. And another scent—fresh bread from the kitchen. Fresh, hot, sweet. The back of her tongue tightened and immediately flooded her mouth with saliva. The rose that stood eighteen inches from her eyes was fragrant too. And it seemed redder than the roses she remembered in Slovakia. Such beauty blossoming from a stalk of thorns. The commandant said something, but she didn't hear it.

What was coming over her? All her own words of new birth and hope and passion were now, at this very moment, being tested. In a way, she was coming alive, wasn't she?

But what if it all was just talk? What if there was no true virtue or meaning in this madness of hers?

She swallowed and looked up at the commandant. "Shall we eat? It smells . . . delightful."

He glared at her, but his shock seemed to have lost its edge. "I could have you both shot for this."

"You could have had us both shot months ago. But you're tired of shooting Jews; you told me that yourself. The challenge is gone, remember? So now I give you a new challenge. Accept a sacrifice in the place of another. You may be the only one in the entire war to have done so."

"You're worthless to me like this!"

She wasn't sure what he could mean by that.

"How can you abandon your own child?" he demanded.

"How can you kill Martha's child?"

"She is a Jew!" he shouted.

"So am I!"

To Braun, the war was a game in which he played god. Anything that elevated his status moved him closer to winning. Anything that diminished that status compromised his power. The fact that the Russians were advancing three hundred miles to the east hardly mattered. His game was here, in Toruń, and in Toruń he was winning.

Ruth pulled out the chair she assumed was hers and sat.

"You really believe that I will hang you and let the others live?" Braun demanded. "That's your understanding of how I work?"

She immediately lost her appetite. It was his use of the word "others." He meant Esther and Martha and Martha's child, and she knew that he was fully capable of hanging her and then marching straight over to the barracks to murder Martha and the children. Esther would be most difficult for him, because he regarded himself as Esther's benefactor. She was his proof that he was still human, merciful.

"I expect you to honor the rules of the game," Ruth said. "You may be a murderer, but you still have honor, don't you?" It was a bold-faced lie, but she knew he believed it.

The commandant pulled out his chair, sat, crossed his legs, and studied her carefully. "You never cease to amaze me," he said. "Honestly, I don't understand you. Are you positive that you're Jewish?"

"Yes." Fear began to work its fingers into her mind. He was going along with this. She knew he would, but she expected more of a fight. Maybe a quick gunshot to her head in a fit of anger. The thought of being hanged by a rope—

"Okay, then. Have it your way. But I'll have to kill your daughter. We can't have a baby here without its mother. Maybe I'll send it to Auschwitz in a potato sack."

Ruth was suddenly moving without a clear understanding of what she was doing. She jumped to her feet. The hot porcelain dish with the ginger chicken was in her hands, and then she was hurling it against the back wall. It smashed into the wood with a horrendous crash.

"No!" She knew this wasn't the way to deal with him. For a moment, she'd taken control of the game, but now he'd trumped her. "Don't you dare touch her! Ever!"

He chuckled. Ruth stood, fists shaking at her sides. Her noble sacrifice felt foolish now. She had to control herself. For Esther's sake.

"You have the spirit of twenty men," Braun said. "But you should know by now that you can't tell me what I can or can't do. If I decide to kill your baby, I will. And if I decide she goes to Auschwitz in a potato sack, she goes. Your pathetic sacrifice means nothing."

Ruth sat hard. She took a deep breath and set her hands, palms down, on the table. "I'm sorry. You struck a raw nerve," she said, and then she swallowed to rid her voice of its tremor.

He was smiling, but she noticed that his upper lip was beaded with sweat. "Understandable," he said.

"Thank you."

Think, Ruth. Say what you came to tell him now, before he ends this game.

"But you shouldn't kill my daughter or Martha. In fact, you should honor them. It follows the cleverness of your method here. You extend hope and then dash it. The problem with butchers like Himmler is that they don't extend any hope. They simply take life, and take life, and take life, until the whole mess becomes meaningless. You've said that yourself."

His smile softened. "And?"

"If after my sacrifice you kill Martha or Esther, you will crush the hope of the others completely. They'll know you no longer play by the rules. The scarf will come, and they won't care. You'll become nothing more than yet one more cog in this killing machine."

He regarded her with a long stare. The truth of her words struck her, and she hesitated, but she would say anything now to keep Esther and Martha alive.

"But if you honor them, you will flood the barracks with hope. The next time your scarf settles on one of their beds, they will be crushed. Killing the body is much easier than crushing the spirit."

"All of this at the expense of your own life?" he said.

Her stomach turned. "Yes."

"You really do love them, don't you?"

"Yes."

"I can't guarantee that they will live."

"Then you aren't as powerful as you think you are."

Braun pushed back from the table, stood, gave her a long look, and walked to the window that overlooked the compound. Abandoned to silence once again, she considered what it would feel like to be hanged by the neck. Would the world go black immediately, or would she choke to death? Would her legs jerk?

Dear God, she was abandoning her baby! Her face flushed hot and she suddenly stood. How could she do such a thing to the beautiful, innocent life she'd given birth to only ten days earlier?

No, but there was Martha and Martha's child. If Martha were standing here right now, two lives would be lost for certain. This was the only chance Martha's child had.

Braun turned from the window, face fixed in a frown. "Have it your way, then." He walked to the phone.

"Then make me a promise," Ruth said.

"You've ruined my plans for the evening," he said. "I'm not interested in giving the others hope. I had my heart set on taking Martha's. You're right about the power of hope. Desperation. Desire. I live for it. But you've disturbed me."

"Promise me that you will let them live," she said.

He picked up the field phone and spoke in a soft voice. "Now. Yes, now." He set the phone back in its cradle.

"Promise me." The tears sprang from her eyes before she knew that she was going to cry. The room swam, and she didn't know what to do. Braun watched her, then walked to a dresser and opened a drawer.

Ruth looked away and closed her eyes. She had run out of smart arguments. The guards were coming up the hill. She'd committed herself to death, and she didn't know what to do.

Except cry. She thought that crying now would be okay, because she'd already been strong enough. What did it matter if she died with tears in her eyes? No one would see except for a few guards, who had probably placed bets on how long she would jerk about on the end of the rope. Either way, she would be dead within the hour.

She let the tears stream, but she didn't make a peep. No, that was too much in front of this monster. And she wouldn't beg anymore, no matter how much she wanted to. Braun would not respond well to a begging woman.

"Look at me."

Braun stood three feet from her. In one hand he held a sharp, thin knife. In the other he held a crystal wine glass. He looked like a demon.

"I will do as you request on one condition."

A wedge of hope. She felt suffocated.

"Anything," she said. A sob. "Anything, I swear, anything."

"I will let them live, Ruth. But I need some of your blood. I want you to give me some of your blood. Willingly."

"My blood?"

"Just a small cut on your wrist."

His request made no sense.

"I need it to verify your child's blood line."

Ruth was beyond caring about his reasoning. She believed him. And with her belief came a flood of hope unlike any she'd felt in a very long time.

She stood, trembling from head to foot. He was blurry from her tears, but she held out her arm, wrist up. "Cut me," she said. "Just save my baby. I beg you to save my baby."

He took her hand gently. Rubbed her palm with his finger, fascinated by her skin. It was the first time he had touched her. "I will. I swear I will let your baby live. And I will let you live as well."

Electricity shot through her veins. Could he mean it?

She felt the cold edge of the blade on her wrist.

"I swear you will survive this war."

He jerked the knife. The blade stung. She gasped. The cut was deeper than she had expected.

Braun twisted her wrist and watched the blood dribble into the glass beneath. His eyes were wild and his lips were parted.

Ruth felt a pang of fear.

He dropped her arm and lifted the glass to his nose. Sniffed it like a delicate flower. For a moment she thought he was going to taste it.

Braun looked at her as if suddenly realizing that she was still in the room. They exchanged stares. Then he smiled.

"There is one force in this universe that rules them all," he said. "It is the power behind war and love and life and death. It is hope. Desire. It is passion. It is what enables a mother to give her life for a child. It is what sends man on his search for God. It is what set Lucifer on his ambitious course. It is heaven and it is hell. The desires and affections of man are in the crosshairs."

She was too shocked to move.

"Like Lucifer, I have entered the fray, my dear."

A knock sounded on the door.

He lifted the glass and swirled the blood like a red wine. Then Gerhard Braun lifted the glass to his lips, tilted it back, and drank it to the last drop. When he lowered his arm, his eyes were closed, his breathing ragged, his lips red.

The blood drained from Ruth's head. "You made a promise . . ."

The door opened.

"Which I have no intention of keeping," Braun said. He set the glass on the table. "Hang her. Now."

Boots clumped.

Ruth's throat had frozen shut with horror. They pulled a black bag over her head and quickly bound her arms behind her back. She gave in to their handling completely.

They pushed her forward, down the stairs she'd climbed so many times. Maybe he would let Esther live. Maybe hanging her would be enough for him.

Father, give my baby hope!

She blinked in the pitch darkness and tried to push the picture of the front gate from her mind. The musty cloth pressed into her nostrils. Did they force this same cloth over all of their victims' heads? She imagined the other women who'd taken this walk, how they must have felt all alone in complete darkness, certain only that their lives were about to end. Did they cry? Was it dried tears that she smelled?

Her breathing quickened.

"Step up!"

She stepped up—a chair or a crate. She could feel the rope as they worked it over her head. The adrenaline came in waves, hot to her skin, slicing through her nerves like a million tiny razor blades, each one urging her to run, run away. But there was nowhere to run.

"Dear God in heaven, I beg you to save the children."

Whoever was working on the rope paused for moment, and then cinched it tight.

"Don't let my death be in vain. Save the children." Her voice rose in pitch and in volume. "Give them love and hope."

MARTHA AWOKE before dawn, disorientated in the dark. A baby lay against her belly.

Ruth's baby.

Ruth!

Dread swept through her chest and she moaned. She could look now if she wanted to. She could climb out of bed, sneak over to the window and have a clear view of the gate to Toruń.

But she couldn't.

She lay still for ten minutes before the need to know compelled her to throw off the covers and hurry for the window. She would have to be strong now; the babies depended on her alone. Part of being strong was facing the truth. Knowing. She had to know.

She edged her head into the window slowly.

Then she knew.

The body hung in silence a hundred yards away. There was a black hood over Ruth's head. Her arms and legs hung limply. So innocent and still there across the yard.

Martha clenched her jaw and swallowed the knot in her throat. No more crying. She now had one objective only. Keep the babies alive. Nothing else mattered. Her life mattered only because the children needed her to survive. The war's end mattered only because such an end would set the children free.

The price that had been paid for the child in her womb demanded her unfailing devotion.

Martha stared at Ruth's body and vowed to live so that Ruth's death would not be in vain.

29

S TEPHEN DREAMED OF LEECHES CRAWLING THROUGH HIS TOES and woke to find the dog licking his bare feet. Brandy matched his stare, whined, and crept up the bed to nuzzle his neck before lying down beside him.

It was the most touching moment in Stephen's recent memory. The dog had returned. He was loved. The world had not ended, despite his conclusion of several hours past.

He drifted back into an exhausted sleep—three days without a decent nap had worn him onionskin thin. He'd gone up to the giant, he'd fought with all of his strength, and he'd been sent home packing. Goliath had not fallen.

Someone shook him. Goliath was mocking him, egging him on for a fifth round.

"Stephen."

Goliath knew his name.

"Wake up, dude."

Stephen jerked up. "What?" Brandy lay across the room on Melissa's lap. Sweeney sat cross-legged beside his bed.

"What's up?"

"Sorry to wake you from such a blissful sleep, but I have something I think we should talk about."

Stephen sat up, groggy. "What's up?"

"I just told you what's up."

"I mean, what do you want to talk about? What time is it?"

"It's time to face the dragon, baby." Sweeney grinned.

What was this guy talking about? This was the problem with bohemians—they were too idealistic to be useful. Poetry was fine, but you couldn't wear it, eat it, or sleep in it.

He wanted to reach out and slap the man for waking him.

"How much is it worth to you to get into that building?" Sweeney asked.

"What do you mean?"

"I mean, how much would you pay?"

Stephen sat up, suddenly awake. "Could you get in?"

"Maybe. Depends. But let's say I did have a way in. I mean, an absolutely guaranteed way in. What would it be worth to you?"

"Just tell me if you have a way in!"

"You think I'd wake you up from such serenity to toss around esoteric hypotheticals?"

"I doubt it's beyond you."

"See, there you go, hurting my feelings again. Just go with me, baby. Give me a figure."

"Okay. A thousand dollars."

Sweeney looked long and hard. "That's it? This whole thing is only worth a thousand dollars to you?"

"You have a thousand dollars now?" Stephen asked.

"I don't want a thousand dollars now."

"So why are you asking?"

Sweeney waved a hand. "Forget it, man. I don't know how to get into the building anyway."

"What do you mean, you don't have a way in? You just sat there and told me you did!"

"What does it matter—it's hardly worth a thing to you, right? A thousand bucks—please, man."

"Okay, ten thousand," Stephen said.

"I have a way in, you know. I really do." Sweeney grinned. "But I was under the impression that this thing really meant a lot to you. I'm hearing numbers like a thousand and ten thousand, and I'm thinking that I was wrong."

Sweeney wasn't bluffing, was he? He actually might have a way in. Stephen scrambled to his knees. "You get me in there, and I'll pay you whatever you want."

Sweeney looked over at Melissa, who was watching quietly. "Hear that, babe? Now we're getting somewhere. But that's not the way it works, Groovy. I need to know what it's worth to *you*. It's not what I want that matters here. It's how much you want whatever's over there that matters. How much will you pay?"

"Twenty thousand."

Sweeney just stared at him.

"Fifty thousand—if you get me in."

"Not enough."

"For crying out loud, then! How much *is* enough?"

"Your desire's bigger than that, Groovy. I've seen it in your eyes. You would sell your soul for whatever's in that building."

Stephen settled to his haunches and looked at the smiling bohemian. A bright moon hung in the window. The traffic from La Brea hummed faintly, even though the sun wasn't up.

"You're asking me what I'll pay you, not what it's worth," he said.

"They're synonymous. You'll pay whatever it's worth. It's worth what you'll pay for it. What price are you willing to pay for this obsession of yours? That's what I want to know."

Stephen looked up at Ruth's picture. The moon cast a soft hue over her face.

"That's an unfair question."

"So few are really willing to put their money where their mouths are, isn't that the truth? That's what sets the greatest apart. Gandhi. Jesus. They gave their lives. All I'm asking for is money."

Stephen wasn't sure if he wanted to hit the man or cry on his shoulder. He had promised Dan Stiller five hundred thousand. He'd spent a hundred on Sparks. He had two hundred to spare.

"A hundred thousand," he said.

"Not enough. Guaranteed access to the building."

"Two hundred."

Sweeney hesitated. "That's it? You would walk away from here if it cost you more?"

"No! I didn't say that!"

"Then stop messing around!" Sweeney yelled.

His fury startled Stephen. Tears welled in his eyes.

"Put your gut into it, man!"

"Five hundred!" Stephen cried. Dan would have to forgive him.

"Stop it, Sweeney!" Melissa said. "That's enough. You're torturing him!"

"This is exactly what he needs. It's what we all need." He reached out and rubbed Stephen on the shoulder. "You did well, my man. You did well."

The man stood up and walked to the window. "How will you pay me?"

Stephen cleared his throat. "You're serious?"

"As a heart attack."

"How do you want it?"

"Cash?"

"The bank doesn't like to give me cash, but I think I can arrange it."

"Just curious—how much money do you have in the bank?"

"Seven hundred thousand."

"See, that leaves you with two hundred thousand. Minus expenses."

"Expenses?"

"We'll need some equipment. Shouldn't cost more than a few thousand. I want twenty thousand in cash, and the rest in a cashier's check made out to the charity of your choice."

"What?" Stephen rose slowly to his feet.

Sweeney shrugged. "I don't really have use for money. Twenty thousand will keep me for a couple of years, high on the hog."

"Then why—" He looked at Melissa; she was smiling.

"You're paying every dime, my friend. If this is worth five hundred thousand, then someone's gonna pay five hundred thousand, and that someone is you. Let's just say I'm legitimizing your desire. Either you'll pay, or you won't. And there's one more thing. You pay even if you don't find what you're looking for. I get you in, that's all."

"But you have to guarantee me access."

"If I can't get you in, I'll tear up the check."

An image of the floor safe with the tin box sitting inside filled Stephen's mind. "Okay, when do we go? How's this work? Can you show me now?"

"First things first. I need the money."

"No, I don't think you get it. We can't wait! I'll get your money, I swear, but the people over there are after the same thing I am. They're tearing down the walls as we speak. For all I know, they might already have it! We have to move."

"This isn't an overnight thing," Sweeney said, eyebrow cocked.

"How long?"

"Two days. Maybe longer. Depends."

"Two days? Come on!"

"Two days. At least."

Stephen paced. "Then we have to start now. I'll get you a check as soon as the bank opens. I'll bump the amount to forty thousand if you'll show me now."

Sweeney looked at Melissa. "Okay. You can keep the extra dough, but you renege, and I go to the police and expose what you're doing down here."

"I'm not going to renege," Stephen said firmly.

Sweeney's eyes twinkled like an excited child's. "You wanna see?"

"Yes! Yes, I want to see!"

"Come on."

THEY HURRIED down the three flights of stairs to the ground floor in near darkness. "Wait here," Sweeney instructed. He returned thirty seconds later holding a makeshift torch. "We'll need light down there," he said.

"Down? I have a flashlight in my bag upstairs," Stephen said.

"Too small." He struck a match and set rags ablaze. Flames licked at the cloth and filled the stairwell with dancing light. "Besides, this is much more exciting, don't you think? Come on!"

He flew down the basement stairs, leading a ribbon of oily smoke. "This building was planned in tandem with the other one," Sweeney said, pushing into the basement. "Same basic layout, same foundation, same utilities. If you ask me, they're both trash, but they haven't caved in yet; I guess that's all some people want."

Stephen recalled that Sweeney studied architecture at UCLA. Stephen's blood pressure surged. They'd entered a basement almost identical to Rachel's. He stopped, fixed on one of the doors directly opposite the stairs.

That was the boiler room. The rest of the basement suddenly faded. Sweeney was saying something, but it sounded distant. They were actually in the basement! This was his mother's basement, and that was the boiler room, and in there was the safe!

Stephen tore for the room, slammed into the door, gripped the knob and yanked it open. Dark.

"Hurry!"

"Stephen—"

"Bring the light!" He motioned frantically and stepped in.

Flame light spread into the room from behind. "What is it?" Melissa asked.

Stephen blinked. No drums. The Germans—

"You see something?" Sweeney asked.

"I . . ." The door was missing from the boiler room. The water heater had been ripped out. "Is this the same?" No, of course it wasn't. What was he thinking? This was the boiler room in Building B. A mixture of relief and disappointment washed over him. "Boy. For a moment there I thought this was Rachel's."

He faced Sweeney and Melissa. Brandy trotted into the room, tested the air with a raised nose. All three looked at Stephen.

"It's in the boiler room?" Sweeney asked. "What you want is in the boiler room across the street?"

No use denying what he'd made painfully obvious. "Yeah. I'm sorry, I just kinda flipped out."

"Boy, are you going to love me," Sweeney said with a big smile.

"Why?"

"I said I could get you into the building. What I didn't tell you was that I could get you into the basement."

"You mean just the basement?"

"You'll see. Come on." He turned, walked out, and stopped in the middle of the basement as if undecided where to lead them next.

"By the way, just out of curiosity"—Sweeney faced him—"I know this thing of yours is a closely guarded secret, but so is what I'm about to show you. So first, what exactly are you after over there?"

A compulsion to tell them surprised Stephen. "A box," he said. Surely, anyone who wanted to donate four hundred eighty thousand dollars to a charity wasn't the kind who would steal to feed their greed.

"And what's in the box? Just curious. Are we talking the Ring here? My precious?"

Stephen stared at Sweeney and then at Melissa. He liked them. He liked these two people very much—at this moment, maybe more than he had ever liked anybody his entire life. That was strange, considering the fact that he hardly knew them. The sentiment choked him up a little and he just stared at them, swimming in this fondness.

"You okay?" Melissa asked.

He nodded. "You guys are pretty neat, you know."

She walked over and rubbed his back. "We think you're neat too. That's why we want to help you. We weren't going to ask for money—that was Sweeney's idea." She flashed Sweeney a glare. "He insisted it would make the whole experience more rewarding for you."

"And it will," Sweeney said. "You're feeling it already, aren't you, Groovy? The more you pay for the diamond, the more you love it. I can feel a whole lot of love in this room right now. You understand what I'm saying?"

Stephen nodded. He wanted to hug them both. "To be honest, I don't know for certain what's in the box," he said. "But I'm sure it came from

Nazi Germany, and I know it belongs to a girl named Esther, the daughter of the woman in the picture upstairs. If she's alive."

"Oh, how sweet," Melissa said, rubbing his back again. "You're doing this for love."

"What's in it could be worth a hundred million dollars," Stephen said, but saying it to these two, the detail seemed insignificant. Silly.

Still, the added detail earned him a moment of silence.

"Even so," Melissa said, "you're doing this for love. I can see it in your eyes." She walked over to Sweeney. "All this talk is making my knees weak, baby."

He took her under one arm and kissed her on the lips. "Love, baby. It's all about love."

They looked over at Stephen, smiling like two jack-o'-lanterns. He let out a short sob-laugh, the kind that mothers cry at weddings, the kind of sound he'd once sworn only a woman could make.

"Ready, Groovy? We don't have all night. I'd hate to get caught down there with a burned-out torch."

"I was born ready."

Sweeney winked and walked for a door. They were in a dingy basement in the middle of the night, headed wherever "down there" was, talking gushy and conquering the world. Sweeney was going to march him into the basement, right to the safe.

They entered a room blackened by coal.

Sweeney had said that it would take two days, but that was because he'd wanted the money up front. Without that caveat to hold them up, they would probably have the box by daybreak.

"What's this?" Stephen asked, looking around.

"This is it, man."

Black lumps lay scattered on the floor or stacked in small piles. "The coal room."

Sweeney walked to one end and kicked at the floor. "No. just watch."

Stephen hurried over. "What?"

"Hold this, honey." Sweeney handed the torch to Melissa, dropped to one knee, and yanked on a steel lid. The metal slab slid free with a loud grate and a clang. A two-foot black hole gaped in the floor.

"I give you a drain," Sweeney said proudly, hand extended in majestic presentation.

"A drain?" Stephen looked up. "Where does this lead?"

"Follow me."

Sweeney plopped to his seat, swung his legs into the hole, mounted what Stephen could now see were iron rungs, and climbed down. "You might want to roll up your pants," he called. "It's a bit wet down here." The announcement was followed by a splash.

Stephen stood in dumbfounded stillness. The dog barked, and he flinched.

"It's okay, puppy," Melissa said, rubbing the dog's head. She turned to Stephen and gave the light to him. "Hand this to me when I get set."

Stephen handed her the torch when she was halfway in and stared down at the glowing hole. There was definitely water in there.

"Come on, dude! We don't have all night."

He thought about rolling up his pants, but neither of them had, so he crawled in after them. Brandy stuck her head into the drain and whined, but she made no attempt to take the plunge.

"Hold on, girl; we'll be back."

Stephen lowered himself gingerly into the sewer drain and turned to face Sweeney and Melissa. The concrete tunnel ran past them into darkness—round, about six feet in diameter. Brown slime covered the walls. He looked down at his feet, but they weren't visible in the murky water. Or whatever it was.

"Don't worry, the city has upgraded," Sweeney said. "This drain isn't in use. They moved the street twenty years ago when they rezoned the neighborhood to accommodate the hordes of people who wanted to live by the sea in bliss. Part of the drain was rerouted, but this section was just cut off. This manhole is the only service entrance. Code. You can't have a drain that's inaccessible, even if it's out of use. A piece of bureaucratic brilliance hard at work."

"How do you know all this? This is the only entrance?"

"I designed two buildings to replace these two as part of an assignment for a design class. So you see, this building has sentimental value to me. I'm not here by accident. I chose it."

"But there's only one manhole?"

"It's all that's left of the old sewer system. Come on, let me show you."

Sweeney turned and plowed up the drain, bent slightly to keep the slime out of his hair. Stephen slogged after them. His mind was still suspended between the romance of their moment up on dry ground and the less-appealing sogginess here. There had to be another service entrance that led up into Rachel Spritzer's apartment.

"Ladies and gentlemen, we have arrived." Sweeney spun around and spread his arms.

"Where?" Stephen looked up. Nothing but slime. "What is it?"

"Another drain," Sweeney said, shoving the torch to his left. A round hole no more than eight inches in diameter exited the side of the sewer.

Stephen looked at the hole, glanced back at a smiling Sweeney, and stared at the hole again, hoping this was not Sweeney's answer. His mind fell free of any romantic threads that had kept it in suspension.

"What's this? It's a hole," he said.

"Well said. A hole that leads into the basement of Rachel Spritzer's apartment."

"But it's tiny. I don't see—"

"It's tiny now." Sweeney had not lost his smile. "When we're done with it, it'll be big."

"How?"

Sweeney lifted up his forefinger. "One word, my bohemian understudy. Jackhammer. Or is that two words?"

"Jackhammer."

"Hammer by Jack. Exactly."

"You're telling me that I just shelled out five hundred thousand dollars for you to point out a tiny hole that you expect me to take a jackhammer to?"

Sweeney's smile faded. He lowered his finger. "It's more than a tiny hole. It's the sewer. It's a way into the basement! It's love and passion and the pot at the end of your rainbow."

"It's crazy!" Stephen's voice echoed down the tunnel.

"What did you expect, Groovy? A rocket ride? I said two days."

"No, I didn't expect a rocket ride, although for five hundred thousand maybe I should have. You think we're dealing with idiots up there? You saw how they sent those soldiers packing. The sound of a jackhammer pounding away down here will echo up every drain in the building. Every sink, every toilet, every shower, booming like machine guns. And even if they are deaf, the whole building could fall in on us!"

Sweeney stared at him in silence, smile gone.

"I told you he might not dig it," Melissa said. "No pun intended."

"This can work, man," Sweeney said. "Where's your suck-it-up, I-gotta-have-it-at-any-cost desperation? I *know* these buildings. There's only seven feet of earth and some concrete between us and where that drain takes a turn for the boiler room. That turn is buried in twelve inches of foundation directly below the coal room. I'll admit, there are a few challenges—like the sound thing—but five hundred thousand dollars says that won't stop us."

Stephen ran a hand through his hair and slopped through the muck in a half circle. Maybe he had expected a rocket ride and maybe he was overreacting to the disappointment. He wanted the safe, and he wanted it tonight.

"How do we deal with the sound?"

"Baffles."

"Brilliant. Baffles," he said cynically. "Why don't we tie some earplugs to a rock and throw it through one of their windows? Who wouldn't turn down a free set of earplugs?"

Melissa giggled. Sweeney looked hurt.

"Sorry," Stephen said. "I . . . I just wasn't expecting this." He stared at the hole. Seven feet. He'd never operated a jackhammer, but surely it could cut its way through seven feet in a day, depending on how much concrete they ran into. Maybe they could baffle the drain. Maybe with all their own hammering, the Germans wouldn't hear. And if they did, they might have trouble identifying the source. Or they could be distracted.

The idea began to take root. Imagine breaking in through the bottom of the safe itself. Like breaking into Fort Knox and taking a hundred million dollars' worth of bullion, only this would be legal. At least the taking part would be legal. The breaking-in part could be a problem.

Stephen grunted.

"I'm telling you, Groovy. This is a lot smarter than going in dressed as a woman."

"You know about that?"

Sweeney winked. "You looked marvelous, although I'll admit it was a bit dark and we were a ways down the street. We saw your exit. The Vega gave you away."

"You know my car?"

"Melissa figured that one out."

"Man. You think anyone else saw me?"

"If they did, they couldn't have put it all together. Your secret's safe with us."

Stephen stared at the hole. This idea might actually be the smartest thing he'd tried yet, though that didn't necessarily put it in the brilliant category. He leaned over and peered into the hole. Couldn't see the end.

"Seven feet. Man, wouldn't that be something if we pulled it off. Come up under them like that. Ha!"

"I said I could get you into the building, and I can. That much we definitely will pull off. Whether or not they will be standing over the hole with guns is another issue altogether."

It could work. Stephen stroked the stubble on his chin. It really could. In fact, in its own way, it *was* brilliant. Braun would *never* expect it.

"Okay," Stephen said, turning from the small drain. Nervous anticipation swept through his nerves. "How do we get power down here?"

"Groovy," Sweeney said.

30

E LECTRIC JACKHAMMERS DON'T FALL OUT OF THE SKY UPON request. This is what Stephen learned Tuesday morning.

Nor do cashier's checks for four hundred eighty thousand dollars, but the fact that Stephen had the bank make it out to the Los Angeles Museum of the Holocaust seemed to earn him some respect. "I'm having a stellar year," he told them. "I need the tax break this donation will give me." Donating such a large sum to the same museum his mother had selected seemed fitting.

He walked out at nine thirty with thirty thousand in cash—twenty for Sweeney, ten for operating expenses—and the cashier's check, to be sent posthaste to the museum.

The jackhammer, on the other hand, proved more difficult. They weren't available at the local five-and-dime, and the only rental company that had an electric one ready to go was all the way out in Riverside. By the time Stephen finally made it to the shop, rented the beast, and returned home, noon bells were ringing. Half a day and they hadn't even started. Meanwhile, Braun was tearing through the walls next door.

Stephen parked in the alley behind the abandoned building and climbed out. Sweeney approached and threw open the back door.

"You get it?"

"Got it. The manager assured me it would cut through concrete like butter. You get the extension cords?"

"Ready to go, man. Lights blazing, just waiting on you."

Stephen popped the trunk, and they gazed upon the mammoth rig together. Bold black letters that had once read "Sledge Master" were worn thin in some spots and off in others. Streaks of crusted tar ran down one side. The bit looked as though it had eaten one too many nails.

"He said the gas one would be better 'cause it's heavier," Stephen said.

"He doesn't know that we're digging up, not down—carburetor wouldn't work at that angle. Besides, without ventilation, the exhaust would kill us."

"You sure we have enough power?"

"I blew a fuse not three minutes ago testing it. Sparky's live. Let me give you a hand with this."

They hauled the tool out of the trunk, each on one end. "You have any idea how this works?" Sweeney asked, squinting in the noon sun.

"No. Don't you?"

"Seems awful heavy. I can't imagine what the gas one must weigh."

"But you do know how these work, right?"

"What I do know is that we're standing still, and my arms are about to drop off. It vibrates, right?" He chuckled. "Just pulling your leg, man. I could operate this monster in my sleep."

"This isn't funny, Sweeney!" Stephen felt a trickle of desperation leak into his mind. What if it didn't work? He stumbled backward for the door and stepped through. "Just how many times have you worked one of these?"

"Awake or in my sleep?"

Stephen stopped. "You're kidding, right?"

"Relax, dude. How hard can it be? We plug it in and chop away."

The desperation swept in like a wave. "If this doesn't work, I swear I'm going to strangle you."

"Watch the steps."

They struggled down the stairs, into the basement, and into the coal room. Both were sweating steadily by the time they set down the jackhammer.

Melissa scrambled up the ladder and stuck out her head. "You get it? Wow, that thing's huge!"

"Get the rope, honey."

She came back up with a coil of rope, which they tied around the handle. "I'll guide it from below," she said.

"Not a chance. This thing drops, and it'll crush you like a ripe tomato," Sweeney said.

"And we're supposed to dig up with it?" Stephen asked.

"Have faith."

They were doomed.

They managed to lower the jackhammer into the hole and lug it up the tunnel, which Sweeney had strung with several lights while he was gone. Stephen felt his frustration grow with each step. "I swear, Sweeney. There's no way this is going to work. Maybe I should let you do this while I try something else."

"Something else like what?"

"I don't know, but we're running out of time."

"Did I ever tell you I graduated from UCLA with honors?"

"Meaning what?"

"Meaning I'm not an idiot."

They came to the hole, and Stephen looked up at a contraption that hung from the sewer's ceiling.

"What's that?"

"That's my genius at work." They propped the jackhammer against the wall.

Stephen examined Sweeney's creation. The rig was pieced together with ropes, pulleys, and springs, all anchored into the concrete above by three large screws. It looked like a huge spider dangling from a web.

"I'm not a mechanical engineer, but I did take several engineering classes," Sweeney said. "The way I figure it, those three anchor bolts I've secured into the concrete will hold a hundred pounds without a problem. Maybe twice that. But we'll have a lot of vibration, and the last thing we need is for the whole thing to come crashing down with one of us under it."

"Ripe tomato."

"Exactly. The beast will hang on two ropes that pass through these pulleys and then attach to this spring, which will absorb most of the vibration. Presto. In my sleep."

A grin crept across Stephen's face.

"And you doubted me," Sweeney said.

"Okay. Never again. Let's try it."

"First, we try the jackhammer."

The extension cord was strung from the ceiling with the lights. Melissa plugged the jackhammer in and eyed them. "Who goes first?"

"I will," Stephen said, stepping forward. His confidence was making a comeback. He dragged the machine upright and examined the two levers, one right, one left. Seemed simple enough. A single knob switched the power on. This done, he stood the jackhammer at an angle in the water, braced himself, and pulled the right-hand lever.

Nothing.

Panicked, he grabbed the left-hand lever.

An awful scream filled the tunnel, and the jackhammer started to jump. The power was fierce, like a bull desperate to buck its rider. Stephen hung on for dear life. The beast bounced away from him, jerking madly down the slippery floor.

Sweeney was yelling something, but the noise swallowed his words. Didn't matter, Stephen knew what he should do. He should let go. But if he let go, the whole machine might fall down, land in the water, and fry its circuits.

It was quick thinking, not panic, that made Stephen hang on to the jackhammer gone berserk. He slipped and splashed in a scramble to keep up with the apparatus, which continued to race away from him.

It died suddenly, and he nearly over ran it. Shrieking laughter echoed down the tunnel from behind. He spun and saw that the cord had come unplugged.

"Quiet!" he yelled.

Melissa lifted a hand over her mouth. "I'm sorry, it's just . . . my goodness."

"They'll hear us!" Stephen yelled.

Of course, that was ridiculous. They were about to pound a hole up their noses with a machine that screamed like a banshee. A little laughter was nothing.

Stephen suddenly began to cackle. Melissa removed her hand and laughed out loud. Sweeney howled. For a solid minute, they were incapacitated with relentless laughter in the bowels of the earth.

"It works," Stephen finally said.

This sent Melissa off again, so much so that Stephen and Sweeney both eventually suggested she'd laughed enough. What would they do if she had a hernia down here? Call an ambulance?

It took them another twenty minutes to hoist the jackhammer into place and fill the pipe with as much insulation as they could stuff up it. The baffling wouldn't stop noise from traveling through the ground, but at least it wouldn't pound through the pipes.

They still had one major test. The hammer was designed to operate with gravity doing the hard labor, like a sledgehammer. Pound at a rock hard enough and long enough, and it would break down. But with the weight now suspended from the ceiling, and only Stephen's or Sweeney's strength to bear on the hammer, would the device exert enough force to break up the concrete?

"Ready?"

"Go for it," Sweeney said.

Stephen braced his lower body against the wall behind him, leaned into the jackhammer, and pulled the lever. The tunnel filled with that awful scream and the machine pounded furiously. Stephen had to clench his jaw to keep his teeth from clacking.

"Come on, baby!" he grunted.

First a chip. Then a tiny chunk. Then a very small slab dislodged and splashed into the water. Stephen let up on the lever. His ears rang. All three stared at the damage. It wasn't much, but it was something.

"Yeehaa!" Sweeney bellowed. "Am I a genius, or am I a genius?"

"I need earplugs," Stephen said.

Sweeney grabbed some insulation, tore off a piece, and stuffed it into his ears. Thirty seconds later, they all had pink fuzzballs sticking from their ears. Stephen pulled on the gloves Sweeney had purchased with the rest of the supplies, and set himself up again.

"Ready?"

"I am," Stephen said and pulled the lever.

The progress was slow, and he had to swap out with Sweeney every ten minutes to realign his jarred bones, but slowly the jackhammer chipped away a two-foot circle of concrete around the small drainpipe. Melissa periodically went up to the fourth floor to see if the Germans were peering out the windows or putting their ears to the sidewalk, seeking the source of any noise they heard. The afternoon passed without any sign of them.

The first foot took ten minutes—nothing but gravel packing.

The next foot took three hours.

Stephen let off the lever and squatted, exhausted. His sopped shirt clung to his chest. He pulled off the goggles and painter's mask Sweeney had insisted they wear, and looked up at the hole. Maybe fourteen inches. They'd cut through the sewer wall and were into some rock.

"We're not going to make it," he said.

Sweeney looked into the hole. "Sure we are."

"You're the genius; do the math. You said seven feet."

"If I remember right. Could have been nine."

"Seven times three is twenty-one hours of straight digging. I don't think I can last that long. And I doubt the hammer will either. I think it's already slowing down."

"Not a chance. We'll have to start letting it cool down every now and then, but—"

"And there's another problem. You said the last foot would be solid concrete. Even if we get that far, the last bit will be three hours of straight banging on the foundation. The whole building will echo like a gong."

"Not necessarily."

"Necessarily."

"You're way too moody, man. Have I let you down yet? I told you I could get you in, and I intend to."

The likely outcome of his situation suddenly struck Stephen. He was in a drainpipe under an apartment complex, digging his way into the basement to break into a safe. San Quentin was full of people who'd executed far better plans.

"Okay, here's the truth," Sweeney said. "The digging will get much easier as soon as we hit the gravel base. These buildings are set on footers that run deep, but here in the center it's all gravel, designed to give with the earthquakes. Digging through the gravel will be quiet, but you're right about the noise when we hit the concrete. We'll have to set up a distraction."

"A distraction."

"You're repeating me. Once we break through, you nab the box and we immediately fill the hole with quick-setting concrete. No one ever knows we were even in there."

Stephen was surprised by Sweeney's forethought. He stood up. "You can do that with quick-set? How long will it take to dry?"

"Couple hours. Won't matter, we'll scatter coal over it—unless someone sweeps the room within a couple of hours, we're home free." He grinned. "See?"

"They have dogs in the garage."

"I'm not sure the dogs survived your friends."

"Okay." Stephen paced. His body quivered, and he doubted it had anything to do with the jackhammer. "This could really work."

"Of course. That's why we're doing it. Why don't you catch a couple hours of sleep? We may be in there by noon tomorrow, and we're definitely going to need you awake."

"Noon, huh?" He could hardly stand the wait. "Why can't we press through tonight? If the gravel is that easy, we could be in by morning!"

"Maybe, but we can't start beating on their floor in the middle of the night when the whole world's asleep. They'll hear us for sure. We need a distraction."

"You could blast music from the sidewalk. You know, just a couple of hippies playing their music too loud."

"I don't have a stereo."

"I'll buy you one."

"Not loud enough."

"You want louder?"

"You want a ring of guys with guns standing over the hole when we come out?"

Stephen paced again. This one small problem could be a spoiler. Maybe he could call Sparks and ask his boys to create a distraction. Not a chance.

Another idea dropped into his mind, a gift from the God who favored the oppressed. He stopped and turned slowly to Sweeney.

"I've got it."

31

Los Angeles
July 24, 1973
Tuesday Night

THE BOY WAS CLOSE. STEPHEN WAS VERY CLOSE. THIS MIGHT BE Roth's last night of hunting.

Tonight he would plan a special surprise for Stephen. He'd decided that the friend named Sylvia would be his next victim. She wasn't exactly a blood relative of Stephen's, but she was a Jew and she was a woman.

He'd considered killing the old man and spent two hours watching Chaim Leveler's house earlier that evening. But breaking protocol could adversely affect the cosmic order of power, so he rejected the idea.

Few people understood that the powers of the air were carefully balanced and even the slightest change could upset this perfection. Rituals had to be performed with precision. If you decided to harvest the souls of Jews, but then switched to Russians, for example, you might lose all of the benefit derived from taking Jews.

This was Gerhard's downfall. He'd broken the rules of his own ritual by allowing Martha and the children to live after selecting them with the scarf.

As a result he'd lost all of his power. A single decision made in a moment of weakness had robbed him of power. Now the only way to restore that power was to kill those who should have been killed in the first place. Gerhard would be vindicated. His power restored.

Then Roth could take that power and kill him.

Roth's present indulgences, on the other hand, weren't a matter of precision. He was simply adding to his pleasure. He was showing the powers of the air that he was the kind of vessel that deserved the might they would pour into him when it was all over, in a matter of days now.

Then again, he could use the woman Sylvia as a pawn against the Stephen. Yes, yes, he could do that. Roth smiled, pleased with himself for thinking so broadly about the challenges that lay before him.

He parked the car in the alley behind her apartment complex. He'd killed eight women since coming to Los Angeles. Eight in six nights. He would decide when he saw her whether she would be the ninth. A part of him was tempted to delay killing so that when he took Stephen, his thirst for blood would be ripe.

Another interesting thought.

Roth pulled out another red silk scarf and pressed it to his nose as he always did. Inhaled. He draped it over his neck and tucked it into his shirt. If anyone saw him strolling the alley with a red scarf, they might connect him immediately to the other killings, and the thought excited him.

He wouldn't be caught, naturally. He might have to change his plans for the night, but they would never catch him.

Roth pulled his black gloves on and stepped into the dark alley.

SYLVIA HAD spent the evening as she had spent the last three evenings—returning to her apartment late from work, eating a meat loaf TV dinner and talking to Chaim about Stephen and the Red Scarf Killer, as they were calling him, before retiring at about eleven.

Chaim had left five messages and then called her from a hotel. He was nearly frantic about something Stephen had told him about danger. And he'd seen a black car parked down his street, so he'd packed up and moved into a hotel room for the night.

Sylvia's first response was one of alarm. The rabbi was overreacting. Stephen was a grown adult, not a child.

If anyone had something to be concerned about, it was Sylvia, she said. The killer was still selecting only single Jewish women. He'd upped his nightly quotient to two.

"Then you must come, Sylvia! Spend the night here with me."

"In the Howard Johnson's?"

"In another room, of course. I insist."

"Please, Rabbi. You're taking all of this too far. What is the likelihood that I would be selected by a serial killer in a city this size? He's never broken into an apartment. I have neighbors on all sides here. And I lock my doors with dead bolts."

"Then come for my benefit. Maybe I am overreacting, but that doesn't change the fact that I'm frightened."

She'd spoken to him for nearly half an hour, and when she finally hung up she wondered if her refusal to go was insensitive. She peered out of her window, but saw nothing but an empty alley and the glow of distant city lights.

The one-bedroom apartment was silent. Kitchen with breakfast bar to her right. Bedroom to her left. What if the killer had sneaked in before she'd returned home?

After a moment of contemplation, she satisfied the ghosts of concern by checking the lock, the closet, even the cupboards in the kitchen.

No killer. Of course not.

She brushed her teeth, washed off her makeup, slipped into a yellow-and-blue-flowered cotton nightgown, and rolled into bed. Bathroom light, on. Kitchen light, on.

Soon thoughts of an intruder were replaced by thoughts of Chaim, wringing his hands in the Howard Johnson's. She should have gone over, she thought. At least to reassure him.

Sleep came quickly.

The first foreign sound came even more quickly. A scratch from deep inside of Sylvia's dream.

She made nothing of it, though it did wake her momentarily. The glowing clock face by her bed read almost 2:00 a.m. She'd been asleep that long?

She rolled, and pulled in her second pillow. Sleep was one of the most wonderful sensations. Blissful sleep.

The sound again. A creak this time.

In the space of two heartbeats, Sylvia's world changed from sweet dreams of sleep to blood-stopping terror. Her eyes snapped open and she caught her breath.

She could hear nothing but silence.

Don't be ridiculous. You hear a single sound and you jump out of your skin. It's nothing. Nothing . . .

"Hello, Sylvia."

The words were whispered behind her, low, so low that she wasn't absolutely sure she'd heard them.

"If you make even a very small sound, I will bury this knife in your temple. Can you hear me?" Still whispering very low.

This time she could not mistake the words, try as she did. Someone was behind her. Someone who knew her name. Someone who had a knife.

Sylvia could not move. Her heart crashed violently. Repeatedly.

"Are you awake? You're awake. Your breathing's changed."

She could hear his heavy breathing now.

"Turn over. Let me see you."

She couldn't. *Dear God, help me!*

A cold blade touched her cheek. She clenched her eyes tight and suppressed a whimper.

"Now, now, no need to ruin things with your fear. I'm not going to kill you. Not necessarily. Unless you make noise; then I will kill you." He paused. "Roll over."

Slowly, as if rolling through thick tar, she turned.

He stood tall over the bed. A black shirt, white face. Built like a bull-dog with short cropped hair above grinning face.

There was a red scarf around his neck and a large silver knife in his gloved hand.

"Sit up," he said.

She sat up without thinking, because her mind was filled with other thoughts. She was going to die. She knew she was going to die because this was the same serial killer who'd killed eight single Jewish women in six nights.

She was a single Jewish woman and it was the seventh night. She was going to die.

The man stood looking at her for a long time, pleased with himself—or with what he was doing, or with her, she didn't know which—but pleased.

He sat down on a chair he'd brought in from the kitchen. He'd been here that long? Maybe he'd climbed the fire escape and broken the window. But why hadn't she heard him? Maybe the neighbors had heard him and called the police already.

"So, I understand that you are a female friend of Stephen's; is that so?"

Stephen? This man knew about Stephen?

"You may speak now," the killer said. "No yelling or loud noises, but you will answer my questions."

"Stephen?" she whispered.

"Stephen Friedman, yes? The Jew. You know him?" German accent.

"Yes."

"Good. What can you tell me about him?"

This killer, for whom the whole city was looking, was interested in Stephen? Maybe the man wasn't going to kill her.

"Then should I just kill you? If you don't answer me, I'll have no choice."

"He's a friend. He's a Realtor."

"Yes, I know. But what drives him? Is he religious?"

"He's . . . he's Jewish."

"But is he a man of faith? You know the difference, don't you? Does he put his hope in powers beyond him, or is he just another self-motivated fool who can't see beyond the night?"

The room felt cold. *You have to be strong. Think of a way out. Keep him happy. Maybe if you keep him happy, he won't kill you.*

"He's not really a man of Jewish faith," she said.

"Then maybe Christian, like the old man he lives with? Does he realize that the power of life is in the blood? That's why the Christians drink the blood of Christ. The power is always in the blood. It's why

I have to cut my victims. It's why I drink their blood. Do you know this?"

"No." She had to keep him talking. He was absorbed by this train of thought, so she had to let him follow it long enough for her to think of a way out of this madness.

"No, of course not. He isn't easily discouraged; that's good."

Stephen again.

"No."

How did this man know Stephen? A disgruntled client? A Jew-hater certainly. But why?

"Do you want to know why I'm doing it? Why I killed all of those Jews?"

She didn't, but she couldn't bring herself to say no.

"Because it makes me strong. Pure. What most Aryan purists won't tell you is that the Jews have more power than any other race—that's a spiritual matter we don't have time to go into. Hitler's solution was to eradicate them. Not a bad plan, but shortsighted. Better to take their power." He sat slightly hunched over. Unbreaking stare.

"Have you ever tasted another person's blood, Sylvia?"

"No."

"Its flavor changes with the donor's mood. Anguish, Sylvia. The greater the anguish, the sweeter the blood."

His talk made her sick. She'd recovered enough to speak in a reasonably normal voice.

"Why are you telling me all of this?"

"Because it excites me."

"Then you're a sick man," she said.

He chuckled. "You remind me of Ruth. She was a strong woman too. So strong, you Jews." He shuddered. "I'm tempted."

Tempted to kill her. Sylvia said nothing.

"I'm playing him like a mouse, Sylvia. He doesn't know, of course. He thinks that he's outwitting me. That's good; I need him to feel like he's outwitting me. It raises his hopes. But in the end I will finish what my father started."

For a long time he just looked at her. She knew she should be saying something, distracting him, stalling him. Instead she held very still and silently cried for him to leave.

She would alert the police. Stephen. Chaim. The serial killer was sitting in her room.

"What's your name?" she asked.

The killer suddenly stood. "Turn around."

She instinctively pulled her sheets tight.

"Face the wall. Now."

"You promised—"

"And if you don't do exactly as I say, I may change my promise."

She faced the wall away from him.

The sound of cloth flapped behind her. He'd pulled the scarf off of his neck and snapped it open. It whooshed over her head and then smothered her face.

She wanted to tear it free, but resisted the impulse.

His gloved hand pulled the cloth down into her mouth. He tied it tight behind her head. She could breathe through her nostrils, but her mouth was effectively gagged.

"Step off the bed."

She followed his order and stood shaking.

He jerked her arms back and bound them together with string. Then he ripped tape from a roll and strapped her wrists. Her hands felt as if they were in a plaster cast.

"Lie down on your back."

Again she did as he instructed. It took him a minute at most to tie her legs to the bed posts and her neck to the headboard. Another strap of tape went over her mouth.

He wasn't taking any chances of her escaping, but that was good, she kept telling herself. That meant he was going to let her live. She lay still and let him finish his work.

When he was done, he stood beside the bed and looked down at her. The moments stretched in a long vacuous silence. He grinned.

"Forgive me, but I've changed my mind," he said.

Then he reached down and flicked his knife across her left wrist. Pain flashed up her arm.

He'd cut her!

"Good-bye, Jew."

His fist came out of nowhere and crashed into her temple.

The room went dark.

32

EVEN FROM HER SMALL ROOM IN THE BASEMENT OF THE commandant's quarters, Martha could hear the faint thunder of the Russian artillery to the east. Braun had been beside himself for a week now, taken to muttering from time to time, scurrying from room to room and always to the room down the hall from her own, "the vault," as he called it, which he kept bolted and locked at all times.

Her door was closed now, but he'd stomped past not ten minutes ago, and she hadn't heard him return. He was in his vault. She sat on her bed, staring at the door, willing it to remain closed. Little Esther slept peacefully in a bundle of wool blankets behind her.

His demands had become more absurd as of late. Wash the floor, wash it again, scrub the walls, scrub them again. Scrub them again. He seemed intent on making her life as difficult as possible. She'd given birth four days after Ruth's hanging, and it was a boy after all. She named him David. The barracks had been flooded with hope, perhaps even more than after Esther's birth. See, the commandant wasn't completely evil. He had allowed Martha and Esther and now little David to live because of Ruth's sacrifice.

For five wonderful days, Martha had nursed and coddled the two babies, Esther and David, giving herself completely to the mandate before her. Save the children. At all costs, save the children.

Then a guard came and told her that she was to leave the barracks and be Braun's personal servant. She was to bring Esther. And David? No, not the boy. The boy would stay with Rachel. Bring only Esther.

She'd kissed her son and left in tears, clinging to Esther.

That night, not knowing what the commandant intended for her, Martha had served dinner to Braun and a woman, Emily, whom she recognized from one of the other barracks. Was he going to hang her in Emily's stead? What would happen to her precious David?

The commandant had dismissed Martha at the end of the meal, but she listened with her ear to the door. Emily had squealed with joy, then gasped in horror not two minutes later. What Braun could have said to cause such a reaction, Martha could hardly guess.

The woman's body hung from the gates the next morning. Then, with full view of the body out the picture window, Martha served Braun breakfast while he made his intentions for her utterly clear. She was alive only because of Ruth's sacrifice. She was to care for Esther, but under no circumstances would she be allowed to see her own child, David, even though David would also be allowed to live. He owed this to Ruth.

It was Braun's twisted method of punishment. Of extending hope while maintaining the power and will to withdraw it at any moment. *Please me here, and I will allow your son to live there.*

She'd served him for five months. Or was it six? And no, she was serving Esther, not the commandant. He beat her with his stick on occasion for not cleaning well enough or quickly enough or burning a batch of buns, but otherwise he never touched her.

His footsteps clumped back down the hall. Martha instinctively put her hand on the baby and slowed her breathing. How many nights had she imagined sneaking upstairs to Braun's bedroom and sticking a knife in his throat? If it weren't for the babies, she might have done it.

The door swung open and the commandant stood in the door frame, face drawn, collar unbuttoned and skewed. He stared at her like a man who wanted consolation. She turned her face away.

"We've received orders to evacuate the prisoners," he said.

She looked back and stood, stunned by the news.

"Those who are able to march will be gone in the hour. The weak and the sick will stay."

Why was he telling her this?

"I have been ordered to stay," he said. "You will stay as well."

Her heart hammered. "David?"

"Rachel will stay. So will your son."

If he'd said that David was going, she might have flown at him. The Russians could break through any week and liberate the camp—surely Braun knew his days as a god were numbered. By the haggard look on his face, he did know.

"Follow me," he said and turned for the stairs.

Martha checked Esther, saw that she was still sleeping, and hurried up the stairs after the commandant. He stood at the picture window overlooking the winter-locked camp. Long lines of prisoners filed through the windblown snow toward the front gate. The wind chill had to be well below zero.

"How far are they going?" Martha asked.

Braun sighed. "Seventy kilometers. Let's put it this way: I am extending your life by making you stay."

The women weren't dressed for a one-kilometer march through the snow, much less seventy. They walked proudly, as if to their freedom, but half of them didn't even have coats or proper shoes. Martha doubted that this was Braun's idea, but it would have fitted his methods perfectly. Give them hope, make them think the day of their deliverance had finally arrived, then march them to their deaths.

The door to her old barracks suddenly opened, and out came a troop of women led by Golda. Golda! Martha stepped closer to the window and searched for Rachel's face. She would be the one holding a bundle, her little David. Others whom she recognized followed.

"It would have been easier to send them all to Auschwitz last month," Braun said bitterly. "I told them that. They are too concerned with covering their tracks. Now even Major Hoppe will be leaving. And who stays behind to cover their backsides?"

The last woman spilled from Martha's old barracks—no Rachel.

"It's inhuman," Martha spat. "For such a proud race, don't the Germans even know how to surrender with honor?" Her words surprised her. It was a bold accusation, something Ruth would say.

Braun only shrugged into his coat and opened the door to a blistering wind. The door slammed shut.

Where would they keep the ones who stayed behind? Maybe the commandant would allow her to see David. Maybe even to care for him!

Martha stared, enraged, at the lines of women marching steadily from the camp. But David was still alive. Esther was sleeping peacefully in the basement. They were her concern. For their sakes and for Ruth's, she couldn't allow herself to do anything stupid in her grief over these other women. Grief was useless anyway. Just because she had a warm bed and plenty of food while the rest marched to their deaths didn't mean she had the power to change any of it. She would put what little power she had into protecting the hope of David and Esther.

She turned from the window, ran down the stairs, and was about to enter her room when she noticed that the padlock to Braun's vault lay open.

Open? He never left the lock unlatched! She glanced into her room, saw that the baby hadn't moved, and stood frozen by indecision. Silence filled the house, empty except for her and Esther. Outside, five thousand women blindly marched to their deaths. What kind of courage would it take for her to step into this room and see what the commandant had hidden for so long?

In the distance, a large gun boomed like thunder.

Martha walked quickly to the door, unlatched the lock, and shoved the door open before she could stop herself. The room was dark. If Braun caught her, she would pay a dreadful price.

She found the light switch and eased it up. Twin incandescent bulbs popped to life, baring a sight that made no sense to her at first. She saw the paintings first—a dozen, maybe two—stacked against one wall. Degas, Cézanne, and Renoir—she recognized them from her father's art books. A fortune. Behind her, the house slept on.

She stepped in and glanced around. To her left stood a writing desk with neat stacks of passports, ledgers, a few books, a typewriter, and a quill pen.

The floor was littered with piles of artifacts. A suit of armor that looked very old, with a large shield and sword, the type she imagined a gladiator might wear. There were piles of china and more paintings and spears and several chests. Shelves lined two of the walls, and on the shelves, carefully sorted relics, gold and silver and bronze. An entire wall of Jewish artifacts.

Museum pieces. Spoils of war! Martha clamped her mouth shut and swallowed. Such wealth! Braun had been busy before his assignment to Toruń.

She stepped up to a shelf and lifted a gold candlestick. If she wasn't mistaken, this very piece came from a collection she'd seen in Hungary, although she couldn't remember which. How was that possible? Had he been in Hungary before coming here?

She caught sight of a small, very old mahogany box, perhaps thirty centimeters square, beside the candlestick. She found it familiar but couldn't say why. She set down the candlestick and lifted the lid. Five golden spheres lay embedded in purple velvet. They varied in size and shape, each a few centimeters in diameter, flat like river-washed stones. Each had a six-pointed star stamped on its surface.

Martha's heart nearly seized in her chest. She knew these! They were the Stones of David! Her father had known the collector, who had secured these very stones just before the war—he'd taken Martha to see them several years ago. Pure gold gilded to the five stones David had chosen to slay Goliath, they said. Over the course of history they'd gone missing for hundreds of years at a time.

She reached out and picked one of them up between her thumb and forefinger. This one Stone in her hand was worth many millions of forints, pounds, dollars—take your pick. The entire collection was worth more than her father's entire estate, he'd told her.

What if she were to slip it into her pocket? Not the entire collection, of course, just the one Stone. With all the relics in this room, Braun surely didn't inspect this box often. He might never notice.

She cupped her left hand around her right to steady it. On the other hand, these five Stones could be the most valuable artifacts in the entire collection. For all she knew, Braun inspected them every day.

She set the stone back in its velvet housing, stepped back, and gazed around, pulse throbbing. A treasure trove worth hundreds of millions. She lifted the lid to one of the trunks. Brilliant jewels. Ancient gold coins. How many museums had he raided for these? And how many of these had been confiscated from Jews? She stared at a diamond necklace with large rubies displayed in a glass case. It alone might be worth several million. And the coins?

Martha took a deep breath and let it out slowly. *What do you think you'll do? Pack all of this in a purse, grab the babies, climb over the fence, and hike to the Baltic Sea?*

She closed the box that held the Stones of David.

But one small Stone . . . What if she were to find a way to keep it in Jewish hands? The reward alone could take care of the children for a very long time.

David and Esther were the true Stones of David. Israel. The seed of Abraham. Ironic that one of the most valuable icons in Jewish history should now be in the hands of their enemy.

She was about to turn when she saw a leather book behind the box. She wasn't sure what made her pick it up and open it. It was a journal, and it contained the names of hundreds of women.

Slowly the meaning of this book came to her. What she held in her hands was a trophy of Gerhard Braun's serial killings. She wanted to throw up.

This was a record of his red-scarf game. Only it wasn't a game. It was a ritual, very different from the mass murders at other camps.

Martha replaced the journal, slipped from the vault, set the latch back exactly as she'd found it, and tiptoed to her room.

She decided then that, at the right time, she would take the journal.

And maybe one of the Stones.

33

Toruń
February 28, 1945
Night

THE WAR WAS COMING TO AN END. YOUNG ROTH BRAUN KNEW that, even though the radio announcers insisted it wasn't. He knew it because he'd heard father talking about it. The Russians were coming, Gerhard said.

Roth had been to Toruń six times since he'd first seen the woman hanging from the gate. If his mother had been more cooperative, he would have gone at least ten or twelve times, but she insisted that his spending time at a labor camp, away from her, was too risky. But with bombs falling on Berlin, her perspective changed.

Each visit had lasted a week. Once ten days, when the supply routes had been clogged by a bomb. Before each visit, he'd spend a month dreaming of what his days at the camp would be like. There were no other boys. No games, nothing to do really, except to watch the camp and dream about what Father did to the women.

There was nothing else in the world he wanted more than to serve the power, and thereby gain more power.

The Jew servant, Martha, lived in the basement with the baby, Esther, and Roth was on his third visit when he first began to think about killing the baby.

He grew more powerful every time Father let him drink the blood and chant the oaths late at night. Gerhard spoke until dawn about how many leaders in the Third Reich secretly followed Adolf Hitler in his fascination with the occult. But it was a privileged membership, a secret society, reserved for the superior even among Germans.

Roth decided on his third visit that he would be one of those superior people. He could hardly think of anything else. He was bursting at the seams to reveal his plans to his friends in Berlin, despite his promise not to tell.

He finally broke down one afternoon and told Hanz that he drank the blood of Jews when he visited the labor camp where his father was the commandant. Hanz had laughed and Roth had beaten his face with his fist. When his hand began to hurt, he grabbed a rock and pounded the boy until he stopped moving.

That night, after lying awake for two hours, still exhilarated from beating Hanz, he decided he would definitely kill Martha's baby. For one thing, she was just a Jew. For another thing, he was sure that there was more to Gerhard's ritual than drinking blood. His father was actually responsible for killing the women. That was a big part of it.

Every night until he returned to Toruń, Roth tossed and turned, dreaming of how he would sacrifice the baby and drink her blood. The fact that Father had allowed the child to live in his house made no sense to him.

Father had told him how he'd selected Martha and her baby to be hanged, and how Ruth had taken her place. But in Roth's mind, Martha had been chosen to die. If she lived, she would be the only Jew chosen by Gerhard to actually survive.

The only Jew to outwit his father. To take back all the power that he'd harvested all these years. This one woman and her child could be the undoing of his father. And, by extension, of Roth.

He despised Martha. She was a Jew—even without the scarf, why would Father allow her to live? He had a weak spot for the baby, and Roth thought it was because Gerhard had had a weak spot for her mother—Ruth.

By killing the baby, Roth would gain power and save his father from his own weakness.

On his fourth visit, he plotted and watched and waited for the opportunity. If his father learned of his plans, he would probably forbid it, saying that he was too young. If he just did it, he was sure Gerhard would see the wisdom of it and praise him.

The closest he got to killing the baby on that visit was when he sneaked down the hall late one night and peeked into the Jew's room. But the servant was asleep with the baby in her arms—he would never be able to take it without waking her. He'd returned to Berlin determined to rethink his strategy.

Three weeks later he returned to Toruń. Three nights had passed and he couldn't wait any longer. He would either kill the baby tonight or be caught trying. Roth was agitated; Gerhard hadn't brought a woman up to the house for three nights.

At dinner, he asked his father why.

"Tomorrow night," Gerhard said. He'd nearly finished a whole bottle of wine. "You have to learn to pace yourself. Control, boy. Control."

Roth thought about that.

"If I wanted to show some of my power, would you let me?"

His father seemed confused by the question. "How?"

"Why can't I have a servant?"

"Well . . . you can, boy."

"Then I want Martha," he said.

"No, not Martha. She has a debt to pay to me."

"What better way to show her your power than making her obey your son?"

Gerhard laughed. "Well, then, since you asked, Martha can be your servant tomorrow."

"Tonight," Roth said.

"Tonight? What can she do for you tonight?"

"Cut some wood. It's cold, and I would like a fire."

Gerhard seemed amused. "So tonight it is, then! She's in the kitchen; call her out."

"Not now. Later, when she's already settled for the night. That will show who the boss is."

His father grinned. "I can see you will make a very good soldier."

Roth waited two hours. His father had drunk himself into a warm stupor in his bedroom, and the house was quiet. He told Father that he would have his fire now. Gerhard laughed and waved him on.

The stairs creaked as he descended into the basement where Martha had gone to bed for the night. He stopped in front of her room and lifted his fist. Should he knock?

The thrill of what he was about to do shook his body. He knew why, of course. He was feeling the power of true hope. The kind of desire that had made Lucifer denounce God. He had the power of Satan in him because he'd stolen the hope of Father's Jews with him. It really did work, just as Gerhard had said.

He knocked, because it seemed like the right thing to do.

The door opened a few seconds later, and Martha stared at him, dressed in a dirty night dress.

"I am cold, and I want a fire," he said. "Go outside and chop some firewood and build me a fire."

She stared at him, confused.

"You have to obey me. I am your master."

"You're just a boy. It's not very cold. It's already late."

"If you question me, then my father will take your baby away from you. I have his authority now."

She looked too shocked to react, and Roth felt the thrill of his power over her. Martha started to say something but thought better of it. She grabbed the tattered German coat Gerhard had given her, stepped into the hall, and pulled the door closed behind her.

Roth marched up the stairs ahead of her. He didn't want to give her any ideas. It was bad enough that his hands were shaking like leaves in anticipation already. He put them in his pockets, hoping she hadn't noticed. The pocketknife he'd sharpened felt cold against his fingers.

As soon as he heard the back door close, Roth tiptoed back down the stairs. He pushed the door to Martha's room open.

The baby lay on the bed, like a lump of laundry.

He could hear her breathing. He could hear himself breathing. The room was nearly dark. Quiet. Peaceful. In a way he couldn't explain, he felt sorry for the baby.

Standing there in the doorway, Roth was suddenly horrified. Could he really kill a baby? What kind of power did that require, really?

It didn't matter. He'd dreamed of this moment and told himself that he'd probably be scared. But it was the power of Lucifer in him that would overpower the weakness he felt.

Roth stepped toward the bed.

He couldn't hear the sound of wood chopping outside, probably because he was in the basement. But he had to hurry.

He stepped to the bed and pulled the wool cover down. The baby lay on her side, facing the wall, breathing steadily.

Roth pulled out the pocketknife and pried the blade out.

There was great power in this baby's life. Esther and others like her were the hope of the Jews. And as Gerhard said, the greatest power in the universe is hope. Without it, no one could become like God.

Killing the baby was Satan's hope.

Saving the baby was God's hope.

In the end, hope was the fuel that empowered both sides, and right now Lucifer was winning.

This was the war.

But standing over the child, Roth couldn't ignore the fact that his heart was hammering with more than hope. What if she cried out? What if he couldn't cut her skin with the blade? Or what if he became too frightened to actually do it?

Give me strength.

He immediately felt a surge of confidence. Father never should have let the child live in the first place. Gerhard should have killed Ruth and Martha and both of the children. Now Roth would finish the job, or at least this part of the job.

He lifted the baby's small wrist and turned it so that he could cut the veins. A terrible shaking overtook Roth's body. He suddenly felt like throwing up.

But he knew that this was only his weakness. It would pass.

He rested the blade against the baby's wrists and whispered another prayer.

Please give me strength to become like you.

"What are you doing?"

Roth whipped around at the sound of the servant's voice. Martha stood in the doorway, eyes white in the dim light. Roth's heart bolted into his throat.

"What are you doing?" Her voice was higher. Louder.

Roth couldn't move.

Martha saw the knife in his hand. She screamed and flew at him like a ghost. Her voice was so loud, so piercing, that Roth thought she might actually be a ghost.

He jumped to the side at the last moment. Her fist beat on his shoulder, but she turned her attention to the baby and scooped it up in her arms.

Cut them! Cut them both now, while her attention is on the baby!

Roth swung his knife at Martha's head. It stuck her arm, but he couldn't tell if he'd cut her. He had to go for her throat. Or the baby's . . .

"What is this?"

Father loomed in the doorway, scowling. He glanced from Roth, who stood with the knife, ready to strike again, and the Jew, who sheltered the baby.

"What is going on?"

"I'm killing the baby, Father."

Silence filled the room. The Jew began to sob softly.

"Get out of here!"

At first Roth thought that Father was yelling at Martha. Leave the baby for my son to kill and get out of here!

But then he saw that Gerhard was glaring at him. Why was he so angry? And in front of the Jew!

Gerhard stretched his arm toward the stairs behind him. "Get out of here!"

"Father—"

"Now!"

Roth felt himself blush.

"You can't let them live," he said. "If you do, they'll be the only ones who escape you. They have to die. Why can't I kill one?"

"Out!" his father screamed.

Roth stared at him, stunned by the anger. Surely his father understood that they had to die.

"I said *out*," Gerhard snapped.

Roth hurried past his father and ran up the stairs. A pile of wood sat by the stove. Maybe it had already been cut. He walked to the window overlooking the camp and stared into the darkness.

He decided then that he hated his father.

If Martha and her child lived, he would hunt them down and kill them. He had to. They had been sentenced by the scarf.

34

C HAIM WASN'T SURE WHY THE BLACK CAR HAD ALARMED HIM
so much. Perhaps because of those three words spoken by Stephen two
days ago: *Be careful, Rabbi.*

What if there really was danger? What if someone else was after what
Stephen was after? And what if he, Chaim Leveler, was about to be squeezed
in the middle?

And what if there was someone in that black car, watching him? Or
watching to see if Stephen came home?

He'd called Sylvia at eight in the morning. No answer. He'd called her
office. She was likely running late and on her way to work.

It was time to put an end to this craziness. If he couldn't find Stephen
himself, he would go to the police.

Chaim approached Rachel Spritzer's old apartment complex, whispering prayers for Stephen's safety. Chaim had no indication that the lad was
anywhere near here, but his fixation on the place made perfect sense. It was,
after all, his mother's home. And Stephen had found a safe.

He drove from the north, toward the front of the building. A repair
crew was working on the corner today. One man with a yellow hard hat
wielded a gas-powered jackhammer in an area cordoned off with orange
caution signs. What a racket that thing made.

He crept past the house—no sign of life. For all he knew, Stephen was
actually in some trouble. Kidnapped, or worse. He couldn't ignore the
possibility any longer.

The construction worker looked at him as he passed, smiled, and returned a wave. A bit odd to see that these days.

The building adjacent to Rachel Spritzer's was another abandoned apartment building. Was it remotely possible that Stephen was in there, watching him drive by at this very moment? He'd said that he was in a hotel, but Chaim wouldn't put this past him.

Chaim *humphed* and parked the car by the alley behind the building. He climbed out and headed for a back door on the off chance it was open. Even here, the jackhammer rattled his ears.

The door stood ajar. He stepped in and let his eyes adjust to the dim light.

"Stephen?"

No answer.

"Stephen!"

His voiced bounced around with the jackhammer. A quick look upstairs wouldn't hurt—he'd come this far. He mounted the steps and made his way up through the floors, calling out Stephen's name at each stop.

Last floor. He poked up his head, saw that it was stripped and vacant, and started back down. What was that across the room there? A picture on the wall next to the window. Someone had been here, maybe not so long ago. The window overlooked Rachel's apartment.

Curious, Chaim climbed up and walked across the room. What he saw stopped him. The photograph was of Ruth, the picture Stephen left in his room for a day before breaking in through his window. A bed lay in the corner, and next to it cans of food—half opened, half still sealed. Beans, corn, cranberry sauce. The area was cordoned off with tires and sections of broken wall.

Chaim had found Stephen's . . . place.

"My, my," he muttered. "My, my, my, my. What have you gone and done, my boy?"

What had come over his Stephen? The boy was obsessed with this treasure.

He turned and called out loudly. "Stephen?"

Still no answer. Wherever Stephen was, it looked as though he intended to return. Chaim walked into the space and turned around in a slow circle, imagining what it would be like to sleep here for a few days. Whatever had taken hold of Stephen, he'd lost himself in this thing. And so quickly!

Chaim looked out the window at Rachel's apartment. Was it possible that the Stones of David really were hidden in there?

"Hello?"

He jerked around. A young woman looked at him from the stairs.

"May I help you?"

"Yes, hello. Yes. Do you know Stephen?"

"Stephen?" She was a petite girl, pretty, with bright eyes and dark braided hair heavy with beads. "There's a lot of Stephens around."

He walked out of the square. "I'm looking for a Stephen who is tall. Thin. Dark hair. A Realtor." He pointed back at the shrine. "This is his place. I am his friend."

She glanced at the picture of Ruth. "Is that so? For all I now you're an old kook looking for a scam."

"Really?" He cocked his right eyebrow. "I strike you as an old kook. Funny, but I've never actually been called that before. I just want to talk to him. He lives with me, you see. If I can't find him, I will have to report him missing to the police. They'll want to search this building."

She stared at him evenly, expression now flat.

"Can you at least tell me if he's okay?"

"He's fine. What's your name?"

"Chaim Leveler. Stephen calls me Rabbi, even though I'm not."

"You only want to talk?"

She knew where he was! "Definitely. Just to know that he's safe."

"You swear not to tell anybody about this place?"

"Of course not."

"Swear it."

For the second time in a week, he broke his vow not to swear. "I swear it."

"Follow me. He isn't going to like this."

—ᴡᴡᴡ—

"THERE IT is again," Lars said. "The sound is different. Faster."

Except for Roth, they all stood with ears pressed against the bared apartment wall, listening intently to the sound of a strange thumping that didn't match the racket outside.

Lars straightened. "He's digging under us."

They'd heard the hum through most of the night, but it was morning before Lars suggested that it might not be traffic. Then the thumping in the street had broken the silence—a lone worker breaking up the sidewalk. After an hour, the worker had made no progress, and they knew that something was wrong.

Roth crossed to the window and peered down at the construction worker again. It did make sense—what better way to cover up a jackhammer underneath the building than to run a second jackhammer on the street.

If so, the Realtor's gall was unprecedented. Roth grinned. *Come to me, Stephen. I've been waiting so long. So very, very long.*

Roth descended the stairs. His men followed. He shoved the basement door open and stepped into the concrete room. A steady thumping echoed softly through the entire structure. He faced the east wall, then the west. It was impossible to pinpoint the source of the sound.

Lars ran his fingers along one wall, listening. "It could be from the street, but I don't think so. It's too loud. I think he's actually planning to break in through the floor."

"Idiot!" Claude said. "He'll come up to a rifle in his mouth."

"No," Roth said. "We can't be sure where he'll come up. Even if we could, he'll drop back down and be gone if he sees us. I want him, and I want him alive."

He walked to the doors lining the basement and opened them one by one. He could feel the vibration run through his feet—stronger on the east side away from the boiler room, if his imagination wasn't playing tricks on him.

The worker on the street was a cover-up. Unless the wrong person happened by, no one would know he wasn't who he seemed to be.

Who would have imagined this, tunneling of all things? Then again, if Roth was in his position, he might have done the same. There must be an old sewer or something below the foundation.

"It is critical that we allow him to enter," he said, turning back. "One man stays in the stairwell—Claude. The rest of you, finish upstairs. The moment he breaks through, key your radio three times. Watch him. Take no other action." Roth frowned and then grunted. "Let the mole dig."

35

I'N THERE?" CHAIM SHOUTED. A HORRENDOUS CLAMOR RANG FROM the hole in the ground.

"It's wet down there, Rabbi. You sure you want to do this?" the girl asked.

"Stephen's down in that hole? Is he a prisoner?"

She laughed. "I suppose that's a matter of perspective. Come on."

The dog that had come home with Stephen last week braved the noise to lick his hand. It whined and backed up several steps.

"It's okay, puppy," the girl said. "We're almost done."

The dog retreated out the door, tail between her legs.

The girl lowered herself into the hole and disappeared.

Chaim took a deep breath and swung his legs into the sewer. "My, my, my. What have you done?"

The tunnel glowed under a string of lights. Muddy water covered his leather shoes. Chaim covered his ears and waded toward the pounding.

At first all he saw was a rear end and legs protruding from a hole in the tunnel's wall. The person was operating a jackhammer or something inside the hole, up at an angle. A strange contraption dangled free from the ceiling.

The girl slapped the person's backside. The hammering stopped.

Chaim didn't recognize the man who pulled himself out of the hole. White dust covered a mask and glasses. He looked freshly buttered and rolled in flour. The man saw Chaim, rubbed the lenses, and then pushed them to his forehead.

"Rabbi?"

He heard the voice and knew immediately. "Stephen! I didn't recognize you. What on earth are you doing down here?"

Stephen looked at the girl.

"He said he was going to call the police if I didn't bring him down," she said.

Stephen looked back into the hole, stricken.

"You're tunneling up?" Chaim asked.

Stephen didn't answer.

"Isn't this city property you're tearing up?"

"We're going to fix it," Stephen said.

Looking at the boy now, Chaim knew that he could not hope to stop him. He wasn't even sure he should try. In fact, he probably *would* do more service to Stephen if he helped him, as Gerik had suggested.

"That's Rachel Spritzer's basement up there, isn't it?"

"Um . . . yes."

"The Stones of David? They really are inside?"

"Well . . . I think so."

"And the front door is no longer open to you?"

"No."

"My, my, my." Chaim shook his head. "I do love your spirit. Could you get arrested for doing this?"

"I . . . I don't think we will. The new owners don't want anything to do with the police. They're after the Stones too."

"I see."

"How . . . how did you find me?"

"Detective work." Chaim tapped his head. "My powers of deduction. I think to myself, where would Stephen seek love and happiness, and I narrow it down to two possibilities. One, in Sylvia's arms, or two, the sewer under Rachel Spritzer's apartment. I checked with Sylvia, and her arms were empty, so I rushed here."

The girl chuckled. A crooked grin twisted Stephen's mouth.

"How can I help?" Chaim asked.

"You're serious?"

"This is about a girl named Esther, isn't it? Love. And about your inheritance. I'm not sure I can operate that monster, but anything else, you name it."

A thought seemed to flip a light switch behind Stephen's eyes. No longer concerned with any threat presented by Chaim's sudden appearance, he stuck his head in the hole and pulled out a large jackhammer. The handle thumped to the ground, and Melissa helped him lean it against the wall. He grabbed a flashlight and dived back into the hole, all but disappearing this time.

"My name's Melissa," the girl said, hand extended.

"Pleased to know you, Melissa. How deep is the hole?"

"Seven feet, about."

"How far to go?"

"I'm surprised he hasn't broken through yet."

Stephen slid out, ignoring the dirt that encrusted his stomach. "I'm eight inches through the floor. If Sweeney's right, that leaves four inches." His eyes darted around. "The drill. Hand me the drill."

Chaim stood back and watched them. Melissa unhooked a large red drill from the ceiling and handed it to Stephen. "How long is this bit?" the boy asked. "Six inches? That should work, right?" His frantic pace would impair his judgment.

He virtually threw himself back into the hole and wiggled up till only his muddy tennis shoes stuck out. His voice echoed back after a moment.

"What's he saying?" Melissa asked.

Chaim stuck his head in. "What?"

"Plug it in," Stephen said. "Power!"

"He says to plug it in," Chaim told Melissa.

"Oh. Suppose that would help." She switched the jackhammer's cord for the drill's and then swatted his shoe.

"What's he doing?" Chaim asked.

"Playing it safe. Despite the distraction, there's a possibility that whoever's in there has heard us. He's drilling a small hole to check it out before he breaks in."

Stephen's feet suddenly wiggled in farther. For a moment they remained still.

"I think he's in." Melissa looked into the hole. "Stephen?"

He suddenly scrambled backward, as if he'd met a brood of vipers. He piled out and stripped off his glasses.

"We got a problem. They're in the basement!"

"They're inside? How do you know?" Melissa demanded.

Stephen took two splashing steps through the water and wheeled back. "Oh, man. Oh, man, this isn't good."

"How do you know?"

"I heard someone cough, that's how I know. And the light's on. You have to get Sweeney."

"You want him to stop?"

"We have to figure this out." He paced, desperate. Chaim felt his own pulse quicken. "Get him!" Stephen snapped.

Melissa ran down the tunnel and up the ladder.

Stephen flexed his jaw and slowly beat his head against the concrete wall. "They heard us. They're in the basement."

"There has to be something you can do," Chaim said.

"They probably have it already."

"Can I go in? The front door?"

Stephen ignored him. He dived back into the hole, pulled himself way in, lay still for a moment, and then slid back out.

"They're definitely in there."

"I'm sorry—"

"Please." Stephen held up a hand and closed his eyes. "Just let me think."

THEY STOOD in silence, feet planted in six inches of water. Sweeney, Stephen, Melissa, and the rabbi. Stephen clenched his teeth, furious. He fought a terrible urge to run across the street and slam through the front door. Maybe the dogs were dead; maybe he could bluff his way in; maybe he could race down the stairs, grab the box, and lock himself in the coal room while Sweeney finished the digging. Another five minutes of hard hammering would surely crack open the hole.

"We have to get them out of the basement," Sweeney said.

"Smoke 'em out," Melissa said.

Stephen glared at her. "Well, sure, that's just brilliant. We could build a fire down here and let the smoke seep through the little hole I drilled."

"Lighten up."

He lowered his head and kneaded his skull.

"There's got to be a way," Sweeney insisted. "Why don't we burn down the building?" They looked at him. "Strike that."

"You need to get them out of that building, correct?" Chaim asked.

"Yes. At least out of the basement."

"For how long?"

"There's about four inches of concrete, but without any support behind, it's going to crack pretty quickly. Maybe fifteen minutes."

"Plus time to repair the damage?" Chaim pressed.

"Forget that—"

"No, hear him out," Sweeney said. "What's on your mind, old man?"

"Maybe nothing, but it might start you thinking. The city has very specific evacuation policies for fires. If a fire breaks out in any building, they immediately evacuate not only that building, but any building next to it. It's the law. They have to verify safety before allowing the occupants back into their homes."

"So what are you saying?" Sweeney asked. "We start a fire?"

"No, we could never do that. But I know the fire department, and I know that if this building were to catch fire, the city would force the evacuation of all the buildings—"

"That's it!" Stephen said. "That's it! Right?" His eyes were like saucers.

Sweeney smiled. "Actually . . ."

Stephen broke for the manhole.

"Stephen? Where are you going?" the rabbi demanded.

"To start a fire," he yelled. "Come on!"

36

"GET THE GUNS," ROTH SAID. "EVERYTHING, IN THE CAR. NOW!" Claude ran for the stairs. Three fire engines had screeched to a halt in front of the building across the street. Thick black smoke boiled out of the windows on the upper floor. He could see no flames, only smoke.

The construction worker had run out to the street, heaved the jackhammer and the signs into the back of a car with the help of an older man, and then careened around the corner.

Still no sign of a breakthrough in the basement.

"He's burned himself out," Lars said. "The fool stumbled over a gas can or something—"

"Quiet," Roth snapped.

The game had escalated. It was more than he'd hoped for. The others had no clue what was happening, but they weren't meant to. This was between him and the Jew.

Naturally there was the possibility of failure, but that was part of the exhilaration—success was still a hope.

Lucifer's hope.

In reality, the possibility of failure was very small. Roth was far too powerful. He just had to bring that power to play in a reasoned, methodical way, as he had last night.

He would be out of the country before anyone figured out that he was connected to the killings. This thought made Roth feel warm.

The streets filled with running people. Firemen quickly strung a hose, yelling at the gathering crowd to stay back. How likely was it that something had caught fire and was forcing the Jew to shut down?

A fist pounded on the front door. "Fire Marshal. Open up!"

Roth took a deep breath and turned from the building. He glanced at the car. Claude slammed the trunk on the last of the equipment they'd retrieved from the third floor and nodded. Roth walked to the door and pulled it open.

A fireman stood in a yellow slicker. "I'm sorry, but you'll have to evacuate this building."

He looked past the fireman and gazed at the fire. "Is everything under control? What happened?"

"We need everyone out. Don't worry, it won't touch this building."

"Then we'll stay here." He began to close the door.

The man leaned forward, barring the door open. "I'm sorry, but you have to leave. City ordinance. No more than half an hour, with any luck. Let's go."

Roth motioned Claude out with a nod. "You won't be entering the building?"

"Just to clear it." The man waited while they filed out. "Anyone else inside?"

"No."

"Wait here." The man ran for the stairwell and disappeared.

"Spread out along the street," Roth ordered his men. "Keep your eyes open. No one enters without my knowing."

The fireman ran out, slammed the door, and stretched a piece of wide yellow tape over to seal it. "This one's clear. Stay back on the street. We'll let you know when it's safe. Unauthorized entry is a crime, understand?"

Roth ignored him and looked at the burning building. Three police cruisers had joined the party. Stephen was up to something.

Think, Roth. Outthink the Jew.

———

"GO, GO!" Sweeney yelled down the manhole. "They're out!"

Stephen turned to the rabbi. "Cut the lights!"

The string of lights went out. He scrambled into the hole, put his full weight into the jackhammer, and squeezed the lever. The machine shook furiously in his hands. Four inches. With any luck, the Germans wouldn't hear the sound now that they had evacuated. Not that it mattered. With a little more luck, the slab he was pounding on would break free along the circle of holes he'd drilled while they waited for the fire trucks to respond.

They were taking three calculated risks, any of which could sink them. The most obvious was the whole arson bit. They'd laid down slabs of old asbestos on the top two floors, piled the slabs with tires, and lit the stacks on fire. Unless the fire department responded slowly, the smoldering tires would be extinguished and the building cleared in short order, though hopefully not too short. The stunt might cost them a slap on the wrist, but they already had their story in place. Sweeney wanted to see how much smoke tires made. He'd taken precautions. If there was a law against burning tires, he was totally unaware of it.

The second risk was possibly being discovered by the fire marshal down in the manhole, operating a jackhammer. To this end, Sweeney had closed the door to the coal room and presumably pulled the mound of insulation over the cover as planned.

The third risk was beyond them entirely. Stephen wasn't positive how many men Braun actually had over there. What if he'd hidden one away in the coal room with a gun?

He would find out soon enough.

So close. So, so close after so much effort. Stephen redoubled his pressure on the jackhammer. "Come on, baby, break. Break!"

He'd drilled twenty holes—surely that had weakened the slab. Sweeney had assured him there was no rebar in the floor, said they would've run into it by now if there was. Man, if there was rebar, they were dead. He would kill—

The jackhammer suddenly surged forward. He released the trigger. Chunks of large concrete lay over the bit. Above, a gray circle of light.

The breakthrough was so sudden, so complete, that Stephen wasn't sure it had actually happened.

"Guys?"

Stephen jerked his head up, slammed it into the ceiling and ducked back down, hardly aware of the pain. He lowered himself back into the sewer. Pitch black.

"Guys?"

"Here," said Sweeney.

"We're in!"

"We're in?"

"We're in!"

Stephen tugged at the jackhammer and jumped out of the way as it hurtled out of the drain.

Splash.

"What was that?" Sweeney asked.

"The jackhammer."

Stephen clambered back up the hole, saw that the broken concrete would need to be removed for him to climb past, and dragged the two largest pieces back down the hole.

Splash, splash.

"What was that?"

"Concrete."

He crawled up again, scooting all the way on knees and elbows. Shoved more debris past him, down the hole. Someone grunted.

"Sorry."

The slab had broken free along the line of holes he'd drilled. "Perfect. Perfect, perfect." He reached up, gripped the floor's edge, and pulled his head out.

The basement.

The sweet, sweet, beautiful basement. Silent and bare past the open door. No guns, no Germans. He could hardly stand such a sight.

Something bumped his foot. "Go, go!" Sweeney called up.

Stephen climbed out of the hole and stood. The door into this room stood open; it had a dead bolt on the inside, which was strange. Maybe it had been a study or hideout once. The bulb out in the basement glared. The cement on the floor was shiny. He ran to the door, poked his head out, and then stepped into the main room. The door to the boiler room was closed.

"Please, please," he breathed. What if they had found it? He couldn't think like that. Not now.

"Take my hand," Sweeney whispered behind him. Stephen glanced back to see Sweeney kneeling over the hole, helping one of the others. He looked up at Stephen. "Hurry, man! We have to do this and get out!"

Stephen walked to the boiler room, cracked the door, peeked into the dark. His heart pumped like that jackhammer, breaking up his confidence. What if the tin was gone?

He hit the light switch, and the lone incandescent bulb snapped to life. The boiler was open. He'd left it closed. The drums looked as if they might have been shifted.

Braun had been here!

Stephen leaped for the boiler, grabbed the empty drum behind with both hands, and sent it crashing to the side. There lay the top of the safe, covered in dirt.

Stephen let out a soft, involuntary cry. For a moment, he felt ruined by relief. Then he dropped to his knees, swept the dirt off, and yanked the lid. Esther's face stared up at him, serene.

He shoved both hands into the safe, latched his fingers around the tin box, and pulled it out.

Surprisingly light. What would four gilded Stones wrapped in cloth weigh? Less than the tin box perhaps. Maybe more. Maybe much more.

He spun around and ran into the rabbi, who had come in unnoticed. "It's here?"

Stephen clutched the box with white fingers. "Yes."

The rabbi looked from the box to Stephen.

"I have it," Stephen said.

"Yes. Yes, I see that." A slight smile formed on Chaim's face.

Stephen rushed past him into the main room, driven by the adrenaline in his blood, not the thoughts in his head. There were no thoughts in his head. He had the box, that was all. The box was in his hands.

"Are you going to open it?" Chaim asked.

He whirled around, caught off guard by the question. "Here? Not here!"

Sweeney and Melissa stood by the coal room, staring. "That's it?" Sweeney asked.

For a moment, they all stared at it. Why? What were they trying to prove with their gawking? Sweeney had already mixed the quick-setting concrete, which sat in a bucket behind him. They should be moving, not gawking.

Sweeney stuck out his hand. "As much as I would love to sit around and look at your five-hundred-thousand-dollar box, the clock is ticking. It's been a pleasure, Groovy. If I don't see you in prison, I'll try to look you up." He grinned. "The concrete's already half-set, so as soon as I wedge the wood in place, you pour. Got it?"

Stephen's legs were numb. He nodded.

"You sure you're all right?"

"'Course." He cleared his throat.

"And you might want to stash the contents of that box in your pockets. It's a bit obvious."

It was Stephen's idea that he should be the one to stay behind, fill the hole, and escape through the garage. After all, it was his treasure, and someone had to do it. The notion struck him as a bit ambitious now.

Melissa kissed him on the cheek. "See you around, Stephen."

"Okay," Sweeney said. "Come on, Rabbi."

"I'll stay with Stephen," Chaim said.

"You have to get out, you know? Two will be harder than one."

"And three will be harder than two escaping from the smoking building. I think I should stay with Stephen."

"Okay, Stephen?"

"Okay."

Sweeney winked, followed Melissa down the tunnel, and wedged a piece of plywood behind him, forming a floor of sorts for the quick mix. He knocked on it from below. "Okay, all set. Good luck."

Stephen kept looking down at the box in his hands. It was an old cookie box, roughly twelve by eight inches. Orange wafers ran around the sides. No tape to seal it. Ruth's picture looked up at him in a surreal silence. He shook it gently once—something thumped softly inside. A knot filled his throat.

Chaim watched Stephen, and then, without a word, dumped the concrete into the hole. He smoothed it as best he could with the bottom of the bucket, and then shoved loose coal over the mess.

Stephen would have helped, but he couldn't bring himself to put down the box. He watched in silence, contemplating Sweeney's advice that he leave the box behind. A box was just a box. He could take the picture off and take out the Stones and leave the box.

Chaim finished in less than a minute. It wouldn't support a man's weight for another half hour, but the coal masked the job well. If Sweeney was as successful at hiding the manhole on his end, their tunnel might never be discovered.

All Stephen and Chaim had to do now was get out.

SOMETHING WAS wrong. Roth had never been so sure of his instincts before. It was the fire—something was wrong about the fire. So much smoke and yet no flames.

He paced the sidewalk, eyes peeled for any sign of a fireman, a policeman, a city inspector, anyone who might look like the Jew or the construction worker. For that matter, he wouldn't have to look like the Jew—Friedman wasn't beyond dressing as a woman. Anyone who approached the building would be suspect.

Ten minutes after their evacuation, he learned why there were no flames. Tires. They were saying that someone had set tires on fire.

The Jew had set the tires on fire knowing it would force an evacuation, resumed his digging, and was now in the building.

Roth ran toward the front doors.

He pulled up. What was he thinking? The authorities had eyes everywhere.

He hurried back to Lars. Panic spread through his limbs, enough to make him want to scream. "They may have tunneled through the floor under cover of the fire. Have Ulrich set fire to one of the cars down the street—I need their eyes away from me. Do you understand what I'm telling you?"

"Start a fire? How?"

"I don't care how!" he yelled, then quickly turned in the event he'd attracted attention. "I don't even care if he's caught. Tell him to stuff a rag into the gas tank and set it on fire. Just do it!" His head swam with emotions he had never experienced before. He might be having a breakdown right here on the street. Control. He had to regain control.

"Hurry!"

"RABBI!" STEPHEN WHISPERED.

Chaim turned from the door that led into the stairwell.

"Maybe I should take them out."

"We have to hurry!" the rabbi said.

"I know, but maybe Sweeney's right. I should hide them somewhere else so that if they take the box, I'll still have the Stones. I think we still have time; it's only been ten minutes—didn't you say we had at least twenty?"

The rabbi looked at the door, then back. "Where would you put them?"

"In my pockets. Or my shoes."

Chaim walked back. "Okay." He looked at the box. "Open it."

"Okay," Stephen said.

He couldn't move his fingers though. They hadn't moved in five minutes.

The rabbi's hand reached out and touched the photograph. "She's very beautiful. Please, Stephen."

"Okay."

He gingerly set the box on the ground, knelt down, wiped his palms on his pants, and pried his fingers under one end of the lid. It came loose with a soft popping sound. Stephen felt such a terrible desperation in that moment that he nearly slammed the lid closed. Desire, of course; yes, desire. But fear as well. Terror!

What if the Stones of David weren't in this box?

He slid the lid over and let it clatter to the floor. Inside was a red bundle. Silk. He scooped it out with trembling hand. Beautiful, soft silk that felt like cream in his hands.

He looked down, thinking there could be more at the bottom of the box. There was. A worn journal. He scooped it out, leafed through it quickly, and handed it to Chaim.

Carefully, he unraveled the silk scarf. It felt empty. Panic crept up his throat. He shook the scarf. A folded letter fell to the floor.

No Stones.

Stephen sank to his haunches, horrified. He could hardly breathe. A red scarf and a folded letter. There had to be more. The safe! The safe had a false bottom!

He leaped to his feet, tore into the boiler room, and plunged his hand into the safe. His knuckles crammed against a hard bottom. He struck at it furiously, but it sounded dull. No false bottom.

Stephen stared into the hole and began to breathe hard, as if he were locked in an overheated sauna, desperate to get out.

"Stephen?"

The truth was unbearable. A mountain on his shoulders, crushing with its dead weight. There was no treasure. The children were the Stones of David. Esther. Ruth's picture flashed through his mind.

"Stephen!"

Chaim was at the door. Stephen turned slowly, senses dulled. The rabbi looked at him, face white. The letter shook in his right hand.

Stephen stood unsteadily. "What?"

"I . . . you should read this." The rabbi held it out.

"It's a letter," Stephen said. "To Esther?"

"Yes. To Esther and David. From Martha."

"Martha?"

"I think you should read it."

Stephen walked forward and took the letter. Written in cursive. The ink was old, and the creases in the paper were worn nearly through.

My dearest son, David, and Esther, for whom you were born:

I've searched the world and cannot find you. I can only pray that someday one of you will find this letter and know the truth.

I have married a good man, Rudy Spritzer, and I call myself Rachel now in honor of the woman who cared for you, David, in the camp. There I was known as Martha. I was able to give birth to you at the labor camp Toruń only because of the sacrifice of Ruth, who had given birth to Esther just weeks earlier. I was chosen by the red scarf to die, but Ruth took the scarf for herself.

The commandant wouldn't let me care for you, David, but I cared for Esther. He took you both before the camp was liberated. I searched for five years and then came to the United States when I learned that many orphans had immigrated. I discovered only that the commandant left my dear David in an orphanage near Ketrzyn and took Esther into Germany.

Please forgive me, but I couldn't let him know that I had taken the journal, or he would hunt me down. It contains enough information to send him to his grave. But you must understand, I could not allow them to prosecute the commandant. He alone may have knowledge of your whereabouts.

I couldn't seek you out publicly, for fear that they would come for you as well. You will know you belong to me and to Ruth because I have marked both of you with half of David's Stone. I tried to find you through the mark—I'm so sorry I could not.

I have prayed every day that God will draw you to me and to each other as he draws a man seeking the pearl of great price. May he fill you with the hope we entrusted in you. You must find each other. Then you will know the real treasure, which makes the Stones look like toys for children. I am sorry, so sorry, dearest children. You are the true Stones of David, and I pray every day that if I cannot find you, you will find each other in good health.

As for the Stones, their hiding place will go to the grave with Ruth and me. Find each other and find God.

Martha
Sept. 1958

"Esther," Stephen said quietly. Tears welled in his eyes, and he was forced to swallow. "Dear God, I have to find her."

He owed his life to a woman named Ruth, and by extension to her daughter. *Esther* was the treasure. Not some ancient Stones covered in gold, but a child of the war. A woman. Esther, for whom he was born.

He couldn't explain what happened next, except to think that a week of madness had finally broken him down to a pulp. Stephen dropped to his knees, covered his face, and yielded to sobs. They started with soft shakes and grew to rob his breath completely. He bobbed on his knees, wanting to shake the emotion that ravaged his body, but it only tightened its grip on his throat and chest.

The photographs from Martha's sunroom flashed across his mind. Girls and boys, wives and mothers and daughters, husbands and fathers and sons. They had died, and he had lived—because of one named Ruth. He owed his every breath to another Jew. And for twenty years, he'd betrayed the memory of their deaths by ignoring their pain.

Chaim tried to comfort him, tried to suggest they must leave, but Stephen sank to the ground, letter clenched in his fist. For a few unbearable moments, he imagined that the picture of the little bald girl from the medical clinic was him. He was there, in Poland. Every day, the Germans carried him down to a room that smelled like alcohol, and they injected different parts of his body with cancer cells. That's how he lost his hair and his teeth.

But he wasn't dead from cancer. He was alive because someone else had died to give him life. Ruth. Esther.

Chaim was shaking Stephen violently. "Someone's coming!"

Stephen scrambled for orientation. "The letter!"

A door slammed somewhere.

Stephen struggled to his feet. They had to get out! He quickly shoved the letter into the ash tray below the boiler.

"You're leaving it?"

"What if they find it on me? We'll come back for it. Hurry!" He ran out, scooped up the tin box with the journal and the scarf, and turned for the door.

"No. Not this time."

Braun stood at the entrance to the stairwell, pistol in his fist. He walked straight for Stephen. The German's gun hand flashed out, and Stephen felt sharp pain shoot through his skull. Something crashed to the concrete. A tin box.

He hit the floor hard and lost consciousness.

38

STEPHEN HAD NO IDEA HOW LONG HE'D BEEN UNCONSCIOUS. He lay in a heap on the basement floor, stripped to his undershirt and briefs. His head pounded, and he lay still for a few minutes, listening to several men talking in German. Slowly, the details of the letter again filled his mind. He had to find Esther.

Stephen straightened his leg. The talking ceased immediately. Thirty seconds later, Braun stood above him.

"Have a seat."

Hands hauled him up from behind. They set him in a chair.

"Where's the rabbi?" Stephen asked.

"The rabbi?" Braun chuckled. "He's no rabbi. Which is a disappointment to me." Braun wore an unbuttoned Nazi SS jacket, revealing a black silk shirt beneath. His slacks and shoes were the same he'd worn before. The red scarf was draped over his left shoulder. He strolled to Stephen's right, drawing on a cigarette.

"I would have killed his worthless soul already, but for the moment he's more useful to me alive. The old ones always go quickly, my father used to say."

Stephen felt a chill snake down his spine. The large blond they called Lars stood by the stairwell, staring without emotion. Claude stood in front of the boiler room.

"Do you like my jacket?" Braun asked. "It was my father's. I wear it sometimes, when I make deals with Jews."

He held up the tin's lid and stared at Ruth's picture. "I want you to tell me where you put the Stones, Mr. Friedman. We found the floor safe. I must say, your juvenile bluffs successfully diverted our attention from the basement. We tore the upper floors to pieces, and all the while you had the safe covered by a drum in the basement. How did you get in?"

"What do you mean?"

"I mean, an hour ago you weren't in, and now you are. How did you get in?"

They hadn't discovered the covered tunnel yet. "Through the garage door."

Roth slapped Stephen hard across the cheek. "I don't have time for lies, Jew."

Stephen caught his balance, put his hand to his tingling face. "We . . . we knew the fire would force your evacuation. In the confusion, we forced the garage door open and walked in. I was dressed like a fireman."

"Where are the clothes?"

"We tossed them outside."

Judging Roth Braun by his expression was impossible. He showed no emotion. "And the jackhammer?"

"We were digging a hole from a sewer that connects the buildings, but the motor burned up. The fire was a last resort." Stephen took a deep breath. "There are no Stones," he said. "Only the scarf."

"And the journal." Braun raised it in one hand and took a drag on the cigarette with the other. "Do you know who this scarf belongs to?"

"Rachel Spritzer."

"You mean Martha. She was my father's personal servant at Toruń. She stole this scarf from my father. I know it well. It was very special to him." He lifted the picture of Ruth, caught Stephen's eye, and sniffed the photograph as if testing her perfume.

Stephen felt sick.

"This is Ruth," Braun said. "Amazing how Esther resembles her."

Stephen's hands were free; he could rush the man and take the picture. But it would only prove that he knew about Esther. He couldn't tip his hand. Braun didn't know about the letter yet.

"You do know Esther?" the German asked, gaze studied.

Stephen didn't respond.

"Ruth's daughter." Braun's lips twitched. "My father sent her into the Alps after the war, to a small village named Greifsman." His eyes twinkled. "She's very beautiful."

She *was* alive! "He . . . I don't understand . . ."

"Why is she alive? Let's just say that Esther is our bargaining chip, in the event we ever found Martha. But her value has now expired, hasn't it?"

Braun grinned. "And you're Martha's son, David. My father made the mistake of allowing you to live as well. He wanted Martha's missing son to haunt her till her death. A good instinct, but fundamentally flawed. After all, you were chosen by the scarf."

"I don't know what you're talking about," Stephen said. He had to distract Braun from this line of thinking. "I knew Rachel Spritzer from an antique shop I used to frequent," he lied. "She purchased some things there. She talked about her Stones of David, but I always thought she meant her children, until I saw that she had donated one to the museum. I looked around and stumbled onto the floor safe. You know the rest."

"Another one of your inventive stories? My father took the Stones of David as spoils from a collection in Hungary, and I'm sure he would like to have them back. But this"—he held up the journal—"interests us the most. If you've seen the contents I'm sure you know why."

It occurred to Stephen that Braun was incriminating himself—something he would never risk if he intended to let Stephen live. A moan seeped from under the door to the coal room.

Chaim.

"I think the Stones were in this box with the journal," Braun said. "I'm willing to wager the old man's life on it. We can begin now, one finger at a time, or you can tell me what you did with them and make this painless."

"There are no Stones! Do whatever you want, but there was only the scarf."

The letter would prove there were no Stones here, but did he dare tell him about the letter?

"Fine." Braun turned to Claude, who stood by the door to the coal room. "Start with a thumb."

Stephen bolted to his feet. "Stop!" He had to stall. "Okay, listen. The scarf must mean something. She left it for a reason. It leads to the Stones. Ask yourself how."

Braun hesitated. "Nothing comes to mind."

"Think about it. She wanted me to find the scarf. Why?" Stephen felt toothless, standing up to this monster while wearing nothing but Fruit of the Loom briefs and a torn T-shirt, but he would bite at any hope. "Because you're right. I am David. The scarf saved my life. She drew me in to find the scarf."

"Cut off his thumb," Braun said to Claude, who turned to enter the room where Chaim moaned.

"Wait, there's a letter! It's in the boiler."

Braun held up his hand to Claude. He glanced through the door into the boiler room.

"Well?"

Claude ran in and emerged a moment later bearing the smudged letter.

Braun took the letter, eyed Stephen, and then read it quickly. His left eye twitched once as he neared the end. Stephen sagged into the chair. Braun would now assume the Stones were hidden somewhere else. *The Stones' hiding place will go to the grave with Ruth and me.*

ROTH WAS having a hard time controlling his exuberance. He was playing the boy like a fiddle. He'd convinced the Jew that he was after the Stones of David as well as the journal. And that Esther was still alive in Germany.

He turned his back to Stephen and reread the letter. The old man called Stephen's name softly once, and Claude thumped the door. "Shut up!" An eerie silence filled the basement.

Roth planted his feet wide and rolled his neck.

"The Stones aren't here," Roth said softly.

He took several deep breaths. He was so taken by his own game that he almost missed the significance of the last line. He'd missed it when he'd first read the letter several days earlier. Now it jumped out at him.

"What could she have possibly . . ." He read the last line out loud. "As for the treasure, its hiding place will go to the grave with Ruth and me."

The implication was what? That Ruth, not only Martha, had known something about the Stones' hiding place.

He turned around and would have grinned wickedly if not for his practiced control.

"Strip him!"

The others hesitated, not expecting the sudden order.

Roth walked to the Jew. "I said *strip* him!" He grabbed the neck of Stephen's T-shirt and jerked it down. The cotton fabric ripped, leaving half of Stephen's chest exposed.

Lars and Ulrich grabbed Stephen and pulled him to his feet.

Roth stared at Stephen's chest. He extended his hand and touched the scar. Traced it.

"David," Roth said. "Isn't it ironic that after all these years, your very survival continues to play into our hands? You've led us to this letter, which says more than Martha meant—I can promise you that. I have to pay our beloved Esther a visit now, so I'm afraid we won't be seeing each other again, but I want you to remember my face. I assure you, I look like my father. Your mother went to her grave with his face stamped in her mind. Why should you go any differently?"

He dropped the letter and walked to the door. "Lars, Ulrich, come with me." He opened the door and turned back to Claude. "Kill the old man and dispose of his body. Keep this other stinking Jew alive until I call. If he tries to escape the basement, kill him. I trust you can manage that."

The instructions were for Stephen's benefit, naturally. The game wasn't over—not yet.

Claude dipped his head, indicating that he'd understood. If he didn't, he would pay with his own life.

—⁓—

THEY WERE going to kill Chaim?

"Cover the stairs," Claude said to Carl. Stephen jerked his head around—Claude was screwing a silencer onto his pistol.

Stephen responded instinctively rather than with any kind of coherent plan. He leaped to his feet, hurled the chair at Claude with a furious grunt, and rushed the man before the chair struck.

Claude absorbed most of the flying chair with his left forearm, but one of the legs struck him square in the forehead. Stephen slammed into the chair, shoving Claude hard against the wall. The German batted at him with a thick hand, struck him on the shoulder, and pushed him into the coal room door.

Stephen grabbed the handle, jerked the door open, and spun inside. He slammed the door, once on Claude's hand, and again after the man sensibly withdrew it. Stephen crammed his palm into the dead bolt he'd seen earlier. It banged home.

Stephen took a step back, trembling from head to foot. He couldn't see—the room was pitch black. Fists pounded on the door. Bitter curses.

"Hello?"

Chaim's voice. From his left. The pounding stopped, and it occurred to Stephen that a bullet could pop through the door as if it were paper.

He dived to his left.

Phwet! Stephen hit the rabbi and both crashed to the floor. *Phwet! Phwet!* Bullets punched round holes of light in the door.

"Uhhh!"

"Down!" Stephen snapped. "Stay down!"

He jerked his eyes back to the door. They seemed to be shooting randomly, hoping for a hit, but it wouldn't take much to blow off the latch. In ten seconds they would be through.

"The tunnel!" Stephen coughed. The quick-drying cement they'd used set up in thirty minutes, but how long before it solidified?

Stephen rolled to his feet and tore for the center of the room. Somehow the spitting bullets missed him as he kicked at the coal they'd scattered over the tunnel. A circle darkened by coal quickly took shape.

"Chaim—"

"Hurry!" The rabbi was beside him, already stomping.

The shooting stopped momentarily, then started again, just below the dead bolt.

"Jump!" Stephen shouted. "Hard!"

He slammed both feet down and was rewarded with a teeth-rattling jolt. It had hardened.

"Together. One, two, three!" He jumped again, but the rabbi's leap came after his. Two more holes popped in the door, up toward the latch.

"Together. Together! One, two, three."

They both leaped; they both slammed into the fresh concrete together; they both fell when the concrete caved.

"Out!" Stephen pushed the rabbi, who quickly crawled out.

Streams of light blazed through the holes in the door. Stephen shoved his hands into the tunnel, grabbed chunks of concrete and wood, and threw them out.

A shot blew away the door latch. But the dead bolt above still held. Someone kicked at the door and swore again.

The tunnel couldn't possibly be clear of all the material Sweeney had used to prop up the concrete, but Stephen had pulled out the large slabs and the plywood. They were out of time.

"Follow me."

He went in headfirst, like a tentative child taking his first daring ride down a slide. His hands struck two-by-fours, and smaller chunks of crumbling cement littered the hole. He shoved them down, ahead of him, praying they wouldn't jam.

Wiggling and squirming, he slid down, plowing the refuse until it splashed into the sewer ahead. He didn't try to slow his exit, but he did tuck and roll the moment his head cleared the tunnel. The sudden cold of sewer water sent waves of relief through him. He wanted to cheer.

The rabbi was spared the bath; he fell on top of Stephen like a huge sack of potatoes. The impact knocked the breath from Stephen's lungs, but the fact was lost to the whine of bullets. Claude was shooting down the hole.

"Hurry!" Chaim gasped.

They ran through the blackness. The shooting stopped, and Stephen knew the German was coming down after them. He hoped Sweeney hadn't heaped bricks on the manhole cover.

Stephen managed to find the ladder, scrambled up first. He heaved on the grate, but it refused to budge. Behind them, Claude swore. He was feeling his way out of the tunnel they'd dug. Stephen pushed again. Not a chance.

"Move it! Move it," the rabbi whispered.

"It's stuck! Shh, quiet!" But even the *shh* carried down the sewer like air brakes.

A huge splash. Claude was in. Stephen swallowed. This was it, then. They were trapped. He gathered all of his strength and crammed his back against the lid above. Nothing.

Far away, a dog barked.

"Brandy?" Stephen's whisper echoed down the tunnel. His question was answered by a sudden sloshing and another big splash, followed by another curse.

Now the dog was barking furiously.

The manhole cover suddenly slid off. Stephen stared up into the round eyes of Sweeney. Brandy attacked his face with a wet tongue.

"No, Brandy. Hurry, get me out!" he cried.

Sweeney and Melissa grabbed his arms and yanked him out of the hole. Brandy stood back, head cocked.

"The rabbi, hurry!"

Up came Chaim.

The sewer filled with splashing and yells. Stephen shoved the cover back over the hole. "How was it braced?"

Sweeney got behind a large timber that he'd found and pushed it back over the cover.

"Good night, what happened?" Sweeney asked.

The cover bounced up.

"More! He's strong."

"There is no more," Sweeney said.

Stephen looked around quickly. The cover rose a full two inches off the hole—he could see the German's gun hand. Without thinking, Stephen jumped up on the timber. The lid clanged back into place.

"Find something." The lid rocked crazily. "Hurry!"

Instead, Sweeney jumped up with him. This time the cover slammed home with confidence. "That'll give him something to think about," Sweeney said. "You're lucky we came back to check out the damage."

"My car's on the street," Stephen said to Chaim. "Spare key's in the gas well. Take Melissa and wait for us."

Chaim needed no encouragement. They left with Brandy bouncing behind.

The timber below them shifted, and Sweeney crouched like a surfer. "That guy's a bull!"

"There's more than one," Stephen said. "We have to get out of here. Four guys with guns could be crossing the street already."

"What went wrong?"

"Long story."

"Did you get it?"

Stephen hesitated. "Sort of."

"You don't have any pants on," Sweeney said.

"I about had my tail shot off. No time for pants."

Sweeney stared at him dumbly.

"Make sure you don't kick the wood off the cover when we push off," Stephen said. "Ready? You go first; I'm right behind. Go!"

Sweeney jumped off and sprinted from the room. Stephen followed on his heels. Behind them, the cover scraped concrete. A single bullet chipped the wall before they made the stairwell. They cleared the building, tore up the alley, and ran straight for Stephen's car, a happening hippie in blue bell-bottoms and a scruffy Realtor in white underwear.

Not until Chaim pulled the car into traffic on La Brea did Stephen feel his pulse ease. But the madness wasn't over, was it? In so many ways, it was just beginning.

For the first time, he knew what was happening; now he just had to follow through. A whole new world had just been opened up to him. He was being drawn by the pearl of great price. The pearl was Esther, for whom he was born.

STEPHEN PACED in the living room, peering repeatedly out the windows on either side of the house. They'd let Sweeney and Melissa off ten blocks down La Brea and returned home the long route. An hour had passed since their narrow escape, but Stephen's nerves still felt taut like piano wires.

They'd called the police who'd dispatched a cruiser to check out Rachel Spritzer's apartment.

"Rabbi—"

"I'm sorry I didn't help you sooner, Stephen. I was afraid you were pulling back into yourself. But I see that you've been reaching out more than withdrawing. You're finding your own identity."

Stephen nibbled at his index fingernail. "I don't think I can hang out here for the police."

"They'll want to take a statement. We were shot at and nearly killed!"

Stephen looked in his eyes. "She's alive, Chaim."

"Who is?"

"Esther."

"She's alive and in a German town called Greifsman." He swallowed. "He's going to kill her. I have to stop him. He said the red scarf had selected—"

"Red scarf?" the rabbi interrupted, paling.

"The red scarf. You saw it. The letter—"

"He's the one behind the killings!"

"That's what the letter said. His father was the commandant in the camp where my mother was held."

"No, now. The killings in Los Angeles."

"What killings?"

"You haven't heard? Of course you haven't!" Chaim quickly filled him in.

"There's no direct link," Stephen said. "Either way, he's gone now. I have to get to Germany, rabbi."

Chaim looked at him blankly.

"Braun's going to kill her, did you hear me? I have to beat him there."

"And maybe that's what he wants."

"Then he would have taken me with him. Or killed me when he had the chance."

"This is very dangerous, Stephen." The rabbi hurried to the phone, dialed a number. "You can't just run off to Germany. Do you even have a passport?"

"Yes. Who are you calling?"

"Sylvia. She's working on the Red Scarf case."

Stephen stared out the window as Chaim spoke on the phone. The possibility that Roth Braun was a killer failed to upstage the revelations of Martha's letter.

"Thank you," Chaim said into the phone. He dialed a second number.

On the other hand, this serial-killer business was extremely important. It meant that Esther was about to die. At least that's how Stephen saw it.

He bumped his forehead with his fist. The emotion that had consumed him for the last few days now felt like a hot branding iron on the brain.

Chaim dropped the receiver in its cradle. "She's not at work. No answer at home."

"I'm going, Rabbi."

They stood in silence for a moment. "Why would Braun want to kill her now, assuming he's known all along where she lives? Does she know where the Stones are?"

"No. I don't know. The letter says that their hiding place would go to the grave with Martha and Ruth."

"And they're both dead."

"Right."

"So what does Braun know?"

"I don't know. But I know he's going after Esther."

"Well, this is terribly dangerous."

"No, this is my life!" Stephen was yelling now. He might burst into tears at any moment. "I have to do this. I can't explain why any more than I can explain why I tunneled into the apartment, but I have to go."

"The police—"

"I can't afford to be questioned by the police. If Roth Braun is the man they're looking for, then the danger for Los Angeles is gone. Let them try to find him, although I can guarantee you that he's already in the air. It'll take time to coordinate any action with the German police."

His words echoed in the small house.

"I have to go now."

"Then I'll go with you."

"No. Stay and fill the police in. Tell Sylvia. Do whatever you need, but please give me a chance to get out of the country."

"They'll want to know—"

"Then tell them. Just don't tell them where I've gone. I'm not the criminal here. They can't hold me, can they?"

"Vandalism."

Stephen knew Chaim had a point, and it infuriated him. He gathered himself.

"I have to go, rabbi," he said quietly. "Please, hear me. I have to go."

Chaim sighed and finally nodded. "Okay. Find her, but please remember what I said, Stephen."

The phone rang. Chaim snatched it up. The police.

In a moment the rabbi set the phone back down and faced Stephen wearing a frown. "You were right—no sign of Braun; no evidence of a crime. Other than a hole in the basement. They want a statement from both of us."

"I'll give mine when I get back."

The rabbi seemed to accept this.

"Obsession is a dangerous business, Stephen. You can't lose sight of virtue or morality for the sake of passion. Just because your intentions are noble, you have no right to break the law. Certainly not to kill or to—"

"I'm not going to kill anyone. I'm going to rescue Esther. God has answered my mother's prayers."

39

THE COMMANDANT'S EYES WERE RED AND WATERY FROM LACK OF sleep. He leaned over the table and sipped at a spoon of the corn chowder Martha had prepared for supper at his request. The china was set on a white cloth, and the commandant was dressed in the uniform he reserved for social events—black, pressed, and starched. For nine months she'd waited on the commandant, while the war slowly ground to a halt throughout the world. Auschwitz had been liberated, Belsen liberated, even Buchenwald in Germany itself liberated. But here in Toruń, just a few miles from Stutthof, the Germans had dug in and were fighting a fierce battle over these last camps. Why? And how could Braun sit so calmly while even now Russian planes flew overhead, armed with bombs for Stutthof?

Martha had long ago lost her fear of Gerhard Braun.

"It's over," she said.

"It will never be over," he answered, not bothering to look up. "You're alive today. Does that mean you'll be alive tomorrow?"

Martha looked away. His threats hardly even registered anymore. Several other facts, however, did register, like glaring lights in her eyes. The first was that David was still alive. She hadn't seen him for nine months, but she knew he survived in the barracks below. The second was that in a matter of days, whatever end awaited them all would come.

And the third was a growing hope—yes, hope—that she could actually affect that end. How many nights had she laid awake, her mind filled with fantasies of revenge, plotting to use Braun's treasures to her advantage? Her only living mission was to save the children; perhaps she could do so with the help of the spoils hidden in the vault.

The only question was how? Anytime now, Braun would evacuate the vault and be gone.

Paper covered the picture window now, obstructing the view of the camp below where her little David lived. Most of the Russian bombs had descended on the main camp at Stutthof, but Toruń had suffered several raids as well. Braun had sent most of the remaining prisoners north to the Baltic nearly two weeks ago to be evacuated by sea, he said. All but a hundred, mostly wounded or sick, were gone. Rachel was among those who remained. Rachel and David. Rachel and David and Martha and Esther, pawns in his game, kept only to make Braun feel powerful.

If only there was a way to speak sense into this pig! "You have no reason to keep us," Martha said. "And you have no reason to kill us. What will any of this prove?"

Braun set his spoon into the empty bowl, dabbed his lips with a serviette, and ran his tongue over his teeth. She wanted to cut off his red lips with a knife. A fantasy as foolish as taking his treasure.

"Don't be a fool," he said softly. "I have more reasons than you can possibly know to kill you." He stood and picked up his hat. "As it turns out, I also have several compelling reasons not to kill you. Killing you would end your misery, and I have no interest in ending your misery. Also, the Allies are evidently frowning on the indiscriminate killing of prisoners—I'll be gone when they come, but I wouldn't want to leave any evidence to fuel their fires."

Martha, confused, watched him walk to the door. It was the part about her misery that sounded wrong. How would her liberation lead to extended misery—except in the memories she would take with her? Such relatively insignificant misery was beneath Braun. He meant to do more.

"I will be leaving in the morning, but the guards at the perimeter will remain. Don't think you can walk out of here."

He reached the door, put on his hat, and turned the handle. "Oh, and I've decided to take the children with me."

Martha's mouth dropped open. "No! No, you can't!" She took three steps toward him and stopped. "You . . . you can't!"

"But I am. What's more, I can promise you that you'll never find them."

Martha ran to him, fell to her knees, and grabbed his hand before considering the consequences of such an action. "No, I beg you!" she cried. "I beg you; they are children! They mean nothing to you!"

He looked at her as a scientist might look at a lab experiment, pleased by such an unusual reaction from her.

"Please, let me keep my child," Martha whispered.

"You don't think that I'd seriously allow Ruth's ridiculous obsession with hope to actually find life outside this camp, do you? There is no hope for the Jews."

He jerked his hand free and stepped out into the darkness. "If you make any attempt to escape, I would be delighted to shoot all three of you. Except Esther. I've taken a liking to the little girl."

"As has your son," Martha said bitterly.

His head snapped up. He glared. The night Roth had tried to kill Esther had been the last time Martha had seen him.

She pushed him, knowing the danger of it. "He's stronger than you."

Gerhard spat. "He's a child who doesn't know that the war is over. Yesterday's indulgences are today's death sentences. If I didn't know you better, I might think you were asking to be killed."

"I have no reason to live without my David."

"Which is the point. You'll live with the horror of this camp your whole life. Roth doesn't understand that death is sometimes the easy way out."

Gerhard made a disgusted, dismissing motion with his right hand and shut the door with a *thump*.

Martha jumped to her feet and ran for the stairs, mindless. Her right foot was already down two steps before the first clear thought forced her attention. She had to get David! The commandant was leaving, and she had to get her baby before then. She spun around, ran for the door, but pulled up without opening it.

What was she thinking? Even if she could get David, she could never escape with two children under her arms. Even alone, she would be killed.

She threw both fists toward the floor, jerked to the window and screamed through gritted teeth, like an animal. For several long seconds she just stood there, tensed from head to foot, trembling with fury. The thought of losing Esther and David was like the thought of dying. Maybe worse. What did he have to gain from this? Nothing!

But she knew that her scream would do nothing for either David or Esther. She forced herself to take a deep breath. Maybe she could still prevent him from taking the children. Or maybe he didn't really mean to carry out this threat. He was playing with her, one last sick joke before running off with this loot of his.

She blinked. The Stones of David. The journal.

Martha walked to the kitchen and then back working quickly through ideas. There *was* no way to save the children. Nothing would prevent Braun from taking them.

She stopped by the kitchen table and stared at the far wall without seeing, never so hopeless since seeing the red scarf on her bed nine months earlier. Whatever Braun planned to do with the children could not be good. He might kill them outside the camp, leaving her with lingering hope and uncertainty.

"No, Martha," she muttered, wiping her eyes. "You have to be strong. You have to be strong."

She returned to an idea she'd massaged for dozens of hours late in the nights. A thread, however thin, of hope for the children.

She ran down the stairs, suddenly consumed with accomplishing this one task before Braun returned. Esther slept in peace—her night started at five, something the commandant had insisted on. He wanted the child asleep before he sat down for a quiet evening meal. Martha had wanted to dump poison in his quiet evening meal when he'd first made the demand, but tonight she was grateful.

First, the vault.

How long would Braun be gone? It could be five minutes, or it could be several hours. She ran back upstairs to his bedroom, to a beautifully engraved, white jewelry box on his nightstand, under which she'd discovered the key to the vault three months earlier while cleaning. Tilting back the box, she snatched up the key and flew to the basement. Most of her plan would require stealth, in the late-night hours after Braun was asleep. This first part, however, she could not do without disturbing the peace.

The idea had first mushroomed in her mind as she contemplated how renowned the Stones of David were. Certainly they were far more important to the world than two Jewish children, even if in her mind David and Esther were the true Stones. If her children were ever to be lost, they would be forgotten forever with untold thousands following the war. But the Stones would always stand as icons, sought by the whole world.

What if she could somehow link both children to the Stones of David? Draw them by association to each other and to her? Rachel's confession in the barracks over a year earlier had haunted Martha. What if she could mark Esther and David as Rachel had done? And what if later she could make it clear in private circles that she was looking for a girl named Esther and a boy named David, both bearing this mark?

She unlocked the door with unsteady hands and stepped into the cool, dark room. It looked just as it had the first time she'd come in. But the journal was gone.

Gone?

Martha hurried to the box and opened it. There, on top of the five stones, lay the leather journal.

She emerged from the vault three minutes later with two green ammunition containers the size of shoe boxes under her right arm. Sweat slicked her palms, but she didn't falter. Not once. She locked the door, slid the boxes under her bed, and returned the key to its place under the commandant's jewelry box.

Returning to the living room window, she peered past a tear in the paper. No sign of him yet. She had to put the mark on Esther before he returned, or her crying would cause a terrible scene. And she would cry. Poor baby, she would cry.

Martha hurried to her room and reached under her thin mattress for the twisted piece of metal. She'd formed the symbol a week ago, using one paper clip, cut and folded back on itself to show the brand she intended.

It would never work! She paused, reconsidering, trying to think of a better way.

There was no time.

The child slept on her back. Martha looked at her supple, innocent body and started to cry silently. She tied the crude brand to the end of a wooden ladle and then bared little Esther's chest. Should she wake her?

Dear God, this was madness! How could she burn a child? She nearly abandoned the plan then, but this was the only way she knew to extend the very hope Ruth had died for. The thought gave her the strength to slowly heat the metal over a candle flame until it was red hot.

She had to clear her eyes of tears twice so she could see. "I'm sorry, dear Esther," she whispered, and then she pressed the metal into the baby's flesh, hard.

Esther did cry. She screamed through Martha's fingers. But thankfully, before the child fully realized she was under assault, the damage was done.

Martha hugged the child tight and rocked her. "Shh, shh, I'm so sorry. I don't mean to hurt you. Shh, shh, you must be quiet."

She dabbed the deep burn with an ointment she'd confiscated from Braun's personal medicine cabinet and then placed a bandage over it. Esther might tear it off, but Martha knew the burn must be hidden from Braun, at least for as long as he had both children.

Surely he wouldn't keep both—it wasn't in his character. He would rid himself of David; why would he keep David? No reason to keep a Jewish boy. The only reason he'd allowed the boy to live was for the sake of his game. He would rid himself of her son within a day or two, maybe sooner.

Martha's thoughts brought her no comfort. Had she burned in vain the child she had promised to care for as her own? Fresh tears streamed down her cheeks, and she lay down with the child, soothing her slowly back to sleep. Exhausted by the pain and tears, Esther finally settled.

She would have to wait now, lying here in bed, cold with sweat. Wait. And doubt.

The door upstairs banged an hour later, and Martha bolted up. Boots clomped on the wood floor, then down the stairs. Many boots, maybe four pair or more. They walked by her door, straight to the vault.

Panicked, she slid from the bed, dropped to her knees, shoved the ammunition boxes all the way under her bed, and then pushed some dirty clothes after it, knowing this cover-up was hopeless. If the commandant discovered anything missing from the vault, he would tear through the entire house, starting with her room, until he found it.

This wasn't just a few coins she'd relieved him of. The journal could destroy him. Dear God, what was she thinking?

They walked by nineteen times, and each time Martha lost a kilo in sweat. And then they didn't return. The house grew quiet. A sudden, terrifying thought struck her: What if he meant to take the children tonight?

She jerked upright. He'd said in the morning, but what if he meant *by* the morning? What if he'd left already to collect David, with the intention of returning for Esther?

Martha threw off the covers and tiptoed up the stairs in her bare feet. Water, if he asked. She was getting a glass of water.

She peeked down the hall and saw his bedroom door closed. A thin line of light ran along the base of the door. She retreated, her bare feet whispering across the concrete. He'd emptied the vault, presumably without noticing anything missing. What kind of good fortune had extended her this grace?

And to what end? She wouldn't be leaving here with the children, much less the treasure. It was nearly midnight, at least eleven. Her plan would be for nothing if she didn't get down to David. She *had* to get to her son. How could she possibly explain this to Rachel?

Martha slipped to her seat and sat in the dark hall, sunk by a terrible hopelessness. What would Ruth do in a situation like this? Ruth would pray. She would cry out to God for his favor and his hope. She would believe that God would preserve the Stones of David. She would believe that God would protect the children without being compelled to explain why he hadn't protected countless others in this horrifying war.

Martha whispered her prayers to God and then assured herself that he would indeed preserve the true Stones of David. Her tears slowly dried, and her resolve returned. She finally took a deep breath and set about to do what she must.

She pulled out the ammunition boxes, rolled them in a blanket, and ascended the stairs. The light was out beneath the commandant's door. So then, what was she waiting for? Ruth had given her life for hope; it was time for Martha to risk hers.

She would need a shovel, and although she had an idea where she could get one, she wasn't sure. This part of the plan she might have to abandon. She had one of the Stones at any rate, stashed in her underclothes. If all else failed, she could call to the children after the war using this one Stone.

Martha took a deep breath and slipped out the back door.

40

Germany
July 27, 1973
Friday

STEPHEN STOOD BY THE VOLKSWAGEN BUS HE'D RENTED IN Hamburg and stared down at the small town of Greifsman. A bird chirped from a grove of trees to his right; the sky was blue and the air was cool. It felt surreal to be here, so far from home, yet so close.

Several children played in the village square; a tall bell tower marked the church around which two or three hundred homes crowded. The village wasn't unlike any small Russian town, a far cry from the sprawling cities of America. For every minute of the past forty-eight hours, he'd imagined this moment, driving into Greifsman and running into Esther's arms, two soul mates finally and miraculously reunited. He'd stared at Ruth's picture for hours, considering every conceivable eventuality.

But the three-dimensional reality dashed his fantasies. If she wasn't here, he was lost. If she was here but refused to go with him, he was lost. If she was here and agreed to go with him, and Braun was also here, they were both lost. For all he knew, she was already dead. Or alive and happily married with twelve children. Even one child. Spoke no English. A dozen other possibilities.

Stephen had contacted Chaim upon his arrival in Germany. The rabbi had terrified him with new details.

Sylvia was dead.

Dead?

Dead.

The news still seemed impossible.

Chaim had gone looking for her after giving the police a statement on the fire. She never had shown up at work.

He found her bound in her apartment on blood-soaked sheets. Gagged with a red scarf. Lifeless.

Chaim blurted the news through tears, demanding that Stephen return immediately. This changed everything. Stephen couldn't return, of course. Another woman's life was at stake.

Esther. Her face was burned into Stephen's head, begging, dying for his help. His love.

They'd already made contact with the German authorities, but Stephen was right—these things took time.

Now standing over the village called Greifsman, Stephen was suddenly sure that the next hour would turn out badly.

In a moment of overwhelming resolve, however, he ran for the Volkswagen, climbed in, and fired up the van. Lack of sleep had made him emotional. He looked over at the picture of Ruth on the passenger's seat. This was insane.

He muscled the gearshift forward, released the clutch, and jerked with the bus. The gravel road was steep, and he found himself wondering how they managed in the winter. Maybe there was another road, although the man at the rental agency had assured him this was the only way to Greifsman, if he absolutely insisted on visiting. No one visited Greifsman. It was nothing but a pile of rubble in the middle of nowhere.

Stephen accelerated and shifted into a higher gear. He would blaze into town; he would search; would find; he would leave.

Honestly, he wasn't sure he actually wanted to find her. Yes, as odd as that sounded, he really wasn't too thrilled about the prospect of searching for someone who was likely married or dead. And he wasn't just telling himself that to keep his hopes from boiling over. Or was he? Either way, he couldn't race through the streets yelling her name, now, could he? The residents might come out of the houses with pitchforks.

No, it would be a calm, collected affair. A simple question here, a suggestion there. He would compare faces against Ruth's picture, show it to others. If he wore his collar up, Braun might not even know he was in town.

He glanced at the picture and took a settling breath. "God help me."

Everyone who saw him drive up the cobblestone street into Greifsman stared. They didn't run out and clap their hands and dance in the streets as if he were the liberating army; they simply stared at him, as if they'd seen this before. The return of the gunslinger. Maybe the car rental man back in the airport knew a few things.

Stephen parked the van by the square and looked around. A bread shop, a butcher, the distant sound of children singing. School. An old man with a wrinkled face sat on a bench ten yards ahead, watching him with casual interest.

Okay, Stephen. Calm, collected, methodical. You've come this far.

He took the photograph, exited the van, and walked straight to the old man.

"Excuse me."

The man cracked a toothless smile and nodded.

"Excuse me, you speak English?"

"Anglesh," the man said.

Apparently not. He held up the picture. "Du yu no vwherr I ken fined dis wooman? Estar?" What was he thinking? He cleared his throat and spoke in normal English. "Do you know where I can find this woman?"

"Nein." The man shook his head and wagged one hand.

"Thank you." He walked up the street where a group of children watched him, smiling.

He held up the picture. "Esther? Anyone know this girl?"

A girl of eight or nine giggled. The rest ran off, squealing with delight.

He walked on, feeling more self-conscious than he had upon exiting the van. Several women were crossing the street to his left. "Excuse me." They ignored him and continued. "Excuse me, does anyone speak English? I'm looking for Esther."

They whispered to each other and moved on without paying him more than a sideways glance. Stephen stopped on the sidewalk, suddenly worried. What if she really wasn't here? Braun might have purposefully thrown Stephen off. He swallowed and hurried toward the bread shop. A woman with a plaid dress covered by a white apron walked out holding a large bag, gave him a quick glance, and moved away quickly. Not a good prospect. He stepped into the shop.

He stumbled out thirty seconds later. Not one of the seven people inside seemed to speak English. Not one showed any recognition when he showed them the picture. She wasn't here! And the people were treating him like a piece of trash that had blown in on the wind.

The calm, collected approach wasn't working.

Stephen ran to the corner and thrust the picture above his head. "Hey!" he yelled. "English! Who speaks English?" His voice rang out over the street. There were several cars, a dozen bicycles, and at least forty people in his field of vision. The bustle paused with his cry. A hundred eyes turned his way.

He had their attention.

"Please, I'm looking for Esther! The girl in this photograph." He pointed at the photo. "Can anyone tell me where I can find her?"

The pause lasted two seconds, and then as one they resumed their bustle, as if he didn't exist here on the corner, bellowing like a fool.

"Hey!"

This time, they ignored him entirely. They were hiding something! Of course! Why would so many people ignore him? Germans were well-known for their friendliness, even more so in the country. If one of them had responded kindly, tried to explain—but no. The whole village was conspiring against him.

The obsession he'd lived with in Los Angeles drove him forward now. Stephen ran down the sidewalk, waving the picture in front of startled villagers. "See her? This is Ruth. Esther's mother. Tell me where she is. Tell me!"

A middle-aged woman scolded him in high-pitched outrage. The only word he caught with certainty was "idiot."

He honestly didn't care whether she thought he was an idiot. If she had any idea what he'd gone through to be here, she would be running around frantically with him.

He showed the picture to at least fifty people, ignoring their blatant denial, gaining steam as he progressed, as much out of anger as hopelessness now. The main street ran for about a hundred yards, and he hurried all the way to its end, begging, yelling, whispering, any and every approach that came to mind. "Show me some respect, for heaven's sake. Look at the picture!"

Except for the occasional vacant or sympathetic stare and several angry lectures, the villagers continued to ignore him. He was doomed. No, he refused to be doomed.

Stephen pulled up and faced the street, beyond himself. "You lying hoard of insensitive—" He jumped up and beat at the air. "Speak to me!"

"They wouldn't tell you if they did know," a voice said behind him. Stephen whirled. A young man leaned against the wall, stroking a black goatee.

"You speak English," Stephen said.

"So do half the people in this town. The younger ones."

"Then why—"

"This town is controlled by the . . . what do you call it? Like German Mafia. Do you want these people to be killed? Only a fool would tell you anything, whether they know or not. And only a fool would run around town yelling at them and jumping in the air. You'll be dead by sunset."

Stephen stared at him.

The man turned away.

"No, wait." Stephen stepped up and grabbed his arm. "Do you know her?" he whispered.

The man stopped. "Let go of my arm."

Stephen did.

"Are you deaf? Do you want a sniper to pop my head like a pumpkin?"

"No."

"Then don't ask again." He walked off. "No, I don't know her," he said so Stephen could hear.

No? No? Stephen scanned the roofs of the buildings, half expecting to see the glimmer of a rifle. Snipers in this tiny village? It had to be a figure of speech.

He hurried for a side street, suddenly feeling like a fool. Okay, so maybe calm and collected would have been better after all. But now he had a problem of incalculable proportions. He had to believe Esther lived here, in this village. He really had no alternative. If no one would tell him where to find Esther, then he would have to find her himself.

Stephen stopped and looked back toward the town square. How many people lived in this place? One thousand? Three thousand? Couldn't be more than three thousand. How long would it take to search thirty streets? He would go door-to-door if he had to. If Esther was here, he would recognize her; he was sure of that.

On the other hand, some of them would surely recognize him from his circus act on Main Street—maybe even report him to the snipers. Half the town had probably seen or heard of him by now. He had to be more discreet. But he also had to hurry; if Braun hadn't taken her already, he couldn't be far behind.

He considered retreating to the van, but one glance at the picture and he discarded the thought. He hid the photograph under his shirt, shoved his hands into his pockets, and walked on. He bought a floppy black hat from a street vendor, hoping it might alter his appearance at least some.

He entered a lazy cobblestone street that ran in front of the towering church. Half a dozen people sat or stood outside as many shops. Someone laughed, but he didn't turn to see if it was directed at him. He glanced as nonchalantly as possible at each face. None of them was Esther. None of them was even a woman.

Another thought struck him. Maybe Esther would find *him*. If it was true that they were soul mates, wouldn't she recognize something special in him? Maybe he should be less concerned about being recognized by the Mafia types and more concerned with letting everyone in the village get a good look at him. He would leave the rest in God's hands, if indeed God was interested.

He glanced up at the church across the street. A woman stood at the side of the building, by the entrance to an alley, arms crossed. She was staring at him.

Stephen stopped. Was . . . was it her?

The same dark hair, the same finely curved cheekbones. Eyes that drilled him with a bright stare. She wore an equally bright blue dress.

He was holding his breath.

He glanced up the street—no one was watching him. Except her. She was still looking at him. His mouth was open, he knew that, but he wasn't thinking clearly enough to close it. Worse, he couldn't move his feet. He just stood there, forty yards away, ogling her as if she were an apparition who'd come to sweep him off to heaven.

This didn't seem to faze her. She continued staring. Or was she glaring?

Stephen regained his composure and headed across the street, straight for her. She let him come. He stopped ten feet from her. This was Esther, the perfect image of Ruth. The same hair, flowing gracefully past smooth cheeks. The same disarming eyes and the same small nose. She was petite, no more than a couple of inches over five feet.

"What are you staring at?" she asked.

"What?"

"You're staring at me as if you were looking at a ghost. Haven't you ever seen a woman before?"

"Of course." His voice cracked, but he didn't bother to correct it. She was reacting out of shock at finally seeing him. Hiding her own need for him with this charade.

"Then stop staring as if you haven't," she said.

He blinked. "You speak English."

"Obviously."

"Do you have twelve children?"

It was her turn to blink. "Do I look like I've had twelve children?"

"No! Sorry." His face flushed. "You're just so beautiful, I had to know . . ."

"If I've had twelve children?"

"Are you married?"

"No."

It was too much for Stephen. He rushed to her and threw his arms around her neck before she could move.

"My name is Stephen. David. I've looked everywhere for you!"

She was stiff like a mannequin. He was overwhelming her. *Get ahold of yourself, Stephen. She's a tender twig; you'll snap her in two. This is no way to introduce yourself.*

He started to pull back and was aided by a shove from her.

She stepped away, horrified and angry. "What on earth do you think you're doing?" she said, eyes darting up the street.

"I'm sorry. I don't know what came over me. You're . . . you're Esther, right?"

"I don't know what you're talking about."

This couldn't be! Was she terrified out here on the street? Of course!

"Maybe we should go to the alley," he said.

She reached out and slapped him. "What do you take me for?"

For the first time, he wondered if he'd made a terrible mistake.

"What do you mean, prancing around the village, making a fool of yourself?" she demanded.

Stephen stepped back. "You saw me?"

"Half the village saw you. If there's an Esther who lives here, I don't know her. Now leave, before you get yourself killed."

She glanced over his shoulder, gave him a parting glare, and walked away.

41

WHO THE MAN WAS, SHE HAD NO IDEA, BUT IF HE CONTINUED with these antics, neither of them would live out the day. She feared as much for him as she did for herself. Perhaps more.

That's why she'd slapped him.

Yes, that's why. Hard enough to really hurt. Tears came to her eyes now as she walked briskly from him. How he knew, she couldn't guess. He'd called her beautiful. She couldn't remember the last time a man had told her she was beautiful. It wasn't permitted.

But this bold fool from America named Stephen David didn't know that. He had maybe seen her somewhere and really thought she was pretty. Now he was coming after her in full daylight. Is this how Americans courted their women?

And yet she found herself undeniably attracted to the tall man with haphazard dark hair. He'd told her she was beautiful. Did he really believe she was beautiful? Was *he* beautiful? He did not fit her preconceived notion of American men. And yet, he could be missing his ears and she might think him beautiful. He desired her.

"Stop it," she whispered harshly. "What do you take yourself for? A whore?" Fresh tears filled her eyes. She bit her bottom lip. Some realities in life couldn't be changed.

The first: no man could love her.

The second: she could love no man, because she certainly could never love the man who'd imprisoned her here.

The third: she was trapped. If she set one foot outside this pathetic village, Braun would kill the only person who meant anything to her.

She rounded the corner and glanced back. No sight of the American. She stopped for a moment, swallowed, and then hurried down the street. Her memories flitted to Hansen. She was eighteen, and he was a strong young man with bright blue eyes and a wide smile. Braun had killed that budding desire. Literally. She'd cried for two straight weeks. Her first and last true love. Braun's decree could not have been more clear. The men stayed away from her after that. And she from them.

Her earliest memories took her back to age six, when she first began to realize that she was different from the other children. She had no mother, no father, only uncles. And her uncles were mean men who cursed often.

When she was eight, the other children seemed to turn on her. She remembered the day on the playground clearly. Freddy had called her a whore in front of all the other children. She didn't even know what a whore was. No one had stood up to him.

She learned the truth of her life when she was twelve—why she had no memory of her parents and lived with mean uncles and aunts.

She caught the eye of Armond across the street, keeping his eternal watch over her. She squared her shoulders.

What would they all say if the American ran up to her again and pronounced his undying love? Was she lovable? Was she not a woman? The American seemed to think so.

She secretly wished that Stephen David would do just that. That he would chase her at a full sprint and fall to his knees and cry out his adoration for all the village to hear.

But that was a foolish fantasy. And a dangerous one.

"Please leave," she whispered. "Leave this town."

STEPHEN LOOKED around. Three men angled toward him, intentions clear. They were coming to the aid of a woman who'd been attacked by a foreigner.

He stepped into the alley, took several long steps until he was sure he was out of their sight, and ran. What had he just done?

The alley ended. He veered to his right and slowed to a walk. How could she not be Esther? What was the probability that a woman who so closely resembled Ruth just happened to live in the very village Braun had named?

On the other hand, Stephen wasn't a student of faces. In the past twenty-four hours, a hundred women who resembled Ruth had made his heart jump. He had seen her face in the clouds, in the rocks, even in the Volkswagen emblem on the van's steering wheel.

Stephen began to run again, terrified by the possibility that he had just let Esther go. He had to at least warn her about Braun. Where could she have gone?

The answer came quickly when she walked out onto the same street, fifty yards ahead. He instinctively threw himself into a doorway. Somehow skipping up to her for another hug didn't strike him as the most effective way to gain her confidence.

He poked his head around the corner and looked both ways. The men had either given up their pursuit or had opted to follow her to safety. The girl who wasn't Esther was walking away, deeper into the village.

He stepped onto the sidewalk, lowered his head, and followed. The floppy black hat was a beacon now; he pulled it off and tossed it in a doorway. Ten paces later, he braved a glance. She wasn't walking as if she was concerned. Even if she wasn't Esther, she was one of the most beautiful women he'd ever laid eyes on. Of course, that was probably because he'd imagined she *was* Esther, and his mind had been ruined by . . .

She began to turn. He leaped to his right, behind a garbage bin, and dropped to a crouch. Someone chuckled, and he turned toward the sound. It had come from an older gentleman seated in a doorway. The man waved, and Stephen waved back, embarrassed.

He sneaked a peek. She was entering another alley, headed back toward the church! Stephen stood, immobilized by indecision. If he ran down the street she'd emerged from a moment ago, he might be able to intercept her.

He ran. If she was Esther, Braun hadn't arrived yet. The thought propelled him into a sprint, legs pumping like a world-class runner. The old man's cackle chased him down the street and around the corner. He ignored a dozen alarmed villagers, took a sharp left at the next corner, and blasted for the alley from which he knew she would emerge.

He slid to a stop at the corner, took one deep breath, and jumped out. Another second and he might have landed on top of her. She jumped back and shrieked.

The leap had been a bit much, he immediately saw. A nonchalant, suave entrance would have accomplished the same thing with far more subtlety.

She held a hand to her chest. "What are you doing, you idiot! Get away from me!"

He held up a finger. "Shh!" Looking into her eyes again, he was sure she was Esther. He felt as though he'd searched for those eyes his entire life.

"Why are you attacking me?"

Her accusation shocked him. "I wouldn't dream of hurting you. How can you say that? I'm here to save you!"

"Throwing yourself at me and then stalking me in broad daylight is your idea of saving me? They'll kill you for sure now."

"Stop it!" he yelled. Footsteps pounded behind him. They'd heard her cry and were coming. Stephen pulled out the photograph and spoke quickly. "Help me, I'm begging you. This is Ruth, Esther's mother. She gave her life for me in the concentration camp at Toruń. There isn't time— Braun's on his way here now. For Esther."

The woman stared. Running feet entered the alley.

"Please," Stephen said quietly. "I swear I thought you were Esther, otherwise I wouldn't have done that. Please, I have to help her."

A rough male voice spoke in German behind Stephen.

The woman hesitated. "I'm okay," she told the man.

The footsteps left.

"Thank you." He was still holding the photograph out to her.

Her eyes searched his for several moments and then lowered to the photograph.

"I wish I could help you," she said. "But I can't."

"You must!"

She stood defiant, but he thought her eyes were misty.

"I don't know who Esther is," she said, "but I do know they will kill you if you continue. Braun's well-known here. He doesn't value life."

"And he's on his way here now."

She stepped around him and hurried for the street.

Stephen walked after her. "Please—"

"You must leave before you get both of us killed."

He ignored the glares of onlookers and hurried to catch her.

"I'm telling you the truth. My name is David. I go by Stephen. I was born in Toruń. My mother's name was Martha. Do you know any of this?"

She veered up the stairs to the church doors. Her jaw was firm, but he saw a tear escape her eye, and the realization nearly crushed him. What had Braun done to make her so terrified?

He followed her into an arching foyer with stained glass high above. "I just came from Los Angeles. Braun was there looking for the Stones of David. Doesn't any of this mean anything to you?"

She spun. "You have no idea!" Her eyes blazed, but she could not hold back another tear that ran down her face. She was Esther after all! She had to be.

"Look at it!" he said, shoving the picture forward. "This is your mother! She gave her life!"

Esther looked at the photo. But her eyes stayed on the image. Surely she saw her own features in it.

"You are Esther!" He turned the photograph over. "Read it!"

Her eyes dropped to the writing.

My dearest Esther, I found this picture in Slovakia after the war. It is your mother, Ruth, one year before your birth.

Not an hour passes without my begging God that you and David will find each other. I will never forget. You are the true Stones of David.

"No. It can't be."

Her lips quivered. Stephen resisted an impulse to take her into his arms again.

Dear Esther, I am so sorry. What have they done to you?

She shook her head. "You have the wrong person."

Stephen grabbed his collar and ripped his shirt open, exposing the scar on his chest, daring her to deny it.

She stared, unable to move her eyes. Her face softened, and the tears began to run unrestricted. She lifted a trembling hand over her heart and slowly, as if in a dream, pulled the neckline of her dress down just enough to reveal the skin below her collarbone. There, burned into her flesh, was an identical scar.

"Esther," he said.

Her eyes rose to meet his. "Yes."

He stepped forward and put his hand on her shoulder. Anything else seemed inappropriate. She slowly rested her forehead on his chest and began to cry.

42

A YEAR HAD PASSED SINCE ROTH LAST VISITED THE VILLAGE. HIS MEN usually did the honors. From the road, the town looked unchanged.

Gerhard had his journal, but the Stones of David were still missing. With the threat posed by the journal behind Gerhard, Roth had little trouble stirring up his father's passion for the Stones.

Gerhard hadn't been so delighted in thirty years. Roth was pleased. And he had a plan.

When he'd received the phone call nearly two hours ago saying the Jew had arrived, Roth had nearly wept for joy.

Stephen had come, as surely as Roth had known in his remarkable judgment he would. The Jew would chase this fantasy of his to hell and back if necessary. Why not? After all, Christ had.

Little did Stephen know.

The danger of playing the game so close to the wire was both thrilling and unnerving to Roth. What if the Jew outwitted him as Martha had out-witted his father? Or worse, what if the Jew had already left?

"Straight to her house, Lars."

"If she's not there?"

"Then we'll find her at the church," he said. "Just hurry."

The car surged forward, down the steep grade.

He lifted his father's old red scarf, pressed it against his nose, and inhaled deeply. It smelled like Ruth, he thought. Like Esther. He glanced over his shoulder. Esther was about to get a wake-up call.

"Faster."

"Any faster, and we'll be off the side," Lars shot back.

Roth took a deep breath. The thought of what lay ahead tested even him.

—–—–—

STEPHEN WATCHED Esther pace behind the last pew, content to study her fiery brown eyes and her blue dress, which flowed lazily with each turn.

Esther. This was Esther. This stunning creature who paced before him was really Esther. He could still hardly believe she was Ruth's daughter.

They'd burned forty minutes in the church, far more than he knew was reasonable considering their predicament. But he was asking her to leave the only home she knew on a moment's notice. Half an hour ago, he was jumping out at her from the alleys; now, he was asking her to head to the hills with him. Unlike her confession, this wasn't something he could force.

He'd walked among the pews and discreetly watched her weigh the choice before her. There wasn't a shred of doubt in Stephen's mind: he was born for this woman. And he would win her love or die trying. No other woman could compare, not even in the smallest way—he was sure of this, though he hardly knew her at all.

Yet he did know some things. She had the spirit of an eagle caged by evil. If ever there was a victim of cruelty, it was her; and yet she endured it with her chin level. Because of this alone, he was utterly in love with her. He would set her free.

And there was more. The flip of her wrist, the darting of her eyes, the smell of her skin, the sound of her voice. She had the skin of a dove. She was his soul mate, created for him. And he for her.

His pearl of great price, as Martha had put it.

His obsession had taken flesh, and he would embrace it. Protect it. Its name was Esther. Gerik was surely right—man was created to obsess.

Despite the danger that now faced them, he could barely keep his mind on the task at hand. Perhaps because the task always had been love. It made sense that he was now as concerned about love as he was about staying alive or finding the Stones of David. Of course, staying alive was a prerequisite to winning Esther's love.

He knew she couldn't possibly feel the same about him. After all, she hardly knew him. But he thought maybe she was warming to him. Her apprehension was understandable. Once they got out of this mess, he'd give her time and space to grow to love him. He'd romance her properly. Candlelight, roses, moonlight strolls on the beach—the lot. She wouldn't be able to resist . . .

He looked over and stopped. She was gone! His heart jumped into his throat.

"Esther?"

"Yes?"

Her voice drifted in from the foyer. He vaulted the pew and ran in. "Don't you ever do that again!"

"Do what?" She stood before a large mirror, looking at her scar. "I walked ten paces. Just because I leave the room doesn't mean I've fled."

"I crossed the ocean to find you."

"And if I would have known about you, I would have done the same," she said.

This was good, right?

"I've been lost my whole life," Stephen said. "Until now."

She didn't respond, but her eyes spoke clearly enough. She was as lonely as he, just as desperate. The only difference was that she hadn't dwelt on the matter for a week as he had.

She looked back at the mirror. Even watching her now, his knees felt weak. He felt completely unreasonable and soft. Really, his whole life had been moving inexorably toward this day.

"Please don't go anywhere without telling me," he said. "Braun's out there somewhere."

"Stephen."

"Yes?"

"Will you come here?"

He walked over, feeling awkward. "Have you decided whether you'll come with me?"

"Yes," she said matter-of-factly.

He stopped. "Yes?"

She looked over at him. "Yes."

"So you'll come with me?"

"I said yes."

"Then we should go now."

She eyed him, amused. "Will you come here for a moment?"

He stepped up next to her in front of the mirror.

"May I see your scar?" she asked.

He exposed the burn on the left side of his chest.

"Come over here, on this side."

His hand that held the shirt open was trembling. He released it. "Please, Esther. If we don't get out now, we may never get out."

"Please," she said softly.

A strange faintness drained Stephen. Her words were a lovely, sedating drug. Just a simple word, *please*, yet he felt he might crumple where he stood!

Stephen swallowed. "Okay."

She guided him to her right side, so they stood shoulder to shoulder, exposing their burns to the mirror. Hers was a full foot lower than his.

"Wait here." She brought a padded stool that sat beside the door. "Here, kneel on this."

He watched her. She did everything with an incredible grace. The way she picked up the stool; the way she carried it over as if it were made of feathers; the way she bent her legs to set it down; the way she said "kneel on this." No woman could move or speak so gracefully.

He knelt on the padded stool. Now they were at roughly the same height.

"It's hard to believe, isn't it?" she said. "Your mother did this to us so we could find each other."

Stephen focused on her scar. Here they were, kneeling in front of a mirror, Esther and David, the two children from the camps, shoulders bared, branded for each other. The sight was so perfect. Terrifying. He jerked his shirt back up to cover his chest.

"Please, Esther, we have to leave."

She covered her shoulder and turned away. Was something wrong? "Esther?"

She walked to the window, peered out, and then turned back. "You have to understand something, Stephen." The fire flashed in her eyes again. "I can't leave here yet. Not as long as Braun is alive."

"What? We don't have time for that! We should be somewhere else. As far away from here as possible. Why can't we just leave? He has nothing to gain by coming after us."

"No. He won't permit me to leave." Her jaw was set.

"What can he possibly do?"

"More than you can know."

"What do you mean? We *have* to leave. Now!"

She closed her eyes and took a deep breath. "I'm a prisoner of Braun." Her eyes snapped open. "Believe me, he'll find us both, and when he does he'll kill us. I can't leave as long as he's alive."

"You have to. We have each other; we can run."

"Where can we go that he will not follow? No. I will not run."

Urgency swelled in Stephen's chest. "He'll kill you if you stay."

"That is why I have to kill him before he gets to me. Leave if you have to, but I can't. There are other reasons."

"I can't leave you!" He placed both palms against his forehead and paced. "That's crazy. If you only knew what I've been through."

"I'm sure it's no more than what I've been through. Or my mother. Or your mother. This doesn't end as long as Braun is alive. The man is obsessed."

Her use of the term stopped Stephen. "And so am I."

"Then go find your obsession."

"I already have."

Her eyebrow arched.

"You," he said. "You're the obsession I've searched for my entire life."

"Really? We met only an hour ago. In an alley, if you recall." She looked deep into his eyes. "To what ends will you go to protect this obsession of yours? Will you kill the beast who threatens her, or will you hide so that he can live to stalk her another day? Believe me, Stephen, there's more here than you can know. I can't leave this place as long as Braun is alive."

He frowned, struck as much by her suggestion that he would do anything less than protect her as by the sudden realization that he had to do exactly that.

He had to kill Braun.

He swallowed. What was he thinking? He had to kill Braun? He had to *run*! With Esther.

"But . . . if we kill him, aren't we becoming like him?"

"No. We're doing what Ruth and Martha would have done if they had the chance."

"Okay. Okay, then maybe we should kill him." Hearing his own words, Stephen felt dizzy. Would he actually kill a man? Should he?

"Just like that?" Esther asked.

"I won't let anybody hurt you. Never again."

She walked up to him, eyes searching. "Are you a dream, Stephen?"

"No."

She was putting on a brave face, but he could see the fear in her eyes. She didn't know if she could trust him. Yet he was giving her no choice. *Dear Esther, what have they done to you?*

She suddenly turned and hurried for the sanctuary.

"Follow me."

43

THE BELL TOWER ROSE HIGH ABOVE THE CHURCH, AND BY THE looks of the aged bricks that lined the bell housing, it had been built long before the war. Stephen stood against one wall, staring at Esther, who scanned the street over an old hidden rifle she'd extracted from the back of the tower's only closet.

"No sign of him," she said.

Her voice rose just above a contralto, impossibly sweet. He knew what was happening. Now that the truth of her identity had settled fully in his mind, the fixation he'd had with the Stones of David had been transferred, heart and soul, to Esther. He felt like a puppy in her presence. He'd followed her up the stairs, lightheaded as much from the scent of her perfume as from the climb, and listened as she explained how she knew the rifle was there. Something about having smuggled it there years ago during a lapse in her captors' attentiveness, but he was more interested in her.

"Stephen?" Esther turned her head.

She'd caught him staring? He jerked his eyes from her, aware of his flushed skin. Could she read his thoughts? No, how could she know his mind by looking at him? He was overreacting, which explained the hot and cold waves that spread over his skull and down his neck.

"Are you okay?" she asked.

"Yes. Yes, of course I'm okay. What are you doing?"

"I'm waiting for Braun—what do you mean, what am I doing?"

"Of course. What I meant was, why? Or . . . what are you thinking?"

Stupid. Stupid question!

Esther turned back to her study of the street without betraying any problem with his question. "I'm thinking that the moment this pig shows himself, his life is going to end."

"Sure. Of course. Makes perfect sense."

Did it? He hadn't been able to think clearly enough to imagine actually killing a man. The whole plan—coming up here to pick Braun off—seemed surreal.

Was he thinking straight?

Another thought occurred to him. How could a preoccupation that impaired his reasoning be a good thing? If God had created man to obsess, had he also created him to trade reason for intuition? Or worse, sacrifice reason for emotion? The rabbi would never agree. Not even Gerik would agree.

Stephen watched her as she peered over the rifle. Her lips were parted slightly, but she was breathing through her nose. A wisp of dark hair rested on her cheek. Her right hand, tender and white, gripped the trigger. This was the image of God before him. He was staring at a piece of God, and he could hardly stand the wonder.

Chaim had often preached passion for God. In this moment, Stephen thought he understood what the rabbi meant. If man could be as obsessed with God as Stephen was with Esther—what a thought.

And if Chaim was right, if man's emotions were only a dim reflection of the Creator's emotions, wouldn't God also have feelings like Stephen had? Was God obsessed? Was he preoccupied with an extravagant love for man?

How reasonable was dancing naked in the streets, as King David had done? How collected was Noah in building his huge boat in the desert? Or the prophets, being fed by birds or crawling around like an animal for years? Whatever had motivated those great shapers of history had been sparked by a moment of the deepest conviction and passion—maybe not so different from his own.

The entire line of reasoning took no more than ten seconds, and Stephen felt his confidence surge as a result of it.

"Are you really going to shoot him?" he asked.

"Do you have a better idea?"

"It just seems so . . . illegal."

"How can you stand there and talk to me about laws? This man kills. His father killed your mother. He will kill you too. And me. What he's done to me is illegal. Foul!"

She straightened and walked three steps to the still bell, then back to the window, tucking a strand of hair behind her ear.

Foul?

Rage blackened Stephen's vision. "What . . ." *No, not now.* He took a deep breath. "You're right; I'm sorry," he said.

"What am I supposed to do? You can run; I can't. He'll hound me!" For a moment, Stephen thought she might cry.

"No, I was wrong," he cried. "Kill him! We'll kill him for sure!" He took two steps toward her, sick that he'd hurt her again. What was his problem?

Chaim's words were burning a hole in his soul, that was his problem. *This obsession business is dangerous, Stephen. You can't break laws in the name of love.*

Esther's eyes darted about the room and briefly settled on his face. She looked like a child caught between terror and hopelessness.

"Esther . . ."

She spun to the window and froze.

"What?"

She leaped forward and crouched at the sill. "He's here!" she whispered.

Stephen sprang forward, saw the black car roll to a halt across the street. How Esther knew it was Braun, he didn't know, but neither did he doubt. One glance at her face, and he knew this man was a living demon to her. Her lips quivered with fury.

Esther brought the rifle to her shoulder and angled the barrel toward the car. She was breathing hard, and the gun wavered with each breath.

The car's rear door swung open. Braun stepped out.

Stephen bent behind Esther, beating back panic. How could he stand here like a mouse while she fought off the beast?

Esther began muttering under her breath. Bitterly.

Stephen stared at the unfolding scene, aghast. *Foul,* she had said. Roth had abused her.

He lunged for the gun; grabbed the barrel. "Wait! I'll do it!"

The gun boomed in the enclosed tower. Stephen jumped back, rifle in hand. Below them, Braun ducked and ran across the street toward the church's entrance.

"What are you doing?" cried Esther, jumping up.

"I should do the shooting," Stephen said.

"You made me miss!" She gaped at him, and he wanted to explain, but words seemed inadequate.

Esther clamped her mouth shut and ran past him. "Hurry, we're sitting ducks up here!" She disappeared through the tower door.

"Esther!"

From the corner of his eye, Stephen saw the driver's door fly open. Lars dived out.

"Hurry, Stephen!" She was calling him.

His lover was calling his name.

"Esther!"

He worked the bolt, pivoted the rifle out the window, lined the sights in the man's direction, and jerked the trigger.

Boom!

Lars staggered.

Stephen ejected the spent cartridge and shot at the large target again. This time, the man turned and hopped back toward the car. He'd hit him! He'd shot at a man through his leg! Or maybe his hip.

Stephen whirled and raced for the stairs. "Esther!"

She was running straight for Braun! Stephen took the stairs three at a time, rifle flailing overhead. His foot missed one of the steps and bounced over the edges of three more before finding purchase on the fourth. The rifle sailed free as he grabbed at the air. It clanged down a flight and came to rest on the floor directly below him.

"Es—" He cut the yell short. Braun would hear him screaming! The thought sent him flying down the stairs for the gun. He had to get into the sanctuary and cut Braun down before the man found Esther, assuming she didn't find him first.

Stephen reached the rifle, grabbed metal, and came up in a run.

The blow came out of nowhere, a sledgehammer that crashed into his head and sent him reeling back to the floor.

Braun, he thought vaguely. *That was Braun.* But his vision had clouded over, and he couldn't make sense of his surroundings. The gun lay on the floor to his right. He was sitting down. Maybe he'd run into the wall.

No, he'd seen movement. He tried to stand, but his muscles weren't cooperating.

Hands grabbed his collar and jerked him to his feet. "Where is she?"

The stench of the man's breath buffeted his face. Stephen's world cleared. He was standing just inside the sanctuary, supported by Braun. The man's white knuckles gripped a fistful of shirt and pressed against Stephen's nose. He nearly opened his mouth and bit the man's fingers but quickly decided that angering Braun more would only make matters worse.

"Where is she?" Braun said.

She'd eluded him! Esther had eluded this monster and, fortunately, Stephen had no clue where she could be. Hopefully halfway up the hill headed for Hamburg.

A hand slapped his face. "Where?" Braun dragged him into the sanctuary.

"She's gone," Stephen said. "She ran away when I told her about Martha. I told her Alaska would—"

"Jews don't run. They wait obediently; don't you know your history?"

"You'll never find her."

Braun dropped him to the floor by the altar and stepped back. He held a pistol in his right hand, angled casually at the ground. But there was nothing casual about the man's grin. Sweat wet his flushed skin, and his nostrils pulled at the air.

He pulled out the red scarf Stephen had found in the safe and wiped his face as he glanced around the sanctuary, searching the dark corners by the confessional and the doorways.

"She's gone," Stephen said. If he could keep the man occupied long enough, Esther could make her escape. Surely she would know to run. Without a gun, she would never confront Braun, no matter how much she despised him.

"I know what happened to the Stones of David," Stephen said. "Esther doesn't, but I do."

The man cast a sideways glance at him. He wasn't buying it.

Stephen cleared his throat and tried again. "She doesn't know because they belonged to my mother, not hers. You think I would tell her? I've been searching for them my whole life—I'm not about to confide in someone I hardly know."

Braun turned to Stephen and watched him for a moment. Slowly his face settled with a cold determination. "You'll tell me where she is," he said.

"Aren't you listening to me?" Stephen demanded. "She's out of this! Me, I alone, have what you want."

"The city inspector has what I want?"

"You think I would lie with a gun to my head? I didn't even know she existed until you told me. I'm after the same thing you are."

Braun's left eye twitched. "I doubt it."

Stephen was pushing—maybe too much.

"I'm just saying that we need each other," Stephen said. "I have what you want, and you have what I want."

"What do I have that you want?"

"My life! Obviously. You're standing over me with a gun. You let me live, and I'll split it with you."

"The Stones of David. Split them. You are more stupid than I thought, inspector. You think I would share the Stones with a Jew?"

"If you kill me, you'll never find the other four Stones."

A grin nudged the big man's lips. "I do not live for the Stones." Braun glanced around the room again. He dropped one end of the scarf so that it hung from his fingers. "I love games. Shall we play a game?"

He walked forward and held the red silk out so that it hung above Stephen. "You've become useless to me. The only reason you're still alive is because there's a slight possibility that the girl is as stupid as her mother. We'll find out soon enough."

Braun dropped the scarf. It spilled over Stephen's shoulder and hung down his chest. "My father selected your mother, Martha, to die. It seems fitting that I should select you. Unless your guardian angel sweeps in to take your place, I will put a bullet in your forehead. Ten seconds." His voice rang throughout the auditorium.

"Let me live, and you can have it all," Stephen said. "I'll show you exactly where the treasure is, and then you can kill me if you want."

"Seven!"

"She's gone! Kill me, and it's over. I have the information."

"Five."

Stephen knew that his prodding had probably sealed his death, but he couldn't just sit here and die. *Dear Esther, what have I done?*

"Three!" Braun raised his revolver.

"Okay, you win," Stephen said. Panic swarmed him. He was going to die. A bullet was about to punch a hole through his head. He sat up, furious. "I said you win! I'll tell you everything!"

"Stop!" Esther's shrill cry echoed through the chamber. Stephen turned toward the sound of her voice. She stood at the entrance to the stairwell, arms limp at her sides, feet together.

44

STEPHEN FELT HIS HEART SINK TO THE FLOOR OF HIS STOMACH. "Leave," he demanded. "Get out! Run!"

Esther regarded him with a casual glance and then stared at Braun. "There's an exit behind me," she said. "If you kill him, I will run, and you should know that I have a way out of this village that no one knows about. You'll never know what I know; I can promise you that."

"I don't need anything you know," Roth said. "And I don't think hiding will be so easy."

"Then let him go, and I'll cooperate." Her voice held a tremor.

"Esther, please," Stephen pleaded.

Esther ignored him. "Let him go."

Braun could hardly hide his excitement. "Like mother, like daughter. Take the scarf, and I won't kill—"

"I know how your disgusting game is played. How do I know you'll keep your word?"

"Did my father kill Martha when Ruth took the scarf?"

Esther shifted her gaze back to Stephen.

"Please, Esther, don't do this," he said. "He'll kill me either way."

"Maybe. Maybe not. But either way, I'm finished." She looked at Braun. "You hear that, you pig? I know that my life is worth something to you. If you kill him, I'll run, and you'll have to shoot me. I don't know what you have planned, but if I had no value to you, you'd have killed me long ago."

Braun tilted his gun up to the ceiling. "You have my word. He'll go free."

"I don't trust your word," Esther said. "Throw me the scarf."

"Come and take it."

"Do I strike you as a fool? You need me alive, so throw me the scarf."

Braun eyed her, clearly caught off guard by her audacity. But she was right. Braun wanted her alive.

Why?

Braun snatched up the scarf and flung it at Esther. She caught the material, looked at it for a moment, and then casually draped it around her neck.

"Stand up, Stephen," she said calmly.

He scrambled to his feet.

"You'll find another exit through those doors behind you," Esther told him. "Walk out."

"No."

"Then my own life will be in vain," she said.

"He'll kill you," Stephen cried. "I couldn't live with myself."

"He'll kill me anyway," Esther said.

"If you run now, you can still make it. He probably won't kill me. I'm an American citizen, and the district attorney in Los Angeles knows I'm here with Roth Braun."

It hadn't occurred to him until he said it, but this did present a potential problem for Braun. Assuming the man cared.

Braun chuckled. Evidently not.

"Why are you arguing with me?" Esther asked, eyes now moist with tears.

"I'm not arguing—I'm trying to help you!"

"Why would you risk your life for me?"

"You're . . . you're Esther," he said.

"I am. I'm Esther, and no one has ever loved me."

Stephen took a step in her direction before remembering that Braun was in the room. "That's not true. *I* love you. I love you more than anything I can imagine."

"You don't even *know* me." Tears began to slip down her cheeks.

"I was *made* for you," Stephen said.

"Enough," Braun said.

Stephen ignored the man. Esther was offering to give her life for him, not because she loved him so dearly, but because she saw her own life as worthless. The few minutes of tenderness he'd shown her were more valuable in her mind than her life.

Dear Esther. My dear Esther! You are willing to throw your life away for a moment's love.

"Don't you see, Esther? Our hearts have been beating together for thirty years. The truth is, I don't think Martha hid the other four Stones of David. *We're* the Stones of David. I . . . I don't think I can live without you. Please, just run."

"I can't just—"

Boom! Stephen jumped. Braun had fired into the air.

Braun waved the gun at Esther. "Come here, please."

"Not until Stephen leaves," she said.

"You think you can outwit me at my own game?"

"Shoot me," she challenged.

The quiver in his fingers told the truth. Their ploy had stalled him. He couldn't kill Esther, not yet.

Braun twisted his head toward the door. "Lars!"

Lars?

It occurred to Stephen that Braun could easily stop Esther. A simple shot to her leg, and she would be powerless. He was either lost to this fact, or he was playing another game altogether.

If Stephen didn't move now, they could both be dead in a matter of seconds.

"Wait." He could hardly stomach the thought of leaving her here with Braun, but he had no choice. "She's right."

Stephen took a step back. "Okay, I'll leave. I'll leave."

———

THE GAME had been played out like chess match: for every move a counter-move, for every victory a defeat, for every hope a helping of despair. Roth could not have hoped for more.

He was quite sure that he could be completely satisfied standing here for hours listening to their desperate ploys. But little did they know. It was just getting good. Really good.

He could toy with them both as if they were made of clay. And compared to him, they were. Next to him, most humans were merely dirt that had been fashioned into walking objects.

Stephen backed toward the door. "I'm leaving. And since I'm an American citizen and people know I'm here, shooting me would be a mistake. I'll go."

Braun swung his gun in line with Stephen and waved at Esther. "I want you here, beside me, before he leaves."

She walked toward him slowly. "I'm coming. Now let him go."

Stephen took another step back, hands up. "Easy. I'm going. I'll be going." His back hit the door, and he felt for the knob.

Braun turned the pistol back on Esther. Stephen pulled the door open, stepped quickly through, and slammed it shut.

45

STEPHEN HEARD A SLAP THAT SOUNDED LIKE ONE OF THOSE TINY firecrackers, followed immediately by Esther's muted cry. The world tipped crazily. He had to go back in. He gripped the doorknob but stopped short. Braun was yelling at her in German.

Time was running out. Stephen turned, bounded for the outer door, and threw it open. A back alley; empty. He had to find his way back to the bell tower.

Hold on, Esther!

Stephen gritted his teeth and tore down the alley toward the door below the bell tower. Tugged on it.

Locked! Dear God, it was locked!

He sprinted around the corner, but he was running farther from her, not to her rescue. What if he couldn't find another way in? Inside, Braun was brutalizing Esther, and her only hope for survival was running in the wrong direction.

The species of panic that swallowed him in that moment was a rare kind, debilitating in dreams and deadly in waking life. His legs felt numb, and he wasn't running nearly as quickly as his heart suggested he was.

He ran straight for the street, barely aware of three women who gawked at him from across the lane. Rough brick tore at his fingers when he grabbed the building's corner for the turn.

The steps leading to the front entrance loomed, gray and empty. No other doors. The steps, the foyer, and then the sanctuary. And in the sanctuary, Esther.

From the corner of his eye, he saw Lars, limping, pulling something from the back of the car.

Stephen took the steps at a full run. A faint cry of pain drifted from the church. He was out of time.

He slammed through the heavy church doors. He crossed the foyer in three long strides and headed up the center aisle at a full sprint.

Braun knelt on the floor, directly ahead, bent over Esther.

A terrifying, throaty scream echoed off the arching walls, and Stephen realized it was his own. He rushed forward, blindly, pushed by the power of his own rage. Braun stared at him, frozen by the sudden intrusion.

Still Stephen ran. Still he screamed.

He was halfway up the line of pews before a thought redirected him, an image of that rifle he'd dropped at the base of the tower stairs.

He veered to his right, vaulted a pew, landed his foot on the seat of a second, and hurdled the pew tops toward the bell tower.

A gunshot boomed, but he didn't duck or stop. His momentum permitted neither.

Another gunshot. Stained glass shattered high above and rained down.

Stephen skipped over the entire bank of pews before his left foot finally betrayed him and came up short on the last bench. He threw himself forward in a dive, banged his shin hard, toppled over the pew, and landed on his side with a tremendous grunt.

Wood splintered above his head—Braun's shots tore at pews that momentarily shielded Stephen. He couldn't breathe. The bell-tower door was open, two yards away.

He clambered for it on his hands and knees.

Click! Click!

The gun-hammer fell on an empty chamber. Braun was out of bullets?

Stephen was still out of breath. He shoved himself to his feet and lunged through the door. The old rifle lay where it had fallen.

He snatched it up.

Chambered a round, desperate for breath.

Whirled back.

Lurched for the doorway, feeling faint.

His reason was making a comeback, and for once it sang in harmony with his passion. Kill Braun. He had to kill Braun.

Still no breath.

Stephen staggered into the doorway, gun extended, trigger halfway through its pull, sights lined for Braun.

But Braun didn't fill the sights. Esther did.

Stephen blinked. Braun had pulled Esther to her feet and stood behind her. A large, shiny blade pressed against her throat.

"Drop it," the German said. "Drop it, or I cut her and drink her blood here before it's time."

Stephen's lungs finally inhaled a pocket of usable air.

"Lower the weapon."

Stephen held the gun as steadily as he could, which amounted to wavering in favor of jerking. He had no chance of picking off Braun's head like they did in the movies. Esther's shoulder was exposed, baring the scar. Her eyes stared at him, glazed with indifference. She'd resigned herself to die.

"Let her go," Stephen said, still gasping.

"Drop the gun, and I'll release her."

Stephen groped for a way out, but came up empty-handed.

"I can't put the gun down, and you know it," Stephen said. "But I can promise you that if you draw blood, I'll take my chances and shoot."

"Then you'll kill her," Braun said.

"You'll kill her anyway."

The front doors crashed open. A woman's muffled cry.

Stephen froze.

A sick grin distorted Braun's mouth.

Lars staggered into the back of the sanctuary. Shoved a woman down the aisle. Her hands were bound. Lars held a gun to her back.

It took Stephen a few seconds to realize who he was looking at, not because she looked any differently than he might have guessed, not because the gray tape over her mouth hid her facial features, but because he simply couldn't understand what he was seeing.

Esther. Only older.

Ruth.

But this couldn't be Ruth.

Ruth was dead.

"Hello, Ruth," Braun said.

46

Toruń
May 8, 1945

MARTHA STEPPED INTO THE YARD BEHIND THE COMMANDANT'S red house and let her eyes adjust to the darkness. Ordinarily, the lights would be blazing from tall posts throughout the camp, but not since the Russians had begun their air raids. Not even the front gate was lighted. It was so dark tonight that Martha had to choose her way carefully. If the perimeter fence wasn't flowing with high-voltage electricity, she might have been able to find a way out with the children under the cover of this darkness.

She made it as far as the tool shed at the edge of the yard before a sound stopped her dead in her tracks.

A cough.

From the shed? Did Braun keep prisoners in the shed? She wouldn't put anything past Braun, but why? Most of the barracks below were empty.

There it was again. The cough.

It didn't matter; she had to keep her mind focused. She had to hurry, or she could endanger the children's lives. The fate of one or two prisoners locked in a concrete cell was no longer her concern. Maybe on the way back she would—

"God forgive me. God forgive me." The voice came now, a soft, mumbling voice that stopped Martha in her tracks. Didn't she know that voice?

She heard it again, coming from a small, barred window to her left. "God forgive me."

Martha held her breath and stepped up to the bars. "Hello?"

Nothing.

"Is anyone in there?" she whispered.

"Martha?"

"Ruth?" A knot tried to choke her off. "Is that you, Ruth?"

Hands grasped the bars. A face pushed up between them. Ruth's face.

"Ruth! Is it you? How . . . ? I thought he—"

"Martha! Thank God, Martha. You're alive!" Ruth frantically searched her face. "The children! Are the children—"

"Yes! Yes—oh, yes. I can't believe it's you! I was so certain that . . . I saw your body!"

"It wasn't me. I don't know who."

"But you're alive!" Martha kissed her fingers, then her forehead. "Oh, I have so much to tell you. So much! Esther is the most beautiful child. He won't let me see David."

"They're here? Can I see them?"

Martha glanced back toward the house. "They're here, but the commandant . . . I can't bring her out. She'll wake up. We are being liberated tomorrow, Ruth!"

"You're sure?"

"Yes! Yes, I'm sure of it." She had to leave; she knew she did. If Gerhard found them . . .

"Listen to me, Ruth. There is so much I will tell you. Tomorrow. If we get separated, then you should know that I've marked Esther, and I am going to mark David. Each with half a circle with a star of David in it. The Stone of David. You know it?"

"Yes."

She stepped back and lifted up the boxes. "I have them. And I am going to hide them. If for some reason we get separated from each other, or from the children, remember this."

Martha told her how she planned to hide the treasure.

"What good will that do? His gold is filthy!"

"Do I care? It's for the children, Ruth."

"They will have each other."

"He's . . ." Should she tell Ruth? She had to. "He's taking the children with him, Ruth."

"No!"

"Yes. I'm so sorry. Don't worry, God will protect them. You said so yourself. As long as he thinks I have stolen his treasure, he won't hurt them. Do you see? He'll keep them alive until he finds it. It's the only solution I have. We must have leverage. I have to go." She kissed Ruth on the forehead and nose.

"Thank you, Ruth. You saved my life. I love you more than I would my own sister. Tomorrow we will talk, okay?"

"Pray that God will draw the children with his hope. Like desperate children seeking the pearl of great price."

"I will, Ruth. I will pray it every day."

"God be with you."

"God be with you."

She hated leaving, but she walked with a new urgency. Ruth had survived! Think of it. A great weight was gone from her shoulders.

It took her half an hour to pick her way through the camp toward the barracks she thought would be David's. The door was unlocked. She slipped in and shut the door quietly. "Rachel?"

Silence.

Louder now. "Rachel?"

"Yes?"

Martha ran past empty bunks toward the sound. "Rachel. It's Martha."

"Martha?"

The woman lay on a lower bunk, one of only a few people in the beds as far as Martha could see. She set her bundle on the bed and threw her arms around the woman, noting Rachel's frailty through the cloth immediately. She was nothing but bones!

"Thank God you're alive."

"Martha?"

"Yes, it's Martha, dear. You have my baby? David. Where is David?"

Rachel shifted to reveal a small lump in the blankets behind her.

"This is David," she said very quietly, almost as if it were a question. The woman's mind was slipping.

Martha stared at the form, afraid to ask anything more. She leaned in and eased back the blanket. There lay a small boy, white chest rising and falling slowly. Dark hair covered his head. Her David.

She lifted her fingers to her mouth to hold back an urge to cry. But this scene was too much for her. She sank to her knees, folded her hands in gratitude to God, and began to shake with soft sobs.

Her son was more beautiful than she had ever imagined in thousands of hours of imagining. He lay with all of his arms and legs and a nose and such tender lips and eyes with long lashes. And he was breathing.

Martha knew she had to hurry, but she hadn't counted on such brutal emotion. The thought that she was about to lose her precious child again, this very night, consumed her.

She couldn't wake him.

Did she dare hold him? If he awoke, she would never have the strength to mark him. If she didn't mark him, she might never see him again. She might never see him again anyway. Shouldn't she just hold him now—her baby in her arms, his soft cheek against hers, his breathing in her ear?

She reached a trembling hand for his body. Touched him lightly on his head, pushed his hair back. He took a deep breath and turned his head toward her, still deep in sleep.

"This is David," Rachel said quietly.

Martha nodded but couldn't speak. There was no possible way for her to take him away from the commandant. Marking her beautiful baby boy might be the only way to find him again.

Martha closed her eyes and gripped her hands to fists. *Strong, Martha. You have to be strong.*

With Rachel and two other gaunt women in nearby bunks now staring on, Martha heated the brand until it glowed. She'd reversed it on the ladle to make it a companion to Esther's mark.

She could barely see to press the hot brand into David's flesh for all her tears. To make matters worse, Rachel began to hit her feebly as soon as the metal made contact. As with Esther, it took a moment for David to wake, but when he did, a scream was already in his throat.

For the first time in nine months, Martha pulled her baby boy to her neck and held him tight. His cries tore at her heart like knives, and she did her best to comfort him. He didn't know who she was, didn't recognize the scent of skin or the tone of her voice. Slowly, he calmed.

"It's my mark, Rachel," she said as she put the salve on David's burn. "Do you understand? My mark. So that later I will be able to find him."

Rachel stared at her with hollow eyes, but Martha thought she might understand, might remember what she had done once for her own son. One of the women looked out the dark window to their left. Martha followed her gaze and froze. A light! A guard was coming!

Now, so late? It couldn't be possible!

She spun to Rachel. "Where's his shirt?"

Rachel blinked.

"His shirt—we must cover this! Hurry!"

The woman picked up a small cotton shirt from the end of the bed, and Martha snatched it from her hands. If the guards caught her in here, all would be lost.

The light approached steadily, swinging at the end of the guard's arm. Had Braun discovered her missing? She began to panic. There was no time. No time!

She handed her child to Rachel. "Lie down! Pretend you're sleeping. Don't let them see!"

She scooped up the ammo boxes, ran to the back around the last bunk, and climbed through a window just as the front door opened. If they would have turned on a light, they might have caught her with one leg still hooked in the window, but with the raids, they couldn't chance the brilliance.

Then Martha fled as fast as she dared in the darkness, pulse hammering in her skull, certain that all was lost.

47

"MOTHER?" ESTHER'S EYES WIDENED.
"Esther?"

Esther stepped forward, but Braun grabbed her collar and yanked her back.

"Drop the gun," Lars said, shoving his pistol into Ruth's back.

Ruth's face wrinkled in empathy. She looked at Stephen. Then at Esther. Her eyes flooded with tears. Ruth began to cry.

"I thought . . ." Stephen didn't know what to say.

"Yes, you thought she was dead," Braun said. "She is. She's been dead for thirty years."

"Mama?" Esther gazed at her mother. There was something between them, Stephen thought. Something they knew that he did not.

The rifle wavered in his hands. "She . . . she's been alive all these years?"

"Naturally," Braun said. "My father's foolishness in allowing any of you to live has created several problems, but it would take too long to explain how the powers of the air work."

He ran a fat tongue over his upper lip. "When he found the journal and the Stones missing, Gerhard was . . . let us say, disturbed. Martha had outwitted him, and Gerhard was forced to keep Ruth alive. In the event we found Martha, she would reveal the location of the Stones if we hung Ruth's life over her head. So we kept Ruth alive, in my father's house."

He paused as if to let comprehension of Ruth's plight sink in.

"And, of course, what better way to keep Ruth in humble service than to let her know that her daughter was also alive, and would remain so only if Ruth stayed faithful? We told Esther the same about her mother. They've never met, as you can see, but they've lived in respect of each other's life."

Braun's smile faded. "You see what happens when you don't follow the rules? My father should have killed Martha when he selected her with the scarf. Instead she stole his power and handed him thirty years of misery. Today I intend to take that power back." He shivered.

"I'm sorry, Mother," Esther said. "I'm so sorry."

"Don't be. God has answered our prayers."

An awkward moment of silence passed.

"Please lower the gun," Braun said.

Stephen's head buzzed. Slowly his rifle came down, as if it had a will of its own.

"Rifle on the floor," Braun said.

"Forgive me, Mama," Esther said.

"Rifle on the floor!"

Stephen set down the rifle and stepped back.

"Don't be sorry," Ruth said. "Never. Every minute of my life has been worth this one."

Braun clasped his hands behind his back and spoke in a low voice. "Go on. Go to your mother." A chill descended over Stephen. Braun's eyes held wickedness.

Esther walked down the aisle, then hurried the last few paces and embraced Ruth. She kissed her graying hair and her cheeks, then turned to Braun.

"Untie her! What kind of animal leads a weak woman around by a rope?"

Braun's eyebrow arched. "The master of that woman. Back!"

Esther hesitated then walked back.

"David. You are such a lovely boy." Ruth looked between them.

It occurred to Stephen that Braun was reloading his pistol. He exchanged a short glance with Esther.

"And Martha?" Ruth asked. "How is my Martha?"

"She . . . she's dead," Stephen said. "She died in America two weeks ago. She died happy, and she led us to you."

"Did she?" Braun snapped the clip home in his pistol. "Let's give Martha credit, but not too much, shall we?"

Meaning what?

"This moment is . . . invigorating, it really is," Braun said. "But I'm afraid we have to shift our attention back to the Stones." He looked at Ruth. "I trust you don't need any more convincing."

Ruth didn't seem to have heard the man. She was captivated by Esther and Stephen.

Braun pressed his gun into Esther's hip. "Or do you?"

Ruth's face settled, and her jaw firmed. Her eyes met Braun's.

"You had us fooled all these years. Bravo. You convinced us that you couldn't possibly have known what Martha did with the Stones. Martha wasn't even aware that you'd survived your little hanging." He pulled the hammer back on his revolver. "But now I know the truth. You know where Martha hid the Stones. Don't you, dear Ruth? Martha's letter has spoken from beyond the grave."

No one moved. Stephen's mind tripped back to the letter. He could see the last sentence in his mind's eye now: *As for the Stones, their hiding place will go to the grave with Ruth and me.*

"As you can see, your daughter is as healthy as an ox. You have five seconds to begin speaking."

One glance at Ruth, and Stephen knew she had the information Braun wanted.

"If you kill her, I won't tell you," Ruth said.

"I will do much worse than kill her."

Braun lifted his pistol to Esther's head. The gun jumped in his hand. Esther jerked and cried out. Blood oozed from a crease in her skin where the bullet had grazed her neck.

Roth wiped the blood from her cheek and then sucked it off his finger. "That was a warning. I imagine she can take ten carefully placed bullets without dying."

Ruth stared at the man for a few seconds. There may have been a day when she would have called his bluff. But today she looked like a woman who'd been beaten down one too many times.

"They are buried at Toruń," Ruth said without batting an eye.

—⁘—

THE SOUND of the words sent a tremor through Roth. The Stones were buried in Toruń. His focused intellect had assumed as much for years. Gerhard had even swept the camp with electronic gear once without success.

Still, Roth knew. He had always known. His whole plan practically depended on Toruń. Which is why hearing that name brought such relief.

Toruń.

Toruń, Roth's spiritual birthing place. Where his father had shown him how to harvest souls.

Toruń, where his father had lost all of his power through one asinine decision.

Toruń, where Roth would finally become a god.

He could barely speak for all of his pleasure. "Where?"

Ruth hesitated. "Under the gates. But I will only show you when you have let her go as agreed."

It was too much! Under the gates! The confession was nothing less than an announcement from Lucifer himself. *Lead them like lambs to the slaughter, and I will deliver myself unto you.*

Roth wanted to shout out his joy, but he held it back in a final act of control. He would have to spread some joy throughout Hamburg to celebrate, but only when he'd finished what his cowardly father had failed to complete himself.

—⁘—

A FIRE had entered Roth Braun's eyes, Stephen thought. His eyes danced; an obscene grin tugged at his lips. Sweat dampened his face.

He walked to Stephen. "I want you to listen carefully, Jew, if you want to live. I'm sure the police in Los Angeles will have a problem with your disappearance, so go set their minds at ease. If you ever look for us,

I'll kill them both. One word to the wrong people, and Esther will pay with her life. Carry that with you to your grave."

The man's arm flashed out. His pistol crashed against Stephen's skull, like bricks hurled from a catapult. He felt himself fall.

Hit the pew. Heard a sob.

Esther's.

Then nothing.

48

ESTHER DRIFTED BETWEEN REALITIES, VAGUELY AWARE THAT something was wrong. Something had happened—something furious and explosive—followed by the smell of a strong medicine, but that was surely a dream.

They were in a dark car, she and Ruth in the back, men's voices in the front. She thought they might have driven through a city some time ago, collected an old man with tubes in his nose, but he was surely a dream. The kind of nightmare the mind fabricated in deep, deep sleep.

In reality, she was driving with Stephen. Stephen and her mother, Ruth. They were going to Poland to deal with Braun, or they were running from him. She wasn't sure which. Mostly, they were just going. Together. In his car. She and Stephen in the front seat, Ruth in the back. Stephen obsessing after her from behind the wheel, she pondering him from the passenger's seat, her mother smiling with approval.

They were passing through the border into Poland, going after the Stones of David.

Stephen smiled and she smiled back, dreamy and hazy.

When the border guard waved them through, Stephen revved up the van and took off with enough acceleration to produce a tiny squeal.

"Slow down." Esther objected. "You're driving as if we've just robbed a bank."

Stephen slowed and glanced in the rearview mirror. "Sorry. We're okay." He grinned. "Peachy."

"Peachy?" It was the American colloquialism he'd used during their long discussion in the church while waiting for Braun.

"Peachy."

"Peachy?" Ruth said. "I love peaches."

Esther chuckled. Her mother was here, safe and together with her for the first time in her memory. She couldn't stop looking at her, this woman who'd given birth to her and then given her life.

Then there was Stephen. Everything about Stephen struck her as a bit funny. Not funny as in comical, but funny as in nice. This man—who'd jumped out of the alley at her, who'd ruined her first good shot at Braun, and then who'd come screaming back into the church for her—made her feel funny. A nice kind of funny.

Esther turned and felt something that smelled like leather press against her face. Was she sitting up front with Stephen, or had she climbed in the back with Ruth?

Up front with Stephen, of course.

She'd never felt this way about a man before. Here was a man who claimed to be obsessed with her, a savior who'd come blazing out of the past to rescue her from her eternal prison. David, who had been born because of her mother's sacrifice and who now seemed willing to give his life for hers in repayment. No, not in repayment. In love.

With each passing minute, the realization that Stephen really did love her grew, until she began to wonder whether she herself was smitten with this obsession of his. For him. How ridiculous! Was his disease contagious?

How could any sane woman find herself so hopelessly attracted to any man in such a short time? This couldn't be love. It must be her irrational response to the first sign of real kindness shown her by any man in years. She'd been smothered by Braun's thick hand since birth, a bird caught in a cage, a tiger whipped into submission, a butterfly snagged in a web. And now she was suddenly free because of these two people. Her mother and her . . .

Her what? That was the question, wasn't it? Here was the kind of man she had longed for all these years. Here was her knight in shining armor.

Here was the one who really did think she was beautiful. How could she possibly resist such a love? She couldn't. And Ruth, her mother, didn't want her to resist either. It was meant to be, and they all knew it. A fairy tale come true. She felt like laughing.

She sat with her hands folded in her lap, smiling, bouncing quietly along, wanting to see if he might be looking at her. She couldn't very well just turn and stare at him, now, could she? When they talked, she would have ample opportunity to look directly at him.

"I can't believe I actually found you," he would say.

Esther would face him. He would make a show of looking at the cattle in the field they were passing. But she could tell that his mind was lost on her. Why else would he swallow like that, or lick his dry lips and then bite them? His hair curled around his ear, dark strands moved by a hidden breeze. He was such a gentle man, beautiful to look at and fascinating to think about. She could still see him running over the pew tops screaming. What kind of man would do that for her?

"Right?" he asked, glancing at her.

He'd caught her staring? But she had the right to look at him because he said something and wanted a response. Still, she'd looked at him too long. Her face flushed. She'd betrayed herself. But she didn't look away.

He'd asked a question. What was the question?

"What?" she asked.

For an eternal moment, they stared deep into each other's eyes. "I was just thinking of how incredible it was that I actually found you," he said.

"Yes." She cleared her throat and looked at the cows he'd pretended to be interested in. "Incredible. Like finding a mouse in a haystack."

"A needle," he said.

Another of his colloquialisms.

"How silly. Whoever heard of losing a needle in a haystack? We say mouse. Have you ever tried to catch a mouse in a haystack?"

"No." He chuckled.

Another good opportunity to look at him. She did so, laughing with him. "What's so funny?"

"You."

"I'm funny?"

"No. You're . . . cute."

She blushed again. "Mice are cute; needles are not."

Why was she disagreeing with him? She should be throwing herself at him and thanking him from the bottom of her heart.

"Touché," he said.

"Yes, touché," Ruth said. They both looked at her and smiled.

"Talk, talk," Ruth said, waving her arms in encouragement. "I've waited my whole life for this moment; please don't spoil it for me. Talk about love."

Tears blurred Esther's vision. She reached a hand back and squeezed her mother's. "I'm so happy. Thank you." She looked at Stephen and touched his arm with her other hand. "Thank you both. Thank you for finding me. I feel . . ." She paused, suddenly unsure of what to tell them. She couldn't say she was falling madly in love with Stephen. That would sound stupid. She couldn't say she was so glad Mother was free. That sounded too plain.

David's right brow went up, urging her to continue.

". . . found," she finally said.

Esther rubbed Ruth's hand and smiled through tears.

David frowned and nodded. "Hmm. Found. Like the treasure in the field. Wow, that's perfect."

It was? *Wow.* The American expression was new, and she liked it.

"If I'm right, he's already on his way," an uncomfortably familiar voice said.

Esther moaned and rolled. Funny how it felt as if she was lying down somewhere. And where was Stephen?

Maybe she was dreaming.

———

A FIERCE odor stung his nostrils. The sound of running feet. Stephen pulled himself from darkness. Slowly, he remembered what had happened. What was happening.

Braun had knocked him out and dumped him in the alley. He'd then taken Esther and Ruth and was on his way to Toruń.

This simple thought was filled with complex details. Details like Braun, the beast, and Esther, the beauty, and Ruth, his savior, and Toruń, the place where the beast played his game with the red scarf and killed the beauties.

Details like the fact that someone had waked him.

He pushed himself off the cobblestones in an attempt to stand. But his muscles weren't ready to execute the maneuver, and he fell flat on his face.

Roth Braun had let him go. Why?

Stephen moaned, rolled, and desperately willed his body's cooperation. Slowly, his arms and legs responded. Then he was tripping down the alley, one hand dragging on the wall, the other flailing for balance.

The panic hadn't abated. Nor could it. Surges of hot and cold swept over his body like storm-driven waves. They had taken Esther. They were taking Esther to Toruń. They were going to kill Esther at Toruń.

Stephen staggered down the alley and began to cry uncontrollably. His sobs echoed off the walls. When he broke into the street, people were staring at him.

"You should be ashamed of yourselves!" he cried.

The statement sounded absurd. Stephen began to run. There was no way to even begin telling them what they had just done. A princess had lived among them, and they had just killed her. Every last one of them should pay for their sin!

His vision was blurry. He overran himself and slammed into the Volkswagen van. He quickly recovered, tore the door open, and slid in.

How much time had passed? What if they weren't going to Toruń?

Pain hollowed his chest, a pain worse than long swords running him through. Nothing could be worse than this. Nothing!

Never had he wanted anything as terribly as he wanted to save Esther. His desire for the safe in Los Angeles paled by comparison.

And he knew that this was precisely what Roth expected. Stephen's reaction was the object of this mad game Roth was playing. He was lifting and dashing hopes as his father had with the women of Toruń.

He knew it, and he was powerless to stop it.

Stephen yelled at the windshield and slammed both hands against the steering wheel, once, twice. He fired the van up and screeched through a U-turn. A man on a bicycle dived for cover.

"Get out of my way!" He was briefly tempted to drive straight over the spinning wheels.

He roared from the village, redlining the VW's small motor before remembering to shift. When he did, he went right through the gears, blasting down the road.

The incline out of the village slowed the van, and he cursed his decision to rent the van over a Porsche.

Somewhere ahead on this very road, another car carried Esther, his dear, precious Esther, bound and taped and being led to her slaughter.

And what if he was wrong? What if Braun was still back in the village, beating the truth out of her?

Stephen shoved the brake pedal to the floor, sending the van into a precarious skid. A few hours had passed, judging by the light. Braun *had* to be on his way to Toruń. Either way, Stephen didn't have time to run through the village searching, while in all likelihood Esther was on the way to Poland.

He gritted his teeth and slammed the accelerator home.

The first fifty kilometers flew by. He didn't encounter any more than three vehicles. But then he pulled onto the autobahn headed east, and cars abounded. He felt lost in a sea of thugs, even though he knew these weren't the thugs. A hundred cars faded in his rearview mirror before it occurred to him that getting pulled over at this speed might actually put him in jail. Then again, he was on an autobahn, wasn't he? The square blue signs said 130 for cars and motorcycles and 80 for trucks.

He pushed the van to 140 km/h.

A hundred scenarios played through his mind. Images of Ruth. Of Esther speaking her mind and putting Braun in his place. Or being gagged and drugged. Or dead.

God, please. I beg you. Whoever you are, whatever your purpose, I beg you, bring Esther back to me.

He still had to cross the border into Poland. Thank God he had a

Russian passport and the twenty thousand dollars he'd brought with him. He only prayed it was enough to buy his way across without the right visa. He still had to reach Toruń; he still had to avoid the police while shredding whatever speed limit lay in his way.

Esther still had to be alive.

Ruth still had to be alive.

And even if they were, what then?

49

E STHER AND STEPHEN AND RUTH HAD A DOZEN EXCHANGES, ALL dreamy, all vivid, all beautiful. And all while they were driving straight for this snake pit once known as Toruń.

What they would find there, she really had no clue, and she really didn't want to discuss the matter. There seemed to be an unspoken agreement between the three of them not to discuss the place, which was strange, considering they were headed straight for it. Stephen's preoccupation with her provided enough of a distraction.

Why were they going after the Stones of David? After all, she and David were the true Stones.

The car slowed, and Esther suddenly realized she was leaning against the door. And to her right, Ruth was also slumped over, sleeping. They apparently had fallen asleep while talking to Stephen.

She sat up and looked outside. Night. It was quiet, dark except for the bright moon. They were driving past a large, abandoned camp that looked like it had been turned into a museum. The sign over the gate . . .

STUTTHOF

Her heart bolted. Tall trees with sparse foliage surrounded the huge complex like shamed sentinels, bared for the whole world to see. Barbed fencing still surrounded the compound, and inside, dozens of identical barracks had fallen into various stages of disrepair.

A motorcycle headed the opposite way rushed past with a whine.

How could anyone live near this place? But then, she'd lived in a place like this since her birth, hadn't she?

". . . after all these years. How can we Germans stand by and let them pretend this is a monument to the Jews?" The man spit in disgust. "It's a monument to the greatest time in history. The Third Reich."

For the first time in many hours, Esther began to realize that not all was as she'd imagined. She wasn't in the front seat. Stephen wasn't sitting next to her. She wasn't even in his car!

"She's awake," someone said. The old man she'd imagined in her dreams.

Adrenaline began to clear Esther's mind. She jerked her arms and found that they were bound behind her back. She cried out, only to discover that her mouth had been taped. And next to her, Ruth lay bound and gagged as well. She was still sedated.

The full reality of her predicament settled on her mind like a massive boulder, crushing any attempt to rise above it. Braun had struck Stephen in the church, maybe leaving him dead, and then left the village with her and Ruth drugged and bound. They'd stopped somewhere and collected the old man, who sat in the passenger seat now, breathing through an oxygen tube. The father. The one who'd hanged the women. With the son behind the wheel and the father in the passenger seat, they'd rolled through Poland, and had just passed Stutthof.

They were going to Toruń.

Esther leaned back, swung her feet up, and kicked at the heads on the other side of the seat. Her right foot struck the old man. She kicked at Roth, but the car swerved and she missed him. She struck out again, screaming through the tape, shutting out their curses.

The son reached up and wrenched her foot. Pain shot up her leg, and she arched her back.

"The next time I will break it," he said, and she had no doubt that he would. The father was silent.

She yelled at Roth through the tape, "What are you doing? Let me out!" But he couldn't understand her, and even if he could, the demand wouldn't generate a response. She knew the answer anyway.

They were taking her to Toruń because that's where the treasure was. Because that's where the hangings were.

The old man slowly twisted around and stared at her, and for a moment she thought he was part animal. Deep lines like canyons ran across his white face. His eyes looked black in the dim light, abysmal holes. She returned his gaze, terrified.

Gerhard turned back without speaking.

Silence settled around her once again. She was in a black car with leather seats, wet with her own sweat, sitting next to Ruth, who was still mercifully separated from consciousness. The drug had affected her older, frail body more severely. Her mother was a fighter to the end, though. Ruth had bought them some time, knowing that the moment she revealed the location of the treasure, their usefulness would end.

Esther forced her mind to dig deep, as deep as it could through the lingering effects of the drug. But she couldn't fathom a way out.

The car crested a small hill, and both men looked to the right. Two hundred yards off the road stood two old wooden posts with a crossbar, and beyond that the ruins of buildings jutting from tall grass. A second hill rose to the right of the dilapidated compound, and on that hill was a very old building that was shedding its red paint and looked to be hardly standing.

A pale moon hovered in the graying dusk sky.

Toruń.

Esther's heart hammered. The gates still stood! She had heard that most camps had been leveled.

They turned onto a gravel drive and drove across the field toward the looming gate.

Roth stopped twenty meters from the gate and turned off the engine.

Silence smothered them.

The engine ticked softly.

Esther stared past the entrance. She could see them now, as ghosts, a thousand starving women, dressed in gray clothing, standing in formation, waiting orders from a ruthless commandant.

"Parts still stand," Gerhard said. He slipped out of his nasal cannula and looked at the gate in wonder. "This is better than I could have hoped for." He faced Roth. "You knew?"

Roth didn't respond. He opened his door and stepped out.

A new sound filled Esther's ears. A field of crickets sawing at their own legs, like an orchestra greeting the new prisoners.

Roth's feet crunched on the gravel as he stepped forward, then stopped by the hood. For a moment he just gazed at the camp, then he lifted his chin, put both hands on his hips and breathed deep.

Gerhard stepped out and walked up to the gate. He touched the wood and brushed his hands together.

The crickets seemed to scream now. All of them.

Finally Roth retreated to the back of the car and pulled something from the trunk. He met Gerhard in front of the gate and they approached the entrance to Toruń together, father limping along slowly on thin legs, son holding a shovel and a large coil of rope.

The shovel was to dig. The rope . . .

Esther leaned back and shifted her gaze. She would not think about the rope. Ruth slept on, nostrils pulling audibly at the air.

When Esther looked back up, they were looking up at the crossbar. Even from here she could see the white mark worn on the wood. A rope mark from hundreds of hangings. Roth threw one end of the rope over the wood, lined it up with the groove, and then stood back.

This was their plumb line, Esther thought with sudden hope. The falling rope marked a spot directly beneath the worn mark. They were going to dig under the spot where they'd hanged their women so many years ago.

But couldn't they as easily estimate the center without a rope?

ROTH BRAUN could feel the power. What he now felt was new. How many souls had he stolen since the war? Too many to count.

These would be different.

These were the ones who'd stolen part of his soul first, a feat far more damaging to him in spiritual terms than any occurrence since.

As he saw it, the only way to undo his father's grievous sin was to return Gerhard's full power to him by beating these Jews in their own game, using as much cunning as Martha had.

Now he would outwit them, not by retrieving the Stones of David—although that was no small accomplishment—but by returning these Jews to the very fate they should have suffered in the first place.

By hanging them and then bleeding their souls.

Roth was in a very good mood.

He glanced at the road that led to the camp. Still no sign of pursuit.

"I know why you insist on the ritual," Gerhard said, "but please remember that the Stones are as important."

Roth's mood dimmed. But he was a patient man who could handle the weakness of others when required.

He couldn't bring himself to speak to the old man. Dealing with him would be the least of his pleasures, certainly not something to dwell on. Tragic how this man who'd introduced him to the great war of life—the struggle between God and Lucifer over the passions of man—now served the lesser master of greed and self-preservation.

But this would not stop Roth.

He turned away from his father and went to get the younger one.

THE SON walked back toward the car. Opened the door. "Get out."

Esther pushed herself away from the door and cocked her legs to protect herself.

"Is that necessary?" he said impatiently. His eyes were dark, emotionless.

He grabbed her foot and pulled roughly. She tried to kick—tried to strike him, even though she knew she would only provoke him—but she could not stop her slide. She landed on her back with a dull *thump*.

"Get up, or I'll drag you. And if you kick at me again, I'll put a bullet in your leg."

Esther rolled over, drew her knees under her belly, and struggled to her feet, her arms still tied behind her back. He prodded her and she walked for the gallows, numb.

Gerhard watched her. "Are you frightened now, little flower?"

Esther felt a lump fill her throat. Mama? She wanted to cry out, but her mouth was still strapped with tape.

Roth Braun took Esther's arm and shoved her to the ground. He quickly wound tape around her legs. Silent. Breathing steadily.

The old man stared at her, fascinated. His hands trembled by his sides, and his eyes glimmered with delight.

Roth fashioned a loop with a heavy knot on one end of the rope.

Esther began to panic again. But before she could even whimper, Roth had pulled her to her feet, spun her so she was facing the road, and shoved the noose over her head. He cinched it tight and tied the rope to the fence so that some pressure, but not too much, pulled on Esther's neck.

Braun walked to the car and shook Ruth awake. It took a minute before he finally helped her out of the backseat. Her mother stood unsteadily, gazing dumbly at the camp. Slowly, her eyes focused.

Braun had more rope in hands, from where, Esther hadn't seen.

Roth pulled the tape from her mouth. "No screaming," he said. "You'll have your chance to speak, but not now. Walk."

He directed Ruth to one side, threw the rope over the crossbar and set a twin loop over Ruth's head.

He threw a third length over the bar on Esther's right.

Ruth looked at Esther. A tear on Ruth's cheek glistened in the moonlight, but she showed no other sign of weakness or sorrow. Her mother's strength gave Esther some courage.

"Are we ready?" Gerhard asked his son.

Roth glanced past the car toward the road and hesitated. He was waiting?

He finally put one hand on the rope and faced Ruth. "If you don't tell us where it is, or if you direct us to the wrong location, your daughter will suffer painfully. If you cooperate, you will both live. Do you believe me?"

No answer.

Roth nodded at his father, who approached Ruth.

"Where did Martha hide the Stones?" Gerhard asked.

Ruth stared at him, emotionless. The moment she told them where the treasure was, they would both die, Esther thought, peering down.

"You're thinking that we will kill you anyway," Roth said. "Then what leverage would I have against Stephen? He would tell the world what he knows and I would have a problem. Your choice is a simple one: Either you tell us where the Stones are and live, or Esther dies first, then you."

He pulled on the rope, lifting Esther to her tiptoes.

"One pace south of the center," Ruth said softly. The words horrified Esther. So quickly! Ruth was too weak to resist.

Roth stared at Ruth for a long time as if caught off guard by her response. He had the look of a disappointed man.

He released the rope so that if Esther continued to stand on her toes, the noose wouldn't cut into her skin.

Roth removed his coat, placed it carefully on the fence, took up the shovel, and buried its blade deep into the earth roughly one pace to Esther's left.

She looked at her mother. Ruth gazed at her, eyes tearful. If Esther could speak past the tape, she would tell her mother that she was okay. That her sacrifice hadn't been in vain. That she loved Ruth more than she loved life itself.

Roth swung his shovel. *Chunk, scrape, chunk.* Metal on dirt. But it wasn't as loud as the sound of her own breathing. Or her heart.

It was louder than the crickets, but barely.

Don't panic, Esther. They won't kill you. He's right, they need you alive to keep Stephen from speaking. They've kept you alive all these years. What's a few more?

But she didn't believe it. She'd never felt such lingering horror.

Maybe someone would come over the hill and discover them. The car and the men were visible from the road. Seeing a man digging a hole at the base of this gate would surely draw the attention of anyone driving by. It had to! But whoever would come out to this dreadful place at night?

The old man stood stooped, dressed in wool pants that rose halfway up his belly and a gray sweater that looked as old as the war. Behind him on the hill stood the house from where he'd kept watch over his women.

Esther glanced at Roth steadily digging. There was only one outcome to this madness. Not three or two, but one.

Gerhard was walking around the hole now, like a vulture, waiting. If she could jump and kick him . . .

The shovel struck something solid. Gerhard stepped forward and stared into the hole. He dropped to his knees, thrust his arms below the dirt, and yanked on something that came loose reluctantly.

A container. Small, like a shoe box, maybe an ammunition holder, though she could barely see it.

They'd found Martha's treasure.

She closed her eyes. She heard a small whimper. From her own throat. Panic edged into her mind.

"Shh, shh, shh," Ruth whispered. "I will hold you in my arms forever, my dear Esther."

"Mama . . ."

"Be strong, Esther."

But Ruth was crying as well.

50

IN ROTH'S MIND, FINDING THE STONES WAS MERELY A BONUS. NOT a small one, but still only a bonus.

Roth's skin buzzed with anticipation now. They'd set the table up ten meters from the gate, directly in front of Esther. It was a small folding table, not the lavish spread Gerhard had used in the war. But they had a white tablecloth and three crystal goblets. One tall bar stool.

And a silver knife.

The ammunition box sat on the ground behind them. Esther teetered on her toes, struggling to keep the rope from choking her. Ruth stood next to her. Gerhard stood by Roth's side before the table.

They were all here except Stephen.

The only thing that dampened Roth's spirits was Gerhard's obvious eagerness to hurry the ritual. The Stones were his prize.

Or were they? He hadn't actually opened the box yet.

Gerhard fidgeted and looked at him. "He may not come."

Roth watched the road. Still no sign.

"What are you waiting for?" Ruth demanded. "You have what you came for, and you're too cowardly to keep your word, so finish it. We've defeated you already."

He would have to be careful with Ruth. She was still capable of lowering the heights to which he anticipated ascending today.

"I have no intention of killing you, Ruth," he said. "Your daughter, perhaps, but not you."

"I don't believe you."

Esther's body was shaking with fatigue.

The road was still empty. Roth's eagerness to move forward forced him into a decision. Although patience was a strength, it had to be balanced against ambition and passion.

On balance it was time to move forward.

Roth picked up the bar stool. He stepped around the table.

"Think about it, Ruth," he said, but he was looking at Esther's frantic eyes now. He'd tried to do this once when she was a sleeping baby. It was immeasurably more satisfying now that she was fully aware.

"As stated, I need Esther alive to keep Stephen under control. And I need you to keep her in line. We really are one big happy family, just as we've always been."

"If you'd wanted to bleed us for your sickening ritual, you could have done that years ago," she said.

"Yes, but not with the same results. Bleeding is pointless unless the subject is in a particular state. I don't expect you to understand."

Esther stared at him with wide eyes.

He set the stool against her legs, ripped the tape off of her mouth, and walked toward the fence where the rope was tied off.

"I'm going to pull . . ." He untied the rope and applied some pressure, forcing her to stretch higher. "I advise you to climb the stool as I pull so that I don't break your neck."

Roth pulled. She stabbed at the stool with her legs and drew it under her. Clambered on the first rungs.

Roth snugged the rope. Watching her filled him with pride. His power was superior to hers. It always had been, but until now he'd never had the true opportunity to express it.

He pulled harder. "That's it. Up. Up, up."

She winced when the rope tightened on her neck, but she managed to get her knees on the round wood seat.

"Up, up."

He helped her by pulling her up, like drawing a caught fish out of the water. One leg under. The stool tipped, nearly spilled. That would have been disappointing. But she was a capable woman. She stood on the stool, trembling like a leaf, coughing and gasping. But standing.

Roth fed out a couple feet of slack and tied the rope off.

He walked to the table, picked up the knife and one of the glasses, then faced Esther, whose wrists were still taped together behind her back. Ruth had said nothing. He would have to watch her.

"I'm just going to cut you, Esther. If you look at your mother's palms, you'll see a scar. She's been cut before. Now it's your turn. The only reason I put you on the stool was to control you. If you try to kick me while I'm bleeding you, the stool will probably tip over and you'll drop."

She was trying so hard to be brave. But her face was white and stretched paper thin. She was balanced on that razor edge that divided hope and fear.

He stepped up to her hanging arms and held the glass under her fingertips. He set the blade against her white wrist, just below the gray tape, and pushed lightly.

She whimpered.

"You're in good company. Another Jew was bled by his enemy. Few think of Jesus Christ as a Jew, but he was. It's why we hate him."

Sweat ran down Roth's lip. His own hand began to shake.

Then Roth couldn't hold himself back any longer. He pressed the sharp silver blade down and slid it toward him.

Esther groaned. Her knees began to buckle, then found strength again.

A thin trail of blood seeped out of the cut, over her palm, down her forefinger, into the glass.

"You are a devil," Ruth said.

"I am," he said.

Roth was temporarily frozen by the moment. Lost in his own glory. A tear slipped down his cheek.

He held the cup out to his father, who took it, mesmerized. Subservient.

"Drink it, Father."

"Not you?"

"She undermined you, not me."

"All of it?"

"All of it."

Gerhard tilted the glass back and swallowed the small pool of blood. Roth trembled with anticipation. He turned to Ruth.

"It's your turn, my dear. Just a little blood."

"You are very sick," Ruth said.

"The power of life is in the blood," he said.

51

STUTTHOF.

Stephen roared by the old camp as the sun slipped closer to the horizon, choking on his own heart. The steering wheel was slippery from his sweat, but that didn't matter—there were no turns in this road. Stutthof was on this road, and Toruń was on this road. Sickness and death, that's all. Sickness and death and lots of buried Jews.

He would do anything to prevent Ruth's and Esther's names from being added to the long list.

Maybe he'd passed them on the autobahn. After an hour at 140, he'd pushed the van to its limit and held it there all the way to Poland. The border crossing had slowed him half an hour, but his money had bought a crossing. He could only hope that the border had slowed them as well.

Assuming they had even come this way.

He was driving blind, praying incessantly, hoping that he hadn't misjudged Braun's intent.

If he reached Toruń before them, he would dig a hole and pretend he'd found the treasure only to hide it again. If . . .

The camp suddenly rose into view like a monster from the sea. A black car was parked in front of the gate. Two people standing.

A body hung from the crossbeam. A second next to it, lower.

Stephen's heart seized. He barely glanced at the shoulder before yanking the van off the road, directing it through a shallow ditch and straight for the camp, two hundred meters off.

The van pounded over clumps of grass, threatening to wrest the wheel from his grasp, but Stephen hardly noticed. His eyes were locked on those bodies, and his mind was screaming bloody murder.

Esther's legs were partially obscured by the black car from this angle. He could no longer see Braun. He was bouncing over the field and whimpering and seeing nothing but red. Red and the black forms, hands tied, neck crooked, dangling on the end of the rope.

A sliver of reason sliced into his consciousness. Other than the knife in his right sock, he had no weapon. But the van was a weapon. They would begin shooting at the onrushing van at any moment—he had to bob and weave and he had to actually hit Braun.

One hundred yards. No shots.

Stephen swung the wheel to the right, sent the van into a fishtail. He began to weave through the grass.

———

AT FIRST, Esther thought the blur on the horizon was a bird, diving into the field for prey. Gerhard Braun was drinking their blood, and there was a bird diving from the road.

A car sliding into the field.

Stephen!

Esther couldn't hear the van streaking for them; her ears were filled with rushing blood and her heart was knocking. The old man might be half-deaf, and Roth too distracted, but sooner or later, they would hear. She had to distract them!

But she was still in shock. Her mind was hardly working, much less her mouth.

The van fishtailed crazily, only a hundred yards off now. She could already hear the racing engine as it bounced.

Behind her, Roth began to chuckle.

"The boy does not disappoint," he said.

———

STEPHEN SAW that the rope around Esther's neck was loose when he was still fifty meters out.

She was alive.

The sudden relief vanished immediately. She was on a stool. If she fell, she would die.

Three choices. He could try to angle directly for Roth Braun. He could ram the car and hope that it ran Braun over. Or he could crash into the gate, hoping to bring the whole thing down, including Esther.

Angling for Braun was a problem because he still couldn't see the man at thirty yards out. Ramming the car could be a problem because the black vehicle looked pretty solid—he might accomplish nothing except his own dismemberment. And rather than saving her, crashing into the gate might turn out to be a deathblow to Esther.

He slammed the brakes and brought the van to a skidding halt three feet from the large Mercedes. Esther stared, white-faced.

Stephen began to scream.

At the top of his lungs, as he threw the door open, as he vaulted the Mercedes' hood. He was nothing more than an enraged savage pushed to his limits by this brutal attack on Esther. His woman. His life.

The rage became awareness in the space of two steps. He pulled up abruptly.

Roth stood beside Esther, gripping one of the stool's legs, ready to yank it out. A gun in the other hand, hanging loosely by his side. Face amused.

"Nice of you to join us," Roth said.

"Stephen?" Esther's voice was breathy. High-pitched.

Ruth stood strung to Esther's left. Only then did he see the third rope, hanging on Esther's right. This was for him?

An old man stood by a small table behind Esther. This was Gerhard, Ruth and Martha's tormentor. There were three glasses on the table. One was stained dark; one held a small puddle of black wine; one was empty.

Then he saw the blood dripping from Esther's bound hands. And Ruth's hands. Their wrists had been cut and still bled.

Their predicament settled into his mind. He heaved and vomited on the hood of Braun's car.

Roth smiled softly. "That's right, the situation is quite hopeless, isn't it? For you, that is. For me . . . I'm pleased to have played you so well."

Stephen's head was reeling. It struck him that Roth would now kill all three of them.

"Played me?"

"Surely you don't think you're here without my approval? I'm after more than the Stones of David. The fact is, I've played you like a fiddle from the moment you showed up at Martha's apartment in Los Angeles, as I knew you would. Assuming you were still alive."

"You were there for the Stones," Stephen said.

"I was there for you. I knew the minute I read the news story in the *Los Angeles Times* that Martha suspected you were alive and was calling out to you. She was, and now here you are. Consider yourself called."

Stephen laughed bitterly.

"I'm here because Martha was one step ahead of your father," Stephen said. "I'm here because I've stayed one step ahead of you." His voice held no conviction.

"Have you? I drew you, Jew boy. I let you find the scarf. Build your hope to the point of a mad obsession."

Roth Braun spoke the words as if tasting each with immense satisfaction. Stephen had underestimated the power of this man.

"How do you think you escaped unharmed from the basement? Why did I let you walk out of the church in Greifsman and have my men wake you in the alley? I had to make you believe it was all your own doing—this fuels courage—but you've done nothing without my allowing it."

Roth glared at him smugly.

"And why am I now telling you this, knowing that the game isn't yet finished? Because I know how it will crush you. I intend to return all of you to the death you should have met thirty years ago. I intend to bleed and hang all three of you."

He swayed slightly on his feet.

"Desperation, do you feel it working on your mind?"

The words bounced around Stephen's skull like a Ping-Pong ball.

"Turn around."

52

EVERYTHING WOULD PROCEED EXACTLY AS ROTH HAD planned now.

All three faced him, Esther on the stool, Ruth and Stephen on either side, necks tight in their nooses, hands bound and bleeding behind them.

Gerhard tipped back the chalice containing Stephen's blood and drained it. The evening air was cool, silent except for the cricket's song, screeching through the fields. Tears stained the faces of all three Jews.

Roth trembled.

His father set the glass on the table, eyes closed, face tilted to the dim sky. *Can you feel it, Father? I have restored your power to you.*

Gerhard said nothing. His frail frame looked white in the moonlight. For a moment Roth couldn't help thinking that he was one of the starving Jews that had filled the camps, a ghost of his former self.

But inside, where it mattered, Gerhard had now recaptured the full power once lost to him by his own stupidity.

Roth walked toward the car slowly, a master committed to the grandest of all ceremonies.

He withdrew a rope from the car and brought it back. Without looking at his father, he slung the noose over the cross bar. It slapped the wood noisily, then swung into place, eight feet from the ground.

Gerhard's eyes grew wide. With wonder though, not fear. He still did not understand.

"How do you feel, Father?"

Gerhard glanced at the rope. "A fourth rope?"

"For Martha," Roth said. "All four have to hang, even if Martha's hanging is only symbolic. How do you feel?"

Red stained the man's lips. He looked dazed. Drunk on the blood.

"You were right," he said. "Forgive me for ever doubting you. I feel alive."

Roth stepped to his side, withdrew the pistol from his belt, and slammed it into Gerhard's temple.

His father slumped, unconscious.

The Jews seemed too shocked to express their surprise. Good.

Roth hefted his father up under the arms, dragged him to the rope, and dropped him on the ground. Working calmly, he strapped Gerhard's wrists with tape as he had the Jews. Then he pulled the noose down, slipped it over his father's head, and drew it tight.

STEPHEN COULD not comprehend the events playing out before his eyes. The ache in his wrist where Roth had cut him faded when Gerhard collapsed in a heap.

The rope was cutting off the circulation in his neck, but he found that if he stood on his tiptoes, the blood flowed freely. This, too, was now only a distraction.

To his right, Esther's knees were shaking on the stool.

To his left, Gerhard Braun lay bound and noosed.

Roth was going to hang them all, including his own father.

"I have decided to let each of you witness a hanging before I hang you," Roth said. "I want you to see the horror on a man's face when he realizes that he has not found freedom and glory. He has to die so that I can take his power."

Roth's face shone with sweat, not from exertion. His eyes fixed on his father.

"I would have to say that it's worked out better this way. You've all spent your lives searching. Whether you knew it or not, seeking, seeking. And tonight you've found your treasure. But it isn't the treasure you were hoping for, is it? Not what Martha had in mind at all. Your hope for love and all that nonsense is now smothered by horror. Emptiness. Death. Hope, on the other hand, will belong to me."

An image of Chaim and Sylvia flashed through Stephen's mind. A week ago he'd been busy trying to convince Dan what a good investment the property in Santa Monica would make. He'd forsaken all that was once dear for the woman who now teetered on a stool beside him.

What had happened to him? He'd lost his mind.

Or had he? No, he'd found his heart.

Esther, I am so sorry.

"If you can see his eyes, watch them carefully," Roth said. "You can see the horror in the eyes."

He looked at Stephen for a moment, and then frowned as if disappointed that, in his current state, Stephen wouldn't be watching Gerhard's eyes, at least not carefully.

Roth suddenly stepped forward, grabbed the end of Gerhard's rope that hung free, and began to haul his father off the ground, headfirst.

The father came to his knees.

Gerhard coughed once, sputtered, and threw his hands around his neck. He clawed at the rope, disoriented. Finally he got his feet under himself and staggered to his feet.

"What . . ." he screeched. He began to cough before he could finish the sentence.

Roth tied his end of the rope around the post, walked to Gerhard, who was now hacking and wheezing in agony, and spread gray tape over the old man's lips. The father's eyes bulged wide and he strained to breathe through flaring nostrils.

Roth uttered a short cry of delight and jumped back to the post. He grabbed the rope with both hands and yanked Gerhard off the ground.

His father began to kick.

"You should have let me kill her, Father," Roth said. "Now look what you've gone and done."

Roth tied the rope off again. Gerhard's struggles eased. His wheezing was choked off. Only the crickets screeched.

Roth bounded behind his father, slipped a silver knife from his belt, and lined it up along the man's wrists.

Another kick from Gerhard.

"Be still!"

Roth cut him. Then jumped back, delighted. He ran to the table, scooped up one of the glass chalices and hurried back to his father. He worked frantically now, driven to drain his father's power and satisfy his obsession.

Gerhard went limp.

Roth lifted the glass and drank.

And then the air went silent again. Even the crickets had momentarily stalled their wails.

All the while Ruth had kept her eyes fixed dead ahead. Esther had followed her mother's cue and stood tall, despite the trembling in her legs.

And Roth . . . Roth stood panting behind them.

Stephen wasn't sure why, but the entire scene suddenly struck him as nothing more than child's play, which was odd because his quest for power certainly wasn't child's play. Still, in context, it now seemed hardly more than silly.

Foolish ambition in the face of far greater power.

What could possibly drive a man to such insane depths? What made one man crave another man's blood?

Obsession. A craving to have what he could not have. Power. Like Lucifer himself defying God in hopes of elevating himself. This moment was nothing less than the collision of two obsessions, theirs and Roth's. God's obsession with man. Lucifer's obsession with himself. Humankind's obsession with God on one hand, or themselves on the other hand.

Stephen turned his head to Esther and Ruth. He smiled. "I love you, Esther. God has given you to me as my obsession, and I love you."

"And I love you, David," Esther said bravely.

"Take courage," Ruth whispered. "God is our deliverer."

—⁓—

THE JEWS were talking, but Roth couldn't make out what they were saying. His head throbbed with an expansive pride that elevated him to a state of heavenly perfection.

It was finished. He had restored his father's power and now taken his soul. Even the Stones of David were now his. The Jews were cowering. He would hang them next. Then he would cut down the bodies and bury them behind the forest.

"Roth!"

The sound of his name cut through his heavy head.

"Roth. Oh, Roth, you do have a problem."

It was the Jew. Stephen. What was he saying?

Roth turned around and stared at them blankly.

"You're drunk on your father's blood, so you may not realize it yet, but you have a very significant problem," Stephen said boldly. Too boldly. "Your plan to harvest souls in anguish has failed."

Roth's mind started to clear. The Jew was trying to sabotage this glorious evening?

"You have not killed our hope. You can't."

———⁓———

THE MOMENT he saw Roth's bewildered expression, Stephen knew he'd struck a chord of fear in the man. This simple yet genuine display of courage undermined him in a way that no physical power could.

Stephen laughed, loudly, deliberately. "Ha! You've lost the upper hand, man. Our simple love overpowers you with a single word. Hang us! Hang us and see that it gains you nothing!"

He felt giddy. Perhaps it was the result of the emotional strain he'd suffered for a week now. Perhaps there was some truth in his claim—surely some of that. But mostly Stephen yelled the words because they really did fill him with a sense of power.

He laughed again, louder this time. "You've taken nothing from us!"

———⁓———

ROTH STARED at him. This was a farce.

Stephen was smiling because he'd gone mad with fear.

Then the Jew looked up at Esther, but continued to address Roth. "You thought you brought me for a death, but instead I have found

love." Stephen faced him and set his jaw. "I love Esther!" he cried, eyes
bright with passion. "I love her. I love her deeply, and I can die easily,
happily knowing that I have found my love."

He kept laughing. A genuine laugh.

Roth was too shaken to move.

"And I have found love," Esther said. "God has given me love instead
of fear."

Roth slammed his fist on the table. "Stop it!"

Ruth was smiling.

This couldn't be! He couldn't hang them while they were in this
frame of mind. It would undermine his whole plan. Anguish! He had to
return them to a state of anguish!

"I am about to hang you fools by the neck until you are dead!" He
thrust a finger toward Gerhard. "Look at my father. Look at his white, dead
face!"

They did not look.

The mother, Ruth, stared at him between the eyes. "You have another
problem," she said. "The box that you believe holds the Stones of David
is empty."

What was she saying?

"Don't be a fool," he said.

"Check it."

"You're lying."

"Check it," Stephen said. "Then hang us if you want. You've lost whatever you came here to gain anyway. We have no regrets, no fear. Only love
at finding each other."

Roth didn't want to check the box. He knew that even considering
their lies was a sign of weakness. But the thought of owning the Stones
had set its claws deeper into his mind than he had guessed.

He walked to the box as slowly as possible.

THE MOMENT Roth turned, Stephen lifted his right heel and grabbed
at his ankle with his bound hands.

He managed to grab his slacks and support his leg with one hand while he groped for the knife in his sock with his other hand. His fingers closed around the handle. Pulled it free.

He lowered his leg. If he dropped the knife now, there would be no retrieving it. He had to saw through the tape that bound his wrists before Roth returned his attention to them.

And if he did, then what?

Yes, then what?

He pointed the knife up and dug at the tape. Missed. Stuck his wrist instead. He ignored the pain and sliced upwards again.

Roth dropped to his knees by the box. He clawed at the lid.

Come on, Stephen.

The lid flew open. Roth stared into the box.

Thrust his hand inside. Pulled out bundled cloth. Stephen recognized it as one of the old shirts issued to prisoners in the camp. Martha had wrapped the Stones in a shirt.

Stephen felt something cutting, but he couldn't tell how much progress he was making. *Come on, Stephen, cut!*

Roth stood slowly to his feet, kneading the cloth, feeling for the Stones.

He turned to Ruth, eyes frenzied. Or delighted?

He let one end of the shirt fall. The cloth unraveled.

Empty.

Ruth was right; the box was empty.

Their tormentor began to moan. He faced them all, eyes darting, arms spread like a gunslinger. A white ghost in the moonlight, living on rage now.

"Where are they?"

Ruth said nothing.

Stephen prayed the German wouldn't see his shaking as he sawed at the tape. But he had no choice. He had to cut himself free now.

"Where are they?" Roth screamed. "Tell me, you filthy Jew!"

Ruth stared at him defiantly. "Now it is you who are in anguish. You've lost all of your power."

Roth rushed forward with surprising speed. He rounded the table, headed straight for Ruth. But he didn't go to Ruth.

He veered toward Esther at the last moment, grabbed the stool with both hands, and yanked it out, just as Stephen felt the tape give way behind his back.

Esther fell a foot before reaching the end of the rope. She bounced and swung three feet off the ground.

He'd hung her!

———

WHEN ESTHER saw Roth veer toward her, she knew the worst was about to happen. She instinctively took a huge gulp of air, tensed her muscles, and clenched her eyes.

Then she was airborne. She hit the bottom and bounced. Pain flashed down her spine. She swung like a piñata.

It took a moment for her to realize that she was alive. Not only was she alive, but her neck, though stretched, wasn't broken. And she could breathe. Barely.

She opened her eyes. She was dangling from the rope above the ground, but fully conscious and fully alive. Was this what it felt like to be hanged? Others' necks were broken by the snap, but hers wasn't. How long would she swing here before dying?

Stephen was swinging too! Had he been hanged as well?

She moved her legs but immediately felt pain stab at her neck. At any minute her neck could break. She wondered if it might be easier to just relax and let the noose take her life quickly. A buzzing began in her ears.

Her vision began to cloud.

———

ROTH LIFTED the stool and smashed it on the ground. It splintered into a heap of sticks.

Stephen wrenched his wrists free from the tape and grabbed the rope above his head for support. He threw his weight forward, lifted both legs as high as he could, and struck out with as much force as he could gather.

Roth spun, stunned by the sudden movement.

Stephen's heel caught him square in the temple. Any smaller of a man and he might have broken his skull. The impact sent a sharp shaft of pain clear up to his hip.

Roth staggered back several steps, fell heavily to his seat, then fell on his side, unconscious.

———

STEPHEN WAS only halfway out of his noose when Roth moved.

Already?

Stephen ripped the noose from his head and dropped to his feet, facing the German, who was now pushing himself up.

Behind Stephen, Esther hung on the end of the rope.

Roth stood, blinking. His eyes darted to the left, and Stephen followed them to a black lump on the earth, behind the table.

His pistol.

Esther began to rasp.

You have time to save her. Not much, but enough.

Stephen spun and grabbed Esther before realizing his mistake. He couldn't turn his back! The snake could easily have a second gun and put a bullet into both of their heads.

He whirled back, Esther in his arms.

Roth was withdrawing a small, snub-nosed revolver from his pocket. The man was still dazed, which slowed him down.

Stephen let Esther go, tore for Roth, and swung his hand, open palmed, for the man's face. The night crackled with a loud snap, like a firecracker.

Stephen's hand flashed with pain.

He formed a fist and drove it into Roth's nose. *Crack!*

Roth grunted and fell back to his seat.

"Stephen!" Ruth was crying out for him. "Esther . . . you have to get Esther."

Esther's rasping had intensified. He grabbed the fallen gun, smashed its butt into Roth's head, and hurled the weapon into the grass as Roth slumped to the ground.

He should have kept the gun, he thought. No time now. He had to get to Esther.

"Stephen!" Ruth cried.

He leaped for Esther and grabbed her legs and shoved her up to ease the pressure on her neck.

"Are you okay?"

She coughed and gasped.

"Are you okay?" he demanded.

"Down!"

Stephen glanced around, suddenly struck with the slight problem of getting her down. Ruth stared at them helplessly. He wasn't quite sure what to do. So he asked her again, "Are you okay?"

"I'm hung!" she barely croaked.

"Are . . . are you hurt somewhere?"

"Everywhere!"

"But not bad?" Surely not a broken neck!

"Bad!" she said.

"Is your neck broken?" he cried in alarm.

She looked down at him and held his gaze. She let out a breath and her face wrinkled, but it was relief, not pain in her eyes.

Stephen's vision blurred with gratitude. "Thank God."

"Stephen?"

"Yes?"

"Free my hands."

"How?"

"Stephen!"

He twisted at Ruth's cry and saw that Braun was struggling to lift his head. Ten yards from him lay the pistol that had fallen free during the confusion.

This was not good. He couldn't let go of Esther. Couldn't get to Braun. Couldn't reach to untie the tape around Esther's wrists. He saw it all, and he knew in a single, dreadful moment what he must do.

Roth slowly pushed himself to his knees.

"Esther, please—"

"Yes!"

"Hold on!" He eased her down, felt the rope take up her weight, felt nauseated. He took two long steps, snatched his fallen knife from the ground, and hurried back. If he thought she could withstand the pressure, he would have gone after Roth before returning to support her.

But the risk of her neck breaking was too high.

He grabbed her legs and shoved her back up. She gasped.

Braun got one leg under himself. Started to rise. Settled back down and tried again.

"Hurry!"

"I'm hurrying!" He held her up with one arm and searched for the tape with a shaking hand. He pressed the blade against it, afraid he might cut her skin.

Braun faltered, then staggered toward the gun.

Esther wheezed a cry.

Stephen sawed, wincing. The tape came apart.

She struggled above him, gripped the noose under her chin, and wrestled with the rope. "Go!"

He ran for Braun like a place-kicker running for a kickoff. His foot landed in the man's rear.

Braun grunted and sprawled to his face.

Stephen flew over him and scooped up the handgun. "Ha!" He spun around, knelt by the killer, and hit him on the head with the butt of the gun.

"Ha!"

This was the third major blow to the man's head. Surely it would keep him out.

In his peripheral vision he saw that Esther was falling.

She'd freed her neck and dropped cleanly to the ground, where she tried to hold her balance and then sank to her seat. She tried to stand, but fell back.

Stephen scrambled to his feet. "Are you okay?"

Esther touched her neck. The bleeding from her wrist had stopped.

Stephen jumped over Braun's prone body and rushed to them. He grabbed the knife and attacked Ruth's bonds. Freed her from the noose.

Dropped the knife.

Faced Esther. They were free.

Stephen sat and took Esther in his arms. She clung to him and began to cry softly.

"It's okay. It's okay, you're safe now."

He wanted to wash away her tears and squeeze her forever. Instead, he took her face in both hands and kissed her.

"I love you."

She couldn't respond for her tears. She didn't need to.

Stephen held her tight, her face planted in his neck as she wept. His eyes swept the camp behind her.

Roth Braun lay still.

This is where we were born. This is where our mothers' lives were once stolen.

He'd never felt so full of life as he did at this moment.

Epilogue

THE AMMUNITION BOX WAS EMPTY FOR GOOD REASON, RUTH told them. Martha had buried two boxes in the event that the treasure's location was forced from them. She would confess taking one Stone and burying an empty canister. When they dug it up and confirmed her story, they would assume someone else had stolen the other four Stones at the end of the war.

But Ruth knew the location of both boxes. Now the second ammunition box sat on the ground—green, dirty, and latched shut. Martha had buried it five paces from the other, directly under the same beam.

They knelt before it in silence.

They'd wrapped their wrists in cloth and then strapped them tight with gray tape. Stephen had gagged and bound Roth like a hog, lowered Gerhard to the ground, and dragged them both around the fence, where the authorities would find them once the call was made. He'd then dug in the spot Ruth had indicated as her best guess.

She'd been right. What thirty years of mystery had covered, five minutes of digging had uncovered.

Ruth unceremoniously reached out, flipped the latch, and pulled open the lid.

On one hand, Stephen wasn't sure he wanted to see what was inside. Considering all the impossible directions the road had taken them these last two weeks, nothing would surprise him. The box might contain the Stones of David. It might just as easily contain a letter. He wasn't sure which he preferred any longer. He had Esther. Didn't he? They had Ruth.

Martha's plan had succeeded. In the end they had beaten the diabolical plan to steal their hope, their love, their very lives.

On the other hand, he was desperate to see what was inside this box.

"It's . . . it's full," Ruth said.

"Full?" Stephen leaned forward.

Gold coins.

His heart pounded.

"Coins?" Esther reached her hand in and pulled out one of the coins.

"It's . . . it's Roman," Stephen said. He was staring at a single coin worth at least a hundred thousand dollars.

He pulled the canister closer and tipped it to one side. Gold clattered from the tin box, the unmistakable sound of priceless metals. The treasure rushed out all at once, gold coins, emeralds, rubies, diamonds, others he couldn't immediately name. There had to be a hundred!

Stephen dropped the box and gawked in silence. There on top of the pile rested a round lump of gold. Imprinted with a six-pointed star. And another . . . three more similar . . .

The Stones of David.

Esther touched one, then lifted it up. "The Stones of David?"

"Yes," he whispered. He cleared his throat and said it again. "Yes."

Her eyes were round and bright, like the diamonds.

"Is this worth very much?"

They both looked back at Ruth. She gazed at them, smiling. She didn't know. She didn't care. Her eyes were on her treasure.

"A . . ." Stephen cleared his throat. "A hundred . . ." He didn't know how much. "Yes."

She set the Stone back on the top of the mound. "Wow," she said.

"Ha."

They looked at each other. A mischievous smile slowly lifted her cheeks. Stephen felt like hollering, like yelling, like screaming for joy. Not simply for the treasure on the ground, but for the treasure before him. For all of it. For the reward that had been bought and paid for by his mother. By Ruth. By Esther. And now by him.

This was their inheritance.

"You are my Stone of David," Esther said.

"You are my Stone of David."

"I was born for you," she said.

"I was born for you."

She leaned forward slowly, then kissed him on the lips.

Beside them, Ruth began to cry.

THE KINGDOM OF HEAVEN IS LIKE A TREASURE HIDDEN IN a field. A certain man learned that the treasure existed and he developed a terrible obsession to possess it. He wasted all of his wealth and secretely sold everything he had to purchase the field so that he could own the treasure.

Again, the kingdom of heaven is like a pearl of great price. When a man found it, he sold all that he had and purchased the pearl.

Unless you, too, obsess after God's kingdom, like this man did over his treasure, you will not find it.

Knock and keep on knocking. Seek and keep on seeking. When they send you away again and again, come back and seek still again. Then you will find the treasure you seek.

Parables of Jesus
Paraphrased and expanded
Found in the book of Saint Matthew

teddekker.com

DEKkER FANTASY

BOOKS OF HISTORY CHRONICLES

THE LOST BOOKS
Chosen
Infidel
Renegade
Chaos

THE CIRCLE TRILOGY
Black
Red
White

THE PARADISE NOVELS
Showdown
Saint
Sinner (SEPTEMBER 2, 2008)

Skin
House (with Frank Peretti)

DEKkER MYSTERY

Kiss (WITH ERIN HEALY—JANUARY 2009)
Blink of an Eye

MARTYR'S SONG SERIES

Heaven's Wager
When Heaven Weeps
Thunder of Heaven
The Martyr's Song

THE CALEB BOOKS
Blessed Child
A Man Called Blessed

DEKkER THRILLER

THR3E
Obsessed
Adam

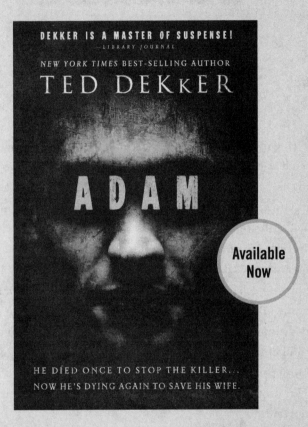

2008

A HOT, STICKY EVENING in Los Angeles. Outside, the city was clogged with traffic and a million souls fighting their way through another rush hour, preoccupied with bloated mortgage payments and impossible social pressures. Inside the FBI's Los Angeles field office, the air conditioner's hum had more significance to Daniel at the moment.

Special Agent Daniel Clark stared across the broad maple desk at Frank Montova's dark eyes, set deep behind puffy cheeks, like raisins. The man's neck bulged over a collar two sizes too small. Of the fifty-six domestic FBI field offices, only four were large enough to be helmed by an assistant director in charge, or an ADIC, as opposed to a special agent in charge. LA was one of those four. The running joke was that Montova fit his professional acronym at times.

"I'm not saying I wouldn't use other resources at our disposal," Daniel said.

"You don't catch a methodical pattern killer who's left a trail of fifteen victims across nine states without a *lot* of help. I don't care how good you are. You go rogue, you break the chain-of-evidence custody, and you'll blow our chances of getting a prosecution altogether, let alone a conviction."

"This isn't just about getting a conviction," Daniel said. "It's about stopping the killer in the Eve case before he kills another woman. It's about getting into the mind of a killer without him knowing it. I think I can do that better alone than with a team. We follow protocol, we may never find him. We have to anticipate him, not just chase him."

"You sure this isn't about Mark White's death?"

Mark was the forensic pathologist who'd worked with Daniel, uncovering what clues they could from the victims' bodies. Two weeks earlier he was killed in a car crash that hadn't yet been ruled accidental. Daniel had considered Mark a friend more than a partner.

"I can understand how you might come to that conclusion, but no. Mark and I had discussed going dark. This is about trying to get an investigation ahead of Eve, not just waiting to catch up with his crime scenes."

"I'd be more concerned with legality and judicial precedence." Montova's lips turned down. "The director doesn't like it. There are reasons why the bureau investigates the way it does."

Daniel took a slow breath, calmed himself. "You're denying my request?"

The chief eyed him carefully. "It's my call. And, yes, I'm leaning that way."

Daniel stood from the green upholstered guest chair and stepped over to the window. Like many of the bureau offices, the furniture was dated, held over from the last round of budget cuts. Two bookcases stuffed with black case logs and leather-bound legal briefs. A fake rubber tree plant in one corner. Round oak conference table with four metal chairs. Gray industrial carpet.

The city towered outside, gray piles of concrete jutting to the sky beyond Wilshire Boulevard like a dusty three-dimensional bar graph.

"Fifteen women are dead because of our bureaucratic inability to do what is necessary. He kills every lunar cycle, which means he already has his next victim. And if pathology's correct, he's already exposed her to the disease. Twenty-eight days is tomorrow. And we have no breaks, am I right?"

"Go on."

"If we get nothing this time, let me go dark. Give me access to whatever information I need—I work strictly through a channel of your choosing. Officially take me off the case. Put a legal layer of protection in play so that we don't endanger the evidence or the case, and then prosecute as you see fit. But let me do what I do best. *Alone.*"

Montova regarded him with a long stare. Shifted his eyes to the bookcase on his left. Daniel followed his gaze. Two spines stood out from the long row of books, a red one and a black one, side by side.

Inside the Criminal Mind

Fixing the Broken Among Us

Both were authored by the same man. Daniel Clark, PhD.

He'd written them after receiving his doctorate at age thirty-five. The subsequent five years of lectures and tours led to his divorce from Heather, after which he requested and received a reassignment to the field. That was nearly two years ago.

At first the Eve case gave him an avenue of escape from the pain of the divorce. But the case soon developed into an obsession because, as Heather insisted, Daniel knew nothing *but* obsession.

It was why he understood the obsessive criminal mind as well as he did. It was why he'd gone back to school for his doctorate. Why he'd ignored his wife in favor of dishing out a hundred lectures on the same subject. It took an obsessive mind to know one.

Behavioral patterns, like forensic evidence, could lead them not only to a conviction but also to a new understanding of the psychology of serial killing. ViCAP, the federal Violent Criminal Apprehension Program, had a continually evolving database about the intrinsic natures of violent criminals. A pebble of prevention against a landslide of future psychopaths.

The Eve killer was a poster child for the conclusions presented in both of Daniel's books if there ever was one.

Montova's eyes were back on him. "Do what you do best, huh?"

"Yes."

"And what *is* it that you do best, Daniel?"

"I work alone best. Without all the distractions that keep me out."

"Out?"

Daniel hesitated. "Of his mind."

"Eve's mind."

"Yes." Few understood the discipline and focus required to enter the criminal mind.

"Isn't that a dangerous thing to do? Alone?"

Daniel shifted in his chair, uncomfortable for the first time. Heather's words came to him. *They're your addiction, Daniel. You live your life in their minds!*

"If not me, then who?" he said. "You want this piece of trash off the streets, you take some risks."

The assistant director clasped his hands on the desk calendar in front of him. His straight hair, normally slicked to one side, curled down over one ear. Montova was a respected man—a throwback to the previous generation, preferring a pen and a calendar to a Palm Pilot. As he liked to put it, the mind was sharper than any brain power a computer could muster.

"You're more concerned about beating Eve at his own game than you are about the victims," Montova said.

Daniel crossed his legs. "You're forgetting that I was on the Diablo case in Utah. I've seen what a compulsive killer can do in the space of seven hours. Don't tell me I don't care about the victims. I care about stopping the killer, not just wandering behind him with a dustpan and filling out Uniform Crime Reports."

"I'm not saying you don't care about the victims. I'm saying they're not what drives you."

Daniel started to object, but the words caught in his throat. "Does it matter?"

"Actually, it does," Montova said.

His desk phone beeped twice.

"It tells me *why* your motivation runs so deep. This isn't just a job to you, and that makes you a risk to this investigation, even a liability. Your allegiance to protocols—I don't care if you wrote them—is critical."

The phone rang twice more before he reached for the receiver and lifted it to his ear. "Yes?" He listened, interrupting once for clarification.

Daniel glanced at the books he'd written. Heather had repeatedly made the same accusation Montova had. The truth of it had cost them their marriage.

Montova hung up and pressed another extension. "Send her in." He set the receiver back into its cradle.

"Send who in?"

The door opened and a woman stepped in. Closed the door behind her.

"Daniel, meet Lori Ames. Lori, meet Daniel Clark, our major crime SAIC."

Daniel stood and shook her hand. "Nice to meet you."

"I know your work," Lori said. "It's great to finally meet you."

Daniel turned to the bureau chief. "I take it this conversation is over. I hope we can—"

"Sit down, Clark," Montova said. To the woman: "Have a seat."

Lori brushed past him, wearing a gentle smile. Soft brown eyes and a slender body wrapped in a dark business suit. Black heels. Blonde hair that hung just past her shoulders.

But it was the way she looked at him that caught Daniel's attention. Like she knew more than he might assume she did.

He followed her back to the guest chairs and sat.

Montova eyed them both and spoke when neither offered comment. "Agent Ames is a pathologist from the Phoenix field office's evidence response team. She knew the fourteenth victim, Amber Riley, and has since become quite familiar with the case. We'd like to reassign her to you."

They were replacing Mark White two weeks after his death. But why not with a local? There were at least five qualified pathologists at the LA field office. He glanced over at her. Skirt tight against one toned leg crossed over the other. Not exactly the dress of a field agent.

"I suppose that's your call, sir."

"It is, and I've made it. She starts now. And I've changed my mind. I'm granting your request. Assuming, that is, you don't object to working through Lori. She'll remain on the case but shadow you in all respects."

Daniel didn't know what to say. "Just like that?"

"Just like that. Working within these new parameters you suggested, of course. Who do you suggest I turn the case over to?"

"Brit Holman," he said without thinking. The man was competent and nearly as familiar with the case as Daniel was. "You're saying you'll let me go dark alone, as long as my sole contact is an agent who's new to the case?"

Montova looked at Lori, who evidently took his stare as an invitation to share.

"The first believed victim was discovered sixteen months ago in the basement of All Saints Catholic Church in Cincinnati, Ohio. Maria Stencho, a twenty-three-year-old tasked with cleaning the church. Her body was bruised and blistered, and traces of a previously unknown bacteria similar to *Streptococcus pneumoniae* were found in her blood. SP is normally associated with meningitis, which infects the fluid surrounding the brain and spinal cord and can kill a host within hours in a manner consistent with Maria Stencho's death. No signs of struggle, no evidence of blunt-force trauma. No evidence of harm caused by any weapon. According to the local medical examiner, cause of death was acute encephalitis, most closely associated with symptoms consistent with ICD-10, code A-85, *meningoencephalitis*. The lab work detailed leukocytes in the cerebrospinal fluid after a lumbar tap, and confirmed that the disease was present and in full effect at the time of death. It was first assumed that Stencho died from a form of meningitis. Shall I go on?"

"I get the point," Daniel said.

But Montova held up his hand. "Please, go on."

"The next victim was found twenty-eight days later in San Diego. A Mormon, age twenty, female. This time in the basement of an LDS church. Nearly identical set of circumstances except this time the name *EVE* was painted in red on the cement wall next to the body. Lab came up with the same results in the spinal fluid, and the local coroner found evidence of the same intracranial pressure, as well as advanced infection of the meninges. She died of brain pressure leading to cerebral hemorrhage. A new victim has been found every new moon—the killer evidently likes the dark. All fifteen have been female, between the ages of nineteen and twenty-four. All found underground: seven in church basements, four in abandoned cellars at abandoned farms, four in natural caverns preselected by the killer."

Lori switched her gaze to Daniel. She was unique, he'd give her that much. Fresh. Her eyes sparkled with an infectious mystery. If he wasn't mistaken, in her late thirties.

"Evidence recovered from each scene includes size 13 shoe impressions—Bigton boots available at any one of several large chains across America. Stride indicates a height of six-six, and indentation puts him between 220 and 250. Different white vans were recovered near two of the sites. Hair and skin cell samples from each identify the killer as Caucasian, blood type B-positive, male. The lab cross-checked him through Combined DNA Index System (CODIS), and his DNA profile has appeared in no other investigations outside of this series. Hair indicates he is in his forties. There were no latent prints. No saliva, blood, semen, or any other fluid that could be traced to any other source than the victim. The killer's not a secretor. He's effectively either a newcomer or a ghost."

A pause. Then she went on delivering the data with practiced precision.